THE MAMMOTH BOOK OF

FAIRY TALES

The Mammoth Book of
FAIRY TALES

Edited by
Mike Ashley

Robinson
LONDON

Robinson Publishing Ltd
7 Kensington Church Court
London W8 4SP

First published in the UK by Robinson Publishing 1997

Illustrations: Alicia Austin p. 545; Ian Miller p. 38;
Clive Sandall pp. 98, 115, 136, 203, 214, 282, 472, 477, 479, 488,
494, 518; David Wyatt pp. 3, 32, 68, 76, 139, 178, 237, 279, 291,
298, 313, 323, 331, 355, 372, 381, 386, 392, 404, 415, 460, 464, 540

A copy of the British Library Cataloguing in Publication data is available
from the British Library

ISBN 1–85487-508-6
Printed and bound in the EC

10 9 8 7 6 5 4 3 2 1

07215350

BZ A/97

Contents

‑ Contents ‑

— Contents —

– Contents –

- Contents -

Introduction

~

WELCOME. Since you've got this far you must have more than a passing interest in fairy tales. I hope so, because this collection seeks to recapture the wonder of the fairy tale for all readers – to be enjoyed by adults as much as by children. Perhaps even more by adults, because we can appreciate what we've lost when we leave childhood behind us. The grown-up world tries to rob us of the sense of wonder we all had as children. Fairy tales not only help to restore that, but remind us of the thrill of discovery and of some of those simple but important messages that they convey so well.

Fairy tales have been written for hundreds, if not thousands of years, and recounted for even longer. The original tales were satires upon society that could be enjoyed in all innocence by children, but held deeper levels of meaning for adults. The fairy tale lost some of that greater significance during the Victorian period, when children became the primary audience, but even then the old tales held something extra for those who cared to listen.

In this collection, I've brought together tales from many different eras. Most are set in that timeless wonderland of once-upon-a-time, but some are set in the age they were written, which could be our own, or a hundred years ago. Nevertheless, even if they are set in modern days there are no computers or televisions here. These stories are designed to provide an escape from such everyday matters into a world where magic works. Anything can happen, and that's part of the fun.

You might ask, what *are* fairy tales? I think it would be a pity to pin them down and try to define them in academic style. The secret of a good fairy tale is that it should touch something deep within us, that we feel rings true, no matter how fantastic it may seem. These stories, and others like them, possess such a quality, and many have been passed down the generations for hundreds of years – and will continue to be passed down for hundreds more.

If you would like to know more about the stories chosen for this volume there is a separate section at the end of the book. However you choose to read the stories, whether you read them to your children or keep them to yourself, I hope you will enjoy them half as much as I have enjoyed collecting them.

Mike Ashley

A Bag of Poetry

❦

Lawrence Schimel

ANYA STRADDLED THE LOW brick wall surrounding the Safeway parking lot, writing poetry in Polish with a thick black marker on the side of her bag of groceries as she waited for the bus to come. A homeless man approached her and asked for change. His dog sniffed her foot. The dog was black with a small brown spot on the side of its face. The spot looked as if it had been balanced on top of the dog's head until one day the dog tripped and it had slid down his face. The man wore red and green Christmas boxers and a long-sleeved shirt – brown plaid, the same color as the dog's spot. His eyes were baby blue, big and wide with wonder, innocent.

Anya reached into the bag of groceries and brought out a loaf of bread and a pound of roast beef, which she gave to the man. She reached in again and tossed a bone to the dog. "God bless," the man said, bowing to her as he backed away down the street. The dog wagged its tail and followed him.

The bus came and Anya boarded. It was empty as she sat down and pulled a book from the bag. When she looked up again it was her stop, and all the seats were full. The woman next to Anya rose when she did. As Anya stepped from the bus this woman, in her haste, bumped into her from behind. The bag fell to the ground, landing on its side. There was a moment of freeze-framed silence as everyone nearby stared at the open end of the bag, waiting for the food to come spilling out, broken and smashed. The moment

I

lasted too long and the silence was broken. The woman took the final step off the bus while seventeen eggs rolled out from the bag and bumped gently to a stop against the building, all uncracked. A flock of pigeons wandered over and pecked at the eggs, eating first the golden insides and then the shells.

Anya bent to retrieve the bag, and when she stood both woman and bus were gone. She tossed a handful of popcorn to the pigeons and walked to her house. Her mother was waiting for her at the door, and followed her into the kitchen to see what she had brought. Anya placed the bag on the counter and began to unpack it.

The first thing Anya drew from the bag was a new job for her brother.

"Pietor!" her mother cried as she rushed to the stairs. "Pietor!"

Anya kept unpacking, placing a bag of potatoes on the counter next to the new job, then a dozen ears of corn, a sack of flour, and three quarts of milk. Her mother came around the counter to where Anya stood and pinned Anya's hands at her side with a big hug. "This is wonderful news," the mother said, smiling. "Pietor!"

Anya pulled the moon from the bag and placed it on the counter. Her mother thought it was a saucer and poured cream into it. Therefore, while her mother knelt to place the saucer of cream on the floor, Anya brought five kittens from the bag.

"What is this?" the mother asked when she stood and saw them on the counter.

"They are kittens," Anya answered as she placed them on the floor to drink the cream.

"Ay! We have too many already," the mother said as cats flooded the room, skidding across the white linoleum as they ran in from the living room or jumped in through the window.

"You can never have too many cats," Anya declared, pulling tomatoes from the bag. Pietor came into the kitchen, sleepy-eyed. Excited, his mother took him and the new job into the living room. Anya continued to put the food away.

When the cats were done with the cream, Anya took the moon into the backyard and placed it in the sky. Her mother walked into the kitchen again and found it empty, save for the bag on the counter. "Surely, it could hold no more," she thought as she looked into it. She

folded the bag, neatly collapsing it along the creases, and, because she could not read the poetry, threw it out.

Beauty and the Beast

~

Jeanne-Marie Leprince de Beaumont

THERE WAS ONCE A very rich merchant who had six children, three boys and three girls. As he was himself a man of great sense, he spared no expense for their education. The three daughters were all handsome, but particularly the youngest; indeed, she was so very beautiful that in her childhood everyone called her the Little Beauty; and, being equally lovely when she was grown up, nobody called her by any other name, which made her sisters very jealous of her.

This youngest daughter was not only more handsome than her sisters, but also was better tempered. The two eldest were vain of their wealth and position. They gave themselves a thousand airs, and refused to visit other merchants' daughters; nor would they condescend to be seen except with persons of quality. They went every day to balls, plays, and public walks, and always made game of their youngest sister for spending her time in reading or other useful employments.

As it was well known that these young ladies would have large fortunes, many great merchants wished to get them for wives; but the two eldest always answered that, for their parts, they had no thoughts of marrying anyone below a duke or an earl at least. Beauty had quite as many offers as her sisters, but she always answered, with the greatest civility, that, though she was much obliged to her lovers, she would rather live some years longer with her father, as she thought herself too young to marry.

It happened that, by some unlucky accident, the merchant suddenly lost all his fortune, and had nothing left but a small cottage in the country. Upon this he said to his daughters, while the tears ran down his cheeks, "My children, we must now go and dwell in the cottage, and try to get a living by labour, for we have no other means of support." The two eldest replied that they did not know how to work, and would not leave town; for they had lovers enough who would be glad to marry them, though they had no longer any fortune.

But in this they were mistaken; for, when the lovers heard what had happened, they said, "The girls were so proud and ill-tempered that all we wanted was their fortune: we are not sorry at all to see their pride brought down: let them show off their airs to their cows and sheep." But everybody pitied poor Beauty, because she was so sweet-tempered and kind to all, and several gentlemen offered to marry her, though she had not a penny; but Beauty still refused, and said she could not think of leaving her poor father in this trouble. At first Beauty could not help sometimes crying in secret for the hardships she was now obliged to suffer; but in a very short time she said to herself, "All the crying in the world will do me no good, so I will try to be happy without a fortune."

When they had removed to their cottage, the merchant and his three sons employed themselves in ploughing and sowing the fields, and working in the garden. Beauty also did her part, for she rose by four o'clock every morning, lighted the fires, cleaned the house, and got ready the breakfast for the whole family. At first she found all this very hard; but she soon grew quite used to it, and thought it no hardship; indeed, the work greatly benefited her health. When she had done, she used to amuse herself with reading, playing her music, or singing while she spun.

But her two sisters were at a loss what to do to pass the time away: they had their breakfast in bed, and did not rise till ten o'clock. Then they commonly walked out, but always found themselves very soon tired; when they would often sit down under a shady tree, and grieve for the loss of their carriage and fine clothes, and say to each other, "What a mean-spirited poor stupid creature our young sister is, to be so content with this low way of life!" But their father thought differently: and loved and admired his youngest child more than ever.

After they had lived in this manner about a year, the merchant received a letter, which informed him that one of his richest ships, which he had thought was lost, had just come into port. This news made the two eldest sisters almost mad with joy; for they thought they should now leave the cottage, and have all their finery again. When they found that their father must take a journey to the ship, the two eldest begged he would not fail to bring them back some new gowns, caps, rings, and all sorts of trinkets. But Beauty asked for nothing; for she thought in herself that all the ship was worth would hardly buy everything her sisters wished for. "Beauty," said the merchant, "how comes it that you ask for nothing: what can I bring you, my child?"

"Since you are so kind as to think of me, dear Father," she answered, "I should be glad if you would bring me a rose, for we have none in our garden." Now Beauty did not indeed wish for a rose, nor anything else, but she only said this that she might not affront her sisters; otherwise they would have said she wanted her father to praise her for desiring nothing.

The merchant took his leave of them, and set out on his journey; but when he got to the ship some persons went to law with him about the cargo, and after a deal of trouble he came back to his cottage as poor as he had left it. When he was within thirty miles of his home, and thinking of the joy of again meeting his children, he lost his way in the midst of a dense forest. It rained and snowed very hard, and, besides, the wind was so high as to throw him twice from his horse.

Night came on, and he feared he should die of cold and hunger, or be torn to pieces by the wolves that he heard howling round him. All at once, he cast his eyes towards a long avenue, and saw at the end a light, but it seemed a great way off. He made the best of his way towards it, and found that it came from a splendid palace, the windows of which were all blazing with light. It had great bronze gates, standing wide open, and fine courtyards, through which the merchant passed; but not a living soul was to be seen. There were stables too, which his poor starved horse, less scrupulous than himself, entered at once, and took a good meal of oats and hay. His master then tied him up, and walked towards the entrance hall, but still without seeing a single creature.

He went on to a large dining-parlour, where he found a good fire, and a table covered with some very nice dishes, but only one plate with a knife and fork. As the snow and rain had wetted him to the skin, he went up to the fire to dry himself. "I hope," said he, "the master of the house or his servants will excuse me, for it surely will not be long now before I see them." He waited some time, but still nobody came: at last the clock struck eleven, and the merchant, being quite faint for the want of food, helped himself to a chicken, and to a few glasses of wine, yet all the time trembling with fear. He sat till the clock struck twelve, and then, taking courage, began to think he might as well look about him: so he opened a door at the end of the hall, and went through it into a very grand room in which there was a fine bed; and, as he was feeling very weary, he shut the door, took off his clothes, and got into it.

It was ten o'clock in the morning before he awoke, when he was amazed to see a handsome new suit of clothes laid ready for him, instead of his own, which were all torn and spoiled. "To be sure," said he to himself, "this place belongs to some good fairy, who has taken pity on my ill luck." He looked out of the window, and instead of the snow-covered wood, where he had lost himself the previous night, he saw the most charming arbours covered with all kinds of flowers. Returning to the hall where he had supped, he found a breakfast table, ready prepared. "Indeed, my good fairy," said the merchant aloud, "I am vastly obliged to you for your kind care of me."

He then made a hearty breakfast, took his hat, and was going to the stable to pay his horse a visit; but as he passed under one of the arbours, which was loaded with roses, he thought of what Beauty had asked him to bring back to her, and so he took a bunch of roses to carry home. At the same moment he heard a loud noise, and saw coming towards him a beast, so frightful to look at that he was ready to faint with fear. "Ungrateful man!" said the beast in a terrible voice, "I have saved your life by admitting you into my palace, and in return you steal my roses, which I value more than

anything I possess. But you shall atone for your fault: you shall die in a quarter of an hour."

The merchant fell on his knees, and, clasping his hands, said, "Sir, I humbly beg your pardon: I did not think it would offend you to gather a rose for one of my daughters, who had entreated me to bring her one home. Do not kill me, my lord!"

"I am not a lord, but a beast," replied the monster: "I hate false compliments: so do not fancy that you can coax me by any such ways. You tell me that you have daughters; now I will suffer you to escape, if one of them will come and die in your stead. If not, promise that you will yourself return in three months, to be dealt with as I may choose."

The tender-hearted merchant had no thoughts of letting any one of his daughters die for his sake; but he knew that if he seemed to accept the beast's terms, he should at least have the pleasure of seeing them once again. So he gave his promise, and was told he might then set off as soon as he liked. "But," said the beast, "I do not wish you to go back empty-handed. Go to the room you slept in, and you will find a chest there; fill it with whatsoever you like best, and I will have it taken to your own house for you."

When the beast had said this, he went away. The good merchant, left to himself, began to consider that as he must die – for he had no thought of breaking a promise, made even to a beast – he might as well have the comfort of leaving his children provided for. He returned to the room he had slept in, and found there heaps of gold pieces lying about. He filled the chest with them to the very brim, locked it, and, mounting his horse, left the palace as sorrowful as he had been glad when he first beheld it.

The horse took a path across the forest of his own accord, and in a few hours they reached the merchant's house. His children came running round him, but, instead of kissing them with joy, he could not help weeping as he looked at them. He held in his hand the bunch of roses, which he gave to Beauty, saying, "Take these roses, Beauty; but little do you think how dear they have cost your poor father;" and then he gave them an account of all that he had seen or heard in the palace of the beast.

The two eldest sisters now began to shed tears, and to lay the blame upon Beauty, who, they said, would be the cause of her father's death. "See," said they, "what happens from the pride of the little wretch: why did not she ask for such things as we did? But, to be sure, Miss must not be like other people; and though she will be the cause of her father's death, yet she does not shed a tear."

"It would be useless," replied Beauty, "for my father shall not die. As the beast will accept of one of his daughters, I will give myself up, and be only too happy to prove my love for the best of fathers."

"No, sister," said the three brothers with one voice, "that cannot be; we will go in search of this monster, and either he or we will perish."

"Do not hope to kill him," said the merchant, "his power is far too great. But Beauty's young life shall not be sacrificed: I am old, and cannot expect to live much longer; so I shall but give up a few years of my life, and shall only grieve for the sake of my children."

"Never, Father!" cried Beauty: "If you go back to the palace, you cannot hinder my going after you: though young, I am not over-fond of life; and I would much rather be eaten up by the monster than die of grief for your loss."

The merchant in vain tried to reason with Beauty, who still obstinately kept to her purpose; which, in truth, made her two sisters glad, for they were jealous of her, because everybody loved her.

The merchant was so grieved at the thoughts of losing his child that he never once thought of the chest filled with gold; but at night, to his great surprise, he found it standing by his bedside. He said nothing about his riches to his eldest daughters, for he knew very well it would at once make them want to return to town: but he told Beauty his secret, and she then said that, while he was away, two gentlemen had been on a visit at their cottage, who had fallen in love with her two sisters. She entreated her father to marry them without delay, for she was so sweet-natured, she only wished them to be happy.

Three months went by, only too fast, and then the merchant and Beauty got ready to set out for the palace of the beast. Upon this, the two sisters rubbed their eyes with an onion, to make believe they were crying; both the merchant and his sons cried in earnest. Only Beauty shed no tears.

They reached the palace in a very few hours, and the horse, without bidding, went into the same stable as before. The merchant and Beauty walked towards the large hall, where they found a table covered with every dainty, and two plates laid ready. The merchant had very little appetite; but Beauty, that she might the better hide her grief, placed herself at the table and helped her father; she then began to eat herself, and thought all the time that to be sure the beast had a mind to fatten her before he ate her up, since he had provided such good cheer for her. When they had done their supper, they heard a great noise, and the good old man began to bid his poor child farewell, for he knew it was the beast coming to them.

When Beauty first saw that frightful form, she was very much terrified, but tried to hide her fear. The creature walked up to her, and eyed her all over – then asked her in a dreadful voice if she had come quite of her own accord.

"Yes," said Beauty.

"Then you are a good girl, and I am very much obliged to you."

This was such an astonishingly civil answer that Beauty's courage rose: but it sank again when the beast, addressing the merchant, desired him to leave the palace next morning, and never return to it again, "And so good night, merchant. And good night, Beauty."

"Good night, beast," she answered, as the monster shuffled out of the room.

"Ah! My dear child," said the merchant, kissing his daughter, "I am half dead already, at the thought of leaving you with this dreadful beast; you shall go back and let me stay in your place."

"No," said Beauty, boldly, "I will never agree to that; you must go home tomorrow morning."

They then wished each other good night, and went to bed, both of them thinking they should not be able to close their eyes; but as soon as ever they had lain down, they fell into a deep sleep, and did not awake till morning. Beauty dreamed that a lady came up to her, who said, "I am very much pleased, Beauty, with the goodness you have shown in being willing to give your life to save that of your father. Do not be afraid of anything; you shall not go without a reward."

As soon as Beauty awoke, she told her father this dream; but, though it gave him some comfort, he was a long time before he could be persuaded to leave the palace. At last Beauty succeeded in getting him safely away.

When her father was out of sight, poor Beauty began to weep sorely; still, having naturally a courageous spirit, she soon resolved not to make her sad case still worse by sorrow, which she knew was vain, but to wait and be patient. She walked about to take a view of all the palace, and the elegance of every part of it much charmed her.

But what was her surprise, when she came to a door on which was written, BEAUTY'S ROOM! She opened it in haste, and her eyes were dazzled by the splendour and taste of the apartment. What made her wonder more than all the rest was a large library filled with books, a harpsichord, and many pieces of music. "The beast surely does not mean to eat me up immediately," said she, "since he takes care I shall not be at a loss how to amuse myself." She opened the library and saw these verses written in letters of gold on the back of one of the books:-

> *Beauteous lady, dry your tears,*
> *Here's no cause for sighs or fears*
> *Command as freely as you may,*
> *For you command and I obey.*

"Alas!" said she, sighing; "I wish I could only command a sight of my poor father, and to know what he is doing at this moment." Just then, by chance, she cast her eyes on a looking-glass that stood near her, and in it she saw a picture of her old home, and her father riding mournfully up to the door. Her sisters came out to meet him, and, although they tried to look sorry, it was easy to see that in their hearts they were very glad. In a short time all this picture disappeared, but it caused Beauty to think that the beast, besides being very powerful, was also very kind.

About the middle of the day she found a table laid ready for her, and a sweet concert of music played all the time she was dining, without her seeing anybody. But at supper, when she was going to seat herself at table, she heard the noise of the beast, and could not help trembling with fear.

"Beauty," said he, "will you give me leave to see you sup?"

"That is as you please," answered she, very much afraid.

"Not in the least," said the beast; "you alone command in this place. If you should not like my company, you need only say so, and I will leave you that moment. But tell me, Beauty, do you not think me very ugly?"

"Why, yes," said she, "for I cannot tell a falsehood; but then I think you are very good."

"Am I?" sadly replied the beast; "yet, besides being ugly, I am also very stupid: I know well enough that I am but a beast."

"Very stupid people," said Beauty, "are never aware of it themselves."

At which kindly speech the beast looked pleased, and replied, not without an awkward sort of politeness, "Pray do not let me detain you from supper, and be sure that you are well served. All you see is your own, and I should be deeply grieved if you wanted for anything."

"You are very kind − so kind that I almost forgot you are so ugly," said Beauty, earnestly.

"Ah, yes!" answered the beast with a great sigh; "I hope I am good-tempered, but still I am only a monster."

"There is many a monster who wears the form of a man; it is better of the two to have the heart of a man and the form of a monster."

"I would thank you, Beauty, for this speech, but I am too senseless to say anything that would please you," returned the beast in a melancholy voice; and altogether he seemed so gentle and so unhappy that Beauty, who had the tenderest heart in the world, felt her fear of him gradually vanish.

She ate her supper with a good appetite, and conversed in her own sensible and charming way, till at last, when the beast rose to depart, he terrified her more than ever by saying abruptly, in his gruff voice, "Beauty, will you marry me?"

Now Beauty, frightened as she was, would speak only the exact truth; besides, her father had told her that the beast liked only to have the truth spoken to him. So she answered, in a very firm tone, "No, beast."

He did not go into a passion, or do anything but sigh deeply, and depart.

When Beauty found herself alone, she began to feel pity for the poor beast. "Oh!" said she, "what a sad thing it is that he should be so very frightful, since he is so good-tempered!"

Beauty lived three months in this palace very well pleased. The beast came to see her every night, and talked with her while she supped; and though what he said was not very clever, yet, as she saw in him every day some new goodness, instead of dreading the time of his coming, she soon began continually looking at her watch, to see if it were nine o'clock; for that was the hour when he never failed to visit her.

One thing only vexed her, which was that every night, before he went away, he always made it a rule to ask her if she would be his wife, and seemed very much grieved at her steadfastly replying "No." At last, one night, she said to him, "You wound me greatly, beast, by forcing me to refuse you so often; I wish I could take such a liking to you as to agree to marry you: but I must tell you plainly that I do not think it will ever happen. I shall always be your friend; so try to let that content you."

"I must," sighed the beast, "for I know well enough how frightful I am; but I love you better than myself. Yet I think I am very lucky in your being pleased to stay with me: now promise me, Beauty, that you will never leave me."

Beauty would almost have agreed to this, so sorry was she for him, but she had that day seen in her magic glass, which she looked at constantly, that her father was dying of grief for her sake.

"Alas!" she said, "I long so much to see my father that if you do not give me leave to visit him, I shall break my heart."

"I would rather break mine, Beauty," answered the beast; "I will send you to your father's cottage: you shall stay there, and your poor beast shall die of sorrow."

"No," said Beauty, crying, "I love you too well to be the cause of your death; I promise to return in a week. You have shown me that my sisters are married, and my brothers are gone for soldiers, so that my father is left all alone. Let me stay a week with him."

"You shall find yourself with him tomorrow morning," replied the beast; "but mind, do not forget your promise. When you wish to return, you have nothing to do but to put your ring on a table when you go to bed. Goodbye, Beauty!" The beast sighed as he said these words, and Beauty went to bed very sorry to see him so much grieved.

When she awoke in the morning, she found herself in her father's cottage. She rang a bell that was at her bedside, and a servant entered;

but as soon as she saw Beauty, the woman gave a loud shriek; upon which the merchant ran upstairs, and when he beheld his daughter he ran to her, and kissed her a hundred times. At last Beauty began to remember that she had brought no clothes with her to put on; but the servant told her she had just found in the next room a large chest full of dresses, trimmed all over with gold, and adorned with pearls and diamonds.

Beauty, in her own mind, thanked the beast for his kindness, and put on the plainest gown she could find among them all. She then desired the servant to lay the rest aside, for she intended to give them to her sisters; but, as soon as she had spoken these words, the chest was gone out of sight in a moment. Her father then suggested perhaps the beast chose for her to keep them all for herself: and, as soon as he had said this, they saw the chest standing again in the same place. While Beauty was dressing herself, a servant brought word to her that her sisters were come with their husbands to pay her a visit.

They both lived unhappily with the gentlemen they had married. The husband of the eldest was very handsome, but was so proud of this that he thought of nothing else from morning till night, and did not care a pin for the beauty of his wife. The second had married a man of great learning; but he made no use of it, except to torment and affront all his friends, and his wife more than any of them. The two sisters were ready to burst with spite when they saw Beauty dressed like a princess, and looking so very charming. All the kindness that she showed them was of no use; for they were vexed more than ever when she told them how happy she lived at the palace of the beast. The spiteful creatures went by themselves into the garden, where they cried to think of her good fortune.

"Why should the little wretch be better off than we?" said they. "We are much handsomer than she is."

"Sister!" said the eldest, "a thought has just come into my head: let us try to keep her here longer than the week for which the beast gave her leave; and then he will be so angry that perhaps when she goes back to him he will eat her up in a moment."

"That is well thought of," answered the other: "but to do this we must pretend to be very kind."

They then went to join her in the cottage, where they showed her so much false love that Beauty could not help crying for joy.

When the week was ended, the two sisters began to pretend such grief at the thought of her leaving them that she agreed to stay a week more: but all that time Beauty could not help fretting for the sorrow that she knew her absence would give her poor beast; for she tenderly loved him, and much wished for his company again. Among all the grand and clever people she saw, she found nobody who was half so sensible, so affectionate, so thoughtful, or so kind.

The tenth night of her being at the cottage, she dreamed she was in the garden of the palace, that the beast lay dying on a grass-plot, and with his last breath put her in mind of her promise, and laid his death to her forsaking him. Beauty awoke in a great fright, and burst into tears: "Am not I wicked," said she, "to behave so ill to a beast who has shown me so much kindness? Why will not I marry him? I am sure I should be more happy with him than my sisters are with their husbands. He shall not be wretched any longer on my account; for I should do nothing but blame myself all the rest of my life."

She then rose, put her ring on the table, got into bed again, and soon fell asleep. In the morning she with joy found herself in the palace of the beast. She dressed herself very carefully, that she might please him the better, and thought she had never known a day pass away so slowly. At last the clock struck nine, but the beast did not come. Beauty, dreading lest she might truly have caused his death, ran from room to room, calling out, "Beast, dear beast;" but there was no answer. At last she remembered her dream, rushed to the grass-plot, and there saw him lying apparently dead beside the fountain. Forgetting all his ugliness, she threw herself upon his body, and, finding his heart still beat, she fetched some water and sprinkled it over him, weeping and sobbing the while.

The beast opened his eyes: "You forgot your promise, Beauty, and so I determined to die; for I could not live without you. I have starved myself to death, but I shall die content since I have seen your face once more."

"No, dear beast," cried Beauty, passionately, "you shall not die; you shall live to be my husband. I thought it was only friendship I felt for you, but now I know it was love."

The moment Beauty had spoken these words, the palace was suddenly lighted up, and all kinds of rejoicings were heard around them, none which she noticed, but hung over her dear beast with the utmost tenderness. At last, unable to restrain herself, she dropped her head over her hands, covered her eyes, and cried for joy; and, when she looked up again, the beast was gone. In his stead she saw at her feet a handsome, graceful young prince, who thanked her with the tenderest expressions for having freed him from enchantment.

"But where is my poor beast? I only want him and nobody else," sobbed Beauty.

"I am he," replied the prince. "A wicked fairy condemned me to this form, and forbade me to show that I had any wit or sense till a beautiful lady should consent to marry me. You alone, dearest Beauty, judged me neither by my looks nor by my talents, but by my heart alone. Take it, then, and all that I have besides, for all is yours."

Beauty, full of surprise, but very happy, suffered the prince to lead her to his palace, where she found her father and sisters, who had been brought there by the fairy-lady whom she had seen in a dream the first night she came.

"Beauty," said the fairy, "you have chosen well, and you have your reward, for a true heart is better than either good looks or clever brains. As for you, ladies," and she turned to the two elder sisters, "I know all your ill deeds, but I have no worse punishment for you than to see your sister happy. You shall stand as statues at the door of her palace, and when you repent of and have amended your faults, you shall become women again. But, to tell you the truth, I very much fear you will remain statues for ever."

The Bells of Carrillon-Land

∾

Edith Nesbit

THERE IS A CERTAIN country where a king is never allowed to reign
while a queen can be found. They like queens much better than
kings in the country. I can't think why. If someone has tried to
teach you a little history, you will perhaps think that this is the Salic
law. But it isn't.

In the biggest city of that odd country there was a great bell-tower
(higher than the clock-tower of the Houses of Parliament, where they
put MPs who forget their manners). This bell-tower had seven bells
in it, very sweet-toned splendid bells, made expressly to ring on the
joyful occasions when a princess was born who would be queen some
day. And the great tower was built expressly for the bells to ring in.
So you see what a lot they thought of queens in that country.

Now, in all the bells there are Bell-people – it is their voices that
you hear when the bells ring. All that about its being the clapper of the
bell is mere nonsense, and would hardly deceive a child. I don't know
why people say such things. Most Bell-people are very energetic, busy
folk, who love the sound of their own voices and hate being idle, and
when nearly two hundred years had gone by, and no princesses had
been born, they got tired of living in bells that were never rung. So
they slipped out of the belfry one fine frosty night, and left the big,
beautiful bells empty, and went off to find other homes.

One of them went to live in a dinner-bell, and one in a school-bell,
and the rest all found homes – they did not mind where – just anywhere,

in fact, where they could find any Bell-person kind enough to give them board and lodging. And everyone was surprised at the increased loudness in the voices of these hospitable bells. For, of course, the Bell-people from the belfry did their best to help in the housework, as polite guests should, and always added their voices to those of their hosts on all occasions when bell-talk was called for. And the seven big beautiful bells in the belfry were left hollow and dark and quite empty, except for the clappers, who did not care about the comforts of a home.

Now, of course a good house does not remain empty long, especially when there is no rent to pay, and in a very short time the seven bells all had tenants, and they were all the kind of folk that no respectable Bell-people would care to be acquainted with.

They had been turned out of other bells – cracked bells and broken bells, the bells of horses that had been lost in snowstorms or of ships that had gone down at sea. They hated work, and they were a glum, silent, disagreeable people, but, as far as they could be pleased about anything, they were pleased to live in bells that were never rung, in houses where there was nothing to do. They sat hunched up under the black domes of their houses, dressed in darkness and cobwebs, and their only pleasure was idleness, their only feasts the thick dusty silence that lies heavy in all belfries where the bells never ring. They hardly ever spoke even to each other, and in the whispers that good Bell-people talk in among themselves and that no one can hear but the bat, whose ear for music is very fine and who has himself a particularly high voice, and when they did speak they quarrelled.

And when at last the bells *were* rung for the birth of a princess the wicked Bell-people were furious. Of course they had to *ring* – a bell can't help that when the rope is pulled – but their voices were so ugly that people were quite shocked.

"What poor taste our ancestors must have had," they said, "to think these were good bells!"

(You remember the bells had not rung for nearly two hundred years.)

"Dear me," said the King to the Queen, "what odd ideas people had in the old days. I always understood that these bells had beautiful voices."

"They're quite hideous," said the Queen. And so they were. Now, that night the lazy Bell-folk came down out of the belfry full of anger against the Princess whose birth had disturbed their idleness. There is no anger like that of a lazy person who is made to work against his will.

And they crept out of the dark domes of their houses, and came down in their dust dresses and cobweb cloaks, and crept up to the palace where everyone had gone to bed long before, and stood round the mother-of-pearl cradle where the baby princess lay asleep. And they reached their seven dark right hands out across the white satin coverlet, and the oldest and hoarsest and laziest said:

"She shall grow uglier every day, except Sundays, and every Sunday she shall be seven times prettier than the Sunday before."

"Why not uglier every day, and a double dose on Sunday?" asked the youngest and spitefullest of the wicked Bell-people.

"Because there's no rule without an exception," said the eldest and hoarsest and laziest, "and she'll feel it all the more if she's pretty once a week. And," he added, "this shall go on till she finds a bell that doesn't ring, and can't ring, and never will ring, and wasn't made to ring."

"Why not for ever?" asked the young and spiteful.

"Nothing goes on for ever," said the eldest Bell-person, "not even ill-luck. And we have to leave her a way out. It doesn't matter. She'll never know what it is. Let alone find it."

Then they went back to the belfry and rearranged as well as they could the comfortable web-and-owls'-nest furniture of their houses which had all been shaken up and disarranged by that absurd ringing of bells at the birth of a princess that nobody could really be pleased about.

When the Princess was two weeks old the King said to the Queen:

"My love – the Princess is not so handsome as I thought she was."

"Nonsense, Henry," said the Queen, "the light's not good, that's all."

Next day – it was Sunday – the King pulled back the lace curtains of the cradle and said:

"The light's good enough now – and you see she's –"

He stopped.

"It *must* have been the light," he said, "she looks all right today."

"Of course she does, a precious," said the Queen.

But on Monday morning His Majesty was quite sure really that the Princess was rather plain, for a princess. And when Sunday came, and the Princess had on her best robe and the cap with the little white ribbons in the frill, he rubbed his nose and said there was no doubt dress did make a great deal of difference. For the Princess was now as pretty as a new daisy.

The Princess was several years old before her mother could be got to see that it really was better for the child to wear plain clothes and a veil on weekdays. On Sundays, of course, she could wear her best frock and a clean crown just like anybody else.

Of course nobody ever told the Princess how ugly she was. She wore a veil on weekdays, and so did everyone else in the palace, and she was never allowed to look in the glass except on Sundays, so that she had no idea that she was not as pretty all the week as she was on the first day of it. She grew up therefore quite contented. But the parents were in despair.

"Because," said King Henry, "it's high time she was married. We ought to choose a king to rule the realm – I have always looked forward to her marrying at twenty-one and to our retiring on a modest competence to some nice little place in the country where we could have a few pigs."

"And a cow," said the Queen, wiping her eyes.

"And a pony and trap," said the King.

"And hens," said the Queen, "yes. And now it can never, never be. Look at the child! I just ask you! Look at her!"

"No," said the King firmly, "I haven't done that since she was ten, except on Sundays."

"Couldn't we get a prince to agree to a 'Sunday only' marriage – not let him see her during the week?"

"Such an unusual arrangement," said the King, "would involve very awkward explanations, and I can't think of any except the true ones, which would be quite impossible to give. You see, we should want a first-class prince, and no really high-toned highness would take a wife on those terms."

"It's a thoroughly comfortable kingdom," said the Queen doubtfully. "The young man would be handsomely provided for for life."

"I couldn't marry Belinda to a time-server or a place-worshipper," said the King decidedly.

Meanwhile the Princess had taken the matter into her own hands. She had fallen in love.

You know, of course, that a handsome book is sent out every year to all the kings who have daughters to marry. It is rather like the illustrated catalogues of Liberty's or Peter Robinson's, only instead of illustrations showing furniture, or ladies' cloaks and dresses, the pictures are all of princes who are of an age to be married and are looking out for suitable wives. The book is called the *Royal Match Catalogue Illustrated* – and besides the pictures of the princes it has little printed bits about their incomes, accomplishments, prospects, and tempers, and relations.

Now, the Princess saw this book – which is never shown to princesses, but only to their parents – it was carelessly left lying on the round table in the parlour. She looked all through it, and she hated each prince more than the one before till she came to the very end, and on the last page of all, screwed away in a corner, was the picture of a prince who was quite as good-looking as a prince has any call to be.

"I like *you*," said Belinda softly. Then she read the little bit of print underneath.

Prince Bellamant, aged twenty-four. Wants princess who doesn't object to a christening curse. Nature of curse only revealed in the strictest confidence. Good-tempered. Comfortably off. Quiet habits. No relations.

"Poor dear," said the Princess. "I wonder what the curse is? I'm sure *I* shouldn't mind!"

The blue dusk of evening was deepening in the garden outside. The Princess rang for the lamp and went to draw the curtain. There was a rustle and a faint high squeak – and something black flopped on to the floor and fluttered there.

"Oh – it's a bat," cried the Princess as the lamp came in. "I don't like bats."

"Let me fetch a dustpan and brush and sweep the nasty thing away," said the parlourmaid.

"No, no," said Belinda, "it's hurt, poor dear," and though she hated bats she picked it up. It was horribly cold to touch; one wing dragged loosely. "You can go, Jane," said the Princess to the parlourmaid.

Then she got a big velvet-covered box, that had had chocolate in it, and put some cotton wool in it and said to the Bat:

"You poor dear, is that comfortable?" and the Bat said:

"Quite, thanks."

"Good gracious," said the Princess, jumping. "I didn't know bats could talk."

"Everyone can talk," said the Bat, "but not everyone can hear other people talking. You have a fine ear as well as a fine heart."

"Will your wing ever get well?" asked the Princess.

"I hope so," said the Bat. "But let's talk about you. Do you know why you wear a veil every day except Sundays?"

"Doesn't everybody?" asked Belinda.

"Only here in the palace," said the Bat. "That's on your account."

"But why?" asked the Princess.

"Look in the glass and you'll know."

"But it's wicked to look in the glass except on Sundays – and besides they're all put away," said the Princess.

"If I were you," said the Bat, "I should go up into the attic where the youngest kitchenmaid sleeps. Feel between the thatch and the wall just above her pillow and you'll find a little round looking-glass. But come back here before you look at it."

The Princess did exactly what the Bat told her to do, and when she had come back into the parlour and shut the door she looked in the little round glass that the youngest kitchenmaid's sweetheart had given her. And when she saw her ugly, ugly, ugly face – for you must remember she had been growing uglier every day since she was born – she screamed and then she said:

"That's not me; it's a horrid picture."

"It *is* you, though," said the Bat, firmly but kindly; "and now you see why you wear a veil all the week and only look in the glass on Sunday."

"But why?" asked the Princess in tears. "Why don't I look like that in the Sunday looking-glasses?"

"Because you aren't like that on Sundays," the Bat replied. "Come," it went on, "stop crying. I didn't tell you the dread secret of your ugliness just to make you cry – but because I know the way for you to be as pretty all the week as you are on Sundays, and since you've been so kind to me I'll tell you. Sit down close beside me, it fatigues me to speak loud."

The Princess did, and listened through her veil and her tears while the Bat told her all that I began this story by telling you.

"My great-great-great-great-grandfather heard the tale years ago," he said, "up in the dark, dusty, beautiful, comfortable, cobwebby belfry, and I have heard scraps of it myself when the evil Bell-people were quarrelling, or talking in their sleep, lazy things!"

"It's very good of you to tell me all this," said Belinda, "but what am I to do?"

"You must find the bell that doesn't ring, and can't ring, and never will ring, and wasn't made to ring."

"If I were a prince," said the Princess, "I could go out and seek my fortune."

"Princesses have fortunes as well as princes," said the Bat.

"But Father and Mother would never let me go and look for mine."

"Think!" said the Bat. "Perhaps you'll find a way."

So Belinda thought and thought. And at last she got the book that had the portraits of eligible princes in it, and she wrote to the prince who had the christening curse – and this is what she said:

"Princess Belinda of Carrillon-Land is not afraid of christening curses. If Prince Bellamant would like to marry her he had better apply to her Royal Father in the usual way.

   "PS – I have seen your portrait."

When the Prince got this letter he was very pleased, and wrote at once for Princess Belinda's likeness. Of course they sent him a picture of her Sunday face, which was the most beautiful face in the world. As soon as he saw it he knew that this was not only the most beautiful face in the world, but the dearest, so he wrote to her father by the next post − applying for her hand in the usual way and enclosing the most respectable references. The King told the Princess.

"Come," said he, "what do you say to this young man?"

And the Princess, of course, said, "Yes, please."

So the wedding-day was fixed for the first Sunday in June.

But when the Prince arrived, with all his glorious following of courtiers and men-at-arms, with two pink peacocks and a crown-case full of diamonds for his bride, he absolutely refused to be married on a Sunday. Nor would he give any reason for his refusal. And then the King lost his temper and broke off the match, and the Prince went away.

But he did not go very far. That night he bribed a page-boy to show him which was the Princess's room, and he climbed up by the jasmine through the dark rose-scented night, and tapped at the window.

"Who's dhere?" said the Princess, inside in the dark.

"Me," said the Prince in the dark outside.

"Thed id wasnd't true?" said the Princess. "They toad be you'd ridded away."

"What a cold you've got, my Princess," said the Prince, hanging on by the jasmine boughs.

"It's not a cold," sniffed the Princess.

"Then . . . oh, you dear . . . were you crying because you thought I'd gone?" he said.

"I suppose so," said she.

He said, "You dear!" again, and kissed her hands.

"*Why* wouldn't you be married on a Sunday?" she asked.

"It's the curse, dearest," he explained, "I couldn't tell anyone but you. The fact is Malevola wasn't asked to my christening so she doomed me to be . . . well, she said 'moderately good-looking all the week, and too ugly for words on Sundays'. So you see! You *will* be married on a weekday, won't you?"

"But I can't," said the Princess, "because I've got a curse too – only I'm ugly all the week and pretty on Sundays."

"How extremely tiresome," said the Prince, "but can't you be cured?"

"Oh, yes," said the Princess, and told him how. "And you," she asked, "is yours quite incurable?"

"Not at all," he answered, "I've only got to stay under water for five minutes and the spell will be broken. But you see, beloved, the difficulty is that I can't do it. I've practised regularly, from a boy – in the sea, and in the swimming bath, and even in my wash-hand basin – hours at a time I've practised – but I never can keep under more than two minutes."

"Oh, dear," said the Princess, "this is dreadful."

"It is rather trying," the Prince answered.

"You're sure you like me," she asked suddenly, "now you know that I'm only pretty once a week?"

"I'd die for you," said he.

"Then I'll tell you what. Send all your courtiers away and take a situation as under-gardener here – I know we want one. And then every night I'll climb down the jasmine and we'll go out together and seek our fortune. I'm sure we shall find it."

And they did go out. The very next night, and the next, and the next, and the next, and the next, and the next. And they did not find their fortunes, but they got fonder and fonder of each other. They could not see each other's faces, but they held hands as they went along through the dark.

And on the seventh night, as they passed by a house that showed chinks of light through its shutters, they heard a bell being rung outside for supper, a bell with a very loud and beautiful voice. But instead of saying . . . "Supper's ready", as anyone would have expected, the bell was saying:

Ding dong dell!
I could tell
Where you ought to go
To break the spell.

Then someone left off ringing the bell, so of course it couldn't say any more. So the two went on. A little way down the road a cow-bell tinkled behind the wet hedge of the lane. And it said not, "Here I am, quite safe," as a cow-bell should, but:

> Ding dong dell
> All will be well
> If you . . .

Then the cow stopped walking and began to eat, so the bell couldn't say any more. The Prince and Princess went on, and you will not be surprised to hear that they heard the voices of five more bells that night. The next was a school-bell. The schoolmaster's little boy thought it would be fun to ring it very late at night – but his father came and caught him before the bell could say any more than:

> Ding dong dell
> You can break up the spell
> By taking . . .

So that was no good.

Then there were the three bells that were the sign over the door of an inn where people were happily dancing to a fiddle, because there was a wedding. These bells said:

> We are the
> Merry three
> Bells, bells, bells.
> You are two
> To undo
> Spells, spells, spells . . .

Then the wind who was swinging the bells suddenly thought of an appointment he had made with a pine forest, to get up an entertaining imitation of sea-waves for the benefit of the forest nymphs who had never been to the seaside, and he went off – so, of course, the bells couldn't ring any more, and the Prince and Princess went on down the dark road.

There was a cottage, and the Princess pulled her veil closely over her face, for yellow light streamed from its open door – and it was a Wednesday.

Inside a little boy was sitting on the floor – quite a little boy – he ought to have been in bed long before, and I don't know why he wasn't. And he was ringing a little tinkling bell that had dropped off a sleigh.

And this little bell said:

> Tinkle, tinkle, tinkle, I'm a little sleigh-bell,
> But I know what I know, and I'll tell, tell, tell.
> Find the Enchanter of the Ringing Well,
> He will show you how to break the spell, spell, spell.
> Tinkle, tinkle, tinkle, I'm a little sleigh-bell,
> But I know what I know . . .

And so on, over and over, again and again, because the little boy was quite contented to go on shaking his sleigh-bell for ever and ever.

"So now we know," said the Prince, "isn't that glorious?"

"Yes, very, but where's the Enchanter of the Ringing Well?" said the Princess doubtfully.

"Oh, I've got *his* address in my pocket-book," said the Prince. "He's my godfather. He was one of the references I gave your father."

So the next night the Prince brought a horse to the garden, and he and the Princess mounted, and rode, and rode, and rode, and in the grey dawn they came to Wonderwood, and in the very middle of that the Magician's Palace stands.

The Princess did not like to call on a perfect stranger so very early in the morning, so they decided to wait a little and look about them.

The castle was very beautiful, decorated with a conventional design of bells and bell ropes, carved in white stone.

Luxuriant plants of American bell-vine covered the drawbridge and portcullis. On a green lawn in front of the castle was a well, with a curious bell-shaped covering suspended over it. The lovers leaned over the mossy fern-grown wall of the well, and, looking down, they could see that the narrowness of the well only lasted for a few feet, and below that it spread into a cavern where water lay in a big pool.

"What cheer?" said a pleasant voice behind them. It was the Enchanter, an early riser, like Darwin was, and all other great scientific men.

They told him what cheer.

"But," Prince Bellamant ended, "it's really no use. I can't keep under water more than two minutes, however much I try. And my precious Belinda's not likely to find any silly old bell that doesn't ring, and can't ring, and never will ring, and was never made to ring."

"Ho, ho," laughed the Enchanter with the soft full laughter of old age. "You've come to the right shop. Who told you?"

"The bells," said Belinda.

"Ah, yes." The old man frowned kindly upon them. "You must be very fond of each other?"

"We are," said the two together.

"Yes," the Enchanter answered, "because only true lovers can hear the true speech of the bells, and then only when they're together. Well, there's the bell!"

He pointed to the covering of the well, went forward, and touched some lever or spring. The covering swung out from above the well, and hung over the grass grey with the dew of dawn.

"*That?*" said Bellamant.

"That," said his godfather. "It doesn't ring, and it can't ring, and it never will ring, and it was never made to ring. Get into it."

"Eh?" said Bellamant, forgetting his manners.

The old man took a hand of each and led them under the bell.

They looked up. It had windows of thick glass, and high seats about four feet from its edge, running all round inside.

"Take your seats," said the Enchanter.

Bellamant lifted his Princess to the bench and leaped up beside her.

"Now," said the old man, "sit still, hold each other's hands and for your lives don't move."

He went away, and next moment they felt the bell swing in the air. It swung round till once more it was over the well, and then it went down, down, down.

"I'm not afraid with you," said Belinda, because she was, dreadfully.

Down went the bell. The glass windows leaped into light. Looking through them, the two could see blurred glories of lamps in the side of the cave, magic lamps, or perhaps merely electric, which, curiously enough, have ceased to seem magic to us nowadays. Then with a plop the lower edge of the bell met the water, and the water rose inside it, a little, then not any more. And the bell went down, down, and above their heads the green water lapped against the windows of the bell.

"You're under water – if we stay five minutes," Belinda whispered.

"Yes, dear," said Bellamant, and pulled out his ruby-studded chronometer.

"It's five minutes for you, but, oh!" cried Belinda, "it's *now* for me. For I've found the bell that doesn't ring, and can't ring, and never will ring, and wasn't made to ring. Oh, Bellamant dearest, it's Thursday. *Have* I got my Sunday face?"

She tore away her veil, and his eyes, fixed upon her face, could not leave it.

"Oh dream of all the world's delight," he murmured, "how beautiful you are."

Neither spoke again till a sudden little shock told them that the bell was moving up again.

"Nonsense," said Bellamant, "it's not five minutes."

But when they looked at the ruby-studded chronometer, it was nearly three-quarters of an hour. But then, of course, the well was enchanted!

"Magic? Nonsense," said the old man when they hung about him with thanks and pretty words. "It's only a diving-bell. My own invention."

*   *   *

So they went home and were married, and the Princess did not wear a veil at the wedding. She said she had had enough veils to last her time.

And a year and a day after that a little daughter was born to them.

"Now, sweetheart," said King Bellamant – he was king now because the old king and queen had retired from the business, and were keeping pigs and hens in the country as they had always planned to do – "dear sweetheart and life's love, I am going to ring the bells with my own hands, to show how glad I am for you, and for the child, and for our good life together."

So he went out. It was very dark, because the baby princess had chosen to be born at midnight.

The King went out to the belfry, that stood in the great, bare, quiet, moonlit square, and he opened the door. The furry-pussy bell-ropes, like huge caterpillars, hung on the first loft. The King began to climb the curly-wurly stone stair. And as he went up he heard a noise, the strangest noises, stamping and rustling and deep breathings.

He stood still in the ringers' loft, where the pussy-furry caterpillary bell-ropes hung, and from the belfry above he heard the noise of strong fighting, and mixed with it the sound of voices angry and desperate, but with a noble note that thrilled the soul of the hearer like the sound of the trumpet in battle. And the voices cried:

> Down, down – away, away,
> When good has come ill may not stay,
> Out, out, into the night,
> The belfry bells are ours by right!

And the words broke and joined again, like water when it flows against the piers of a bridge. "Down, down . . . ill may not stay . . ." ". . . Good has come . . ." ". . . Away, away . . ." And the joining came like the sound of the river that flows free again.

> Out, out, into the night,
> The belfry bells are ours by right!

And then, as King Bellamant stood there, thrilled, and yet, as it were, turned to stone, by the magic of this conflict that raged above him, there came a sweeping rush down the belfry ladder. The lantern he carried showed him a rout of little, dark, evil people, clothed in dust and cobwebs, that scurried down the wooden steps gnashing their teeth and growling in the bitterness of a deserved defeat. They passed and there was silence. Then the King flew from rope to rope, pulling lustily, and from above the bells answered in their own clear, beautiful voices − because the good Bell-folk had driven out the usurpers and had come to their own again:

> Ring-a-ring-a-ring-a-ring-a-ring! Ring, bell!
> A little baby comes on earth to dwell. Ring, bell!
> Sound bell! Sound! Swell!
> Ring for joy and wish her well!
> May her life tell
> No tale of ill-spell!
> Ring, bell! Joy, bell! Love, bell!
> Ring!

"But I don't see," said King Bellamant, when he had told Queen Belinda all about it, "how it was that I came to hear them. The Enchanter of the Ringing Well said that only lovers could hear what the bells had to say, and then only when they were together."

"You silly dear boy," said Queen Belinda, cuddling the baby princess close under her chin, "we *are* lovers, aren't we? And you don't suppose I wasn't with you when you went to ring the bells for our baby − my heart and soul anyway − all of me that matters!"

"Yes," said the King, "of course you were. That accounts!"

The Birthday Battle

❧

Louise Cooper

MOST OF THE BEST stories begin with "Once upon a time". However, the thing that was happening in this story didn't just happen once. In fact it has happened every year for the past four thousand years, which when you think about it is a lot of "upon a times".

The thing in question was a birthday. For the grand old Yew that was the oldest tree in Wych Wood was soon to be four thousand years old.

That sort of birthday is, of course, a very special occasion indeed, and all the inhabitants of the Wood agreed that a grand celebration should be held. They would have liked to ask the Spirit of the Yew, who lived deep in the tree's ancient trunk, exactly what kind of celebration he would best enjoy. However, that presented a problem – because Yew Spirit was asleep, and would not wake until the birthday itself arrived.

Perhaps I should explain a little about the reason for this. Most trees live to a very great age, given the chance, and Yew trees are among the longest-lived of all. When Yew Spirit was young, Stonehenge had only just been built, and by the time Julius Caesar came to conquer Britain, Yew Spirit was downright middle-aged. These days, he was what the creatures of Wych Wood politely called "an elderly gentleman" (though this annoyed the Elder trees, who found it confusing).

Elderly gentlemen like to sleep a lot, and Yew Spirit was no exception. Since the reign of King Alfred (the one who burnt the

34

cakes) he had slept a very great deal, and now he woke up only once every hundred years, to celebrate special birthdays.

So, as they could not wake Yew Spirit to ask him, the inhabitants of Wych Wood gathered together to decide for themselves what sort of festivities to put on. There was a great deal of argument, which the older creatures, like the Oak Spirits, and one particular Tawny Owl who claimed to be over a hundred years old (though no one believed him), said was only to be expected. The songbirds' and bees' suggestion of a grand concert was objected to by creatures who could only sing badly or not at all, while the ants' idea of a marching display, together with a fly-past by the Gnat and Midge squadrons, was scorned as being much too dull. The voles squeaked excitedly that everyone should do everything they could, all at once and very fast. But no one listened to them. No one ever did.

Before long the argument started to get out of hand, and at last the being who was, so to speak, chairing the meeting (though actually he wasn't sitting on a chair, but on the knee of Oak Spirit's tree) clapped his hands and called for order. As he did so a cloud scudded across the sun, and there was a flicker of lightning and grumble of thunder. Everyone promptly fell silent – even the voles stopped squeaking, which was a very rare thing indeed.

"That's *better*." Summer, who was one of the four Seasons and who was dressed in sky-blue and had hair as yellow and mellow as ripe corn, smiled at the company. The cloud cleared, the thunder stopped, and there was a scent of roses in the Wood. "Now, perhaps I can make a suggestion of my own?" Summer continued. "After all, this is *my* Season." He waved a hand around, indicating the flowers and the green canopy of leaves and the warm air buzzing with insects. "So we should plan something with a summery theme. Also, it seems to me that all the suggestions that have been made so far aren't very original. We *always* have concerts and marching displays and so on for Yew Spirit. I think this time we should do something different."

The other creatures looked at each other.

"Sounds sensible to me," said a badger gruffly.

"*We* like the idea," chimed in the wild flowers.

"Defzzzinitely," agreed the bees.

Then from the shadows between two tall Sycamore trees a new voice, which sounded like a stream chuckling, said, "*Ha!*"

Everyone turned round in surprise as, with a rushing, dancing breeze, a newcomer appeared. She was dressed in the palest green and her hair was the colour of daffodils, flowing over her shoulders like water. Skipping into the middle of the clearing, she looked around, then put her hands on her hips and said, "Well? What are you all staring at? Anyone would think you'd never seen me before!"

Summer jumped to his feet, outraged. "What do *you* want, Spring?"

Spring stuck her tongue out at him. A shower of rain pattered down through the leaves overhead. "I've come to make the arrangements for Yew Spirit's birthday," she said.

"But this is my Season, not yours!" Summer protested. "You've had your turn – go away. Go back to sleep!"

"Ha!" Spring said again, and tossed her hair. "There's my dear brother for you – trying to keep me away from the biggest party Wych Wood has ever seen!"

"But you *can't* come! It isn't the right time of year!"

"Then perhaps it should be," Spring said crossly. "I've been listening to you going on and on about doing something original for Yew Spirit – well, what would be *really* original would be to change the Season to mine!" She clasped her hands together and twirled round. "Spring, with the sap rising in his branches, and all his tiny flowers full of golden pollen, and the weather just right for him. Not boring, dusty Summer, when he gets hot and dry and uncomfortable and pestered by more insects than he can shake a branch at –"

"Hey!" the caterpillars and earwigs interrupted. "Do you mind?"

Spring wrinkled her nose and ignored them. "What *I* say," she continued, "is that we should have a Spring Festival! Then Yew Spirit can –"

She got no further, for another voice interrupted her. "And who, Sister Spring, says that *you* know what's best for Yew Spirit?"

With another lively gust of wind, a brown-haired figure whose gown rustled like fallen leaves and whose cheeks were as rosy as ripe apples appeared among them. Several squirrels yawned, and a cluster of leaves abruptly turned brown and fell, much to the surprise of the Hazel tree who owned them.

Autumn – for that was the new visitor – gazed graciously around and said, "Well, this is a pretty gathering! And what about *my* part in the celebrations? Yew Spirit is very fond of my mellow and peaceful Season; he has said so on many occasions."

Summer and Spring exploded furiously together. "He's done no such thing!" Summer cried, and "*Ha!*" snorted Spring, yet again.

"Scoff if you like," said Autumn in a superior tone, "but everyone knows that *I* am Yew Spirit's favourite Season. I am a time for dreaming, and for thinking of pleasant things. I am the Season in which Yew Spirit can relax, be comfortable, settle down –"

"And what, Sister Autumn, follows that settling down? Answer me that!"

The air turned so cold that every single creature in the Wood shivered. And Winter, tall and thin and stately, with frost-silver hair and a beard like icicles, stood among them.

Three hedgehogs curled themselves up into prickly balls and hibernated on the spot. A stoat (whose fur had suddenly turned white) nudged them, but only hurt his paw, and the hedgehogs flatly refused to unroll. Winter frowned sternly at everyone, but most especially at Summer, and said, "Yew Spirit likes *my* Season best of all. I bring him peace and comfort, the cold that cleanses his roots and branches. The chance to rest and sleep –"

"He's done nothing *but* sleep for the past hundred years," Summer interrupted sourly. There was another flicker of lightning. "And when he *does* wake up, he certainly won't want to see the land all freezing grey and white, without a scrap of colour anywhere. Face the truth, Winter. You're *boring*."

"Until you get in a bad temper," said Autumn huffily. "Then you make life miserable for everyone."

"Yes," Spring agreed. "You don't know anything about peace, Winter! Gales, blizzards, sleet – if you knew the *mess* I have to clear up after you every year –"

"Oh, you're a fine one to talk about mess!" Summer growled. "You and those floods you're so fond of! And with you it's hot one

minute, cold the next – you can never stick to anything for more than five minutes!"

"Well, you can all argue as much as you like," Winter announced, "but *I* know what Yew Spirit would like, and *I'm* going to make sure he has it." He drew himself up to his full height, and the sky turned to the strange, pink-tinged purple colour that heralds snow. "When Yew Spirit wakes, it will be Winter!"

Fat, cold, white flakes began to drift down from above. The flowers squealed and hid, pulling their heads and their leaves under the earth. Squirrels bolted for their dreys, the insects fled, and *all* the hedgehogs in Wych Wood fell sound asleep.

"Now, wait a minute, Winter!" Summer shouted – or rather stammered, for his teeth were chattering. "You can't just walk grandly in here and take over! This is *my* Season!"

"Well, it shouldn't be," said Autumn, whose apply cheeks looked a bit pinched now. "And it shouldn't be *his*," she glared at Winter, "or *hers*," with a scowl at Spring. "Yew Spirit wants *me*!"

Spring cried, "*Ha!*" again, but this time so loudly that the smaller creatures blocked their ears. The snow turned to rain, soaking everyone. Clumps of snowdrops and daffodils appeared, shaking their heads in puzzlement, and several hedgehogs woke up, mumbling, "Whazzat? Whass going on?"

"Now, *look*!" said Summer. The sun came out.

The snowdrops and daffodils said, "Please will you make your *minds* up!" as the dog-roses jostled them out of the way while the hedgehogs started snuffling for something to eat.

Autumn opened her mouth to protest, but before she could say a word Summer continued. "It's perfectly simple," he told the other Seasons. "I have a right to be here, and you don't. So you can just go away until it's your proper time to wake up. Go on, all of you. *Shoo!*"

"Listen to him," sniffed Autumn.

"La-di-da!" Spring stuck her tongue out again.

"You can't make me go away," said Winter with a sly smile. "I'm stronger than you are."

Summer said, "Ha!" then scowled, annoyed that he'd caught the habit from Spring. "Prove it."

"I shall."

"And what about us?" cried Spring and Autumn together. "We're strong – we can beat you both!"

"I can beat you all," added Autumn.

Spring pulled a hideous face at her. "Can't!"

"Can!"

"Can't!"

"Can, so there!"

The creatures of Wych Wood had so far listened in uneasy silence, but at last Oak Spirit felt he couldn't keep quiet any longer. "Ladies, gentlemen, *please*!" he beseeched. "You mustn't quarrel like this – it's very confusing for the rest of us, you know." Which indeed it was, for at that moment the Oak tree had buds, acorns and bare branches all at once, and couldn't decide whether his roots felt cold and soggy or hot and thirsty.

Autumn turned and looked at him in annoyance. "Keep out of this," she said. "It's none of your business."

"But it is," Oak Spirit protested, and from his topmost branch Tawny Owl hooted agreement. "*We* were the ones who wanted to arrange a welcome for Yew Spirit, and I think we should have some say in the matter."

"Nonsense," said Winter. "What do you know about it? You're only a tree."

Under Winter's withering stare, all Oak Spirit's acorns and remaining leaves fell to the ground with a *whump*. A group of voles, who were underneath, squeaked in protest, and Oak Spirit said sadly, "But this squabbling is getting us nowhere."

"There I agree with you," replied Winter. "So there's only one thing for it – Spring and Summer and Autumn and I must challenge each other to battle. And the winner will be the one to greet Yew Spirit when he wakes on his birthday."

The creatures of Wych Wood looked at each other in dismay. They were already having a taste of what happened when the Seasons quarrelled, and a full-scale fight didn't bear thinking about. But when they turned to Summer for help – after all, it was his rightful Season, as he had said – they saw that Summer was quite keen on the idea.

"Right, then," he said briskly. His eyes sparkled blue as a cloudless sky and a wave of heat went through the Wood, melting the icicles that now hung from poor Oak Spirit's branches. "I accept your challenge, Winter."

"But . . ." pleaded Oak Spirit; and, "Oh, *no* . . ." groaned the other creatures. The Seasons ignored them. They were all excited now.

"Let's not waste any more time," said Winter. He raised one finger as if it were a starting-gun. "On the count of three . . . One, two, three – *go!*"

So the Birthday Battle began – and such mayhem and chaos had never been known in Wych Wood before. As Tawny Owl said later, it was like trying to live four different lives all at once – and he freely admitted that he didn't have it half as bad as some of the other creatures. Take the squirrels, for instance. One moment they were curled up sound asleep in their dreys while a blizzard raged outside, then suddenly Autumn got the upper hand and they were racing hither and thither in a frantic search for nuts to hide away – only there weren't any nuts, for the next instant it was Spring, and there were a baffling number of young, green shoots to nibble.

The birds were in a tizzy of confusion. Swallows and swifts and cuckoos were puffed out with starting on their long flights southward, only to find themselves turning round in mid-air and coming back again every five minutes. And the rest complained that it was no fun to be feasting happily on a lovely Autumn glut of blackberries and elder-berries and rowanberries, then seconds later to find the berries gone and the whole nuisance business of nest-building starting all over again when they'd only just taught the last clutch of fledglings to fly.

The plants had the worst of it. The trees sprouted brown leaves, green leaves, catkins and a layer of snow all together (and a heavy weight that added up to, they grumbled), while bluebells and anemones were buried by showers of beech nuts and the summer flowers got frostbite.

Some creatures, such as the hedgehogs and dormice (there were a few dormice in Wych Wood, though they tended to keep themselves to themselves), simply gave up, found quiet corners to hide in, and snored through the whole thing. But for most of the inhabitants the Battle was a time to be remembered – and one which they would have much preferred to forget.

At last, at Oak Spirit's urging, Tawny Owl called an emergency meeting in the clearing where the first gathering had taken place. It was late, in fact it was nearly midnight, and this had been the most confusing day of all – for Sun had set early, only to pop up over the horizon again as the freezing, wintry afternoon turned into a balmy summer evening. Now Moon rode high in a cloudless sky scattered with stars while snow fell thickly (how snow could fall out of a cloudless sky no one knew, but no one had the energy left to ask). And it was hot.

As many creatures as could turned up to the meeting. Most, though, were either too tired or too dizzy with the constant switching and swapping, so it was a fairly small and sorry company that gathered in a half-circle at the Oak tree's feet.

Oak Spirit gave his report, but it wasn't a happy one. All his efforts to make the Seasons see sense had failed, and now they wouldn't even speak to him. Nor, he added, was there any sign that any one of them would ever win the battle, for they were all too evenly matched.

A badger, who had been enjoying a meal of fallen crabapples until they had suddenly vanished right under his nose, looked up and blinked through the snow. "But that's awful!" he said. "If none of them can win, then this disorder will just go on and on for ever!" He frowned, staring suspiciously at the place where the crabapples had been. "I don't *like* disorder."

"None of us likes it," said Oak Spirit, ignoring the voles, who had started to squeak that they didn't mind. "But as to how we can stop it . . . I have to confess I'm stumped."

"Tree-stumped?" asked a magpie with a chattering laugh, but no one else appreciated the joke.

"The trouble is," Oak Spirit went on, "we need the advice of someone older than we are. Someone who might remember if anything like this has ever happened before and so would know what to do about it." He sighed. "We thought of asking Sun – after all, he's been around longer than anyone. But when the skylarks flew up and tried to talk to him, he only sulked and told them to go away and not bother him until all this silliness had stopped."

A vixen with a bedraggled tail (her cubs kept getting Spring fever and biting it) spoke up. "If Sun won't help us, what about Moon? She's nearly as old as he is, and very wise."

Oak Spirit hadn't thought of that, for the sky had been in such a muddle since the Battle began that Moon had hardly been seen. Tonight, though, she was out . . .

"Well . . ." Oak Spirit said. "We could *try* . . ."

"Vixen could ask her," Tawny Owl put in. "She does her best barking by Moon's light. And I do my best flying by Moon, so I'll go with her."

Everyone agreed that this seemed a good idea, so Vixen and Tawny Owl set off to the edge of the wood, from where they could call to Moon without the trees getting in the way. The others waited for them to come back, shivering one moment, fanning themselves and panting the next. A nightingale started to sing, but gave up when icicles formed on her beak.

At last a flutter of wings and a rustle in the undergrowth announced the return of Vixen and Tawny Owl.

"What happened?" they were asked eagerly. "Did Moon answer you?"

"Oh, she answered," said Tawny Owl. "She isn't sulking; in fact she doesn't seem the least bit bothered by any of it. But she wasn't much help."

"She just said, 'What will be, will be'," added Vixen with a sniff, and cuffed a cub who tried to pounce on her twitching tail-tip as a clump of daffodils popped up beside her.

"Fat lot of use I call that," grumbled Badger. "So: *now* what? Anyone else got any bright ideas?"

It seemed no one had, for an embarrassed silence fell. Vixen and Tawny Owl were disappointed at their failure. Oak Spirit and all the other trees were deep in thought. And then, just as one of the voles was about to open his mouth and suggest that maybe if everyone ran round and round in circles, very fast and all at the same time, it might . . . there was a sudden change in the air. Change was hardly unusual now, of course, and they were all thoroughly sick of it – but this was *different*. For the air in the Wood grew very, very still. And there was a feeling of . . . *something* . . . about to happen. Something very . . . *important* . . .

Tawny Owl was the first to suspect the truth. His eyes opened very wide and he said, "Does anyone know . . . what time it is?"

They didn't, for sure, but Badger abruptly realized what Tawny Owl was getting at. "I think," he whispered, "that it could be just about . . . midnight . . ."

Midnight. A new day. And today was –

There came a soft, deep rustling, the sound of thousands and thousands of tiny, green needles moving gently together, and a strong, heady, resiny scent wafted through Wych Wood. Slowly, fearfully, the gathering turned their heads to look. And there in the heart of the Wood, where the shadows were at their darkest, they saw him. He was gnarled and stately, with the oldest and wisest eyes that anyone had ever seen, and he sat high up in his tree, where the great trunk had divided into three, as though he were a king seated on a throne.

The day of the birthday had come, and Yew Spirit had woken from his hundred years of sleep.

"Children, children!" Yew Spirit's voice was slow and strong and awe-inspiring. "It is good to see you all again."

"Yew Spirit . . ." Oak Spirit's voice was filled with respect, even though it felt very strange to him to be called a child. "We . . . we had planned a special welcome . . ."

"To wish you a happy birthday," added Tawny Owl.

"Yes. Yes – happy birthday! Um . . ."

"And many happy returns, of course. Oh, dear . . ."

Then, like a storm breaking, every single creature at the gathering started babbling at once as they all tried to tell Yew Spirit what they had meant to do and how everything had gone so horribly wrong.

"Spring started it! She –"

"But Summer was as bad, because he got all excited about the challenge and –"

"They won't even *talk* to us –"

"We're freezing!"

"Boiling!"

"Hungry!"

"Sleepy!"

And at last, in one great chorus: *"We're fed up!"*

"*Children!*" Yew Spirit's voice rushed through the Wood like a huge, soft gale, and instantly the clamour stopped. A vole squeaked, once, but one of the wood-ants nipped him before he could do it again.

"I understand what has happened," Yew Spirit continued. "Sit still, all of you, and stop worrying. I will deal with this Birthday Battle!"

He drew a vast breath and called out, "Spring! Summer! Autumn! Winter! *I am awake!*"

With a warm, whirling breeze that made the exhausted daffodils struggle above ground yet again, Spring came dancing into the clearing.

"Welcome, Yew Spirit!" she cried delightedly. "See – your favourite Season is here to greet you!"

"Oh, no, you don't!" another voice shouted, and a yellow-haired figure rushed in on her heels, brandishing a long strand of honeysuckle with which he tried to trip her up. "Happy birthday, Yew Spirit! It's Summer – the Season you like best!"

"*I* am the Season Yew Spirit enjoys!" cried Autumn, running at Summer and pelting him with conkers so that he yelped. "Hello, Yew Spirit – welcome to your special day!"

"Silly fools, with your frivolous games!" roared Winter, marching into the clearing with a swathe of crackling frost behind him. "Greetings, noble Yew Spirit – *I* am here to bring you the solemn peace you desire!"

The four Seasons started to argue again. They shouted at the tops of their voices, they threw things at each other, they stamped their feet with rage, until the whole of Wych Wood quaked with their quarrelling. Moon, still floating high above it all, said, "Well, *really!*" but no one heard her above the din. And even Sun came out of his sulk and peered in astonishment over the horizon.

Then Yew Spirit's voice rang out once more.

"Stop this *at once!*"

To the surprise of all the woodland creatures, the Seasons *did* stop, and stood very still, looking at Yew Spirit. Spring pouted and tossed her hair. Summer looked ashamed of himself. Autumn's cheeks were very, very pink. And Winter put his hands behind his back and whistled a little tune, as if the row had been nothing to do with him.

"I am ashamed of you all," said Yew Spirit sternly. "This is supposed to be a celebration, not a fight! And it is most certainly *not* the kind of birthday I want!"

The Seasons shuffled their feet. "We only thought . . ." Autumn began.

"I know what you thought, and you are all extremely conceited," said Yew Spirit. "Why should I prefer any one of you to the others? I enjoy *every* Season – but only at its proper time. And the creatures of Wych Wood agree with me." Squeaks, rustles, barks, twitters and buzzes of agreement followed this.

"But," said Winter, "we thought that as this is such a special birthday you should choose which Season you wanted. Just this once."

"Then why didn't you wait until I woke up, and ask me?" demanded Yew Spirit.

"Um . . ." said Winter. He didn't have an answer to that.

Yew Spirit sighed. "All right. I see that you meant well, so I *shall* choose. Do you agree to abide by my decision?"

"Oh, yes!" the Seasons chorused. "We promise!"

An odd little smile appeared on Yew Spirit's gnarled face. "Then I choose . . . *none* of you."

Their faces fell. "What?" said Summer, and, "You can't do that!" protested Spring.

"Oh, I can. Now, don't argue. You promised, remember? You can't break a promise. So – go away. All of you. Now!"

The Seasons looked at each other in dismay. Then, all together, they vanished.

And here the story does become just *once* upon a time. As the four disappeared, the strangest, eeriest and most awful thing that had ever happened in Wych Wood took place. For suddenly there was no Season at all.

That is very, very hard to imagine, but I'll try to describe it as best I can. It wasn't at all cold, yet it wasn't at all warm. It wasn't really dark, but then again it wasn't really light. There wasn't any rain, yet somehow there wasn't any dry, either. No leaves or flowers, yet no snow or frost. No buds. No fruit. No birdsong, no chuckle of water, no squeaking voles; no sound whatever. Everyone felt tired, yet no one could sleep. There was just . . . *nothing* in the whole of Wych Wood.

The creatures of the Wood looked slowly and fearfully around. What they saw frightened them. It wasn't natural. It wasn't *right.* At last Tawny Owl dared to turn his head towards Yew Spirit, and spoke in a quavering voice.

"Please, Yew Spirit . . . we don't like this . . ."

"Of course you don't," said Yew Spirit gently. "And I won't make it last. I just wanted to teach those silly, squabbling Seasons a lesson, and I think they've learned it now." He raised his voice and called out to the still, grey, *nothing* air.

"All of you. Come back now."

The Seasons appeared one by one. They, too, had seen what had happened, and their eyes were as wide and frightened as the eyes of the woodland creatures.

Spring whispered, "We're sorry. We didn't mean . . ."

"It was my fault," mumbled Winter. "I started it."

"The rest of us were as bad," said Autumn.

Summer only stared down at his own feet, until Yew Spirit spoke to him. "Say a friendly goodbye to your brother Summer," he said. "This is his Season, and the rest of you must go back to sleep until your proper turn comes."

Spring started to look sullen, and a single daffodil appeared at her feet. Yew Spirit frowned warningly. Spring shrugged, and with a sigh of relief the daffodil vanished again.

"Goodbye, Summer," said Spring. She kissed his cheek and vanished.

Autumn said, "Just *one* branch of crabapples, Yew Spirit . . . ? Badger was so enjoying them . . . Oh, very well. Goodbye, Summer. I'll be back to take over from you." And she too kissed him and was gone.

Winter was much too dignified to kiss anyone, so he just bowed stiffly, and said, "I wish you well, brother Summer. Goodbye."

Then only Summer was left. And the relief that the creatures of Wych Wood felt as the air grew warmer, and the leaves sprang to life, and the honeysuckle and dandelions and roses and mallows and valerians and all the other flowers of the *proper* season appeared, was so enormous that they felt they would burst with it.

Young birds in their nests clamoured for food and started trying their wings. The bees hummed contentedly. The fox cubs stopped biting their mother's tail and chased each other instead. The hedgehogs woke up. And the voles, of course, started to squeak with all the energy they had.

Later, Yew Spirit thought, he would have a quiet word with Summer. Not in front of the others, for it would be unkind to embarrass him in public. But he would make quite sure that Summer had learned his lesson . . . and that he would be especially kind to Wych Wood this year. First, though, there was something else to be settled, and he called the creatures around him, hushing their eager thanks for coming to their rescue.

"If you want to repay me," he said, "then what about putting on a splendid birthday celebration? What did you have in mind before all this trouble started?"

The creatures looked at each other. "Er . . ." they said. And: "Well, you see, we were just going to decide when . . ."

"I understand," said Yew Spirit. "Well, how about a nice concert from the songbirds and bees? And you ants – I know how much you like marching, so why not show me your best display? If the gnats and midges want to make a fly-past, too, that will please me enormously. And the sight and sound of all the voles running around and making as much noise as they can is *very* enjoyable . . ."

As Yew Spirit continued to list the things he would like – which were exactly the same things that the creatures of Wych Wood had done for four thousand years – Oak Spirit and Tawny Owl wished that they *had* been able to arrange something original for this very special occasion. But then they thought of the Birthday Battle, and how it had started . . . and they decided that perhaps it was just as well they hadn't.

Blue Roses

❧

Netta Syrett

THE PRINCESS AMELOTTE was the most exasperating princess in the world. The Queen said so frequently, and, as she remarked, "If a mother doesn't know her own daughter, who should?"

"She is not a bit like other princesses," she complained. And indeed she was not. Other princesses waited till they were addressed by tolerant and condescending princes. Amelotte, to their utter confusion and bewilderment, often spoke first. It was even rumoured that she was clever; but that was scarcely fair, since even if it had been true the Princess had wit enough to disguise it.

Still, she was reckless; there was no doubt of that.

Other princesses, for instance, had no sense of humour, or if they had, on being warned that it was an unbecoming possession, they lost no time in suppressing it. Amelotte, on the contrary, laughed at many things, and, as every wise queen knows, there is nothing a prince dislikes so much in a princess as a sense of humour. For it is a well-known fact among princes that princesses *have* no sense of humour. "Therefore to confront them with the impossible," as the Queen justly remarked, "is silly, and only makes them angry." But Amelotte either would or could not take advice, and so it happened that the Queen had the constant mortification of seeing more discreet but quite inferior princesses united to eligible and modest princes, who, after all, only wanted "someone to look up to them."

It was hard on the Queen, for she had spared no pains to render the Princess acceptable, even to the humblest prince. Potent fairies had dowered her with beauty, while fairies still more powerful were kept constantly employed in checking her intellect. Eloquent professors instructed her in the Art of Pleasing; and though, when she chose, no one could flatter a prince better than Amelotte, it sometimes happened that after she had spent a whole afternoon in assuring one of them how wise he was, and how good, he would go away with a puzzled expression and decide upon plain little Princess Yolande, or Violetta, after all.

So, as the Queen often said, "There was something wrong somewhere, and, unless Amelotte's behaviour became more princess-like, princes would continue to view her with disapproval, and it was even possible –" But here the august lady generally turned pale, and never finished the sentence.

"If your Majesty had only taken my advice about the christening," sighed Amelotte's old nurse.

"Yes, that was all the King's obstinacy," replied the Queen.

And in truth the Princess's christening had been a strange affair. The King, who was then young and romantic, had insisted that it should take place out of doors, in the midst of a wood; for he wanted the baby Princess to have the flower fairies as godmothers, and, as everyone knows, the flower fairies can never be persuaded to enter a human dwelling. But it was dangerous, the nurse said – very dangerous.

"Why is it dangerous to be christened out of doors?" the Princess often asked.

"Because sometimes the spirits of wild woodland things enter the baby's heart, and then it never rests," the nurse always replied, and more than this she either would or could not say.

But at last the Queen rejoiced, for the Prince of a neighbouring kingdom cast a favourable eye upon Amelotte, whom he had met at a State ball, and the next day he rode to the palace, a suitor for her hand.

"With all my heart!" exclaimed the King, a little too hurriedly, as the Queen's glance informed him.

"The happiness of our daughter is all the world to us," she said. "It is terrible to lose her," and she wiped her eyes with her royal handkerchief. The King began to look anxious, but cheered up when she added, "But, Prince, to whom could we entrust her future so confidently as to you?"

Prince Fortunas bowed, murmured a suitable reply, and the Queen hurried away to have a little private talk with Amelotte. The result was satisfactory. The Prince had danced well, he was handsome, his manners were good. Amelotte, tired of reproaches, consented to receive him, and in a few days the whole Court went mad with joy and excitement over the betrothal of Princess Amelotte and Prince Fortunas.

The night before the Princess's next birthday, a great ball was given at the palace. The crystal chandeliers sparkled with lights, the marble floors gleamed. Perfumed fountains played in the courtyards; the scent of flowers filled the air, and the most ravishing music floated out into the still darkness of the night.

Anything prettier than the little Princess, in her white dress and her little white cap edged with seed pearls, it would be impossible to conceive, and the Prince regarded her with approval, and almost forgot that her expression was rather too startling for a princess.

Amelotte regarded *him* dubiously. It was intensely foolish of her, but she did not feel quite happy. No one would have guessed this, however, for her laugh was gay, and all the princes with whom she danced found her very amusing.

Prince Fortunas noticed this fact before long, and, giving the Princess his hand, he led her from the ballroom, to offer a few words of advice and admonition. He was fond of both, and Amelotte was becoming just a little restive.

"You seem to find Prince Charming an interesting companion, Princess," he began.

"I find him almost worthy of his name, which is far better," she returned.

"May I suggest that your remark is scarcely worthy of a princess?" he somewhat haughtily replied.

"Certainly you may," said Amelotte, cheerfully, "though I cannot agree with you. If *you* said Princess Violetta was charming, I might deplore your taste, but I shouldn't say it was a remark unworthy of a prince."

"That would be quite a different matter."

"Of course it would," returned the Princess calmly, "because Violetta, though a good girl —"

"You do not gather my meaning," interrupted the Prince.

Amelotte laughed mischievously, and seated herself on the marble edge of a fountain they were passing.

"There are certain things not unbecoming in princes, which in princesses are disgraceful," her lover continued, standing in front of her.

"How do you know?" enquired the Princess, with breathless interest.

"A prince always knows about such things," he assured her.

"Why? I have known some quite silly princes."

"A prince is a prince for all that," returned Fortunas, who, if he had not lived in fairy times, would have been a Scotchman.

Amelotte looked up at him, and smiled bewitchingly.

"My Prince," she said, "it *is* nice of you to be jealous. If you go on in this way I shall certainly fall in love with you."

"But I'm *not* jealous!" the Prince hastened to assure her. "Jealousy is an unworthy passion. I am merely looking at the matter in the abstract —"

"That's what is wrong with you," murmured Amelotte, as though pleased at the discovery. "You look at everything in the abstract."

"I do not like your mood, Princess," declared the Prince.

"I'm sorry, but I can change it in a moment, if you wish," returned the Princess obligingly. "I have an enormous number of them."

"So I am aware. A princess of many moods —"

"Must be very annoying to a prince with none," agreed Amelotte sympathetically.

"I think I may say you will always find me the same," said the Prince, with proud humility.

"Oh, no, no! You mustn't take such a gloomy view," begged Amelotte.

At that moment there was a flourish of trumpets, and the King and Queen, attended by their retinue, swept past on their way to the banqueting-room. The Queen kissed her hand to the young couple, and sighed sentimentally. "Love's young dream!" she murmured.

"What was that you said, my dear?" enquired the King, who was getting a little deaf. It was owing to this circumstance, perhaps, that he could scarcely believe his ears when, after the banquet, he sat listening to a few pointed words from Prince Fortunas, who had requested a private audience.

"It's no use," wailed the Queen. "She must have been bewitched at the christening."

"It was the best christening," muttered the King feebly.

"Yes, but some sprites must have got in as well," returned the Queen. "I *told* you not to have it in the open air."

In the meantime, Amelotte was sitting in her bedroom, whither after the ball she had instantly retired. She sat quite still, and did not know whether to be glad or sorry at her freedom.

"On the whole I'm glad," she reflected, finally. "It would have been *too* dull. And yet to settle down, and be a queen, would save a lot of trouble. Why can't I? Why don't I? Perhaps Nanina is right, and it's something to do with the christening after all."

Springing up impatiently, she walked restlessly up and down till, finding even her beautiful big room too small, she opened the door softly, and began to wander about the palace. The dawn was breaking, and anything more cheerless than the great empty marble rooms, with their big windows and their dying flowers, it would be impossible to imagine. The Princess felt very miserable.

"Oh! I hate it all, and I hate myself," she cried, looking round her. "What do I want? The stars out of the sky? The sun out of heaven?"

And she thought suddenly of the old nurse's words: "*Sometimes the spirits of wild woodland things enter the baby's heart, and then it never rests.*"

"Is that why, I wonder?" she thought. "Is that why ordinary things, however charming, won't do for me? Is that why I want blue roses?"

The memory of roses of any sort gave her a sudden longing to get out into the air, and, gathering up her gleaming dress over one arm, she ran through the dim, mournful rooms, of which she had begun to be afraid, and never stopped till she found herself in the garden.

*   *   *

The palace garden was beautiful as a dream. Its lawns were soft as velvet; its great trees, arching over winding paths, gave pleasant shade at noon; its flowers glowed like fairy jewels; and through its midst flowed a river, murmuring as it slid between grassy banks on its way to the sea.

The garden was beautiful at noonday, when the splendid sun drew from its flowers a cloud of perfume. It was beautiful at sunset, when long shadows lay across the grass, when the birds' voices were sweet, and the spires and pinnacles of the palace were flushed with rose. But perhaps it was most beautiful in the moonlight, for then the lawns were washed with silver and flecked with exquisite shadows, and the river, singing a lullaby in its sleep, held the stars entangled among the rushes, and rocked them all together.

It was while the moonlight still flooded the palace garden that a boat now slid between islands of bending rushes, now floated into soft darkness under willow trees, and again emerged where the stream ran free, a silver pathway bordered by forget-me-nots and the tall spikes of willow-herb.

A faint splash of oars broke the silence of the night, and the gentle lap and ripple of water. The rower sat upright and, as the boat moved on, looked from side to side over the moon-charmed garden, with the alert glance of one who revisits a familiar scene. Sometimes, in passing a big tree or a wooded glade, or at some particular bend of the river, a quick smile sprang to his lips, the smile which only happy memory brings. And so for hours, while the Princess danced in her lighted palace, the boat floated down the river under the faint stars. The great trees dreamt on the lawns, asleep in pools of shadows. The air thrilled with the voices of nightingales; the river sang to the dream-stars hidden deep in its waters; and the moon rained light through all the sky. Then the hush became more profound. The nightingales ceased to sing; the moonlight grew dim. Darkness fell, and a profound silence, in which every leaf, every blade of grass, listened – listened intently and waited. The rower drew in his oars and waited too. Slowly, gradually, into the blackness there stole a ghostly grey. It spread and widened, and presently the garden lay newly enchanted in the earliest glimmer of dawn. In the dim half-light, a little glade was visible, which sloped from the hillside almost to the river's edge; and while the rower sat watching the trees taking shape out of the darkness the air grew suddenly sweet with the scent of flowers – with the perfume of lilies and roses. Almost at the same moment he noticed that the glade was full of dim thronging figures. Every now and then he caught a glimpse of stately forms, white of limb, gold of hair; of others with rose-flushed faces and garments of fluttering green. And he heard their voices, which sounded like the sighing of wind-stirred leaves. But mingled with the tones of the flower fairies there were other and different voices: some wild, like the startled cry of birds, some mocking, some mischievous, some altogether evil. Straining his eyes to find whence these sounds came, he could only see dimly, in the ghostly light, indefinite forms, shadowy flying things with whirring wings and bright, restless eyes. The glade was full of perfume and colour and mingled whispering voices, so confusing that only a little of their meaning reached the listener's brain, and only disjointed, incoherent sentences remained to his after recollection.

"Her birthday," said the Spirit of the lilies. "We gave her beauty; her white body, her golden hair."

"But they are snares. We have made them snares," laughed the evil voices.

"We gave her life and charm, and power to love," whispered the rose fairies.

"Ah! But we lay curled up in the heart of your roses – and we laughed, we laughed!" answered the mocking voices.

"She should have grown sweet and calm and simple, as we grow in the quiet sunshine," sighed the lilies.

"But we would not let her rest! We could not let her rest!" came the answer of the wild, startled things.

And so the confused sighing and whispering and crying went on, in the glade where years ago the Princess had been christened.

And as he looked at the swaying, restless throng, and saw its glitter and colour and perfume, its terror, its ugliness, and its beauty, and as he heard the murmur of its many voices, the listener in the boat said, half-aloud, "Oh, my poor little Princess! It makes things difficult when the fairies come to the christening!"

For some minutes he sat with downcast eyes, thinking very hard about many things, and when at last he raised his head there were streaks of amber light in the east, the birds had begun to sing, and, except for one or two rabbits who were early risers, the glade was empty. But only for a moment. There was a rustling in the tall bracken which grew near the water's edge; it was pushed aside, and between its branching fronds stood the Princess, her white gleaming dress thrown over one arm, her little white shoes drenched with dew.

She started, and then stood quite still, looking at the man in the boat.

"I thought one of the lily fairies had come back," he said at last, softly.

She looked puzzled at first, and then suddenly smiled. "Do you think so now?"

"No," he returned, meeting her glance.

"Why not?"

"Because of the sprites in your eyes."

At this she laughed aloud. "Who are you?" she asked.

"I am a Discoverer."

"But are you a prince?"

"*You* must be the discoverer now."

"That's rather a good idea," said the Princess thoughtfully.

"I am full of them," he returned.

"You are trespassing, as I suppose you know," observed the Princess, with dignity.

"Certainly. It is one of my best ideas."

"What have you come for?" she demanded weakly.

"For you."

The Princess gasped. "But I don't know you."

"That doesn't matter. No one knows anyone. But if you mean you've never seen me before – Oh! You silly Lottchen!"

Amelotte started violently. Only one person had ever called her by that name, and he was the forester's little boy, with whom she'd used to play, and from whom, after angry tears and wild protests, she had at length been parted.

"*Hugo!*" she cried, and coming down to the water's edge she perched herself on the branch of a tree which overhung his boat.

"I told you I should come back one day and take you to my kingdom. Did you forget?"

"Your kingdom? I didn't know you had a kingdom," faltered the Princess.

"I've made one," returned the Discoverer grimly. "Come!" And he held out his hand.

The Princess drew back in dismay. "Oh! But this is ridiculous!" she protested.

The Discoverer shrugged his shoulders. "We'll discuss it if you please, but it's a waste of time," he said.

"I don't in the least know what you're like now!" declared Amelotte. "You were a very annoying little boy," she added.

"You were a most exasperating little girl, and I'm sure you haven't improved," he replied. "On the whole, I think my risk is greater than yours."

"You are not polite!"

"No," Hugo readily agreed.

"Would you trust me?" began Amelotte, with the air of a princess of noble character.

"Quite as much as you trust yourself."

And Amelotte hung her head.

"Would you be jealous of me?" she went on after a moment, in a different voice.

"Yes. But no more jealous of you than you will be of me."

Amelotte began to feel interested, but all she said was a rather faint, "Oh!"

"I don't think you're the ideal of a young prince at all," she added.

"I'm quite sure I'm not. Think how you would hate me if I were."

Amelotte smiled in spite of herself, and Hugo laughed outright. "Don't be a humbug," he said.

"You'd be shocked if I wasn't," she murmured, looking down at the points of her shoes.

"A Discoverer is never shocked. He makes too many discoveries."

"I don't think I should be *bored* with you," said the Princess slowly.

"You must admit that's something."

The Princess gave a long sigh, and looked at him with troubled eyes.

"Should I find blue roses in your kingdom?" she asked.

"No," said the Discoverer gently. "But there will be nothing to prevent you from looking for them."

"You wouldn't think me mad?" asked the Princess in surprise.

"No," replied Hugo, "I shall know you can't help it. The fairies came to your christening."

Amelotte looked long at the Discoverer, and the longer she looked the more she liked him. But still she hesitated.

Then all at once he sprang on to the bank, put his arms round her, and kissed her lips. "Will you come now?" he asked.

"Yes," said the Princess promptly, and stepped into the boat beside him.

Hugo laughed as he pushed off from the shore, and just at that moment the sun's rim appeared above the horizon.

Higher and higher it rose, till the river was a golden pathway between its fringes of willow-herb and forget-me-not; and the Princess's hair was as golden as the river, and her dress shone whiter than the lilies as the boat darted towards the sunrise.

In the palace there was naturally great commotion at first. The Queen wept and blamed the King. The King kept out of the way as much as possible, and took things quietly. The old nurse sighed and lamented the christening. But as nothing lasts long, and no one's affairs are of much importance, except to themselves, the palace settled down in time, and in the Discoverer's self-made kingdom the Princess was as happy as anyone who seeks blue roses has the right to expect.

The Boy Who Plaited Manes

~

Nancy Springer

THE BOY WHO PLAITED the manes of horses came, fittingly enough, on the day of the Midsummer Hunt: when he was needed worst, though Wald the head groom did not yet know it.

The stable was in a muted frenzy of work, as it had been since long before dawn, every groom and apprentice vehemently polishing. The lord's behest was that all the horses in his stable should be brushed for two hours every morning to keep the fine shine and bloom on their flanks, and this morning could be no different. Then there was also all the gear to be tended to.

Though old Lord Robley of Auberon was a petty manor lord, with only some hundred of horses and less than half the number of grooms to show for a lifetime's striving, his lowly status made him all the more keen to present himself and his retinue grandly before the more powerful lords who would assemble for the Hunt. Himself and his retinue and his lovely young wife.

Therefore it was an eerie thing when the boy walked up the long stable aisle, past men possessed with work, men so frantic they took no notice at all of the stranger, up the aisle brick-paved in chevron style until he came to the stall where the lady's milk-white palfrey stood covered withers to croup with a fitted sheet tied on to keep the beast clean, and the boy swung open the heavy stall door and walked in without fear, as if he belonged there, and went up to the palfrey to plait its mane.

60

He was an eerie boy, so thin that he seemed deformed, and of an age difficult to guess because of his thinness. He might have been ten, or he might have been seventeen with something wrong about him that made him beardless and narrow-shouldered and thin. His eyes seemed too gathered for a ten-year-old, gray-green and calm yet feral, like woodland. His hair, dark and shaggy, seemed to bulk large above his thin, thin face.

The palfrey's hair was far better cared for than his. Its silky mane, coddled for length, hung down below its curved neck, and its tail was bundled into a wrapping, to be let down at the last moment before the lady rose, when it would trail on the ground and float like a white bridal train. The boy did not yet touch the tail, but his thin fingers flew to work on the palfrey's mane.

Wald, the head groom, passing nearly at a run to see to the saddling of the lord's hot-blooded hunter, stopped in his tracks and stared. And to be sure it was not that he had never seen plaiting before. He himself had probably braided a thousand horses' manes, and he knew what a time it took to put even a row of small looped braids along a horse's crest, and how hard it was to get them even, and how horsehair seems like a demon with a mind of its own. He frankly gawked, and other grooms stood beside him and did likewise, until more onlookers stood gathered outside the palfrey's stall than could rightly see, and those in the back demanded to know what was happening, and those in the front seemed not to hear them, but stood as if in a trance, watching the boy's thin, swift hands.

For the boy's fingers moved more quickly and deftly than seemed human, than seemed possible, each hand by itself combing and plaiting a long, slender braid in one smooth movement, as if he no more than stroked the braid out of the mane. That itself would have been wonder enough, as when a groom is so apt that he can curry with one hand and follow after with the brush in the other, and have a horse done in half the time. A shining braid forming out of each hand every minute was wonder enough – but that was the least of it. The boy interwove them as he worked, so that they flowed into each other in a network, making of the mane a delicate shawl, a veil, that draped the palfrey's fine neck. The ends of the braids formed a silky hem, curving down to a point at the shoulder, and at the point the boy spiraled the remaining mane into an uncanny horsehair flower. And all the time, though it was not tied and was by no means a cold-blooded beast, the palfrey had not moved, standing still as stone.

Then Wald the head groom felt fear prickling at the back of his astonishment. The boy had carried each plait down to the last three hairs. Yet he had fastened nothing with thread or ribbon, but merely pressed the ends between two fingers, and the braids stayed as he had placed them. Nor did the braids ever seem to fall loose as he was working, or hairs fly out at random, but all lay smooth as white silk, shimmering. The boy, or whatever he was, stood still with his hands at his sides, admiring his work.

Uncanny. Still, the lord and lady would be well pleased . . . Wald jerked himself out of amazement and moved quickly. "Get back to your work, you fellows!" he roared at the grooms, and then he strode into the stall.

"Who are you?" he demanded. "What do you mean coming in here like this?" It was best, in a lord's household, never to let anyone know you were obliged to them.

The boy looked at him silently, turning his head in the alert yet indifferent way of a cat.

"I have asked you a question! What is your name?"

The boy did not speak, or even move his lips. Then or thereafter, as long as he worked in that stable, he never made any sound.

His stolid manner annoyed Wald. But, though the master groom could not yet know that the boy was a mute, he saw something odd in his face. A halfwit, perhaps. He wanted to strike the boy, but even worse he wanted the praise of the lord and lady, so he turned abruptly and snatched the wrapping off the palfrey's tail, letting the cloud of white hair float down to the clean straw of the stall. "Do something with that," he snapped.

A sweet, intense glow came into the boy's eyes as he regarded his task. With his fingers he combed the hair smooth, and then he started a row of small braids above the bone.

Most of the tail he left loose and flowing, with just a cluster of braids at the top, a few of them swinging halfway to the ground. And young Lady Aelynn gasped with pleasure when she saw them, and with wonder at the mane, even though she was a lord's daughter born and not unaccustomed to finery.

It did not matter, that day, that Lord Robley's saddle had not been polished to a sufficient shine. He was well pleased with his grooms. Nor did it matter that his hawks flew poorly, his hounds were unruly and his clumsy hunter stumbled and cut its knees. Lords and ladies looked again and again at his young wife on her white palfrey, its tail trailing and shimmering like her blue silk gown, the delicate openwork of its mane as dainty as the lace kerchief tucked between her breasts or her slender gloved hand that held the caparisoned reins. Every hair of her mount was as artfully placed as her own honey-gold hair looped in gold-beaded curls atop her fair young head. Lord Robley knew himself to be the envy of everyone who saw him for the sake of his lovely wife and the showing she made on her white mount with the plaited mane.

And when the boy who plaited manes took his place among the lord's other servants in the kitchen line for the evening meal, no one gainsaid him.

Lord Robley was a hard old man, his old body hard and hale, his spirit hard. It took him less than a day to pass from being well pleased to being greedy for more: no longer was it enough that the lady's palfrey should go forth in unadorned braids. He sent a servant to Wald with silk ribbons in the Auberon colors, dark blue and crimson, and commanded that they should be plaited into the palfrey's mane and tail. This the stranger boy did with ease when Wald ordered him to, and he used the ribbon ends to tie tiny bows and love knots and leave a few shimmering tendrils bobbing in the forelock. Lady Aelynn was enchanted.

Within a few days Lord Robley had sent to the stable thread of silver and of gold, strings of small pearls, tassels, pendant jewels, and fresh-cut flowers of every sort. All of these things the boy who plaited manes used with ease to dress the lady's palfrey when he was bid. Lady Aelynn went forth to the next hunt with tiny bells of silver and gold chiming at the tip of each of her mount's dainty ribbon-decked braids, and eyes turned her way wherever she rode. Nor did the boy ever seem to arrange the mane and tail and forelock twice in the same way, but whatever way he chose to plait and weave and dress it seemed the most perfect and poignant and heartachingly beautiful way a horse had ever been arrayed. Once he did the palfrey's entire mane in one great, thick braid along the crest, gathering in the hairs as he went, so that the neck seemed to arch as mightily as a destrier's, and he made the braid drip thick with flowers, roses and great lilies and spires of larkspur trailing down, so that the horse seemed to go with a mane of flowers. But another time he would leave the mane loose and floating, with just a few braids shimmering down behind the ears or in the forelock, perhaps, and this also seemed perfect and poignant, and the only way a horse should be adorned.

Nor was it sufficient, any longer, that merely the lady's milk-white palfrey should go forth in braids. Lord Robley commanded that his hot-blooded hunter also should have his mane done up in stubby ribboned braids and rosettes in the Auberon colors, and the horses of his retinue likewise, though with lesser rosettes. And, should his wife choose to go out riding with her noble guests, all their mounts were to be prepared like hers, though in lesser degree.

All these orders Wald passed on to the boy who plaited manes, and the youngster readily did as he was bid, working sometimes from before dawn until long after dark, and never seeming to want more than what food he could eat while standing in the kitchen. He slept in the hay and straw of the loft and did not use even a horseblanket for covering until one of the grooms threw one on him. Nor did he ask for clothing, but Wald, ashamed of the boy's shabbiness, provided him with the clothing due to a servant. The master groom said nothing to him of a servant's pay. The boy seemed content without it. Probably he would have been content without the clothing as well. Though in fact it was hard to tell what he was thinking or feeling, for he never spoke and his thin face seldom moved.

No one knew his name, the boy who plaited manes. Though many of the grooms were curious and made inquiries, no one could tell who he was or where he had come from. Or even what he was, Wald thought sourly. No way to tell if the young snip was a halfwit or a bastard or what, if he would not talk. No way to tell what sort of a young warlock he might be, that the horses never moved under his hands – even the hot-blooded hunter standing like a stump for him. Scrawny brat. He could hear well enough; why would he not talk?

It did not make Wald like the strange boy that he did at once whatever he was told and worked so hard and so silently. In particular he did not like the boy for doing the work for which Wald reaped the lord's praise; Wald disliked anyone to whom he was obliged. Nor did he like the way the boy had arrived, as if blown in on a gust of wind, and so thin that it nearly seemed possible. Nor did he like the thought that any day the boy might leave in like wise. And, even disliking that thought, Wald could not bring himself to give the boy the few coppers a week which were his due, for he disliked the boy more. Wald believed there was something wrong-headed, nearly evil, about the boy. His face seemed wrong, so very thin, with the set mouth and the eyes both wild and quiet, burning like a steady candle flame.

Summer turned into autumn, and many gusts of wind blew, but the boy who plaited manes seemed content to stay, and if he knew of Wald's dislike he did not show it. In fact he showed nothing. He braided the palfrey's mane with autumn starflowers and smiled ever so slightly as he worked. Autumn turned to the first dripping and dismal, chill days of winter. The boy used bunches of bright feathers instead of flowers when he dressed the palfrey's mane, and he did not ask for a winter jerkin, so Wald did not give him any. It was seldom enough, anyway, that the horses were used for pleasure at this season. The thin boy could spend his days huddled under a horseblanket in the loft.

Hard winter came, and the small pox season.

Lady Aelynn was bored in the wintertime, even more so than during the rest of the year. At least in the fine weather there were walks outside, there was riding and hunting and people to impress. It would not be reasonable for a lord's wife, nobly born (though a younger child, and female), to wish for more than that. Lady Aelynn knew full well that her brief days of friendships and courtships were over. She had wed tolerably well, and Lord Robley counted her among his possessions — a beautiful thing to be prized like his gold and his best horses. He was a manor lord and she was his belonging, his lady, and not for others to touch even with their regard. She was entirely his.

So there were walks for her in walled gardens, and pleasure riding and hunting by her lord's side, and people to impress.

But in the wintertime there were not even the walks. There was nothing for the Lady Aelynn to do but tend to her needlework and her own beauty, endlessly concerned with her clothes, her hair, her skin, even though she was so young, no more than seventeen ‒ for she knew in her heart that it was for her beauty that Lord Robley smiled on her, and for no other reason. And though she did not think of it, she knew that her life lay in his grasping hands.

Therefore she was ardently uneasy, and distressed only for herself, when the woman who arranged her hair each morning was laid abed with smallpox. Though, as befits a lady of rank, Aelynn hid her dismay in vexation. And it did not take her long to discover that none of her other tiring-women could serve her nearly as well.

"Mother of God!" she raged, surveying her hair in the mirror for perhaps the tenth time. "The groom who plaits the horses' manes in the stable could do better!" Then the truth of her own words struck her, and desperation made her willing to be daring. She smiled. "Bring him hither!"

Her women stammered and curtseyed and fled to consult among themselves and exclaim with the help in the kitchen. After some few minutes of this, a bold kitchen maid was dispatched to the stable and returned with a shivering waif: the boy who plaited manes.

It was not to be considered that such a beggar should go in to the lady. Her tiring-women squeaked in horror and made him bathe first, in a washbasin before the kitchen hearth, for there was a strong smell of horse and stable about him. They ordered him to scrub his own hair with strong soap and scent himself with lavender, and while some of them giggled and fled, others giggled and stayed, to pour water for him and see that he made a proper job of his ablutions. All that was demanded of him the boy who plaited manes did without any change in his thin face, any movement of his close mouth, any flash of his feral eyes. At last they brought him clean clothing, jerkin and woolen hose only a little too large, and pulled the things as straight as they could on him, and took him to the tower where the lady waited.

He did not bow to the Lady Aelynn or look into her eyes for his instructions, but his still mouth softened a little and his glance, calm and alert, like that of a woodland thing, darted to her hair. And at once, as if he could scarcely wait, he took his place behind her and lifted her tresses in his hands. Such a soft, fine, honey-colored mane of hair as he had never seen, and combs of gold and ivory lying at hand on a rosewood table, and ribbons of silk and gold – everything he could have wanted, his for the sake of his skill.

He started at the forehead, and the lady sat as if in a trance beneath the deft touch of his hands.

Gentle, he was so gentle; she had never felt such a soft and gentle touch from any man, least of all from her lord. When Lord Robley wanted to use one of his possessions he seized it, not so hard as to hurt, but still firmly enough to take control. But this boy touched her as gently as a woman, no, a mother, for no tiring-woman or maid had ever gentled her so . . . Yet unmistakably his was the touch of a man, though she could scarcely have told how she knew. Part of it was power; she could feel the gentle power in his touch, she could feel – uncanny, altogether eerie and uncanny, what she was feeling. It was as if his quick fingers called to her hair in soft command and her hair obeyed just for the sake of the one quick touch, all the while longing to embrace . . . She stayed breathlessly still for him, like the horses.

He plaited her hair in braids thin as bluebell stems, only a wisp of hairs to each braid, one after another with both his deft hands as if each was as easy as a caress, making them stay with merely a touch of two fingers at the end, until all her hair lay in a silky cascade of them, catching the light and glimmering and swaying like a rich drapery when he made her move her head. Some of them he gathered and looped and tied up with the ribbons which matched her dress, blue edged with gold. But most of them he left hanging to her bare back and shoulders. He surveyed his work with just a whisper of a smile when he was done, then turned and left without waiting for the lady's nod, and she sat as if under a spell and watched his thin back as he walked away. Then she tossed her head at his lack of courtesy. But the swinging of her hair pleased her.

She had him back to dress her hair the next day, and the next, and many days thereafter. And, so that they would not have to be always bathing him, her tiring-women found him a room within the

manor house doors, and a pallet and clean blankets, and a change of clothing, plain coarse clothing, such a servants wore. They trimmed the heavy hair that shadowed his eyes, also, but he looked no less the oddling with his thin, thin face and his calm burning glance and his mouth that seemed scarcely ever to move. He did as he was bid, whether by Wald or the lady or some kitchen maid, and every day he plaited Lady Aelynn's hair differently. One day he shaped it all into a bright crown of braids atop her head. On other days he would plait it close to her head so that the tendrils caressed her neck, or in a haughty crest studded with jewels, or in a single soft feathered braid at one side. He always left her tower chamber at once, never looking at the lady to see if he had pleased her, as if he knew that she would always be pleased.

Always, she was.

Things happened. The tiring-woman who had taken smallpox died of it, and Lady Aelynn did not care – not for the sake of her cherished hair and most certainly not for the sake of the woman herself. Lord Robley went away on a journey to discipline a debtor vassal, and Lady Aelynn did not care except to be glad, for there was a sure sense growing in her of what she would do.

When even her very tresses were enthralled by the touch of this oddling boy, longing to embrace him, could she be otherwise?

When next he had plaited her mane of honey-colored hair and turned to leave her without a glance, she caught him by one thin arm. His eyes met hers with a steady, gathered look. She stood – she was taller than he, and larger, though she was as slender as any maiden. It did not matter. She took him by one thin hand and led him to her bed, and there he did as he was bid.

Nor did he disappoint her. His touch – she had never been touched so softly, so gently, so deftly, with such power. Nor was he lacking in manhood, for all that he was as thin and hairless as a boy. And his lips, after all, knew how to move, and his tongue. But it was the touch of his thin hands that she hungered for, the gentle, tender, potent touch that thrilled her almost as if – she were loved . . .

He smiled at her afterward, slightly, softly, a whisper of a smile in the muted half-light of her curtained bed, and his lips moved.

"You are swine," he said, "all of you nobles."

And he got up, put on his plain, coarse clothing and left her without a backward glance.

It terrified Lady Aelynn that he was not truly a mute. Terrified her even more than what he had said, though she burned with mortified wrath whenever she thought of the latter. He, of all people, a mute, to speak such words to her and leave her helpless to avenge herself . . . Perhaps for that reason he would not betray her. She had thought it would be safe to take a mute as her lover . . . Perhaps he would not betray her.

In fact, it was not he who betrayed her to her lord, but Wald.

Her tiring-women suspected, perhaps because she had sent them on such a long errand. She had not thought they would suspect – who would think that such a wisp of a beardless boy could be a bedfellow? But perhaps they also had seen the wild glow deep in his gray-green eyes. They whispered among themselves, and with the kitchen maids, and the bold kitchen maid giggled with the grooms, and Wald heard.

Even though the boy who plaited manes did it all, Wald considered the constant plaiting and adorning of manes and tails a great bother. The whole fussy business offended him, he had decided, and he had long since forgotten the few words of praise it had garnered from the lord at first. Moreover, he disliked the boy so vehemently that he was not thinking clearly. It seemed to him that he could be rid of the boy and the wretched onus of braids and rosettes all in one stroke. The day the lord returned from his journey, Wald hurried to him, begged private audience, bowed low and made his humble report.

Lord Robley heard him in icy silence, for he knew pettiness when he saw it; it had served him often in the past, and he would punish it if it misled him. He summoned his wife to question her. But the Lady Aelynn's hair hung lank, and her guilt and shame could be seen plainly in her face from the moment she came before him.

Lord Robley's roar could be heard even to the stables.

He strode over to her where she lay crumpled and weeping on his chamber floor, lifted her head by its honey-gold hair and slashed her across the face with his sword. Then he left her, screaming and stinging her wound with fresh tears, and he strode to the stable with his bloody sword still drawn, Wald fleeing before him all the way; when the lord burst in all the grooms were scattered but one. The boy Wald had accused stood plaiting the white palfrey's mane.

Lord Robley hacked the palfrey's head from its braid-bedecked neck with his sword, and the boy who plaited manes stood by with something smoldering deep in his unblinking gray-green eyes, stood calmly waiting. If he had screamed and turned to flee, Lord Robley would with great satisfaction have given him a coward's death from the back. But it unnerved the lord that the boy awaited his pleasure with such mute – what? Defiance? There was no servant's boy in this one, no falling to the soiled straw, no groveling. If he had groveled he could have been kicked, stabbed, killed out of hand also . . . But this silent, watchful waiting, like the alertness of a wild thing – on the hunt or being hunted? It gave Lord Robley pause, like the pause of the wolf before the standing stag or the pause of the huntsman before the thicketed boar. He held the boy at the point of his sword – though no such holding was necessary, for the prisoner had not moved even to tremble – and roared for his men-at-arms to come take the boy to the dungeon.

There the nameless stranger stayed without water or food, and aside from starving him Lord Robley could not decide what to do with him.

At first the boy who plaited manes paced in his prison restlessly – he had that freedom, for he was so thin and small that the shackles were too large to hold him. Later he lay in a scant bed of short straw and stared narrow-eyed at the darkness. And yet later, seeing the thin cascades of moonlight flow down through the high, iron-barred window and puddle in moon-glades on the stone floor, he got up and began to plait the moonbeams.

They were far finer than any horsehair, moonbeams, finer even than the lady's honey-colored locks, and his eyes grew wide with wonder and pleasure as he felt them. He made them into braids as fine as silk threads, flowing together into a lacework as close as woven cloth, and when he had reached as high as he could, plaiting, he stroked as if combing a long mane with his fingers and pulled more moonlight down out of sky – for this stuff was not like any other stuff he had ever worked with; it slipped and slid worse than any hair, there seemed to be no beginning or end to it except the barriers that men put in its way. He stood plaiting the fine, thin plaits until he had raised a shimmering heap on the floor, and then he stepped back and allowed the moon to move on. His handiwork he laid carefully aside in a corner.

The boy who plaited moonbeams did not sleep, but sat watching for the dawn, his eyes glowing greenly in the darkened cell. He saw the sky lighten beyond the high window and waited stolidly, as the wolf waits for the gathering of the pack, as a wildcat waits for the game to pass along the trail below the rock where it lies. Not until the day had neared its mid did the sun's rays thrust through the narrow spaces between the high bars, wheel their shafts down to where he could reach them. Then he got up and began to plait the sunlight.

Guards were about, or more alert in the daytime, and they gathered at the heavy door of his prison, peering in between the iron bars of its small window, gawking and quarreling with each other for turns. They watched his unwavering eyes, saw the slight smile come on his face as he worked, though his thin hands glowed red as if seen through fire. They saw the shining mound he raised on the floor, and whispered among themselves and did not know what to do, for none of them dared to touch it or him. One of them requested a captain to come look. And the captain summoned the steward, and the steward went to report to the lord. And from outside the cries began to sound that the sun was standing still.

After the boy had finished, he stood back and let the sun move on, then sat resting on his filthy straw. Within minutes the dungeon door burst open and Lord Robley himself strode in.

Lord Robley had grown weary of mutilating his wife, and he had not yet decided what to do with his other prisoner. Annoyed by the reports from the prison, he expected that an idea would come to him when he saw the boy. He entered with drawn sword. But all thoughts of the thin young body before him were sent whirling away from his mind by what he saw laid out on the stone floor at his feet.

A mantle, a kingly cloak – but no king had ever owned such a cloak. All shining, the outside of it silver and the inside gold – but no, to call it silver and gold was to insult it. More like water and fire, flow and flame, shimmering as if it moved, as if it were alive, and yet it had been made by hands; he could see the workmanship, so fine that every thread was worth a gasp of pleasure, the outside of it somehow braided and plaited to the lining, and all around the edge a fringe of threads like bright fur so fine that it wavered in the air like flame. Lord Robley had no thought but to settle the fiery gleaming thing on his shoulders, to wear that glory and be finer than any king. He seized it and flung it on –

And screamed as he had not yet made his wife scream, with the shriek of mortal agony. His whole hard body glowed as if it had been placed in a furnace. His face contorted, and he fell dead.

The boy who plaited sunbeams got up in a quiet, alert way and walked forward, as noiseless on his feet as a lynx. He reached down and took the cloak off the body of the lord, twirled it and placed it on his own shoulders, and it did not harm him. But in that cloak he seemed insubstantial, like something moving in moonlight and shadow, something nameless roaming in the night. He walked out of the open dungeon door, between the guards clustered there, past the lord's retinue and the steward, and they all shrank back from him, flattened themselves against the stone walls of the corridor so as not to come near him. No one dared take hold of him or try to stop him. He walked out through the courtyard, past the stable, and out the manor gates with the settled air of one whose business is done. The men-at-arms gathered atop the wall and watched him go.

Wald the master groom lived to old age sweating every night with terror, and died of a weakened heart in the midst of a nightmare. Nothing else but his own fear harmed him. The boy who plaited – mane of sun, mane of moon – was never seen again in that place, except that children sometimes told the tale of having glimpsed him in the wild heart of a storm, plaiting the long lashes of wind and rain.

The Castle

❧

George MacDonald

ON THE TOP OF a high cliff, forming part of the base of a great mountain, stood a lofty castle. When or how it was built, no man knew; nor could anyone pretend to understand its architecture. Everyone who looked upon it felt that it was lordly and noble; and where one part seemed not to agree with another, the wise and modest dared not to call them incongruous, but presumed that the whole might be constructed on some higher principle of architecture than they yet understood. What helped them to this conclusion was that no one had ever seen the whole of the edifice; that, even of the portion best known, some part or other was always wrapt in thick folds of mist from the mountain; and that, when the sun shone upon this mist, the parts of the building that appeared through the vaporous veil were strangely glorified in their indistinctness, so that they seemed to belong to some aerial abode in the land of the sunset; and the beholders could hardly tell whether they had ever seen them before, or whether they were now for the first time partially revealed.

Nor, although it was inhabited, could certain information be procured as to its internal construction. Those who dwelt in it often discovered rooms they had never entered before; yea, once or twice whole suites of apartments, of which only dim legends had been handed down from former times. Some of them expected to find, one day, secret places, filled with treasures of wondrous jewels, amongst which they hoped to light upon Solomon's ring, which had for ages disappeared from the earth, but which had controlled the spirits, and the possession of which made a man simply what a man should be, the king of the world. Now and then, a narrow, winding stair, hitherto untrodden, would bring them forth on a new turret, whence new prospects of the circumjacent country were spread out before them. How many more of these there might be, or how much loftier, no one could tell.

Nor could the foundations of the castle in the rock on which it was built be determined with the smallest approach to precision. Those of the family who had given themselves to exploring in that direction found such a labyrinth of vaults and passages, and endless successions of down-going stairs, out of one underground space into a yet lower, that they came to the conclusion that at least the whole mountain was perforated and honeycombed in this fashion. They had a dim consciousness, too, of the presence, in those awful regions, of beings whom they could not comprehend. Once, they came upon the brink of a great black gulf, in which the eye could see nothing but darkness: they recoiled in horror; for the conviction flashed upon them that that gulf went down into the very central spaces of the earth, of which they had hitherto been wandering only in the upper crust; nay, that the seething blackness before them had relations mysterious, and beyond human comprehension, with the far-off voids of space, into which the stars dare not enter.

At the foot of the cliff whereon the castle stood lay a deep lake, inaccessible save by a few avenues, being surrounded on all sides with precipices, which made the water look very black, although it was as pure as the night sky. From a door in the castle, which was not to be otherwise entered, a broad flight of steps, cut in the rock, went down to the lake, and disappeared below its surface. Some thought the steps went to the very bottom of the water.

Now in this castle there dwelt a large family of brothers and sisters. They had never seen their father or mother. The younger had been educated by the elder, and these by an unseen care and ministration, about the sources of which they had, somehow or other, troubled themselves very little, for what people are accustomed to they regard as coming from nobody; as if help and progress and joy and love were the natural crops of Chaos or old Night. But Tradition said that one

day – it was utterly uncertain *when* – their father would come, and leave them no more; for he was still alive, though where he lived nobody knew. In the meantime all the rest had to obey their eldest brother, and listen to his counsels.

But almost all the family was very fond of liberty, as they called it; and liked to run up and down, hither and thither, roving about, with neither law nor order, just as they pleased. So they could not endure their brother's tyranny, as they called it. At one time they said that he was only one of themselves, and therefore they would not obey him; at another that he was not like them, and could not understand them, and *therefore* they would not obey him. Yet, sometimes, when he came and looked them full in the face, they were terrified, and dared not disobey, for he was stately, and stern and strong. Not one of them loved him heartily, except the eldest sister, who was very beautiful and silent, and whose eyes shone as if light lay somewhere deep behind them. Even she, although she loved him, thought him very hard sometimes; for when he had once said a thing plainly, he could not be persuaded to think it over again. So even she forgot him sometimes, and went her own ways, and enjoyed herself without him.

Most of them regarded him as a sort of watchman, whose business it was to keep them in order; and so they were indignant and disliked him. Yet they all had a secret feeling that they ought to be subject to him; and, after any particular act of disregard, none of them could think, with any peace, of the old story about the return of their father to his house. But indeed they never thought much about it, or about their father at all; for how could those who cared so little for their brother, whom they saw every day, care for their father whom they had never seen?

One chief cause of complaint against him was that he interfered with their favourite studies and pursuits; whereas he only sought to make them give up trifling with earnest things, and seek for truth, and not for amusement, from the many wonders around them. He did not want them to turn to other studies, or to eschew pleasures; but, in those studies, to seek the highest things most, and other things in proportion to their true worth and nobleness. This could not fail to be distasteful to those who did not care for what was higher than they. And so matters went on for a time. They thought they could do better without their brother; and their brother knew they could not do at all without him, and tried to fulfil the charge committed into his hands.

At length, one day, for the thought seemed to strike them simultaneously, they conferred together about giving a great entertainment in their grandest rooms to any of their neighbours who chose to come, or indeed to any inhabitants of the earth or air who would visit them. They were too proud to reflect that some company might defile even the dwellers in what was undoubtedly the finest palace on the face of the earth. But what made the thing worse was that the old tradition said that these rooms were to be kept entirely for the use of the owner of the castle. And, indeed, whenever they entered them, such was the effect of their loftiness and grandeur upon their minds that they always thought of the old story, and could not help believing it. Nor would the brother permit them to forget it now; but, appearing suddenly amongst them, when they had no expectation of being interrupted by him, he rebuked them, both for the indiscriminate nature of their invitation, and for the intention of introducing anyone, not to speak of some who would doubtless make their appearance on the evening in question, into the rooms kept sacred for the use of the unknown father.

But by this time their talk with each other had so excited their expectations of enjoyment, which had previously been strong enough, that anger sprung up within them at the thought of being deprived of their hopes, and they looked each other in the eyes; and the look said: "We are many, and he is one – let us get rid of him, for he is always finding fault, and thwarting us in the most innocent pleasures; – as if we would wish to do anything wrong!" So, without a word spoken, they rushed upon him; and although he was stronger than any of them, and struggled hard at first, yet they overcame him at last. Indeed some of them thought he yielded to their violence long before they had the mastery of him; and this very submission terrified the more tender-hearted among them. However, they bound him, carried him down many stairs, and, having remembered an iron staple in the wall of a certain vault, with a thick rusty chain attached to it, they bore him thither, and made the chain fast around him. There they left him, shutting the great gnarring brazen door of the vault as they departed for the upper regions of the castle.

Now all was in a tumult of preparation. Everyone was talking of the coming festivity; but no one spoke of the deed they had done. A sudden paleness overspread the face, now of one, and now of another; but it passed away, and no one took any notice of it; they only plied the task of the moment the more energetically. Messengers were sent far and near, not to individuals or families, but publishing in all places of concourse a general invitation to any who chose to come on a certain day, and partake for certain succeeding days, of the hospitality of the dwellers in the castle. Many were the preparations immediately begun for complying with the invitation. But the noblest of their neighbours refused to appear; not from pride, but because of the unsuitableness and carelessness of such a mode. With some of them it was an old condition in the tenure of their estates, that they should go to no one's dwelling except visited in person, and expressly solicited. Others, knowing what sorts of persons would be there, and that, from a certain physical antipathy, they could scarcely breathe in their company, made up their minds at once not to go. Yet multitudes, many of them beautiful and innocent as well as gay, resolved to appear.

Meanwhile the great rooms of the castle were got in readiness – that is, they proceeded to deface them with decorations; for there was a solemnity and stateliness about them in their ordinary condition which was at once felt to be unsuitable for the lighthearted company so soon to move about in them with the self-same carelessness with which men walk abroad within the great heavens and hills and clouds. One day, while the workmen were busy, the eldest sister, of whom I have already spoken, happened to enter; she knew not why. Suddenly the great idea of the mighty halls dawned upon her, and filled her soul. The so-called decorations vanished from her view, and she felt as if she stood in her father's presence. She was at once elevated and humbled. As suddenly the idea faded and fled, and she beheld but the gaudy festoons and draperies and paintings which disfigured the grandeur. She wept and sped away.

Now it was too late to interfere, and things must take their course. She would have been but a Cassandra-prophetess to those who saw but the pleasure before them. She had not been present when her brother was imprisoned; and indeed for some days had been so wrapt in her own business that she had taken but little heed of anything that was going on. But they all expected her to show herself when the company was gathered; and they had applied to her for advice at various times during their operations.

At length the expected hour arrived, and the company began to assemble. It was a warm summer evening. The dark lake reflected the rose-coloured clouds in the west, and through the flush rowed many gaily-painted boats, with various coloured flags, towards the massy rock on which the castle stood. The trees and flowers seemed already asleep, and breathing forth their sweet dream-breath. Laughter and low voices rose from the breast of the lake to the ears of the youths and maidens looking forth expectant from the lofty windows. They went down to the broad platform at the top of the stairs in front of the door to receive their visitors.

By degrees the festivities of the evening commenced. The same smiles flew forth both at eyes and lips, darting like beams through the gathering crowd. Music, from unseen sources, now rolled in billows, now crept in ripples through the sea of air that filled the lofty rooms. And in the dancing halls, when hand took hand, and form and motion were moulded and swayed by the indwelling music, it governed not these alone, but, as the ruling spirit of the place, every new burst of music for a new dance, swept before it a new and accordant odour, and dyed the flames that glowed in the lofty lamps with a new and accordant stain. The floors bent beneath the feet of the time-keeping dancers. But twice in the evening some of the inmates started, and the pallor occasionally common to the household overspread their faces, for they felt underneath them a counter-motion to the dance, as if the floor rose slightly to answer their feet.

And all the time their brother lay below in the dungeon, like John the Baptist in the castle of Herod, when the lords and captains sat around, and the daughter of Herodias danced before them. Outside, all around the castle, brooded the dark night unheeded; for the clouds had come up from all sides, and were crowding together overhead. In the unfrequent pauses of the music, they might have heard, now and then, the gusty rush of a lonely wind, coming and going no one could know whence or whither, born and dying unexpected and unregarded.

But when the festivities were at their height, when the external and passing confidence which is produced between superficial natures by a common pleasure was at the full, a sudden crash of thunder quelled the music, as the thunder quells the noise of the uplifted sea. The windows were driven in, and torrents of rain, carried in the folds of a rushing wind, poured into the halls. The lights were swept away; and the great rooms, now dark within, were darkened yet more by the dazzling shoots of flame from the vault of blackness overhead. Those that ventured to look out of the windows saw, in the blue brilliancy of the quick-following jets of lightning, the lake at the foot of the rock, ordinarily so still and so dark, lighted up, not on the surface only, but down to half its depth; so that, as it tossed in the wind, like a tortured set of writhing flames or incandescent half-molten serpents of brass, they could not tell whether a strong phosphorescence did not issue from the transparent body of the waters, as if earth and sky lightened together, one consenting source of flaming utterance.

Sad was the condition of the late plastic mass of living form that had flowed into shape at the will and law of the music. Broken into individuals, the common transfusing spirit withdrawn, they stood drenched, cold, and benumbed, with clinging garments; light, order, harmony, purpose departed, and chaos restored; the issuings of life turned back on their sources, chilly and dead. And in every heart reigned that falsest of despairing convictions, that this was the only reality, and that was but a dream.

The eldest sister stood with clasped hands and down-bent head, shivering and speechless, as if waiting for something to follow. Nor did she wait long. A terrible flash and thunderpeal made the castle rock; and in the pausing silence that followed, her quick sense heard the rattling of a chain far off, deep down; and soon the sound of heavy footsteps, accompanied with the clanking of iron, reached her ear. She felt that her brother was at hand. Even in the darkness, and amidst the bellowing of another deep-bosomed cloud-monster, she knew that he had entered the room.

A moment after, a continuous pulsation of angry blue light began, which, lasting for some moments, revealed him standing amidst them, gaunt, haggard, and motionless; his hair and beard untrimmed, his face ghastly, his eyes large and hollow. The light seemed to gather around him as a centre. Indeed, some believed that it throbbed and radiated from his person, and not from the stormy heavens above them. The lightning had rent the wall of his prison, and released the iron staple of his chain, which he had wound about him like a girdle. In his hand he carried an iron fetter-bar, which he had found on the floor of the vault. More terrified at his aspect than at all the violence of the storm, the visitors, with many a shriek and cry, rushed out into the tempestuous night. By degrees, the storm died away. Its last flash revealed the forms of the brothers and sisters lying prostrate, with their faces on the floor, and that fearful shape standing motionless amidst them still.

Morning dawned, and there they lay, and there he stood. But at a word from him they arose and went about their various duties, though listlessly enough. The eldest sister was the last to rise; and when she did it was only by a terrible effort that she was able to reach her room, where she fell again on the floor. There she remained lying for days. The brother caused the doors of the great suite of rooms to be closed, leaving them just as they were, with all the childish adornment scattered about, and the rain still falling in through the shattered windows. "Thus let them lie," said he, "till the rain and frost have cleansed them of paint and drapery: no storm can hurt the pillars and arches of these halls."

The hours of this day went heavily. The storm was gone, but the rain was left; the passion had departed, but the tears remained behind. Dull and dark, the low misty clouds brooded over the castle and the lake, and shut out all the neighbourhood. Even if they had climbed to the loftiest known turret, they would have found it swathed in a garment of clinging vapour, affording no refreshment to the eye, and no hope to the heart. There was one lofty tower that rose sheer a hundred feet above the rest, and from which the fog could have been seen lying in a grey mass beneath; but that tower they had not yet discovered, nor another close beside it, the top of which was never seen, nor could be, for the highest clouds of heaven clustered continually around it. The rain fell continuously, though not heavily, without; and within, too, there were clouds from which dropped the tears which are the rain of the spirit. All the good of life seemed for the time departed, and their souls lived but as leafless trees that had forgotten the joy of the summer, and whom no wind prophetic of spring had yet visited. They moved about mechanically, and had not strength enough left to wish to die.

The next day the clouds were higher, and a little wind blew through such loopholes in the turrets as the false improvements of the inmates had not yet filled with glass, shutting out, as the storm, so the serene visitings of the heavens. Throughout the day, the brother took various opportunities of addressing a gentle command, now to one and now to another of his family. It was obeyed in silence. The wind blew fresher through the loopholes and the shattered windows of the great rooms, and found its way, by unknown passages, to faces and eyes hot with weeping. It cooled and blessed them. When the sun arose the next day, it was in a clear sky.

By degrees, everything fell into the regularity of subordination. With the subordination came increase of freedom. The steps of the more youthful of the family were heard on the stairs and in the corridors more light and quick than ever before. Their brother had lost the terrors of aspect produced by his confinement, and his commands were issued more gently, and oftener with a smile, than in all their previous history. By degrees his presence was universally felt through the house. It was no surprise to anyone at his studies to see him by his side when he lifted up his eyes, though he had not before known that he was in the room. And, although some dread still remained, it was rapidly vanishing before the advances of a firm friendship. Without immediately ordering their labours, he always influenced them, and often altered their direction and objects.

The change soon evident in the household was remarkable. A simpler, nobler expression was visible on all the countenances. The voices of the men were deeper, and yet seemed by their very depth more feminine than before; while the voices of the women were softer and sweeter, and at the same time more full and decided. Now the eyes had often an expression as if their sight was absorbed in the gaze of the inward eyes; and when the eyes of two met, there passed between those eyes the utterance of a conviction that both meant the same thing. But the change was, of course, to be seen more clearly, though not more evidently, in individuals.

One of the brothers, for instance, was very fond of astronomy. He had his observatory on a lofty tower, which stood pretty clear of the others, towards the north and east. But, hitherto, his astronomy, as he had called it, had been more of the character of astrology. Often, too, he might have been seen directing a heaven-searching telescope to catch the rapid transit of a fiery shooting star, belonging altogether to the earthly atmosphere, and not to the serene heavens. He had to learn that the signs of the air are not the signs of the skies. Nay, once, his brother surprised him in the act of examining through his longest tube a patch of burning heath upon a distant hill. But now he was diligent from morning till night in the study of the laws of the truth that have to do with stars; and when the curtain of the sunlight was about to rise from before the heavenly worlds which it had hidden all day long, he might be seen preparing his instruments with that solemn countenance with which it becometh one to look into the mysterious harmonies of Nature. Now he learned what law and order and truth are, what consent and harmony mean; how the individual may find his own end in a higher end, where law and freedom mean the same thing, and the purest certainty exists without the slightest constraint. Thus he stood on the earth, and looked to the heavens.

Another, who had been much given to searching out the hollow places and recesses in the foundations of the castle, and who was often to be found with compass and ruler working away at a chart of the same which he had been in process of constructing, now came to the conclusion that only by ascending the upper regions of his abode could he become capable of understanding what lay beneath; and that, in all probability, one clear prospect, from the top of the highest attainable turret, over the castle as it lay below, would reveal more of the idea of its internal construction, than a year spent in wandering through its subterranean vaults. But the fact was that the desire to ascend wakening within him had made him forget what was beneath; and, having laid aside his chart for a time at least, he was now to be met in every quarter of the upper parts, searching and striving upward, now in one direction, now in another; and seeking, as he went, the best outlooks into the clear air of outer realities.

And they began to discover that they were all meditating different aspects of the same thing; and they brought together their various discoveries, and recognized the likeness between them; and the one thing often explained the other, and combining with it helped to a third. They grew in consequence more and more friendly and loving; so that, every now and then, one turned to another and said, as in surprise, "Why, you are my brother!" "Why, you are my sister!" And yet they had always known it.

The change reached to all. One, who lived on the air of sweet sounds, and who was almost always to be found seated by her harp or some other instrument, had, till the late storm, been generally merry and playful, though sometimes sad. But for a long time after that she was often found weeping, and playing little simple airs which she had heard in childhood – backward longings, followed by fresh tears. Before long, however, a new element manifested itself in her music. It became yet more wild, and sometimes retained all its sadness, but it was mingled with anticipation and hope. The past and the future merged in one; and while memory yet brought the raincloud, expectation threw the rainbow across its bosom – and all was uttered in her music, which rose and swelled, now to defiance, now to victory; then died in a torrent of weeping.

As to the eldest sister, it was many days before she recovered from the shock. At length, one day, her brother came to her, took her by the hand, led her to an open window, and told her to seat herself by it, and look out. She did so; but at first saw nothing more than an unsympathizing blaze of sunlight. But as she looked the horizon widened out, and the dome of the sky ascended, till the grandeur seized upon her soul, and she fell on her knees and wept. Now the heavens seemed to bend lovingly over her, and to stretch out wide cloud-arms to embrace her; the earth lay like the bosom of an infinite love beneath her, and the wind kissed her cheek with an odour of roses. She sprang to her feet, and turned, in an agony of hope, expecting to behold the face of the father, but there stood only her brother, looking calmly though lovingly on her emotion. She turned again to the window. On the hilltops rested the sky: Heaven and Earth were one; and the prophecy awoke in her soul that from betwixt them would the steps of the father approach.

Hitherto she had seen but Beauty; now she beheld truth. Often had she looked on such clouds as these, and loved the strange ethereal curves into which the winds moulded them; and had smiled as her little pet sister told her what curious animals she saw in them, and tried to point them out to her. Now they were as troops of angels, jubilant over her new birth, for they sang, in her soul, of beauty, and truth, and love. She looked down, and her little sister knelt beside her.

She was a curious child, with black, glittering eyes, and dark hair; at the mercy of every wandering wind; a frolicsome, daring girl, who laughed more than she smiled. She was generally in attendance on her sister, and was always finding and bringing her strange things. She never pulled a primrose, but she knew the haunts of all the orchis tribe, and brought from them bees and butterflies innumerable, as offerings to her sister. Curious moths and glowworms were her greatest delight; and she loved the stars, because they were like the glowworms. But the change had affected her too; for her sister saw that her eyes had lost their glittering look, and had become more liquid and transparent. And from that time she often observed that her gaiety was more gentle, her smile more frequent, her laugh less bell-like; and, although she was as wild as ever, there was more elegance in her motions, and more music in her voice. And she clung to her sister with far greater fondness than before.

The land reposed in the embrace of the warm summer days. The clouds of heaven nestled around the towers of the castle; and the hearts of its inmates became conscious of a warm atmosphere – of a presence of love. They began to feel like the children of a household when the mother is at home. Their faces and forms grew daily more and more beautiful, till they wondered as they gazed on each other. As they walked in the gardens of the castle, or in the country around, they were often visited, especially the eldest sister, by sounds that no one heard but themselves, issuing from woods and waters; and by forms of love that lightened out of flowers, and grass, and great rocks.

Now and then the young children would come in with a slow, stately step, and, with great eyes that looked as if they would devour all the creation, say that they had met the father amongst the trees, and that he had kissed them; "And," added one of them once, "I grew so big!" But when others went out to look, they could see no one. And some said it must have been the brother, who grew more and more beautiful, and loving, and reverend, and who had lost all traces of hardness, so that they wondered they could ever have thought him stern and harsh. But the eldest sister held her peace, and looked up, and her eyes filled with tears. "Who can tell," thought she, "but the little children know more about it than we?"

Often, at sunrise, might be heard their hymn of praise to their unseen father, whom they felt to be near, though they saw him not. Some words thereof once reached my ear through the folds of the music in which they floated, as in an upward snowstorm of sweet sounds. And these are some of the words I heard – but there was much I seemed to hear which I could not understand, and some things which I understood but cannot utter again.

"We thank thee that we have a father, and not a maker; that thou hast begotten us, and not moulded us as images of clay; that we have come forth of thy heart, and have not been fashioned by thy hands. It *must* be so. Only the heart of a father is able to create. We rejoice in it, and bless thee that we know it. We thank thee for thyself. Be what thou art – our root and life, our beginning and end, our all in all. Come home to us. Thou livest; therefore we live. In thy light we see. Thou art – that is all our song."

Thus they worship, and love, and wait. Their hope and expectation grow ever stronger and brighter, that one day, ere long, the Father will show himself amongst them, and thenceforth dwell in his own house for evermore. What was once but an old legend has become the one desire of their hearts.

And the loftiest hope is the surest of being fulfilled.

Cinderella or
the Little Glass Slipper

❧

Charles Perrault

ONCE THERE WAS A gentleman who married, for his second wife, the proudest and most haughty woman that was ever seen. She had, by a former husband, two daughters of her own humour, who were, indeed, exactly like her in all things. He had likewise, by another wife, a young daughter, but of unparalleled goodness and sweetness of temper, which she took from her mother, who was the best creature in the world.

No sooner were the ceremonies of the wedding over but the stepmother began to show herself in her true colours. She could not bear the good qualities of this pretty girl, and the less because they made her own daughters appear the more odious. She employed her in the meanest work of the house: she scoured the dishes, tables, etc., and rubbed madam's chamber, and those of the misses, her daughters; she lay up in a sorry garret, upon a wretched straw bed, while her sisters lay in fine rooms, with floors all inlaid, upon beds of the very newest fashion, and where they had looking-glasses so large that they might see themselves at their full length from head to foot.

The poor girl bore all patiently, and dared not tell her father, who would have rattled her off; for his wife governed him entirely. When she had done her work, she used to go into the chimney-corner, and sit down among cinders and ashes, which made her commonly be called

Cinderwench; but the youngest, who was not so rude and uncivil as the eldest, called her Cinderella. However, Cinderella, notwithstanding her mean apparel, was a hundred times handsomer than her sisters, though they were always dressed very richly.

It happened that the King's son gave a ball, and invited all persons of fashion to it. Our young misses were also invited, for they cut a very grand figure among the quality. They were mightily delighted at this invitation, and wonderfully busy in choosing out such gowns, petticoats, and head-clothes as might become them. This was a new trouble to Cinderella; for it was she who ironed her sister's linen, and plaited their ruffles; they talked all day long of nothing but how they should be dressed.

"For my part," said the eldest, "I will wear my red velvet suit with French trimming."

"And I," said the youngest, "shall have my usual petticoat; but then, to make amends for that, I will put on my gold-flowered manteau, and my diamond stomacher, which is far from being the most ordinary one in the world."

They sent for the best tire-woman they could get to make up their head-dresses and adjust their double pinners, and they had their red brushes and patches from Mademoiselle de la Poche.

Cinderella was likewise called up to them to be consulted in all these matters, for she had excellent notions, and advised them always for the best, nay, and offered her services to dress their heads, which they were very willing she should do. As she was doing this, they said to her:

"Cinderella, would you not be glad to go to the ball?"

"Alas!" said she, "you only jeer me; it is not for such as I am to go thither."

"Thou art in the right of it," replied they; "it would make the people laugh to see a Cinderwench at a ball."

Anyone but Cinderella would have dressed their heads awry, but she was very good, and dressed them perfectly well. They were almost two days without eating, so much they were transported with joy. They broke above a dozen of laces in trying to be laced up close, that they might have a fine slender shape, and they were continually at their looking-glass. At last the happy day came; they went to Court, and Cinderella followed them with her eyes as long as she could, and when she had lost sight of them, she fell a-crying.

Her godmother, who saw her all in tears, asked her what was the matter.

"I wish I could – I wish I could –" She was not able to speak the rest, being interrupted by her tears and sobbing.

This godmother of hers, who was a fairy, said to her, "Thou wishest thou couldst go to the ball; is it not so?"

"Y – es," cried Cinderella, with a great sigh.

"Well," said her godmother, "be but a good girl, and I will contrive that thou shalt go." Then she took her into her chamber, and said to her, "Run into the garden, and bring me a pumpkin."

Cinderella went immediately to gather the finest she could get, and brought it to her godmother, not being able to imagine how this pumpkin could make her go to the ball. Her godmother scooped out all the inside of it, having left nothing but the rind; which done, she struck it with her wand, and the pumpkin was instantly turned into a fine coach, gilded all over with gold.

She then went to look into her mouse-trap, where she found six mice, all alive, and ordered Cinderella to lift up a little the trap-door, when, giving each mouse, as it went out, a little tap with her wand, the mouse was that moment turned into a fine horse, which altogether made a very fine set of six horses of a beautiful mouse-coloured dapple-grey.

Being at a loss for a coachman, "I will go and see," says Cinderella, "if there is never a rat in the rat-trap – we may make a coachman of him."

"Thou art in the right," replied her godmother; "go and look."

Cinderella brought the trap to her, and in it there were three huge rats. The fairy made choice of one of the three which had the largest beard, and, having touched him with her wand, he was turned into a fat, jolly coachman, who had the smartest whiskers eyes ever beheld. After that, she said to her:

"Go again into the garden, and you will find six lizards behind the watering-pot; bring them to me."

She had no sooner done so but her godmother turned them into six footmen, who skipped up immediately behind the coach, with their liveries all bedaubed with gold and silver, and clung as close behind each other as if they had done nothing else their whole lives. The Fairy then said to Cinderella:

"Well, you see here an equipage fit to go to the ball with; are you not pleased with it?"

"Oh! Yes," cried she; "but must I go thither as I am, in these nasty rags?"

Her godmother only just touched her with her wand, and, at the same instant, her clothes were turned into cloth of gold and silver, all beset with jewels. This done, she gave her a pair of glass slippers, the prettiest in the whole world. Being thus decked out, she got up into her coach; but her godmother, above all things, commanded her not to stay till after midnight, telling her, at the same time, that if she stayed one moment longer, the coach would be a pumpkin again, her horses mice, her coachman a rat, her footmen lizards, and her clothes become just as they were before.

She promised her godmother she would not fail of leaving the ball before midnight; and then away she drives, scarce able to contain herself for joy. The King's son, who was told that a great princess, whom nobody knew, was come, ran out to receive her; he gave her his hand as she alighted out of the coach, and led her into the hall, among all the company. There was immediately a profound silence, they left off dancing, and the violins ceased to play, so attentive was everyone to contemplate the singular beauties of the unknown newcomer. Nothing was then heard but a confused noise of:

"Ha! How handsome she is! Ha! How handsome she is!"

The King himself, old as he was, could not help watching her, and telling the Queen softly that it was a long time since he had seen so beautiful and lovely a creature.

All the ladies were busied in considering her clothes and head-dress, that they might have some made next day after the same pattern, provided they could meet with such fine materials and as able hands to make them.

The King's son conducted her to the most honourable seat, and afterwards took her out to dance with him; she danced so very gracefully that they all more and more admired her. A fine collation was served up, whereof the young prince ate not a morsel, so intently was he busied in gazing on her.

She went and sat down by her sisters, showing them a thousand civilities, giving them part of the oranges and citrons which the Prince had presented her with, which very much surprised them, for they did not know her. While Cinderella was thus amusing her sisters, she heard the clock strike eleven and three-quarters, whereupon she immediately made a courtesy to the company and hasted away as fast as she could.

Being got home, she ran to seek out her godmother, and, after having thanked her, she said she could not but heartily wish she might go next day to the ball, because the King's son had desired her.

As she was eagerly telling her godmother whatever had passed at the ball, her two sisters knocked at the door, which Cinderella ran and opened.

"How long you have stayed!" cried she, gaping, rubbing her eyes and stretching herself as if she had been just waked out of her sleep; she had not, however, any manner of inclination to sleep since they went from home.

"If thou hadst been at the ball," says one of her sisters, "thou wouldst not have been tired with it. There came thither the finest princess, the most beautiful ever was seen with mortal eyes; she showed us a thousand civilities, and gave us oranges and citrons."

Cinderella seemed very indifferent in the matter; indeed, she asked them the name of that princess; but they told her they did not know it, and that the King's son was very uneasy on her account and would give all the world to know who she was. At this Cinderella, smiling, replied:

"She must, then, be very beautiful indeed; how happy you have been! Could not I see her? Ah! Dear Miss Charlotte, do lend me your yellow suit of clothes which you wear every day."

"Ay, to be sure!" cried Miss Charlotte; "lend my clothes to such a dirty Cinderwench as thou art! I should be a fool."

Cinderella, indeed, expected well such answer, and was very glad of the refusal; for she would have been sadly put to it if her sister had lent her what she asked for jestingly.

The next day the two sisters were at the ball, and so was Cinderella, but dressed more magnificently than before. The King's son was always by her, and never ceased his compliments and kind speeches to her; to whom all this was so far from being tiresome that she quite forgot what her godmother had recommended to her; so that she, at last, counted the clock striking twelve when she took it to be no more than eleven; she then rose up and fled, as nimble as a deer. The Prince followed, but could not overtake her. She left behind one of her glass slippers, which the Prince took up most carefully. She got home, but quite out of breath, and in her nasty old clothes, having nothing left her of all her finery but one of the little slippers, fellow to that she dropped. The guards at the palace gate were asked: If they had not seen a princess go out.

Who said: They had seen nobody go out but a young girl, very meanly dressed, and who had more the air of a poor country wench than a gentlewoman.

When the two sisters returned from the ball Cinderella asked them: If they had been well diverted, and if the fine lady had been there.

They told her: Yes, but that she hurried away immediately when it struck twelve, and with so much haste that she dropped one of her little glass slippers, the prettiest in the world, which the King's son had taken up; that he had done nothing but look at her all the time at the ball, and that most certainly he was very much in love with the beautiful person who owned the glass slipper.

What they said was very true; for a few days after the King's son caused it to be proclaimed, by sound of trumpet, that he would marry her whose foot this slipper would just fit. They whom he employed began to try it upon the princesses, then the duchesses and all the Court, but in vain; it was brought to the two sisters, who did all they possibly could to thrust their foot into the slipper, but they could not effect it. Cinderella, who saw all this, and knew her slipper, said to them, laughing:

"Let me see if it will not fit me."

Her sisters burst out a-laughing, and began to banter her. The gentleman who was sent to try the slipper looked earnestly at Cinderella, and, finding her very handsome, said: It was but just that she should try, and that he had orders to let everyone make trial.

He obliged Cinderella to sit down, and, putting the slipper to
her foot, he found it went on very easily, and fitted her as if it
had been made of wax. The astonishment her two sisters were in
was excessively great, but still abundantly greater when Cinderella
pulled out of her pocket the other slipper, and put it on her foot.
Thereupon, in came her godmother, who, having touched with her

wand Cinderella's clothes, made them richer and more magnificent than any of those she had before.

And now her two sisters found her to be that fine, beautiful lady whom they had seen at the ball. They threw themselves at her feet to beg pardon for all the ill-treatment they had made her undergo. Cinderella took them up, and, as she embraced them, cried: That she forgave them with all her heart, and desired them always to love her.

She was conducted to the young Prince, dressed as she was; he thought her more charming than ever, and, a few days after, married her. Cinderella, who was no less good than beautiful, gave her two sisters lodgings in the palace, and that very same day matched them with two great lords of the Court.

The Fortress Unvanquishable, Save for Sacnoth

∿

Lord Dunsany

IN A WOOD OLDER than record, a foster-brother of the hills, stood the village of Allanthurion; and there was peace between the people of that village and all the folk who walked in the dark ways of the wood, whether they were human or of the tribes of the beasts or of the race of the fairies and the elves and the little sacred spirits of trees and streams. Moreover, the village people had peace among themselves and between them and their lord, Lorendiac. In front of the village was a wide and grassy space, and beyond this the great wood again, but at the back the trees came right up to the houses, which, with their great beams and wooden framework and thatched roofs, green with moss, seemed almost to be a part of the forest.

Now, in the time I tell of there was trouble in Allathurion, for of an evening fell dreams were wont to come slipping throught the tree trunks and into the peaceful village; and they assumed dominion of men's minds and led them in watches of the night through the cindery plains of Hell. Then the magician of that village made spells against those fell dreams; yet still the dreams came flitting through the trees as soon as the dark had fallen, and led men's minds by night into terrible places and caused them to praise Satan openly with their lips.

And men grew afraid of sleep in Allathurion. And they grew worn and pale, some through the want of rest, and others from fear of the things they saw on the cindery plains of Hell.

Then the magician of the village went up into the tower of his house, and all night long those whom fear kept awake could see his window high up in the night glowing softly alone. The next day, when the twilight was far gone and night was gathering fast, the magician went away to the forest's edge, and uttered there the spell that he had made. And the spell was a compulsive, terrible thing, having a power over evil dreams and over spirits of ill; for it was a verse of forty lines in many languages, both living and dead, and had in it the word wherewith the people of the plains are wont to curse their camels, and the shout wherewith the whalers of the north lure the whales shoreward to be killed, and a word that causes elephants to trumpet; and every one of the forty lines closed with a rhyme for "wasp".

And still the dreams came flitting through the forest, and led men's souls into the plains of Hell. Then the magician knew that the dreams were from Gaznak. Therefore he gathered the people of the village, and told them that he had uttered his mightiest spell – a spell having power over all that were human or of the tribes of the beasts; and that since it had not availed the dreams must come from Gaznak, the greatest magician among the spaces of the stars. And he read to the people out of the book of Magicians, which tells the comings of the comet and foretells his coming again. And he told them how Gaznak rides upon the comet, and how he visits Earth once in every two hundred and thirty years, and makes for himself a vast, invincible fortress and sends out dreams to feed on the minds of men, and may never be vanquished but by the sword Sacnoth.

And a cold fear fell on the hearts of the villagers when they found that their magician had failed them.

Then spake Leothric, son of the Lord Lorendiac, and twenty years old was he: "Good Master, what of the sword Sacnoth?"

And the village magician answered: "Fair Lord, no such sword as yet is wrought, for it lies as yet in the hide of Tharagavverug, protecting his spine."

Then said Leothric: "Who is Tharagavverug, and where may he be encountered?"

And the magician of Allathurion answered: "He is the dragon-crocodile who haunts the Northern marshes and ravages the homesteads by their marge. And the hide of his back is of steel, and his under parts are of iron; but along the midst of his back, over his spine, there lies a narrow strip of unearthly steel. This strip of steel is Sacnoth, and it may be neither cleft nor molten, and there is nothing in the world that may avail to break it, nor even leave a scratch upon its surface. It is of the length of a good sword, and of the breadth thereof. Shouldst thou prevail against I Tharagavverug, his hide may be melted away from Sacnoth in a furnace; but there is only one thing that may sharpen Sacnoth's edge, and this is one of Tharagavverug's own steel eyes; and the other eye thou must fasten to Sacnoth's hilt, and it will watch for thee. But it is a hard task to vanquish Tharagavverug, for no sword can pierce his hide, his back cannot be broken, and he can neither burn nor drown. In one way only can Tharagavverug die, and that is by starving."

Then sorrow fell upon Leothric, but the magician spoke on:

"If a man drive Tharagavverug away from his food with a stick for three days, he will starve on the third day at sunset. And though he is not vulnerable, yet in one spot he may take hurt, for his nose is only of lead. A sword would merely lay bare the uncleavable bronze beneath, but if his nose be smitten constantly with a stick he will always recoil from the pain, and thus may Tharagavverug, to left and right, be driven away from his food."

Then Leothric said: "What is Tharagavverug's food?"

And the magician of Allathurion said: "His food is men."

But Leothric went straightway thence, and cut a great staff from a hazel tree, and slept early that evening. But the next morning, awaking from troubled dreams, he arose before the dawn, and, taking with him provisions for five days, set out through the forest northwards towards the marshes. For some hours be moved through the gloom of the forest, and when he emerged from it the sun was above the horizon, shining on pools of water in the waste land. Presently he saw the claw-marks of Tharagavverug deep in the soil, and the track of his tail between them like a furrow in a field. Then Leothric followed the tracks till he heard the bronze heart of Tharagavverug before him, booming like a bell.

And Tharagavverug, it being the hour when he took the first meal of the day, was moving towards a village with his heart tolling. And all the people of the village were come out to meet him, as it was their wont to do; for they abode not the suspense of awaiting Tharagavverug and of hearing him sniffing brazenly as he went from door to door, pondering slowly in his metal mind what habitant he should choose. And none dared to flee, for in the days when the villagers fled from Tharagavverug, he, having chosen his victim, would track him tirelessly, like a doom. Nothing availed them against Tharagavverug. Once they climbed the trees when he came, but Tharagavverug went up to one, arching his back and leaning over slightly, and rasped against the trunk until it fell.

And when Leothric came near, Tharagavverug saw him out of one of his small steel eyes and came towards him leisurely, and the echoes of his heart swirled up through his open mouth. And Leothric stepped sideways from his onset, and came between him and the village and smote him on the nose, and the blow of the stick made a dint in the soft lead. And Tharagavverug swung clumsily away, uttering one fearful cry like the sound of a great church bell that had become possessed of a soul that fluttered upward from the tombs at night – an evil soul, giving the bell a voice. Then he attacked Leothric, snarling, and again Leothric leapt aside, and smote him on the nose with his stick. Tharagavverug uttered like a bell howling. And whenever the dragon-crocodile attacked him, or turned, towards the village, Leothric smote him again.

So all day long Leothric drove the monster with a stick, and he drove him farther and farther from his prey, with his heart tolling angrily and his voice crying out for pain.

Towards evening Tharagavverug ceased to snap at Leothric, but ran before him to avoid the stick, for his nose was sore and shining; and in the gloaming the villagers came out and danced to cymbal and psaltery. When Tharagavverug heard the cymbal and psaltery, hunger and anger came upon him, and he felt as some lord might feel who was held by force from the banquet in his own castle and heard the creaking spit go round and round and the good meat crackling on it. And all that night he attacked Leothric fiercely, and ofttimes nearly caught him in the darkness; for his gleaming eyes of steel could see as well by night as by day.

And Leothric gave ground slowly till the dawn, when the light came they were near the village again; yet not so near to it as they had been when they encountered, for Leothric drove Tharagavverug farther in the day than Tharagavverug had forced him back in the night. Then Leothric drove him again with his stick till the hour came when it was the custom of the dragon-crocodile to find his man. One third of his man he would eat at the time he found him, and the rest at noon and evening. But when the hour came for finding his man a great fierceness came on Tharagavverug, and he grabbed rapidly at Leothric, but could not seize him, and for a long while neither of them would retire. But at last the pain of the stick on his leaden nose overcame the hunger of the dragon-crocodile, and he turned from it, howling. From that moment Tharagavverug weakened. All that day Leothric drove him with his stick, and at night both held their ground; and when the dawn of the third day was come the heart of Tharagavverug beat slower and fainter. It was as thought a tired man was ringing a bell. Once Tharagavverug nearly seized a frog, but Leothric snatched it away just in time.

Towards noon the dragon-crocodile lay still for a long while, and Leothric stood near him and leaned on his trusty stick. He was very tired and sleepless, but had more leisure now for eating his provisions. With Tharagavverug the end was coming fast, and in the afternoon his breath came hoarsely, rasping in his throat. It was as the sound of many huntsmen blowing blasts on horns, and towards evening his breath came faster but fainter, like the sound of a hunt going furious to the distance and dying away, and he made desperate rushes towards the village; but Leothric still leapt about him, battering his leaden nose. Scarce audible now at all was the sound of his heart: it was like a church bell tolling beyond hills for the death of some one unknown and far away. Then the sun set and flamed in the village windows, and a chill went over the world, and in some small garden a woman sang; and Tharagavverug lifted up his head and starved, and his life went from his invulnerable body, and Leothric lay down beside him and slept.

And later in the starlight the villagers came out and carried Leothric, sleeping, to the village, all praising him in whispers as they went. They laid him down upon a couch in a house, and danced outside in silence, without psaltery or cymbal. And the next day, rejoicing, to Allathurion they hauled the dragon-crocodile. And Leothric went with them, holding his battered staff; and a tall, broad man, who was smith of Allathurion, made a great furnace, and melted Tharagavverug away until only Sacnoth was left, gleaming among the ashes. Then he took one of the small eyes that had been chiselled out, and filed an edge on Sacnoth, and gradually the steel eye wore away facet by facet, but ere it was quite gone it had sharpened redoubtably Sacnoth. But the other eye they set in the butt of the hilt, and it gleamed there bluely.

And that night Leothric arose in the dark and took the sword, and went westwards to find Gaznak; and he went through the dark forest till the dawn, and all the morning and till the afternoon. But in the afternoon he came into the open and saw in the midst of The Land Where No Man Goeth the fortress of Gaznak, mountainous before him, little more than a mile away.

And Leothric saw that the land was marsh and desolate. And the fortress went up all white out of it, with many buttresses, and was broad below but narrowed highter up, and was full of gleaming windows with the light upon them. And near the top of it a few white clouds were floating, but above them some of its pinnacles reappeared. Then Leothric advanced into the marshes, and the eye of Tharagavverug looked out warily from the hilt of Sacnoth; for Tharagavverug had known the marshes well, and the sword nudged Leothric to the right or pulled him to the left away from the dangerous places, and so brought him safely to the fortress walls.

And in the wall stood doors like precipices of steel, all studded with boulders of iron, and above every window were terrible gargoyles of stone; and the name of the fortress shone on the wall, writ large in letters of brass: "The Fortress Unvanquishable, Save For Sacnoth."

Then Leothric drew and revealed Sacnoth, and all the gargoyles grinned, and the grin went flickering from face to face right up into the cloud-abiding gables.

And when Sacnoth was revealed and all the gargoyles grinned, it was like the moonlight emerging from a cloud to look for the first time upon a field of blood and passing swiftly over the wet faces of the slain that lie together in the horrible night. Then Leothric advanced towards a door, and it was mightier than the marble quarry, Sacremona, from which of old men cut enormous slabs to build the Abbey of the Holy

Tears. Day after day they wrenched out the very ribs of the hill until the Abbey was builded, and it was more beautiful than anything in stone. Then the priests blessed Sacremona, and it had rest, and no more stone was ever taken from it to build the houses of men. And the hill stood looking southwards lonely in the sunlight, defaced by that mighty scar. So vast was the door of steel. And the name of the door was The Porte Resonant, the Way of Egress for War.

Then Leothric smote upon the Porte Resonant with Sacnoth, and the echo of Sacnoth went ringing through the halls, and all the dragons in the fortress barked. And when the baying of the remotest dragon had faintly joined in the tumult, a window opened far up among the clouds below the twilit gables, and a woman screamed, and far away in Hell her father heard her and knew that her doom was come.

And Leothric went on smiting terribly with Sacnoth, and the grey steel of the Porte Resonant, the Way of Egress for War, that was tempered to resist the swords of the world, came away in ringing slices.

Then Leothric, holding Sacnoth in his hand, went in through the hole that he had hewn in the door, and came into the unlit, cavernous hall.

An elephant fled, trumpeting. And Leothric stood still, holding Sacnoth. When the sound of the feet of the elephant had died away in the remoter corridors, nothing more stirred, and the cavernous hall was still.

Presently the darkness of the distant halls became musical with the sound of bells, all coming nearer and nearer.

Still Leothric waited in the dark, and the bells rang louder and louder, echoing through the halls, and there appeared a procession of men on camels riding two by two from the interior of the fortress, and they were armed with scimitars of Assyrian make and were all clad with mail, and chain-mail hung from their helmets about their faces, and flapped as the camels moved. And they all halted before Leothric in the cavernous hall, and the camel bells clanged and stopped. And the leader said to Leothric:

"The Lord Gaznak has desired to see you die before him. Be pleased to come with us, and we can discourse by the way of the manner in which the Lord Gaznak has desired to see you die."

And as he said this he unwound a chain of iron that was coiled upon his saddle, and Leothric answered:

"I would fain go with you, for I am come to slay Gaznak."

Then all the camel-guard of Gaznak laughed hideously, disturbing the vampires that were asleep in the measureless vault of the roof. And the leader said:

"The Lord Gaznak is immortal, save for Sacnoth, and weareth armour that is proof even against Sacnoth himself, and hath a sword the second most terrible in the world."

Then Leothric said: "I am the Lord of the sword Sacnoth."

And he advanced towards the camel-guard of Gaznak, and Sacnoth lifted up and down in his hand as though stirred by an exultant pulse. Then the camel-guard of Gaznak fled, and the riders leaned forward and smote their camels with whips, and they went away with a great clamour of bells through colonnades and corridors and vaulted halls, and scattered into the inner darkness of the fortress.

When the last sound of them had died away, Leothric was in doubt which way to go, for the camel-guard was dispersed in many directions, so he went straight on till he came to a great stairway in the midst of the hall. Then Leothric set his foot in the middle of a wide step, and climbed steadily up the stairway for five minutes. Little light was there in the great hall through which Leothric ascended, for it only entered through arrow slits here and there, and in the world outside evening was waning fast. The stairway led up to two folding doors, and they stood a little ajar, and through the crack Leothric entered and tried to continue straight on, but could get no farther, for the whole room seemed to be full of festoons of ropes which swung from wall to wall and were looped and draped from the ceiling. The whole chamber was thick and black with them. They were soft and light to the touch, like fine silk, but Leothric was unable to break any one of them, and though they swung away from him as he pressed forward, yet by the time he had gone three yards they were all about him like a heavy cloak.

Then Leothric stepped back and drew Sacnoth, and Sacnoth divided the ropes without a sound, and without a sound the severed pieces fell to the floor. Leothric went forward slowly, moving Sacnoth in front of him up and down as he went. When he was come into the middle of the chamber, suddenly, as he parted with Sacnoth a great hammock of strands, he saw a spider before him that was larger than a ram, and the spider looked at him with eyes that were little, but in which there was much sin, and said:

"Who are you that spoil the labour of years all done to the honour of Satan?"

And Leothric answered: "I am Leothric, son of Lorendiac."

And the spider said: "I will make a rope at once to hang you with."

Then Leothric parted another bunch of strands, and came nearer to the spider as he sat making his rope, and the spider, looking up from his work, said: "What is that sword which is able to sever my ropes?"

And Leothric said: "It is Sacnoth."

Thereat the black hair that hung over the face of the spider parted to left and right, and the spider frowned; then the hair fell back into its place, ad hid everything except the sin of the little eyes which went on gleaming lustfully in the dark. But before Leothric could reach him, he climbed away with his hands, going up by one of his ropes to a lofty rafter, and there sat, growling. But, clearing his way with Sacnoth, Leothric passed through the chamber, and came to the farther door; and, the door being shut, and the handle far up out of his reach, he hewed his way through the Porte Resonant, the Way of Egress for War.

And so Leothric came into a well-lit chamber, where Queens and Prices were banquetting together, all at a great table; and thousands of candles were glowing all about, and their light shone in the wine that the Princes drank and on the huge gold candelabra, and the royal faces were irradiant with the glow, and the white table-cloth and the silver plates and the jewels in the hair of the Queens, each jewel having a historian all to itself, who wrote no other chronicles all his days. Between the table and the door there stood two hundred footmen in two rows of one hundred facing one another. Nobody looked at Leothric as he entered through the hole in the door, but one of the Princes asked a question of a footman, and the question was passed from mouth to mouth by all the hundred footmen till it came to the last one nearest Leothric; and he said to Leothric, without looking at him:

"What do you seek here?"

And Leothric answered: "I seek to slay Gaznak."

And footman to footman repeated all the way to the table: "He seeks to slay Gaznak."

And another question came down the line of footmen: "What is your name?"

And the line that stood opposite took his answer back.

Then one of the Princes said: "Take him away where we shall not hear his screams."

And footman repeated it to footman till it came to the last two, and they advanced to seize Leothric.

Then Leothric showed to them his sword, saying, "This is Sacnoth," and both of them said to the man nearest: "It is Sacnoth," then screamed and fled away.

And two by two, all up the double line, footman to footman repeated, "It is Sacnoth," then screamed and fled, till the last two gave the message to the table, and all the rest had gone. Hurriedly then arose the Queens and Princes, and fled out of the chamber. And the goodly table, when they were all gone, looked small and disorderly and awry. And to Leothric, pondering in the desolate chamber by what door he should pass onwards, there came from far away the sounds of music, and he knew that it was the magical musicians playing to Gaznak while he slept.

Then Leothric, walking towards the distant music, passed out by the door opposite to the one through which he had cloven his entrance, and so passed into a chamber vast as the other, in which were many women, weirdly beautiful. And they all asked him of his quest, and when they heard that it was to slay Gaznak, they all besought him to tarry among them, saying that Gaznak was immortal, save for Sacnoth, and also that they had need of a knight to protect them from the wolves that rused round and round the wainscot all the night and sometimes broke in upon them through the mouldering oak. Perhaps Leothric had been tempted to tarry had they been human women, for theirs was a strange beauty, but he perceived that instead of eyes they had little flames that flickered in their sockets, and knew them to be the fevered dreams of Gaznak. Therefore he said:

"I have a business with Gaznak and with Sacnoth," and passed on through the chamber.

And at the name of Sacnoth those women screamed, and the flames of their eyes sank low and dwindled to sparks.

And Leothric left them, and, hewing with Sacnoth, passed through the farther door.

Outside he felt the night air on his face, and found that he stood upon a narrow way between two abysses. To left and right of him, as far as he could see, the walls of the fortress ended in a profound precipice, though the roof still stretched above him; and before him lay the two abysses full of stars, for they cut their way through the whole Earth and revealed the under sky; and threading its course between them went the way, and it sloped upward and its sides were sheer. And beyond the abysses, where the way led up to the farther chambers of the fortress, Leothric heard the musicians playing their magical tune. So he stepped on to the way, which was scarcely a stride in width, and moved along it holding Sacnoth naked. And to and fro beneath him in each abyss whirred the wings of vampires passing up and down, all giving praise to Satan as they flew. Presently he perceived the dragon Thok lying upon the way, pretending to sleep, and his tail hung down into one of the abysses.

And Leothric went towards him, and when he was quite close Thok rushed at Leothric.

And he smote deep with Sacnoth, and Thok tumbled into the abyss, screaming, and his limbs made a whirring in the darkness as he fell, and he fell till his scream sounded no louder than a whistle and then he could be heard no more. Once or twice Leothric saw a star blink for an instant and reappear again, and this momentary eclipse of a few stars was all that remained in the world of the body of Thok. And Lunk, the brother of Thok, who had lain a little behind him, saw that this must be Sacnoth and fled lumbering away. And all the while that he walked between the abysses, the mighty vault of the roof of the fortress still stretched over Leothric's head, all filled with gloom. Now, when the farther side of the abyss came into view, Leothric saw a chamber that opened with innumerable arches upon the twin abysses, and the pillars of the arches went away into the distance and vanished in the gloom to left and right.

Far down the dim precipice on which the pillars stood he could see windows small and closely barred, and between the bars there showed at moments, and disappeared again, things that I shall not speak of.

There was no light here except for the great Southern stars that shown below the abysses, and here and there in the chamber through the arches lights that moved furtively without the sound of footfall.

Then Leothric stepped from the way, and entered the great chamber.

Even to himself he seemed but a tiny dwarf as he walked under one of those colossal arches.

The last faint light of evening flickered through a window painted in sombre colours commemorating the achievements of Satan upon Earth. High up in the wall the window stood, and the streaming lights of candles lower down moved stealthily away.

Other light there was none, save for a faint blue glow from the steel eye of Tharagavverug that peered restlessly about it from the hilt of Sacnoth. Heavily in the chamber hung the clammy odour of a large and deadly beast.

Leothric moved forward slowly, with the blade of Sacnoth in front of him feeling for a foe, and the eye in the hilt of it looking out behind.

Nothing stirred.

If anything lurked behind the pillars of the colonnade that held aloft the roof, it neither breathed nor moved.

The music of the magical musicians sounded from very near.

Suddenly the great doors on the far side of the chamber opened to left and right. For some moments Leothric saw nothing move, and waited, clutching Sacnoth. Then Wong Bongerok came towards him, breathing.

This was the last and faithfullest guard of Gaznak, and came from slobbering just now his master's hand.

More as a child than a dragon was Gaznak wont to treat him, giving him often in his fingers tender pieces of man all smoking from his table.

Long and low was Wong Bongerok, and subtle about the eyes, and he came breathing malice against Leothric out of his faithful breast, and behind him roared the armoury of his tail, as when sailors drag the cable of the anchor all rattling down the deck.

And well Wong Bongerok knew that he now faced Sacnoth, for it had been his wont to prophesy quietly to himself for many years as he lay curled at the feet of Gaznak.

And Leothric stepped forward into the blast of his breath, and lifted Sacnoth to strike.

But when Sacnoth was lifted up, the eye of Tharagavverug in the butt of the hilt beheld the dragon and perceived his subtlety.

For he opened his mouth wide, and revealed to Leothric the ranks of his sabre teeth, and his leather gums flapped upwards. But while Leothric made to smite at his head, he shot forward scorpion-wise over his head the length of his armoured tail. All this the eye perceived in the hilt of Sacnoth, who smote suddenly sideways. Not with the edge smote Sacnoth, for, had he done so, the severed end of the tail had still come hurtling on, as some pine tree that the avalanche has hurled point foremost from the cliff right through the broad breast of some mountaineer. So had Leothric been transfixed; but Sacnoth smote sideways with the flat of his blade, and sent the tail whizzing over Leothric's left shoulder; and it rasped upon his armour as it went, and left a groove upon it. Sideways then at Leothric smote the foiled tail of Wong Bongerok, and Sacnoth parried, and the tail went shrieking up the blade and over Leothric's head. Then Leothric and Wong Bongerok fought sword to tooth, and the sword smote as only Sacnoth can, and the evil faithful life of Wong Bongerok the dragon went out through the wide wound.

Then Leothric walked on past that dead monster, and the armoured body still quivered a little. And for a while it was like all the ploughshares in a county working together in one field behind tired and struggling horses; then the quivering ceased, and Wong Bongerok lay still to rust.

And Leothric went on to the open gates, and Sacnoth dripped quietly along the floor.

By the open gates through which Wong Bongerok had entered, Leothric came into a corridor echoing with music. This was the first place from which Leothric could see anything above his head, for hitherto the roof had ascended to mountainous heights and had stretched indistinct in the gloom. But along the narrow corridor hung huge bells low and near to his head, and the width of each brazen bell was from wall to wall, and they were one behind each other. And as he passed under each the bell uttered, and its voice was mournful and deep, like to the voice of a bell speaking to a man for the last time when he is newly dead. Each bell uttered once as Leothric came under it, and their voices sounded solemnly and wide apart at ceremonious intervals. For if he walked slow, these bells came closer together, and when he walked swiftly they moved farther apart. And the echoes of each bell tolling above his head went on before him, whispering to the others. Once when he stopped they all jangled angrily till he went on again.

Between these slow and boding notes came the sound of the magical musicians. They were playing a dirge now very mournfully.

And at last Leothric came to the end of the Corridor of the Bells, and beheld there a small black door. And all the corridor behind him was full of the echoes of the tolling, and the dirge of the musicians came floating slowly through them like a procession of foreign elaborate guests, and all of them boded ill to Leothric.

The black door opened at once to the hand of Leothric, and he found himself in the open air in a wide court paved with marble. High over it shone the moon, summoned there by the hand of Gaznak.

There Gaznak slept, and around him sat his magical musicians, all playing upon strings. And, even sleeping, Gaznak was clad in armour, and only his wrists and face and neck were bare.

But the marvel of that place was the dreams of Gaznak; for beyond the wide court slept a dark abyss, and into the abyss there poured a white cascade of marble stairways, and widened out below into terraces and balconies with fair white statues on them, and descended again in a wide stairway, and came to lower terraces in the dark, where swart uncertain shapes went to and fro. All these were the dreams of Gaznak, and issued from his mind, and, becoming gleaming marble, passed over the edge of the abyss as the musicians played. And all the while out of the mind of Gaznak, lulled by that strange music, went spires and pinnacles beautiful and slender, ever ascending skywards. And the marble dreams moved slow in time to the music. When the bells tolled and the musicians played their dirge, ugly gargoyles came out suddenly all over the spires and pinnacles, and great shadows passed swiftly down the steps and terraces, and there was hurried whispering in the abyss.

When Leothric stepped from the black door, Gaznak opened his eyes. He looked neither to left nor right, but stood up at once, facing Leothric.

Then the magicians played a deathspell on their strings, and there arose a humming along the blade of Sacnoth as he turned the spell aside. When Leothric dropped not down, and they heard the humming of Sacnoth, the magicians arose and fled, all wailing, as they went, upon their strings.

Then Gaznak drew out screaming from its sheath the sword that was the mightiest in the world except for Sacnoth, and slowly walked towards Leothric; and he smiled as he walked, although his own dreams had foretold his doom. And when Leothric and Gaznak came together, each looked at each, and neither spoke a word; but they smote both at once, and their swords met, and each sword knew the other and from whence he came. And whenever the sword of Gaznak smote on the blade of Sacnoth it rebounded gleaming, as hail from off slated roofs; but whenever it fell upon the armour of Leothric, it stripped it off in sheets. And upon Gaznak's armour Sacnoth fell oft and furiously, but ever he came back snarling, leaving no mark behind, and as Gaznak fought he held his left hand hovering close over his head.

Presently Leothric smote fair and fiercely at his enemy's neck, but Gaznak, clutching his own head by the hair, lifted it high aloft, and Sacnoth went cleaving through an empty space. Then Gaznak replaced his head upon his neck, and all the while fought nimbly with his sword; and again and again Leothric swept with Sacnoth at Gaznak's bearded neck, and ever the left hand of Gaznak was quicker than the stroke, and the head went up and the sword rushed vainly under it.

And the ringing fight went on till Leothric's armour lay all round him on the floor and the marble was splashed with his blood, and the sword of Gaznak was notched like a saw from meeting the blade of Sacnoth. Still Gaznak stood unwounded and smiling still.

At last Leothric looked at the throat of Gaznak and aimed with

Sacnoth, and again Gaznak lifted his head by the hair; but not at his throat flew Sacnoth, for Leothric struck instead at the lifted hand, and through the wrist of it went Sacnoth whirring, as a scythe goes through the stem of a single flower.

And, bleeding, the severed hand fell to the floor; and at once blood spurted from the shoulders of Gaznak and dripped from the fallen head, and the tall pinnacles went down into the earth, and the wide fair terraces all rolled away, and the court was gone like the dew, and a wind came and the colonnades drifted thence, and all the colossal halls of Gaznak fell. And the abysses closed up suddenly as the mouth of a man who, having told a tale, will for ever speak no more.

Then Leothric looked around him in the marshes where the night mist was passing away, and there was no fortress nor sound of dragon or mortal, only beside him lay an old man, wizened and evil and dead, whose head and hand were severed from his body.

And gradually over the wide lands the dawn was coming up, and ever growing in beauty as it came, like to the peal of an organ played by a master's hand, growing louder and lovelier as the soul of the master warms, and at last giving praise with all its mighty voice.

Then the birds sang, and Leothric went homeward, and left the marshes and came to the dark wood, and the light of the dawn ascending lit him upon his way. And into Allathurion he came ere noon, and with him brought the evil wizened head, and the people rejoiced, and their nights of trouble ceased.

This is the tale of the vanquishing of The Fortress Unvanquishable, Save For Sacnoth, and of its passing away, as it is told and believed by those who love the mystic days of old.

Others have said, and vainly claim to prove, that a fever came to Allathurion, and went away; and that this same fever drove Leothric into the marshes by night, and made him dream there and act violently with a sword.

And others again say that there hath been no town of Allathurion, and that Leothric never lived.

Peace to them. The gardener hath gathered up this autumn's leaves. Who shall see them again, or who wot of them? And who shall say what hath befallen in the days of long ago?

The Cloak of Friendship

~

Laurence Housman

THERE WAS ONCE upon a time a king of Finland who had two sons; and when he came to die he did not know which of them it were best to leave his crown to, for though one was the elder, the other might be the fitter; and in that country the King alone had the right to say who should be king after him.

So as he lay dying he bethought him of a way to prove them. Then he called his sons to him and said: "In a short while I shall be gone, and one of you must be king after me; which is it to be?" His sons remained in respectful silence, waiting on what they perceived he had yet to say to them; and, after observing them for a time thoughtfully, the King went on:

"Though you are equally dear to me as sons, yet I may not divide the kingdom between you to weaken it; how then shall I know which of you will make the better ruler when I am gone? This is what I will do. I will show you all my secret treasures, and let each of you choose one of them: and the one that makes the best choice shall be king after me."

So the King led his sons into his treasury, and there showed them all his wealth and means of government; and especially he showed them the three chief treasures by which he maintained the strength and peace and security of his realm. The first was the Sword of Sharpness, whose property was to slay the King's enemies; there was no man so strong that he might stand against it. "It has won me my wars," said the King.

The second was the Cap of Darkness, whose property was to make the wearer of it invisible: by means thereof the King might go to and fro unperceived of any man, and search out those that were in secret his enemies or plotters against the welfare of the state. "It has brought me to old age," said the King.

The third was the Cloak of Friendship. "It has brought me friends," said the King: "but its properties can only be learned by him who wears it; moreover, it is yet in the making, and secures not all friendships, else would there be no wars and no plotters against the good estate of the realm. Now I have shown you my treasures, and it is for you to make choice."

Then the elder son spoke quick, saying: "The Sword of Sharpness! For with that, while I have life, I shall be strong and feared, being secure of victory." And he looked sharply at his younger brother, to whom also, "Make choice," said the King.

Then said the younger son: "My brother's choice deprives me of nothing that I wish for. Let the sword be his, and the crown with it. I choose the Cloak of Friendship."

The King said: "Your choice is the better one. After my death you shall be king."

So when the King died, his younger son, though still a child, was set upon the throne, while the elder, with the Sword of Sharpness, went to offer his services wherever war was, and to win fame; and great news of him came from all the countries around, while the young King sat in peace at home, with the Cloak of Friendship for his possession.

Now this cloak, of which the old King had told that it was yet a-making but not made, was fashioned in this wise: of every kind of animal in the world it contained one hair, and of every kind of bird under heaven it contained one feather; but it contained not the hair of a man. For whatever gave hair or feather to the weaving of that cloak must give life also, and freely, knowing the cost beforehand. Therefore was the cloak woven from the covering of all living kinds under heaven, saving of man; for no man would give his life freely to let one hair of his head carry with it the virtue of self-sacrifice to the weaving of the Cloak of Friendship.

Now, when the old King gave the cloak to his son, he told him also its story: how a great wizard, learned in the speech of all living

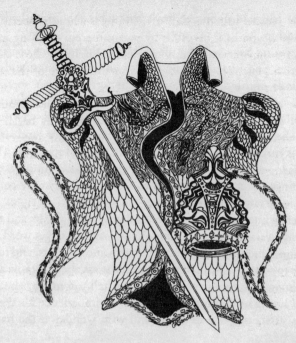

creatures upon earth, had in the making of it spent a long lifetime. For, going first to one and then to another of the tribes of feather and fur, he had said to each: "Find out one of you willing to die that he may have part in the Cloak of Friendship." Then they asked him: "What is this cloak, that we should die to have part in it?" And the wizard told them: "It is a cloak that will bring those that have share in it to be in friendship and understanding with man." And when they heard that, out of every tribe one was found ready to give up life for that friendship and understanding between them and man which had been lost since Adam and Eve were driven out of Eden.

So the cloak came into making, but was not yet made, because as yet no man had been found to give up his life that through him with mankind the bond of friendship might be made whole. Even the wizard when he was dying would not give up one day of his life that its work might become accomplished. So had it been with the old King: "The less we have of life, little son," said he, "the more we cling to it. Thou art full of life, but do not die yet." And so saying he had laid upon the boy's shoulders the unfinished Cloak of Friendship.

The young King wearing the cloak felt the motions of its virtue within him, and had a friendly eye for all living things; and of the lower kinds nothing feared him; he understood their speech and they his, nor were any of their ways strange to him. He knew why the starlings flock and are off again as at a word, and why the wild geese make always the same shape together in flight, and why the dog turns three times in his kennel before he lies down, and why the fallow deer wags his tail before he lifts up his head from grass; and many things we have not the wits to see and hear that are common to all life, he saw and heard.

Thus he knew that on Christmas night, when the ox and the ass are talking in stall, there are others out and seeking to get word, while the Divine rumour runs between the earth and the stars, and to learn what the joy means of which the ox and the ass already know a little. But he knew also that it was well not to tell too much, else might the kind hearts of dumb things break with impatience for the relief which is surely one day to come, and with wonder at the hardness of men's hearts.

One Christmas night it was dark, though the ground was covered with snow; and the little King put on his cloak of feather and fur, and stole out to the fields. And all round him in the air he felt the rumour of the Divine Birth moving to give rest to the hearts of men. Going where the track grew lost on the open down, he met a lame hare limping heavily over the snow.

"Grey hare, grey hare, where are you going so fast?" cried the young King.

And the hare answered: "Whither I go I know not, but danger is behind, and being lame I cannot go fast; yet it seemed to me that I should find shelter this night."

Then the King threw open his cloak, and let it blow wide about his feet. "Come under the Cloak of Friendship," he said, "and you shall be safe."

And the hare limped under the hem of the King's cloak, and cried: "There are multitudes of us here, yet I see none!"

"Wait and see!" said the King. So they went on.

Presently came a ferret running low on the scent of its prey. "Whither away, ferret?" said the King.

"To my supper," answered the ferret, "for I am cold and supperless, and tonight I smell good food ahead if I can only get to it."

"Turn in here," said the King, "and you shall have supper presently." And, spreading his cloak wider, he let the ferret come under it.

"Good even to you, brother!" said the ferret, seeing the hare running close with him at the King's heels; and "Good even, brother!" said the hare. So together the three went on.

A little further and they met a fox; his thick tail brushed the snow as his feet sank in. "Red fox, red fox, where are you going tonight?" asked the King.

"Over the hill to the next farm," answered the fox. "There, under a rick, sleep three white geese, and I mean to have one of them, for tonight the farmer's dog has gone to a christening."

"What christening is that?" asked the King.

"Nay, I know not," answered the fox, "but I heard him today telling the shepherd's dog that tonight there was meat and a warm bed for them both, because of that christening feast. Thus I too profit," said the fox.

"Come under the Cloak of Friendship," said the King, "and you shall fare better than you think."

So the fox ran in alongside of the ferret and the hare, and they exchanged greetings all, and together went on.

"Here be three courses at least," said the fox, sniffing prophetic.

"And three mouths for the same," said the hare, quite as hungry as the rest.

Presently as they went further they met a wolf. "Wolf, wolf," said the King, "where are you going this night?"

"Over the hill, beyond the farm, to the fold," answered the wolf. "A good fat lamb is waiting for me there; and the shepherds will not see me tonight, for with good cheer and song they keep watch carelessly."

"Come under my cloak," said the King, "and you shall sup better with me."

So the wolf went in along with the others under the cloak, and

"Merry company," cried he, seeing them all there, "luck be with us!" So they went on, and whatever they met by the way the King gathered under the Cloak of Friendship and led them on towards the farm. "For," thought he, "since I have saved the farmer a lamb and a goose, he may well feed us!"

There with his friendly rabble he knocked at the door. Out ran the farmer's dog and the sheepdog, barking; but the King had but to call them once, and they too came to heel like the rest.

"God shield us!" cried the farmer, all agape as he beheld the wolf and the fox and the ferret with all the other beasts crowding behind. "What Noah's ark is this that is being loosed upon us now?"

"God be with you," said the young King.

"Amen!" said the farmer; "but for that get you gone!"

"Nay, we are hungry," said the King, "and tonight is peace on earth. Do not send all these away empty."

"Why should *I* feed them?" cried the farmer. "They steal food of me often enough; but tonight they bring their own meal with them: let them but look right and left! And as for you – let go my dogs; you are a wizard, I say. Out, out, else we will try fire on you!" And, while some of those within caught up pitchforks, others drew out brands from the hearth and came running to the door to drive off such unwelcome applicants.

The King drew back from the threshold and let the door be closed. "Alas! little ones," said he to his friends, "I promised you food and warmth: yet now we must go further before we find it. Are you too cold or too hungry to come?"

"Nay, master," said the fox, "for under this cloak of yours I smell good meats ahead. We will yet come with you." And all the others said the same.

So the King turned back towards the city, and brought them all under the Cloak of Friendship right up to the doors of the palace. Great was the astonishment of all there when they saw those strange guests. And the King ordered food and drink in abundance to be set before them: so they ate till they were filled; and after that the king sent them back in peace to their own homes, promising in a year's time the same welcome to all who would come.

On the morrow he noticed that people looked at him strangely;

they crooked their thumbs behind their backs whenever his eye rested on them, and seemed fearful of coming near him. For, because of his strange guests of the night before, all thought him a wizard, a dealer in black magic, even as the farmer had done. Then, had he bethought him of the Cap of Darkness, which lay still in the King's treasury, he could have learned much of what was plotted behind his back; but his heart was full of friendship for all men, and he thought not of such means for guarding himself from danger.

So it was with joy that he heard soon after how his brother was returning from all the wars that he had been waging in other countries, to visit once more the realm of which he would have been King, had not his brother's preferment ousted him.

"Ah, brother!" cried the young King, going out to welcome him. "Sheath your sword for a while, and live in peace with me; you have made wars too many, and stayed too long away from home."

The other answered him coldly: "Brother, long ago your choice of peace seemed good to our father, when he made you to be king: but my choice of the sword seems good to me now. Strange friendship you seem to have made; but your crown you must give up to me."

"Alas! brother," said the King, "has all your fame left you room to be jealous of me and my office? Yet it may well be that for a year you may wish to taste rule over a peaceful kingdom. So, if you will, take mine; but let me keep still this Cloak of Friendship which our father's own hands put on me before he died."

"You may keep it," said his brother; "but go not with it into strange places, nor do any more of the strange things you have done. Take heed, and let my word to you be law!"

So the elder brother took up the crown and ruled; and the other with little ado let it go, and went his own way peacefully, coming and going with little notice from men. And of all his kindly appurtenances the Cloak of Friendship was now the only one that was left to him. That kept his heart warm, and gave employment to his mind during the year that followed his deposition. But often he would look at the frayed edge where it lacked finish because no man would give his life that the bond of friendship between man and beast might be made whole, and would wonder if ever it could be right for a man with a soul that lives to give up life for the sake of the beasts that perish.

So the year went round, and by no sign did the dethroned King show envy of the brother who had usurped his place; but often, beholding him, his heart grew sorrowful, for the Sword of Sharpness would not stay sheathed, and the land had no longer its former rest; and "Alas! brother," cried younger to elder, "now you make great wars: but when Christmas comes I will show you peace."

"What is peace?" enquired the other, scornfully.

"It is the Cloak of Friendship," he answered.

Now, when Christmas was near, it was told to the elder brother how in his own house the younger was preparing a great feast without tables; and the tale of the Christmas before was revived. When the King heard of it, "Make no hindrance," said he, "but at the last bring me word, and my brother shall know which of us rules now and gives law."

On Christmas night, as soon as it was dark, the younger put on the Cloak of Friendship and set out to find his friends. And on the hillside he met them coming, for they all remembered his word to them, and with them they brought others, so that the ground was quick under them, and the snow dark with the trampling of their feet. To him came red deer and wild boar, fox and wolf, marten and stoat, polecat and badger, and with them also came the gentler and more timid kinds; and in greeting to them he said: "Peace be with you!" and spread the Cloak of Friendship wide that all might come under. So host and guests together turned and went back to the city. "This night," he said to them, "is the night of peace: fear no man!"

"What is peace?" asked the fox. "We know little thereof."

"It is the Cloak of Friendship," answered the young King. "Once it was so wide that it covered the whole world; but now it is shorn in pieces and shredded with age and rough usage, and only here and there can one find it. Nevertheless on this night, many years ago, He that wore it whole was born. So in memory of Him there is peace tonight through nature wherever goes understanding of Him. Come under the Cloak of Friendship with me, and you shall be filled."

Not long afterwards word was brought to the elder brother in his palace that wizardry was at work once more, and that the ways of the city swarmed with wild beasts, all going peaceably towards the feast that had been prepared without tables. "Let the city gates be shut," said the King, "and wait you for my word."

And straight upon on that entered to him his brother, who kneeled to him and said: "Fair brother, tonight is the night of Christ's Birth. Come with me, and I will show you peace."

"Nay, brother," answered the King coldly. "I have heard tell already of this brave hunting-ground that you have prepared. So now, come with me and I will show you sport."

Quick with sudden fear, the younger cried: "Brother, you will not kill?"

"As I choose," answered the other.

"Nay, for my honour is pledged to them! I have promised that they shall get no hurt."

"Make good thy promise!" said his brother, laughing; and, without more ado, he gave orders for the archers and the huntsmen with their hounds to make ready.

"Nay, nay, brother!" cried the other, distraught. "For if one of them is harmed I am dishonoured for ever."

"Thy dishonour is in making promises thou canst not perform," replied the King.

Whereat the other, speaking low and all heavy of heart, answered: "Nay, brother, for what I promised that I will perform. Yet, since thus we must part, first give me the kiss of peace that afterwards it may be known that there was love and not hate between us upon this night which is the joy of all Christian souls."

Then he took up the unfinished and frayed edge of the Cloak of Friendship, and wove therein one hair of a man's head, even his own; and he stretched it wide, and drew it about his brother's shoulder, so that the same cloak enfolded both. And so standing in bond to his brother he saw his face change and grow merciful, and knew that the gift had been granted, so that he need fear no longer for the lives of the guests he had brought in with him for that night.

So he kissed him and said: "Fair brother, is it not peace?"

"Nay, what is peace?" cried the elder brother in sudden fear, beholding him so pale; and catching him in his arms he felt his flesh cold as a dead man's.

"It is the Cloak of Friendship," answered the young King; and straightway he kissed death, and his heart stopped from its work, having come to a good end.

The Cotton-Wool Princess

∾

Luigi Capuani

A THOUSAND YEARS AGO there lived a king and a queen. They had only one daughter, who was dearer to them than all the world. Now, when the King of France sent to their Court to request the hand of the Princess, neither father nor mother would part from their beloved daughter, and they said to the Ambassador: ·

"She is still too young!"

But as the girl became every day more beautiful, the next year the King of Spain's Ambassador appeared to request the girl's hand for his Sovereign. And again the parents answered:

"She is still too young!"

Both the Kings were very angry at this refusal, and resolved to revenge themselves on the poor Princess.

As they were not able themselves to carry out their wicked resolve, they summoned a Magician, and said to him:

"You must devise for us some charm to be used against the Princess – and the worse it is the greater shall be your reward!"

With the words:

"In one month your wish shall be fulfilled!" the Magician departed.

Before the four weeks were over, he appeared again in the castle of the King of Spain.

"Your Majesty, here is the charm!" he cried. "Give her this ring as a present, and when she has worn it on her finger for four-and-twenty hours, you shall see the effect!"

Now the two Kings consulted together as to how they should get the ring to the Princess, for they were no longer friendly with her parents, who would, consequently, become suspicious of any present sent by them. What was to be done?

"I have it! I have it!" the King of Spain cried, suddenly.

Then he disguised himself as a goldsmith, set out on a journey, and took up his position just opposite the palace where the Princess lived. The Queen noticed him from her window, and as she happened at that time to be wanting to buy some jewellery she sent for him. After she had bought from the stranger various bracelets, chains, and ear-rings, she said to her daughter:

"And you will not choose anything among all these fine things for yourself, little daughter?"

Then the Princess answered:

"I see nothing especially beautiful among them."

Then the disguised King took the ring out of his case, which he had up to the present kept hidden, made it sparkle in the sun, and said:

"Your Majesty, here is still a very rare jewel; this ring has not its equal in the world for beauty. And it does not please you?"

"Oh, how splendid! Oh, how beautifully it sparkles and gleams!" cried the Princess, entranced. "How much does it cost?"

"The ring has no price; I shall be contented with whatever you give me for it."

Then a great sum of money was paid to him, and he went his way. The Princess put the ring on her finger, and could not turn her eyes away from it, so charmed was she with its brilliancy. But four-and-twenty hours had not passed – it was just evening – when the poor girl uttered a terrible cry of anguish.

"Oh, dear! Oh, dear!" sounded through the whole palace.

The King, the Queen, and all the ladies of the Court ran, white with terror, and with candles in their hands, to see what had happened.

"Take away your candles! Take them away! Take them away!" cried the Princess, beside herself with despair. "Do you not see that I have turned into cotton-wool?"

And her body had, indeed, suddenly changed into cotton-wool. The King and Queen were inconsolable at this terrible misfortune, and they at once summoned the wisest men of the kingdom to consult with them as to what was to be done in this extremity.

"Your Majesties," the councillors concluded, after long deliberation, "have it proclaimed in all countries that whoever restores your daughter may wed her."

And then messengers with drums and trumpets went round the whole kingdom and far beyond it, and proclaimed:

"He who restores the Princess to health may become the King's son-in-law."

About this time there lived in a small town the son of a shoemaker. There was great want in his father's house, and one day, when not even a crust of bread remained, and both would have had to die of hunger, the son said:

"Father, give me your blessing; I will go out into the world to seek my fortune."

"May Heaven be gracious to you, my son!" said the father, and the youth took his staff and set out on his journey.

He had already left the fields of his native district far behind him when he met a band of rough boys, who were making a fearful uproar and throwing stones at a toad to kill it.

"What harm has the poor animal done you? Is it not as much God's creature as you are? Let it live!" he exclaimed, indignantly. But when he saw that the hard-hearted fellows paid no attention to his words, and did not desist from their intention, he rushed angrily at them and gave one a sound box on the ears and another a mighty punch in his ribs. The boys scattered in a tumult, and the toad quickly used the opportunity to slip into a hole in the wall.

Then the youth went farther and farther on his way. Suddenly the sound of trumpets and the roll of drums came to his ear. And listen! Is not some proclamation being made? He listened attentively, and distinctly heard the words:

"He who restores the Princess to health may become the King's son-in-law!"

"What is the matter with her?" he asked a passer-by.

"Don't you know? She has turned into cotton-wool."

He thanked his informant and continued his travels. Now, by the time night had sunk upon the earth, he had come to a great desert, and he determined to lay himself down to sleep. But how terrified he was when, on turning his head to look once again at the way he had come, he saw a tall, beautiful woman standing at his side. He was about to spring quickly away when she said:

"Do not be afraid of me. I am a Fairy, and have come to thank you."

"To thank me? And what for?" the youth asked, in confusion.

"You saved my life! My fate ordains that I shall be a toad by day and a fairy by night. Now I am at your service."

"Good Fairy," then said the youth, "I have just heard of a Princess who has turned into cotton-wool, and whoever heals her may become her husband. Teach me how to restore her to health. That is my most ardent wish!"

Then the Fairy said:

"Take this sword in your hand and walk straight on until you come to a dense forest, full of snakes and wild animals. However, you must not be afraid of them, but must bravely continue your journey until you stand in front of the Magician's palace. As soon as you have reached it, knock three times at the great gate . . ." And she described to him fully what he was to do. "If you ever need my help, come to this place at this same hour, and you will find me here!" And, giving him her white hand in farewell, she disappeared before the youth could open his mouth to thank her.

Without pausing to consider, the cobbler's son set out and went straight on, according to his instructions. He had already gone a good way when his path led him into a dark forest, into the midst of wild animals. That was awful! They filled the air with fearful roars, gnashed their teeth blood-thirstily, and hungrily opened their jaws. Though the poor youth's heart thumped, he went straight on, making as if he did not notice them. At last he reached the Magician's palace, and knocked three times at the great gate.

Then a voice came from the interior of the castle:

"Woe to you, rash stranger, who have the boldness to come to me! What is your wish?"

"If you really are the Magician, come out and fight with me!" cried the youth.

The Magician, in a great fury at this audacity, rushed out, armed to the teeth, to accept the challenge. But as soon as he saw the sword in the youth's hand, he broke out into pitiable lamentation, and, sinking trembling on to his knees, cried:

"Oh, woe to me, unfortunate creature that I am! At least spare my life!"

Then the youth said:

"If you will release the Princess from the spell, your life shall be spared."

Then the Magician took a ring out of his pocket and said:

"Take this ring and put it on the little finger of her left hand and she shall be well again."

Not a little rejoiced at the success of his journey, the youth hastened to the King and asked, just to satisfy himself of the truth of what he had been told:

"Your Majesty, is it true that he who restores the Princess to health will be your son-in-law?"

"It is verily true," the anxious King assured him.

"Well, then, I am ready to accomplish the task."

Then the poor Princess was brought in, and all the ladies of the Court, as well as the servants, stood round her to witness the miracle.

But no sooner had she put the ring on her little finger than she burst into bright flame and stood there, uttering heart-rending cries. Everything was plunged into confusion, and the horrified youth seized the opportunity of escaping from the scene of the disaster as fast as his legs would carry him. His one wish was to get to the Fairy, and he did not stop running until he had come to the place where he had seen her the first time.

"Fairy, where are you?" he cried, all in a tremble.

"I am at your service," was the answer.

Then he told the Fairy of the misfortune which had happened to him.

"You have allowed yourself to be deceived! Take this dagger and go again to the Magician. See that he does not fool you this time!"

Then she gave him all sorts of good advice for his dangerous journey, and bestowed on him her blessing. Arrived at the great gate of the palace, he knocked three times. Then the Magician cried, as before:

"Woe to you, bold stranger! What is your wish?"

"If you are really the Magician, you are to fight with me!"

The Magician, armed to his teeth, came rushing out in a rage. But when he saw the dagger he sank trembling on his knees, and begged piteously:

"Oh, spare my life."

"Good-for-nothing Magician!" the youth cried, angrily; "you have deceived me! Now I will keep you in chains until the Princess is freed from the spell!"

Then he put him in chains, stuck the dagger into the earth, and fastened the chain to it so that the Magician could not move.

"You are mightier than I! Now I realize it!" cried the enchained Magician, gnashing his teeth. "Take the goldsmith's ring from the Princess's finger, and she will be released from the spell."

Not until the youth had learnt that the Princess had escaped with only a few burns on her hands, owing to the promptness of the bystanders in extinguishing the flames, did he summon up enough courage to appear before the King again.

"Your Majesty, I implore your pardon!" he said. "The treacherous Magician, not I, was the cause of the disaster. Now I have completely overcome him, and my remedy will succeed. I have only to draw the goldsmith's ring from your daughter's finger and she will be all right again."

And so it happened. As soon as the ring was taken off, the Princess at once changed back to what she had been before. But who would believe it to be possible? Her tongue, eyes, and ears were missing; they had been consumed by the flames! The youth's perplexity at this new disaster was indescribable. Again he applied to his guardian Fairy for help.

"You have let him make a fool of you a second time!" she said, again giving him advice to help him towards the fulfilment of his wish of becoming the King's son-in-law.

When he came to the Magician he shouted at him:

"You miserable deceiver! Now my patience is at an end! But eye for eye, tongue for tongue, ear for ear!"

With these words he seized the Magician to strangle him.

But the latter cried, in the utmost peril of death:

"Have mercy! Have mercy! Let me live! Go to my sisters, who live a little farther back than this."

Then he gave him the necessary directions so that he might find the way there without delay, and also the magic word which he had to pronounce at the gate. After some hours he came to the gate of a palace, which was in every respect like that of the Magician. He knocked, and in answer to the question:

"Who are you, and what do you want here?"

He answered:

"I want the little gold horn."

"I perceive that my brother has sent you to me. What does he want of me?"

"He wants a little piece of red cloth; he has torn a hole in his cloak."

"Here's a piece, and now get you gone from here!" a woman in the palace cried angrily, at the same time throwing into his opened hands a little piece of red cloth, which she had cut in the shape of a tongue.

He journeyed on for several hours, and at last came to the foot of a high mountain. On a spur of rock was a castle, which looked exactly like that of the Magician. Then he knocked at the great gate, and a voice came from the interior, saying:

"Who are you, and what is your desire?"

"I want the little gold hand."

"That's all right. I perceive that my brother has sent you. What does he want from me?"

"He wants two lentil-grains for soup."

"What rubbish! Here, take them and make yourself scarce!"

Then the owner of the castle threw him two little lentil-grains wrapped in a piece of paper, and noisily closed the window.

At last he came to a wide plain, in the middle of which a castle exactly like the Magician's was built. When he knocked he was asked what he wanted, and answered:

"I want the little gold foot."

"Ah! My brother has sent you to me! And what does he wish from me?"

"He wishes you to send him two snails for his supper."

"Here they are, but now leave me in peace!" a woman called out, ungraciously, from the window, at the same time throwing him the two snails he desired.

Now the youth returned with the things he had collected to the Magician, and said:

"Here I bring you what you wished for."

Then the Magician gave him all the necessary instructions as to the use of the three things. But when the youth turned his back to go away, the captive cried, imploringly:

"And you are going to leave me lying here?"

"It would be no more than you deserve. However, I will release you. But woe betide you if you have deceived me again."

After the youth had released the Magician from his chains, he hurried away to appear before the Princess.

Opening her mouth, he put in it the little piece of red

stuff which he had brought with him, and she at once had a tongue.

But the first words which came from her mouth were:

"Miserable cobbler! Out of my sight! Begone!"

The poor youth was motionless with painful amazement, and said to himself:

"This is once more the work of the faithless Magician."

But he would not let this bitter ingratitude prevent him from completing the good work. Then, taking the two little lentil-grains, he put them into the blind pupils of the girl's eyes, and at once she was able to see as before. But no sooner had she turned her eyes upon him than she covered her face with her hands and cried scornfully:

"Oh, how ugly mankind is! How horribly ugly!"

The poor youth's courage nearly vanished, and again he said to himself:

"The worthless Magician has done this for me!"

But he would not allow himself to be put out. Taking the empty snail-shells from his pocket, he put them very skilfully where the girl's ears had once been, and behold! the Princess had back again her sweet little ears.

Then the youth turned to the King and said:

"Your Majesty, now I am your son-in-law!"

But when the Princess heard these words she began to weep like a spoilt child, sobbing:

"He called me a witch! He said I was an old witch!"

That was too much ingratitude for the poor youth. Without saying a word, he hurriedly left the castle to seek out his Fairy.

"Fairy, where are you?" he cried, still trembling with anger and vexation.

"I am at your service."

Then he told her how shamefully he had been treated by the Princess, who was now restored to health.

The Fairy said, laughing:

"You probably forgot to take the Magician's other ring from her little finger?"

"Oh, dear! I did not think of that in my confusion," exclaimed the youth, seizing his head between his two hands in mingled terror and shame.

"Now hasten and repair the mistake!" advised the Fairy.

Sooner than he had thought possible, he was standing in front of the Princess and drew the evil ring from her little finger. Then a lovely smile spread over her beautiful features, and she thanked him so sweetly and kindly that he became red with embarrassment.

Then the King said, solemnly:

"This is your husband."

And the youth and the Princess embraced one another in the sight of all, and a few days afterwards the wedding was celebrated.

The Drawing School

~

J. Muñez Escomez

ONCE THERE WAS A BOY so fond of spoiling walls, doors, and windows with grotesque drawings that there was no way of stopping him from practising his silly cleverness wherever he was. And I say silly, because from his hand came forth some primitive dolls, with heads as round as a billiard ball, eyes and nose forming a sort of cork, and arms and legs like thin thread, terminating in hands and feet which required an inscription in order not to be taken for scourges.

One afternoon he approached the very wall of the school, and there, with the greatest coolness, commenced to draw with a piece of charcoal some of his strange figures. Perico, for so the boy was called, traced the figure of the head of a puppet, made the eyes and the mouth, and, oh, how strange! The doll began to wink and open its mouth and put its tongue out like anything.

Perico was not timid, and therefore the moving of the eyes and mouth did not startle him, and so without paying attention continued with his sketching the arms and the rest of the body. But he had hardly finished when the doll's hand came out and gave him such a tremendous knock that it made him lose his balance, and he would even have fallen to the ground if another blow with the other hand and on the opposite cheek had not kept him on his feet. And as if this was not enough, the legs sprang out of the wall, and two vigorous kicks that Perico received in the pit of the stomach quite convinced him that there was one too many, and he was the one.

Thus convinced, he was about to run away when the whole doll came away from the stone, and at a bound leapt on his shoulders and began to bite him in the back of the head.

Perico ran towards his house like a greyhound, feeling on his neck the weight of that unexpected load, when the latter grew heavy, as if, instead of a charcoal picture, he had to deal with a bronze statue.

The poor little boy sank to the ground, and on getting up saw at his side, in the middle of the square, the doll in question, as tall as a giant and changed into a motionless iron statue.

He tried to fly, but the statue caught him with its great hands by the neck and, raising him up, placed him on its shoulders, and this being done commenced to run in the direction of the country. Its footsteps produced a very disagreeable noise of ironmongery, something like a sack of nails being shaken up.

It was night-time and our giant, with Perico on its shoulders, ran as fast as anything to a neighbouring mountain, until he came to a dark grotto into which he penetrated without any need of matches, because intense lights shone from his eyes.

During all this Perico, needless to mention, was more afraid than ashamed, and did not know, nor could even imagine, how it was going to end.

At length, after some minutes' walk in the grotto, the iron man straightened himself, and turning the light of his eyes towards a corner, lighted up by a glance the lamp which hung down from the rocky ceiling, and, this being done, took Perico down from his shoulders and sat down.

"You do not know who I am," said the doll, opening his mouth with a horrible smile; "but when you do know, it will make your hair stand on end from fright."

"I am sure it won't," said the lad, "because it is already doing so; and as I cannot be any more afraid than I am now, on account of being so much afraid, the fear which I felt is passing away."

"Well, then, I am the magician Adefesio, and I am tired of your drawing me so ugly and so similar to all the boys. The thing which puts me out most is that you draw my eyes without pupils and my nose without nostrils. Moreover, the ears which you sketch look like jug handles, and I am sick of my portrait going about the world so disfigured and so badly done. Could you not have learnt to draw a little before commencing these pictures? Well, the punishment that I reserve for you is to draw your portrait every day."

"What a punishment!" exclaimed Perico.

"The fact is that I do not know how to draw either," answered the man of iron, "and the worst of it all is that while I am drawing you, you will grow like my sketch, so that in a twinkling you will be disfigured. There, does not that seem a severe punishment to you? Well, you will see!"

And, seizing Perico by one arm, he pulled the lamp which hung down. Then a hole opened in the ceiling and the lamp went up, dragging the doll and Perico through the air.

The light continued to rise through a sort of well which was lighted up, and whose walls were lined with books full of badly-made drawings, spoilt plans, pieces of forms with engravings made with penknives, and table-covers destroyed through having been drawn on. That was the museum of the man of iron, and each time he saw it he was filled with anger towards the young draughtsmen who spoilt everything.

Soon they found themselves in a spacious room decorated in Arabian style and furnished most luxuriously. In the background there was an easel of great size, and on it a blackboard on which were drawn a lot of dolls of the same sort that Perico drew.

"Dear me, how fine!" said the boy, looking at the sketches; "it seems that I did them."

"Well, now you will see the consequences," and snapping his fingers he produced a metallic sound, and immediately a multitude of boys of different ages came through a door. But what funny boys! All had round heads, eyes like fishes, flat noses, and mouths like letter boxes, wide open and showing teeth like saws. Their arms were thin as wire, ending in long fingers without joints. Perico was not startled when they came in.

"Well, that is how you will look in a little while," said the iron man.

"He always exaggerates!" exclaimed Perico aside. "But seeing is believing."

The man of iron seized a piece of chalk, and going near to the

board began to draw Perico's head; but the latter called the doll's attention, and when he looked the other way rubbed out what he had drawn.

The man could not have seen very well because he went on drawing very tranquilly, and Perico continued rubbing out what the other drew; and when he thought that he had finished he caught up the boy, brought him to the light, and imagine his surprise on seeing him the same as before. He went back, full of rage, to the blackboard; but Perico tripped him up, and did it so well that he fell down. Then he threw the board and easel on him, and, climbing on top, began to jump on the doll, and calling to his companions, shouted:

"Come here so that he will not be able to run away!"

The boys drew near and, climbing on the blackboard, by their weight prevented the iron doll from moving.

But things did not rest thus, because Perico was a very daring boy, and, taking up a rope, which was close at hand, hung the iron man by the neck to the lamp, and, pulling on the other end of the rope, hauled him up with the help of his companions.

As he was made of iron he was not choked, but hanging up he could do nothing except make grimaces like a jack-in-the-box, which was just what he looked like hanging in the air.

"Let me down!" shouted the unhappy man. "And you may draw whatever you like."

"That won't do, my friend," answered Perico, laughing at the doll's movements. "I should not be so stupid as to let you escape."

So that, as the song says:

> "Here, sirs, came to an end
> The life of Don Crispin."

"Do you think I have forgotten the punch you gave me?"

The other boys tied the rope to a sofa, so as not to get tired, and led by Perico began to explore the rooms of the cave. They were all beautiful save that the ornaments on the walls were of dolls as grotesque as the master.

The way out of the grotto could not be seen anywhere. And the reason was simple, as the means of exit was by the lamp to which the doll was hanging; but the boys did not like the idea of going down one by one, with a great risk of breaking their heads.

Perico, now uneasy, recommenced to run about the rooms, and, troubled by seeing on the walls what recalled his unfortunate adventure, pulled out his handkerchief and rubbed out all the drawings, seeing, with extraordinary surprise, that the boys recovered their original shapes. On rubbing out the last drawing, a formidable noise was heard: the iron man vanished as if he were smoke, the palace disappeared, and they found themselves at the entrance to the cave. From there they marched to the town, where their parents were anxiously waiting for them, and there they related what had occurred.

All returned, thanks to God, and promised not to draw dolls again anywhere.

Perico became a very honourable man, devoted himself to drawing, and became a great artist, but he never forgot those dolls, which might have cost him so dear.

The Dutch Cheese

❧

Walter de la Mare

ONCE – ONCE UPON A TIME – there lived, with his sister Griselda, in a little cottage near the Great Forest, a young farmer whose name was John. Brother and sister, they lived alone, except for their sheep-dog, Sly, their flock of sheep, the numberless birds of the forest, and the "fairies". John loved his sister beyond telling; he loved Sly; and he delighted to listen to the birds singing at twilight round the darkening margin of the forest. But he feared and hated the fairies. And, having a very stubborn heart, the more he feared, the more he hated them; and the more he hated them, the more they pestered him.

Now these were a tribe of fairies, sly, small, gay-hearted and mischievous, and not of the race of fairies noble, silent, beautiful and remote from man. They were a sort of gipsy-fairies, very nimble and of aery and prankish company, and partly for mischief and partly for love of her they were always trying to charm John's dear sister Griselda away, with their music and fruits and trickery. He more than half believed it was they who years ago had decoyed into the forest not only his poor old father, who had gone out faggot-cutting in his sheepskin hat with his ass; but his mother too, who soon after had gone out to look for him.

But fairies, even of this small tribe, hate no man. They mocked him and mischiefed him; they spilt his milk, rode astraddle on his rams, garlanded his old ewes with sow-thistle and bryony, sprinkled water on his kindling wood, loosed his bucket into the well, and hid

his great leather shoes. But all this they did, not for hate – for they came and went like evening moths about Griselda – but because in his fear and fury he shut up his sister from them, and because he was sullen and stupid. Yet he did nothing but fret himself. He set traps for them, and caught starlings; he fired his blunderbuss at them under the moon, and scared his sheep; he set dishes of sour milk in their way, and sticky leaves and brambles where their rings were green in the meadows; but all to no purpose. When at dusk, too, he heard their faint, elfin music, he would sit in the door blowing into his father's great bassoon till the black forest re-echoed with its sad, solemn, wooden voice. But that was of no help either. At last he grew so surly that he made Griselda utterly miserable. Her cheeks lost their scarlet and her eyes their sparkling. Then the fairies began to plague John in earnest – lest their lovely, loved child of man, Griselda, should die.

Now one summer's evening – and most nights are cold in the Great Forest – John, having put away his mournful bassoon and bolted the door, was squatting, moody and gloomy, with Griselda, on his hearth beside the fire. And he leaned back his great hairy head and stared straight up the chimney to where high in the heavens glittered a host of stars. And suddenly, while he lolled there on his stool moodily watching them, there appeared against the dark sky a mischievous elvish head secretly peeping down at him; and busy fingers began sprinkling dew on his wide upturned face. He heard the laughter too of the fairies miching and gambolling on his thatch, and in a rage he started up, seized a round Dutch cheese that lay on a platter, and with all his force threw it clean and straight up the sooty chimney at the faces of mockery clustered above. And after that, though Griselda sighed at her spinning-wheel, he heard no more. Even the cricket that had been whistling all through the evening fell silent, and John supped on his black bread and onions alone.

Next day Griselda woke at dawn and put her head out of the little window beneath the thatch, and the day was white with mist.

"'Twill be another hot day," she said to herself, combing her beautiful hair.

But when John went down, so white and dense with mist were the fields, that even the green borders of the forest were invisible, and the whiteness went to the sky. Swathing and wreathing itself, opal and white as milk, all the morning the mist grew thicker and thicker about the little house. When John went out about nine o'clock to peer about him, nothing was to be seen at all. He could hear his sheep bleating, the kettle singing, Griselda sweeping, but straight up above him hung only, like a small round fruit, a little cheese-red beamless sun – straight up above him, though the hands of the clock were not yet come to ten. He clenched his fists and stamped in sheer rage. But no one answered him, no voice mocked him but his own. For when these idle, mischievous fairies have played a trick on an enemy they soon weary of it.

All day long that little sullen lantern burned above the mist, sometimes red, so that the white mist was dyed to amber, and sometimes milky pale. The trees dripped water from every leaf. Every flower asleep in the garden was neckleted with beads; and nothing but a drenched old forest crow visited the lonely cottage that afternoon to cry: "Kah, Kah, Kah!" and fly away.

But Griselda knew her brother's mood too well to speak of it, or to complain. And she sang on gaily in the house, though she was more sorrowful than ever.

Next day John went out to tend his flocks. And wherever he went the red sun seemed to follow. When at last he found his sheep they were drenched with the clinging mist and were huddled together in dismay. And when they saw him it seemed that they cried out with one unanimous bleating voice:

"O ma-a-a-ster!"

And he stood counting them. And a little apart from the rest stood his old ram, Soll, with a face as black as soot; and there, perched on his back, impish and sharp and scarlet, rode and tossed and sang just such another fairy as had mocked John from the chimney-top. A fire seemed to break out in his body, and, picking up a handful of stones, he rushed at Soll through the flock. They scattered, bleating, out into the mist. And the fairy, all-acockahoop on the old ram's back, took its small ears between finger and thumb, and as fast as John ran, so fast jogged Soll, till all the young farmer's stones were thrown, and he found himself alone in a quagmire so sticky and befogged that it took him till afternoon to grope his way out. And only Griselda's singing over her broth-pot guided him at last home.

Next day he sought his sheep far and wide, but not one could he find. To and fro he wandered, shouting and calling and whistling to Sly, till, heartsick and thirsty, they were both wearied out. Yet bleatings seemed to fill the air, and a faint, beautiful bell tolled on out of the mist; and John knew the fairies had hidden his sheep, and he hated them more than ever.

After that he went no more into the fields, brightly green beneath the enchanted mist. He sat and sulked, staring out of the door at the dim forests far away, glimmering faintly red beneath the small red sun. Griselda could not sing any more; she was too tired and hungry. And just before twilight she went out and gathered the last few pods of peas from the garden for their supper.

And while she was shelling them, John, within doors in the cottage, heard again the tiny timbrels and the distant horns, and the odd, clear, grasshopper voices calling and calling her, and he knew in his heart that, unless he relented and made friends with the fairies, Griselda would surely one day run away to them and leave him forlorn. He scratched his great head, and gnawed his broad thumb. They had taken his father, they had taken his mother, they might take his sister – but he *wouldn't* give in.

So he shouted, and Griselda in fear and trembling came in out of the garden with her basket and basin and sat down in the gloaming to finish shelling her peas.

And as the shadows thickened and the stars began to shine, the malevolent singing came nearer, and presently there was a groping and stirring in the thatch, a tapping at the window, and John knew the fairies had come – not alone, not one or two or three, but in their company and bands – to plague him, and to entice away Griselda. He shut his mouth and stopped up his ears with his fingers, but when, with great staring eyes, he saw them capering like bubbles in a glass, like flames along straw, on his very doorstep, he could contain himself no longer. He caught up Griselda's bowl and flung it – peas, water and all – full in the snickering faces of the Little Folk! There came a shrill, faint twitter of laughter, a scampering of feet, and then all again was utterly still.

Griselda tried in vain to keep back her tears. She put her arms round John's neck and hid her face in his sleeve.

"Let me go!" she said. "Let me go, John, just a day and a night, and I'll come back to you. They are angry with us. But they love me; and if I sit on the hillside under the boughs of the trees beside the pool and listen to their music just a little while, they will make the sun shine again and drive back the flocks, and we shall be as happy as ever. Look at poor Sly, John dear, he is hungrier even than I am.' John heard only the mocking laughter and the tap-tapping and the rustling and crying of the fairies and he wouldn't let his sister go.

And it began to be marvellously dark and still in the cottage. No stars moved across the casement, no waterdrops glittered in the candleshine. John could hear only one low, faint, unceasing stir and rustling all around him. So utterly dark and still it was that even Sly woke from his hungry dreams and gazed up into his mistress's face and whined.

They went to bed; but still, all night long, while John lay tossing on his mattress, the rustling never ceased. The old kitchen clock ticked on and on, but there came no hint of dawn. All was pitch-black and now all was utterly silent. There wasn't a whisper, not a creak, not a sigh of air, not a footfall of mouse, not a flutter of moth, not a settling of dust to be heard at all. Only desolate silence. And John at last could endure his fears and suspicions no longer. He got out of bed and stared from his square casement. He could see nothing. He tried to thrust it open; it would not move. He went downstairs and unbarred the door and looked out. He saw, as it were, a deep, clear, green shade, from behind which the songs of the birds rose faint as in a dream.

And then he sighed like a grampus and sat down, and knew that the fairies had beaten him. Like Jack's beanstalk, in one night had grown up a dense wall of peas. He pushed and pulled and hacked with his axe, and kicked with his shoes, and buffeted with his blunderbuss. But it was all in vain. He sat down once more in his chair beside the hearth and covered his face with his hands. And at last Griselda, too, awoke, and came down with her candle. And she comforted her brother, and told him if he would do what she bade she would soon make all right again. And he promised her.

So with a scarf she bound tight his hands behind him; and with a rope she bound his feet together, so that he could neither run nor throw stones, peas or cheeses. She bound his eyes and ears and mouth with a napkin, so that he could neither see, hear, smell, nor cry out. And, that done, she pushed and pulled him like a great bundle, and at last rolled him out of sight into the chimney-corner against the wall. Then she took a small sharp pair of needlework scissors that her godmother had given her, and snipped and snipped, till at last there came a little hole in the thick green hedge of peas. And putting her mouth there she called softly through the little hole. And the fairies drew near the doorstep and nodded and nodded and listened.

And then and there Griselda made a bargain with them for the forgiveness of John – a lock of her golden hair; seven dishes of ewes' milk; three and thirty bunches of currants, red, white and black; a bag of thistledown; three handkerchiefs full of lambs' wool; nine jars of honey; a peppercorn of spice. All these (except the hair) John was to bring himself to their secret places as soon as he was able. Above all, the bargain between them was that Griselda would sit one full hour each evening of summer on the hillside in the shadow and greenness that slope down from the great forest towards the valley, where the fairies' mounds are, and where their tiny brindled cattle graze.

Her brother lay blind and deaf and dumb as a log of wood. She promised everything.

And then, instead of a rustling and a creeping, there came a rending and a crashing. Instead of green shade, light of amber; then white. And as the thick hedge withered and shrank, and the merry and furious dancing sun scorched and scorched and scorched, there came, above the singing of the birds, the bleatings of sheep – and behold sooty Soll and hungry Sly met square upon the doorstep; and all John's sheep shone white as hoar-frost on his pastures; and every lamb was garlanded with pimpernel and eyebright; and the old fat ewes stood still, with saddles of moss; and their laughing riders sat and saw Griselda standing in the doorway in her beautiful yellow hair.

As for John, tied up like a sack in the chimney-corner, down came his cheese again, crash upon his head, and, not being able to say anything, he said nothing.

The Elves

~

Ludwig Tieck

"WHERE IS OUR LITTLE Mary?" said the father.

"She is playing out upon the green there, with our neighbour's boy," replied the mother.

"I wish they may not run away and lose themselves," said he; "they are so thoughtless."

The mother looked for the little ones, and brought them their evening luncheon. "It is warm," said the boy; "and Mary had a longing for the red cherries."

"Have a care, children," said the mother, "and do not run too far from home, and not into the wood; Father and I are going to the fields."

Little Andres answered, "Never fear, the wood frightens us; we shall sit here by the house, where there are people near us."

The mother went in, and soon came out again with her husband. They locked the door, and turned towards the fields to look after their labourers, and see their hay-harvest in the meadow. Their house lay upon a little green height, encircled by a pretty ring of paling, which likewise enclosed their fruit and flower garden. The hamlet stretched somewhat deeper down, and on the other side lay the castle of the count. Martin rented the large farm from this nobleman, and was living in contentment with his wife and only child; for he yearly saved some money, and had the prospect of becoming a man of substance by his industry, for the ground was productive, and the count not illiberal.

As he walked with his wife to the fields, he gazed cheerfully round, and said, "What a different look this quarter has, Brigitta, from the place we lived in formerly! Here it is all so green; the whole village is bedecked with thick-spreading fruit-trees; the ground is full of beautiful herbs and flowers; all the houses are cheerful and cleanly, the inhabitants are at their ease: nay, I could almost fancy that the woods are greener here than elsewhere, and the sky bluer; and, so far as the eye can reach, you have pleasure and delight in beholding the bountiful earth."

"And, whenever you cross the stream," said Brigitta, "you are, as it were, in another world, all is so dreary and withered; but every traveller declares that our village is the fairest in the country far and near."

"All but that fir-ground," said her husband; "do but look back to it, how dark and dismal that solitary spot is, lying in the gay scene; the dingy fir-trees with the smoky huts behind them, the ruined stalls, the brook flowing past with a sluggish melancholy."

"It is true," replied Brigitta; "if you but approach that spot, you grow disconsolate and sad; you know not why. What sort of people can they be that live there, and keep themselves so separate from the rest of us, as if they had an evil conscience?"

"A miserable crew," replied the young farmer: "gipsies, seemingly, that steal and cheat in other quarters, and have their hoard and hiding-place here. I wonder only that his lordship suffers them."

"Who knows," said the wife, with an accent of pity, "but perhaps they may be poor people, wishing, out of shame, to conceal their poverty; for, after all, no one can say aught ill of them; the only thing is that they do not go to church, and none knows how they live; for the little garden, which indeed seems altogether waste, cannot possibly support them; and fields they have none."

"God knows," said Martin, as they went along, "what trade they follow; no mortal comes to them, for the place they live in is as if bewitched and excommunicated, so that even our wildest fellows will not venture into it."

Such conversation they pursued while walking to the fields. That gloomy spot they spoke of lay aside from the hamlet. In a dell, begirt with firs, you might behold a hut, and various ruined office-houses; rarely was smoke seen to mount from it, still more rarely did men appear there; though at times curious people venturing somewhat nearer, had perceived upon the bench before the hut some hideous women, in ragged clothes, dandling in their arms some children equally dirty and ill-favoured; black dogs were running up and down upon the boundary; and, of an evening, a man of monstrous size was seen to cross the foot-bridge of the brook, and disappear in the hut; and in the darkness various shapes were observed, moving like shadows round a fire in the open air. This piece of ground, the firs, and the ruined huts, formed, in truth, a strange contrast with the bright green landscape, the white houses of the hamlet, and the stately new-built castle.

The two little ones had now eaten their fruit: it came into their heads to run races; and the little nimble Mary always got the start of the less active Andres. "It is not fair," cried Andres, at last; "let us try it for some length, then we shall see who wins."

"As thou wilt," said Mary; "only to the brook we must not run."

"No," said Andres; "but there, on the hill, stands the large pear-tree, a quarter of a mile from this. I shall run by the left, round past the fir-ground; thou canst try it by the right, over the fields; so we do not meet till we get up, and then we shall see which of us is swifter."

"Done," cried Mary, and began to run; "for we shall not mar one another by the way; and my father says it is as far to the hill by that side of the gipsies' house as by this."

Andres had already started, and Mary, turning to the right, could no longer see him. "It is very silly," said she to herself: "I have only to take heart, and run along the bridge, past the hut, and through the yard, and I shall certainly be first." She was already standing by the brook and the clump of firs. "Shall I? No: it is too frightful," said she. A little white dog was standing on the farther side, and barking with might and main. In her terror, Mary thought the dog some monster, and sprang back. "Fy! Fy!" said she: "the dolt is gone halfway by this time, while I stand here considering." The little dog kept barking, and, as she looked at it more narrowly, it seemed no longer frightful, but, on the contrary, quite pretty: it had a red collar round its neck, with a glittering bell; and as it raised its head, and shook itself in barking, the little bell sounded with the finest tinkle. "Well, I must risk it!" cried she: "I will run for life; quick, quick, I am through; certainly to Heaven! They cannot eat me up alive in half a minute!" And with this, the gay, courageous little Mary sprang along the foot-bridge, passed the dog, which ceased its barking and began to fawn on her, and in a moment she was standing on the other bank, and the black firs all round concealed from view her father's house and the rest of the landscape.

But what was her astonishment when here! The loveliest, most variegated flower-garden lay round her; tulips, roses, and lilies were glittering in the fairest colours; blue and gold-red butterflies were wavering in the blossoms; cages of shining wire were hung on the espaliers, with many-coloured birds in them, singing beautiful songs; and children, in short white frocks, with flowing yellow hair and brilliant eyes, were frolicking about: some playing with lambkins, some feeding the birds or gathering flowers, and giving them to one another; some, again, were eating cherries, grapes, and ruddy apricots. No hut was to be seen; but instead of it a large fair house, with a brazen door and lofty statues, stood glancing in the middle of the space. Mary was confounded with surprise, and knew not what to think; but, not being bashful, she went right up to the first of the children, held out her hand, and wished the little creature good even.

"Art thou come to visit us, then?" said the glittering child; "I saw thee running, playing on the other side, but thou wert frightened for our little dog."

"So you are not gipsies and rogues," said Mary, "as Andres always told me! He is a stupid thing, and talks of much he does not understand."

"Stay with us," said the strange little girl; "thou wilt like it well."

"But we are running a race."

"Thou wilt find thy comrade soon enough. There, take and eat."

Mary ate, and found the fruit more sweet than any she had ever tasted in her life before; and Andres, and the race, and the prohibition of her parents were entirely forgotten.

A stately woman, in a shining robe, came towards them, and asked about the stranger child. "Fairest lady," said Mary, "I came running hither by chance, and now they wish to keep me."

"Thou art aware, Zerina," said the lady, "that she can be here but for a little while; besides, thou shouldst have asked my leave."

"I thought," said Zerina, "when I saw her admitted across the bridge, that I might do it; we have often seen her running in the fields, and thou thyself hast taken pleasure in her lively temper. She will have to leave us soon enough."

"No, I will stay here," said the little stranger; "for here it is so beautiful, and here I shall find the prettiest playthings, and stores of berries and cherries. On the other side it is not half so grand."

The gold-robed lady went away with a smile; and many of the children now came bounding round the happy Mary in their mirth, and twitched her, and incited her to dance; others brought her lambs, or curious playthings; others made music on instruments, and sang to it.

She kept, however, by the playmate who had first met her; for Zerina was the kindest and loveliest of them all. Little Mary cried and cried again: "I will stay with you for ever; I will stay with you, and you shall be my sisters"; at which the children all laughed and embraced her. "Now we shall have a royal sport," said Zerina. She ran into the palace, and returned with a little golden box, in which lay a quantity of seeds, like glittering dust. She lifted of it with her little hand, and scattered some grains on the green earth. Instantly the grass began to move, as in waves; and, after a few moments, bright rose-bushes started from the ground, shot rapidly up, and budded all at once, while the sweetest perfume filled the place.

Mary also took a little of the dust, and, having scattered it, she saw white lilies, and the most variegated pinks, pushing up. At a signal from Zerina, the flowers disappeared, and others rose in their room. "Now," said Zerina, "look for something greater." She laid two pine-seeds in the ground, and stamped them in sharply with her foot. Two green bushes stood before them. "Grasp me fast," said she; and Mary threw her arms about the slender form. She

felt herself borne upward; for the trees were springing under them with the greatest speed; the tall pines waved to and fro, and the two children held each other fast embraced, swinging this way and that in the red clouds of the twilight, and kissed each other; while the rest were climbing up and down the trunks with quick dexterity, pushing and teasing one another with loud laughter when they met; if anyone fell down in the press, it flew through the air, and sank slowly and surely to the ground. At length Mary was beginning to feel frightened; and the other little child sang a few loud tones, and the trees again sank down, and set them on the ground as gradually as they had lifted them before to the clouds.

They next went through the brazen door of the palace. Here many fair women, elderly and young, were sitting in the round hall, partaking of the fairest fruits, and listening to glorious invisible music. In the vaulting of the ceiling, palms, flowers, and groves stood painted, among which little figures of children were sporting and winding in every graceful posture; and with the tones of the music, the images altered and glowed with the most burning colours; now the blue and green were sparkling like radiant light, now these tints faded back in paleness, the purple flamed up, and the gold took fire; and then the naked children seemed to be alive among the flower-garlands, and to draw breath, and emit it through their ruby-coloured lips, so that by fits you could see the glance of their little white teeth, and the lighting up of their azure eyes.

From the hall, a stair of brass led down to a subterranean chamber. Here lay much gold and silver, and precious stones of every hue shone out between them. Strange vessels stood along the walls, and all seemed filled with costly things. The gold was worked into many forms, and glittered with the friendliest red. Many little dwarfs were busied sorting the pieces from the heap, and putting them in the vessels; others, hunch-backed and bandy-legged, with long red noses, were tottering slowly along, half bent to the ground, under full sacks, which they bore as millers do their grain; and, with much panting, shaking out the gold-dust on the ground. Then they darted awkwardly to the right and left, and caught the rolling balls that were like to run away; and it happened now and then that one in his eagerness overset the other, so that both fell heavily and clumsily to the ground. They made angry faces, and looked askance, as Mary laughed at their gestures and their ugliness. Behind them sat an old, crumpled little man, whom Zerina reverently greeted; he thanked her with a grave inclination of his head. He held a sceptre in his hand, and wore a crown upon his brow, and all the other dwarfs appeared to regard him as their master, and obey his nod.

"What! More wanted?" asked he, with a surly voice, as the children came a little nearer. Mary was afraid, and did not speak; but her companion answered, they were only come to look about them in the chambers. "Still your old child's tricks!" replied the dwarf; "will there never be an end to idleness?" With this, he turned again to his employment, kept his people weighting and sorting the ingots; some he sent away on errands, some he chid with angry tones.

"Who is the gentleman?" said Mary.

"Our Metal-Prince," replied Zerina, as they walked along.

They seemed once more to reach the open air, for they were standing by a lake, yet no sun appeared, and they saw no sky above their heads. A little boat received them, and Zerina steered it diligently forward. It shot rapidly along. On gaining the middle of the lake, the strangers saw that multitudes of pipes, channels, and brooks were spreading from the sea in every direction. "These waters to the right," said Zerina, "flow beneath your garden, and this is why it blooms so freshly; by the other side we get down into the great stream."

On a sudden, out of all the channels, and from every quarter of the lake, came a crowd of little children swimming up: some wore garlands of sedge and water-lily; some had red stems of coral; others were blowing on crooked shells; a tumultuous noise echoed merrily from the dark shoes; among the children might be seen the fairest women sporting in the waters, and often several of the children sprang about some one of them, and with kisses hung upon her neck and shoulders. All saluted the strangers; and these steered onward through the revelry out of the lake into a little river, which grew narrower and narrower. At last the boat came aground. The strangers took their leave, and Zerina knocked against the cliff. This opened like a door, and a female form, all red, assisted them to mount. "Are you all brisk here?" enquired Zerina.

"They are just at work," replied the other, "and happy as they could wish; indeed, the heat is very pleasant."

They went up a winding stair, and on a sudden Mary found herself in a most resplendent hall, so that, as she entered, her eyes were dazzled by the radiance. Flame-coloured tapestry covered the walls with a purple glow; and when her eye had grown a little used to it, the stranger saw, to her astonishment, that in the tapestry there were figures moving up and down in dancing joyfulness; in form so beautiful, and of so fair proportions, that nothing could be seen more graceful: their bodies were as of red crystals, so that it appeared as if the blood were visible within them, flowing and playing in its courses. They smiled on the stranger, and saluted her with various bows; but as Mary was about approaching nearer them, Zerina plucked her sharply back, crying, "Thou wilt burn thyself, my little Mary, for the whole of it is fire."

Mary felt the heat. "Why do the pretty creatures not come out," said she, "and play with us?"

"As thou livest in the Air," replied the other, "so are they obliged to stay continually in Fire, and would faint and languish if they left it. Look, now how glad they are, how they laugh and shout; those down below spread out the fire-floods everywhere beneath the earth, and thereby the flowers, and fruits, and vine are made to flourish; these red streams, again, are to run beside the brooks of water; and thus the fiery creatures are kept ever busy and glad. But for thee it is too hot here; let us return to the garden."

In the garden the scene had changed since they left it. The moonshine was lying on every flower; the birds were silent, and the children were asleep in complicated groups among the green groves. Mary and her friend, however, did not feel fatigue, but walked about in the warm summer night, in abundant talk, till morning.

When the day dawned they refreshed themselves on fruit and milk, and Mary said, "Suppose we go, by way of change, to the firs, and see how things look there?"

"With all my heart," replied Zerina; "thou wilt see our watchmen, too, and they will surely please thee; they are standing up among the trees on the mound." The two proceeded through the flower garden by pleasant groves full of nightingales; then they ascended a vine-hill;

and at last, after long following the windings of a clear brook, arrived at the firs, and the height which bounded the domain. "How does it come," said Mary, "that we have to walk so far here, when, without, the circuit is so narrow?"

"I know not," said her friend; "but so it is."

They mounted to the dark firs, and a chill wind blew from without in their faces; a haze seemed lying far and wide over the landscape. On the top were many strange forms standing, with mealy, dusty faces, their misshapen heads not unlike those of white owls; they were clad in folded cloaks of shaggy wool; they held umbrellas of curious skins stretched out above them; and they waved and fanned themselves incessantly with large bat's wings, which flared out curiously beside the woollen roquelaures.

"I could laugh, yet I am frightened," cried Mary.

"These are our good, trusty watchmen," said her playmate; "they stand here and wave their fans, that cold anxiety and inexplicable fear may fall on every one that attempts to approach us. They are covered so, because without it is now cold and rainy, which they cannot bear. But snow, or wind, or cold air never reaches down to us – here is an everlasting spring and summer; yet, if these poor people on the top were not frequently relieved, they would certainly perish."

"But who are you, then?" said Mary, while again descending to the flowery fragrance; "or have you no name at all?"

"We are called the Elves," replied the friendly child; "people talk about us in the Earth, as I have heard."

They now perceived a mighty bustle on the green. "The fair bird is come!" cried the children to them. All hastened to the hall. Here, as they approached, young and old were crowding over the threshold, all shouting for joy, and from within resounded a triumphant peal of music. Having entered, they perceived the vast circuit filled with the most varied forms, and all were looking upward to a large bird with glancing plumage, that was sweeping slowly round in the dome, and in its stately flight describing many a circle. The music sounded more gaily than before; the colours and lights alternated more rapidly. At last the music ceased; and the bird, with a rustling noise, floated down upon a glittering crown that hung hovering in air under the high window, by which the hall was lighted from above. His plumage was purple and green, and shining golden streaks played through it; on his head there waved a diadem of feathers, so resplendent that they glanced like jewels. His bill was red, and his legs of a glancing blue. As he moved, the tints gleamed through each other, and the eye was charmed with their radiance. His size was as that of an eagle. But now he opened his glittering beak, and sweetest melodies came pouring from his moved breast, in finer tones than the lovesick nightingale gives forth; still stronger rose the song, and streamed like floods of light, so that all, the very children themselves, were moved by it to tears of joy and rapture. When he ceased, all bowed before him; he again flew round the dome in circles, then darted through the door, and soared into the light heaven, where he shone far up like a red point, and then soon vanished from their eyes.

"Why are ye all so glad?" enquired Mary, bending to her fair playmate, who seemed smaller than yesterday.

"The King is coming!" said the little one; "many of us have never seen him, and whithersoever he turns his face, there is happiness and mirth; we have long looked for him, more anxiously than you look for spring when winter lingers with you; and now he has announced, by his fair herald, that he is at hand. This wise and glorious bird, that has been sent to us by the King, is called Phoenix; he dwells far off in Arabia, on a tree which there is no other that resembles on earth, as in like manner there is no second Phoenix. When he feels himself grown old, he builds a pile of balm and incense, kindles it, and dies singing; and then from the fragrant ashes soars up the renewed Phoenix, with unlessened beauty. It is seldom he so wings his course that men behold him; and when once in centuries this does occur, they note it in their annals, and expect remarkable events. But now, my friend, thou and I must part; for the sight of the King is not permitted thee."

Then the lady with the golden robe came through the throng, and, beckoning Mary to her, led her into a sequestered walk. "Thou must leave us, my dear child," said she; "the King is to hold his court here for twenty years, perhaps longer; and fruitfulness and blessings will spread far over the land, but chiefly here beside us; all the brooks and rivulets will become more bountiful, all the fields and gardens richer, the wine more generous, the meadows more fertile, and the woods more fresh and green; a milder air will blow, no hail shall hurt, no flood shall threaten. Take this ring, and think of us; but beware of telling anyone of our existence; or we must fly this land, and thou and all around will lose the happiness and blessing of our neighbourhood. Once more kiss thy playmate, and farewell."

They issued from the walk: Zerina wept, Mary stooped to embrace her, and they parted. Already she was on the narrow bridge; the cold air was blowing on her back from the firs; the little dog barked with all its might, and rang its little bell; she looked round, then hastened over, for the darkness of the firs, the bleakness of the ruined huts, the shadows of the twilight, were filling her with terror.

"What a night my parents must have had on my account!" said she to herself, as she stepped on the green; "and I dare not tell them where I have been, or what wonders I have witnessed, nor indeed would they believe me." Two men passing by saluted her, and as they went along, she heard them say, "What a pretty girl! Where can she come from?" With quickened steps she approached the house; but the trees which were hanging last night loaded with fruit, were now standing dry and leafless; the house was differently painted, and a new barn had been built beside it. Mary was amazed, and thought she must be dreaming. In this perplexity she opened the door, and behind the table sat her father, between an unknown woman and a stranger youth. "Good God! Father," cried she, "where is my mother?"

"Thy mother!" said the woman, with a forecasting tone, and sprang towards her: "Ha! Thou surely canst not – Yes, indeed, indeed thou art my lost, long-lost, dear, only Mary!" She had recognized her by a little brown mole beneath the chin, as well as by her eyes and shape. All embraced her, all were moved with joy, and the parents wept. Mary was astonished that she almost reached to her father's stature; and she could not understand how her mother had become so changed and faded. She asked the name of the stranger youth. "It is our neighbour's Andres," said Martin. "How comest thou to us again, so unexpectedly, after seven long years? Where hast thou been? Why didst thou never send us tidings of thee?"

"Seven years!" said Mary, and could not order her ideas and recollections. "Seven whole years?"

"Yes, yes," said Andres, laughing, and shaking her trustfully by the hand; "I have won the race, good Mary; I was at the pear-tree and back again seven years ago, and thou, sluggish creature, art but just returned!"

They again asked, they pressed her; but, remembering her instruction, she could answer nothing. It was they themselves chiefly that, by degrees, shaped a story for her: How, having lost her way, she had been taken up by a coach, and carried to a strange, remote part, where she could not give the people any notion of her parents' residence; how she was conducted to a distant town, where certain worthy persons brought her up, and loved her; how they had lately died, and at length she had recollected her birthplace, and so returned. "No matter how it is!" exclaimed her mother; "enough that we have thee again, my little daughter, my own, my all!"

Andres waited supper, and Mary could not be at home in anything she saw. The house seemed small and dark; she was astonished at her dress, which was clean and simple, but appeared quite foreign; she looked at the ring on her finger, and the gold of it glittered strangely, enclosing a stone of burning red. To her father's question, she replied that the ring also was a present from her benefactors.

She was glad when the hour of sleep arrived, and she hastened to her bed. Next morning she felt much more collected; she had now arranged her thoughts a little, and could better stand the questions of the people in the village, all of whom came in to bid her welcome. Andres was there too, with the earliest, active, glad, and serviceable beyond all others. The blooming maiden of fifteen had made a deep impression on him: he had passed a sleepless night. The people of the castle likewise sent for Mary, and she had once more to tell her story to them, which was now grown quite familiar to her. The old Count and his lady were surprised at her good breeding; she was modest, but not embarrassed; she made answer courteously in good phrases to all their questions; all fear of noble persons and their equipage had passed away from her; for when she measured these halls and forms by the wonders and the high beauty she had seen with the Elves in their hidden abode, this earthly splendour seemed dim to her; the presence of men was almost mean. The young lords were charmed with her beauty.

It was now February. The trees were budding earlier than usual; the nightingale had never come so soon; the spring rose fairer in the land than the oldest men could recollect it. In every quarter, little brooks gushed out to irrigate the pastures and meadows; the hills seemed heaving, the vines rose higher and higher, the fruit-trees blossomed as they had never done, and a swelling, fragrant blessedness hung suspended heavily in rosy clouds over the scene. All prospered beyond expectation; no rude day, no tempest injured the fruits; the vine flowed blushing in immense grapes; and the inhabitants of the place felt astonished, and were captivated as in a sweet dream. The next year was like its forerunner; but the men had become accustomed to the marvellous. In autumn, Mary yielded to the pressing entreaties of Andres and her parents; she was betrothed to him, and in winter they were married.

She often thought with inward longing of her residence beyond the fir-trees; she continued serious and still. Beautiful as all that lay around her was, she knew of something yet more beautiful; and from the remembrance of this a faint regret attuned her nature to soft melancholy. It smote her painfully when her father and mother talked about the gipsies and vagabonds that dwelt in the dark spot of the ground. Often she was on the point of speaking out in defence of those good beings, whom she knew to be the benefactors of the land, especially to Andres, who appeared to take delight in zealously abusing them; yet still she repressed the word that was struggling to escape her bosom. So passed this year; in the next she was solaced by a little daughter, whom she named Elfrida, thinking of the designation of her friendly Elves.

The young people lived with Martin and Brigitta, the house being large enough for all, and helped their parents in conducting their now extended husbandry. The little Elfrida soon displayed peculiar faculties and gifts, for she could walk at a very early age, and could speak perfectly before she was a twelvemonth old; and, after some few years, she had become so wise and clever, and of such wondrous beauty, that all people regarded her with astonishment; and her mother could not keep away the thought that her child resembled one of those shining little ones in the space behind the firs.

Elfrida cared not to be with other children, but seemed to avoid, with a sort of horror, their tumultuous amusements, and liked best to be alone. She would then retire into a corner of the garden, and read, or work diligently with her needle; often, also, you might see her sitting, as if deep sunk in thought, or violently walking up and down the alleys, speaking to herself. Her parents readily allowed her to have her will in these things, for she was healthy, and waxed apace; only her strange, sagacious answers and observations often made them anxious. "Such wise children do not grow to age," her grandmother Brigitta many times observed; "they are too good for this world; the child, besides, is beautiful beyond nature, and will never find its proper place on earth."

The little girl had this peculiarity, that she was very loath to let herself be served by anyone, but endeavoured to do everything herself. She was almost the earliest riser in the house; she washed herself carefully, and dressed without assistance. At night she was equally careful; she took special heed to pack up her clothes and washed with her own hands, allowing no one, not even her mother, to meddle with her articles. The mother humoured her in this caprice, not thinking it of any consequence. But what was her astonishment when, happening one holyday to insist, regardless of Elfrida's tears and screams, on dressing her out for a visit to the castle, she found upon her breast, suspended by a string, a piece of gold of a strange form, which she directly recognized as one of that sort she had seen in such abundance in the subterranean vault! The little thing was greatly frightened, and at last confessed that she had found it in the garden, and, as she liked it much, had kept it carefully; she at the same time prayed so earnestly and pressingly to have it back that Mary fastened it again on its former place, and, full of thoughts, went out with her in silence to the castle.

Sideward from the farmhouse lay some offices for the storing of produce and implements, and behind these there was a little green, with an old grove, now visited by no one, as, from the new arrangement of the buildings, it lay too far from the garden. In this solitude Elfrida delighted most; and it occurred to nobody to interrupt her there, so that frequently her parents did not see her for half a day. One afternoon her mother chanced to be in these buildings, seeking for some lost article among the lumber, and she noticed that a beam of light was coming in, through a chink in the wall. She took a thought of looking through this aperture, and seeing what her child was busied with; and it happened that a stone was lying loose, and could be pushed aside, so that she obtained a view right into the grove.

Elfrida was sitting there on a little bench, and beside her the well-known Zerina; and the children were playing and amusing one another in the kindliest unity. The Elf embraced her beautiful companion, and said mournfully, "Ah! dear little creature, as I sport with thee, so have I sported with thy mother, when she was a child; but you mortals so soon grow tall and thoughtful! It is very hard; wert thou but to be a child as long as I!"

"Willingly would I do it," said Elfrida; "but they all say I shall come to sense, and give over playing altogether; for I have great gifts, as they think, for growing wise. Ah! And then I shall see thee no more, thou dear Zerina! Yet it is with us as with the fruit-tree flowers: how glorious the blossoming apple-tree, with its red bursting buds! It looks so stately and broad, and everyone that passes under it thinks, surely something great will come of it; then the sun grows hot, and the buds come joyfully forth; but the wicked kernel is already there, which pushes off and casts away the fair flower's dress; and now, in pain and waxing, it can do nothing more, but must grow to fruit in harvest. An apple, to be sure, is pretty and refreshing, yet nothing to the blossom of spring. So is it with us mortals: I am not glad in the least at growing to be a tall girl. Ah! Could I but once visit you!"

"Since the King is with us," said Zerina, "it is quite impossible; but I will come to thee, my darling, often, often, and none shall see me either here or there. I will pass invisible through the air, or fly over to thee like a bird: oh! we will be much, much together, while thou art still little. What can I do to please thee?"

"Thou must like me very dearly," said Elfrida, "as I like thee in my heart: but come, let us make another rose."

Zerina took the well-known box from her bosom, threw two grains from it on the ground, and instantly a green bush stood before them, with two deep-red roses, bending their heads as if to kiss each other. The children plucked them, smiling, and the bush disappeared. "Oh, that it would not die so soon!" said Elfrida; "this red child, this wonder of the earth!"

"Give it me here," said the little Elf; then breathed thrice upon the budding rose, and kissed it thrice. "Now," said she, giving back the rose, "it will continue fresh and blooming till winter."

"I will keep it," said Elfrida, "as an image of thee; I will guard it in my little room, and kiss it night and morning, as it were thyself."

"The sun is setting," said the other; "I must home." They embraced again, and Zerina vanished.

In the evening Mary clasped her child to her breast with a feeling of alarm and veneration. She henceforth allowed the good little girl more liberty than formerly, and often calmed her husband, when he came to search for the child, which for some time he was wont to do, as her retiredness did not please him, and he feared that, in the end, it might make her silly, or even pervert her understanding. The mother often glided to the chink, and almost always found the bright Elf beside her child, employed in sport or in earnest conversation.

"Wouldst thou like to fly?" enquired Zerina, once.

"Oh, well! How well!" replied Elfrida; and the fairy clasped her mortal playmate in her arms, and mounted with her from the ground, till they hovered above the grove. The mother, in alarm, forgot herself, and pushed out her head in terror to look after them; when Zerina, from the air, held up her finger, and threatened, yet smiled; then descended with the child, embraced her, and disappeared. After this it happened more than once that Mary was observed by her; and every time, the shining little creature shook her head, or threatened, yet with friendly looks.

Often, in disputing with her husband, Mary had said in her zeal, "Thou dost injustice to the poor people in the hut!" But when Andres pressed her to explain why she differed in opinion from the whole village, nay, from his lordship himself, and how she could understand it better than the whole of them, she still broke off, embarrassed, and became silent. One day, after dinner, Andres grew more violent than ever, and maintained that, by one means or another, the crew must be packed away, as a nuisance to the country; when his wife in anger said to him, "Hush! For they are benefactors to thee and to every one of us."

"Benefactors!" cried the other, in astonishment: "these rogues and vagabonds!"

In her indignation, she was now at last tempted to relate to him, under promise of the strictest secrecy, the history of her youth; and as Andres at every word grew more incredulous, and shook his head in mockery, she took him by the hand and led him to the chink, where, to his amazement, he beheld the glittering Elf sporting with his child, and caressing her in the grove. He knew not what to say; an exclamation of astonishment escaped him, and Zerina raised her eyes. On the instant she grew pale and trembled violently; not with friendly but with indignant looks, she made the sign of threatening, and then said to Elfrida, "Thou canst not help it, dearest heart; but they will never learn sense, wise as they believe themselves." She embraced the little one with stormy haste; and then, in the shape of a raven, flew with hoarse cries over the garden towards the firs.

In the evening the little one was very still: she kissed her rose with tears. Mary felt depressed, and frightened, Andres scarcely spoke. It grew dark. Suddenly there went a rustling through the trees; birds flew to and fro with wild screaming; thunder was heard to roll, the earth shook, and tones of lamentation moaned in the air. Andres and his wife had not courage to rise; they shrouded themselves within the curtains, and with fear and trembling awaited the day. Towards morning it grew calmer; and all was silent when the sun, with his cheerful light, rose over the wood.

Andres dressed himself, and Mary now observed that the stone of the ring upon her finger had become quite pale. On opening the door, the sun shone clear on their faces, but the scene around them they could scarcely recognize. The freshness of the wood was gone; the hills were shrunk, the brooks were flowing languidly with scanty streams, the sky seemed grey; and when you turned to the firs, they were standing there, no darker or more dreary than the other trees. The huts behind them were no longer frightful; and several inhabitants of the village came and told about the fearful night, and how they had been across the spot where the gipsies had lived; how these people must have left the place at last, for their huts were standing empty, and within had quite a common look, just like the dwellings of other poor people: some of their household gear was left behind.

Elfrida, in secret, said to her mother, "I could not sleep last night; and, in my fright at the noise, I was praying from the bottom of my heart, when the door suddenly opened, and my playmate entered to take leave of me. She had a travelling-pouch slung round her, a hat on her head, and a very large staff in her hand. She was very angry at thee, since on thy account she had now to suffer the severest and most painful punishments, as she had always been so fond of thee; for all of them, she said, were very loath to leave this quarter."

Mary forbade her to speak of this; and now the ferryman came across the river, and told them new wonders. As it was growing dark, a stranger man of large size had come to him, and hired his boat till sunrise; and with this condition; that the boatman should remain quiet in his house – at least, not cross the threshold of his door. "I was frightened," continued the old man, "and the strange bargain would not let me sleep. I slipped softly to the window, and looked towards the river. Great clouds were driving restlessly through the sky, and the distant woods were rustling fearfully; it was as if my cottage shook, and moans and lamentations glided round it. On a sudden I perceived a white, streaming light, that grew broader and broader, like many thousands of falling stars: sparkling and waving, it proceeded forward from the dark fir-ground, moved over the fields, and spread itself along towards the river. Then I heard a trampling, a jingling, a bustling and rushing, nearer and nearer; it went forward to my boat, and all stepped into it, men and women, as it seemed, and children; and the tall stranger ferried them over. In the river were by the boat swimming many thousands of glittering forms; in the air, white clouds and lights were wavering; and all lamented and bewailed that they must travel forth so far, far away, and leave their beloved dwelling. The noise of the rudder and the water creaked and gurgled between whiles, and then suddenly there would be silence. Many a time the boat landed, and went back, and was again laden; many heavy casks, too, they took along with them, which multitudes of horrid-looking little fellows carried and rolled; whether they were devils or goblins, Heaven only knows. Then came, in waving brightness, a stately freight: it seemed an old man mounted on a small, white horse, and all were crowding round him. I saw nothing of the horse but its head, for the rest of it was covered with costly glittering cloths and trappings. On his brow the old man had a crown so bright that as he came across I thought the sun was rising there, and the redness of the dawn was glimmering in my eyes. Thus it went on all night. I at last fell asleep in the tumult, half in joy, half in terror. In the morning all was still; but the river is, as it were, run off, and I know not how I am to steer my boat in it now."

The same year there came a blight; the woods died away, the springs ran dry; and the scene, which had once been the joy of every traveller, was in autumn standing waste, naked, and bald, scarcely showing here and there, in the sea of sand, a spot or two where grass, with a dingy greenness, still grew up. The fruit-trees all withered, the vines faded away, and the aspect of the place became so melancholy, that the Count, with his people, next year left the castle, which in time decayed and fell to ruins.

Elfrida gazed on her rose day and night with deep longing, and thought of her kind playmate; and as it drooped and withered, so did she also hang her head; and before the spring, the little maiden had herself faded away. Mary often stood upon the spot before the hut, and wept for the happiness that had departed. She wasted herself away like her child, and in a few years she too was gone. Old Martin, with his son-in-law, returned to the quarter where he had lived before.

The Enchanted Watch

∾

Charles Deulin

ONCE UPON A TIME there lived a rich man who had three sons. When they grew up, he sent the eldest to travel and see the world, and three years passed before his family saw him again. Then he returned, magnificently dressed, and his father was so delighted with his behaviour that he gave a great feast in his honour, to which all the relations and friends were invited.

When the rejoicings were ended, the second son begged leave of his father to go in his turn to travel and mix with the world. The father was enchanted at the request, and gave him plenty of money for his expenses, saying, "If you behave as well as your brother, I will do honour to you as I did to him." The young man promised to do his best, and his conduct during three years was all that it should be. Then he went home, and his father was so pleased with him that his feast of welcome was even more splendid than the one before.

The third brother, whose name was Jenik, or Johnnie, was considered the most foolish of the three. He never did anything at home except sit over the stove and dirty himself with the ashes; but he also begged his father's leave to travel for three years. "Go if you like, you idiot; but what good will it do you?"

The youth paid no heed to his father's observations as long as he obtained permission to go. The father saw him depart with joy, glad to get rid of him, and gave him a handsome sum of money for his needs.

Once, as he was making one of his journeys, Jenik chanced to cross a meadow where some shepherds were just about to kill a dog. He entreated them to spare it, and to give it to him instead, which they willingly did, and he went on his way, followed by the dog. A little further on he came upon a cat, which someone was going to put to death. He implored its life, and the cat followed him. Finally, in another place, he saved a serpent, which was also handed over to him, and now they made a party of four – the dog behind Jenik, the cat behind the dog, and the serpent behind the cat.

Then the serpent said to Jenik, "Go wherever you see me go," for in the autumn, when all the serpents hide themselves in their holes, this serpent was going in search of his king, who was king of all the snakes.

Then he added: "My king will scold me for my long absence, everyone else is housed for the winter, and I am very late. I shall have to tell him what danger I have been in, and how, without your help, I should certainly have lost my life. The King will ask what you would like in return, and be sure you beg for the watch which hangs on the wall. It has all sorts of wonderful properties; you only need to rub it to get whatever you like."

No sooner said than done. Jenik became the master of the watch, and the moment he got out he wished to put its virtues to the proof. He was hungry, and thought it would be delightful to eat in the meadow a loaf of new bread and a steak of good beef washed down by a flask of wine, so he scratched the watch, and in an instant it was all before him. Imagine his joy!

Evening soon came, and Jenik rubbed his watch and thought it would be very pleasant to have a room with a comfortable bed and a good supper. In an instant they were all before him. After supper he went to bed and slept till morning, as every honest man ought to do. Then he set forth for his father's house, his mind dwelling on the feast that would be awaiting him. But as he returned, in the same old clothes in which he went away, his father flew into a great rage, and refused to do anything for him. Jenik went to his old place near the stove, and dirtied himself in the ashes without anybody minding.

The third day, feeling rather dull, he thought it would be nice to see a three-storey house filled with beautiful furniture, and with vessels of silver and gold. So he rubbed the watch, and there it all was. Jenik went to look for his father, and said to him: "You offered me no feast of welcome, but permit me to give one to you, and come and let me show you my plate."

The father was much astonished, and longed to know where his son had got all this wealth. Jenik did not reply, but begged him to invite all their relations and friends to a grand banquet.

So the father invited all the world, and everyone was amazed to see such splendid things, so much plate, and so many fine dishes on the table. After the first course Jenik prayed his father to invite the King, and his daughter the Princess. He rubbed his watch and wished for a carriage ornamented with gold and silver, and drawn by six horses, with harness glittering with precious stones. The father did not dare to sit in this gorgeous coach, but went to the palace on foot. The King and his daughter were immensely surprised with the beauty of the carriage, and mounted the steps at once to go to Jenik's banquet. Then Jenik rubbed his watch afresh, and wished that for six miles the way to the house should be paved with marble. Who ever felt so astonished as the King? Never had he travelled over such a gorgeous road.

When Jenik heard the wheels of the carriage, he rubbed his watch and wished for a still more beautiful house, four storeys high, and hung with gold, silver, and damask; filled with wonderful tables, covered with dishes such as no king had ever eaten before. The

King, the Queen, and the Princess were speechless with surprise. Never had they seen such a splendid palace, nor such a high feast! At dessert, the King asked Jenik's father to give him the young man for a son-in-law. No sooner said than done! The marriage took place at once, and the King returned to his own palace, and left Jenik with his wife in the enchanted house.

Now Jenik was not a very clever man, and at the end of a very short time he began to bore his wife. She enquired how he managed to build palaces and to get so many precious things. He told her all about the watch, and she never rested till she had stolen the precious talisman. One night she took the watch, rubbed it, and wished for a carriage drawn by four horses; and in this carriage she at once set out for her father's palace. There she called to her own attendants, bade them follow her into the carriage, and drove straight to the sea-side. Then she rubbed her watch, and wished that the sea might be crossed by a bridge, and that a magnificent palace might arise in the middle of the sea. No sooner said than done. The Princess entered the house, rubbed her watch, and in an instant the bridge was gone.

Left alone, Jenik felt very miserable. His father, mother, and brothers, and, indeed, everybody else, all laughed at him. Nothing remained to him but the cat and dog whose lives he had once saved. He took them with him and went far away, for he could no longer live with his family. He reached at last a great desert, and saw some crows flying towards a mountain. One of them was a long way behind, and when he arrived his brothers enquired what had made him so late. "Winter is here," they said, "and it is time to fly to other countries." He told them that he had seen in the middle of the sea the most wonderful house that ever was built.

On hearing this, Jenik at once concluded that this must be the hiding-place of his wife. So he proceeded directly to the shore with his dog and his cat. When he arrived on the beach, he said to the dog: "You are an excellent swimmer, and you, little one, are very light; jump on the dog's back and he will take you to the palace. Once there, he will hide himself near the door, and you must steal secretly in and try to get hold of my watch."

No sooner said than done. The two animals crossed the sea; the dog hid near the house, and the cat stole into the chamber. The

Princess recognized him, and guessed why he had come; and she took the watch down to the cellar and locked it in a box. But the cat wriggled its way into the cellar, and the moment the Princess turned her back, he scratched and scratched till he had made a hole in the box. Then he took the watch between his teeth, and waited quietly till the Princess came back. Scarcely had she opened the door when the cat was outside, and the watch into the bargain.

The cat was no sooner beyond the gates than he said to the dog:

"We are going to cross the sea; be very careful not to speak to me."

The dog laid this to heart and said nothing; but when they approached the shore he could not help asking, "Have you got the watch?"

The cat did not answer – he was afraid that he might let the talisman fall. When they touched the shore the dog repeated his question.

"Yes," said the cat.

And the watch fell into the sea. Then our two friends began each to accuse the other, and both looked sorrowfully at the place where their treasure had fallen in. Suddenly a fish appeared near the edge of the sea. The cat seized it, and thought it would make them a good supper.

"I have nine little children," cried the fish. "Spare the father of a family!"

"Granted," replied the cat; "but on condition that you find our watch."

The fish executed his commission, and they brought the treasure back to their master. Jenik rubbed the watch and wished that the palace, with the Princess and all its inhabitants, should be swallowed up in the sea. No sooner said than done. Jenik returned to his parents, and he and his watch, his cat and his dog, lived together happily to the end of their days.

The Enchanted Whistle

❧

Alexandre Dumas

THERE WAS ONCE A rich and powerful king, who had a daughter remarkable for her beauty. When this princess arrived at an age to be married, he caused a proclamation to be made by sound of a trumpet, and by placards on all the walls of his kingdom, to the effect that all those who had any pretension to her hand were to assemble in a widespread meadow.

Her would-be suitors being in this way gathered together, the Princess would throw into the air a golden apple, and whoever succeeded in catching it would then have to resolve three problems, after doing which he might marry the Princess, and, the King having no son, inherit the kingdom.

On the day appointed the meeting took place. The Princess threw the golden apple into the air, but not one of the first three who caught it was able to complete the easiest task set him, and neither of them attempted those which were to follow.

At last the golden apple, thrown by the Princess into the air for the fourth time, fell into the hands of a young shepherd, who was the handsomest, but, at the same time, the poorest of all the competitors.

The first problem given him to solve – certainly as difficult as a problem in mathematics – was this:

The King had caused one hundred hares to be shut up in a stable; he who should succeed in leading them out to feed upon the meadow where the meeting was being held, the next morning, and conduct them all back to the stable the next evening, would have resolved the first problem.

When this proposition was made to the young shepherd he asked to be allowed a day to reflect upon it; the next day he would say "yes" or "no" to it.

The request appeared so just to the King that it was granted to him.

He immediately took his way to the forest, to meditate there on the means of accomplishing the task set him.

With down-bent head he slowly traversed a narrow path running beside a brook, when he came upon a little old woman with snow-white hair, but sparkling eyes, who enquired the cause of his sadness.

The young shepherd replied, shaking his head, "Alas! Nobody can be of any assistance to me, and yet I greatly desire to wed the King's daughter."

"Don't give way to despair so quickly," replied the little old woman; "tell me all about your trouble, and perhaps I may be able to get you out of your difficulty."

The young shepherd's heart was so heavy that he needed no entreaty to tell her his story.

"Is that all?" said the little old woman; "in that case you have not much to despair about."

And she took from her pocket an ivory whistle and gave it to him.

This whistle was just like other whistles in appearance; so the shepherd, thinking that it needed to be blown in a particular way, turned to ask the little old woman how this was, but she had disappeared.

Full of confidence, however, in what he regarded as a good genius, he went next day to the palace, and said to the King, "I accept, sir, and have come in search of the hares to lead them to the meadow."

On hearing this, the King rose, and said to his Minister of the Interior, "Have all the hares turned out of the stable."

The young shepherd placed himself on the threshold of the door to count them; but the first was already far away when the last was set at liberty; so much so, that when he reached the meadow he had not a single hare with him.

He sat himself down pensively, not daring to believe in the virtue of his whistle. However, he had no other resource, and placing the whistle to his lips he blew into it with all his might.

The whistle gave forth a sharp and prolonged sound.

Immediately, to his great astonishment, from right and left, from before him and behind him – from all sides, in fact – leapt the hundred hares, and set to quietly browsing on the meadow around him.

News was brought to the King, how the young shepherd had probably resolved the problem of the hares.

The King conferred on the matter with his daughter.

Both were greatly vexed; for if the young shepherd succeeded with the two other problems as well as he had with the first, the Princess would become the wife of a simple peasant, than which nothing could be more humiliating to royal pride.

"You think over the matter," said the Princess to her father, "and I will do the same."

The Princess retired to her chamber, and disguised herself in such a way as to render herself unrecognizable; then she had a horse brought for her, mounted it, and went to the young shepherd.

The hundred hares were frisking joyously about him.

"Will you sell me one of your hares?" asked the young Princess.

"I would not sell you one of my hares for all the gold in the world," replied the shepherd; "but you may gain one."

"At what price?" asked the Princess.

"By dismounting from your horse and sitting by me on the grass for a quarter of an hour."

The Princess made some objections, but as there was no other means of obtaining the hare, she descended to the ground, and seated herself by the young shepherd.

The hundred hares leaped and bounded around him.

At the end of a quarter of an hour, during which the young shepherd said a hundred tender things to her, she rose, and claimed her hare, which the shepherd, faithful to his promise, gave her.

The Princess joyfully shut it in a basket which she carried at the bow of her saddle, and rode back towards the palace.

But hardly had she ridden a quarter of a league, when the young shepherd placed his whistle to his lips and blew into it; and, at this imperative call, the hare forced up the lid of the basket, sprang to the ground, and made off as fast as his legs would carry him.

A moment afterwards, the shepherd saw a peasant coming towards him, mounted on a donkey. It was the old King, also disguised, who had quitted the palace with the same intention as his daughter.

A large bag hung from the donkey's saddle.

"Will you sell me one of your hares?" he asked of the young shepherd.

"My hares are not for sale," replied the shepherd; "but they may be gained."

"What must one do to gain one?"

The shepherd considered for a moment.

"You must kiss three times the tail of your donkey," he said.

This strange condition was greatly repugnant to the old King, who tried his hardest to escape it, going so far as to offer fifty thousand francs for a single hare, but the young shepherd would not budge from the terms he had named. At last the King, who held absolutely to getting possession of one of the hares, submitted to the conditions, humiliating as they were for a king. Three times he kissed the tail of his donkey, who was greatly surprised at a king doing him so much honour; and the shepherd, faithful to his promise, gave him the hare demanded with so much insistence.

The King tucked his hare into his bag, and rode away at the utmost speed of his donkey.

But he had hardly gone a quarter of a league, when a shrill whistle sounded in the air, on hearing which the hare nibbled at the bag so vigorously as speedily to make a hole, out of which it leapt to the ground and fled.

"Well?" enquired the Princess, on seeing the King return to the palace.

"I hardly know what to tell you, my daughter," replied the King. "This young shepherd is an obstinate fellow, who refused to sell me one of his hares at any price. But don't distress yourself; he'll not get so easily through the two other tasks as he has done with this one."

It need hardly be said that the King made no allusion to the conditions under which he had for a moment had possession of one of his hares, nor that the Princess said nothing about the terms of her similar unsuccess.

"That is exactly my case," she remarked; "I could not induce him to part with one of his hares, neither for gold nor silver."

When evening came, the shepherd returned with his hares; he counted them before the King; there was not one more or one less. They were given back to the Minister of the Interior, who had them driven into the stable.

Then the King said, "The first problem has been solved; the second now remains to be accomplished. Pay great attention, young man."

The shepherd listened with all his ears.

"Up yonder, in my granary," the King went on, "there are one hundred measures of grey peas, and one hundred measures of lentils; lentils and peas are mixed together; if you succeed tonight, and without light, in separating them, you will have solved the second problem."

"I'll do my best," replied the young shepherd.

And the King called his Minister of the Interior, who conducted the young man up to the granary, locked him in, and handed the key to the King.

As it was already night, and as, for such a labour, there was no time to be lost, the shepherd put his whistle to his lips, and blew a long, shrill note.

Instantly five thousand ants appeared, and set to work separating the lentils from the peas, and never stopped until the whole were divided into two heaps.

The next morning the King, to his great astonishment, beheld the work accomplished. He tried to raise objections, but was unable to find any ground whatever.

All he could now do was to trust to the third trial, which, after the shepherd's success in the other two trials, he found to be not very hopeful. However, as the third was the most difficult of all, he did not give way to despair.

"What now remains for you to do," he said, "is to go into the bread-room, and, in a single night, eat the whole week's bread, which is stored there. If tomorrow morning not a single

crumb is to be found there, I will consent to your marrying my daughter."

That same evening the young shepherd was conducted to the bread-room of the palace, which was so full of bread that only a very small space near the door remained unoccupied.

But, at midnight, when all was quiet in the palace, the shepherd sounded his whistle. In a moment ten thousand mice fell to gnawing at the bread in such a fashion that the next morning not a single crumb remained in the place.

The young man then hammered at the door with all his might, and called out –

"Make haste and open the door, please, for I'm hungry!"

The third task was thus victoriously accomplished, as the others had been.

Nevertheless, the King tried hard to get out of his engagement.

He had a sack, big enough to hold six measures of wheat, brought; and, having called a good number of his courtiers about him, said:

"Tell us as many falsehoods as will fill this sack, and when it is full you shall have my daughter."

Then the shepherd repeated all the falsehoods he could think of; but the day was half spent, and he was at the end of his fibs, and still the sack was far from being full.

"Well," he went on, "while I was guarding my hares the Princess came to me disguised as a peasant, and, to get one of my hares, permitted me to kiss her."

The Princess, who, not in the least suspecting what he was going to say, had not been able to close his mouth, became as red as a cherry; so much so that the King began to think that the young shepherd's tarradiddle might possibly be true.

"The sack is not yet full, though you have just dropped a *very* big falsehood into it," cried the King. "Go on."

The shepherd bowed and continued: "A moment after the Princess was gone, I saw His Majesty, disguised as a peasant and mounted on a donkey. His Majesty also came to buy one of my hares; seeing, then, what an eager desire he had to obtain a hare from me, what do you imagine I compelled him to do?"

"Enough! enough!" cried the King; "the sack is full."

A week later, the young shepherd married the Princess.

The Fairy Gift

~

Charlotte Brontë

ONE COLD EVENING in December 17–, while I was yet but a day labourer, though not even at that time wholly without some aspirations after fame and some intimations of future greatness, I was sitting alone by my cottage fire engaged in ambitious reveries of *l'avenir*, and amusing myself with wild and extravagant imaginations. A thousand evanescent wishes flitted through my mind, one of which was scarcely formed when another succeeded it; then a third, equally transitory, and so on.

While I was thus employed with building castles in the air my frail edifices were suddenly dissipated by an emphatic "Hem!" I started, and raised my head. Nothing was visible, and, after a few minutes, supposing it to be only fancy, I resumed my occupation of weaving the web of waking visions. Again the "Hem!" was heard; again I looked up, when lo! sitting in the opposite chair I beheld the diminutive figure of a man dressed all in green. With a pretty considerable fluster I demanded his business, and how he had contrived to enter the house without my knowledge.

"I am a fairy," he replied, in a shrill voice; "but fear nothing; my intentions are not mischievous. On the contrary, I intend to gift you with the power of obtaining four wishes, provided that you wish them at different times; and if you should happen to find the fruition of my theme not equal to your anticipations, still you are at liberty to cast it aside, which you must do before another wish is granted."

When he had concluded this information he gave me a ring, telling me that by the potency of the spell with which it was invested my desires would prove immediately successful.

I expressed my gratitude for this gift in the warmest terms, and then enquired how I should dispose of the ring when I had four times arrived at the possession of that which I might wish.

"Come with it at midnight to the little valley in the uplands, a mile hence," said he, "and there you will be rid of it when it becomes useless."

With these words he vanished from my sight. I stood for some minutes incredulous of the reality of that which I had witnessed, until at last I was convinced by the green-coloured ring set in gold that sparkled in my hand.

By some strange influence I had been preserved from any feeling of fear during my conversation with the fairy, but now I began to feel certain doubts and misgivings as to the propriety of having any dealings with supernatural beings. These, however, I soon quelled, and began forthwith to consider what should be the nature of my first wish. After some deliberation I found the desire for beauty was uppermost in my mind, and therefore formed a wish that next morning when I arose I should find myself possessed of surpassing loveliness.

That night my dreams were filled with anticipations of future grandeur, but the gay visions which my sleeping fancy called into being were dispelled by the first sounds of morning.

I awoke lightsome and refreshed, and springing out of bed glanced half-doubtingly into the small looking-glass which decorated the wall of my apartment, to ascertain if any change for the better had been wrought in me since the preceding night.

Never shall I forget the thrill of delighted surprise which passed through me when I beheld my altered appearance. There I stood, tall, slender, and graceful as a young poplar tree, all my limbs moulded in the most perfect and elegant symmetry, my complexion of the purest red and white, my eyes blue and brilliant, swimming in liquid radiance under the narrow dark arches of two exquisitely-formed eyebrows, my mouth of winning sweetness, and, lastly, my hair clustering in rich black curls over a forehead smooth as ivory.

In short, I have never yet heard or read of any beauty that could at all equal the splendour of comeliness with which I was at that moment invested.

I stood for a long time gazing at myself in a trance of admiration while happiness such as I had never known before overflowed my heart. That day happened to be Sunday, and accordingly I put on my best clothes and proceeded forthwith towards the church. The service had just commenced when I arrived, and as I walked up the aisle to my pew I felt that the eyes of the whole assembly were upon me, and that proud consciousness gave an elasticity to my gait which added stateliness and majesty to my other innumerable graces. Among those who viewed me most attentively was Lady Beatrice Ducie. This personage was the widow of Lord Ducie, owner of the chief part of the village where I resided and nearly all the surrounding land for many miles, who, when he died, left her the whole of his immense estates. She was without children and perfectly at liberty to marry whomsoever she might chance to fix her heart on, and therefore, though her ladyship had passed the meridian of life, was besides fat and ugly, and into the bargain had the reputation of being a witch, I cherished hopes that she might take a liking for me, seeing I was so very handsome; and by making me her spouse raise me at once from indigence to the highest pitch of luxury and affluence.

These were my ambitious meditations as I slowly retraced my steps homeward.

In the afternoon I again attended church, and again Lady Ducie favoured me with many smiles and glances expressive of her admiration. At length my approaching good fortune was placed beyond a doubt, for while I was standing in the porch after service was over she happened to pass, and, inclining her head towards me, said: "Come to my house tomorrow at four o'clock." I only answered by a low bow and then hastened back to my cottage.

On Monday afternoon I dressed myself in my best, and, putting a Christmas rose in the buttonhole of my coat, hastened to the appointed rendezvous.

When I entered the avenue of Ducie Castle a footman in rich livery stopped me and requested me to follow him. I complied, and we proceeded down a long walk to a bower of evergreens, where sat her ladyship in a pensive posture. Her stout, lusty figure was arrayed in a robe of purest white muslin, elegantly embroidered. On her head she wore an elaborately curled wig, among which borrowed tresses was twined a wreath of artificial flowers, and her brawny shoulders were enveloped in a costly Indian shawl. At my approach she arose and saluted me. I returned the compliment, and when we were seated, and the footman had withdrawn, business summarily commenced by her tendering me the possession of her hand and heart, both which offers, of course, I willingly accepted.

Three weeks after, we were married in the parish church by special licence, amidst the rejoicings of her numerous tenantry, to whom a sumptuous entertainment was that day given.

I now entered upon a new scene of life. Every object which met my eyes spoke of opulence and grandeur. Every meal of which I partook seemed to me a luxurious feast. As I wandered through the vast halls and magnificent apartments of my new residence I felt my heart dilating with gratified pride at the thought that they were my own.

Towards the obsequious domestics that thronged around me I behaved with the utmost respect and deference, being impelled thereto by a feeling of awe inspired by their superior breeding and splendid appearance.

I was now constantly encompassed by visitors from among those who moved in the highest circles of society. My time was passed in the enjoyment of all sorts of pleasures; balls, concerts, and dinners were given almost every day at the castle in honour of our wedding. My evenings were spent in hearing music, or seeing dancing and gormandizing; my days in excursions over the country, either on horseback or in a carriage.

Yet, notwithstanding all this, I was not happy. The rooms were so numerous that I was often lost in my own house, and sometimes got into awkward predicaments in attempting to find some particular apartment. Our high-bred guests despised me for my clownish manners and deportment. I was forced to bear patiently the most humiliating jokes and sneers from noble lips. My own servants insulted me with impunity; and, finally, my wife's temper showed itself every day more and more in the most hideous light. She became terribly jealous, and would hardly suffer me to go out of her sight a moment. In short, before the end of three months I sincerely wished myself separated from her and reduced again to the situation of a plain and coarse but honest and contented ploughboy.

This separation was occasioned by the following incident sooner than I expected. At a party which we gave one evening there chanced to be present a young lady named Cecilia Standon. She possessed no mean share of beauty, and had besides the most graceful demeanour I ever saw. Her manner was kind, gentle, and obliging, without any of that haughty superciliousness which so annoyed me in others of my fashionable acquaintances. If I made a foolish observation or transgressed against the rules of politeness she did not give vent to her contempt in a laugh or suppressed titter, but informed me in a whisper what I ought to have done, and instructed me how to do it.

When she was gone I remarked to my wife what a kind and excellent lady Miss Cecilia Standon was. "Yes," exclaimed she, reddening, "everyone can please you but me. Don't think to elude my vigilance. I saw you talking and laughing with her, you low-born creature whom I raised from obscurity to splendour. And yet not one spark of gratitude do you feel towards me. But I will have my revenge." So saying, she left me to meditate alone on what that revenge might be.

The same night, as I lay in bed restless, I heard suddenly a noise of footsteps outside the chamber door. Compelled by irresistible curiosity, I rose and opened it without making any sound. My surprise was great on beholding the figure of my wife stealing along on tiptoe with her back towards me, and a lighted candle in her hand. Anxious to know what could be her motive for walking about the house at this time of night, I followed softly, taking care to time my steps so as to coincide with hers.

After proceeding along many passages and galleries which I had never before seen, we descended a very long staircase that led us underneath the coal and wine cellars to a damp, subterraneous vault. Here she stopped and deposited the candle on the ground. I shrank instinctively, for the purpose of concealment, behind a massive stone pillar which upheld the arched roof on one side.

The rumours which I had often heard of her being a witch passed with painful distinctness across my mind, and I trembled violently. Presently she knelt with folded hands and began to mutter some indistinguishable words in a strange tone. Flames now darted out of the earth, and huge smouldering clouds of smoke rolled over the slimy walls, concealing their hideousness from the eye.

At length the dead silence that had hitherto reigned unbroken was dissipated by a tremendous cry which shook the house to its centre, and I saw six black, indefinable figures gliding through the darkness bearing a funeral bier on which lay arranged, as I had seen her the previous evening, the form of Cecilia Standon. Her dark eyes were closed, and their long lashes lay motionless on a cheek pale as marble. She was quite stiff and dead.

At this appalling sight I could restrain myself no longer, and uttering a loud shriek I sprang from behind the pillar. My wife saw me. She started from her kneeling position, and rushed furiously towards where I stood, exclaiming in tones rendered tremulous by excessive fury: "Wretch, wretch, what demon has lured thee hither to thy fate?" With these words she seized me by the throat and attempted to strangle me.

I screamed and struggled in vain. Life was ebbing apace when suddenly she loosened her grasp, tottered, and fell dead.

When I was sufficiently recovered from the effects of her infernal grip to look around I saw by the light of the candle a little man in a green coat striding over her and flourishing a bloody dagger in the air. In his sharp, wild physiognomy I immediately recognized the fairy who six months ago had given me the ring.

That was the occasion of my present situation. He had stabbed my wife through the heart, and thus afforded me opportune relief at the moment when I so much needed it.

After tendering him my most ardent thanks for his kindness I ventured to ask what we should do with the dead body.

"Leave that to me," he replied. "But now as the day is dawning, and I must soon be gone, do you wish to return to your former rank of a happy, honest labourer, being deprived of the beauty which has been the source of so much trouble to you, or will you remain as you are? Decide quickly, for my time is limited."

I replied unhesitatingly, "Let me return to my former rank," and no sooner were the words out of my mouth than I found myself standing alone at the porch of my humble cottage, plain and coarse as ever, without any remains of the extreme comeliness with which I had been so lately invested.

I cast a glance at the tall towers of Ducie Castle which appeared in the distance faintly illuminated by the light reflected from rosy clouds hovering over the eastern horizon, and then, stooping as I passed beneath the lowly lintel, once more crossed the threshold of my parental hut.

A day or two after, while I was sitting at breakfast, a neighbour entered and, after enquiring how I did, etc., asked me where I had been for the last half-year. Seeing it necessary to dissemble, I answered that I had been on a visit to a relation who lived at a great distance. This satisfied him, and I then enquired if anything had happened in the village since my departure.

"Yes," said he, "a little while after you were gone Lady Ducie married the handsomest young man that was ever seen, but nobody knew where he came from, and most people thought he was a fairy; and now about four days ago Lady Ducie, her husband, and Lord Standon's eldest daughter all vanished in the same night and have never been heard of since, though the strictest search has been made after them. Yesterday her ladyship's brother came and took possession of the estate, and he is trying to hush up the matter as much as he can."

This intelligence gave me no small degree of satisfaction, as I was now certain that none of the villagers had any suspicion of my dealings with the fairy.

But to proceed. I had yet liberty to make three more wishes; and, after much consideration, being convinced of the vanity of desiring such a transitory thing as my first, I fixed upon "superior talent" as the aim of my second wish; and no sooner had I done so than I felt an expansion, as it were, of soul within me.

Everything appeared to my mental vision in a new light. High thoughts elevated my mind, and abstruse meditations racked my brain continually. But you shall presently hear the upshot of this sudden *ećlaircissement*.

One day I was sent to a neighbouring market town, by one Mr Tenderden, a gentleman of some consequence in our village, for the purpose of buying several articles in glass and china.

When I had made my purchases I directed them to be packed up in straw, and then with the basket on my back trudged off homeward. But ere I was halfway night overtook me. There was no moon, and the darkness was also much increased by a small mizzling rain. Cold and drenched to the skin, I arrived at The Rising Sun, a little wayside inn, which lay in my route.

On opening the door my eyes were agreeably saluted by the light of a bright warm fire, round which sat about half a dozen of my acquaintance.

After calling for a drop of something to warm me, and carefully depositing the basket of glass on the ground, I seated myself amongst them. They were engaged in a discussion as to whether a monarchical or republican form of government was the best. The chief champion of the republican side was Bob Sylvester, a blacksmith by trade, and of the largest loquacity of any man I ever saw. He was proud of his argumentative talents, but by dint of my fairy gift I soon silenced him, amid cheers from both sides of the house.

Bob was a man of hot temper, and not calculated for lying down quietly under a defeat. He therefore rose and challenged me to single combat. I accepted, and a regular battle ensued. After some hard hits he closed in furiously, and dealt me a tremendous left-handed blow. I staggered, reeled, and fell insensible. The last thing I remember was a horrible crash, as if the house was tumbling in about my ears.

When I recovered my senses I was laid in bed in my own house, all cut, bruised, and bloody. I was soon given to understand that the basket of glass was broken, and Mr Tenderden, being a miserly, hard-hearted man, made me stand to the loss, which was upwards of five pounds.

When I was able to walk about again I determined to get rid of my ring forthwith in the manner the fairy had pointed out, seeing that it brought me nothing but ill-luck.

It was a fine clear night in October when I reached the little valley in the uplands before mentioned. There was a gentle frost, and the stars were twinkling with the lustre of diamonds in a sky of deep and cloudless azure. A chill breeze whistled dreamily in the gusty passes of the hills that surrounded the vale, but I wrapped my cloak around me and standing in a sheltered nook boldly awaited the event.

After about half an hour of dead silence I heard a sound as of many voices weeping and lamenting at a distance. This continued for some time until it was interrupted by another voice, seemingly close at hand. I started at the contiguity of the sound, and looked on every side, but nothing was visible. Still the strain kept rising and drawing nearer. At length the following words, sung in a melancholy though harmonious tone, became distinctly audible:

> Hearken, O Mortal! to the wail
> > Which round the wandering night-winds fling,
> Soft-sighing 'neath the moonbeams pale,
> > How low! how old! its murmuring!
>
> No other voice, no other tone,
> > Disturbs the silence deep;
> All, saving that prophetic moan,
> > Are hushed in quiet sleep.
>
> The moon and each small lustrous star,
> > That journey through the boundless sky,
> Seem, as their radiance from afar
> > Falls on the still earth silently,
>
> To weep the fresh descending dew
> > That decks with gems the world:
> Sweet teardrops of the glorious blue
> > Above us wide unfurled.
>
> But, hark! again the sighing wail
> > Upon the rising breeze doth swell.
> Oh! hasten from this haunted vale,
> > Mournful as a funeral knell!
>
> For here, when gloomy midnight reigns,
> > The fairies form their ring,

And, unto wild unearthly strains,
  In measured cadence sing.

No human eye their sports may see.
  No human tongue their deeds reveal;
The sweetness of their melody
  The ear of man may never feel.

But now the elfin horn resounds,
  No longer mayst thou stay;
Near and more near the music sounds,
  Then, Mortal, haste away!

Here I certainly heard the music of a very sweet and mellow horn. At that instant the ring which I held in my hand melted and became like a drop of dew, which trickled down my fingers and, falling on the dead leaves spread around, vanished.

Having now no further business, I immediately quitted the valley and returned home . . .

Being very tired and sleepy I retired to bed. As I have no doubt my reader is by this time in much the same state, I bid him goodbye.

The Forest Fairy

~

Lord Brabourne

SOME PEOPLE THINK that there are no Fairies now-a-days. There are so many large towns, full of dust and smoke, and so many railroads, on which trains run snorting and screaming through the pretty, lonely country-places, where the Fairies used to be found, that a great many people fancy these things have quite driven the Fairies out of England, and that we must cross the seas, and go to distant countries, if we want to see or hear any more of the dear little creatures.

But indeed this is not the case. It is not so easy to get rid of the Fairies. Even in the dark, dull towns, there are gleams of Fairy brightness to be seen sometimes, and scenes of Fairy-land float before the eyes of many a child whose heart is light and whose spirit is pure; and the Fairies come in dreams, and take it away to dance and play with them for a while, and forget the toils and hardships of its everyday life. Ay, and even when the railway-train whistles and screeches through the woods where the Fairies used to hold their midnight meetings, and over the soft meadows where they danced so often in the Fairy-ring, it cannot drive the little Elves away for good and all. They stop their ears sometimes, and go further away from the harsh, screeching sound, but they do not quite desert the place; and they never will desert dear old England, as long as there are warm and tender hearts to love their kind ways, and eager little ears to hear all the pretty stories of which Fairy-land is full, and which help to make it so pleasant.

But there was no big town and no railroad in that part of the country where dwelt the Fairy of whom I am going to tell you. There was a large wood, full of very tall trees, so thick with their beautiful foliage that the rays of the sun could scarcely force their way through in the brightest summer day; but underneath the boughs it was right pleasant to walk, for there you found beautiful shade, and the mossy turf beneath your feet was soft as velvet. And when the calm pale moon shed her mild rays over the earth, peeping in through the thick foliage, she gave a quiet, holy light to the wood here and there, and you felt as if you were in some sacred spot, where you were only inclined to speak in whispering tones, lest you should disturb the solemn silence of the place.

One tree – much larger than most of its companions – stood in the middle of the wood. It was very old, but yet it was not quite hollow, for its wood was stout and tough. Its great roots ran out on all sides of it, and you could not look upon it without confessing at once that it was a Royal tree. And in the crown of this tree dwelt the loveliest little Fairy that anyone ever set eyes upon. She was about seven inches high, of perfect face and form, and with a queenly look about her which inspired respect, just as her beauty and sweet manners compelled people to love the very sight of her.

But that forest was her kingdom, and that was her palace; and she wore the lightest, prettiest dress you can imagine. Madame Elise never turned out a dress so elegant and lovely – and that is saying a great deal, because everybody knows that Madame Elise is almost a Fairy herself in the way she produces beautiful dresses! But nothing could equal my Fairy: and, moreover, she was as kind at heart as she was beautiful. Her great pleasure was to do good wherever she could. If any of the animals in the forest were hurt, they would often come moaning up to the tree, and seldom indeed was it that they did not receive assistance; and many of the poor people who lived near that forest had felt the kindness of the Fairy, and had had pieces of good luck happen to them, which you may be very sure were all of her doing.

She usually drove about the forest in a little wicker carriage, drawn by six squirrels; and it was the prettiest sight imaginable to see her drive the dear little creatures, well broken-in as they were, and dart about through the trees in the most graceful manner possible. This was her favourite conveyance; but sometimes she would ride about on the back of a squirrel or a rabbit, and now and then took a flight on a wood-pigeon; for she was not at all a stay-at-home Fairy, but loved to roam about the country, and see what there was to be seen.

Now it happened that at no great distance from the forest lived an old man, in a small cottage which was still older than himself, and was therefore in a sad state of decay. This old man was by trade a faggot-seller, for he had the right of cutting wood in the forest; and he used to cut faggots and sell them to the people around, by which means he earned enough to keep the pot boiling. His only companion was his little granddaughter, who was everything in the world to him, for he had no other relation or friend. She was as good a little girl as you will find anywhere, and very fond of her old grandfather, who, on his side, was tenderly attached to her.

Every morning she would be up early enough to light the fire and get his bit of breakfast ready for him before he went out to his work; and when he was gone, she would sweep the room, and put the place tidy; and then, when she had finished, it was time to get his dinner ready, and she would prepare it very carefully, and then take it out to him in the forest in a little basket – and right glad was the old man to see his little Lilian (for so was the child called) coming along under the shady trees. He would listen to her pretty prattle while he ate his dinner; and often she would bring her knitting out, and sit there, in the fine summer afternoons, until he had finished his work and they could walk home together.

It was a pretty sight to see the old man and the young child walking hand-and-hand, her large, loving blue eyes turned up to his old, weather-beaten face, and her little tongue asking him questions about the forest, and the big world beyond it, of which he knew but little more than she did; for the old man had passed nearly all his life in the cottage where he lived, and the little he knew of the wide world was gathered from conversations now and then with neighbours as poor as himself, but who had been tempted, from time to time, to roam further from home.

Very happily and very contentedly did Lilian and her grandfather live for some time, till she grew to be about eleven years old, and the old man's strength began to fail. He could no longer do such a long day's work as he used to do, and seemed to get more tired of an evening, and less and less inclined to get up early in the morning. But worse than that – for troubles seldom come alone – he could no longer sell his faggots so easily as in the old days. People had taken more and more to burning coal, and he had to go far and wide to gather the few pence which his faggots would bring him. No other occupation could he get; and all this time the old cottage got worse and worse.

The rain came in, and the cold got through the walls; and when the high winds blew, it often seemed as if the whole cottage would be blown down – the windows rattled in their casements, and the walls seemed to shake; and everything showed that the place was hardly fit to be lived in. But what distressed the old man more than anything else in these hard times was the thought of his little grandchild. What would become of her if he was to be taken away from her? She could not live alone in the cottage, even if it were better and stronger and safer. How would she live, and where would she go to? These thoughts greatly troubled his mind, and he hardly dared to look forward to the future.

Still times got worse – meat became a scarce article in the cottage, and, save as they could, there was so little to save from that their prospects were very bad. Winter came on, and the old man felt his heart grow heavier, and heavier, as he thought of the joyous days of his boyhood, when Christmas-time brought lightness of heart and gladness of spirit to him, and all seemed so mirthful and happy. Why should Christmas-time be so different to his little Lilian? Not that she was wanting in cheerfulness, for she was a light-hearted, lively child; but she had little to make her so, and he could do so little for her!

These thoughts were in his heart as he sallied forth the day before Christmas-Day, and walked slowly into the forest. He came to the place where he had been working last, and determined that he would try and cut and make up a few faggots, and forget his cares in the healthy work before him. At it he went, and worked steadily on till past twelve o'clock. The leaves were crisp under his feet, and the air was fresh; for there was frost abroad, but not hard enough to be very cold; such weather it was as makes folks genial and happy in their hearts, and tingles their fingers without making them more than *just* so cold that a hearty rub sends the warm blood through the veins, and makes them warm and glowing again. And the old man looked up from his work, and put down his axe, and rubbed his hands, as he saw Lilian coming slowly along the wood with her little basket. On she came, till she got close to him, and then she said –

"Poor Gran, there isn't much dinner today – only potatoes and a crust of bread: but the salt will make the potatoes taste nice; and then, how many poor people have no bread at all!"

This was the most cheerful thing that poor Lilian could say, and she was quite right in reminding her grandfather how many people were worse off than he was. For I think all of us are much too fond of comparing ourselves with those who are *better off* than we are; and this makes us discontented; whereas, if we would only think how very many more there are who are worse off, we should find we had great reason to be contented with our lot.

The old man sighed: but he did not wish to seem sad before Lilian; so he tried to put on a cheerful tone, and proposed that they should stroll down into the forest and find a sheltered nook where they might eat their dinner. So they walked down a little way, carrying the basket, till they came to a large oak, which seemed to offer the very shelter which they sought. Accordingly, they sat down close to it, made themselves as comfortable as they could, and began to open the basket and take out its contents. But scarcely had the cloth been spread upon the ground and disclosed the potatoes that were in it, and scarcely had Lilian produced the dark-coloured brown bread which was to aid the meal, when a clear little silvery voice above their heads said, very distinctly –

"Who is it that eats bread and potatoes for dinner on Christmas-Eve?"

Lilian and her grandfather both looked up, but could see nothing but a pretty brown squirrel munching a nut in the boughs above them; so they looked at each other and stared; and then each thought it must have been a mistake, and the grandfather put out his hand to take a potato. But, wonder of wonders! the potato, which to all appearance was a vegetable of unblemished character, duly baked and only wanting to be eaten, deliberately rolled away of its own accord, and was immediately followed by all the others.

Lilian and her grandfather were too much astonished to try and prevent them, but the old man, being uncommonly hungry after his work, made a rapid snatch at the bread. Back, however, he drew his hand more quickly than he had put it out, for instead of the brown loaf there was only a hedgehog, who scuttled off as fast he could towards a neighbouring rabbit-hole, while, at the same time, the identical voice again exclaimed –

"*Not* bread and potatoes on Christmas-Eve, *I* think!" and both Lilian and her grandfather jumped up in the greatest astonishment. There, on a large bough of the oak, immediately above their heads, stood the Forest Fairy. She was dressed in her winter cloak of moleskin; but so elegantly was it made that you could tell at once that it belonged to a Fairy, even if you had not seen the beautiful diamond buttons, and the gold and silver braid all over it. She had a branch of mistletoe in her hand, and a squirrel sat on each side of her, whilst she stood on the oak-bough and spoke to her visitors below. The latter, though startled at first, felt that no harm was intended, for they had only to look upon the kind expression on the face of the Forest Fairy to be quite sure that she had the most friendly feeling towards them.

"Why have you come to my palace, good people?" she asked; and the grandfather opened his mouth very wide, as some people always do when they are asked a question by a person of higher rank than themselves. But Lilian clasped her little hands and said at once to the Fairy –

"Oh, do not be angry, dear Lady, for we did not know – Gran and I – that this was your palace, and we came down here to eat our dinner quietly under the oak-boughs. And as to our having only bread and potatoes, indeed that isn't our choice, but we can get nothing else; for we are poor, very poor, Gran and I, and we hardly know on one day whether we can look forward to any dinner at all on the next. But it is *my* fault bringing Gran down under the Oak; so pray don't be angry with *him*!"

Then the Fairy smiled sweetly upon the child, and she said –

"Lilian!" (for Fairies know children's names by instinct, and, if they are good children, are very partial to them,) "I am not angry,

nor are you so very, very poor; for no one is very poor who has a loving heart like yours, and tries to be contented. But you shall not dine off bread and potatoes today. I am obliged to go away on business; but when you and your grandfather are hungry, look the other side of the oak, and if you want anything, rap three times on the old tree."

When she had done speaking, the Fairy gracefully bent her head, and disappeared immediately. The old man looked at Lilian, and Lilian looked at the old man, till at last the former said –

"But how about our victuals? I'm precious hungry."

"Oh, Gran!" said Lilian. "Let's trust the beautiful Lady, and look the other side of the oak."

So they walked round the other side of the oak, and what do you think they saw? A plain deal table, firmly fixed in the ground, with a chair on each side of it. Upon it was a snowy-white table-cloth, and opposite each chair was a plate, a knife and fork, a piece of bread, and a mug. But, glorious to behold, in the middle of the table was a magnificent sirloin of beef, done to a turn, with the fat still crackling from the fire, and a perfect pool of rich, good gravy all round it, not to mention delicately-white horseradish strewn upon it in profusion. On one side of it was a dish of smoking-hot potatoes, and on the other one of tempting-looking Yorkshire pudding, whilst a large carving-knife and fork lay by the dish, and seemed by their appearance and attitude to invite the strangers to make use of them without further delay.

Gran wanted no second invitation: seating himself at the table without the loss of a moment, he only waited until Lilian had said grace for both of them, before he commenced a vigorous attack upon the joint before him. You never saw an old man with such an appetite! Consider, this was the third day he had had no meat, and the clear, cold air, together with the exercise of chopping wood, had given him a capacity for eating which few aldermen could equal and which a Lord mayor himself could scarcely surpass. Lilian, too, enjoyed her beef thoroughly, though she continually stopped, and her eyes glistened with pleasure, as she saw her dear old grandfather so supremely happy. Presently, however, he stopped, and, looking round, perceived a foaming jug of ale upon the table, which he had not observed before. He instantly filled both the mugs, and they drank the Fairy's health with three times three.

However, in this world nothing lasts for ever, and after a while they seemed to have had as much beef as they wanted. Lilian, who had only had half a mugful of the ale, thought she should like a glass of water, and modestly knocked three times at the oak, according to the Fairy's directions. Instantly there appeared, to her great surprise, four Rabbits in the livery of the Fairy; that is to say, white breeches with light-blue stripes, and silver jackets with gold embroidery. In their hands they bore a large dish, and, having removed the beef and vegetables from the table, they deposited upon it an enormous plum-pudding, and stood bowing around the table as if to invite the company to fall to at once.

This was not to be resisted, and although Lilian resisted all her grandfather's entreaties to do more than just taste the pudding, the old gentleman fell to with a relish in which no one could have believed who had seen him previously tackle the beef. The pudding removed (from which he parted with a sigh), the attendant Rabbits at once produced cheese and celery, of which, however, the old man could partake but sparingly, and in a few moments the dinner was over.

When Lilian had said grace, she was not quite sure what to do next, for it seemed very ungrateful to go away without thanking the kind Fairy who had given them so good a dinner in exchange for their bread and potatoes. There was no Fairy, however, to be seen, and the Rabbits stood there bowing so politely that neither Lilian nor her grandfather felt it right to be sitting there so long and keeping them out in the cold. They slowly rose, therefore, and left the table, which almost immediately afterwards disappeared, and the Rabbits also. The well-dined couple stood looking at the oak a little time with a look of lingering affection, and then walked slowly back to the place where the old man had been at work.

All of a sudden, Lilian remembered that she had left her basket behind her, with the cloth which had held the potatoes. So she ran back as quickly as she could, but neither cloth nor basket could she see. She looked about everywhere, but in vain, and felt quite inclined to cry; but, having always been taught to make the best of everything, she tried to hope that these little articles had been picked up by someone still poorer and in greater distress than her grandfather and she, and that they might be of great service to them. Still, she could not help being sorry to have lost her property. Her grandfather, however, was not angry with her, partly because he was too fond of her for *that*, and partly because he had eaten such a good dinner, which put him, as a good dinner puts most people, in a particularly good humour.

He did not do much more work that day, and when Lilian and he walked home together, the old boy was in better spirits than he had been for many a long day. He cracked a joke or two, and laughed at his own jokes (which is generally the sign of a contented disposition), and even went so far as to sing a verse or two of a merry old song, which quite delighted both the child and himself.

As they got near home, however, and he began to think how differently things would look there to what they had done under the oak-tree, a kind of heaviness seemed to steal over him, which Lilian strove to chase away by cheerful conversation: and so they journeyed on until they turned a corner which brought them fun in view of their cottage home.

But what a strange sight met their eyes! How changed the appearance of everything! The fence round the garden in front of the cottage, which had been quite broken down, had disappeared altogether, and a spick and span iron rail-fence stood there in its place. The weeds which Lilian had not had time to finish plucking up were gone, every weed of them, and the garden was as neat and tidy as if a regular gardener had been looking after it every day in the week. And then the house! Instead of leaning a little on one side, as it used to do — tempting the cruel wind to drive the cold rain against it and to try to turn it quite over — there it was, upright and firm as any new model cottage of them all. No casements shook, all were firmly fixed; and the brown paper with which many broken panes of glass had been from time to time replaced had all disappeared, and new panes appeared in every window. The door, too, had its broken latch mended, and instead of the wind whistling under it as before, a stout, thick bit of list, carefully nailed on, quite put a stop to *that*; and as to the roof! why there wasn't a broken tile left upon it, but every tile was as straight and new as if it had just been put on, and put on well too.

The whole place was so altered that the old grandfather opened his mouth nearly wide enough to have swallowed it down, cottage and all, while Lilian darted forward with a scream of delight, crying out –

"Oh, the Fairy! The Fairy – the dear, good Fairy! I am sure it is she who has been here."

The old man stood stock-still in amazement, until another cry from Lilian, who had now opened the door, woke him up. He hurried on to the cottage, and entered after her. What do you think he saw? In the middle of the room in which they usually lived was a brand-new table, whilst four new chairs were placed about in different parts of the room – which had also been newly papered, and had a nice new carpet of a common, but strong and useful sort.

Everything appeared to have been changed, as if by magic, from being old and worn out to new and strong, and there was an air of comfort about the whole place which was perfectly delightful. Nor were the wonders to cease here. They opened the door which led into the kitchen behind the living room, and a sight met their eyes which caused them both to start back with astonishment. There, indeed, was the kitchen the same as ever, but the grate was evidently new; new saucepans, a bright and clean row, hung by the side of the wall; a new set of crockery was ranged upon the shelves; and even the big kitchen-poker was bright and clean, and evidently prepared to start upon a new life fit for any work that might be required of him.

But, more marvellous than all, in the middle of the kitchen, as much at home as if it had been born and bred there, stood the identical table which had borne the welcome meal which Lilian and her grandfather had enjoyed under the Fairy's Oak – yes! there was no mistake about it – and a neat white table-cloth upon it, marked in the corner "F.F.," which plainly stood for "Forest Fairy," showed whence it came. Nor was the table empty – the remainder of that noble sirloin of beef was there, and the magnificent plum-pudding stood by its side, so tempting as almost to induce the old man to attack it again at once. There it was, and there were the knives and forks they had used in the forest, and the very crumbs of the bread and cheese they had left; for the table seemed to have been transported just as it was from beneath the oak-tree, except that the beef and plum-pudding, which the Rabbit-footmen had taken away, had been put back upon it. And oh! joy of joys ! upon the kitchen dresser, lo and behold! stood Lilian's basket, safe and sound.

"O my dear old basket!" cried the child, and ran up and took hold of it; when, on lifting up the lid, what do you think she saw? The cloth was there in which the potatoes had been wrapped; but, instead of potatoes, there was a fat goose, all trussed ready for roasting, with a stuffing of sage and onions which it made your mouth water to look at; while close by, carefully wrapped up in a cloth of its own, was perhaps the richest-looking mince-pie that ever gladdened the eyes of a hungry schoolboy.

A little parcel lay upon the top of the cloth, to which was tied a slip of paper, and on it was written, "A Christmas-box for Lilian." She eagerly opened it, and what do you think was in it? A neat little work-box, with cotton, needles, scissors, and everything that could make a work-box complete; and, not only this, but a warm winter shawl wrapped carefully round the work-box, but which would be more useful, as the old grandfather wisely observed, when it was wrapped round Lilian's shoulders on a cold winter's day.

Two such happy faces as those of Lilian and her grandfather are not to be seen every day in the week, I can assure you. It was altogether such a happy change from the condition in which they had left the cottage in the morning, that they hardly knew how to believe their own eyes.

"Oh, Grandfather!" exclaimed the child. "The Fairy, the dear, good, kind Fairy! I know it is all her doing. How I should like to thank her!"

"So you shall, Lilian," said a pleasant voice at that moment; and, looking out of the window, they saw the Forest Fairy in her squirrel-carriage standing at the garden-gate. "You may thank me, Lilian," she went on to say; "but you may thank yourself too. All that I have done for you and for your good grandfather today has been done for your sake, because you have a tender, loving heart, and a contented disposition, so that it is a real pleasure to make you happy. If it had not been so, I could have done nothing for you, because we Fairies have only power to help grateful, loving people, who try to help themselves and each other. You have done this and you have been a good and attentive child to your old grandfather;

and so you see there has come a reward to you when you did not expect it."

And the Fairy smiled, oh, so sweetly! upon Lilian; and then she kissed her hand to her, and cracked her little whip, the handle of which was of the whitest ivory, and the lash made of skeins of gold thread; and off darted the squirrels and carried their mistress back to the green forest and the ancient oak.

And from that day forward Lilian and her grandfather found that everything went well with them, so that they lived together as happily as possible, and always remembered with joy and gratitude that merry Christmas dinner under the Fairy's Oak.

Ah! You will say that we do not see these little Fairies now. I am not so sure about *that*, and I know that people, small and great, who have loving, tender hearts, who make sunshine around them by their pleasant ways, are grateful for the blessings they have, and always make the best of everything, these are the people most likely to see kind Fairies, and it is on them that misfortune falls most lightly; their troubles fly away like magic, and they seem to have found out some secret of being happy, which is every bit as good and useful as any that could have been told them by the Forest Fairy.

The Forest of Dreams

~

Lawrence Schimel

THE WOODS OF IRELAND were filled with mystery. Walking beneath the branches of the trees, Sean might be anything. He made up stories as he roamed, stories of the animals and people he saw, but mostly stories of the faery folk which his grandmother had told him lived there long ago. Who, some said, lived there still.

Sean's grandmother knew many stories about the faery folk, the magical Sidhe. He always looked forward to the autumn, when his family would travel to Ireland and stay with her. When she wasn't telling him about the countryside, Sean wandered through it, looking for the creatures from her tales. He looked into the river for a Pookah. He could never find one when he looked directly into the water, searching. But sometimes, as he walked along the river, from the corner of his eyes he would catch sight of a horse made of water matching pace with him. It was always gone when he turned to look at it, melting back into the swift current, but he was sure it was there, just as his grandmother had told him.

Sean turned from the water and walked among the trees again, imagining he was a powerful Druid, caretaker of the forest. He picked berries and fed them to birds, holding so still that the birds were not afraid and landed on his hand to eat from his palm. He sat down at the base of an ancient oak and watched the forest. Sean's head pressed against the rough bark, and his thoughts seemed to slip into the wood, travelling down into the trunk and out through the roots.

The tree pulled him back to the time when the Sidhe roamed above ground and wove beautiful magicks . . .

He almost lost himself to such memories, but the tree, wishing to dream its own dreams, brought him back. Sean swam into reality and opened his eyes to see the pale moon watching him. One of the sacred times was drawing near; Samhain, the feast of the dead. His grandmother had explained to him how the ceremony of Samhain had become the Hallowe'en that was celebrated today. She had also explained how, tonight, the boundaries between this world and the next would become thin. Sean rose from his seat and prepared for the ceremony to honour his ancestors who, tonight, would roam freely in the lands of the living again. He began the chant, which he knew without ever having read or heard it before. It wasn't something his grandmother had taught him, either; he simply knew it. He was halfway through the chant when he heard the harp. He knew he shouldn't stop in the middle, but the music . . .

The harpist came into view, or maybe it was Sean who had moved, following the notes until he stood in front of the musician. The music was like the wind, cushioning soft like a zephyr and bearing wonderful treasures on it as the wind carried smells, memories of long ago. And looking at the harpist's hands Sean saw that it was the wind playing those hauntingly sweet melodies. He ran from there, breaking through the circle of white forms that had silently surrounded him. He caught glimpses of them as he ran: a beautiful face with sad eyes that reached into him and made him feel pity; men bearing shields which boasted the symbols from many a clan; well-worn weapons and faces which stated they well knew how to use the weapons they held; torcs proclaiming the ranks of the individuals who wore them.

Horns sounded, and from somewhere in the forest hounds began yapping. All took up the chase as Sean passed them; men and women alike. The Wild Hunt was on and Sean knew that there was no hope; once begun, The Hunt would not rest until they had caught their quarry. But he ran faster nonetheless, wishing for something to cross his path and lead The Hunt away. The trees got in his way; where was the end of this accursed forest? It must be just to the left; beyond that next copse. But Sean was running in the lands of the Sidhe and

the forest never ended; the path he was on led right through the heart of the forest and from there no mortal ever returned.

Sean glanced over his shoulder at his pursuers. There seemed to be hundreds of them! Every spirit they passed got sucked into the chase, and they were all after him! Sean put on a new burst of speed. He didn't know what he could do; he was no match for trained warriors, who would outrun him easily in no time. Already they were gaining ground quickly. On an impulse, Sean veered off the path as he passed a large oak tree. A branch caught on his sweater, and snapped as he plunged deeper into the forest, thinking the trees themselves were after him now. But the opposite was true; the snapped branch, and the noise of The Hunt had awakened Arafel, the Lady of the Trees. She saw Sean and the danger he was heading towards; danger both from the forest ahead of him and the Sidhe who chased him. She took pity on him, and diverted him back to the mortal world. The Hunt followed after him, but the sun was rising now. Time flowed differently between the two worlds and Arafel had sent him back at the time when The Hunt must relinquish its prey and return to their resting places. The Sidhe faded into the fog rising from a nearby bog and they slipped unnoticed back into the hearts of the trees.

"Mist!" Sean said in disbelief, as he struggled to catch his breath. "They were just mist." He laughed at himself. "Nothing but mist . . ."

But in the hearts of the trees something also laughed, for they knew better.

The Girl Who Loved the Wind

∾

Jane Yolen

ONCE MANY YEARS AGO, in a country far to the east, there lived a wealthy merchant. He was a widower and had an only daughter named Danina. She was dainty and beautiful, and he loved her more than he loved all of his treasures.

Because Danina was his only child, the merchant wanted to keep her from anything that might hurt or harm her in any way, and so he decided to shut her away from the world.

When Danina was still an infant, her father brought her to a great house which he had built on the shore of the sea. On three sides of the house rose three huge walls. And on the fourth side was the sea itself.

In this lovely, lonely place Danina grew up, knowing everything that was in her father's heart, but nothing of the world.

In her garden grew every kind of fair fruit and flower, for so her father willed it. And on her table was every kind of fresh fish and fowl, for so her father ordered. In her room were the finest furnishings. Gaily-coloured books and happy music, light dancing and bright paintings filled her days. And the servants were instructed always to smile, never to say no, and to be cheerful all through the year. So her father wished it, and so it was done. And, for many years, nothing sad touched Danina in any way.

Yet one spring day, as Danina stood by her window gazing at the sea, a breeze blew salt across the waves. It whipped her hair about her face. It blew in the corners of her room. And, as it moved, it whistled a haunting little tune.

Danina had never heard such a thing before. It was sad, but it was beautiful. It intrigued her. It beguiled her. It caused her to sigh and clasp her hands.

"Who are you?" asked Danina.

And the wind answered:

> "Who am I?
> I call myself the wind.
> I slap at ships and sparrows.
> I sough through broken windows.
> I shepherd snow and sandstorms.
> I am not always kind."

"How peculiar," said Danina. "Here you merely rustle the trees and play with the leaves and calm the birds in their nests."

"*I am not always kind,*" said the wind again.

"Everyone here is always kind. Everyone here is always happy."

"*Nothing is always,*" said the wind.

"My life is always," said Danina. "Always happy."

"*But life is not always happy,*" said the wind.

"Mine is," said Danina.

"*How sad,*" whispered the wind from a corner.

"What do you mean?" asked Danina. But the wind only whirled through the window, carrying one of her silken scarves, and before she could speak again, he had blown out to sea.

Days went by, happy days. Yet sometimes in her room, Danina would try to sing the wind's song. She could not quite remember the words or recall the tune, but its strangeness haunted her.

Finally, one morning, she asked her father: "Why isn't life always happy?"

"Life *is* always happy," replied her father.

"That's what I told him," said Danina.

"Told who?" asked her father. He was suddenly frightened, frightened that someone would take his daughter away.

"The wind," said Danina.

"The wind does not talk," said her father.

"He called himself the wind," she replied.

But her father did not understand. And so, when a passing fisherman found Danina's scarf far out at sea and returned it to the merchant's house, he was rewarded with a beating, for the merchant suspected that the fisherman was the one who called himself the wind.

Then one summer day, weeks later, when the sun was reflected in the petals of the flowers, Danina strolled in her garden. Suddenly the wind leaped over the high wall and pushed and pulled at the tops of the trees. He sang his strange song, and Danina clasped her hands and sighed.

"Who are you?" she whispered.

"*Who am I?*" said the wind, and he sang:

> "Who am I?
> I call myself the wind.
> I've worked the sails of windmills.
> I've whirled the sand in deserts.
> I've wrecked ten thousand galleons.
> I am not always kind."

"I knew it was you," said Danina. "But no one believed me."

And the wind danced around the garden and made the flowers bow.

He caressed the birds in the trees and played gently with the feathers on their wings.

"You say you are not always kind," said Danina. "You say you have done many unkind things. But all I see is that you are gentle and good."

"*But not always,*" reminded the wind. "*Nothing is always.*"

"Is it sad, then, beyond the wall?"

"*Sometimes sad and sometimes happy,*" said the wind.

"But different each day?" asked Danina.

"*Very different.*"

"How strange," Danina said. "Here things are always the same. Always beautiful. Happy. Good."

"*How sad,*" said the wind. "*How dull.*" And he leaped over the wall and blew out into the world.

"Come back," shouted Danina, rushing to the wall. But her voice was lost against the stones.

Just then her father came into the garden. He saw his daughter standing by the wall and crying to the top. He ran over to her.

"Who are you calling? Who has been here?" he demanded.

"The wind," said Danina, her eyes bright with memory. "He sang me his song."

"The wind does not sing," said her father. "Only men and birds sing."

"This was no bird," said his daughter.

"Then," thought her father, "it must have been a man." And he resolved to keep Danina from the garden.

Locked out of her garden, Danina began to wander up and down the long corridors of the house, and what once had seemed like a palace to her began to feel like a prison. Everything seemed false. The happy smiles of the servants she saw as smiles of pity for her ignorance. The gay dancing seemed to hide broken hearts. The paintings disguised sad thoughts. And soon Danina found herself thinking of the wind at every moment, humming his song to the walls, his song about the world – sometimes happy, sometimes sad, but always full of change and challenge.

Her father, who was not cruel but merely foolish, could not keep her locked up completely. Once a day, for an hour, he allowed Danina to walk along the beach. But three maidservants walked before her. Three manservants walked behind. And the merchant himself watched from a covered chair.

One chilly day in the fall, when the tops of the waves rolled in white to the shore, Danina strolled on the beach. She pulled her cape around her for warmth. And the three maidservants before her and the three manservants behind shivered in the cold. Her father in his covered chair pulled his blanket to his chin and stared out to sea. He was cold and unhappy, but he was more afraid to leave Danina alone.

Suddenly the wind blew across the caps of the waves, tossing foam into the air.

Danina turned to welcome him, stretching out her arms. The cape billowed behind her like the wings of a giant bird.

"Who are you?" thundered Danina's father, jumping out of his chair.

The wind spun around Danina and sang:

> "Who am I?
> I call myself the wind.
> I am not always happy.
> I am not always kind."

"Nonsense," roared Danina's father. "Everyone here is always happy and kind. I shall arrest you for trespassing." And he shouted, "*Guards!*"

But, before the guards could come, Danina had spread her cape on the water. Then she stepped onto it, raised one corner, and waved goodbye to her father. The blowing wind filled the cape's corner like the sail of a ship.

And before Danina's father had time to call out, before he had time for one word of repentance, she was gone. And the last thing he saw was the billowing cape as Danina and the wind sailed far to the west into the ever-changing world.

The Glass Dog

❧

L. Frank Baum

AN ACCOMPLISHED WIZARD once lived on the top floor of a tenement house and passed his time in thoughtful study and studious thought. What he didn't know about wizardry was hardly worth knowing, for he possessed all the books and recipes of all the wizards who had lived before him; and, moreover, he had invented several wizardments himself.

This admirable person would have been completely happy but for the numerous interruptions to his studies caused by folk who came to consult him about their troubles (in which he was not interested), and by the loud knocks of the iceman, the milkman, the baker's boy, the laundryman and the peanut woman. He never dealt with any of these people; but they rapped at his door every day to see him about this or that or to try to sell him their wares. Just when he was most deeply interested in his books or engaged in watching the bubbling of a cauldron there would come a knock at his door. And after sending the intruder away he always found he had lost his train of thought or ruined his compound.

At length these interruptions aroused his anger, and he decided he must have a dog to keep people away from his door. He didn't know where to find a dog, but in the next room lived a poor glass-blower with whom he had a slight acquaintance; so he went into the man's apartment and asked:

"Where can I find a dog?"

"What sort of a dog?" enquired the glass-blower.

"A good dog. One that will bark at people and drive them away. One that will be no trouble to keep and won't expect to be fed. One that has no fleas and is neat in his habits. One that will obey me when I speak to him. In short, a good dog," said the wizard.

"Such a dog is hard to find," returned the glass-blower, who was busy making a blue glass flowerpot with a pink glass rosebush in it, having green glass leaves and yellow glass roses.

The wizard watched him thoughtfully.

"Why cannot you blow me a dog out of glass?" he asked, presently.

"I can," declared the glass-blower; "but it would not bark at people, you know."

"Oh, I'll fix that easily enough," replied the other. "If I could not make a glass dog bark I would be a mighty poor wizard."

"Very well; if you can use a glass dog I'll be pleased to blow one for you. Only, you must pay for my work."

"Certainly," agreed the wizard. "But I have none of that horrid stuff you call money. You must take some of my wares in exchange."

The glass-blower considered the matter for a moment.

"Could you give me something to cure my rheumatism?" he asked.

"Oh, yes; easily."

"Then it's a bargain. I'll start the dog at once. What color of glass shall I use?"

"Pink is a pretty color," said the wizard, "and it's unusual for a dog, isn't it?"

"Very," answered the glass-blower; "but it shall be pink."

So the wizard went back to his studies and the glass-blower began to make the dog.

Next morning he entered the wizard's room with the glass dog under his arm and set it carefully upon the table. It was a beautiful pink in color, with a fine coat of spun glass, and about its neck was twisted a blue glass ribbon. Its eyes were specks of black glass and sparkled intelligently, as do many of the glass eyes worn by men.

The wizard expressed himself pleased with the glass-blower's skill and at once handed him a small vial.

"This will cure your rheumatism," he said.

"But the vial is empty!" protested the glass-blower.

"Oh, no; there is one drop of liquid in it," was the wizard's reply.

"Will one drop cure my rheumatism?" enquired the glass-blower, in wonder.

"Most certainly. That is a marvelous remedy. The one drop contained in the vial will cure instantly any kind of disease even known to humanity. Therefore it is especially good for rheumatism. But guard it well, for it is the only drop of its kind in the world, and I've forgotten the recipe."

"Thank you," said the glass-blower, and went back to his room.

Then the wizard cast a wizzy spell and mumbled several very learned words in the wizardese language over the glass dog. Whereupon the little animal first wagged its tail from side to side, then winked his left eye knowingly, and at last began barking in a most frightful manner – that is, when you stop to consider the noise came from a pink glass dog. There is something almost astonishing in the magic arts of wizards; unless, of course, you know how to do the things yourself, when you are not expected to be surprised at them.

The wizard was as delighted as a schoolteacher at the success of his spell, although he was not astonished. Immediately he placed the dog outside his door, where it would bark at anyone who dared knock and so disturb the studies of its master.

The glass-blower, on returning to his room, decided not to use the one drop of wizard cure-all just then.

"My rheumatism is better today," he reflected, "and I will be wise to save the medicine for a time when I am very ill, when it will be of more service to me."

So he placed the vial in his cupboard and went to work blowing more roses out of glass. Presently he happened to think the medicine might not keep, so he started to ask the wizard about it. But when he reached the door the glass dog barked so fiercely that he dared not knock, and returned in great haste to his own room. Indeed, the poor man was quite upset at so unfriendly a reception from the dog he had himself so carefully and skillfully made.

The next morning, as he read his newspaper, he noticed an article stating that the beautiful Miss Mydas, the richest young lady in town, was very ill, and the doctors had given up hope of her recovery.

The glass-blower, although miserably poor, hard-working and homely of feature, was a man of ideas. He suddenly recollected his precious medicine, and determined to use it to better advantage than relieving his own ills. He dressed himself in his best clothes, brushed his hair and combed his whiskers, washed his hands and tied his necktie, blackened his shoes and sponged his vest, and then put the vial of magic cure-all in his pocket. Next he locked the door, went downstairs and walked through the streets to the grand mansion where the wealthy Miss Mydas resided.

The butler opened the door and said:

"No soaps, no chromos, no vegetables, no hair oil, no books, no baking powder. My young lady is dying and we're well supplied for the funeral."

The glass-blower was grieved at being taken for a peddler.

"My friend," he began, proudly; but the butler interrupted him, saying:

"No tombstones, either; there's a family graveyard and the monument's built."

"The graveyard won't be needed if you will permit me to speak," said the glass-blower.

"No doctors, sir; they've given up my young lady, and she's given up the doctors," continued the butler, calmly.

"I'm no doctor," returned the glass-blower.

"Nor are the others. But what is your errand?"

"I called to cure your young lady by means of a magical compound."

"Step in, please, and take a seat in the hall. I'll speak to the housekeeper," said the butler, more politely.

So he spoke to the housekeeper and the housekeeper mentioned the matter to the steward and the steward consulted the chef and the chef kissed the lady's maid and sent her to see the stranger. Thus are the very wealthy hedged around with ceremony, even when dying.

When the lady's maid heard from the glass-blower that he had a medicine which would cure her mistress, she said:

"I'm glad you came."

"But," said he, "if I restore your mistress to health she must marry me."

"I'll make enquiries and see if she's willing," answered the maid, and went at once to consult Miss Mydas.

The young lady did not hesitate an instant.

"I'd marry any old thing rather than die!" she cried. "Bring him here at once!"

So the glass-blower came, poured the magic drop into a little water, gave it to the patient, and the next minute Miss Mydas was as well as she had ever been in her life.

"Dear me!" she exclaimed; "I've an engagement at the Fritters' reception tonight. Bring my pearl-colored silk, Marie, and I will begin my toilet at once. And don't forget to cancel the order for the funeral flowers and your mourning gown."

"But, Miss Mydas," remonstrated the glass-blower, who stood by, "you promised to marry me if I cured you."

"I know," said the young lady, "but we must have time to make proper announcement in the society papers and have the wedding cards engraved. Call tomorrow and we'll talk it over."

The glass-blower had not impressed her favorably as a husband, and she was glad to find an excuse for getting rid of him for a time. And she did not want to miss the Fritters' reception.

Yet the man went home filled with joy; for he thought his stratagem had succeeded and he was about to marry a rich wife who would keep him in luxury forever afterward.

The first thing he did on reaching his room was to smash his glassblowing tools and throw them out of the window.

He then sat down to figure out ways of spending his wife's money.

The following day he called upon Miss Mydas, who was reading a novel and eating chocolate creams as happily as if she had never been ill in her life.

"Where did you get the magic compound that cured me?" she asked.

"From a learned wizard," said he; and then, thinking it would interest her, he told how he had made the glass dog for the wizard, and how it barked and kept everybody from bothering him.

"How delightful!" she said. "I've always wanted a glass dog that could bark."

"But there's only one in the world," he answered, "and it belongs to the wizard."

"You must buy it for me," said the lady.

"The wizard cares nothing for money," replied the glass-blower.

"Then you must steal it for me," she retorted. "I can never live happily another day unless I have a glass dog that can bark."

The glass-blower was much distressed at this, but said he would see what he could do. For a man should always try to please his wife, and Miss Mydas had promised to marry him within a week.

On his way way home he purchased a heavy sack, and when he passed the wizard's door and the pink glass dog ran out to bark at him he threw the sack over the dog, tied the opening with a piece of twine, and carried him away to his own room.

The next day he sent the sack by a messenger boy to Miss Mydas, with his compliments, and later in the afternoon he called upon her in person, feeling quite sure he would be received with gratitude for stealing the dog she so greatly desired.

But when he came to the door and the butler opened it, what was his amazement to see the glass dog rush out and begin barking at him furiously.

"Call off your dog," he shouted, in terror.

"I can't, sir," answered the butler. "My young lady has ordered the glass dog to bark whenever you call here. You'd better look out, sir," he added, "for if it bites you, you may have glassophobia!"

This so frightened the poor glass-blower that he went away hurriedly. But he stopped at a drug store and put his last dime in the telephone box so he could talk to Miss Mydas without being bitten by the dog.

"Give me Pelf 6742!" he called.

"Hello! What is it?" said a voice.

"I want to speak with Miss Mydas," said the glass-blower.

Presently a sweet voice said: "This is Miss Mydas. What is it?"

"Why have you treated me so cruelly and set the glass dog on me?" asked the poor fellow.

"Well, to tell the truth," said the lady, "I don't like your looks. Your cheeks are pale and baggy, your hair is coarse and long, your eyes are small and red, your hands are big and rough, and you are bow-legged."

"But I can't help my looks!" pleaded the glass-blower; "and you really promised to marry me."

"If you were better looking I'd keep my promise," she returned. "But under the circumstances you are no fit mate for me, and unless you keep away from my mansion I shall set my glass dog on you!" Then she dropped the phone and would have nothing more to say.

The miserable glass-blower went home with a heart bursting with disappointment and began tying a rope to the bedpost by which to hang himself.

Someone knocked at the door, and, upon opening it, he saw the wizard.

"I've lost my dog," he announced.

"Have you, indeed?" replied the glass-blower, tying a knot in the rope.

"Yes; someone has stolen him."

"That's too bad," declared the glass-blower, indifferently.

"You must make me another," said the wizard.

"But I cannot; I've thrown away my tools."

"Then what shall I do?" asked the wizard.

"I do not know, unless you offer a reward for the dog."

"But I have no money," said the wizard.

"Offer some of your compounds, then," suggested the glass-blower, who was making a noose in the rope for his head to go through.

"The only thing I can spare," replied the wizard, thoughtfully, "is a Beauty Powder."

"What!" cried the glass-blower, throwing down the rope. "Have you really such a thing?"

"Yes, indeed. Whoever takes the powder will become the most beautiful person in the world."

"If you will offer that as a reward," said the glass-blower, eagerly, "I'll try to find the dog for you, for above everything else I long to be beautiful."

"But I warn you the beauty will only be skin-deep," said the wizard.

"That's all right," replied the happy glass-blower; "when I lose my skin I shan't care to remain beautiful."

"Then tell me where to find my dog and you shall have the powder," promised the wizard.

So the glass-blower went out and pretended to search, and by-and-by he returned and said:

"I've discovered the dog. You will find him in the mansion of Miss Mydas."

The wizard went at once to see if this were true, and, sure enough, the glass dog ran out and began barking at him. Then the wizard spread out his hands and chanted a magic spell which sent the dog fast asleep, when he picked him up and carried him to his own room on the top floor of the tenement house.

Afterward he carried the Beauty Powder to the glass-blower as a reward, and the fellow immediately swallowed it and became the most beautiful man in the world.

The next time he called upon Miss Mydas there was no dog to bark at him, and when the young lady saw him she fell in love with his beauty at once.

"If only you were a count or a prince," she sighed, "I'd willingly marry you."

"But I am a prince," he answered; "the Prince of Dogblowers."

"Ah!" said she; "then if you are willing to accept an allowance of four dollars a week I'll order the wedding cards engraved."

The man hesitated, but when he thought of the rope hanging from his bedpost he consented to the terms.

So they were married, and the bride was very jealous of her husband's beauty and led him a dog's life. So he managed to get into debt and made her miserable in turn.

As for the glass dog, the wizard set him barking again by means of his wizardness and put him outside his door. I suppose he is there yet, and am rather sorry, for I should like to consult the wizard about the moral to this story.

The Green Bird

❧

Laurence Housman

THERE WAS ONCE a Prince whose palace lay in the midst of a wonderful garden. From gate to gate was a day's journey, where spring, summer and autumn stayed captive; for warm streams flowed, bordering its ways, through marble conduits; and warm winds, driven by brazen fans, blew over it out of great furnaces that were kept alive through the cold of winter.

And day by day, when no sun shone in heaven, a ball of golden fire rose from the palace roof and passed down to the west, sustained invisibly in mid-air, and giving light and warmth to the flowers below. And after it, by night, went a lamp of silver flame, that changed its

quarters as the moon changes hers in heaven, and threw a silver light over the lawns and the flowered avenues.

All these things were, so that the Prince might have delight and beauty ever around him. To his eyes, summer was perpetual, without end, and nothing died save to give out new life on the morrow. So through many morrows he lived, and trod the beautiful soft ways devised for him by cunning hands, and did not know that there was winter, or cold, or hunger to be borne in the world; for he never crossed the threshold of his enchanted garden, but stayed lapped in the luxury of its bright colours and soft airs.

One day he was standing by a bed of large white bell-lilies. Their great bowls were full of water, and inside among the yellow stamens, gold fish went darting to and fro.

While he watched he saw, mirrored in the water, the breast of a green bird flying towards the trees of the garden.

It had come from a far country, surely, for its shape and colour were strange to him; and the most curious thing of all was that it carried its nest in its beak.

Its flight came keen as a sword's edge through those bowery spaces, till its wings closed with a shock that sent the golden fruit tumbling from the branches where it had lodged; and through the whole garden went a crashing sound as of soft thunder.

The Prince waited long, hoping to hear the bird sing, but it hid itself silently among the thickest of the leaves, and never moved or uttered a sound. He went back to the palace, a little sorry not to have heard the Green Bird sing; "But at least," he said to himself, "I shall hear it tomorrow."

That night he dreamed that something came and tapped at his heart, and that his heart tapped back saying; "Go away; if I let you in, there will be sorrow!'

In the morning, on the window-sill he saw a green feather lying; but as he opened the window a puff of wind lifted it, and carried it up into the air and high out of sight.

All that day the Prince saw nothing of the Green Bird, nor heard a note of its singing. "Strange," thought he to himself, "I have never heard its song, yet somehow I know quite well that it sings most beautifully."

At dusk, when the lilies began to close their globes round the gold fish and the yellow stamens, he went back to the palace, and before long to bed, and slept.

Once more he heard in dreams someone tapping at his heart, and this time his heart answered, "Who is there?"

Then a voice answered back, "The Green Bird"; but his heart said, "Go away, for if I let you in there will be sorrow!"

Now it had been foretold of the Prince, at his birth, that if he ever knew sorrow, his wealth and his estate and his power would all go from him. Therefore, from his childhood, he had been shut up in a beautiful palace with miles and miles of enchanted gardens, so that sorrow might not get near him, and it was said that if ever sorrow came to him, the palace and the enchanted gardens would suddenly fall into ruins and disappear, and he would be left standing alone to beg his way through the world. Therefore it was for this that his heart said in his dream: "Go away! For if I let you in there will be sorrow."

In the morning a green feather lay on the window-sill, but as he opened the window, the wind took it up and carried it away. So the next night, as soon as his attendants were gone, the Prince got up softly and opened the window, calling "Green Bird!" Then all at once he felt something warm against his heart, and suddenly his heart began to ache; and there was the Green Bird with its wings spread gently about him, keeping time ever so softly to the beating of his heart.

Then the Prince said, "Beautiful Green Bird, what have you brought me!" and the Green Bird answered; "I have brought you dreams, out of a far-off country, of things you never saw; if you will come and sleep in my nest you shall dream them."

So the Prince went out by the window and along the balcony, and so away into the garden, and up into the heart of the great tree where the Green Bird had its nest. There he lay down, and the Green Bird spread its wings over him, and he fell fast asleep.

Now as he slept he dreamed that the Green Bird put into his hand three grains of seed, saying, "Take these and keep them until you come to the right place to sow them in. And, as soon as one is sown, go on till you come to the place where

the next one must be sown, following the signs which I now
tell you.

"The first you must not sow till you find yourself in a white
country, where the trees and the grass are white."

(And the Prince said in his heart, "Where can I find that?")

"And the second one you must not sow till you see a thing like
a tortoise put out a small white hand."

("And where," said the Prince, "can I meet with that wonder?")

"And when you have seen the second sprout up through the ground, go on till you come again to the land you have lost, and the place where you first knew sorrow."

("And what is sorrow?" said the Prince to his heart.)

"Then, when you have sown the third seed and watched it sprout, you will know perfect happiness, and will be able to hear the song which I sing."

Then the Green Bird lifted its wings and flew away through the night; and out of the darkness came three notes that filled him with wonderful delight.

But afterwards, when they ceased, came sorrow.

Now, when the Prince woke, he was in his own bed; and he rose much puzzled by the dream which had seemed so true.

Then came to him one of the pages, who said, "There was a strange bird flying over the palace about dawn, and a watchman on the high tower shot it, so I have brought it for you to see." And as he spoke, the page showed him the Green Bird lying dead between his hands.

The Prince took it without a word, and kissed it before them all, afterwards burying it where the white lilies full of gold fish grew, wherein he had first seen the image of its green breast fly. And as he stood sorrowing, the garden faded before his eyes, and a cold wind blew; and the palace, which had its foundations on happiness, crumbled away to ruin; and snow came down, kissing the earth and making it white.

He opened his hand, and found in it three grains of seed, and then he saw some of his dream already coming to pass. For the whole world with all the trees and grass was turning white before his eyes. Therefore he sowed the first grain of seed over the grave that he had made, and set out, over hill and dale, to fulfil the dream that the Green Bird had given him.

"But the Green Bird I shall see no more," he said, and wept.

For a year he went on through a desolate and waste country, meeting no man, nor discerning any sign. Till one day as he was coming down a mountain, he saw at the bottom a hut with a round roof like a great tortoise; and when he got quite near, out of the door came a small white hand, palm upwards, feeling to know if it rained.

Then all at once he remembered the word of the Green Bird; and, as he dropped the second seed into the ground, it seemed to him that he heard again the three notes of his song.

A young girl looked out of the hut; "What do you want?" she said, when she saw the Prince.

He saw her eyes, how blue and smiling they were, and it seemed as if he dreamed of them once. "Let me stay here for a while," he said, "and rest."

"If you will rest one day and work the next, you may," she answered.

So he rested that day, and the next he worked at her bidding in a small patch of ground that was before the hut.

When the day was over and he returned to the hut for the night, he looked again at the young girl, and, seeing how beautiful she was, said, "Why are you here all alone with no one to protect you?"

And she answered, "I have come from my own country, which is very far away, in search of a beautiful Green Bird which while it was mine I loved greatly, and which one day flew away, promising to return. When you came, something made me think the bird was with you; but perhaps tomorrow it will return."

At that the Prince sighed in his heart, for he knew that the bird was dead. Then also she told him how in her own country she had been a Princess; so now, she from whom the Green Bird had flown, and he to whom it had come, were living there together like beggars in a hut.

For a whole year he toiled and waited, hoping for the second seed to sprout; and at last one day, just where he had planted it, he saw a little spring rising out of the ground.

When the Princess saw it, she clapped her hands; "Oh," she cried, "it is the sign I have waited for! If we follow it, it will take us to the Green Bird." But the Prince sighed, for in his heart he knew that the Green Bird was dead.

Yet he let her take his hand; and they two went on following the course of the spring till they came to a wild, desolate place full of ruins; and as soon as they came to it, the spring disappeared into the ground.

Then the Prince began to look about him, and saw that he was

standing once more on the land that he had lost; above the very spot in the enchanted garden where he had buried the Green Bird and sorrowed over it. Then he stooped down and set the last grain of seed into the ground; and, as he did so, surely from below came the three sweet notes of a song!

Then all at once the earth opened, and out of it grew a tree, tall and green and waving; and out of the midst of the tree, flew the Green Bird with its nest in its beak.

The sun was setting; in the east rose a full red moon; grey mists climbed out of the grass. The bird sang and sang and sang; every note had the splendour of palace walls, and towers, and gardens, and falling fountains. The Princess ran fast and let herself be caught in the Prince's arms while she listened. Many times they hung together and kissed, and all the time the bird sang on.

"I see the palace walls grow," said the Princess. "They are as high as the hills, and the garden covers the valleys, and the sun and the moon lighten it."

And, in truth, round them a new palace had grown, and the Green Bird was building his nest in the roof.

The Happy Prince

~

Oscar Wilde

HIGH ABOVE THE CITY, on a tall column, stood the statue of the Happy Prince. He was gilded all over with thin leaves of fine gold, for eyes he had two bright sapphires, and a large red ruby glowed on his sword-hilt.

He was very much admired indeed. "He is as beautiful as a weathercock," remarked one of the Town Councillors who wished to gain a reputation for having artistic tastes; "only not quite so useful," he added, fearing lest people should think him unpractical, which he really was not.

"Why can't you be like the Happy Prince?" asked a sensible mother of her little boy, who was crying for the moon. "The Happy Prince never dreams of crying for anything."

"I am glad there is someone in the world who is quite happy," muttered a disappointed man as he gazed at the wonderful statue.

"He looks just like an angel," said the Charity Children as they came out of the cathedral in their bright scarlet cloaks, and their clean white pinafores.

"How do you know?" said the Mathematical Master. "You have never seen one."

"Ah! but we have, in our dreams," answered the children; and the Mathematical Master frowned and looked very severe, for he did not approve of children dreaming.

One night there flew over the city a little Swallow. His friends had gone away to Egypt six weeks before, but he had stayed behind, for he was in love with the most beautiful Reed. He had met her early in the spring as he was flying down the river after a big yellow moth, and had been so attracted by her slender waist that he had stopped to talk to her.

"Shall I love you?" said the Swallow, who liked to come to the point at once, and the Reed made him a low bow. So he flew round and round her, touching the water with his wings, and making silver ripples. This was his courtship, and it lasted all through the summer.

"It is a ridiculous attachment," twittered the other Swallows, "she has no money, and far too many relations"; and indeed the river was quite full of Reeds. Then, when the autumn came, they all flew away.

After they had gone he felt lonely, and began to tire of his lady-love. "She has no conversation," he said, "and I am afraid that she is a coquette, for she is always flirting with the wind." And certainly, whenever the wind blew, the Reed made the most graceful curtsies. "I admit that she is domestic," he continued, "but I love travelling, and my wife, consequently, should love travelling also."

"Will you come away with me?" he said finally to her; but the Reed shook her head, she was so attached to her home.

"You have been trifling with me," he cried, "I am off to the Pyramids. Goodbye!" and he flew away.

All day long he flew, and at night-time he arrived at the city. "Where shall I put up?" he said; "I hope the town has made preparations."

Then he saw the statue on the tall column. "I will put up there," he cried; "it is a fine position with plenty of fresh air." So he alighted just between the feet of the Happy Prince.

"I have a golden bedroom," he said softly to himself as he looked round, and he prepared to go to sleep; but just as he was putting his head under his wing a large drop of water fell on him. "What a curious thing!" he cried. "There is not a single cloud in the sky, the stars are quite clear and bright, and yet it is raining. The climate in the north of Europe is really dreadful. The Reed used to like the rain, but that was merely her selfishness."

Then another drop fell.

"What is the use of a statue if it cannot keep the rain off?" he said; "I must look for a good chimney-pot," and he determined to fly away.

But before he had opened his wings, a third drop fell, and he looked up, and saw – Ah! what did he see?

The eyes of the Happy Prince were filled with tears, and tears were running down his golden cheeks. His face was so beautiful in the moonlight that the little Swallow was filled with pity.

"Who are you?" he said.

"I am the Happy Prince."

"Why are you weeping, then?" asked the Swallow; "you have quite drenched me."

"When I was alive and had a human heart," answered the statue, "I did not know what tears were, for I lived in the Palace of Sans-Souci, where sorrow is not allowed to enter. In the daytime I played with my companions in the garden, and in the evening I led the dance in the Great Hall. Round the garden ran a very lofty wall, but I never cared to ask what lay beyond it, everything about me was so beautiful. My courtiers called me the Happy Prince, and happy indeed I was, if pleasure be happiness. So I lived, and so I died. And now that I am dead they have set me up here so high that I can see all the ugliness and all the misery of my city, and though my heart is made of lead yet I cannot choose but weep."

"What, is he not solid gold?" said the Swallow to himself. He was too polite to make any personal remarks out loud.

"Far away," continued the statue in a low, musical voice, "far away in a little street there is a poor house. One of the windows is open, and through it I can see a woman seated at a table. Her face is thin and worn, and she has coarse, red hands, all pricked by the needle, for she is a seamstress. She is embroidering passion-flowers on a satin gown for the loveliest of the Queen's maids-of-honour to wear at the next Court ball. In a bed in the corner of the room her little boy is lying ill. He has a fever, and is asking for oranges. His mother has nothing to give him but river water, so he is crying. Swallow, Swallow, little Swallow, will you not bring her the ruby out of my sword-hilt? My feet are fastened to this pedestal and I cannot move."

"I am waited for in Egypt," said the Swallow. "My friends are flying up and down the Nile, and talking to the large lotus-flowers. Soon they will go to sleep in the tomb of the great King. The King is there himself in his painted coffin. He is wrapped in yellow linen, and embalmed with spices. Round his neck is a chain of pale green jade, and his hands are like withered leaves."

"Swallow, Swallow, little Swallow," said the Prince, "will you not stay with me for one night, and be my messenger? The boy is so thirsty, and the mother so sad."

"I don't think I like boys," answered the Swallow. "Last summer, when I was staying on the river, there were two rude boys, the miller's sons, who were always throwing stones at me. They never hit me, of course; we swallows fly far too well for that, and besides, I come of a family famous for its agility; but still, it was a mark of disrespect."

But the Happy Prince looked so sad that the little Swallow was sorry. "It is very cold here," he said; "but I will stay with you for one night, and be your messenger."

"Thank you, little Swallow," said the Prince.

So the Swallow picked out the great ruby from the Prince's sword, and flew away with it in his beak over the roofs of the town.

He passed by the cathedral tower, where the white marble angels were sculptured. He passed by the palace and heard the sound of dancing. A beautiful girl came out on the balcony with her lover. "How wonderful the stars are," he said to her, "and how wonderful is the power of love!"

"I hope my dress will be ready in time for the State ball," she answered; "I have ordered passion-flowers to be embroidered on it; but the seamstresses are so lazy."

He passed over the river, and saw the lanterns hanging to the masts of the ships. He passed over the Ghetto, and saw the old Jews bargaining with each other, and weighing out money in copper scales. At last he came to the poor house and looked in. The boy was tossing feverishly on his bed, and the mother had fallen asleep, she was so tired. In he hopped, and laid the great ruby on the table beside the woman's thimble. Then he flew gently round the bed, fanning the boy's forehead with his wings. "How cool I feel," said the boy, "I must be getting better"; and he sank into a delicious slumber.

Then the Swallow flew back to the Happy Prince, and told him what he had done. "It is curious," he remarked, "but I feel quite warm now, although it is so cold."

"That is because you have done a good action," said the Prince. And the little Swallow began to think, and then he fell asleep. Thinking always made him sleepy.

When day broke he flew down to the river and had a bath. "What a remarkable phenomenon," said the Professor of Ornithology as he was passing over the bridge. "A swallow in winter!" And he wrote a long letter about it to the local newspaper. Everyone quoted it, it was full of so many words that they could not understand.

"Tonight I go to Egypt," said the Swallow, and he was in high spirits at the prospect. He visited all the public monuments, and sat a long time on top of the church steeple. Wherever he went the Sparrows chirruped, and said to each other, "What a distinguished stranger!" so he enjoyed himself very much.

When the moon rose he flew back to the Happy Prince. "Have you any commissions for Egypt?" he cried; "I am just starting."

"Swallow, Swallow, little Swallow," said the Prince, "will you not stay with me one night longer?"

"I am waited for in Egypt," answered the Swallow. "Tomorrow my friends will fly up to the Second Cataract. The river-horse couches there among the bulrushes, and on a great granite throne sits the God Memnon. All night long he watches the stars, and when the morning star shines he utters one cry of joy, and then he is silent. At noon the yellow lions come down to the water's edge to drink. They have eyes like green beryls, and their roar is louder than the roar of the cataract."

"Swallow, Swallow, little Swallow," said the Prince, "far away across the city I see a young man in a garret. He is leaning over a desk covered with papers, and in a tumbler by his side there is a bunch of withered violets. His hair is brown and crisp, and his lips are red as a pomegranate, and he has large and dreamy eyes. He is trying to finish a play for the Director of the Theatre, but he is too cold to write any more. There is no fire in the grate, and hunger has made him faint."

"I will wait with you one night longer," said the Swallow, who really had a good heart. "Shall I take him another ruby?"

"Alas! I have no ruby now," said the Prince; "my eyes are all that I have left. They are made of rare sapphires, which were brought out of India a thousand years ago. Pluck out one of them and take it to him. He will sell it to the jeweller, and buy food and firewood, and finish his play."

"Dear Prince," said the Swallow, "I cannot do that"; and he began to weep.

"Swallow, Swallow, little Swallow," said the Prince, "do as I command you."

So the Swallow plucked out the Prince's eye, and flew away to the student's garret. It was easy enough to get in, as there was a hole in the roof. Through this he darted, and came into the room. The young man had his head buried in his hands, so he did not hear the flutter of the bird's wings, and when he looked up he found the beautiful sapphire lying on the withered violets.

"I am beginning to be appreciated," he cried; "this is from some great admirer. Now I can finish my play," and he looked quite happy.

The next day the Swallow flew down to the harbour. He sat on the mast of a large vessel and watched the sailors hauling big chests out of the hold with ropes. "Heave a-hoy!" they shouted as each chest came up. "I am going to Egypt!" cried the Swallow, but nobody minded, and when the moon rose he flew back to the Happy Prince.

"I am come to bid you goodbye," he cried.

"Swallow, Swallow, little Swallow," said the Prince, "will you not stay with me one night longer?"

"It is winter," answered the Swallow, "and the chill snow will soon be here. In Egypt the sun is warm on the green palm-trees, and the crocodiles lie in the mud and look lazily about them. My companions are building a nest in the Temple of Baalbec, and the pink and white doves are watching them, and cooing to each other. Dear Prince, I must leave you, but I will never forget you, and next spring I will bring you back two beautiful jewels in place of those you have given away. The ruby shall be redder than a red rose, and the sapphire shall be as blue as the great sea."

"In the square below," said the Happy Prince, "there stands a little match-girl. She has let her matches fall in the gutter, and they

are all spoiled. Her father will beat her if she does not bring home some money, and she is crying. She has no shoes or stockings, and her little head is bare. Pluck out my other eye, and give it to her, and her father will not beat her."

"I will stay with you one night longer," said the Swallow, "but I cannot pluck out your eye. You would be quite blind then."

"Swallow, Swallow, little Swallow," said the Prince, "do as I command you."

So he plucked out the Prince's other eye, and darted down with it. He swooped past the match-girl, and slipped the jewel into the palm of her hand. "What a lovely bit of glass," cried the little girl; and she ran home, laughing.

Then the Swallow came back to the Prince. "You are blind now," he said, "so I will stay with you always."

"No, little Swallow," said the poor Prince, "you must go away to Egypt."

"I will stay with you always," said the Swallow, and he slept at the Prince's feet.

All the next day he sat on the Prince's shoulder, and told him stories of what he had seen in strange lands. He told him of the red ibises, who stand in long rows on the banks of the Nile, and catch gold fish in their beaks; of the Sphinx, who is as old as the world itself, and lives in the desert, and knows everything: of the merchants, who walk slowly by the side of their camels, and carry amber beads in their hands; of the King of the Mountains of the Moon, who is as black as ebony, and worships a large crystal; of the great green snake that sleeps in a palm-tree, and has twenty priests to feed it with honey-cakes; and of the pygmies who sail over a big lake on large flat leaves, and are always at war with the butterflies.

"Dear little Swallow," said the Prince, "you tell me of marvellous things, but more marvellous than anything is the suffering of men and of women. There is no Mystery so great as Misery. Fly over my city, little Swallow, and tell me what you see there."

So the Swallow flew over the great city, and saw the rich making merry in their beautiful houses while the beggars were sitting at the gates. He flew into dark lanes, and saw the white faces of starving children looking out listlessly at the black streets. Under the archway of a bridge two little boys were lying in one another's arms to try and keep themselves warm. "How hungry we are!" they said. "You must not lie here," shouted the Watchman, and they wandered out into the rain.

Then he flew back and told the Prince what he had seen.

"I am covered with fine gold," said the Prince, "you must take it off leaf by leaf, and give it to my poor; the living always think that gold can make them happy."

Leaf after leaf of the fine gold the Swallow picked off, till the Happy Prince looked quite dull and grey. Leaf after leaf of the fine gold he brought to the poor, and the children's faces grew rosier, and they laughed and played games in the street. "We have bread now!" they cried.

Then the snow came, and after the snow came the frost. The streets looked as if they were made of silver, they were so bright and glistening; long icicles like crystal daggers hung down from the eaves of the houses, everybody went about in furs, and the little boys wore scarlet caps and skated on the ice.

The poor little Swallow grew colder and colder, but he would not leave the Prince; he loved him too well. He picked up crumbs outside the baker's door when the baker was not looking, and tried to keep himself warm by flapping his wings.

But at last he knew that he was going to die. He had just strength to fly up to the Prince's shoulder once more. "Goodbye, dear Prince!" he murmured. "Will you let me kiss your hand?"

"I am glad that you are going to Egypt at last, little Swallow," said the Prince, "you have stayed too long here; but you must kiss me on the lips, for I love you."

"It is not to Egypt that I am going," said the Swallow. "I am going to the House of Death. Death is the brother of Sleep, is he not?"

And he kissed the Happy Prince on the lips, and fell down dead at his feet.

At that moment a curious crack sounded inside the statue, as if something had broken. The fact is that the leaden heart had snapped right in two. It certainly was a dreadfully hard frost.

Early the next morning the Mayor was walking in the square below in company with the Town Councillors. As they passed the column he looked up at the statue: "Dear me! How shabby the Happy Prince looks!" he said.

"How shabby indeed!" cried the Town Councillors, who always agreed with the Mayor, and they went up to look at it.

"The ruby has fallen out of his sword, his eyes are gone, and he is golden no longer," said the Mayor; "in fact, he is little better than a beggar!"

"Little better than a beggar," said the Town Councillors.

"And here is actually a dead bird at his feet!" continued the Mayor. "We must really issue a proclamation that birds are not to be allowed to die here." And the Town Clerk made a note of the suggestion.

So they pulled down the statue of the Happy Prince. "As he is no longer beautiful he is no longer useful," said the Art Professor at the University.

Then they melted the statue in a furnace, and the Mayor held a meeting of the Corporation to decide what was to be done with the metal. "We must have another statue, of course," he said, "and it shall be a statue of myself."

"Of myself," said each of the Town Councillors, and they quarrelled. When I last heard of them they were quarrelling still.

"What a strange thing!" said the overseer of the workmen at the foundry. "This broken lead heart will not melt in the furnace. We must throw it away." So they threw it on a dust-heap where the dead Swallow was also lying.

"Bring me the two most precious things in the city," said God to one of His Angels; and the Angel brought Him the leaden heart and the dead bird.

"You have rightly chosen," said God, "for in my garden of Paradise this little bird shall sing, for evermore, and in my city of gold the Happy Prince shall praise me."

How Wry-Face
Played a Trick on One-Eye

❦

Agnes Grozier Herbertson

ONE DAY, AS Oh-I-Am the Wizard went over Three-Tree Common, his shoe became unstringed, and he bent down to refasten it. Then he saw Wry-Face, the gnome, hiding among the bracken and looking as mischievous as anything. In one hand he held a white fluff-feather. Now, these feathers are as light as anything, and will blow in the wind; and whatever they are placed under, whether light or heavy, they are bound to topple over as soon as the wind blows.

As Oh-I-Am tied his shoe he saw Wry-Face place his fluff-feather carefully in the roadway; and at the same moment there came along One-Eye, the potato-wife, with her cart full of potatoes. The cart went rumble, crumble, crack, crack, crack, over the leaves and twigs, and One-Eye sang to her donkey:

> "Steady, steady,
> We're always ready,"

in a most cheerful voice.

Then the cart came to the fluff-feather, and over it went – crash, bang, splutter; and the potatoes flew everywhere, like rain.

Wry-Face, the gnome, laughed to himself so that he ached, and

he rolled over the ground with mirth. Then he flew away, laughing as he went.

But One-Eye, the potato-wife, was not laughing. Her tears went drip-drip as she started to gather her potatoes together. And as to getting her cart straight again, she did not know how she was to do it.

But when she turned round from gathering together the potatoes, she found that the cart was all right again, since Oh-I-Am the Wizard had straightened it for her, and the donkey was standing on his legs, none the worse for his fall.

Oh-I-Am looked stern and straight in his brown robe which trailed behind him. He said:

"One-Eye, have you got all your potatoes together?"

One-Eye still wept. She said, "No, I have not found all of them, for some have wandered far. And I must not seek farther, for this is market-day, and I must away to the town."

And she began to gather up the potatoes, and drop them into the cart, thud, thud, thud.

Oh-I-Am stooped, then, and he, too, gathered up the potatoes; and he threw them into the cart splish-splash-splutter!

"Alas!" said One-Eye, "if you throw them into the cart, splish-splash-splutter, you will bruise and break them. You must throw them in gently, thud, thud, thud."

So Oh-I-Am held back his anger, and he threw the potatoes in gently, thud, thud, thud. But when the potato-wife had gone on her way, he flew off to his Brown House by the Brown Bramble; and he began to weave a spell.

He put into it a potato, and a grain of earth, and a down from a pillow, and a pearl, and an apple-pip from a pie. And when the spell was ready, he lay down, and fell asleep.

Wry-Face had gone round to all the neighbours to tell them the grand joke about One-Eye, the potato-wife. Sometimes he told it through the window, and sometimes he stood at the door. Sometimes he told it to a gnome who was fine and feathery, and sometimes to one who was making bread. But all the time he laughed, laughed, laughed, till he was scarcely fit to stand.

Now, he did not call at Oh-I-Am's fine house to tell *him*, not he! And it was quite unnecessary, since Oh-I-Am knew the joke already, every bit.

Oh-I-Am had hidden the spell in his cupboard. When it was evening-time, he stole out and laid it by Wry-Face's door. Then he went home, and went to bed.

Wry-Face was making a pie for his supper. Suddenly the room became dark as dark. The darkness was not night coming on, for this was summer-time and night never came on as quickly as all that.

"Dear me, what can be the matter?" thought Wry-Face; for he could hardly see to finish making his pie.

Then he heard a little voice from his window, crying, "Here I am, Wry-Face, here I am!" But he could not go out to see what it was yet awhile.

Then the apple-pie was finished, and in the oven; and Wry-Face ran outside as fast as he could. But he did not see the spell which Oh-I-Am had placed by his door.

What he did see was a great potato-plant which had sprung up suddenly close to his window, and was springing up farther still, high, high, and higher.

"Good gracious me!" cried Wry-Face in a rage. "I never planted a potato-plant there, not in my whole life! Now I should just like to know what you are doing by my window?"

The potato-plant took no notice, but went on climbing high, high, and higher; and ever so far above he heard a tiny, faint voice crying:

"Here I am, Wry-Face, here I am!"

"Well, I never did!" cried Wry-Face, and he began to weep; for he saw that the potato-plant would climb up to his roof and round his chimney and he would never be able to get rid of it.

And he wept and wept.

At last he went in, and took his pie out of the oven, and set it in the pantry, for it was quite done. And he found a spade, and went out, and began to dig and dig at the root of the potato-plant. But his digging did not seem to make any difference; and the evening began to grow darker.

Wry-Face fetched his little lamp, which is named Bright-Beauty, and which always burns without flickering. Then he went on digging, and he dug, and dug, and dug.

And when he had dug for hours and hours, so that he was tired to death, the potato-plant began suddenly to dwindle and dwindle. It dwindled as fast as anything, the leaves disappeared, and the stem disappeared and all the horrid stretching arms. They sank down, down, and down, till at last there was nothing left at all but – a big brown potato!

"Well, I do declare!" cried Wry-Face. "I should like to know what you have to do with my fine garden!"

The potato replied, "I jumped here from the cart of One-Eye, the potato-wife, and it is quite certain that, unless I am taken back to her immediately, I shall start again, growing, and growing, and growing!"

"Dear potato, you must not start growing again!" cried Wry-Face, in a great way. "Tonight I am so tired I cannot do anything, but if you will but wait till tomorrow I will take you back to One-Eye, the potato-wife – I will, indeed!"

At first the potato would not listen to this at all; but after a while it said, "Well, well, I will wait till tomorrow. But remember, if tomorrow you do not carry me home to One-Eye, the potato-wife, I shall grow into a potato-*tree*, without a doubt!"

So Wry-Face carried the potato into his house, and stored it in his bin. But he never noticed the spell which Oh-I-Am had placed by his door.

*   *   *

"I am so tired, I can hardly yawn," said Wry-Face. "It is quite time I had my supper, and went to bed."

So he fetched the apple-pie from the pantry, and set it upon the table; and presently he sat down to his meal.

And he forgot for a moment how tired he was, thinking how delightful it was to sit down to a supper of apple-pie.

Then he lifted his knife and fork to cut off a large piece; but alas, the fork stuck fast. As for the knife, it would not move either, not an inch. Wry-Face began to weep.

"Alack, what has happened to my apple-pie?" cried he; and his tears fell round as round.

Then he got upon his feet, and he caught hold of the knife and fork and pulled, and pulled, and pulled. And with the last pull the top of the apple-pie came off, sticking to the knife and fork, and Wry-Face saw that within the pie there was not one piece of apple, but – a big brown potato!

Wry-Face wept again with horror at the sight.

"I should like to know," cried he, "what you are doing in my fine apple-pie."

But the brown potato replied, as cool as cool, "I am one of the potatoes belonging to One-Eye, the potato-wife, and I turned the apples out that I might hide here a while. But this I must tell you, my Wry-Face, unless you take me home immediately to the potato-wife, here, in this pie-dish, I intend to remain."

"Alas," cried Wry-Face, "tonight I am so tired I could never find One-Eye; but if you will but wait till tomorrow, I will carry you home to the potato-wife – I will indeed!"

At first the potato would not agree to this at all, but after a while it said, "Very well, I will wait till tomorrow. But remember, my Wry-Face, if tomorrow you do not carry me home to One-Eye, I will creep into every pie you make; and you will die at last of starvation without a doubt!"

So Wry-Face stored the potato in the potato-bin, and he went supperless to bed. And he knew nothing of the spell which Oh-I-Am had placed by his door.

Now he got into bed, and thought he would go to sleep; but, oh, how hard the mattress was! Wry-Face lay this way, then that, but no matter what way he lay, he found a great lump just beneath him which was as hard, and as nobbly as could be.

Wry-Face tossed and tossed till it was nearly morning; and his bones were so sore that he could lie no longer.

Then he pulled the mattress from the bed and cut a great hole in it, and when he had searched and searched he found in the middle of the mattress – a big brown potato!

"This," cried Wry-Face, "is why I have not slept the whole night through!" and he wept like anything.

But the potato was as cool as cool.

"I belong," it said, "to One-Eye, the potato-wife; and let me tell you, my little gnome, unless you take me to her immediately, I shall climb into your mattress again; and there I shall remain!"

"Alas," cried Wry-Face, "I have tossed about for hours and hours, and am too tired to do anything. But if you will wait till tomorrow, dear potato, I will carry you to One-Eye, the potato-wife – I will, indeed!"

At first the potato was unwilling to listen to this, but after a while it said: "Very well, then, I will wait till the morning. But this much I know, my Wry-Face, if you do not carry me then to One-Eye, the potato-wife, I shall get into your mattress and roll again *every night*!"

So Wry-Face put the potato in the bin. When he had done that he went back to bed, and slept, and slept.

When the sun was shining he awakened, and he remembered that he had to carry the potatoes back to One-Eye, the potato-wife; and he was as cross as anything.

"Well, I suppose I must!" he said. And when he had had his breakfast, he went to his cupboard to get a sack.

Then he found that his sack was full of pearls which he had gathered together for Heigh-Heavy the Giant, whose daughter So-Small he wished to marry.

So he thought, "First of all I will carry the pearls to Heigh-Heavy, for that is more important." And away he went with the sack upon his back. And he never saw the spell which Oh-I-Am had placed beside his door.

When he reached the Most-Enormous-House of Heigh-Heavy the Giant, there the giant was, sitting in his parlour lacing his shoes.

So Wry-Face cried out in a gay little voice, "Here I am, Heigh-Heavy, here I am! And here is a bag of pearls which I have brought you in exchange for your beautiful daughter, So-Small!"

When Heigh-Heavy heard this, he stopped lacing his shoes, and he said, "You must bring me in exchange for my daughter So-Small as many pearls as will cover my palm."

Then Wry-Face skipped forward, and he tipped up the sack; and he shook out all that it held into the hand of Heigh-Heavy the Giant, standing high upon his toes.

Now all that it held was – one brown potato!

Wry-Face the gnome stared, and stared, and stared, his eyes growing rounder and rounder; but he had no time to weep on account of Heigh-Heavy the Giant, who had fallen into a rage terrible to see.

"Now there is one thing quite certain," said Heigh-Heavy, "and that is that you shall never marry my daughter So-Small; for, my Wry-Face, I will turn you into a brown potato, and a brown potato you shall remain your whole life through!"

When Wry-Face heard this terrible threat he took to his heels, and ran from the Most-Enormous-House of Heigh-Heavy the Giant. And he ran, and ran, till his coat was torn and his ears were red. And he never rested till he reached his cottage door, and got inside.

Heigh-Heavy laughed till he cried to see the little gnome run. "He will play no tricks on *me*!" said he. And he went in and shut the door.

But Wry-Face said to himself as, weeping, he carried the potatoes to the potato-wife:

"I will never play a trick on *anyone* again, not as long as I live!"

Jack and the Beanstalk

∾

Anonymous

ONCE UPON A TIME there was a poor widow who lived in a little cottage with her only son Jack. Jack was a giddy, thoughtless boy, but very kind-hearted and affectionate. There had been a hard winter, and after it the poor woman had suffered from fever and ague. Jack did no work as yet, and by degrees they grew dreadfully poor. The widow saw that there was no means of keeping Jack and herself from starvation but by selling her cow; so one morning she said to her son, "I am too weak to go myself, Jack, so you must take the cow to market for me, and sell her."

Jack liked going to market to sell the cow very much; but as he was on the way he met a butcher who had some beautiful beans in his hand. Jack stopped to look at them, and the butcher told the boy that they were of great value and persuaded the silly lad to sell the cow for these beans.

When he brought them home to his mother instead of the money she expected for her nice cow, she was very vexed and shed many tears, scolding Jack for his folly. He was very sorry, and mother and son went to bed very sadly that night; their last hope seemed gone.

At daybreak Jack rose and went out into the garden.

"At least," he thought, "I will sow the wonderful beans. Mother says that they are just common scarlet-runners, and nothing else; but I may as well sow them."

So he took a piece of stick, made some holes in the ground, and put in the beans. That day they had very little dinner, and went sadly to bed, knowing that for the next day there would be none, and Jack, unable to sleep from grief and vexation, got up at day-dawn and went out into the garden.

What was his amazement to find that the beans had grown up in the night, and climbed up and up till they covered the high cliff that sheltered the cottage, and disappeared above it! The stalks had twined and twisted themselves together till they formed quite a ladder.

"It would be easy to climb it," thought Jack.

And, having thought of the experiment, he at once resolved to carry it out, for Jack was a good climber. However, after his late mistake about the cow, he thought he had better consult his mother first.

So Jack called his mother, and they both gazed in silent wonder at the Beanstalk, which was not only of great height, but was thick enough to bear Jack's weight.

"I wonder where it ends," said Jack to his mother; "I think I will climb up and see."

His mother wished him not to venture up this strange ladder, but Jack coaxed her to give her consent to the attempt, for he was certain there must be something wonderful in the Beanstalk; so at last she yielded to his wishes. Jack instantly began to climb, and went up and up till everything he had left behind him – the cottage, the village, and even the tall church tower – looked quite little, and still he could not see the top of the Beanstalk.

Jack felt a little tired, and thought for a moment that he would go back again; but he was a very persevering boy, and he knew that the way to succeed in anything was not to give up. So after resting for a moment he went on.

After climbing higher and higher, till he grew afraid to look down for fear he should be giddy, Jack at last reached the top of the Beanstalk, and found himself in a beautiful country, finely wooded, with beautiful meadows covered with sheep. A crystal stream ran through the pastures; not far from the place where he had got off the Beanstalk stood a fine, strong castle.

Jack wondered very much that he had never heard of or seen this castle before; but when he reflected on the subject, he saw that it was as much separated from the village by the perpendicular rock on which it stood as if it were in another land.

While Jack was standing looking at the castle, a very strange-looking woman came out of the wood, and advanced towards him. She wore a pointed cap of quilted red satin turned up with ermine, her hair streamed loose over her shoulders, and she walked with a staff. Jack took off his cap and made her a bow.

"If you please, ma'am," said he, "is this your house?"

"No," said the old lady. "Listen, and I will tell you the story of that castle. Once upon a time there was a noble knight, who lived in this castle, which is on the borders of Fairyland. He had a fair and beloved wife and several lovely children: and as his neighbours, the little people, were very friendly towards him, they bestowed on him many excellent and precious gifts. Rumour whispered of these treasures; and a monstrous giant, who lived at no great distance, and who was a very wicked being, resolved to obtain possession of them. So he bribed a false servant to let him inside the castle, when the knight was in bed and asleep, and he killed him as he lay. Then he went to the part of the castle which was the nursery, and also killed all the poor little ones he found there. Happily for her, the lady was not to be found. She had gone with her infant son, who was only two or three months old, to visit her old nurse, who lived in the valley; and she had been detained all night there by a storm.

"The next morning, as soon as it was light, one of the servants at the castle, who had managed to escape, came to tell the poor lady of the sad fate of her husband and her pretty babes. She could scarcely believe him at first, and was eager at once to go back and share the fate of her dear ones; but the old nurse, with many tears, besought her to remember that she had still a child, and that it was her duty to preserve her life for the sake of the poor innocent.

"The lady yielded to this reasoning, and consented to remain at her nurse's house as the best place of concealment; for the servant told her that the giant had vowed, if he could find her, he would kill both her and her baby. Years rolled on. The old nurse died, leaving her cottage and the few articles of furniture it contained to her poor lady, who dwelt in it, working as a peasant for her daily bread. Her spinning-wheel and the milk of a cow, which she had purchased with the little money she had with her, sufficed for the scanty subsistence of herself and her little son. There was a nice little garden attached to the cottage, in which they cultivated peas, beans and cabbages, and the lady was not ashamed to go out at harvest time, and glean in the fields to supply her little son's wants.

"Jack, that poor lady is your mother. This castle was once your father's, and must again be yours."

Jack uttered a cry of surprise.

"My mother! Oh, madam, what ought I to do? My poor father! My dear mother!"

"Your duty requires you to win it back for your mother. But the task is a very difficult one, and full of peril, Jack. Have you courage to undertake it?"

"I fear nothing when I am doing right," said Jack.

"Then," said the lady in the red cap, "you are one of those who slay giants. You must get into the castle, and if possible possess yourself of a hen that lays golden eggs, and a harp that talks. Remember, all the giant possesses is really yours." As she ceased speaking the lady suddenly disappeared, and of course Jack knew she was a fairy.

Jack determined at once to attempt the adventure; so he advanced, and blew the horn which hung at the castle portal. The door was opened in a minute by a frightful giantess, with one great eye in the middle of her forehead. As soon as Jack saw her he turned to run away, but she caught him, and dragged him into the castle.

"Ho, ho!" she laughed terribly. "You didn't expect to see *me* here, that is clear! No, I shan't let you go again. I am weary of my life. I am so overworked, and I don't see why I should not have a page as well as other ladies. And you shall be my boy. You shall clean the knives, and black the boots, and make the fires, and help me generally when the giant is out. When he is at home I must hide you, for he has eaten up all my pages hitherto, and you would be a dainty morsel."

While she spoke she dragged Jack right into the castle. The poor boy was very frightened. But he remembered that fear disgraces a man; so he struggled to be brave and make the best of things.

"I am quite ready to help you, and do all I can to serve you, madam," he said, "only I beg you will be good enough to hide me from your husband, for I should not like to be eaten at all."

"That's a good boy," said the Giantess, nodding her head; "it is lucky for you that you did not scream out when you saw me, as the other boys who have been here did, for if you had done so my husband would have awakened and have eaten you, as he did them, for breakfast. Come here, child; go into my wardrobe: he never ventures to open *that*; you will be safe there."

And she opened a huge wardrobe which stood in the great hall, and shut him into it. But the keyhole was so large that it admitted plenty of air, and Jack could see everything that took place through it. By and by he heard a heavy tramp on the stairs, like the lumbering along of a great cannon, and then a voice like thunder cried out:

> "Fe, fa, fi-fo-fum,
> I smell the breath of an Englishman.
> Let him be alive or let him be dead,
> I'll grind his bones to make my bread."

"Wife," cried the Giant, "there is a man in the castle. Let me have him for breakfast."

"You are grown old and stupid," cried the lady in her loud tones. "It is only a nice fresh steak off an elephant, that I have cooked for you, which you smell. There, sit down and make a good breakfast."

When he had breakfasted he went out for a walk; and then the Giantess opened the door, and made Jack come out to help her.

The Giant came in to supper. Jack watched him through the keyhole, and was amazed to see him put half a fowl at a time into his capacious mouth. When the supper was ended he bade his wife bring him his hen that laid the golden eggs. The Giantess returned with a little brown hen. The Giant took up the brown hen and said to her:

"Lay!" And she instantly laid a golden egg.

"Lay!" said the Giant again. And she laid another.

"Lay!" he repeated the third time. And again a golden egg lay on the table. Now Jack was sure this hen was that of which the fairy had spoken. By-and-by the Giant put the hen down on the floor, and soon after went fast asleep, snoring so loud that it sounded like thunder.

Directly Jack perceived that the Giant was fast asleep, he pushed open the door of the wardrobe and crept out; picking up the hen, he made haste to quit the apartment and flew back to the Beanstalk, which he descended as fast as his feet would move.

When his mother saw him enter the house she wept for joy, for she had feared that the fairies had carried him away, or that the Giant had found him. But Jack put the brown hen down before her, and told her how he had been in the Giant's castle, and all his adventures. She was very glad to see the hen, which would make them rich once more.

Jack made another journey up the Beanstalk to the Giant's castle one day while his mother had gone to market; but first he dyed his hair and disguised himself. The old woman did not know him again, and dragged him in as she had done before, to help her to do the work; but she heard her husband coming, and hid him in the wardrobe, not thinking that it was the same boy who had stolen the hen. She bade him stay quite still there or the Giant would eat him. Then the Giant came in saying:

> "Fe, fa, fi-fo-fum,
> I smell the breath of an Englishman.
> Let him be alive or let him be dead,
> I'll grind his bones to make my bread."

"Nonsense!" said the wife, "it is only a roasted bullock that I thought would be a tit-bit for your supper; sit down and I will bring it up at once."

As soon as they had finished their meal, the Giant rose and said: "Bring me my money bags, that I may count my golden pieces before I sleep." The Giantess obeyed. She soon returned with two large bags which she put down by her husband.

"There," she said; "that is all that is left of the knight's money. When you have spent it you must go and take another baron's castle."

"That he shan't, if I can help it," thought Jack.

The Giant, when his wife was gone, took out heaps of golden pieces, and counted them, and put them in piles, till he was tired of the amusement. Then he swept them all back into their bags, and, leaning back in his chair, fell fast asleep, snoring so loud that no other sound was audible.

Jack stole softly out of the wardrobe, and, taking up the bags of money, he ran off, and, with great difficulty descending the Beanstalk, laid the bags of gold on his mother's table. She had just returned from town, and was crying at not finding Jack.

"There, Mother, I have brought you the gold that my father lost."

"Oh, Jack! You are a very good boy, but I wish you would not risk your precious life in the Giant's castle. Tell me how you came to go there again."

And Jack told her all about it. Jack's mother was very glad to get the money, but she did not like him to run any risk for her.

But after a time Jack made up his mind to go again to the Giant's castle.

So he climbed the Beanstalk once more, and blew the horn at the Giant's gate. The Giantess soon opened the door; she was very stupid, and did not know him again, but she stopped a minute before she took him in. She feared another robbery; but Jack's fresh face looked so innocent that she could not resist him, and so she bade him come in, and again hid him away in the wardrobe.

By-and-by the Giant came home, and as soon as he had crossed the threshold he roared out;

> "Fe, fa, fi-fo-fum,
> I smell the breath of an Englishman.
> Let him be alive or let him be dead,
> I'll grind his bones to make my bread."

"You stupid old Giant," said his wife, "you only smell a nice sheep which I have grilled for your dinner."

And the Giant sat down, and his wife brought up a whole sheep for his dinner. When he had eaten it all up, he said: "Now bring me my harp, and I will have a little music while you take your walk."

The Giantess obeyed, and returned with a beautiful harp. The framework was all sparkling with diamonds and rubies, and the strings were all of gold.

"This is one of the nicest things I took from the knight," said the Giant. "I am very fond of music, and my harp is a faithful servant." So he drew the harp towards him, and said: "Play!"

And the harp played a very soft, sad air.

"Play something merrier!" said the Giant.

And the harp played a merry tune.

"Now play me a lullaby," roared the Giant; and the harp played a sweet lullaby, to the sound of which its master fell asleep.

Then Jack stole softly out of the wardrobe, and went into the huge kitchen to see if the Giantess had gone out; he found no one there, so he entered the Giant's room and seized the harp and ran away with it; but as he jumped over the threshold the harp called out: "MASTER! MASTER!" And the Giant woke up.

With a tremendous roar he sprang from his seat, and in two strides had reached the door.

But Jack was very nimble. He fled like lightning with the harp, talking to it as he went, and telling it he was the son of its old master.

Still the Giant came on so fast that he was quite close to poor Jack, and had stretched out his great hand to catch him. But, luckily, just at that moment he stepped upon a loose stone, stumbled, and fell flat on the ground, where he lay at his full length.

This accident gave Jack time to get on the Beanstalk and hasten down it; but just as he reached their own garden he beheld the Giant descending after him.

"Mother!" cried Jack. "Make haste and give me the axe."

His mother ran to him with a hatchet in her hand, and Jack with one tremendous blow cut through all the Beanstalks except one.

"Now, Mother, stand out of the way!" said he.

Jack's mother shrank back, and it was well she did so, for, just as the Giant took hold of the last branch of the Beanstalk, Jack cut the stem quite through and darted from the spot.

Down came the Giant with a terrible crash, and as he fell on his head, he broke his neck, and lay dead at the feet of the woman he had so much injured.

Before Jack and his mother had recovered from their alarm and agitation, a beautiful lady stood before them.

"Jack," said she, "you have acted like a brave knight's son, and deserve to have your inheritance restored to you. Dig a grave and bury the Giant, and then go and kill the Giantess."

"But," said Jack, " I could not kill anyone unless I were fighting with him; and I could not draw my sword upon a woman. Moreover, the Giantess was very kind to me."

The Fairy smiled on Jack.

"I am very much pleased with your generous feeling," she said. "Nevertheless, return to the castle, and act as you will find needful."

Jack asked the Fairy if she would show him the way to the castle, as the Beanstalk was now down. She told him that she would drive him there in her chariot, which was drawn by two peacocks. Jack thanked her, and sat down in the chariot with her.

The Fairy drove him a long distance round, till they reached a village which lay at the bottom of the hill. Here they found a number of miserable-looking men assembled. The Fairy stopped her carriage and addressed them:

"My friends," said she, "the cruel giant who oppressed you and ate up all your flocks and herds is dead, and this young gentleman was the means of your being delivered from him, and is the son of your kind old master, the knight."

The men gave a loud cheer at these words, and pressed forward to say that they would serve Jack as faithfully as they had served his father. The Fairy bade them follow her to the castle, and they marched thither in a body, and Jack blew the horn and demanded admittance. The old Giantess saw them coming from the turret loop-hole. She was very much frightened, for she guessed that something had happened to her husband; and as she came downstairs very fast she caught her foot in her dress, and fell from the top to the bottom and broke her neck. When the people outside found that the door was not opened to them, they took crowbars and forced the portal. Nobody was to be seen, but on leaving the hall they found the body of the Giantess at the foot of the stairs.

Thus Jack took possession of the castle. The Fairy went and brought his mother to him, with the hen and the harp. He had the Giantess buried, and endeavoured as much as lay in his power to do right to those whom the Giant had robbed.

Before her departure for fairyland, the Fairy explained to Jack that she had sent the butcher to meet him with the beans, in order to try what sort of lad he was.

"If you had looked at the gigantic Beanstalk and only stupidly wondered about it," she said, "I should have left you where misfortune had placed you, only restoring her cow to your mother. But you showed an enquiring mind, and great courage and enterprise, therefore you deserve to rise; and when you mounted the Beanstalk you climbed the Ladder of Fortune."

She then took her leave of Jack and his mother.

The Knave and the Fool

Juliana H. Ewing

A FOOL AND A KNAVE once set up house together: which shows what a fool the Fool was.

The Knave was delighted with the agreement; and the Fool thought himself most fortunate to have met with a companion who would supply his lack of mother-wit. As neither of them liked work, the Knave proposed that they should live upon their joint savings as long as these should last; and, to avoid disputes, that they should use the Fool's share till it came to an end, and then begin upon the Knave's stocking.

So, for a short time, they lived in great comfort at the Fool's expense, and were very good company; for easy times make easy tempers.

Just when the store was exhausted, the Knave came running to the Fool with an empty bag and a wry face, crying, "Dear friend, what shall we do? This bag, which I had safely buried under a gooseberry-bush, has been taken up by some thief, and all my money stolen. My savings were twice as large as yours; but now that they are gone, and I can no longer perform my share of the bargain, I fear our partnership must be dissolved."

"Not so, dear friend," said the Fool, who was very good-natured; "we have shared good luck together, and now we will share poverty. But, as nothing is left, I fear we must seek work."

"You speak very wisely," said the Knave. "And what, for instance, can you do?"

"Very little," said the Fool; "but that little I do well."

"So do I," said the Knave. "Now can you plough, or sow, or feed cattle, or plant crops?"

"Farming is not my business," said the Fool.

"Nor mine," said the Knave; "but no doubt you are a handicraftsman. Are you clever at carpentry, mason's work, tailoring, or shoemaking?"

"I do not doubt that I should have been, had I learned the trades," said the Fool, "but I never was bound apprentice."

"It is the same with myself," said the Knave; "but you may have finer talents. Can you paint, or play the fiddle?"

"I never tried," said the Fool; "so I don't know."

"Just my case," said the Knave. "And now, since we can't find work, I propose that we travel till work finds us."

The two comrades accordingly set forth, and they went on and on, till they came to the foot of a hill, where a merchantman was standing by his wagon, which had broken down.

"You seem two strong men," said he, as they advanced; "if you will carry this chest of valuables up to the top of the hill, and down to the bottom on the other side, where there is an inn, I will give you two gold pieces for your trouble."

The Knave and the Fool consented to this, saying, "Work has found us at last;" and they lifted the box on to their shoulders.

"Turn, and turn about," said the Knave; "but the best turn between friends is a good turn; so I will lead the way up-hill, which is the hardest kind of travelling, and you shall go first down-hill, the easy half of our journey."

The Fool thought this proposal a very generous one, and, not knowing that the lower end of their burden was the heavy one, he carried it all the way. When they got to the inn, the merchant gave each of them a gold piece, and, as the accommodation was good, they remained where they were till their money was spent. After this, they lived there awhile on credit; and when that was exhausted, they rose one morning whilst the landlord was still in bed, and pursued their journey, leaving old scores behind them.

They had been a long time without work or food, when they came upon a man who sat by the roadside breaking stones, with a quart of porridge and a spoon in a tin pot beside him.

"You look hungry, friends," said he, "and I, for my part, want to get away. If you will break up this heap, you shall have the porridge for supper. But when you have eaten it, put the pot and spoon under the hedge, that I may find them when I return."

"If we eat first, we shall have strength for our work," said the Knave; "and as there is only one spoon, we must eat by turns. But fairly divide, friendly abide. As you went first the latter part of our journey, I will begin on this occasion. When I stop, you fall to, and eat as many spoonfuls as I ate. Then I will follow you in like fashion, and so on till the pot is empty."

"Nothing could be fairer," said the Fool; and the Knave began to eat, and went on till he had eaten a third of the porridge. The Fool, who had counted every spoonful, now took his turn, and ate precisely as much as his comrade. The Knave then began again, and was exact to a mouthful; but it emptied the pot. Thus the Knave had twice as much as the Fool, who could not see where he had been cheated.

They then set to work.

"As there is only one hammer," said the Knave, "we must work, as we supped, by turns; and as I began last time, you shall begin this. After you have worked awhile, I will take the hammer from you, and do as much myself whilst you rest. Then you shall take it up again, and so on till the heap is finished."

"It is not everyone who is as just as you," said the Fool; and, taking up the hammer, he set to work with a will.

The Knave took care to let him go on till he had broken a third of the stones, and then he did as good a share himself; after which the Fool began again, and finished the heap.

By this means the Fool did twice as much work as the Knave, and yet he could not complain.

As they moved on again, the Fool perceived that the Knave was taking the can and the spoon with him.

"I am sorry to see you do that, friend," said he.

"It's a very small theft," said the Knave. "The can cannot have cost more than sixpence, when new."

"That was not what I meant," said the Fool, "so much as that I fear the owner will find it out."

"He will only think the things have been stolen by some vagrant," said the Knave, "which, indeed, they would be if we left them. But, as you seem to have a tender conscience, I will keep them myself."

After a while they met with a farmer, who offered to give them supper and a night's lodging, if they would scare the birds from a field of corn for him till sunset.

"I will go into the outlying fields," said the Knave, "and as I see the birds coming, I will turn them back. You, dear friend, remain in the corn, and scare away the few that may escape me."

But, whilst the Fool clapped and shouted till he was tired, the Knave went to the other side of the hedge, and lay down for a nap.

As they sat together at supper, the Fool said, "Dear friend, this is laborious work. I propose that we ask the farmer to let us tend sheep, instead. That is a very different affair. One lies on the hillside all day. The birds do not steal sheep; and all this shouting and clapping is saved."

The Knave very willingly agreed, and next morning the two friends drove a flock of sheep on to the downs. The sheep at once began to nibble, the dog sat with his tongue out, panting, and the Knave and Fool lay down on their backs, and covered their faces with their hats to shield them from the sun.

Thus they lay till evening, when, the sun being down, they uncovered their faces, and found that the sheep had all strayed away, and the dog after them.

"The only plan for us is to go separate ways in scarch of the flock," said the Knave; "only let us agree to meet here again." They accordingly started in opposite directions; but when the Fool was fairly off, the Knave returned to his place, and lay down as before.

By and by the dog brought the sheep back; so that, when the Fool returned, the Knave got the credit of having found them; for the dog scorned to explain his part in the matter.

As they sat together at supper, the Fool said, "The work is

not so easy as I thought. Could we not find a better trade yet?"

"Can you beg?" said the Knave. "A beggar's trade is both easy and profitable. Nothing is required but walking and talking. Then one walks at his own pace, for there is no hurry, and no master, and the same tale does for every door. And, that all may be fair and equal, you shall beg at the front door, whilst I ask an alms at the back."

To this the Fool gladly agreed; and as he was as lean as a hunted cat, charitable people gave him a penny or two from time to time. Meanwhile, the Knave went round to the back yard, where he picked up a fowl, or turkey, or anything that he could lay his hands upon.

When he returned to the Fool, he would say, "See what has been given to me, whilst you have only got a few pence."

At last this made the Fool discontented, and he said, "I should like now to exchange with you. I will go to the back doors, and you to the front."

The Knave consented, and at the next house the Fool went to the back door; but the mistress of the farm only rated him, and sent him away. Meanwhile, the Knave, from the front, had watched her leave the parlour, and, slipping in through the window, he took a ham and a couple of new loaves from the table, and so made off.

When the friends met, the Fool was crestfallen at his ill luck, and the Knave complained that all the burden of their support fell upon him. "See," said he, "what they give me, where you get only a mouthful of abuse!" And he dined heartily on what he had stolen; but the Fool only had bits of the bread-crust, and the parings of the ham.

At the next place the Fool went to the front door as before, and the Knave secured a fat goose and some plums in the back yard, which he popped under his cloak. The Fool came away with empty hands, and the Knave scolded him, saying, "Do you suppose that I mean to share this fat goose with a lazy beggar like you? Go on, and find for yourself." With which he sat down and began to eat the plums, whilst the Fool walked on alone.

After a while, however, the Knave saw a stir in the direction of the farm they had left, and he quickly perceived that the loss of the

goose was known, and that the farmer and his men were in pursuit of the thief. So, hastily picking up the goose, he overtook the Fool, and pressed it into his arms, saying, "Dear friend, pardon a passing ill humour, of which I sincerely repent. Are we not partners in good luck and ill? I was wrong, dear friend; and, in token of my penitence, the goose shall be yours alone. And here are a few plums with which you may refresh yourself by the wayside. As for me, I will hasten on to the next farm, and see if I can beg a bottle of wine to wash down the dinner, and drink to our good-fellowship." And before the Fool could thank him, the Knave was off like the wind.

By and by the farmer and his men came up, and found the Fool eating the plums, with the goose on the grass beside him.

They hurried him off to the justice, where his own story met with no credit. The woman of the next farm came up also, and recognized him for the man who had begged at her door the day she lost a ham and two new loaves. In vain he said that these things also had been given to his friend. The friend never appeared; and the poor Fool was whipped and put in the stocks.

Towards evening the Knave hurried up to the village green, where his friend sat doing penance for the theft.

"My dear friend," said he, "what do I see? Is such cruelty possible? But I hear that the justice is not above a bribe, and we must at any cost obtain your release. I am going at once to pawn my own boots and cloak, and everything about me that I can spare, and if you have anything to add, this is no time to hesitate."

The poor Fool begged his friend to draw off his boots, and to take his hat and coat as well, and to take his hat and coat as well, and to make all speed on his charitable errand.

The Knave took all that he could get, and, leaving his friend sitting in the stocks in his shirt-sleeves, he disappeared as swiftly as one could wish a man to carry a reprieve.

For those good folks to whom everything must be explained in full, it may be added that the Knave did not come back, and that he kept the clothes.

It was very hard on the Fool; but what can one expect if he keeps company with a Knave?

Little Red Riding Hood

❧

Laura Valentine

ONCE UPON A TIME, in an ancient forest of Brittany, there dwelt a woodman and his wife, who had one only child – a little daughter.

She was so very beautiful, so good, so tender, and so kind, that everybody loved her. Her grandmother, who dwelt in the midst of the wood, made her a little red cloak and hood, which became her glossy black hair and sparkling hazel eyes so well that people used to call her Little Red Riding Hood.

She dwelt in a pleasant home: green glades stretched all round it, beautiful wild flowers grew under the trees, silvery may, bluebells, wild thyme, oxlips and cowslips, primroses – all in their season; and, in the ripe autumn, hazel-nuts and blackberries. And the birds and the squirrels were Red Riding Hood's playfellows, in addition to the great wolfhound, Bran, called after the King himself, who loved her dearly, and was seldom happy when she was out of his sight.

Little Red Riding Hood was the kindest child that ever was known. She delighted in doing good. She shared her dinner with Bran. She saved all the crumbs for the birds. Everything in the forest loved her.

When she took her father's dinner to him at noon, she went with quite a procession. Bran walked gravely by her side; on her shoulder sat a cushat dove; a raven hopped along on the side opposite to the dog; a soft, grey pussy crept along in front, rubbing herself at times against her little mistress, and getting a gentle chiding for nearly throwing her down.

And Hugh, the woodman, would say to her father: "Here comes sweet Red Riding Hood; she is like a little sunbeam in the green wood."

Then they would all sit down together under a great oak, and Red Riding Hood's father, Hugh, the child, the dog, the dove, the raven, the cat, and the two men would eat their dinner.

And she never failed to give a bit of all she had to Bran, and to the raven, and the dove, and pussy, if it were only a crumb.

When they had dined – they were allowed an hour for dinner – the woodmen would repay their little attendant for her trouble by telling her stories, wonderful tales of the cruel wolves and dark dreadful creatures that haunted the lonely woods. And as Little Red Riding Hood walked home again she would talk to Bran about it, and tell the dog what *her* idea of a wolf was.

"It must be a dreadful monster, Bran! Very big! Oh, as tall as the house nearly, and with great flaming eyes just like red-hot coals. When it walks it must quite shake the woods, and its paws could crush you and me, Bran, at a single blow."

"Bow-wow-wow," said Bran indignantly. He could not tell her that she was quite mistaken, because dogs can't learn to speak men's language, having, in fact, very little occasion for words to tell you what they think or wish, they have such a wonderful way of making you understand them.

One fine sunshiny day, when Red Riding Hood came down to breakfast, she was surprised to see her father all dressed in his best green suit, which he only wore on Sundays.

"Oh, Father!" cried she, "where are you going? It is not Sunday."

"No, my child, but there is a great archery show today, and our chief desires me to attend it."

"Is Hugh going?" asked Little Red Riding Hood.

"No," said her father, laughing; "he will stay in the forest to drive away the wolves."

And then the woodman gave his little daughter a good kiss on her rosy cheek, and went away.

By-and-by Red Riding Hood's mother said to her:

"Red Riding Hood, as Father is gone out, you will not have

to carry his dinner into the wood today. I shall send you to your grandmother's instead."

"Oh, Mother dear, I shall be so glad to go!" said the little one.

"The dear old lady has been very ill for a long time now," added Red Riding Hood's mother, "and never, I think, gets up; she is quite bedridden. Winifred, her little servant, has asked leave to go to the archery show today, and poor Granny is all alone. So I thought that you could go and stay with her a little while, and take a basket of nice things to her from me."

"That I will gladly," said the little girl. "I dearly love Granny, and she loves me. She will be so happy. Make haste, Mother, to pack the basket."

And Red Riding Hood's mother made haste, and put some new-laid eggs and a few pats of butter into a basket; and she laid some cheesecakes and gingerbread at the top of all.

"There, my dear," she said; "this basket is for your grandmamma, and this little packet at the top for yourself. You will be hungry, I daresay, before you get there, and you will find in it some bread and butter and cold meat. Get your red cloak and hood, dear, and I will tie it on."

Little Red Riding Hood obeyed. And her mother tied on her scarlet hood, and kissed her, and gave her the basket and told her to go. And Red Riding Hood set off on her errand.

Now I really think it was very imprudent of her mother to send her alone; but people get used to dangers, and then they cease to fear them; and Red Riding Hood's mother did not care the least for a wolf, and had nearly forgotten that they were dangerous.

She watched her little daughter, however, till she was out of sight, not from any fears as to her safety, but because she was very proud of the poor child's beauty; for a sweeter little creature you never saw, trotting along in her red hood, with the dove perched on it, and the raven half hopping and half flying beside her.

It was still early. The gossamer dew was all over the grass, sparkling in the sunshine like diamonds, and the lark was singing sweetly quite low down. He had not had time to get up in the sky out of sight.

And Red Riding Hood peeped about to see if she could find his nest in the grass, but she could not.

Then she saw a bee buzzing about close to her; and she followed it and watched it gathering honey from the thyme.

By-and-by she came to a glade full of foxgloves, pink and white; and, as she dearly loved flowers, she gathered a great bunch of them.

"They will make Grandmamma's chamber look quite gay, and remind her of the beautiful summer out of doors," she thought. "Ah, and there are violets down among the moss. I must have some of these."

And she gathered a lovely bouquet while Ralph, the raven, picked about finding worms, and Lily, the dove, sat on a bough close by and cooed softly to please her.

And then, when she had gathered as many flowers as she liked, Red Riding Hood ran on, and, turning down another path, came upon Hugh and his fellow-woodman.

"Halloa, little woman!" said the worthy fellow; "where are *you* going so early?"

"I am going to see my grandam, Hugh," she said, smiling sweetly at him; "and I am taking her a present."

"'Tis a long way for a babe like you," said Hugh; "have you got the dog? Where is he?"

"He is gone to the archery show with Father," she replied. "I am all by myself, except Lily and Ralph."

"Caw, caw! Craw, craw!" said the raven solemnly, as if to say, "Yes, *I* am here; I can take care of Red Riding Hood."

"Well," said Hugh, "make haste, and don't tarry in the forest. I and Caleb shall be coming in that direction before long."

"Goodbye," said Red Riding Hood. "I will make haste."

And she ran on, and the woodmen's axes resounded the next minute on the gnarled old trunk.

Meantime Little Red Riding Hood ran gaily on. She had not advanced ten yards from the spot where the woodmen were (though she was out of sight, being hidden by the trees) when a large dog, something like Bran, came trotting towards her, and came up to her and said:

"Good-morning, Little Red Riding Hood."

"Good-morning," said the little girl.

The supposed dog – alas! it was really a wolf – turned and trotted along by the side of her, although the raven croaked and gave his heels a sly bite.

"Where are you going, Little Red Riding Hood?" asked the wolf.

"I am going to see Grandmamma," replied the child. "She lives at the cottage beneath the elms in the forest."

"Ah, I know her!" said the wolf. "Rather an old lady, is she not?"

"Yes," said Little Red Riding Hood, "and such a dear, kind, gentle granny. I wish she were not so feeble, and that she could run and jump as well as I can."

"Can't she?" said the sly wolf.

"No; she is obliged always to be in bed, and so she has a little girl called Winifred – old David the woodman's daughter – to clean her house, and cook her dinner, and take care of her."

"The little girl will be very glad to see you, Red Riding Hood," said the cunning wolf.

"She always is when she is at home," said Red Riding Hood; "but today she is gone out to the archery show; and as my mother fears that Grandmamma may be dull, she has sent me to be with her, and I am carrying her a basket of nice things as a present."

"Is there any meat in it?" asked the wolf, putting his nose to the side of the basket.

"Oh, no! Granny does not care for meat. She eats nothing but eggs, and cakes, and soft bread."

"I suppose she has no teeth, then?"

"I don't know," replied Red Riding Hood innocently. "It is so long since I have seen her that I quite forget."

"But how will she let you in if her nurse is out?" asked the wolf.

"Oh, very easily. I shall rap and she will say, 'Pull the string and the latch will come up.' Then I shall do so and go in."

"That is very convenient," said the wolf. And he longed to eat Red Riding Hood up; but Hugh and Caleb were working in that direction, and he could hear their axes. He feared if he flew at Red Riding Hood that she would scream, and that they would hurry to her assistance. So he thought of another plan. "Well, Red Riding Hood," he said, "I am obliged to make haste home, as I have a great deal to do. Good-morning, I wish you a pleasant walk."

"Goodbye," said Red Riding Hood, and the wolf trotted off very fast. "I wish our Bran could talk like that dog," thought Red Riding Hood. "He seemed very wise, only he has an ugly voice."

"Caw, craw!" said the raven; "Co-o-o!" said the dove. They were both glad to see the wolf run away.

And now Red Riding Hood was hungry, so she sat down under the trees and opened her packet, and took out her bread and cold venison (which she had forgotten when the wolf's nose was at her basket), and began to eat her dinner, sharing it, of course, with Ralph and Lily. Ralph liked a bit of meat now and then; but Lily would only accept a few crumbs of the bread.

By the time Little Red Riding Hood had dined, the sun was high above the trees, and she knew it was getting late, so she rose and set off again. But alas for her good resolutions!

Just at that moment a beautiful golden butterfly, just like a flying primrose, she thought, rose from the grass before her, and she could not help trying to catch it.

But that was not an easy task, for it flew so fast, fluttering first to one flower and then to another, that she grew quite tired and breathless in her chase after it.

Then three or four more butterflies appeared, crimson, and brown, and cornflower-blue, and she danced along after them with delight, forgetting that time flies faster even than butterflies.

The sun was high in heaven, the red deer crouched in the shade, the birds twittered languidly, and Red Riding Hood was tired. She sat down again to rest, and the bees buzzed round her, and the leaves lightly shivered, and everything seemed to say, "Go to sleep," so Little Red Riding Hood's dark eyelashes fell on her rosy cheeks, and she went off into a gentle slumber. And Ralph stood by the basket, to take care of it and of his little mistress; and Lily cooed a lullaby to the child.

Meantime, the wicked wolf trotted heavily on till he reached the cottage in the wood. He tapped at the door.

"Who is there?" said a feeble voice inside.

"Little Red Riding Hood," replied the wolf, feigning the child's tones.

"Come in, my love. Pull the string and the latch will come up," said the aged woman from her bed. And the wicked wolf went in.

It was a neat little chamber into which he trotted. The floor was clean and newly sanded. Winny had put everything to rights before she left. There was a great four-post bed with curtains on one side of the room, and in it lay the poor old woman, looking very meek, and patient, and nice.

A round table, with a cup and spoon on it, stood near her pillow.

She was dreadfully frightened, as you may suppose, when she saw the wolf come in instead of her little grandchild. But the savage creature did not give her time to wonder. He jumped upon the bed, and ate her all up. But he did not hurt her so much as you would think, and as she was a very good old woman, it was better for her to die than to live in pain; but still it was very dreadful of the wolf to eat her.

The sum was near setting when Red Riding Hood awoke. She jumped up, feeling very sorry for having slept so long.

"Oh, dear, Lily," she said to the Dove, "I shall have very little time with poor Granny, after all. What a foolish child I have been! But I didn't mean to fall asleep I am sure, and I wish I had not! I had a horrid dream of a wolf, and I feel quite cold and stiff."

"Crass, crass!" croaked the Raven reprovingly.

"Well, I must make haste on now," said Red Riding Hood. "Come along, Ralph." And the three went on again. By-and-by Red Riding Hood reached the cottage.

Now, the wicked wolf, who had had plenty of time, peeping out of the window, saw Little Red Riding Hood at the door and made haste to put on the poor old woman's cap, and lie down in the bed, intending to deceive the little girl; for he feared if she saw him when first she opened the door, she would scream out and the woodmen would hear her; but if she shut the door, and he could make her get into bed, he thought no one could hear her; but he had not noticed that there was a pane of glass broken in the window. Red Riding Hood tapped at the door.

"Who is there?" said the wolf, trying to speak like her grandmother; but his voice was very hoarse – "who is there?"

"Little Red Riding Hood, Grandmamma."

"Pull the string, and the latch will come up," squeaked the wolf. And Little Red Riding Hood went in. Poor child! if she had only known that it was a wolf!

"I have brought you a present from my mother, Grandmamma," said Red Riding Hood, putting her basket on the table. "Some eggs, and a little butter, and a few cheesecakes."

"Thank you, my dear. Shut the door, please; I am afraid of catching cold."

"Indeed, you are a little hoarse," said Red Riding Hood as she obeyed. But, as she closed the door, Lily flew over her head and went out at it, and Ralph hopped out also. They were not deceived by the wolf.

"Red Riding Hood," said the wolf, "take off your cloak and hood and get into bed, that I may talk to you."

And Red Riding Hood obeyed. She took off her little hood and laid it down, and put her basket on one side, and got into bed with the wolf. And the red sunlight stole in at the window, and fell on the ugly face on the pillow. And Little Red Riding Hood thought how strange her grandmamma looked, and what a great deal of hair had grown on her face.

"Grandmamma," said little Red Riding Hood softly, "what great eyes you have got!"

"All the better to see you with, my dear," said the wolf.

"Grandmamma, what great arms you have got!" said the child.

"All the better to fold you in, my love," said the wolf.

"Grandmamma, what great ears you have got!"

"All the better to hear your sweet voice with, my dear," said the wolf.

"And what a long nose!" added Red Riding Hood wonderingly.

"All the better to smell the sweet flowers, my dear."

"And, oh, Grandmamma," added the little one, growing very frightened (for she felt sure it was *not* her dear grandmamma), "what a large mouth and great teeth you have!"

"All the better for eating you with, my dear," snarled the wolf;

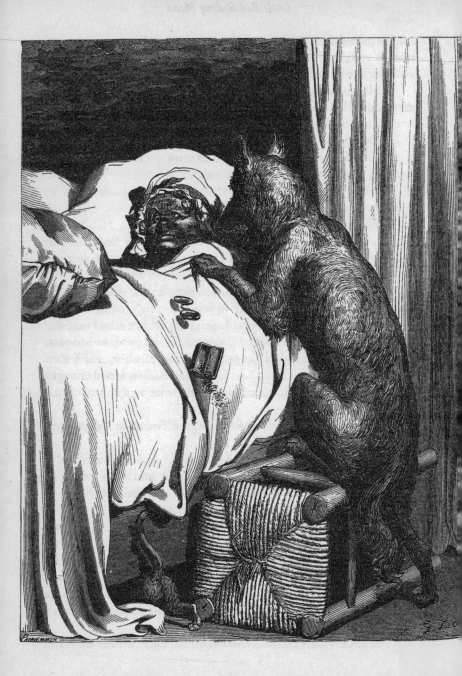

and he raised himself in order to crunch her all up, but the old woman's nightdress, fortunately, entangled his limbs, and he rolled awkwardly over, while Red Riding Hood's cries rent the air.

Meantime Hugh and Caleb had been working slowly in the direction of the cottage.

"I am not happy in my mind about Red Riding Hood," said Hugh. "One can never tell where those wolves lurk."

Just at that moment a fluttering of wings was heard, and Lily flew right on Hugh's shoulder; while Ralph perched on Caleb's arm. The feathers of both the birds were much ruffled.

"Coo, coo," moaned Lily loudly.

"Crass, crass," croaked the raven.

"Hallo!" said Hugh. "What is the meaning of this? Caleb, Caleb, hasten man! Red Riding Hood is killed, or these faithful creatures would not have left her. Let us hasten to avenge her fate."

And, seizing his axe, and calling his dog, he darted through the wood, followed by Caleb. Just as they came in sight of the cottage, Red Riding Hood's screams rang on the air. They rushed on; beat in the door with their axes; and the wolf left his prey to stand at bay. But they cut him down with their axes, while Tray, their dog, held him by the throat; and then, when the monster was dead, they turned to little Red Riding Hood. She was sitting in a corner, crying bitterly.

"My poor grandmamma! My poor grandmamma! I shall never see her again."

"That you will not," said Hugh tenderly, "poor innocent! But you may be thankful that you have escaped yourself. How came the wolf to be in a nightcap and nightdress, or rather the tatters of a nightdress?"

"I don't know," sobbed Red Riding Hood. "I think it was Grandmamma's. He had it rolled round him so that he could not get up, and so I jumped out of bed, and screamed. And, oh! I am so glad you came and killed the wicked dog."

"Dog? It is a wolf, Red Riding Hood. It was lucky for you that he had so chained himself, or we should have been too late."

And then Hugh sat down and took the child on his knee and

soothed her, and gathered from her sobbing words the whole story of that eventful day.

"You see, my darling," he said gently, as she paused, "that one should never loiter on an errand, nor tell one's affairs to strangers, for many a wolf looks like an honest dog. But I had best carry you home now, for I doubt not your mother is very uneasy about you."

So he carried Red Riding Hood in his arms, through the wood, to her home. And by-and-by they heard a loud barking, and Bran ran forward to greet his dear little mistress. And next her father appeared. He had won the prize at the archery, and had returned early; and he was greatly alarmed at finding that his wife had sent Red Riding Hood to her grandmother's.

"For I hear," he said, "that there is a large, fierce wolf in the wood."

And he took his axe, and called Bran, and went out to find or to meet his child. I cannot tell you how glad he was to see her safe, and how much obliged he was to the brave woodmen. He could never thank them enough. And Red Riding Hood's mother, when she heard the tale, and clasped her darling to her heart, shed tears of joy for the child's safety, and of sorrow for the death of the poor grandmamma.

All the wolves are killed now, and no little girl, in this land of ours, need be afraid of such a fate as that which threatened little Red Riding Hood.

Little Snowdrop; or, Snow White and the Seven Dwarfs

The Brothers Grimm

ONCE UPON A TIME, in the middle of winter, when the flakes of snow fell like feathers from the sky, a queen sat at a window set in an ebony frame, and sewed. While she was sewing and watching the snow fall, she pricked her finger with her needle, and three drops of blood dropped on the snow. And because the crimson looked so beautiful on the white snow, she thought, "Oh that I had a child as white as snow, as red as blood, and as black as the wood of this ebony frame!"

Soon afterwards she had a little daughter, who was as white as snow, as red as blood, and had hair as black as ebony. And when the child was born, the Queen died.

After a year had gone by, the King took another wife. She was a handsome lady, but proud and haughty, and could not endure that anyone should surpass her in beauty. She had a wonderful mirror, and whenever she walked up to it, and looked at herself in it, she said:

> "Little glass upon the wall,
> Who is fairest among us all?"

Then the mirror replied:

> "Lady Queen, so grand and tall,
> Thou art the fairest of them all."

And she was satisfied, for she knew the mirror always told the truth. But Snowdrop grew ever taller and fairer, and at seven years old was beautiful as the day, and more beautiful than the Queen herself. So once, when the Queen asked of her mirror:

> "Little glass upon the wall,
> Who is fairest among us all?"

it answered:

> "Lady Queen, you are grand and tall,
> But Snowdrop is fairest of you all."

Then the Queen was startled, and turned yellow and green with envy. From that hour she so hated Snowdrop that she burned with secret wrath whenever she saw the maiden. Pride and envy grew apace, like weeds in her heart, till she had no rest day or night. So she called a huntsman and said, "Take the child out in the forest, for I will endure her no longer in my sight. Kill her, and bring me her lungs and liver as tokens that you have done it."

The huntsman obeyed, and led the child away; but when he had drawn his hunting-knife, and was about to pierce Snowdrop's innocent heart, she began to weep, and said, "Ah! dear huntsman, spare my life, and I will run deep into the wild forest, and never more come home."

The huntsman took pity on her, because she looked so lovely, and said, "Run away then, poor child!" – "The wild beasts will soon make an end of thee," he thought; but it seemed as if a stone had been rolled from his heart, because he had avoided taking her life; and as a little bear came by just then, he killed it, took out its liver and lungs, and carried them as tokens to the Queen. She made the cook dress them with salt, and then the wicked woman ate them, and thought she had eaten Snowdrop's lungs and liver.

The poor child was now all alone in the great forest, and she felt frightened as she looked at all the leafy trees, and knew not what to do. So she began to run, and ran over the sharp stones, and through the thorns; and the wild beasts passed close to her, but did her no harm. She ran as long as her feet could carry her, and, when evening closed in, she saw a little house, and went into it to rest herself. Everything in the house was very small, but I cannot tell you how pretty and clean it was.

There stood a little table, covered with a white tablecloth, on which were seven little plates (each little plate with its own little spoon) − also seven little knives and forks, and seven little cups. Round the walls stood seven little beds close together, with sheets as white as snow. Snowdrop, being so hungry and thirsty, ate a little of the vegetables and bread on each plate, and drank a drop of wine from every cup, for she did not like to empty one entirely.

Then, being very tired, she laid herself down in one of the beds, but could not make herself comfortable, for one was too long, and another too short. The seventh, luckily, was just right; so there she stayed, said her prayers, and fell asleep.

When it was grown quite dark, home came the masters of the house, seven dwarfs, who delved and mined for iron among the mountains. They lighted their seven candles, and, as soon as there was a light in the kitchen, they saw that someone had been there, for it was not quite so orderly as they had left it.

The first said, "Who has been sitting on my stool?"

The second, "Who has eaten off my plate?"

The third, "Who has taken part of my loaf?"

The fourth, "Who has touched my vegetables?"

The fifth, "Who has used my fork?"

The sixth, "Who has cut with my knife?"

The seventh, "Who has drunk out of my little cup?"

Then the first dwarf looked about, and saw that there was a slight hollow in his bed, so he asked, "Who has been lying in my little bed?"

The others came running, and each called out, "Someone has also been lying in my bed."

But the seventh, when he looked in his bed, saw Snowdrop there, fast asleep. He called the others, who flocked round with cries of surprise, fetched their seven candles, and cast the light on Snowdrop.

"Oh, heaven!" they cried. "What a lovely child!" And were so pleased that they would not wake her, but let her sleep on in the little bed. The seventh dwarf slept with all his companions in turn, an hour with each, and so they spent the night. When it was morning, Snowdrop woke up, and was frightened when she saw the seven dwarfs. They were very friendly, however, and enquired her name.

"Snowdrop," answered she.

"How have you found your way to our house?" further asked the dwarfs.

So she told them how her stepmother had tried to kill her, how the huntsman had spared her life, and how she had run the whole day through, till at last she had found their little house.

Then the dwarfs said, "If thou wilt keep our house, cook, make the beds, wash, sew and knit, and make all neat and clean, thou canst stay with us, and shalt want for nothing."

"I will, right willingly," said Snowdrop. So she dwelt with them and kept their house in order. Every morning they went out among the mountains, to seek iron and gold, and came home ready for supper in the evening.

The maiden being left alone all day long, the good dwarfs warned her, saying, "Beware of thy wicked stepmother, who will soon find out that thou art here; take care that thou lettest nobody in."

The Queen, however, after having, as she thought, eaten Snowdrop's lungs and liver, had no doubt that she was again the first and fairest woman in the world; so she walked up to her mirror, and said:

> "Little glass upon the wall,
> Who is fairest among us all?"

The mirror replied:

> "Lady Queen, so grand and tall,
> Here, you are fairest of them all;

But over the hills, with the seven dwarfs old,
Lives Snowdrop, fairer a hundredfold."

She trembled, knowing the mirror never told a falsehood; she felt sure that the huntsman had deceived her, and that Snowdrop was still alive. She pondered once more, late and early, early and late, how best to kill Snowdrop; for envy gave her no rest, day or night, while she herself was not the fairest lady in the land. When she had planned what to do, she painted her face, dressed herself like an old pedlar-woman, and altered her appearance so much that no one could have known her. In this disguise she went over the seven hills, to where the seven dwarfs dwelt, knocked at the door, and cried, "Good wares, cheap! Very cheap!"

Snowdrop looked out of the window and cried, "Good morning, good woman: what have you to sell?"

"Good wares, smart wares," answered the Queen—"bodice laces of all colours;" and drew out one which was woven of coloured silk.

"I may surely let this honest dame in!" thought Snowdrop; so she unfastened the door, and bought for herself the pretty lace.

"Child," said the old woman, "what a figure thou art! Let me lace thee for once properly." Snowdrop feared no harm, so stepped in front of her, and allowed her bodice to be fastened up with the new lace.

But the old woman laced so quick and laced so tight, that Snowdrop's breath was stopped, and she fell down as if dead. "Now I am fairest at last," said the old woman to herself, and sped away.

The seven dwarfs came home soon after, at eventide, but how alarmed were they to find their poor Snowdrop lifeless on the ground! They lifted her up, and, seeing that she was laced too tightly, cut the lace of her bodice; she began to breathe faintly, and slowly returned to life. When the dwarfs heard what had happened, they said, "The old pedlar-woman was none other than the wicked Queen. Be careful of thyself, and open the door to no one if we are not at home."

The cruel stepmother walked up to her mirror when she reached home, and said:

"Little glass upon the wall,
Who is fairest among us all?"

To which it answered, as usual:

"Lady Queen, so grand and tall,
Here, you are fairest of them all;
But over the hills, with the seven dwarfs old,
Lives Snowdrop, fairer a hundredfold."

When she heard this, she was so alarmed that all the blood rushed to her heart, for she saw plainly that Snowdrop was still alive.

"This time," said she, "I will think of some means that shall destroy her utterly;" and with the help of witchcraft, in which she was skilful, she made a poisoned comb. Then she changed her dress and took the shape of another old woman.

Again she crossed the seven hills to the home of the seven dwarfs, knocked at the door, and cried, "Good wares, very cheap!"

Snowdrop looked out and said, "Go away – I dare let no one in."

"You may surely be allowed to look!" answered the old woman, and she drew out the poisoned comb and held it up. The girl was so pleased with it that she let herself be cajoled, and opened the door.

When the bargain was struck, the dame said, "Now let me dress your hair properly for once." Poor Snowdrop took no heed, and let the old woman begin; but the comb had scarcely touched her hair before the poison worked, and she fell down senseless.

"Paragon of beauty!" said the wicked woman, "all is over with thee now," and went away.

Luckily, it was near evening, and the seven dwarfs soon came home. When they found Snowdrop lifeless on the ground, they at once distrusted her stepmother. They searched, and found the poisoned comb; and, as soon as they had drawn it out, Snowdrop came to herself, and told them what had happened. Again they warned her to be careful, and open the door to no one.

The Queen placed herself before the mirror at home and said:

"Little glass upon the wall,
Who is fairest among us all?"

But it again answered:

"Lady Queen, so grand and tall,
Here, you are fairest of them all;
But over the hills, with the seven dwarfs old,
Lives Snowdrop, fairer a thousandfold."

When she heard the mirror speak thus, she quivered with rage. "Snowdrop shall die," she cried, "if it costs my own life!"

Then she went to a secret and lonely chamber, where no one ever disturbed her, and compounded an apple of deadly poison. Ripe and rosy-cheeked, it was so beautiful to look upon that all who saw it longed for it; but it brought death to any who should eat it. When the apple was ready, she painted her face, disguised herself as a peasant-woman, and journeyed over the seven hills to where the seven dwarfs dwelt. At the sound of the knock, Snowdrop put her head out of the window, and said, "I cannot open the door to anybody, for the seven dwarfs have forbidden me to do so."

"Very well," replied the peasant-woman; "I only want to be rid of my apples. Here, I will give you one of them!"

"No!" said Snowdrop. "I dare not take it."

"Art thou afraid of being poisoned?" asked the old woman. "Look here; I will cut the apple in two, and you shall eat the rosy side, and I the white."

Now the fruit was so cunningly made that only the rosy side was poisoned. Snowdrop longed for the pretty apple; and, when she saw the peasant-woman eating it, she could resist no longer, but stretched out her hand and took the poisoned half. She had scarcely tasted it when she fell lifeless to the ground.

The Queen, laughing loudly, watched her with a barbarous look, and cried, "O thou who art white as snow, red as blood, and black as ebony, the seven dwarfs cannot awaken thee this time!"

And when she asked the mirror at home:

"Little glass upon the wall,
Who is fairest among us all?"

the mirror at last replied:

"Lady Queen, so grand and tall,
You are the fairest of them all."

So her envious heart had as much repose as an envious heart can ever know.

When the dwarfs came home in the evening, they found Snowdrop lying breathless and motionless on the ground. They lifted her up, searched whether she had anything poisonous about her, unlaced her, combed her hair, washed her with water and with wine; but all was useless, for they could not bring the darling back to life. They laid her on a bier, and all the seven placed themselves round it, and mourned for her three long days. Then they would have buried her, but that she still looked so fresh and life-like, and had such lovely rosy cheeks.

"We cannot lower her into the dark earth," said they; and caused a transparent coffin of glass to be made, so that she could be seen on all sides, and laid her in it, writing her name outside in letters of gold, which told that she was the daughter of a king. Then they placed the coffin on the mountain above, and one of them always stayed by it and guarded it. But there was little need to guard it, for even the wild animals came and mourned for Snowdrop: the birds likewise ‒ first an owl, and then a raven, and afterwards a dove.

Long, long years did Snowdrop lie in her coffin unchanged, looking as though asleep, for she was still white as snow, red as blood, and her hair was black as ebony. At last the son of a king chanced to wander into the forest, and came to the dwarfs' house for a night's shelter. He saw the coffin on the mountain with the beautiful Snowdrop in it, and read what was written there in letters of gold. Then he said to the dwarfs, "Let me have the coffin! I will give you whatever you like to ask for it."

But the dwarfs answered, "We would not part with it for all the gold in the world."

He said again, "Yet give it me; for I cannot live without seeing

Snowdrop, and, though she is dead, I will prize and honour her as my beloved."

Then the good dwarfs took pity on him, and gave him the coffin. The Prince had it borne away by his servants. They happened to stumble over a bush, and the shock forced the bit of poisoned apple which Snowdrop had tasted out of her throat. Immediately she opened her eyes, raised the coffin-lid, and sat up alive once more. "Oh, heaven!" cried she. "Where am I?"

The Prince answered joyfully, "Thou art with me," and told her what had happened, saying, "I love thee more dearly than anything else in the world. Come with me to my father's castle, and be my wife."

Snowdrop, well pleased, went with him, and they were married with much state and grandeur.

The wicked stepmother was invited to the feast. Richly dressed, she stood before the mirror, and asked of it:

> "Little glass upon the wall,
> Who is fairest among us all?"

The mirror answered:

> "Lady Queen, so grand and tall,
> Here, you are fairest among them all;
> But the young Queen over the mountains old,
> Is fairer than you a thousandfold."

The evil-hearted woman uttered a curse, and could scarcely endure her anguish. She first resolved not to attend the wedding, but curiosity would not allow her to rest. She determined to travel, and see who that young queen could be, who was the most beautiful in all the world. When she came, and found that it was Snowdrop alive again, she stood petrified with terror and despair. Then two iron shoes, heated burning hot, were drawn out of the fire with a pair of tongs, and laid before her feet. She was forced to put them on, and to go and dance at Snowdrop's wedding – dancing, dancing on these red-hot shoes till she fell down dead.

The Mad-Hatter's Tea Party

∾

Lewis Carroll

ALICE HAD NOT GONE far before she came in sight of the house of the March Hare: she thought it must be the right house, because the chimneys were shaped like ears and the roof was thatched with fur. It was so large a house that she did not like to go nearer till she had nibbled some more of the left-hand bit of mushroom, and raised herself to about two feet high: even then she walked up towards it rather timidly, saying to herself "Suppose it should be raving mad after all! I almost wish I'd gone to see the Hatter instead!"

There was a table set out under a tree in front of the house, and the March Hare and the Hatter were having tea at it: a Dormouse was sitting between them, fast asleep, and the other two were using it as a cushion, resting their elbows on it, and talking over its head. "Very uncomfortable for the Dormouse," thought Alice; "only as it's asleep, I suppose it doesn't mind."

The table was a large one, but the three were all crowded together at one corner of it. "No room! No room!" they cried out when they saw Alice coming. "There's plenty of room!" said Alice indignantly, and she sat down in a large arm-chair at one end of the table.

"Have some wine," the March Hare said in an encouraging tone.

Alice looked all round the table, but there was nothing on it but tea. "I don't see any wine," she remarked.

"There isn't any," said the March Hare.

"Then it wasn't very civil of you to offer it," said Alice angrily.

"It wasn't very civil of you to sit down without being invited," said the March Hare.

"I didn't know it was *your* table," said Alice: "it's laid for a great many more than three."

"Your hair wants cutting," said the Hatter. He had been looking at Alice for some time with great curiosity, and this was his first speech.

"You should learn not to make personal remarks," Alice said with some severity: "It's very rude."

The Hatter opened his eyes very wide on hearing this; but all he *said* was, "Why is a raven like a writing desk?"

"Come, we shall have some fun now!" thought Alice. "I'm glad they've begun asking riddles – I believe I can guess that," she added aloud.

"Do you mean that you think you can find out the answer to it?" said the March Hare.

"Exactly so," said Alice.

"Then you should say what you mean," the March Hare went on.

"I do," Alice hastily replied; "at least – at least I mean what I say – that's the same thing, you know."

"Not the same thing a bit!" said the Hatter. "Why, you might just as well say that 'I see what I eat' is the same thing as 'I eat what I see'!"

"You might just as well say," added the March Hare, "that 'I like what I get' is the same thing as 'I get what I like'!"

"You might just as well say," added the Dormouse, which seemed to be talking in its sleep, "that 'I breathe when I sleep' is the same thing as 'I sleep when I breathe'!"

"It *is* the same thing with you," said the Hatter, and here the conversation dropped, and the party sat silent for a minutes, while Alice thought over all she could remember about ravens and writing-desks, which wasn't much.

The Hatter was the first to break the silence. "What day of the month is it?" he said, turning to Alice: he had taken his watch out of his pocket, and was looking at uneasily, shaking it every now and then, and holding to his ear.

Alice considered a little, and then said, "The fourth."

"Two days wrong!" sighed the Hatter. "I told you butter wouldn't suit the works!" he added, looking angrily at the March Hare.

"It was the *best* butter," the March Hare meekly replied.

"Yes, but some crumbs must have got in as well," the Hatter grumbled: "you shouldn't have put it in with the bread-knife."

The March Hare took the watch and looked at it gloomily: then he dipped it into his cup of tea, and looked at it again: but he could think of nothing better to say than his first remark, "It was the *best* butter, you know."

Alice had been looking over his shoulder with some curiosity. "What a funny watch!" she remarked. "It tells the day of the month, and doesn't tell what o'clock it is!"

"Why should it?" muttered the Hatter. "Does *your* watch tell you what year it is?"

"Of course not," Alice replied very readily: "but that's because it stays the same year for such a long time together."

"Which is just the case with *mine*," said the Hatter.

Alice felt dreadfully puzzled. The Hatter's remark seemed to her to have no sort of meaning in it, and yet it was certainly English. "I don't quite understand you," she said, as politely as she could.

"The Dormouse is asleep again," said the Hatter, an he poured a little hot tea upon its nose.

The Dormouse shook its head impatiently, and said, without

opening its eyes, "Of course, of course: just what I was going to remark myself."

"Have you guessed the riddle yet?" the Hatter said, turning to Alice again.

"No, I give it up," Alice replied. "What's the answer?"

"I haven't the slightest idea," said the Hatter.

"Nor I," said the March Hare.

Alice sighed wearily. "I think you might do something better with the time," she said, "than wasting it in asking riddles that have no answers."

"If you knew Time as well as I do," said the Hatter, "you wouldn't talk about wasting *it*. It's *him*."

"I don't know what you mean," said Alice.

"Of course you don't!" the Hatter said, tossing his head contemptuously. "I dare say you never even spoke to Time!"

"Perhaps not," Alice cautiously replied; "but I know I have to beat time when I learn music."

"Ah! That accounts for it," said the Hatter. "He won't stand beating. Now, if you only kept on good terms with him, he'd do almost anything you liked with the clock. For instance, suppose it were nine o'clock in the morning, just time to begin lessons: you'd only have to whisper a hint to Time, and round goes the clock in twinkling! Half past one, time for dinner!"

"I only wish it was," the March Hare said to itself in a whisper.

"That would be grand, certainly," said Alice thoughtfully; "but then − I shouldn't be hungry for it, you know."

"Not at first, perhaps," said the Hatter: "but you could keep it to half-past one as long as you liked."

"Is that the way *you* manage?" Alice asked.

The Hatter shook his head mournfully. "Not I!" he replied. "We quarrelled last March − just before *he* went mad, you know −" (pointing with his teaspoon at the March Hare) "− it was at the great concert given by the Queen of Hearts, and I had to sing:

> *'Twinkle, twinkle, little bat!*
> *How I wonder what you're at!'*

You know the song, perhaps?"

"I've heard something like it," said Alice.

"It goes on, you know," the Hatter continued, "in this way:

> '*Up above the world you fly.*
> *Like a tea-tray in the sky.*
> *Twinkle, twinkle –*'

Here the Dormouse shook itself, and began singing in its sleep "*Twinkle, twinkle, twinkle, twinkle –*" and went on so long that they had to pinch it to make it stop.

"Well, I'd hardly finished the first verse," said the Hatter, "when the Queen bawled out, 'He's murdering the time! Off with his head!'"

"How dreadfully savage!" exclaimed Alice.

"And ever since that," the Hatter went on in a mournful tone, "he won't do a thing I ask! It's always six o'clock now."

A bright idea came into Alice's head. "Is that the reason so many tea-things are put out here?" she asked.

"Yes, that's it," said the Hatter with a sigh: "it's always tea-time, and we've no time to wash the things between whiles."

"Then you keep moving round, I suppose?" said Alice.

"Exactly so," said the Hatter: "as the things get used up."

"But what happens when you come to the beginning again?" Alice ventured to ask.

"Suppose we change the subject," the March Hare interrupted, yawning. "I'm getting tired of this. I vote the young lady tells us a story."

"I'm afraid I don't know one," said Alice, rather alarmed at the proposal.

"Then the Dormouse shall!" they both cried. "Wake up, Dormouse!" And they pinched it on both sides at once.

The Dormouse slowly opened its eyes. "I wasn't asleep," it said in a hoarse, feeble voice, "I heard every word you fellows were saying."

"Tell us a story!" said the March Hare.

"Yes, please do!" pleaded Alice.

"And be quick about it," added the Hatter, "or you'll be asleep again before it's done."

"Once upon a time there were three little sisters," the Dormouse began in a great hurry; "and their names were Elsie, Lacie, and Tillie; and they lived at the bottom of a well —"

"What did they live on?" said Alice, who always took a great interest in questions of eating and drinking.

"They lived on treacle," said the Dormouse, after thinking a minute or two.

"They couldn't have done that, you know," Alice gently remarked. "They'd have been ill."

"So they were," said the Dormouse; "*very* ill."

Alice tried a little to fancy to herself what such an extraordinary way of living would be like, but it puzzled her too much: so she went on: "But why did they live at the bottom of a well?"

"Take some more tea," the March Hare said to Alice, very earnestly.

"I've had nothing yet," Alice replied in an offended tone: "so I can't take more."

"You mean you can't take *less*," said the Hatter: "it's very easy to take *more* than nothing."

"Nobody asked *your* opinion," said Alice.

"Who's making personal remarks now?" the Hatter asked triumphantly.

Alice did not quite know what to say to this: so she helped herself to some tea and bread-and-butter, and then turned to the Dormouse, and repeated her question. "Why did they live at the bottom of a well?"

The Dormouse again took a minute or two to think about it, and then said "It was a treacle-well."

"There's no such thing!" Alice was beginning very angrily, but the Hatter and the March Hare went "Sh! Sh!" and the Dormouse sulkily remarked "If you can't be civil, you'd better finish the story for yourself."

"No, please go on!" Alice said very humbly. "I won't interrupt you again. I dare say there may be *one*."

"One, indeed!" said the Dormouse indignantly. However, he

consented to go on. "And so these three little sisters – they were learning to draw, you know –"

"What did they draw?" said Alice, quite forgetting her promise.

"Treacle," said the Dormouse, without considering at all, this time.

"I want a clean cup," interrupted the Hatter: "let's all move one place on."

He moved on as he spoke, and the Dormouse followed him: the March Hare moved into the Dormouse's place, and Alice rather unwillingly took the place of the March Hare. The Hatter was the only one who got any advantage from the change; and Alice was a good deal worse off than before, as the March Hare had just upset the milk-jug into his plate.

Alice did not wish to offend the Dormouse again, so she began very cautiously: "But I don't understand. Where did they draw the treacle from?"

"You can draw water out of a water-well," said the Hatter; "so I should think you could draw treacle out of a treacle-well – eh, stupid?"

"But they were *in* the well," Alice said to the Dormouse, not choosing to notice this last remark.

"Of course they were," said the Dormouse: "well in."

This answer so confused poor Alice that she let the Dormouse go on for some time without interrupting it.

"They were learning to draw," the Dormouse went on, yawning and rubbing its eyes, for it was getting very sleepy; "and they drew all manner of things – everything that begins with an M –"

"Why with an M?" said Alice.

"Why not?" said the March Hare.

Alice was silent.

The Dormouse had closed its eyes by this time, and was going off into a doze; but, on being pinched by the Hatter it woke up again with a little shriek, and went on: "– that begins with an M, such as mouse-traps, and the moon, and memory, and muchness – you know you say things are 'much of a muchness' – did you ever see such a thing as a drawing of a muchness?"

"Really, now you ask me," said Alice, very much confused, "I don't think —"

"Then you shouldn't talk," said the Hatter.

This piece of rudeness was more than Alice could bear: she got up in great disgust, and walked off: the Dormouse fell asleep instantly, and neither of the others took the least notice of her going, though she looked back once or twice, half hoping that they would call after her: the last time she saw them, they were trying to put the Dormouse into the teapot.

"At any rate I'll never go *there* again!" said Alice, as she picked her way through the wood. "It's the stupidest tea-party I ever was at in all my life!"

The Mistreated Fellow

❦

Jessica Amanda Salmonson

ONCE UPON A TIME there had never been a story told that began with once upon a time. Since that primordial age there have been nine-hundred-ninety-nine-thousand-nine-hundred-ninety-nine such tales written down. This is the millionth.

Long ago in a certain place, meaning I don't know when and I don't know where, there was a dwarf named Theofald. He was bowlegged and round and had a gigantic forehead which, alas, did not denote intelligence; but Theofald, as a decent man, did not merit the stares, insults, and stone-throwing which he suffered. Eventually he gave up the towns, forsook his dreams of camaraderie, and repaired to a mountain retreat.

Theofald was half-blind as well as short and misshapen. There is no limit to the misery God in his generosity is apt to visit on a little man like that.

Theofald could see well enough to get around, but that was about all. He recognized people by their voices or not at all, for their faces were like a blur. If he came to a flower, or some fruit upon a tree, he had to put his nose right up next to it to be sure what it was.

As nobody had ever been kind to him, or taught him much, Theofald had no idea that other people could see better than he.

As he lived alone on the mountain, people began to think he was a mountain spirit and not a man at all. "He doesn't *look* like a man,"

289

would say the woodcutters and hunters and pilgrims, or whoever noticed him outside his hut made with bark walls and mossy shingle roof. But Theofald was a human being much as any other, for all his odd appearance.

His poor vision was a blessing, though a pathetic one, for Theofald was at least unable to see how ugly he was. On sunny days he would go down to the pond and look at his reflection. He could not see what it was other people thought repellent or laughable, except, perhaps, that he had no hair.

What is sadder than a dwarf if not a bald dwarf? Theofald set out one day to see what could be done about his baldness. He met a man in the woods whose job it was to collect sap from the lacquer trees. He begged a cupful of lacquer. Later, with a brush made of leaves, Theofald lacquered the top of his head.

This made all the difference, thought Theofald. With his head lacquered on the top and around the ears, it looked as though he had a lot of pitch-black hair. At least, that was how it looked to half-blind Theofald, who saw his reflection in the quiet pond at twilight. To others, it looked as though half his head was a bowling ball, and his deep-set eyes and little round mouth were just right for a bowler's fingers. Theofald also smudged on eyebrows, then said to his reflection, "What a good-looking fellow! Now, if only I could find a wife to live with me on this mountain, I would be a happy man."

One day a father and his daughter came to the mountain in the middle of the night. The daughter was sixteen or seventeen years of age, but small for that, and finished with growing. She was not much larger than Theofald. He heard them pass by his hut, though they traveled furtively. He came out and, in secret, followed the sound of their feet. Then, in a moonlit clearing, he saw them faintly, like ghosts to his bad vision; but he heard them plainly.

The father said to his daughter: "Forgive me, little one, but I cannot help the way I feel. Now that your mother is dead, I shall not be the one to keep you. I cannot bear to. I leave your fate to God." Then the old father shambled off, having made his daughter understand she was not to move until he was out of sight. When he was gone, the girl began to cry.

"How odd that is," said Theofald to himself, "that she was spoken

to like a child when she is bigger than I." He crept nearer but could not make out her features because he never could make out anyone's features. If he could have seen her, he would have noted the shape of her eyes was like that of people far in the East of the world, though she had not an ounce of Asian blood. She was sallow and rather fat-faced, and drooled as she cried. She was unable to talk much and moved about clumsily.

"What a pretty girl!" thought Theofald, and for all he could see, she was. He stepped boldly into the clearing with his black-lacquered pate shining in the moonlight. He bowed politely, saying, "Sweet maiden! I am in love with you at first sight! As your family has had done with you, come live in my shack!"

The foolish girl wailed as though she saw a monster standing before her.

A good many stories of this kind end with happily ever after; and really there should be no reason to end this tale in a cruel manner. A mistreated man who never asked to be a dwarf and a severely retarded woman who needed constant care from someone truly concerned with her wellbeing might well live happily in the mountains, away from the glowering or laughing faces of unkind folk. But is it honest to say people live happily ever after when so few do?

A good-looking prince and a beautiful princess are apt to quarrel their whole lives and have misbehaving children and truly hate each other a great deal; and if such healthy, handsome people cannot find happiness, how can a dwarf and a retarded girl? Well, maybe some other dwarf found happiness somewhere, and some other witless girl. But this girl was so frightened that she dashed off into the night and fell over a cliff. Theofald made a cairn over her body, and sat beside it weeping. A week later, he died from an infection caused by the lacquer stuck to his head; for lacquer, as everyone but Theofald knew, is poison to the skin.

Mother-of-All

❧

F. Gwynplaine MacIntyre

THERE IS A FARAWAY LAND which we call Long Ago, but the people who dwell in that land call it Now. In the country of Now, in the province of Often, in the village of Frequently, there lived a maiden whose name was Kate Bobbin. But everyone called her Lazy Kate, because she had never seen hard work except from a distance.

"Up, lazy thing!" said Mistress Bobbin, Kate's mother, coming into Kate's room with a broom in her hand. "The bright morning sun has arisen to greet you. Get up! Get to work! Or I'll certainly beat you! A girl who is lazy is probably dull. Get up! Get to work! Or I'll fracture your skull!"

Lazy Kate woke up. She yawned and stretched, and – with an effort – she sat up in bed and opened her eyes. As soon as her eyes were open, Lazy Kate could see all of the work that she had left unfinished: there was a cow half-milked, some butter half-churned, and a stack of holes that Kate had never finished mending. Worst of all: by the hearth there was a spinning-wheel which Lazy Kate had never touched, and beside it there waited a mountain of raw flax which Kate had neglected to spin into yarn.

"I will spin the flax tomorrow," said Lazy Kate Bobbin, for tomorrow was the place where she liked to do all her work.

"Tomorrow, is it?" Mistress Bobbin screeched. "If you are going to tomorrow, let me give you a journey-present to carry along on the trip with you. Take *this*!" said Mistress Bobbin, using her broom to give Lazy Kate's skull a good whackety-thwack. "And *this*!" said Mistress Bobbin, using her broom to give Lazy Kate's shoulders a smackety-whack. "And don't forget to take *this*!" said Mistress Bobbin, adding a rosy glow to Kate's cheeks while the broomstick went thwackety-smack. "And take *this* and *this* and *this*, which you may add to your collection!" screeched Mistress Bobbin, beginning a whackety-thwack-smack attack on Kate's back. "You'll spin your flax or win more thwacks!"

And Lazy Kate cried, "Ow! *Ow! OW!*" But she got beaten anyhow.

Now it chanced that Her Royal Majesty, Queen Repugna, was riding through this very village. For twice a year at six-month intervals it pleased Her Majesty to look upon the wretched and unfortunate peasants who dwelt in her domain. (The Queen had no intention of doing anything to help them, but she enjoyed looking at them.) As the Queen rode forth, she sang a merry tune:

> "*I derive my daily pleasance*
> *From the presence of the peasants.*
> *For whenever I can see one*
> *I am happy not to be one.*"

"Ow! *Ow! Ow!*" cried Lazy Kate, joining in the chorus unintentionally, while her mother's broom went whackety-smack.

"Hark!" said the Queen. "One of my subjects is being beaten, and I am not there to see it. I must ride closer, for there is no melody so soothing to me as the sweet music of one of my peasants receiving a well-deserved beating. It is my favourite tune."

So Queen Repugna rode towards the sounds, and soon she came to the cottage where Mistress Bobbin was thrashing Lazy Kate. "How now, good woman?" asked the Queen, looking in through the window.

"This is how, Your Majesty," said Mistress Bobbin, tugging her forelock with one hand whilst she used the broomstick in her other hand to comb her daughter's hair. "You may perhaps be wondering why I am thrashing the daylights out of my ungrateful daughter."

"The thought had crossed my mind, yes," said the Queen.

Mistress Bobbin's arm was getting tired. So she put her broom down, and stopped beating her daughter while the Queen awaited an explanation.

Now Mistress Bobbin had a sore dilemma. She was ashamed to tell the Queen that her daughter Kate was the laziest wretch on nine continents. Still, *some* sort of explanation was clearly in order. Just then, Mistress Bobbin saw her daughter's unused spinning-wheel sitting by the hearth, and she thought of a tale to tell the Queen.

"I am beating my daughter because she is selfish, and she takes all the work for herself," Mistress Bobbin lied sweetly. "Yesterday was market-month, and I came home with ten wainloads of flax, which is enough to keep all the girls and women in the village busy spinning yarn for a fortnight. But my greedy daughter Kate has selfishly taken all of the flax for her own spinning-wheel, and in a single day she has spun all ten wainloads of flax into yarn!" said Mistress Bobbin, spinning quite a bit of yarn herself.

"Has she, now?" said the Queen. "Ten wainloads of flax in a day! Such a talented girl is wasted in this hideous village. Therefore, I shall take your daughter away with me."

"Yes," said Lazy Kate, overcoming just enough of her laziness to manage a curtsey to the Queen. "Yes, Your Majesty, please take me away with you."

"You shall live in the palace with me," said the Queen. "And wear fine clothes, and feast upon sweetmeats."

"Gladly, Your Majesty," said Lazy Kate, who was fond of fine clothes and good sweetmeats, even though she had never actually had them.

"You will live in the room next-door over from mine," said the Queen.

"Yes, Your Majesty," curtseyed Lazy Kate.

"And each morning," said the Queen, "my servants will bring you ten wainloads of flax."

"Er, wait a minute . . ." Lazy Kate began.

"And each day," said the Queen, ignoring Kate's interruption, "each day you will spin ten wainloads of flax into yarn, in the room next to mine. Through the wall, the sound of your spinning-wheel creaking and turning at its daily task will soothe me, for there is no melody so pleasing to my ears as the sound of hard work . . . so long as someone other than myself is doing it. The song of the spinning-wheel is my favourite tune."

"I had thought, Your Majesty," said Lazy Kate, curtseying again, "that the sound of a peasant getting beaten was your favourite tune."

"It is indeed," the Queen nodded. "So from now on I will hear your spinning-wheel, or I will hear you getting beaten. And see that you spin ten wainloads of flax every day, girl, or else I shall hear the sound of the Lord High Headsman as he chops off your head with his axe. And that, *too*, is my favourite tune!"

And so Lazy Kate was taken to the Queen's palace. The Queen's handmaidens gave Lazy Kate fine garments to wear, and the Queen's servants gave Lazy Kate delicious sweetmeats to eat. And, so long as the minstrels kept fiddling, it seemed to Lazy Kate that perhaps this new life would be pleasant after all. But then the Queen's minions brought Lazy Kate to a room containing nothing but a hard iron bed, and a hard wooden chair, and an old spinning-wheel. And heaped and piled in every corner of the room were heaps and piles and hills and mountains of raw golden flax to be spun into yarn.

"Behold tomorrow's work set out for you today," said Queen Repugna, while – through the iron bars of the room's only window – Lazy Kate could see the evening sun begin to set while the Queen spoke: "Sleep well, my girl, for tomorrow either you or the headsman will have work to do. It matters not to me which one is busier: the flax, or the axe."

Then Lazy Kate was locked into her cell, with a spinning-wheel and ten mountains of flax, and no living creature to keep her company except a spider spinning its web in the corner.

Lazy Kate moaned and wept and pulled her hair. She knew nothing at all about spinning-wheels. With one timid forefinger she touched the rim of the wheel, expecting something to happen. The wheel turned slightly, chuckling to itself. Then it stopped again. That was all.

Lazy Kate knelt on the cold stone floor and picked up a handful of flax. The long golden-white fibres were harsh and stiff to her touch, and they ungentled her fingers.

Lazy Kate touched wheel to flax, and flax to wheel, as if hoping that some miracle would chance itself. Nothing happened.

Lazy Kate let the flax fall to the floor, and she lay there weeping floodwaters of grief. Even the spider had crept away, leaving only the tapestry of its web, and Lazy Kate was alone.

Presently, in the darkness outside her window, Lazy Kate heard a peculiar noise coming towards her. It sounded like this: Tappety-*thump*! Slippety-*slap*! Crickety-crackety-*creak*! And so on, again, coming closer and louder. Lazy Kate looked out through the bars of her window, and in the darkened courtyard she saw three weirdly-shaped creatures coming towards her. Now she saw that they were three *old women*. But the women were bent and hunched into shapes such as Lazy Kate had never seen before.

The first old woman's right foot was ten times larger and broader than her left one, and it was the sound of these two different feet walking forward – one dainty, one huge – that Kate had heard tappety-thumping.

The second old woman had a lower lip and a tongue that dangled past her chin and nearly to her bosom, and it was the sound of this wet tongue and sloppy lip dangle-slobbering against each other that Kate had heard slippety-slapping.

The third old woman had two huge hands that were twisted and gnarled, with long spidery fingers that twitched and beckoned convulsively as if longing to clutch unseen things. And it was the sounds of the joints in this old woman's hands creak-a-cracking that Kate heard outside her window.

Now Kate called out to the three ugly ancients: "Who are you?"

And the three twisted old women together replied: "*We are Mother-of-All.*"

"You are none of you *my* mother," said Lazy Kate Bobbin. "Although the three of you together are certainly as ugly as she is."

"We are your mother," said Mother-of-All. "Your mother, aye, and your aunt, and grandmother, and cousin. We are your daughter, and your niece as well. Each woman and all. We are *you*."

"You are drunk," said Kate Bobbin, who had seen a tavern standing hard by the Queen's palace on her way here.

"Please yourself, then," said Mother-of-All. "But you are in trouble, dear sister, and we have come to help you as sisters would and sisters should."

Now Kate was proud as well as lazy, and her pride was her guide as she idly replied: "I don't need help from anyone, and you aren't my sisters."

"It is wonderful to be a woman who needs no help from anyone," said the three ancient uglies. "But we are your sisters all the same, and there are times when every woman needs a sister to assist her."

Now the moonrise glinted on the heaping mounds of flax, reminding Kate that she very much needed help indeed, in large quantities. "What do you want, then?" she called out to the three, and they answered:

"You must ask us to help you, as a sister should and a sister would."

"Very well, then," said Kate. "Please help me."

Nothing happened, except that the moon rose a bit higher and cast its gleam upon the giant mounds of flax. In the courtyard, the three old maids waited.

"Please help me, *sisters*," said Kate.

"*We are here*," said three voices behind her.

Kate turned round, and now she saw that in her moonlit cell – which somehow had become as bright as day – the three ugly old women had joined her.

"Let us introduce ourselves," said the peculiar trio, speaking sometimes each one in her turn and sometimes all three together. "I am Clothilde; I cast the yarn. I am Lackeasy; I spin the yarn. And I am Atropina; I draw off the yarn."

Then, in the puddle of moonlight, all three women shifted and changed. They melted into each other, and joined, and became a single woman with two legs and six arms – like a spider – who spoke: "*I am Mother-of-All.*"

Then Mother-of-All went to the spinning-wheel and sat down in the chair beside it, quite as if chair and wheel were her own property. "I will teach you to spin, daughter-sister," said Mother-of-All to Kate Bobbin. "But you must watch, and you must learn, for you must do. For the thread is your own as well as mine."

And Kate Bobbin agreed.

Now Mother-of-All took a double handful of raw flax. "This is how to draught the yarn." She pinched the fibres, pressing them against her knee with one long-boned finger. She drew the fibres up her thigh towards her hip, allowing them to *roll* beneath her touch yet at the same time pressing them tightly with her finger, so that the fibres *twisted* round each other in a winding spiral of thread. Her other hand clasped this, and pinched it, drawing the ends of the newly-made yarn apart from each other. To her knee again, she pressed with thumb and rolled towards the thigh. Then clasp and pinch and draw again, but this time the yarn was thinner and finer and stronger all together . . . and *longer*, as well, because each time she did this the old woman's hands were able to pull the ends farther apart without breaking the thread. Then again and again – knee, thumb, thigh; clasp, pinch, draw – as the thread grew longer-stronger until she held it up for Kate to see.

"Behold the thread," said Mother-of-All.

Kate Bobbin touched the twisting fibres with her hand. The raw flax had felt stiff and sharp to her before, but now its fibres had gentled themselves in the sure touch of Mother-of-All. The twist of the yarn looked familiar. Now Kate tried to remember enough of her schooling to recall the name of this twist-a-turn shape that entwined in her hands. "It is . . . a *spiral*," she decided.

"Not a spiral," said Mother-of-All. "Daughter-sister, the shape of our thread is a *helix,* from beginning to end. Now it is *your* turn, daughter, to lengthen the thread I have made."

So Kate tried now to draught the yarn. But she was standing, for Mother-of-All had taken the chair by the spinning-wheel. And as Kate rolled the flax in her hands she discovered that this was a task best done sitting down: for her thigh and bent knee were partners in the task as well. So Kate sat on the bed, and rolled yarn.

Mother-of-All took the tip of the long flaxen twine. "Cotton and wool may be spun when dry," said Mother-of-All. "But flax must be spun *wet,* or else it will brittle and snare." She lifted the twine in her hands, and with her long tongue she moistened the tip of the yarn.

"This is the *flyer,*" said Mother-of-All, feeding the moistened yarn into a hole – above the treadle and below the band – in the right side of the spinning-wheel. Then she seized one of the spokes of the wheel and turned it gently, and her right foot danced up and down on the treadle. The wheel began to revolve, and as it did this a rod at the side of the wheel rose and fell.

"Here is the *footman,*" said Mother-of-All, touching this. As she spoke, her toe came down a bit more lightly on the treadle. The footman rose and fell again, but this time more slowly. Mother-of-All pressed the treadle more firmly this time, and this time as the wheel revolved the footman rose and fell more swiftly at his task.

Kate Bobbin watched, and she saw that Mother-of-All used the treadle to vary the spin of the wheel, trying various speeds: faster, slower. Kate dared not breathe, but Mother-of-All's breath was calm and unhurried as she tested the speeds of the wheel. The old woman's bosom rose and fell in a steady unvarying rhythm as she tested the treadle and wheel. Now she found a pace that suited her at last. The wheel revolved again, and now Kate saw – because the wooden footman rose and fell, rose and fell in steady unison with the rising and falling bosom of Mother-of-All – that the old woman made the wheel revolve at the very same rate that she breathed, in and out. The spinning-woman made the wheel dance to the rhythm of herself.

Now the beginning of the long moistened flax – no longer crude hand-rolled yarn, but a finely-drawn *thread* – emerged from a hole in the shaft like the eye of a needle, and Mother-of-All guided this between two wooden handles, side by side, which she manipulated so as to adjust the tension of the growing thread as she skeined it. "These two who stand together, side by side, are the *maidens*," said Mother-of-All. "Now let us cast on, and spin."

The yarn flew through the wheel. Mother-of-All held the yarn at an angle to the shaft, so that it did not slip off, while the wheel clucked and clicked and revolved. The maidens squeaked in protest, but did their task. And the treadle creak-squeaked, up and down, up and down, joining into its song with the dance of the wheel:

> "*The wheel, the wheel, the rolling reel,*
> *The maidens rise and fall.*
> *Come pedal the treadle, and then all the thread'll*
> *Unite in the Mother-of-All.*"

"It almost looks like a game," said Kate Bobbin.

"It *is* a game, in its way," answered Mother-of-All. "It is pleasure and task both at once. A woman's mind has many rooms, and in some of those rooms she must work while in other rooms she dances. But after a woman learns the spinning-craft, then it is work and relaxation both together. For she can keep the spinning-wheel turning in one special place in her mind, while leaving the rest of her brain free to work or to play as it pleases: making heavy decisions or spinning sweet daydreams." And, as Mother-of-All said these words, the treadle nodded up and down in agreement, and the spinning-wheel chuckled and clicked its approval.

"May I try it?" asked Lazy Kate Bobbin.

"Perhaps not," said the old woman. Her left hand and her foot on the treadle kept the wheel ever-turning while her right hand's expert fingertips joined in sisterhood with her knee and her thigh – clasp, pinch, draw; clasp, pinch, draw – to twist another handful of yarn. Her tongue moistened the tip of the yarn, slipping it into the flyer so that it could *wind on*: adding itself to the long, unending legacy of thread. She raised her left hand from its duties at the wheel, licked her fingertips, and then with these fingertips moistened the flax as it spun through the maidens. "If I let you try this, you might break the thread."

"I will not break the thread," said Kate Bobbin. "Now that I see how it's done, this looks easy."

"It is easy for *me*," said old Mother-of-All. "It would be difficult for *you*."

"That's not fair," said Kate Bobbin. "It's only easier for you because you have six hands."

"Have I, sister?" asked Mother-of-All. And in the moonlight, Kate saw that the old woman – formerly spider-shaped – now had only two arms and two legs, just like Kate herself. The old woman used one hand to draught the yarn, one hand for winding on, while her right foot worked the treadle and her left foot stayed in contact with the ground, steadying her body and her chair. After a while her feet switched tasks, so that her treadle-foot could rest, and touch the earth, and refresh itself while its sister foot worked the treadle instead. It looked so easy to Kate, and so restful . . . and yet it looked like a challenge as well.

"I can do this," said Kate.

"Oh, sister; oh, cousin," sighed Mother-of-All, while her thread whistled out in its infinite helix. "For as long as the wheel has been turning, this thread has been passed on from woman to girl. You might break it."

"I will not break the thread," said Kate Bobbin.

"The thread goes ever on," said Mother-of-All, "but not every woman is obliged to join the task. I must pass on the thread to another, yet she need not be *you*."

"Let me try," said Kate Bobbin.

"Ah, cousin; ah, sister," sighed Mother-of-All, while she spun out the infinite thread. "Beware the law of the spinning-wheel. No woman need add to the thread. But she who agrees to continue the task must not drop the thread, nor break it, until her spinning is done."

"I will not break the thread," said Kate Bobbin. "Let me try."

"If I pass the thread to you, daughter," said Mother-of-All, "then what will you give me in return?"

"What do you wish?" Kate asked, and the steady clackety-click of the wheel was so reassuring that she would have agreed to nearly anything.

"This is our wish," said three voices at once in the room, as the three portions of Mother-of-All – Clothilde, and Lackeasy, and Atropina – spoke all together. "When you are married, you must invite us to the wedding-feast, and welcome us, and introduce us to all the guests assembled as your sisters. Do you promise?"

"That I will," said Kate Bobbin.

"And afterwards," said the three, "you must allow us to witness the birth of your eldest daughter. When the she-child is born, we will cut the cord that links her body to your own loins. Then we will take that cord away with us, for a keepsake."

"But if I have no child?" Kate asked.

"The thread will be broken," said Mother-of-All.

"And if my womb bears only sons?" Kate asked.

"The thread will be dropped," said the Mother-of-All.

"And if no cord passes from me to a daughter?"

"The thread will be lost," said the Mother-of-All.

"I will do my best," said Kate Bobbin. "Sister, give me the thread."

So then Mother-of-All let Kate Bobbin take her place at the treadle and wheel. And then Mother-of-All showed Kate Bobbin the craft of the wheel. Kate discovered that – by slowing the pace of her treadling, then hastening it, so that the wooden footman rose and fell less swiftly than the wheel revolved – the spinning-wheel would actually *reverse* directions, then return to its original course so rapidly that Kate might think the wheel had never stopped at all. This varied the clickety-clack of the wheel, allowing Kate to unwind the thread and cast it off when she had completed a skein.

Mother-of-All showed her pupil that there were several different ways for hand and wheel to fashion thread. She taught Kate how to do the long draw, the double-draw, the spin from the fold, and the push-me-pull. Then Mother-of-All stepped away from the wheel, so that Kate could handle the task by herself.

In the courtyard a cock crowed. Kate looked up, and she saw through the iron-barred window that dawn had arrived. "We have been spinning all night!" remarked Kate in surprise to the old woman standing behind her.

There was no answer.

Kate turned. There was no one there, except a spider climbing back into its web, and renewing its tapestry. And round about the room were folds and stacks of golden flax, all neatly spun in linen skeins.

After a leisurely breakfast in bed, Queen Repugna refreshed herself and rose to meet the day. Although her bed was soft and thick, the Queen had tossed and turned fitfully through the night . . . for she had been kept half-awake by the endless click-clack of the spinning-wheel in the room adjacent to her own.

"It hardly matters, anyway," said the Queen to her handmaids, as she selected a silken gown from her capacious wardrobe and permitted her handmaids to dress her. "For the little peasant-girl has undertaken a task that cannot possibly come off . . . and so her *head* must come off instead." Queen Repugna laughed. "The Lord High Headsman will earn his wage-packet today, and the little peasant-girl's head will dance a merry gavotte across the stones of my courtyard. I must remember to sit well back from the chopping-block, so as not to stain my gown when her blood spurts." The Queen yawned. "Perhaps, if I am *very* lucky, the little peasant-girl has actually managed to give me one or two skeins of useful thread."

Stepping forth from her chamber, Queen Repugna gestured to a guard to unlock the door of the room beyond. She stepped into the room, and . . .

Kate Bobbin curtseyed prettily, while she gestured towards ten wainloads' worth of spun linen. "Have I done well, Your Majesty?"

"Indeed," said the Queen, after she had regained consciousness, and sent word to the Lord High Headsman that his services would not be required after all. "She who spins ten wainloads of flax in a night is worthy of the highest prize that I can bestow: she must marry my son. Welcome, *daughter*! You shall marry Prince Uggworth, my son and my heir. Nor need you bring any dowry to the marriage. For your bride-price, you have only to spin ten wainloads of flax every night, for the rest of your life."

"Er, wait a minute . . ." Kate began.

And so Kate was introduced to Prince Uggworth, for this was one of the more up-to-date countries, in which two people were actually introduced to each other before they got married. As luck would have it, Prince Uggworth – despite all rumours to the contrary – turned out to be a fine young man indeed. He fell in love with Kate Bobbin as soon as he met her, and she as instantly with him. The Queen made immediate plans for their wedding.

"Grant me only one boon," said Kate Bobbin to her betrothed. "I have three sisters, whom I dearly love. They are coarse and unsightly, and have peasant ways, but they must be welcome at our wedding, and they must sit with us at the wedding-feast."

"*Peasants* at a royal wedding?" screeched Queen Repugna. "Pish and tosh! And likewise pooh!" As she spoke, the Queen tried to step on a nearby spider . . . but it scuttled safely into a hole in the wall.

"Whatever pleases my bride is my will," said Prince Uggworth. "Your sisters will be welcome, dearest Kate."

And so three seats were reserved in the front pew for the royal wedding, and three chairs at the head of the banquet-hall were reserved at the wedding-feast. But the three seats went empty at the wedding, which otherwise proceeded quite as planned. And the three seats likewise went empty at the wedding-feast. But no one noticed this, because Princess Kate – for such she was now – had been the centre of attention through all of the festivities, until the moment when her husband-prince arose to give the wedding-toast.

"My lords, ladies and gentlemen," said the Prince. "I give you . . ."

What he gave them, no one ever heard. For at that moment, a peculiar noise arose in the chamber outside the banquet-hall: Tappety-thump! Slippety-slap! Crickety-crackety-creak!

Into the banquet-hall came three old women.

The first old woman's right foot was ten times larger and broader than her left one. Tappety-*thump*!

The second old woman had a lower lip and a tongue that dangled past her chin and nearly to her bosom. Slippety-*slap*!

The third old woman had two huge hands that were twisted and gnarled. Crickety-crackety-*creak*!

"Behold," said Princess Kate to all her wedding-guests. "Behold and welcome them: these women are my sisters."

The Prince was goggling in astonishment. "What hideous malady has done these things to you?" he asked the three old ugly women.

Clothilde lifted her ghastly foot. "All my days this foot has treadled the spinning-wheel," she answered. "To spin flax, to make linen . . . so that babies, drawn hot from the womb, may wear swaddling-garments."

Lackeasy shook her head, so that her huge tongue and her long lower lip wambled and wimbled grotesquely. "All my days this tongue and lip have moistened the thread of the spinning-wheel," she answered. "To spin flax, to make linen . . . so that the bride, going fresh to her groom, may have petticoats on her wedding-day and bedsheets on her wedding-night."

Atropina raised her clacketing hands, and to the noise of their music she spoke: "All my days these hands have been busy twisting and drawing the thread of the spinning-wheel," she replied. "To spin flax, to make linen . . . so that the dead, taken cold to the tomb, may wear shrouds."

"Then your spinning is ended," said Queen Repugna, as she raised a crystal goblet to her lips and smugly quaffed her wine. "For know you all that, henceforward, my daughter-in-law Kate must spin all the flax that my household requires."

"*Never!*" said the Prince, pounding the banquet-table with such unexpected fury that his mother the Queen promptly choked on her wine and dropped dead on the spot. "If *this* is what spinning-wheels do to womenfolk, then I decree that henceforth my wife will spin only so much as she pleases . . . and no more!"

And so it was done. And Princess Kate became Queen Kate: for her husband was heir to the throne, and the previous queen was even now turning blue on the carpet. And Queen Kate and her husband ruled happily till the end of their lives, and when they died their daughter ruled wisely and well, and *her* daughter after. And the thread goes ever on.

The Necklace of Tears

∾

Mrs Egerton Eastwick

ONCE, MANY YEARS AGO, there lived in Ombrelande a most beautiful princess. Now, Ombrelande is a country which still exists, and in which many strange things still happen, although it is not to be found in any map of the world that I know of.

The Princess, at the time the story begins, was little more than a child, and while her growing beauty was everywhere spoken of she was unfortunately still more noted for her selfish and disagreeable nature. She cared for nothing but her own amusement and pleasure, and gave no thought to the pain she sometimes inflicted on others in order to gratify her whims. It must be mentioned, however, as an excuse for her heartlessness, that, being an only child, she had been spoilt from her babyhood, and always allowed to have her own way, while those who thwarted her were punished.

One day the Princess Olga, that was her name, escaped from her governess and attendants, and wandered into the wood which joined the gardens of the palace. It was her fancy to be alone; she would not even allow her faithful dachshund to bear her company.

The air was soft with the coming of spring; the sun was shining, the songs of the birds were full of gratitude and joy; the most lovely flowers, in all imaginable hues, turned the earth into a jewelled nest of verdure.

Olga threw herself down on a bank, bright with green moss and soft as a downy pillow. The warmth and her wanderings had already wearied her. She had neglected her morning studies, and left her singing-master waiting for her in despair in the music-room of the palace, that she might wander into the wood, and already the pleasure was gone.

She threw herself down on the bank and wished she was at home. There was one thing, however, of which she never tired, and that was her own beauty; so now, having nothing to do, and finding the world and the morning exceedingly tiresome and tame and dull, she unbound her long golden hair, and spread it all around her like a carpet over the moss and the flowers, that she might admire its softness and luxuriance, by way of a change.

She held up the yellow meshes in her hands and drew them through her fingers, laughing to see the golden lights that played among the silky waves in the sunlight; then she fell to admiring the small white hands which held the treasure, holding them up against the light to see their almost transparent delicacy, and the pretty rose-pink lines where the fingers met. Certainly she made a charming picture, there in the sunshine among the flowers: the picture of a lovely innocent child, if she had been less vain and self-conscious.

Presently she heard a slight rustle of boughs behind her, and looking round she saw that she was no longer alone. Not many paces away, gazing at her with admiring wonder, stood a youth in the dress of a beggar, and over his shoulder looked the face of a young girl, which Olga was forced to acknowledge as lovely as her own. Now, the forest was the private property of the King, and the presence of these poor-looking people was certainly an intrusion.

"What are you doing here?" said Olga, haughtily. "Don't you know that you are trespassing? This wood belongs to the King, and is forbidden to tramps and beggars."

"We are no beggars, lady," said the youth. He spoke with great gentleness, but his voice was strong and sweet as a deep-toned bell. "To us no land is forbidden – and we owe allegiance to no one."

"My father will have you put in prison," said Olga, angrily. "What is your name?"

"My name is Kasih."

"And that girl behind you – she is hiding – why does she not come forward?"

"It is Kasukah – my sister," he said, looking round with a smile; "she is shy, and frightened, perhaps."

"What outlandish names! You must be gipsies," said Olga, rudely, "and perhaps thieves."

"Indeed, lady, you are mistaken – on the contrary, it is in our power to bestow upon you many priceless gifts. But we have travelled far to find you, and are weary; only bid us welcome – let us go with you to the castle to rest – Kasukah –"

"How dare you speak so to me?" interrupted Olga, in a fury. "To the castle, indeed – what are you thinking of? There is a poor-house somewhere, I have heard the people say, maintained by my father's bounty out of the taxes – you can go there. Go at once – or –"

She raised the little silver-handled dog-whip which hung at her girdle. To do her justice, she was no coward. Kasukah had quite disappeared; the boy stood alone, looking at Olga with sad, reproachful eyes. For a moment she thought what a pity he was so poor and shabby; he had the face and bearing of a king. But she was too proud to change her tone.

"Or what?" he said.

"I will drive you away," she said, defiantly. Still Kasih did not move, and the next moment she had struck him smartly across the cheek with the whip.

He made no effort at self-defence or retaliation, only it seemed to her that she herself felt the pain of the wound. For a few instants she saw his sorrowful face grown white and stern, and the red, glowing scar which her whip had caused; then like Kasukah, he seemed to vanish, and disappeared among the trees, while where he had stood a sunbeam crossed the grass.

Olga felt rather scared. She had been certainly very audacious, and it was odd that the boy should have shown no resentment. After all, she rather wished she had asked both him and his sister to stay; they might have proved amusing.

However, it was too late now; she could not call them back; so she thought she would return to the castle; she was beginning to feel hungry. So she went leisurely home, and, for the remainder of the day, proved a little more tractable than usual. She did not forget Kasih and his sister, and for a time wondered if they would ever seek her again; but the months went by and she saw them no more.

Now, as Olga grew older, of course the question arose of finding for her a desirable husband. And one suitor came and another, but none pleased her; and, indeed, more than one highly eligible young prince was frightened away by her haughty manners and violent temper.

The truth was that in secret she had not forgotten the face of Kasih, and she sometimes told herself that if she could find among her suitors one who was at all like him, and was also rich and powerful enough to give her all she desired in other ways, him she would choose. Kasih was certainly very handsome, in spite of his beggar's clothes; and suitably dressed he would have been quite adorable. Also, it would be delightful to find a husband with such a gentle, yielding disposition, who never thought of resenting anything she said or did.

And one day a suitor came to the palace who really made her heart beat a little faster than usual at first; he was so like the lost Kasih. But unfortunately he was only the younger son of a Royal Duke, and could offer her nothing better than a small, insignificant Principality and an income hardly sufficient to pay her dressmaker's bills. So it was no use thinking about him, and he was dismissed with the others. Olga's father began to think his daughter would never find all she required in a husband, but would remain for ever in the ancestral castle: as every year she grew more disagreeable, the prospect did not afford him entire satisfaction.

At length, however, appeared a very powerful prince, who peremptorily demanded her hand. He was a big, strong man, and carried on his wooing in such a masterful manner that even Olga was a little afraid of him. At the same time he loaded her with jewels and beautiful presents of all kinds, brought from his own country. He was said to possess fabulous wealth: and, partly because she feared him, and partly because of her pride and ambition, haughty Olga surrendered and promised to become his wife. Having once gained her consent, Hazil would brook no delay.

The date was immediately fixed, and the grandest possible preparations made for the wedding. No expense was spared, innumerable guests were invited, while those less favoured among the people came from far and near to see the bride's wedding clothes and to bring her presents. Indeed, the King of Ombrelande was forced to add a new suite of rooms to the castle to contain the wedding gifts and display them to the best advantage.

Such a sight as the bridal train had never been seen before, for it was spangled all over with diamonds so closely that Olga when she moved looked like a living jewel – and her veil was sprinkled with diamond dust, which sparkled like a myriad of tiny stars.

The evening before the wedding day Olga sat alone in her chamber, thinking of the magnificence that awaited her, also a little of Hazil, the bridegroom. She had that day seen Hazil, in a passion, punish, with his own hands, a servant for disobedience, and the sight had displeased her. It had been an ugly and unpleasant exhibition, but, worse than all, the sight of the poor man's wounds had recalled that livid mark across the fair cheek of Kasih which she herself had wrought. The boy's gentle face, which had become so stern when they parted, the laughing eyes of Kasukah, quite haunted her tonight. She thought she would like to make amends for her rudeness; if she knew where they were, she would ask brother and sister to her wedding. And, just as she was so thinking, a soft tap sounded at the door, and before she could ask who was there (she thought it must surely be the Queen, her mother, come to bid her a last goodnight, and felt rather displeased at the interruption) the door opened, and a stranger entered the room.

Olga saw a tall figure, draped from head to foot in a soft darkness that shrouded her like a cloud, obscuring even her face.

"Who are you?" said Olga. "And what do you want in my private apartments? Who dared admit you without my leave?"

"I asked admittance of no one, for none can refuse me or bar my way," answered the stranger, in a voice like the sighing of soft winds at night. "My name is Kasuhama – I am the foster-sister of Kasukah and Kasih, of whom you were just now thinking, and I come to bring you a wedding gift."

She withdrew her veil slightly as she spoke, and Olga saw a pale, serene face, sorrowful in expression, and framed with snow-white hair, but yet bearing a likeness, that was like a memory, to Kasih and Kasukah.

"I wish," said Olga, petulantly, "that Kasih had brought it tomorrow and been present at our feast. I would have seen that he was properly attired for the occasion. Your sad face is hardly suitable for a wedding feast. Shall I ever see him again?"

"As to that, I cannot answer," said Kasuhama, gravely; "but your wedding is no place either for him or Kasukah. As for me – I go everywhere. I am older in appearance than the others, you see, though, in reality, it is not so. But that is because they have immortal souls and I have none. The time will come when I must bid them farewell. We but journey together for a time."

The air of the room seemed to have become strangely chill and cold, and Olga shivered. "I am tired," she said, "and I wish to rest. Will you state your business and leave me?"

Experience had made her less abruptly rude than when she dismissed Kasih in the wood; also this cold, pale, soulless woman struck her with something like awe.

"Yes – I will say farewell to you now. In the future you will know me better and perhaps learn not to fear me – but I will leave with you the present I came to bring."

She held out a necklace of pearls more wonderful than even Olga had ever seen. They were large and round, lustrous and fair, but as Olga took them in her hands it seemed to her that, in their mysterious depths, each jewel held imprisoned a living soul.

"Wear them," said Kasuhama; "by them you will remember me."

Almost involuntarily Olga raised her hands and fastened the necklace around her slender throat. The clasps just met, and the pearls glistened like dewdrops on her bosom – or were they tears?

But in the centre of the necklace was a vacant space.

"There is one lost!" she said.

"Not lost, but missing," answered Kasuhama, softly. "One day the place will be filled, and the necklace will be complete." And with these words she waved her hand to Olga, and, drawing her dusky veil around her, quitted the room as quietly as she had entered.

The ceremonies of the following day passed off without let or hindrance, and Olga, dazzled by her grandeur, would have thought little of her visitor of the previous night – would indeed have believed

the incident a dream, a trick of the imagination – but for the necklace. It still circled her throat, for her utmost efforts proved unavailing to unfasten the clasps, and everyone stared and marvelled at the wonderful pearls which seemed endowed with a curious fascination.

Only Prince Hazil was displeased; for he could not bear his bride to wear jewels not his gift, and that outshone by their lustre any he could produce; also, he was jealous of the unknown giver. When the wedding was over, and they were travelling away to the distant castle where the first weeks of Olga's new life were to be spent, he tried to take the jewels from their resting-place. Olga smiled, for she knew that even his great strength would be unavailing, and so it proved; and although on reaching their destination Hazil sent for all the Court jewellers, neither then nor at any other time could the most experienced among them loosen Kasuhama's magic gift from its place.

The months rolled by, and Olga reigned as Queen in her husband's country, but her life was a sad one. Hazil was often cruel, and it seemed as though he were bent upon heaping upon her all the contumely and harshness she had shown to others. Still her proud spirit refused to yield. She met him with defiance in secret, and openly bore herself with so much cold haughtiness that no one dared to hint at her trouble, much less to offer her any sympathy.

But when alone in her chamber she saw again the faces of Kasih and Kasukah; but more often that of Kasuhama. For the necklace was still there to remind her; the pearls still shone with mysterious, undimmed lustre; indeed, they seemed to grow more numerous, and to be woven into more delicate and intricate designs, as time went on. Still, however, the place for the central jewel remained unfilled. Often Olga herself tried with passionate, almost agonizing effort to break their fatal chain, for every day their weight grew heavier, until she seemed to bear fetters of iron about her fair throat, and when the pearls touched her they burned, as though the iron were molten.

Still, in public they were universally admired, and gratified vanity enabled her to bear the pain and inconvenience without open complaint.

But one day was placed in her arms another treasure – a beautiful living child. And she was so fair that they called her Pearl, but the

Queen hated the name. The child, however, found a soft place in Hazil's rough nature; indeed, he idolized her; but Olga rarely saw her little daughter, and left her altogether to the care of the nurses and attendants.

So little Pearl grew very fragile, and had a wistful look in her blue eyes, as though waiting for something that never came; for in her grand nurseries and among all her beautiful playthings she found no mother-love to perfect and nourish her life.

And all this time Olga had seen no more of Kasih or Kasukah: had, indeed, almost forgotten what their faces were like. But one night, at the close of a grand entertainment, she was summoned in haste to the nursery. The Court physician came to tell her that little Pearl was ill.

Olga was very weary. Never had the necklace seemed so heavy a burden as that night, or the Court functions so endless. She rose, however, and followed the physician at once. Hazil, the King, was far away, visiting a distant part of his great territory; he would be terribly angry if anything went wrong with little Pearl during his absence.

She reached the room where the child lay on her lace-covered pillows, very white and small, but with a happy smile on her tiny face, a happy light in her blue eyes, which looked satisfied at last. But Olga knew that the smile was not for her, that the child did not recognize her, would never know her any more.

Someone else stood beside the couch: a stranger with bent head and loving, outstretched arms, and little Pearl prattled in baby language of playthings and flowers and sunlight and green fields. Olga drew near and watched, helpless and terrified, with a strange despair at her heart. And soon the little voice grew weaker – but the happy smile deepened as the blue eyes closed.

And there was a great silence in the nursery. The stranger lifted the little form in his arms, and as he raised his head Olga saw his face, and she knew that it was Kasih come at last, for across his cheek still glowed the red line of the wound which her hand had dealt many years before. His eyes met hers with the same stern sadness of reproach as when they had parted – then she remembered no more.

When the Queen recovered from her swoon they told her that

her little daughter was dead; but she knew that Kasih had taken her. She said no word, and showed few signs of grief, but remained outwardly proud and cold, though her heart was wrung with pain and fear she could not understand. She was full of wrath against Kasih, who, she thought, had taken this way of avenging the old insult she had offered him. Yet the sorrowful look in his eyes haunted her.

The pearls about her neck pressed upon her with a heavier weight, and in her sleep she saw them as in a vision, and in their depths she discerned strange pictures: faces she had known years ago and long since forgotten, the faces of those whom her pride and harshness had caused to suffer, who had appealed to her for love and pity and were denied.

And then in her dream she understood that the pearls were in truth the tears of those she had made sorrowful, kept and guarded by Kasih in his treasure-house, but given to her by Kasuhama to be her punishment.

Before many days had passed, the King Hazil returned, and, when he learned that his little daughter was dead, he summoned the Queen to his presence. Olga went haughtily, for she dared not altogether disobey. Then Hazil loaded her with reproaches, and in his anger he told her many, many hard things, and the words sank deep into her heart. It seemed, presently, that she could bear no more, and, hardly knowing what she did, she cast herself at his feet and prayed for mercy.

She asked him to remember that the child had been hers also — that she had loved it. But Hazil, in his bitterness, laughed in her face and told her she was a monster, that it was for lack of her love that the child had died; that she had never loved anything — not even herself. He turned away to nurse his own grief, and Olga dragged herself up and went away to the silent room, and knelt by the little couch where she had seen Kasih take away her child.

And there at length the blessed tears fell, for she was humbled at last, and sorry, and quite desolate and alone. And it seemed to her that through her tears she once more saw Kasih, and that he held towards her the little Pearl, more beautiful than ever, and the child put its arms about her neck, and she was comforted.

Well, from that day the life of the Queen was changed. When

next she looked at the pearl necklace she found that a jewel, more beautiful than any of the others, had been added to it: and she knew that the tear of her humiliation had filled the vacant place.

And henceforth she often saw the face of Kasih: near the bed of the dying, beside all who needed consolation, kindness and love, there she met him constantly. Near him sometimes she caught a glimpse of bright Kasukah, but, for a while, more often of Kasuhama.

The face of the white-haired sister, however, had grown very gentle and kind, and she whispered of a time when Kasukah should take her place for ever – for Love and Joy are eternal, but Sorrow has an end. And with every act of unselfish kindness and love that the Queen Olga performed the weight and burden of the necklace grew less, until the day that it fell from her of its own accord, and she was able to give it back to Kasuhama. And Hazil, the King, seeing how greatly Olga was changed, in time grew gentle towards her, and loved her; for Kasuhama softened his heart.

The Night the Stars were Gone

❧

Joan Aiken

THERE WAS ONCE A boy called Tony whose father had a tree farm.
Young trees of every sort in the world grew on this farm – oaks,
palms, banyans, gum trees, coal trees, and Christmas trees. When
the trees had reached a certain size they were sold and taken away to be
planted in parks, or in gardens, or to make avenues, or plantations.

Tony worked with his father and helped him feed and water the
trees, and clip and trim and prune them so that they grew straight and
sturdy. When people bought trees it was often Tony who carefully
dug them up and wrapped them in wet cloth and loaded them into
a pony-cart and drove them to wherever they were to be planted.
Very often it was he who planted the trees in their new places, so
as to be sure they had a proper start.

One day Tony had to take five young handkerchief trees to be
planted in the garden of Lord Stone, a very wealthy man who lived
in the nearby town.

As it happened, Tony had never been in Lord Stone's garden
before. When he arrived there he thought that it was a very strange
place. A huge iron gate was opened for him, so that he could drive
through. The garden was hidden inside a wall as high as a house.
And it was all paved with stone; there were no lawns or flowers, not
a single blade of grass. Trees grew here and there, in small square
spaces, with ivy covering the soil round their roots. But the trees were
not beautiful; they seemed like sad, stooped people, all twisted and

knotted and gnarled; they looked as if they were not comfortable in Lord Stone's garden.

Tony felt unhappy for his five little handkerchief trees, with their big white leaves, which looked as if they were meant for blowing noses on, or for fluttering in the breeze. He did not think they would like it in this silent, windless spot. But Lord Stone had bought the trees, and paid for them, so Tony planted them as carefully as possible, spreading out the roots and giving them plenty of tree-food, in the five new square spaces that had been made ready among the stone paving slabs.

While he was working, Tony noticed that a swing, hanging from one of the twisted trees, was all studded with real pearls. And he could see a gold-paved swimming-pool, and a silver climbing-frame, and a seesaw with ruby seats. But, in spite of these treasures, Tony thought that the garden was an ugly and gloomy place.

Then a girl came out of the house and watched him plant the last tree. She was younger than Tony, but very fat. She carried an emerald-studded hoop and a pair of roller-skates with diamond buckles, but she did not roll the hoop or skate on the skates. She sat down on an iron chair and scowled at Tony, who thought she looked very bad-tempered.

"My father is much richer than *your* father," she said. "He is the richest man in the town."

"I know," said Tony.

"He is probably the richest man in the world."

"Fancy that," said Tony.

"He bought those trees to remind him of my mother, who is dead," said the girl.

"I'm sorry about that," said Tony, but the girl took no notice of his words.

"This whole garden is in memory of my mother," she said.

Tony did not know what to say to that. He loaded his tools into the cart.

"My name is Ann," said the girl.

"Oh," said Tony. She did not seem to want to know *his* name, so he did not tell it.

"Well? Do you like our garden?" said Ann.

"No, not very much," said Tony.

"Then I think you are very rude," said Ann, frowning till her eyebrows nearly touched her fat cheeks.

A tall thin man came out of the house to inspect the trees. His face reminded Tony of the stone pavement, it was so set and flat and grey; his eyes seemed to look through holes like the holes in a mask.

"Don't talk to the garden boy, Ann," he said.

Ann put out her tongue at Tony and walked slowly towards the house. As she passed the cart she gave the pony a thump with her hoop. Tony thought she was the fattest and most disagreeable girl he had ever seen. He was glad to leave the garden and go home to his father's farm.

But, after that, whenever his errands took him though the town, he tried to drive past Lord Stone's gates, so as to look through the bars, and see how his little handkerchief trees were getting on. They grew, but very slowly, and their white leaves hung down sadly. The wall round the garden was so high that the trees growing there were nearly always in shadow; the sun shone down on them only for an hour at noon.

As time passed, Tony noticed that many new treasures were brought into the garden: a rainbow in a glass box, a fountain of red wine, a rocking-horse carved from white marble with a gold saddle; a table carved from mother-of-pearl; an ivory summerhouse with beautiful pictures painted on its walls; and a garden parasol made from green jade and peacocks' feathers; but still Tony thought that the garden was a strange sad place.

Sometimes, when he drove slowly past on his cart, fat Ann would come and put her tongue out at him through the bars of the gate. But she never said anything to him. Once or twice Tony saw Lord Stone, wandering slowly about the garden, or going into the house. Often Tony wondered what the inside of the house could be like; if there were such precious and costly things in the garden, what kind of furniture could they have indoors?

One evening Tony was driving home just at sunset, down the long gentle hill that led through the town to the valley where his father's farm lay.

Tony loved this road at this time, for usually the sunset sky would be all pink and red and scarlet, with clouds like rose-coloured or golden feathers. But on this evening the sky was strangely grey and empty, and the sun dropped out of sight with none of the usual sunset colours.

Tony might not have thought more about this if he had not happened to notice, when he passed Lord Stone's gate and looked through, that the windows of the big house, generally so dark and blank, were today all filled with pink light, as if they reflected the sunset sky.

And yet there were no sunset colours in the sky.

"That's queer," Tony thought.

But he drove home, and did not think about the matter again until the next evening, when he stepped out of doors just after dark to take the pony her night feed.

There was the moon, shining white up above, but there were no stars in the dark blue; not a single star to be seen anywhere in the sky.

"Father!" called Tony in a fright. "Come and see! Someone's taken the stars!"

"Nonsense," said his father, looking out for a moment and then going back indoors, "it's cloudy, that's all. Come and get your supper."

Tony went in, but he was sure that something was wrong.

The next night the stars were still missing, and the night after.

Tony asked several people in the town if they had noticed that there were no stars.

"Oh," said one, "we've been having a lot of mist lately, that's all it is."

"It's the time of the month," said another.

"It's the time of the year," said a third.

"It's heat-haze," said a fourth.

"Don't be silly," said a fifth. "You can't have looked properly. The stars are always there."

But the stars were not there in the sky, and Tony thought he could guess where they might be.

So on the following night he climbed quietly out of bed at

midnight, when everybody was fast asleep, and he put on his clothes and walked across the town to Lord Stone's iron gates, and looked through.

What a sight he saw.

The garden was full of stars: they hung in the boughs of the trees, quite weighing them down. They lay sparkling in the little square plots of ivy round the trunks of the trees. They were floating in the gold swimming-pool, thick as breadcrumbs; and hundreds of them had collected, like midges, on the peacock-feathered parasol.

By the flickering, twinkling light they gave, Tony could see that fat Ann was sitting on her iron chair among all those stars, and she saw Tony.

She walked to the gate and opened it and let him in.

"Well?" she said proudly. "Do you like our garden now?"

Tony saw that the windows of the house were all pink, still, with reflected sunset, although it was the middle of the night. Up above, the white moon hung in the empty sky.

"How did you get all the stars down out of the sky?" Tony asked.

"A travelling man sold my father a pair of long black gloves. If you put them on, you can reach anything that you want, anything in the world. So my father put them on, and reached up, and scraped all the stars down out of the sky."

"He shouldn't have done that," said Tony.

"What business is it of yours?" Ann said angrily. "The stars don't belong to you."

Then she started. "Oh!" she whispered. "Here's Father coming. He'll be angry that I let you in. Go away, quick!"

But Tony did not want to go. He waited till Lord Stone came up to them.

"Sir," he said. "You should not have taken the stars."

Lord Stone looked grey and tired in the flickering star-light.

"Be quiet, boy," he said. "I am not interested in what you think."

He did not seem surprised, or angry, at finding Tony in the garden, so late at night. He kept rubbing and twisting his hands, pulling at the fingers of the long black gloves he wore, which went right up to his elbows.

"These gloves are too tight," he said. "As you are here, boy, you can help me pull them off."

Tony pulled at the gloves. But they were so tight that they seemed almost like skin. They would not come off. Lord Stone cried out with pain.

"Stop! My hands feel as if they were burning!"

"If you put your hands in the pool and wetted the gloves, that might stretch them," suggested Tony.

"I wish I had never bought the gloves," Lord Stone muttered. He dipped his hands in the pool, among all the floating stars. "What good does it do, anyway, to have all these stars in the garden? They don't bring my wife back. What is the use of them?"

Tony pulled again at the wet black gloves. But still they clung as tight as skin and would not come off.

"Now I remember," Lord Stone said. "The man from whom I bought the gloves said that if I wanted to get rid of them, I must sell them again, at the same price I gave for them. Boy, will *you* buy them?"

Tony did not want the gloves at all, but still, he felt sorry for Lord Stone. Very slowly, he said, "What price did you give for the gloves, sir?"

"All the money I had in the world," said Lord Stone.

"All I have in the world is a shilling," said Tony, "as I help my father for nothing. But you can have that, if you like." He took the shilling out of his pocket and handed it to Lord Stone.

Then they were able to pull the gloves off.

But Lord Stone's hands were still very painful: they burned and stung as if he had laid them on hot iron.

"Oh, if only there were some snow here," he cried. "If I could dip them in snow, I believe they might get better. Boy, you could reach out in the gloves and get me a bit of snow."

"No, sir," said Tony. "I bought the gloves from you, but I am not going to put them on. You must find your own snow."

"I'll go to the mountains," said Lord Stone. "I'll get out my car and drive there. Ann," he said to the girl, "will you come with me?"

"No," she said sulkily. "I don't want to go."

Lord Stone rolled up an ebony door in the wall, and got out his enormous car, and drove away in it without looking back.

The two long black gloves lay on the pavement like lizards between Tony and Ann.

"Why don't you put them on?" said Ann. "You could have anything in the world that you want to reach for."

"I don't want anything," said Tony.

He tied the gloves round a dead branch that had dropped from one of the trees, and carried them back through the moonlit streets to the edge of the town, to the corner of the valley where he and his father burned all their dead leaves, and prunings, and weeds, and garden rubbish. A great fire was always slowly smouldering there, with a red-hot heart and a plume of blue smoke drifting away from it into the air.

Tony poked the dead branch, with the gloves wound round it, right into the middle of the bonfire, and covered them with dry leaves and grass. They caught light at once and burned fiercely, with a green flame and a black smoke. They went on burning for a long, long time. As the green flame slowly died down, Tony noticed something out of the corner of his eye. He looked up, and was just in time to see a single star spring into the sky. Then three more suddenly sparked out as if they had been switched on. Then thirty. Then three hundred. Then three hundred thousand.

Next week a neighbour said to Tony's father,

"Have you heard? No one has seen Lord Stone for a week. He went off in his car and hasn't come back."

Tony began to wonder if Ann was all right. "Perhaps I should go and see," he thought. He had to take two tree-lupins to a house on the far side of the town that afternoon, so he came back by way of Lord Stone's gates, and looked through.

He noticed that grass had broken through the stone pavement. The slabs were cracked, as if they were hundreds of years old. Spring bulbs, snowdrops and daffodils were poking through. Some of the trees were in blossom.

The gate stood open, so he went in.

All the garden's treasures were gone – the pearl swing and the marble rocking-horse, the summerhouse and the rainbow in a glass box. The pool water was rusty and full of dead leaves. But the five little handkerchief trees looked sturdy and well; they were covered with new buds.

Tony walked up to the windows of the house, which were no longer full of pink light, but were just plain glass, some of them cracked. He looked through and saw that the rooms inside were empty and bare: no tables, no chairs, no rugs, no pictures, nothing. Ann sat inside on the floor.

When she saw him she came out of the house.

"What did you do with the gloves?" she asked.

"I burned them," he said. "In our bonfire."

"What is a bonfire?" she asked.

"Haven't you ever seen one?"

"No, never," she said. "Can I come and see it?"

"Of course," Tony said. "You can ride in the cart."

So he drove her back to the farm, and Ann looked at the bonfire, and the sheds full of tools, and the plough, and all the little growing trees.

Tony said, "Would you like to stay with us? Until your father comes back?"

"Could I?" said Ann. "Wouldn't your father mind?"

"No, of course not!" said Tony. "Come along in to supper."

He stabled the pony and took Ann up to the farmhouse. As he opened the back door, Ann said, "What is your name?"

Old Pipes and the Dryad

❦

Frank R. Stockton

A MOUNTAIN BROOK RAN through a little village. Over the brook there was a narrow bridge, and from the bridge a footpath led out from the village and up the hillside to the cottage of Old Pipes and his mother. For many, many years Old Pipes had been employed by the villagers to pipe the cattle down from the hills. Every afternoon, an hour before sunset, he would sit on a rock in front of his cottage and play on his pipes. Then all the flocks and herds that were grazing on the mountains would hear him, wherever they might happen to be, and would come down to the village – the cows by the easiest paths, the sheep by those not quite so easy, and the goats by the steep and rocky ways that were hardest of all.

But now, for a year or more, Old Pipes had not piped the cattle home. It is true that every afternoon he sat upon the rock and played upon his familiar instrument; but the cattle did not hear him. He had grown old, and his breath was feeble. The echoes of his cheerful notes, which used to come from the rocky hill on the other side of the valley, were heard no more; and twenty yards from Old Pipes one could scarcely tell what tune he was playing. He had become somewhat deaf, and did not know that the sound of his pipes was so thin and weak that the cattle did not hear him. The cows, the sheep, and the goats came down every afternoon as before, but this was because two boys and a girl were sent up after them. The villagers did not wish the good old man to know that his piping was no longer of any use, so they paid him his little salary every month and said nothing about the two boys and the girl.

Old Pipes's mother was, of course, a great deal older than he was and as deaf as a gate – posts, latch, hinges, and all – and she never knew that the sound of her son's pipes did not spread over all the mountainside and echo back strong and clear from the opposite hills. She was very fond of Old Pipes, and proud of his piping; and, as he was so much younger than she was, she never thought of him as being very old. She cooked for him and made his bed and mended his clothes; and they lived very comfortably on his little salary.

One afternoon, at the end of the month, when Old Pipes had finished his piping, he took his stout staff and went down the hill to the village to receive the money for his month's work. The path seemed a great deal steeper and more difficult than it used to be; and Old Pipes thought that it must have been washed by the rains and greatly damaged. He remembered it as a path that was quite easy to traverse either up or down. But Old Pipes had been a very active man, and, as his mother was so much older than he was, he never thought of himself as aged and infirm.

When the Chief Villager had paid him and he had talked a little with some of his friends, Old Pipes started to go home. But when he had crossed the bridge over the brook and gone a short distance up the hillside, he became very tired and sat down upon a stone. He had not been sitting there half a minute when along came two boys and a girl.

"Children," said Old Pipes, "I'm very tired tonight, and I don't believe I can climb up this steep path to my home. I think I shall have to ask you to help me."

"We will do that," said the boys and the girl, quite cheerfully; and one boy took him by the right hand and the other by the left, while the girl pushed him in the back. In this way he went up the hill quite easily and soon reached his cottage door. Old Pipes gave each of the three children a copper coin, and then they sat down for a few minutes' rest before starting back to the village.

"I'm sorry that I tired you so much," said Old Pipes.

"Oh, that would not have tired us," said one of the boys, "if we had not been so far today after the cows, the sheep, and the goats.

They rambled high up on the mountain, and we never before had such a time in finding them."

"Had to go after the cows, the sheeps, and the goats!" exclaimed Old Pipes. "What do you mean by that?"

The girl, who stood behind the old man, shook her head, put her hand on her mouth, and made all sorts of signs to the boy to stop talking on this subject; but he did not notice her and promptly answered Old Pipes.

"Why, you see, good sir," said he, "that as the cattle can't hear your pipes now, somebody has to go after them every evening to drive them down from the mountain, and the Chief Villager has hired us three to do it. Generally it is not very hard work, but tonight the cattle had wandered far."

"How long have you been doing this?" asked the old man.

The girl shook her head and clapped her hand on her mouth more vigorously than before, but the boy went on.

"I think it is about a year now," he said, "since the people first felt sure that the cattle could not hear your pipes; and from that time we've been driving them down. But we are rested now and will go home. Goodnight, sir."

The three children then went down the hill, the girl scolding the boy all the way home. Old Pipes stood silent a few moments, and then he went into his cottage.

"Mother," he shouted, "did you hear what those children said?"

"Children!" exclaimed the old woman. "I did not hear them. I did not know there were any children here."

Then Old Pipes told his mother, shouting very loudly to make her hear, how the two boys and the girl had helped him up the hill and what he had heard about his piping and the cattle.

"They can't hear you?" cried his mother. "Why, what's the matter with the cattle?"

"Ah, me!" said Old Pipes. "I don't believe there's anything the matter with the cattle. It must be with me and my pipes that there is something the matter. But one thing is certain: if I do not earn the wages the Chief Villager pays me, I shall not take them. I shall go straight down to the village and give back the money I received today."

"Nonsense!" cried his mother. "I'm sure you've piped as well as you could, and no more can be expected. And what are we to do without the money?"

"I don't know," said Old Pipes; "but I'm going down to the village to pay it back."

The sun had now set, but the moon was shining very brightly on the hillside, and Old Pipes could see his way very well. He did not take the same path by which he had gone before, but followed another, which led among the trees upon the hillside, and, although longer, was not so steep.

When he had gone about halfway, the old man sat down to rest, leaning his back against a great oak tree. As he did so, he heard a sound like knocking inside the tree, and then a voice distinctly said, "Let me out! Let me out!"

Old Pipes instantly forgot that he was tired and sprang to his feet. "This must be a dryad tree!" he exclaimed. "If it is, I'll let her out."

Old Pipes had never, to his knowledge, seen a dryad tree, but he knew there were such trees on the hillsides and the mountains and that dryads lived in them. He knew, too, that in the summertime, on those days when the moon rose before the sun went down, a dryad could come out of her tree if anyone could find the key which locked her in and turn it. Old Pipes closely examined the trunk of the tree, which stood in the full moonlight. "If I see that key," he said, "I shall surely turn it." Before long, he perceived a piece of bark standing out from the tree, which appeared to him very much like the handle of a key. He took hold of it and found he could turn it quite around. As he did so, a large part of the side of the tree was pushed open, and a beautiful dryad stepped quickly out.

For a moment she stood motionless, gazing on the scene before her – the tranquil valley, the hills, the forest, and the mountainside, all lying in the soft, clear light of the moon. "Oh, lovely! Lovely!" she exclaimed. "How long it is since I have seen anything like this!" And then, turning to Old Pipes, she said, "How good of you to let me out! I am so happy and so thankful that I must kiss you, you dear old man!" And she threw her arms around the neck of Old Pipes and kissed him on both cheeks. "You don't know," she then went on to

say, "how doleful it is to be shut up so long in a tree. I don't mind it in the winter, for then I am glad to be sheltered, but in summer it is a rueful thing not to be able to see all the beauties of the world. And it's ever so long since I've been let out. People so seldom come this way; and when they do come at the right time they either don't hear me, or they are frightened and run away. But you, you dear old man, you were not frightened, and you looked and looked for the key, and you let me out, and now I shall not have to go back till winter has come and the air grows cold. Oh, it is glorious! What can I do for you, to show you how grateful I am?"

"I am very glad," said Old Pipes, "that I let you out, since I see that it makes you so happy; but I must admit that I tried to find the key because I had a great desire to see a dryad. But if you wish to do something for me, you can, if you happen to be going down toward the village."

"To the village!" exclaimed the Dryad. "I will go anywhere for you, my kind old benefactor."

"Well, then," said Old Pipes, "I wish you would take this little bag of money to the Chief Villager and tell him that Old Pipes cannot receive pay for the services which he does not perform. It is now more than a year that I have not been able to make the cattle hear me when I piped to call them home. I did not know this until tonight; but now that I know it, I cannot keep the money, and so I send it back." And, handing the little bag to the Dryad, he bade her goodnight and turned toward his cottage.

"Goodnight," said the Dryad. "And I thank you over and over and over again, you good old man!"

Old Pipes walked toward his home, very glad to be saved the fatigue of going all the way down to the village and back again. "To be sure," he said to himself, "this path does not seem at all steep, and I can walk along it very easily; but it would have tired me dreadfully to come up all the way from the village, especially as I could not have expected those children to help me again." When he reached home, his mother was surprised to see him returning so soon.

"What!" she exclaimed. "Have you already come back? What did the Chief Villager say? Did he take the money?"

Old Pipes was just about to tell her that he had sent the money to the village by a dryad when he suddenly reflected that his mother would be sure to disapprove such a proceeding, and so he merely said he had sent it by a person whom he had met.

"And how do you know that the person will ever take it to the Chief Villager?" cried his mother. "You will lose it, and the villagers will never get it. Oh, Pipes! Pipes! When will you be old enough to have ordinary common sense?"

Old Pipes considered that as he was already seventy years of age he could scarcely expect to grow any wiser, but he made no remark on this subject; and, saying that he doubted not that the money would go safely to its destination, he sat down to his supper. His mother scolded him roundly, but he did not mind it; and after supper he went out and sat on a rustic chair in front of the cottage to look at the moonlit village and to wonder whether or not the Chief Villager really received the money. While he was doing these two things, he went fast asleep.

When Old Pipes left the Dryad, she did not go down to the village with the little bag of money. She held it in her hand and thought about what she had heard. "This is a good and honest old man," she said; "and it is a shame that he should lose this money. He looked as if he needed it, and I don't believe the people in the village will take it from one who has served them so long. Often, when in my tree, have I heard the sweet notes of his pipes. I am going to take the money back to him." She did not start immediately, because there were so many beautiful things to look at; but after a while she went up to the cottage, and, finding Old Pipes asleep in his chair, she slipped the little bag into his coat pocket and silently sped away.

The next day Old Pipes told his mother that he would go up the mountain and cut some wood. He had a right to get wood from the mountain, but for a long time he had been content to pick up the dead branches which lay about his cottage. Today, however, he felt so strong and vigorous that he thought he would go and cut some fuel that would be better than this. He worked all the morning, and when he came back he did not feel at all tired, and he had a very good appetite for his dinner.

Now, Old Pipes knew a good deal about dryads, but there was one thing which, although he had heard, he had forgotten. This was that a kiss from a dryad made a person ten years younger. The people of the village knew this, and they were very careful not to let any child of ten years or younger go into the woods where the dryads were supposed to be; for, if they should chance to be kissed by one of these tree nymphs, they would be set back so far that they would cease to exist. A story was told in the village that a very bad boy of eleven once ran away into the woods and had an adventure of this kind; and when his mother found him, he was a little baby of one year old. Taking advantage of her opportunity, she brought him up more carefully than she had done before, and he grew to be a very good boy indeed.

Now, Old Pipes had been kissed twice by the Dryad, once on each cheek, and he therefore felt as vigorous and active as when he was a hale man of fifty. His mother noticed how much work he was doing and told him that he need not try in that way to make up for the loss of his piping wages; for he would only tire himself out and get sick. But her son answered that he had not felt so well for years and that he was quite able to work. In the course of the afternoon Old Pipes, for the first time that day, put his hand in his coat pocket, and there, to his amazement, he found the little bag of money.

"Well, well!" he exclaimed, "I am stupid, indeed! I really thought that I had seen a dryad; but when I sat down by that big oak tree, I must have gone to sleep and dreamed it all; and then I came home thinking I had given the money to a dryad, when it was in my pocket all the time. But the Chief Villager shall have the money. I shall not take it to him today, but tomorrow I wish to go the village to see some of my old friends; and then I shall give up the money."

Toward the close of the afternoon Old Pipes, as had been his custom for so many years, took his pipes from the shelf on which they lay and went out to the rock in front of the cottage.

"What are you going to do?" cried his mother. "If you will not consent to be paid, why do you pipe?"

"I am going to pipe for my own pleasure," said her son. "I am used to it, and I do not wish to give it up. It does not matter now whether the cattle hear me or not, and I am sure that my piping will injure no one."

When the good man began to play upon his favorite instrument, he was astonished at the sound that came from it. The beautiful notes of the pipes sounded clear and strong down into the valley and spread over the hills and up the sides of the mountain beyond, while, after a little interval, an echo came back from the rocky hill on the other side of the valley.

"Ha ha!" he cried. "What has happened to my pipes? They must have been stopped up of late, but now they are as clear and good as ever."

Again the merry notes went sounding far and wide. The cattle on the mountain heard them, and those that were old enough remembered how these notes had called them from their pastures every evening, and so they started down the mountainside, the others following.

The merry notes were heard in the village below, and the people were much astonished thereby. "Why, who can be blowing the pipes of Old Pipes?" they said. But, as they were all very busy, no one went up to see. One thing, however, was plain enough: the cattle were coming down the mountain. And so the two boys and the girl did not have to go after them and had an hour for play, for which they were very glad.

The next morning Old Pipes started down to the village with his money, and on the way he met the Dryad. "Oh, ho!" he cried. "Is that you? Why, I thought my letting you out of the tree was nothing but a dream."

"A dream!" cried the Dryad. "If you only knew how happy you have made me, you would not think it merely a dream. And has it not benefited you? Do you not feel happier? Yesterday I heard you playing beautifully on your pipes."

"Yes, yes," cried he. "I did not understand it before, but I see it all now. I have really grown younger. I thank you, I thank you, good Dryad, from the bottom of my heart. It was the finding of the money in my pocket that made me think it was a dream."

"Oh, I put it in when you were asleep," she said, laughing, "because I thought you ought to keep it. Goodbye, kind, honest man. May you live long and be as happy as I am now."

Old Pipes was greatly delighted when he understood that he was really a younger man; but that made no difference about the money, and he kept on his way to the village. As soon as he reached it, he was eagerly questioned as to who had been playing his pipes the evening before, and when the people heard that it was himself, they were very much surprised. Thereupon, Old Pipes told what had happened to him, and then there was greater wonder, with hearty congratulations and handshakes; for Old Pipes was liked by everyone. The Chief Villager refused to take his money, and, although Old Pipes said that he had not earned it, everyone present insisted that, as he would now play on his pipes as before, he should lose nothing because for a time he was unable to perform his duty.

So Old Pipes was obliged to keep his money, and after an hour or two spent in conversation with his friends he returned to his cottage.

There was one individual, however, who was not at all pleased with what had happened to Old Pipes. This was an echo-dwarf who lived on the hills on the other side of the valley, and whose duty it was to echo back the notes of the pipes whenever they could be heard. There were a great many other echo-dwarfs on these hills, some of whom echoed back the songs of maidens, some the shouts of children, and others the music that was often heard in the village. But there was only one who could send back the strong notes of the pipes of Old Pipes, and this had been his sole duty for many years. But when the old man grew feeble and the notes of his pipes could not be heard on the opposite hills, this echo-dwarf had nothing to do, and he spent his time in delightful idleness; and he slept so much and grew so fat that it made his companions laugh to see him walk.

On the afternoon on which, after so long an interval, the sound of the pipes was heard on the echo hills, this dwarf was fast asleep behind a rock. As soon as the first notes reached them, some of his companions ran to wake him. Rolling to his feet, he echoed back the merry tune of Old Pipes. Naturally, he was very much annoyed and indignant at being thus obliged to give up his life of comfortable leisure, and he hoped very much that this pipe-playing would not occur again.

The next afternoon he was awake and listening, and, sure enough, at the usual hour, along came the notes of the pipes as clear and strong as they ever had been; and he was obliged to work as long as Old Pipes played. The echo-dwarf was very angry. He had supposed, of course, that the pipe-playing had ceased forever, and he felt that he had a right to be indignant at being thus deceived. He was so much disturbed that he made up his mind to go and try to find out whether this was to be a temporary matter or not. He had plenty of time, as the pipes were played but once a day, and he set off early in the morning for the hill on which Old Pipes lived. It was hard work for the fat little fellow, and when he had crossed the valley and had gone some distance into the woods on the hillside, he stopped to rest, and in a few minutes the Dryad came tripping along.

"Ho, ho!" exclaimed the dwarf. "What are you doing here, and how did you get out of your tree?"

"Doing!" cried the Dryad. "I am being happy; that's what I am doing. And I was let out of my tree by the good old man who plays the pipes to call the cattle down from the mountain. And it makes me happier to think that I have been of service to him. I gave him two kisses of gratitude, and now he is young enough to play his pipes as well as ever."

The echo-dwarf stepped forward, his face pale with passion. "Am I to believe," he said, "that you are the cause of this great evil that has come upon me and that you are the wicked creature who has again started this old man upon his career of pipe-playing? What have I ever done to you that you should have condemned me for years and years to echo back the notes of those wretched pipes?"

At this the Dryad laughed loudly.

"What a funny little fellow you are." she said. "Anyone would think you had been condemned to toil from morning till night; while what you really have to do is merely to imitate for half an hour every day the merry notes of Old Pipes's piping. Fie upon you, Echo-dwarf! You are lazy and selfish; and that is what is the matter with you. Instead of grumbling at being obliged to do a little wholesome work, which is less, I am sure, than that of any other echo-dwarf upon the rocky hillside, you should rejoice at the good fortune of the old man who has regained so much of his strength and vigor. Go home and learn to be just and generous; and then perhaps you may be happy. Goodbye."

"Insolent creature!" shouted the dwarf, as he shook his fat little fist at her. "I'll make you suffer for this. You shall find out what it is to heap injury and insult upon one like me and to snatch from him the repose that he has earned by long years of toil." And, shaking his head savagely, he hurried back to the rocky hillside.

Every afternoon the merry notes of the pipes of Old Pipes sounded down into the valley and over the hills and up the mountainside; and every afternoon, when he had echoed them back, the little dwarf grew more and more angry with the Dryad. Each day, from early morning till it was time for him to go back to his duties upon the rocky hillside, he searched the woods for her. He intended, if he met her, to pretend to be very sorry for what he had said, and he thought he might be able to play a trick upon her which would avenge him well.

One day, while thus wandering among the trees, he met Old Pipes. The Echo-dwarf did not generally care to see or speak to ordinary people; but now he was so anxious to find the object of his search that he stopped and asked Old Pipes if he had seen the Dryad. The piper had not noticed the little fellow, and he looked down on him with some surprise.

"No," he said, "I have not seen her, and I have been looking everywhere for her."

"You!" cried the dwarf. "What do you wish with her?"

Old Pipes then sat down on a stone, so that he should be nearer the ear of his small companion, and he told what the Dryad had done for him.

When the Echo-dwarf heard that this was the man whose pipes he was obliged to echo back every day, he would have slain him on the spot had he been able; but, as he was not able, he merely ground his teeth and listened to the rest of the story.

"I am looking for the Dryad now," Old Pipes continued, "on account of my aged mother. When I was old myself, I did not notice how very old my mother was; but now it shocks me to see how feeble and decrepit her years have caused her to become; and I am looking for the Dryad to ask her to make my mother younger, as she made me."

The eyes of the Echo-dwarf glistened. Here was a man who might help him in his plans.

"Your idea is a good one," he said to Old Pipes, "and it does you honor. But you should know that a dryad can make no person younger but one who lets her out of her tree. However, you can manage the affair very easily. All you need do is to find the Dryad, tell her what you want, and request her to step into her tree and be shut up for a short time. Then you will go and bring your mother to the tree; she will open it, and everything will be as you wish. Is not this a good plan?"

"Excellent!" cried Old Pipes; "and I will go instantly and search more diligently for the Dryad."

"Take me with you," said the Echo-dwarf. "You can easily carry me on your strong shoulders; and I shall be glad to help you in any way that I can."

"Now, then," said the little fellow to himself, as Old Pipes carried him rapidly along, "if he persuades the Dryad to get into a tree – and she is quite foolish enough to do it – and then goes away to bring his mother, I shall take a stone or a club, and I will break off the key to that tree, so that nobody can ever turn it again. Then Mistress Dryad will see what she has brought upon herself by her behavior to me."

Before long they came to the great oak tree in which the Dryad had lived, and at a distance they saw that beautiful creature herself coming toward them.

"How excellently well everything happens!" said the dwarf. "Put me down, and I will go. Your business with the Dryad is more important than mine; and you need not say anything about my having suggested your plan to you. I am willing that you should have all the credit of it yourself."

Old Pipes put the Echo-dwarf upon the ground, but the little rogue did not go away. He concealed himself between some low, mossy rocks, and he was so much of their color that you would not have noticed him if you had been looking straight at him.

When the Dryad came up, Old Pipes lost no time in telling her about his mother and what he wished her to do. At first the Dryad answered nothing, but stood looking very sadly at Old Pipes.

"Do you really wish me to go into my tree again?" she said. "I should dreadfully dislike to do it, for I don't know what might happen. It is not at all necessary, for I could make your mother younger at any time if she would give me the opportunity. I had already thought of making you still happier in this way; and several times I have waited about your cottage, hoping to meet your aged mother, but she never comes outside, and you know a dryad cannot enter a house. I cannot imagine what put this idea into your head. Did you think of it yourself?"

"No, I cannot say that I did," answered Old Pipes. "A little dwarf whom I met in the woods proposed it to me."

"Oh!" cried the Dryad. "Now I see through it all. It is the scheme of that vile Echo-dwarf – your enemy and mine. Where is he? I should like to see him."

"I think he has gone away," said Old Pipes.

"No, he has not," said the Dryad, whose quick eyes perceived the Echo-dwarf among the rocks. "There he is. Seize him and drag him out, I beg of you."

Old Pipes perceived the dwarf as soon as he was pointed out to him, and, running to the rocks, he caught the little fellow by the arm and pulled him out.

"Now, then," cried the Dryad, who had opened the door of the great oak, "just stick him in there, and we will shut him up. Then I shall be safe from his mischief for the rest of the time I am free."

Old Pipes thrust the Echo-dwarf into the tree; the Dryad pushed the door shut; there was a clicking sound of bark and wood, and no one would have noticed that the big oak had ever had an opening in it.

"There," said the Dryad; "now we need not be afraid of him. And I assure you, my good piper, that I shall be very glad to make your mother younger as soon as I can. Will you not ask her to come out and meet me?"

"Of course I will," cried Old Pipes; "and I will do it without delay."

And then, the Dryad by his side, he hurried to his cottage. But when he mentioned the matter to his mother, the old woman became very angry indeed. She did not believe in dryads; and if they really did exist she knew they must be witches and sorceresses, and she would have nothing to do with them. If her son had ever allowed himself to be kissed by one of them, he ought to be ashamed of himself. As to its doing him the least bit of good, she did not believe a word of it. He felt better than he used to feel, but that was very common.

She had sometimes felt that way herself, and she forbade him ever to mention a dryad to her again.

That afternoon Old Pipes, feeling very sad that his plan in regard to his mother had failed, sat down upon the rock and played upon his pipes. The pleasant sounds went down the valley and up the hills and mountain, but, to the great surprise of some persons who happened to notice the fact, the notes were not echoed back from the rocky hillside but from the woods on the side of the valley on which Old Pipes lived. The next day many of the villagers stopped in their work to listen to the echo of the pipes coming from the woods. The sound was not as clear and strong as it used to be when it was sent back from the rocky hillside, but it certainly came from among the trees. Such a thing as an echo changing its place in this way had never been heard of before, and nobody was able to explain how it could have happened.

Old Pipes, however, knew very well that the sound came from the Echo-dwarf shut up in the great oak tree. The sides of the tree were thin, and the sound of the pipes could be heard through them, and the dwarf was obliged by the laws of his being to echo back those notes whenever they came to him. But Old Pipes thought he might get the Dryad in trouble if he let anyone know that the Echo-dwarf was shut up in the tree, and so he wisely said nothing about it.

One day the two boys and the girl who had helped Old Pipes up the hill were playing in the woods. Stopping near the great oak tree, they heard a sound of knocking within it, and then a voice plainly said, "Let me out! Let me out!"

For a moment the children stood still in astonishment, and then one of the boys exclaimed, "Oh, it is a dryad, like the one Old Pipes found! Let's let her out!"

"What are you thinking of?" cried the girl. "I am the oldest of all, and I am only thirteen. Do you wish to be turned into crawling babies? Run! Run! Run!"

And the two boys and the girl dashed down into the valley as fast as their legs could carry them. There was no desire in their youthful hearts to be made younger than they were. And, for fear that their parents might think it well that they should commence their careers anew, they never said a word about finding the dryad tree.

As the summer days went on, Old Pipes's mother grew feebler and feebler. One day when her son was away – for he now frequently went into the woods to hunt or fish, or down into the valley to work – she arose from her knitting to prepare the simple dinner. But she felt so weak and tired that she was not able to do the work to which she had been so long accustomed. "Alas! Alas!" she said. "The time has come when I am too old to work. My son will have to hire someone to come here and cook his meals, make his bed, and mend his clothes. Alas! Alas! I had hoped that as long as I lived I should be able to do these things. But it is not so. I have grown utterly worthless, and someone else must prepare the dinner for my son. I wonder where he is." And, tottering to the door, she went outside to look for him. She did not feel able to stand, and, reaching the rustic chair, she sank into it, quite exhausted, and soon fell asleep.

The Dryad, who had often come to the cottage to see if she could find an opportunity of carrying out Old Pipes's affectionate design, now happened by; and, seeing that the much desired occasion had come, she stepped up quietly behind the old woman and gently kissed her on each cheek and then as quietly disappeared.

In a few minutes the mother of Old Pipes awoke, and, looking up at the sun, she exclaimed, "Why, it is almost dinner time! My son will be here directly, and I am not ready for him." And, rising to her feet, she hurried into the house, made the fire, set the meat and vegetables to cook, laid the cloth; and by the time her son arrived the meal was on the table.

"How a little sleep does refresh one," she said to herself as she was bustling about. She was a woman of very vigorous constitution and at seventy had been a great deal stronger and more active than her son was at that age. The moment Old Pipes saw his mother, he knew that the Dryad had been there; but, while he felt as happy as a king, he was too wise to say anything about her.

"It is astonishing how well I feel today," said his mother; "and either my hearing has improved or you speak much more plainly than you have done of late."

The summer days went on and passed away; the leaves were falling from the trees, and the air was becoming cold.

"Nature has ceased to be lovely," said the Dryad, "and the night winds chill me. It is time for me to go back into my comfortable quarters in the great oak. But first I must pay another visit to the cottage of Old Pipes."

She found the piper and his mother sitting side by side on the rock in front of the door. The cattle were not to go to the mountain any more that season, and he was piping them down for the last time. Loud and merrily sounded the pipes of Old Pipes, and down the mountainside came the cattle — the cows by the easiest paths, the sheep by those not quite so easy, and the goats by the most difficult ones among the rocks — while from the great oak tree were heard the echoes of the cheerful music.

"How happy they look, sitting there together," said the Dryad; "and I don't believe it will do them a bit of harm to be still younger." And, moving quietly up behind them, she first kissed Old Pipes on his cheek and then his mother.

Old Pipes, who had stopped playing, knew what it was, but he did not move, and said nothing. His mother, thinking that her son had kissed her, turned to him with a smile and kissed him in return. And then she arose and went into the cottage, a vigorous woman of sixty, followed by her son, erect and happy and twenty years younger than herself.

The Dryad sped away to the woods, shrugging her shoulders as she felt the cool evening wind.

When she reached the great oak, she turned the key and opened the door. "Come out," she said to the Echo-dwarf, who sat blinking within. "Winter is coming on, and I want the comfortable shelter of my tree for myself. The cattle have come down from the mountain for the last time this year; the pipes will no longer sound, and you can go to your rocks and have a holiday until next spring."

Upon hearing these words, the dwarf skipped quickly out, and the Dryad entered the tree and pulled the door shut after her. "Now, then," she said to herself, "he can break off the key if he likes. It does not matter to me. Another will grow out next spring. And, although the good piper made me no promise, I know that when the warm days arrive next year, he will come and let me out again."

The Echo-dwarf did not stop to break the key of the tree. He was too happy to be released to think of anything else, and he hastened as fast as he could to his home on the rocky hillside.

The Dryad was not mistaken when she trusted in the piper. When the warm days came again, he went to the oak tree to let her out. But to his sorrow and surprise he found the great tree lying upon the ground. A winter storm had blown it down, and it lay with its trunk shattered and split. And what became of the Dryad, no one ever knew.

The Pied Piper of Hamelin

∿

Charles Marelles

A VERY LONG TIME ago the town of Hamelin in Germany was invaded by bands of rats, the like of which had never been seen before nor will ever be again.

They were great black creatures that ran boldly in broad daylight through the streets, and swarmed so, all over the houses, that people at last could not put their hand or foot down anywhere without touching one. When dressing in the morning they found them in their breeches and petticoats, in their pockets and in their boots; and when they wanted a morsel to eat, the voracious horde had swept away everything from cellar to garret. The night was even worse. As soon as the lights were out, these untiring nibblers set to work. And everywhere, in the ceilings, in the floors, in the cupboards, at the doors, there was a chase and a rummage, and so furious a noise of gimlets, pincers, and saws, that a deaf man could not have rested for one hour together.

Neither cats nor dogs, nor poison nor traps, nor prayers nor candles burnt to all the saints – nothing would do anything. The more they killed the more came. And the inhabitants of Hamelin began to go to the dogs (not that *they* were of much use), when one Friday there arrived in the town a man with a queer face, who played the bagpipes and sang this refrain:

"Qui vivra verra:
Le voilà,
Le preneur des rats."

He was a great gawky fellow, dry and bronzed, with a crooked nose, a long rat-tail moustache, and two great yellow piercing and mocking eyes, under a large felt hat set off by a scarlet cock's feather. He was dressed in a green jacket with a leather belt and red breeches, and on his feet were sandals fastened by thongs passed round his legs in the gipsy fashion.

That is how he may be seen to this day, painted on a window of the cathedral of Hamelin.

He stopped on the great market-place before the town hall, turned his back on the church and went on with his music, singing:

"Who lives shall see:
This is he,
The ratcatcher."

The town council had just assembled to consider once more this plague of Egypt, from which no one could save the town.

The stranger sent word to the councillors that, if they would make it worth his while, he would rid them of all their rats before night, down to the very last.

"Then he is a sorcerer!" cried the citizens with one voice; "we must beware of him."

The Town Councillor, who was considered clever, reassured them.

He said: "Sorcerer or no, if this bagpiper speaks the truth, it was he who sent us this horrible vermin that he wants to rid us of today for money. Well, we must learn to catch the devil in his own snares. You leave it to me."

"Leave it to the Town Councillor," said the citizens one to another.

And the stranger was brought before them.

"Before night," said he, "I shall have despatched all the rats in Hamelin if you will but pay me a *gros* a head."

"A *gros* a head!" cried the citizens, "but that will come to millions of florins!"

The Town Councillor simply shrugged his shoulders and said to the stranger:

"A bargain! To work; the rats will be paid one *gros* a head as you ask,"

The bagpiper announced that he would operate that very evening when the moon rose. He added that the inhabitants should at that hour leave the streets free, and content themselves with looking out of their windows at what was passing, and that it would be a pleasant spectacle. When the people of Hamelin heard of the bargain, they too exclaimed: "A *gros* a head! But this will cost us a deal of money!"

"Leave it to the Town Councillor," said the town council with a malicious air. And the good people of Hamelin repeated with their councillors, "Leave it to the Town Councillor."

Towards nine at night the bagpiper reappeared on the marketplace. He turned, as at first, his back to the church, and the moment the moon rose on the horizon, "Trarira, trari!" the bagpipes resounded.

It was first a slow, caressing sound, then more and more lively and urgent, and so sonorous and piercing that it penetrated as far as the farthest alleys and retreats of the town.

Soon, from the bottom of the cellars, the top of the garrets, from under all the furniture, from all the nooks and corners of the houses, out come the rats, search for the door, fling themselves into the street, and trip, trip, trip, begin to run in file towards the front of the town hall, so squeezed together that they cover the pavement like the waves of flooded torrent.

When the square was quite full the bagpiper faced about, and, still playing briskly, turned towards the river that runs at the foot of the walls of Hamelin.

Arrived there, he turned round; the rats were following.

"Hop! hop!" he cried, pointing with his finger to the middle of the stream, where the water whirled and was drawn down as if through a funnel. And hop! hop! Without hesitating, the rats took the leap, swam straight to the funnel, plunged in head foremost and disappeared.

The plunging continued thus without ceasing till midnight.

At last, dragging himself with difficulty, came a big rat, white with age, and stopped on the bank.

It was the king of the band.

"Are they all there, friend Blanchet?" asked the bagpiper.

"They are all there," replied friend Blanchet.

"And how many were they?"

"Nine hundred and ninety thousand, nine hundred and ninety-nine."

"Well reckoned?"

"Well reckoned."

"Then go and join them, old sire, and *au revoir*."

Then the old white rat sprang in his turn into the river, swam to the whirlpool and disappeared.

When the bagpiper had thus concluded his business he went to bed at his inn. And for the first time during three months the people of Hamelin slept quietly through the night.

The next morning, at nine o'clock, the bagpiper repaired to the town hall, where the town council awaited him.

"All your rats took a jump into the river yesterday," said he to the councillors, "and I guarantee that not one of them comes back. They were nine hundred and ninety thousand, nine hundred and ninety-nine, at one *gros* a head. Reckon!"

"Let us reckon the heads first. One *gros* a head is one head the *gros*. Where are the heads?"

The ratcatcher did not expect this treacherous stroke. He paled with anger and his eyes flashed fire.

"The heads!" cried he. "If you care about them, go and find them in the river."

"So," replied the Town Councillor, "you refuse to hold to the terms of your agreement? We ourselves could refuse you all payment. But you have been of use to us, and we will not let you go without a recompense," and he offered him fifty crowns.

"Keep your recompense for yourself," replied the ratcatcher proudly. "If you do not pay me I will be paid by your heirs."

Thereupon he pulled his hat down over his eyes, went hastily out of the hall, and left the town without speaking to a soul.

When the Hamelin people heard how the affair had ended they rubbed their hands, and, with no more scruple than their Town Councillor, they laughed over the ratcatcher, who, they said, was caught in his own trap. But what made them laugh above all was his threat of getting himself paid by their heirs. Ha! They wished that they only had such creditors for the rest of their lives.

Next day, which was a Sunday, they all went gaily to church, thinking that after Mass they would at last be able to eat some good thing that the rats had not tasted before them.

They never suspected the terrible surprise that awaited them on their return home. No children anywhere; they had all disappeared!

"Our children! Where are our poor children?" was the cry that was soon heard in all the streets.

Then through the east door of the town came three little boys, who cried and wept, and this is what they told:

While the parents were at church a wonderful music had resounded. Soon all the little boys and all the little girls that had been left at home had gone out, attracted by the magic sounds, and had rushed to the great market-place. There they found the ratcatcher playing his bagpipes at the same spot as the evening before. Then the stranger had begun to walk quickly, and they had followed, running, singing and dancing to the sound of the music, as far as the foot of the mountain which one sees on entering Hamelin. At their approach the mountain had opened a little, and the bagpiper had gone in with them, after which it had closed again. Only the three little ones who told the adventure had remained outside, as if by a miracle. One was bandy-legged and could not run fast enough; the other, who had left the house in haste, one foot shod the other bare, had hurt himself against a big stone and could not walk without difficulty; the third had arrived in time, but in hurrying to go in with the others had struck so violently against the wall of the mountain that he fell backwards at the moment it closed upon his comrades.

At this story the parents redoubled their lamentations. They ran with pikes and mattocks to the mountain, and searched till evening to find the opening by which their children had disappeared, without being able to find it. At last, the night falling, they returned desolate to Hamelin.

But the most unhappy of all was the Town Councillor, for he lost three little boys and two pretty little girls, and, to crown all, the people of Hamelin overwhelmed him with reproaches, forgetting that the evening before they had all agreed with him.

What had become of all these unfortunate children?

The parents always hoped they were not dead, and that the ratcatcher, who certainly must have come out of the mountain, would have taken them with him to his country. That is why for several years they sent in search of them to different countries, but no one ever came on the trace of the poor little ones.

It was not till much later that anything was to be heard of them.

About one hundred and fifty years after the event, when there was no longer one left of the fathers, mothers, brothers or sisters of that day, there arrived one evening in Hamelin some merchants of Bremen returning from the East, who asked to speak with the citizens. They told that they, in crossing Hungary, had sojourned in a mountainous country called Transylvania, where the inhabitants only spoke German, while all around them nothing was spoken but Hungarian. These people also declared that they came from Germany, but they did not know how they chanced to be in this strange country. "Now," said the merchants of Bremen, "these Germans cannot be other than the descendants of the lost children of Hamelin."

The people of Hamelin did not doubt it; and since that day they regard it as certain that the Transylvanians of Hungary are their country folk, whose ancestors, as children, were brought there by the ratcatcher. There are more difficult things to believe than that.

The Pot of Gold

～

Horace E. Scudder

Chrif begins the Search

ONCE UPON A TIME there stood by the roadside an old red house. In this house lived three people. They were an old grandmother; her grandchild, Rhoda; and a boy named Christopher. Christopher was no relation to Rhoda and her grandmother. He was called Chrif for short.

The grandmother earned her living by picking berries. Every day in fair weather she went to the pastures. But she did not take the children with her. They played at home.

Rhoda had a flower garden in an old boat. The boat was filled with earth. There grew larkspur and sweet-william. Rhoda loved her flowers and tended them faithfully.

Chrif did not care much for flowers. He preferred to sail boats. He would cut them out of wood with his jack-knife, and load them with stones and grass. Then he would send the boats down the little stream that flowed past the old red house.

"This ship is going to India," he would say to Rhoda. "She carries gold and will bring back pearls and rice."

"How much you know, Chrif," said Rhoda.

"I mean to go to India some day," said Chrif. "People ride on elephants there."

Rhoda would sail little twigs in the stream. Her boats were small, but they sometimes went farther than Chrif's. His were loaded so heavily that they often overturned.

One day the children were sailing boats when a thunder-storm arose. How fast the rain fell! And how fast they ran to the house!

"Poor Grandmother will be all wet!" said Rhoda. She and Chrif were watching the falling rain from the window.

Suddenly the sun came out. A little rain was still falling, but the children ran into the yard.

"Look, there's a rainbow!" cried Chrif. "What pretty colours! And how ugly our old red house looks! I wish I were where the rainbow is."

"I see just the colour of my larkspur in the rainbow," said Rhoda.

"O pooh!" said Chrif. "Only a flower! That's not much. Now, if I were only rich, I wouldn't stay here. I'd go off into the world. How grand it must be over there beyond the rainbow."

"One end is quite near us," said Rhoda.

"Are ye looking for a Pot of Gold, children?" said a voice behind them. It was the old broom-woman. She had a little house in the woods and sold brooms for a living.

"A Pot of Gold!" cried Chrif. "Where is it?"

"It's at the foot of the rainbow," said the broom-woman. "If ye get to the foot of the rainbow and then dig and dig, ye'll come to a Pot of Gold."

"Rhoda! Let's go quick!" said Chrif.

"No," said Rhoda, "I ought to weed my flowers."

"Ye must hurry," laughed the old broom-woman. "The rainbow won't stay for lazy folks."

"I'm off!" cried Chrif; and away he went in search of the Pot of Gold. Rhoda watched him out of sight. Then she turned to weed the boat-garden.

When her grandmother came from the berry pasture, Rhoda told her where Chrif had gone. "We shall all be rich when he comes back with his Pot of Gold," said the little girl.

"He will not find it," said the grandmother. Rhoda, however, was not so sure.

Chrif in the New Land

Chrif ran straight across the fields towards the glowing rainbow. One end of the lovely arch seemed to touch the top of a distant hill. Chrif climbed the hill, but the rainbow was no longer there. It rested on the far side of a valley. He hurried down the hill and into the valley. When he reached the spot where the end of the rainbow had rested, the rainbow was gone. Chrif could see it nowhere.

The lad stopped and looked around him. Not far away a flock of sheep were feeding. A shepherd-boy lay on the ground near them. He was reading a book.

Chrif crept to the shepherd-boy's side and read over his shoulder. This is what he read: "Beyond the setting of the sun lies the New Land. Here are mountains, forests, and mighty rivers. The sands of the streams are golden; the trees grow wonderful fruit; the mountains hide strange monsters. Upon a high pillar near the coast is the famous Pot of Gold."

"Oh, where is this country?" cried Chrif.

"Will you go?" asked Gavin, the shepherd-boy.

"Go! That I will," said Chrif. "The Pot of Gold is there, and that is what I have set out to find."

"Yes," said Gavin, "the Pot of Gold is there and many other things. I long to see them all. Let us hurry on our way."

The two boys first went through a forest. Then they came out upon the ocean side. The sun was setting in the sea. A path of gold lay across the water.

A gay ship was about to set sail. Her white canvas was spread; her oars were in place. Her deck was crowded with lads. They were all starting for the wonderful New Land across the sea.

Chrif and Gavin climbed on board and the ship bounded from the land.

On and on they went, straight into the sunset. The rowers sang as they worked. Gavin tried to read his book, but Chrif looked eagerly ahead. How he longed to see the new country to which they were going!

And very soon the New Land came in sight. Then a party landed; Chrif, Gavin, and a boy named Andy were among them.

They walked some distance and then night darkened down around them. The mountains looked cruel; the fields barren. "Let us return to the ship," said many.

But Chrif would not turn back. "I must find the Pot of Gold," he said, "it cannot now be far away." And Gavin and Andy went with him.

"I should like to dip my fingers into your Pot of Gold," said Andy.

"You shall have your share," said Chrif. "It is on the top of a pillar not far from the coast. If you'll stand below, I'll get on your shoulders, and then perhaps I can reach it."

"Only don't let it drop on my head," said Andy, with a laugh.

They walked along the shore in silence. After a time Chrif cried out with joy, "Here is a path leading into the woods. And I do believe I see the pillar!"

"Hurrah!" cried Andy. "Let's push on!"

And now the three stood at the foot of the pillar and looked up to the top. By the faint light of the moon they saw the Pot of Gold.

"Climb on Andy's shoulders, Gavin, and then I will stand on yours," said Chrif.

"I don't want the Pot of Gold," said Gavin. "I have seen it; that is enough. I will go to see the Magic Fountain." And Gavin turned into the forest.

The other two friends stood by the pillar. "I must have that Pot of Gold. I want it for Rhoda and the old grandmother."

As Chrif spoke, he looked at the pillar. Lo! a picture was on its side. He saw the old red house, the grandmother at the window, and Rhoda in the garden. Rhoda was watering the flowers in the dear old boat. Now and then she would turn her head and look up the road. She seemed hoping that Chrif would come.

The pillar and the Pot of Gold faded away; then the picture of home went too. Chrif was left in darkness.

Then Andy spoke. "Hark!" he whispered. "I hear something."

Chrif at the Palace

Chrif listened and he too heard distant music. Its notes were very sweet.

"Come, let us go where the music is!" said Andy.

Chrif and Andy made their way through the woods and entered a shining city. Every street was blazing with lights; the fronts of the houses were hung with lanterns; fireworks were being set off in the public squares. All the people wore their finest clothes.

"How gay they all are! I wonder why?" said Andy.

"Hush!" cried Chrif.

A man on a prancing horse had just come in sight. He reined in his horse and blew a horn. Then he cried with a loud voice these words: "This night there is a ball in the palace. All are welcome. The Pot of Gold will be given to the one with whom the Princess shall dance."

"Hurrah!" cried the people. "Hurrah! Hurrah!" cried Chrif, louder than them all.

When Chrif and Andy entered the palace, they saw the Princess upon her throne. Dancing was going on, but the Princess did not dance. She was waiting for the handsomest dancer. All who thought themselves good-looking stood in a row not far from the Princess. Each lad was trying to look handsomer than the others in the line.

Over the throne was a pearl clock. It was that kind of clock called a cuckoo clock. When the hours struck, a golden cuckoo would come out of a little door. He would cuckoo as many times as there were hours and then go back, shutting the door after him.

When Chrif and Andy entered the hall, the Princess saw them at once. "Those two are the handsomest of all," she thought, "and one of them is handsomer than the other."

She looked at Chrif again. Then she stepped down from the throne.

"Dance with me," she said, "and you shall have the Pot of Gold," and she held out her hand to Chrif.

"What was I to do with it?" asked Chrif. "Oh, I know. I was to take it home to Rhoda."

That moment the little bird burst open the pearl door. "Cuckoo! Cuckoo! Cuckoo!" he cried.

But to Chrif he seemed to say: "Rhoda sits by the window watching for Chrif. The flowers are dead in the boat-garden. 'Chrif will never come back,' says Grandmother, 'he cares nothing for us.'"

Again Chrif saw the beautiful hall and the Princess standing before him. Then, suddenly, the music grew harsh; the palace walls fell; the dancers were gone. Chrif was all alone.

Chrif and his Books

When day dawned, Chrif was walking over a wide plain. On the far side of the plain stood a ruined house. Between a row of poplar-trees a path led to the door.

Chrif knocked, but no one came. Then he pushed open the door and entered. An old man sat at a table. The table was covered with great books and many papers. Overhead a lamp burned dimly.

The old man was bent over the books. He seemed to study busily, but when Chrif went near, he saw that the old man was dead.

There were two doors to this room. One was the door by which

Chrif had entered. The other was opposite. This door was of stone. On it was written: "Behind this door is the Pot of Gold. To open you must first read the words written below."

The words written below were strange; the letters too were strange.

"These books may help me read the writing," thought Chrif. "This old man has spent his life in the search. Shall I be more successful, I wonder?"

Then he buried the old man, lighted the lamp, and read the books. Weeks passed and even months. Chrif ate little and slept less.

At last, one day, he lifted a shining face. 'I have found the secret!" he cried. "The letters are plain."

Then, stepping to the door, he read: "Knock and this door will open."

Chrif knocked once, and the door flew open. One shining spot he saw in the darkness. It was the Pot of Gold.

Chrif put out his hand to take it, when lo! burning words shone on its side. And Chrif read:

"I am the Pot of Gold; I can give thee all things save one. If thou hast me, thou canst not have that. Close thine eyes. Then, if thou choosest me, open them again."

Chrif closed his eyes. He saw the old red house dark and cold. No one lived there now. The boat-garden was hidden under the snow. Someone in white passed him by. She was weeping bitterly. "Rhoda!" he cried, and followed in her steps.

Suddenly a warm hand fell upon his shoulder.

"Chrif, dear Chrif!"

He opened his eyes, and O joy! Rhoda stood beside him.

Chrif's Return

"I have come to look for you," said Rhoda. "Why, Chrif, you have been gone three years!"

"Three years!" gasped Chrif.

"When Grandmother died, last winter, I was so lonely, I said, 'When spring comes I will find Chrif.'"

"Grandmother dead! Why, it was but yesterday that I left home!"

"Ah, no," answered Rhoda. And she looked at Chrif and smiled.

And so they came again to the old red house. There was the dear old boat-garden. Sweet-peas were in bloom and morning-glories climbed up the side of the house. It was very pleasant.

As they stood by the boat-garden, a voice called to them. The old broom-woman stood in the road.

"Have ye found the Pot of Gold?" she asked.

"No; but I have found something else far better!" said Chrif. "I have found home."

Princess Crystal; or,
The Hidden Treasure

❧

Isabel Bellerby

THERE WERE THE FOUR kings: the King of the North, the region of perpetual snow; the King of the South, where the sun shines all the year round; the King of the East, whence the cold winds blow; and the King of the West, where the gentle zephyrs breathe upon the flowers and coax them to open their petals while the rest of the world is still sleeping.

And there was the great Dragon, who lived on top of a high mountain in the centre of the universe. He could see everything that happened everywhere by means of his magic spectacles, which enabled him to look all ways at once, and to see through solid substances; but he could only see, not hear, for he was as deaf as a post.

Now the King of the North had a beautiful daughter called Crystal. Her eyes were bright like the stars; her hair was black like the sky at night; and her skin was as white as the snow which covered the ground outside the palace where she lived, which was built entirely of crystals clear as the clearest glass.

And the King of the South had a son who had been named Sunshine on account of his brightness and warmth of heart.

The King of the East had a son who, because he was always up early and was very industrious, had been given the name of Sunrise.

The King of the West also had a son, perhaps the handsomest of the three, and always magnificently dressed; but as it took him all day to make his toilette, so that he was never seen before evening, he received the name of Sunset.

All three Princes were in love with the Princess Crystal, each hoping to win her for his bride. When they had the chance they would go and peep at her as she wandered up and down in her glass palace. But she liked Prince Sunshine best, because he stayed longer than the others, and was always such excellent company. Prince Sunrise was too busy to be able to spare her more than half an hour or so: and Prince Sunset never came until she was getting too tired and sleepy to care to see him.

It was of no use, however, for her to hope that Sunshine would be her husband just because she happened to prefer him to the others. Her father – the stern, blusterous old King, with a beard made of icicles so long that it reached to his waist and kept his heart cold – declared that he had no patience for such nonsense as likes and dislikes; and one day he announced, far and wide, in a voice that was heard by the other three Kings, and which made the earth shake so that the great green Dragon immediately looked through his spectacles to see what was happening:

"He who would win my daughter must first bring me the casket containing the Hidden Treasure, which is concealed no man knows where!"

Of course the Dragon was none the wiser for looking through his spectacles, because the words – loud though they were – could not be heard by his deaf ears.

But the other Kings listened diligently; as did the young Princes. And poor Princess Crystal trembled in her beautiful palace lest Sunrise, who was always up so early, should find the treasure before Sunshine had a chance: she was not much afraid of the indolent Sunset, except that it might occur to him to look in some spot forgotten by his rivals.

Very early indeed on the following morning did Prince Sunrise set to work; he glided along the surface of the earth, keeping close to the ground in his anxiety not to miss a single square inch. He knew he was not first in the field; for the Northern King's proclamation had been made towards evening on the previous day, and Prince Sunset had bestirred himself for once, and had lingered about rather later than usual, being desirous of finding the treasure and winning the charming Princess.

But the early morning was passing, and very soon the cheery, indefatigable Sunshine had possession of the entire land, and flooded Crystal's palace with a look from his loving eyes which bade her not despair.

Then he talked to the trees and the green fields and the flowers, begging them to give up the secret in return for the warmth and gladness he shed so freely on them. But they were silent, except that the trees sighed their sorrow at not being able to help him, and the long grasses rustled a whispered regret, and the flowers bowed their heads in grief.

Not discouraged, however, Prince Sunshine went to the brooks and rivers, and asked their assistance. But they, too, were helpless. The brooks gurgled out great tears of woe, which rushed down to the rivers, and so overcame them – sorry as they were on account of their own inability to help – that they nearly overflowed their banks, and went tumbling into the sea, who, of course, wanted to know what was the matter: but, when told, all the sea could do was to thunder a loud and continuous "No!" on all its beaches. So Prince Sunshine had to pass on and seek help elsewhere.

He tried to make the great Dragon understand; but it could not hear him. Other animals could, though, and he went from one to another, as cheerful as ever, in spite of all the "Noes" he had met with: until, at last, he knew by the twittering of the birds that he was going to be successful.

"We go everywhere and learn most things," said the swallows, flying up and down in the air, full of excitement and joy at being able to reward their beloved Sunshine for all his kindness to them. "And we know this much, at any rate: the Hidden Treasure can only be found by he who looks at its hiding-place through the Dragon's magic spectacles."

Prince Sunshine exclaimed that he would go at once and borrow these wonderful spectacles; but a solemn-looking old owl spoke up:

"Be not in such a hurry, most noble Prince! The Dragon will

slay anyone — even so exalted a personage as yourself — who attempts to remove those spectacles while he is awake; and, as is well known, he never allows himself to sleep, for fear of losing some important sight."

"Then what is to be done?" asked the Prince, beginning to grow impatient at last, for the afternoon was now well advanced, and Prince Sunset would soon be on the war-path again.

A majestic eagle came swooping down from the clouds.

"There is only one thing in all the world," said he, "which can send the Dragon to sleep, and that is a caress from the hand of the Princess Crystal."

Sunshine waited to hear no more. Smiling his thanks, he hastened away to put his dear Crystal's love to the test. She had never yet ventured outside the covered gardens of her palace. Would she go with him now, and approach the great Dragon, and soothe its savage watchfulness into the necessary repose?

As he made the request, there stole into the Princess's cheeks the first faint tinge of colour that had ever been seen there.

"My robe is of snow," she faltered; "if I go outside these crystal walls into your radiant presence it will surely melt."

"You look as if you yourself would melt at my first caress, you beautiful, living snowflake," replied the Prince; "but have no fear; see, I have my own mantle ready to enfold you. Come, Princess, and trust yourself to me."

Then, for the first time in her life, Princess Crystal stole out of her palace, and was immediately wrapped in Prince Sunshine's warm mantle, which caused her to glow all over; her face grew quite rosy, and she looked more than usually lovely, so that the Prince longed to kiss her; but she was not won yet, and she might have been offended at his taking such a liberty.

Therefore, he had to be content to have her beside him in his golden chariot with the fiery horses, which flew through space so quickly that they soon stood on the high mountain, where the Dragon sat watching them through his spectacles, wondering what the Princess was doing so far from home, and what her father would think if he discovered her absence.

It was no use explaining matters to the Dragon, even had they wished to do so; but of course nothing was further from their intention.

Holding Prince Sunshine's hand to give her courage, the Princess approached the huge beast and timidly laid her fingers on his head.

"This is very nice and soothing," thought the Dragon, licking his lips; "very kind of her to come, I'm sure; but – dear me! – this won't do! I'm actually – going – to – sleep!"

He tried to rise, but the gentle hand prevented that. A sensation of drowsiness stole through all his veins, which would have been delightful but for his determination never to sleep. As it was, he opened his mouth to give a hiss that would surely have frightened the poor Princess out of her wits: but he fell asleep before he could so much as begin it: his mouth remained wide open: but his eyes closed, and his great head began to nod in a very funny manner.

Directly they were satisfied that he really slept, Prince Sunshine helped himself to the Dragon's spectacles, requesting the Princess not to remove her hand, lest the slumber should not last long enough for their purpose.

Then he put on the spectacles, and Princess Crystal exclaimed with fear and horror when – as though in result of his doing so – she saw her beloved Prince plunge his right hand into the Dragon's mouth.

Prince Sunshine had stood facing the huge beast as he transferred the spectacles to his own nose, and, naturally enough, the first thing he saw through them was the interior of the Dragon's mouth, with the tongue raised and shot forward in readiness for the hiss which sleep had intercepted; and under the tongue was the golden casket containing the Hidden Treasure!

The spectacles enabled the Prince to see through the cover; so he learned the secret at once, and knew why the King of the North was so anxious to possess himself of it, the great treasure being a pair of spectacles exactly like those hitherto always worn by the Dragon, and by him alone – which would keep the King informed of all that was going on in every corner of his kingdom, so that he could always punish or reward the right people and never make mistakes; also he could learn a great deal of his neighbours' affairs, which is pleasant, even to a King.

The Princess was overjoyed when she knew the casket was already found; she very nearly removed her hand in her eagerness to inspect it; but, fortunately, she remembered just in time, and kept quite still until Prince Sunshine had drawn his chariot so close that they could both get into it without moving out of reach of the Dragon's head.

Then, placing the spectacles, not in their accustomed place, but on the ground just beneath, and laying the golden casket on the Princess's lap, the Prince said, as he gathered up the reins:

"Now, my dearly beloved Crystal – really mine at last – take away your hand, and let us fly, without an instant's delay, to the Court of the King, your royal father."

It is well they had prepared for immediate departure. Directly the Princess's hand was raised from the Dragon's head his senses returned to him, and, finding his mouth open ready for hissing, he hissed with all his angry might, and looked about for his spectacles that he might pursue and slay those who had robbed him; for, of course, he missed the casket at once.

But he was a prisoner on that mountain and unable to leave it, though he flapped his great wings in terrible wrath when he saw the Prince and Princess, instead of driving down the miles and miles of mountainside as he had hoped, being carried by the fiery horses right through the air, where he could not reach them.

They only laughed when they heard the hiss and the noise made by the useless flapping of wings. Prince Sunshine urged on his willing steeds, and they arrived at the Court just as the King, Crystal's father, was going to dinner; and he was so delighted at having the treasure he had so long coveted, that he ordered the marriage to take place at once.

Prince Sunset called just in time to be best man, looking exceedingly gorgeous and handsome, though very disappointed to have lost the Princess: and the festivities were kept up all night, so that Prince Sunrise was able to offer his good wishes when he came early in the morning, flushed with the haste he had made to assure Prince Sunshine that he bore him no ill-will for having carried off the prize.

Princess Crystal never returned to her palace, except to peep at it occasionally. She liked going everywhere with her husband, who, she found, lived by no means an idle life, but went about doing good

– grumbled at sometimes, of course, for some people will grumble even at their best friend – but more generally loved and blessed by all who knew him.

Princess Sansu

∿

Tanith Lee

THE ONLY TROUBLE WITH Princess Sansu's hair was that it simply wasn't long enough. There was nothing else wrong. It was fine and shining, and a most beautiful golden colour, but it only reached to her waist. The King and Queen's other four daughters all had hair that reached to the back of their knees, and so did the Queen, and so did Sansu's grandmother.

Every morning the King would come into the dining room, and the Queen and the grandmother and the five Princesses would all sit down. The King would walk along behind their chairs and see that they were all sitting on their hair, except, that was, for poor Sansu. Then he would take out his tape-measure, measure her hair, sigh, put it back again, and then sit down and push away his plate of bacon and eggs.

"No," he would say, in a sad voice. "I'm not very hungry today."

Sansu privately thought it was all a bit silly. She didn't like being a disappointment to her parents, but really there didn't seem to be any hope. At one time she'd used to tie herself to the top of the banisters with three or four old woolly socks knotted together, and ask her two pet dogs to take half the ends of her hair each in their mouths, and pull very hard. She had thought it might stretch, but it didn't. What actually happened was that the banister post, eventually weakened by so much pulling, came loose, and Sansu and the dogs fell over, and rolled all the way downstairs, all jumbled up in the hair and the three or four woolly socks.

The King said please, would she not do it again, as it gave him a headache. Sansu promised she wouldn't.

One morning, however, the King, instead of coming into breakfast looking sad, ran in smiling.

"Dear Sansu," he said, "our troubles are at an end. I have written to the witch who lives over the mountain about your hair, and she says she can do something for us. She will be here in time for tea."

Unfortunately, this was the worst thing he could have done. The King didn't know, but this witch was a dreadful old thing called Night-Mary, who never did anything good if she could help it. The trouble was that ever since she could remember she had been trying to win the Best Bad Witch of the Year Award. To get first prize you not only had to do something really awful, but something which had never been done before. This was pretty difficult. Every year Night-Mary had rushed around turning people into frogs and pillars of rock, or getting princesses to fall into hundred-year sleeps, only to find that it had already been done. But this year she was determined to win. She had printed a big red notice which read:

NIGHT-MARY
FOR BEST BAD
WITCH OF THE YEAR

and pinned it up in her mountain cave, facing her bed, where she could see it the moment she woke up.

When Night-Mary got the King's letter about Sansu's hair she had a marvellous idea, so she kicked an old raven out of bed and made it fly to the King, and say she would be on her way at once. Then she put on her black witch's robe – she usually wore an old dressing-gown and an apron about the cave – and her witch's hat, and jumped on her flying crocodile. It wasn't a real crocodile; it was made of magic cardboard, had big wings, and a tail that occasionally fell off. Sometimes a real flying crocodile would go past and laugh and make the poor thing terribly embarrassed.

"Well," said Night-Mary, as they flew over Sansu's father's kingdom, "what a pleasant spot, just by the sea. Couldn't be better." And she gave the cardboard crocodile a kick because she was pleased. The crocodile snivelled.

The King and the Queen and the five Princesses and their grandmother and the two pet dogs were all outside in the palace garden having tea when the witch flew down. The moment she got off the cardboard crocodile it ran up to the table and started gobbling up the fruit salad and cream. Night-Mary never gave it anything nice to eat. Everyone jumped up and screamed, and Night-Mary gave it a good kick. It went off and sat under an elm tree with its back to them.

"Do take a seat, madam," said the King. "I'm afraid I can't offer you any tea." The crocodile had upset the tea-pot. "Or any lemonade, either," he added. It had upset that too.

"Let's get down to business," said Night-Mary. "Which one is Sansu?"

Sansu thought the witch was rather rude, but she came and stood in front of her and said: "I am."

"Good, good," said Night-Mary. "We'll get started at once, then."

She took out some red chalk and drew a nasty, messy circle on the King's lawn, and made Sansu stand in the middle of it. Then she threw coloured powders about, most of which fell on the sandwiches, and said little pieces of poetry, such as:

> "Griddle me riddle and fiddle de dee,
> Oceans of porridge run down to the sea,"

and:

> "Hair-em, scare-em, give 'em a fright,
> Measles by day and mumps at night."

None of these sounded either very sensible or very nice, but Night-Mary seemed pleased. Eventually she produced a dusty,

sticky-looking wand, wiped it on the King's tablecloth, and hit
Sansu on the head with it. There was a flash of gold lightning.

"There!" cried Night-Mary. Then she hugged herself, and chortled
merrily, "Who's going to be Best Bad Witch of the Year?"

"Er," began the King rather nervously, "will Sansu's hair
grow now?"

"Oh, yes!" cried Night-Mary. "And so fast it won't know itself."
Then her face took on a really unpleasant look, and she said, "It will
grow and grow and grow, and nothing can stop it, and the moment
it touches the ground – " She paused dramatically.

"Yes?" everyone asked anxiously.

"A great tidal wave will sweep in from the sea, and cover your
kingdom," Night-Mary finished.

"Oh!" cried the Queen, turning pale.

Sansu's two dogs ran into the palace to pack their dog-biscuits
and bones in waterproof bags.

"This is disgraceful," declared the King.

"Isn't it?" agreed Night-Mary happily.

"I shall cut Sansu's hair before it reaches the ground," said Sansu's
grandmother, but that was no good either.

"You'll find nothing can cut through Sansu's hair," said the
witch. "I've put a spell on it. Try if you like."

So the King ran hurriedly indoors, colliding with the two dogs,
who were digging up their last bones from the rose-beds, and got a
pair of scissors. Everyone tried to cut Sansu's thick hair: the King,
the Queen, the grandmother, and the four Princesses, but nobody
could. The scissor-blades seemed to go through, but somehow
they didn't.

"Isn't there anything that will do it?" cried the King.

"Oh, yes," said the witch. "I've got a pair of magic scissors at
home. They're the only pair I've got, but they can cut through
anything. They'd do it, and what's more, if you cut the hair with
them, it would go back to normal and stop growing. But you won't
be able to get at those. They're in my cave, in a magic box, and only
I know the right spell to open it." So saying, with a nasty laugh, she
jumped on to the cardboard crocodile and they rose into the sky.

"Whatever shall we do?" cried the King. Then he noticed that

Sansu's golden hair was already growing fast, and had nearly reached her ankles. "Get up on the table, dear," he said hastily.

Sansu did, and soon they had put a chair on the table, and she had to stand on that.

It really was an awful situation.

Soon Sansu was standing on three chairs on top of four tables, and her hair was growing all the time. And then the sun sank and it began to get cold.

"There's no help for it," said Sansu's grandmother, who was a practical old lady. "Sansu will have to go into the tower at the bottom of the garden."

The tower was very tall, with an outside stone staircase leading up to a little round room in the top. It was damp and draughty, and the roof had blown away long ago. Still, it couldn't be helped.

The grandmother and the Princesses formed a line and took hold of Sansu's hair and held it very carefully above the ground, while the King lifted her down. Still holding it, like a sort of train, they followed Sansu to the tower and up the stairs. In the room, they let it fall on the floor, but it soon piled up, and had to be hung out of a window.

Meanwhile the Queen had hurriedly got together as many quilts and shawls and hot-water bottles as she could, and came and wrapped Sansu up in them. Then everyone except Sansu went down the stairs again and looked at the hair hanging out of the window.

"By morning it will be at least halfway down," said the King worriedly.

"Well," said the grandmother, "you'll just have to get a team of men together to make a wooden section to fit on top of the tower, and some more stairs. Sansu will go and sit in that, and then they will make another one to fit on top of the first one, and so on. Sansu will just keep going upstairs until we think of something else."

And so this was what they did.

Poor Sansu!

All day long the garden was full of the sound of men hammering together the next section of the tower, and grumbling, but at night it got dreadfully quiet and lonely. The King or the Queen or one of

Sansu's sisters were continually running up and down the stairs. At dinnertime the King brought up her dinner, but it was always cold by the time he reached the tower room.

Soon Sansu could see over the tops of the trees and out to sea. The sailors thought the tower was a funny sort of new lighthouse, and couldn't understand why there was no light in it. The birds who lived in the elms and oaks round the tower wrote a rude letter to the King, complaining that since it had got so tall it shut the sun out of their nests, and an elderly crow, who lived in the tower itself, wrote a worse letter, saying he had not asked for a lodger, and he was going to complain to somebody about it.

The King had messengers ride around the land to see if anyone had any bright ideas about what they could do, but no one had.

It rained, and the wooden roof leaked, and Sansu's two dogs, who always tried to get up to see her at least once a week (it took them almost a week to get up and down the stairs), brought her an umbrella to sit under.

Sansu, meanwhile, was racking her brains for a way to get out of the tower. She'd been very good about the whole thing, but it really was a bit much to expect her to stay up there for ever. She tried to talk it over with the crow, but it rudely told her that lodgers were bad enough, but noisy lodgers were intolerable. So she had to think in silence.

And the tower grew and grew. Soon Sansu could see the clouds outside the window.

Then one morning Sansu was woken up by the most awful crash.

"Must you make such a din?" complained the crow.

"It wasn't me," said Sansu. "And someone is pulling my hair."

"Of course it was, and of course there isn't," said the crow. "Noisy lodgers are intolerable, but noisy lodgers who tell lies are even worse," and it fluffed out its feathers.

Just then an angry face with a long grey beard and bushy eyebrows appeared at the window.

"I would like you to know, madam," said the face to Sansu, "that I am Wizard Busy, and I've just had a nasty accident with your beastly tower. Your tower is a public menace, madam. It's too tall, and you can't see it through the cloud. I have just driven my winged chariot right slap bang into it, and now both it and I are tangled up in all this hair you have so inconsiderately hung out of your window."

Sansu apologized and, going out on to the staircase, she managed to untangle the wizard, who in turn untangled the chariot. The wizard still seemed so annoyed that Sansu gave him some lemonade, and explained to him all about the tower, and how her hair kept on growing, and the dreadful witch, Night-Mary. Finally she added, rather wistfully: "I suppose you can't think of any way for me to stop it growing and get it back to normal, so that I can come down?"

"No," admitted the wizard, "I can't. As Night-Mary said, the only way to do that is to cut it with her magic scissors. *Then* it will go back to its normal length, and not otherwise. But," he added, "I can tell you why Night-Mary did it."

And he explained about the Best Bad Witch of the Year Competition.

"And now," he finished, "I expect Night-Mary is sitting in her cave, waiting for someone to come along and say she's won, and give her first prize. Only she hasn't, and they won't, because your hair hasn't touched the ground yet, and the tidal wave hasn't happened, after all. Well, well, must dash off now." And off he rode.

And that was when Sansu suddenly thought of an idea. She took the horn she had to blow whenever she wanted anything, and blew it with all her might. The crow clapped its wings over its ears and scowled.

A few hours later, when everybody had reached the top of the tower, Sansu told them what she was going to do.

The first thing Sansu did was to ask the King to get everyone in the kingdom to come to the tower, and then spread out in a huge chain. This started at the foot of the staircase and stretched across the garden, out into the town, along the beach to the outskirts of a big wood, and then back from the wood to the beach to the town, from the town to the palace and across the gardens to the foot of the tower again.

Sansu dressed herself in a very old smock with the hood dyed black, a black pointed witch's hat made of cardboard, a nasty false nose, and a pair of thick spectacles. Her hair was hidden under the hat, the hood and the smock, and appeared again at the bottom like a silly sort of golden tail.

Next she picked up a large brown paper parcel and tucked it under one arm.

Then she came out of her room and stepped slowly down the staircase, lowering her golden hair ahead of her. As soon as this got near enough, the first person in the chain grabbed it and, as more of it cascaded downwards, he passed his bit to the next person and held the new lot. In this way the hair was passed right along the chain, and when it came to the very last pair of hands, which happened to be those of an old blacksmith in a temper, Sansu was at the bottom of the tower, and took the final hand-over herself, which was the very ends of her hair, from the blacksmith, with some difficulty, as he didn't want to let go. In no place did the hair touch the ground.

"Now," said Sansu, "we must set out for the mountain." But everyone began to ask where was the Princess, and she had quite a job explaining that she was in disguise.

When she had eventually convinced everybody that she really *was* the Princess, and all the children who were frightened had stopped crying, they set out.

The journey to the mountain took a long time, but the people had brought plenty of food with them. Of course, Sansu's hair was still growing, but whenever it got too near the ground, somebody would wind it round and round himself to hold it up a bit higher. This worked very well, except that the women kept losing their knitting in it, and several birds flew down and built their nests in it, and a very small mouse, called Cuthbert, somehow got caught up in it and couldn't find the way out. He later wrote a book about his experiences, from which it was quite clear that he thought Sansu's hair was a cornfield.

Anyway, somehow or other, the chain made its way up the mountain, Sansu leading them in her black hat, and false nose and spectacles, still carrying the parcel under her arm and the ends of her hair in the other hand.

It was dusk when they came to the edge of a little wood and saw Night-Mary's cave in the mountain-face just in front of them. Sansu asked everybody to be very quiet, and then she took the ends of her long, long, long hair, plaited them into four thick plaits, and tied them round the large brown paper parcel. She did them up with some very complicated, awkward knots, and then asked the nearest people to unwind themselves a little, and as they did, she was able to go forward until she reached the cave mouth.

She knocked on the door.

"Go away!" said a bad-tempered voice from inside the cave. Night-Mary was feeling very angry that she hadn't heard about winning the Best Bad Witch Award yet.

"Night-Mary," said Sansu, in a funny cracked voice, rather like Night-Mary's own, "do let me in. I've got something for you."

Night-Mary couldn't ignore that. She flung open the cave door at once.

"May I congratulate you," croaked Sansu, "on being this year's Best Bad Witch. Here is your prize." And she held out the brown paper parcel, tied up with her own hair. Her smock hid the rest of the hair, and it was very dark in the cave.

"I'll hold it for you, dear," rasped Sansu, "while you undo the string."

Night-Mary did her best. She fumbled and scrabbled at the knots, but in vain.

"Bother this string," she said at last. "I'll have to cut it. What was that?" she added. "I thought I heard a baby crying." And she peered out of the cave, but it was so dark she couldn't see anything, even though there seemed to be a lot more trees about than she remembered. She was too excited to worry, however. "I'll just get my magic scissors," she told Sansu, and she turned to a cupboard and took out a big black box. She threw some pink powder at it, and yelled:

> "*Darned socks, hollyhocks,*
> *Spring locks, open box.*"

The box opened, Night-Mary pulled out the magic scissors, and the next moment she had cut through all four of Sansu's plaits.

At once a great cheer went up from the wood.

Sansu's hair had vanished completely, except for her own golden curls which hung to her waist. Out of the hair which had vanished had fallen knitting and nests and a lot of birds and paper bags and some teaspoons and Cuthbert.

Sansu took off the false nose and spectacles, and the hat and the hood, looked Night-Mary in the eye, and cried: "Boo!"

The witch began to threaten all sorts of nasty things, but the old blacksmith, who was still in a bad temper, chased her back into the cave, and she shut and bolted the door.

Just then the cardboard crocodile, who had been hiding in some bushes, came out and begged Sansu to take it with her.

"The witch has always been unbearable," it said, "but now I don't know what she'll do."

So Sansu rode back to the palace on it, and never kicked it once.

"Well," said the King when she got home, "I'm glad all that's over; and I shan't mind your hair being too short any more. I won't ever measure it again."

But Sansu had her own ideas. The cardboard crocodile had convinced her that she ought to go to witch-school, and then she might be able to win the Best Good Witch of the Year Award, or something like that. She rode off on the crocodile a few days later with the two pet dogs, who had decided to go to witch-school, too.

Everyone missed her very much, and the old crow left the tower, and insisted on living with the King and Queen. It confessed that unasked-for, noisy lodgers who told lies were better than no lodgers at all.

The Rat that Could Speak

❧

Charles Dickens

THERE WAS ONCE A shipwright, and he wrought in a Government Yard, and his name was Chips. And his father's name before him was Chips, and *his* father's name before *him* was Chips, and they were all Chipses. And Chips the father had sold himself to the Devil for an iron pot and a bushel of tenpenny nails and half a ton of copper and a rat that could speak; and Chips the grandfather had sold himself to the Devil for an iron pot and a bushel of tenpenny nails and a half a ton of copper and a rat that could speak; and Chips the great-grandfather had disposed of himself in the same direction on the same terms; and the bargain had run in the family for a long long time. So, one day, when young Chips was at work in the dock slip all alone, down in the dark hold of an old Seventy-four that was hauled up for repairs, the Devil presented himself, and remarked:

> A Lemon has pips,
> And a Yard has ships,
> And *I*'ll have Chips!

Chips looked up when he heard the words, and there he saw the Devil with saucer eyes that squinted. And whenever he winked his eyes showers of blue sparks came out, and his eyelashes made a clattering like flints and steels striking lights. And hanging over one of his arms by the handle was an iron pot, and under that arm was a bushel of tenpenny nails, and under his other arm was half a ton of copper, and sitting on one of his shoulders was a rat that could speak. So, the Devil said again:

A Lemon has pips,
And a Yard has ships,
And *I*'ll have Chips!

So, Chips answered never a word, but went on with his work. "What are you doing, Chips?" said the rat that could speak. "I am putting in new planks where you and your gang have eaten old away," said Chips.

"But we'll eat them too," said the rat that could speak; "and we'll let in the water and drown the crew, and we'll eat them too."

Chips, being only a shipwright, and not a man-of-war's man, said, "You are welcome to it." But he couldn't keep his eyes off the half a ton of copper or the bushel of tenpenny nails; for nails and copper are a shipwright's sweethearts, and shipwrights will run away with them whenever they can.

So, the Devil said, "I see what you are looking at, Chips. You had better strike the bargain. You know the terms. Your father before you was well acquainted with them, and so were your grandfather and great-grandfather before him."

Says Chips, "I like the copper, and I like the nails, and I don't mind the pot, but I don't like the rat."

Says the Devil, fiercely, "You can't have the metal without him – and *he's* a curiosity. I'm going."

Chips, afraid of losing the half a ton of copper and the bushel of nails, then said, "Give us hold!" So, he got the copper and the nails and the pot and the rat that could speak, and the Devil vanished.

Chips sold the copper, and he sold the nails, and he would have sold the pot; but whenever he offered it for sale the rat was in it, and the dealers dropped it, and would have nothing to say to the bargain. So, Chips resolved to kill the rat, and, being at work in the Yard one day with a great kettle of hot pitch on one side of him and the iron pot with the rat in it on the other, he turned the scalding pitch into the pot, and filled it full. Then he kept his eye upon it till it cooled and hardened, and then he let it stand for twenty days, and then he heated the pitch again and turned it back into the kettle, and then he sank the pot in water for twenty days more, and then he got the smelters to put it in the furnace for twenty days more, and then they gave it him out, red-hot, and looking like red-hot glass instead of iron – yet there was the rat in it, just the same as ever! And it said with a jeer:

> A Lemon has pips,
> And a Yard has ships,
> And *I*'ll have Chips!

Now, as the rat leaped out of the pot when it had spoken, and made off, Chips began to hope that it wouldn't keep its word. But, a terrible thing happened next day. For, when dinner time came, and the dock bell rang to strike work, he put his rule into the long pocket at the side of his trousers, and there he found a rat – not that rat, but another rat. And in his hat, he found another; and in his pocket handkerchief, another. And from that time he found himself so frightfully intimate with all the rats in the Yard that they climbed up his legs when he was at work, and sat on his tools while he used them. And they could all speak to one another, and he understood what they said. And they got into his lodging, and into his bed, and into his teapot, and into his beer, and into his boots. And he was going to be married to a corn chandler's daughter; and when he gave her a workbox he had himself made for her, a rat jumped out of it; and when he put his arm round her waist, a rat clung about her; so the marriage was broken off, though the banns were already twice put up – which the parish clerk well remembers, for, as he handed the book to the clergyman for the second time of asking, a large fat rat ran over the leaf.

You may believe that all this was very terrible for Chips; but even all this was not the worst. He knew, besides, what the rats were doing, wherever they were. So, sometimes he would cry aloud, when he was at his club at night, "Oh! Keep the rats out of the convicts' burying ground! Don't let them do that!" Or, "There's one of them at the cheese downstairs!" Or, "There's two of them smelling at the baby

in the garret!" Or, other things of that sort. At last, he was voted mad, and lost his work in the Yard, and could get no other work. But, King George wanted men, so before very long he got pressed for a sailor. And so he was taken off in a boat one evening to his ship, lying at Spithead, ready to sail. And so the first thing he made out in her as he got near her, was the figure-head of the old Seventy-four, where he had seen the Devil. She was called the *Argonaut*, and they rowed right under the bowsprit where the figurehead of the *Argonaut*, with a sheepskin in his hand and a blue gown on, was looking out to sea; and sitting staring on his forehead was the rat who could speak, and his exact words were these: "Chips ahoy! Old boy! We've pretty well eaten them too, and we'll drown the crew, and will eat them too!"

The ship was bound for the Indies; and if you don't know where that is, you ought to, and angels will never love you. The ship set sail that very night, and she sailed, and sailed, and sailed. Chips's feelings were dreadful. Nothing ever equalled his terrors. No wonder. At last, one day he asked leave to speak to the Admiral. The Admiral giv' leave. Chips went down on his knees in the Great State Cabin. "Your Honour, unless your Honour, without a moment's loss of time, makes sail for the nearest shore, this is a doomed ship, and her name is the Coffin!"

"Young man, your words are a madman's words."

"Your Honour, no; they are nibbling us away."

"They?"

"Your Honour, them dreadful rats. Dust and hollowness where solid oak ought to be! Rats nibbling a grave for every man on board! Oh! Does your Honour love your lady and your pretty children?"

"Yes, my man, to be sure."

"Then, for God's sake, make for the nearest shore, for at this present moment the rats are all stopping in their work, and are all looking straight towards you with bare teeth, and are all saying to one another that you shall never, never, never, never, see your lady and your children more."

"My poor fellow, you are a case for the doctor. Sentry, take this man!"

So, he was bled and he was blistered, and he was this and that, for six whole days and nights. So, then he again asked leave to speak to the Admiral. The Admiral giv' leave. He went down on his knees in the Great State Cabin. "Now, Admiral, you must die! You took no warning; you must die! The rats are never wrong in their calculations, and they make out that they'll be through at twelve tonight. So, you must die! With me and all the rest!"

And so at twelve o'clock there was a great leak reported in the ship, and a torrent of water rushed in and nothing could stop it, and they all went down, every living soul. And what the rats – being water rats – left of Chips, at last floated to shore, and sitting on him was an immense overgrown rat, laughing, that dived when the corpse touched the beach and never came up. And there was a deal of seaweed on the remains. And if you get thirteen bits of seaweed,

and dry them and burn them in the fire, they will go off like in these
thirteen words as plain as plain can be:

> A Lemon has pips,
> And a Yard has ships,
> And *I*'ve got Chips!

Rumpelstiltskin

❧

The Brothers Grimm

THERE WAS ONCE A miller who was very poor, but he had a beautiful daughter. Now, it happened that he came to speak to the King, and, to give himself importance, he said to him, "I have a daughter who can spin straw into gold."

The King said to the miller, "That is a talent that pleases me well; if she be as skilful as you say, bring her tomorrow to the palace, and I will put her to the proof."

When the maiden was brought to him, he led her to a room full of straw, gave her a wheel and spindle, and said, "Now set to work, and if by the morrow this straw be not spun into gold, you shall die." He locked the door, and left the maiden alone.

The poor girl sat down disconsolate, and could not for her life think what she was to do; for she knew not – how could she? – the way to spin straw into gold; and her distress increased so much that at last she began to weep. All at once the door opened, and a little man entered and said, "Good evening, my pretty miller's daughter; why are you weeping so bitterly?"

"Ah!" answered the maiden. "I must spin straw into gold, and know not how to do it."

The little man said, "What will you give me if I do it for you?"

"My neckerchief," said the maiden.

He took the kerchief, sat down before the wheel, and grind, grind, grind – three times did he grind – and the spindle was full:

384

then he put another thread on, and grind, grind, grind, the second was full; so he spun on till morning; when all the straw was spun, and all the spindles were full of gold.

The King came at sunrise, and was greatly astonished and overjoyed at the sight; but it only made his heart the more greedy of gold. He put the miller's daughter into another much larger room, full of straw, and ordered her to spin it all in one night, if life were dear to her. The poor helpless maiden began to weep, when once more the door flew open, the little man appeared, and said, "What will you give me if I spin this straw into gold?"

"My ring from my finger," answered the maiden.

The little man took the ring, began to turn the wheel, and, by the morning, all the straw was spun into shining gold.

The King was highly delighted when he saw it, but was not yet satisfied with the quantity of gold; so he put the damsel into a still larger room full of straw, and said, "Spin this during the night; and if you do it you shall be my wife." "For," he thought, "if she's only a miller's daughter, I shall never find a richer wife in the whole world."

As soon as the damsel was alone the little man came the third time and said, "What will you give me if I again spin all this straw for you?"

"I have nothing more to give you," answered the girl.

"Then promise, if you become queen, to give me your first child."

"Who knows how that may be, or how things may turn out between now and then?" thought the girl, but in her perplexity she could not help herself: so she promised the little man what he desired, and he spun all the straw into gold.

When the King came in the morning, and saw that his orders had been obeyed, he married the maiden, and the beautiful miller's daughter became a queen. After a year had passed she brought a lovely baby into the world, but quite forgot the little man, till he walked suddenly into her chamber, and said, "Give me what you promised me." The Queen was frightened, and offered the dwarf all the riches of the kingdom if he would only leave her her child; but he answered, "No; something living is dearer to me than all the treasures of the world."

Then the Queen began to grieve and to weep so bitterly that the little man took pity upon her and said, "I will give you three days; if in that time you can find out my name, you shall keep the child."

All night long the Queen thought over every name she had ever heard, and sent a messenger through the kingdom to enquire what names were usually given to people in that country. When, next day, the little man came again, she began with Caspar, Melchior, Balthazar, and repeated, each after each, all the names she knew or had heard of; but at each one the little man said, "That is not my name."

The second day she again sent round about in all directions, to ask how the people were called, and repeated to the little man the strangest names she could hear of or imagine: to each he answered always, "That is not my name."

The third day the messenger returned and said: "I have not been able to find a single new name; but as I came over a high mountain by a wood, where the fox and the hare bid each other goodnight, I saw a little house, and before the house was burning a little fire, and round the fire danced a very funny little man, who hopped upon one leg, and cried out:

> "Today I brew, tomorrow I bake,
> Next day the Queen's child I shall take;
> How glad I am that nobody knows
> My name is Rumpelstiltskin!"

You may guess how joyful the Queen was at hearing this; and when, soon after, the little man entered and said, "Queen, what is my name?" she asked him mischievously: "Is your name Kunz?"

"No."

"Is your name Carl?"

"No."

"Are you not sometimes called Rumpelstiltskin?"

"A witch has told you that – a witch has told you!" shrieked the poor little man, and stamped so furiously with his right foot that it sunk into the earth up to the hip; then he seized his left foot with both hands with such violence that he tore himself right in two.

The Seekers

❧

H. E. Bates

I

ON A CERTAIN NIGHT when the sky was as black as if the moon had gone into mourning for some lost star, a little swallow, with a sudden, despairing burst of wings, flew to the top of a great hill and settled there with a sigh. Then, after looking over the dark masses of land ahead, it rose upward again, twittered brightly and called down the hill: "Here is a land which I never remember seeing before! Oh! come quickly!"

This it called several times before receiving an answer, which when it came was as faint as if its speaker were dying and no more than a brief, "In a little while, swallow, in a little while."

To which the swallow replied insistently: "But, Prince, this is a discovery most wonderful! Oh! come quickly!"

But it was a long time before there crawled over the edge of the cliff a young man, shabbily dressed and looking as if he had not slept for many nights, and whose eyes shone with tiredness as he searched the sky for the restless swallow.

Unable to find it he called it feebly, at which it settled on his breast as he lay staring up at the sky.

"Prince, oh, Happy Prince!" it whispered to him. "Cannot you see that this is a new land, a land we have never seen before? Let us make haste and go down to it."

The Prince smiled.

"I have no strength," he said. "I could no more go down this hill than I could fly as you do."

"But, oh, master! It may be a rich land, or a beautiful one!" The swallow touched the face of the Prince. "We must go," it said earnestly, "we must go. Something tells me that there we should never be tired again."

"But I am tired now," replied the man – "so tired it seems to me that I am going to be tired for ever."

"Do you mean you are tired of wandering?"

"Yes, of wandering. Since they cast me out of my own town I have been a little wearier every day."

The swallow pressed its breast against the Prince's throat, and in the deep silence whispered: "But already the air is sweeter and fresher. Come down!"

The Prince, however, shook his head.

"I must sleep," he muttered, closing his eyes.

Suddenly, however, he opened them again, very bright, as if he had dreamed happily, and, taking the swallow into his hands, said: "But you can go. In a little while you could find out everything."

The swallow struggled with joy.

"I will go," it told him, "and you may sleep!"

And, breaking from the Prince's hold, it cut with its white bosom into the dark air and flew madly away, calling "Adieu! Adieu!"

The prince, however, neither heard nor spoke, for he was already asleep.

II

The swallow flew swiftly and with a new vigour. For some time he travelled far above the land, as if afraid of some danger lurking in its darkness, but by and by found that the hills were so near to him as almost to touch his breast. Then he found they were smooth, and not only smooth but warm; but he did not descend, and flying quickly he passed over lakes where people were singing and weeping on the white shores. Beyond these the hills grew more gigantic, stretching out into terrible darkness, so that the swallow became afraid and flew faster and faster, searching for the faintest spot of light in the land beneath.

At last he saw what looked to him like two little lamps set in the hills to guide him, and, descending, settled on a sharp ridge between them, wondering who had set them there.

But as he sat there they went out, then as suddenly shone again, brighter than ever. He trembled. The next moment, as if to show him that he was not alone in his trembling, the whole mountain shook beneath his feet. Somewhere afar off a dark shape explored the air and disappeared again, while beneath his feet was set up a great growl that shot him fearfully into the sky.

From there he looked down on what he had thought were hills, but which he now knew was some sleeping giant.

Then the swallow knew that he must have alighted on the nose of a giant in the Valley of Giants (of which his mother had told him) and had mistaken his eyes for lamps.

As he continued his journey it grew colder – though it might have been fear which chilled him – and he began to wish for the warm hand of the Prince he had left on the hill behind. Yet he dare not fly low, because of the giant he had disturbed and the wolves which he now heard barking across the valleys. So he turned his course slightly towards his left leg.

Almost at once the air grew warmer. The swallow flew on in comfort. The wind no longer dug its cold nails into his feathers. But suddenly, with a burst of heat like that when an oven is opened, he found himself over a land of great fires which cast their orange reflections up into his face, the heat from whose flames scorched his feet and singed his precious wings.

Then the swallow knew that he must be passing over the Valley of Fire (about which his mother had warned him), and, with his feet tucked as close to him as possible, flew on and on, scarcely aware of pain and still less aware of time, so that he did not know how long had passed since he had said "Adieu" to the Prince on the mountain.

III

So the swallow came to where he could hear the sea complaining as its own waves tangled themselves up with each other, and could see the great Beacons reflected in its water.

And that night (though he could not of course know it) he must have passed over the mouth of the Dream River, near the Castle of Seven Towers, and across the wood of witches, by Castle Warlock and the Valley of Dragons, where the air became hot again, and over the strange places where the Rocs build their dark enormous nests – for only by passing that way could he have come to where the cliffs of Diamond glisten in the hard morning sun.

It was actually a little farther on from there that he at last alighted – for the first time since he had perched between the giant's eyes – and looked about him.

The place he had chosen was a grassy cliff, cut with little holes like caves. From some of these, before long, one or two little men appeared, scratching their long, untidy beards with wakefulness and stretching their sleepy arms to the sun. Never had the swallow seen men so small; and he was puzzled – indeed puzzled enough to ask: "Can you tell me who you are – and where I am?"

In answer, and at the same time tossing his beard, as if to keep all intruders at a distance, the little man cried: "Don't you know by this time that you are in Fairyland?" He laughed. "Why! – you must know – I can see through your wings. Your wings have the fairy look about them and are like gossamer!"

At which the swallow looked at his wings and felt a new joy, for he could certainly see the green earth through them. But all he could say was: "So this is Fairyland!"

"Yes!" replied the dwarf. "And if you doubt me fly on, over the Great Wall and the forests until you come to the sea again." And with what was for him a majestic gesture he waved his hand to west of where the moon lay invisible and disappeared.

Surprised, but joyful too, the swallow flew on over the Great Wall of which the dwarf had spoken; and in a moment or two he was able to see it, glinting like a great curved shell in the morning sun. And he flew on more swiftly than ever as the sun climbed the sky.

That day he saw many strange things and (though he could not of course know it) must have passed over the whole of Elfland, by Cock Robin's grave, by Deidre's house, and by the homes of a hundred people of which his mother had told him (just as your mother has told you) – past the great gate of Ivory, over the River of White Nymphs and the Pool of the Nereids which lies at the feet of the great forests, and on and on (just as the little whiskered dwarf had told him) until he came to the sea again.

There the sun was already setting, throwing gold on his wings and the waves he could see through his wings; and, on the sails of the ships he saw in the harbour there, bright colours that grew richer and deeper as the sun fell nearer the water. On those sails he saw the imprint of strange things – quaint birds and shields and the heads of animals he had never seen before.

They waved their sleepy folds; they whispered to him: "This is the Harbour of Dreamland and we are its ships."

He felt sleepy there. The ships seemed to beckon him to ride out over the shadowy sea; and it was only the thought of the Prince on the mountain that made him pass on.

Once out of the Harbour of Dreamland the way grew bright again, as if the harbour had been nothing but a dream itself, and the sun shone again, burning his dark back. And this time he passed over the Field of Centaurs, and the shores where the sirens lie on the warm rocks, over the beach where thousands of pearls lay as carelessly as if children had scattered them there, and finally across the Garden of Proserpine, where the scent of flowers made him faint and drop to earth.

And as he lay there in the dark silence of his swoon, a voice asked: "Who are you? Why do you lie there looking as if you are dead?"

The swallow fluttered and, opening his eyes, saw before him a quaint little boy, who laughed: "The flowers have been too much for you."

He bent and kissed the swallow.

"My name is Puck," he said. "Fly on again. I have given you the Kiss of Youth!"

And, thanking him, though not quite understanding, and still with a drowsy wonder in his eyes, the swallow flew up and away. And in this flight he must have passed over the great forest of Lyonnesse and the Holy Mountain of Monsalvat, for only by going this way could he have come to Honeymouth Cove, and through the Never Never Land into the open sea, over which the moon was already beginning to chase the first timid stars into the darkening sky.

Passing over here, he looked down with amazement, for it seemed to him that many of the ships he saw there floating like curled leaves across the path of the moon were those he had seen waving their sails in the Harbour of Dreamland.

He knew then that the end of his journey must be near.

But a strange thing happened. The air grew suddenly cold, great rainbows appeared mysteriously in the sky, looking like the perfect reflections of each other, twilight descended, mighty winds blew his body hither and thither, and the sky itself thundered and thundered. Below him only a solitary ship slid across the lonely water, as if frightened.

And the swallow too was frightened, imagining he might never see the Prince again, but almost before he was aware of it he found that the wind had blown him out of reach of the thunder and that where the rainbows had been were only quiet untroubled stars. The hills lay pale and friendly beneath him, and in the distance a lake shone up at him like a clear blue stone with a light in its breast.

He grew giddy with joy at having crossed that strange sea, and began to fall as he had fallen in the Garden of Proserpine. For what seemed an age he fell through the air. Below him were confused shouts, and in the direction of the lake a sound as of someone singing. But all this ceased when his fall ceased, and he lay for a moment bewildered.

In the silence he opened his eyes . . . Then he saw he had fallen again into the arms of the Happy Prince.

IV

After he had lain there for some minutes he became aware of many voices chattering and looked up at the Prince as if to say: "Who are these people?"

(And he wrinkled up his feathers just as you wrinkle up your brows.)

The Prince laughed.

"Oh!" he said, "all these have come since you flew away; and each of them is like me – a wanderer and tired of wandering. Each is looking for a happy land in which to rest and abide."

Then the swallow turned a somersault, the first since his previous birthday, and cried out: "Then I can help them! I can help them! The land down there" – and he pointed away to the pale hills and the sea – "is Fairyland!"

Immediately the Prince and his friends set up a great shout. Some laughed also, one played on a pipe he had, some sang, one stood on his head and sang, "Merrily, merrily shall I live now," and another, who was something like a quaint little monkey, ran up the nearest tree he could find and chattered.

The swallow, bewildered, looked at the Prince for explanation.

"Don't be afraid," said the Prince in assurance, "I'll introduce you."

"But," protested the swallow, "I haven't washed. I haven't combed my wings!"

"All of which," answered the Prince kind-heartedly, "doesn't matter with the best people."

"Of course not," suddenly said a little girl with not very many clothes on. "I shan't mind, for one. That is, I shan't if I can be introduced first." And without more ceremony she introduced herself, "Taffimai Metallumai – is me," she declared.

"Meaning," said the Prince, as the swallow gasped, "small-person-without-any-manners-who-ought-to-be-spanked!"

"Which you can always shorten to Taffy if the worst comes to the worst," explained the owner of that name. "Now you know."

The swallow, thanking her, said he would not forget.

But he did forget almost immediately, for during the next ten minutes or so he became so flurried by being introduced to that throng which had gathered on the hill-top that he could scarcely remember their faces, let alone their names.

They were a very mixed crowd up there. Besides the little girl Taffy were three other children, who played constantly with a great cat that seemed to belong to a queer old lady with a hat like a tea-cosy and a face like the face of a duchess – and unmistakably so, since she was a duchess and was called "Duchess", and awed the swallow much, after the manner of duchesses. But the children, whose names the swallow discovered were Sylvie, Bruno, and Nixie (who would talk about an Uncle Paul), were not the slightest bit afraid. Nor were a sailor named Sinbad, and a lovely woman named Gulnarè, who talked often of the sea, and the strange one, Aladdin, who carried a little lamp he would allow no one to touch.

Oh! no – none were afraid of the Duchess, as who, knowing a duchess, would be? On the contrary, these people would stand together in little groups talking and making friends with each other, and pointing to them the Prince would say, "This is the Princess Lirazel and this the youth Alveric," or whomever it might be.

Soon the swallow came to know, besides these, the little fairy-like girl Tourmelise, who said he might sometimes call her Maia instead, and threw him a flower, which he caught in his beak and cherished for many days; and then those three who were never silent (and never will be silent while there are children like you and men like me), the boy with a pipe who is called the Pied Piper, another fairy thing who spoke in soft bewitching tones, and a sprite who danced to the tune of the pipe and sang till the air quivered; and these two were called respectively Melmillo and Ariel.

Contrasted against that merriment was the quietness of a tall, beautiful girl with short hair, and a little pale-faced Friar, who took the swallow in his hand, and said: "This is Joan and I am Francis. Don't be afraid."

Thus the swallow knew that all these, even the monkey Nod (who wasn't a monkey really but a Mulla-mulgar, which is very different), were friends to him. And he was able to perch in peace.

At last the Prince said "Hush!" to all the chatter, and asked of the company: "Where is it we all desire to go?"

And everyone answered with a shout: "Down to the land where the swallow has been!"

"Agreed?" queried the Prince.

"Agreed!" said everyone, as solemnly as town councillors.

"But," the prince warned them, "you forget we know nothing of this land."

To which everyone chorused like children in school: "But the swallow can tell us."

But the little bird blushed, and would have flown away had not Francis called it back again.

"Tell us?" he asked quietly.

And, unable to resist this little man, who treated him as he had never been treated before, even more sweetly than the Prince had done, he told the company what he had seen in the new land.

"You can go day after day and night after night, and your legs and wings will not be tired," he said at the end.

At this everyone applauded, most of them like you and me, with hands, but one or two, like Ariel, by standing on their heads or dancing.

"Ah! But," said the Mulla-mulgar Nod, "are there nuts?"

"There are forests," replied the swallow.

"And are there flowers?" asked Maia.

"There is a garden by the sea," replied the bird, "whose scents will make you drowsier than a forest of white poppies."

"And are there ships?" asked Sinbad.

"There is a harbour whose ships are like sunset-clouds that have been caught and moored there, sodden with colours."

"Wonderful!" said all.

"But, remember," warned the swallow seriously, being now a creature of importance, because he was also a creature of experience, "there are also witches and dragons and wolves and bogles and ghosts and monsters and giants and tempests and ogres and nightmares and sirens and — " here he must pause for a puff or two of breath " — and — fire!"

There was a solemn silence.

"Valleys of Fire," emphasized the swallow.

The silence became awful. Then the maid Joan said quietly: "I am no longer afraid of fire."

"Nor I," said Francis. "He is our friend."

So everyone brightened. At that point Ariel asked: "Did you ever in your travels see a fellow named Puck?"

"I did," replied the swallow. "When the scent of flowers overcame me he restored me by the kiss of youth."

"Excellent!" cried Ariel. "We began life together. Now, if I could find him we might persuade him to make clear the way into this wonderful land, for otherwise it is surely going to be extremely difficult to gain entrance."

"Horribly difficult," broke in the Duchess. "And the moral of that is . . ."

"Almost impossible," interrupted Sinbad.

"Oh! But nothing is impossible," declared Aladdin, holding up his strange lamp. "Nothing is impossible."

"That is so," agreed the Prince. "Therefore let us send Ariel to find this Puck with whom he began life."

"Ariel! Ariel!" called everyone at once. "Let us send Ariel!"

But he had vanished, and only his friend Melmillo knew that he had already begun that journey, for only to her had he confided his secret before departing.

V

The secret journey of Ariel came to an end quickly, and within five minutes those on the hill-crest were watching him return, dropping like a bright leaf through the sky. They watched him anxiously, as bearers of uncertain tidings are always watched, and questioned him when he alighted among them with a smile. And they had nothing to ask but: "Where is Puck? where is Puck?"

Ariel was playfully scornful in his sudden shout: "You weren't so foolish as to expect Puck would ever come out of Fairyland again, were you?"

They shook shameful heads at him.

"Oh! no, that's altogether impossible," went on Ariel. He lowered his voice. "But he is over there, sitting on the edge of a cloud till I return" – he flung out a toe in the direction from which he had just come – "just within the borders of his own land."

Everyone looked.

"But you will not see him," Ariel assured them. "It's many leagues away yet."

"Then what can we do?" asked the Prince.

"Write him a letter," suggested Taffy.

"Nonsense," said the Duchess, after the manner of duchesses. "You can't do that sort of thing here. You can't write letters to Puck. It's not done."

"Nonsense in one way," agreed Ariel. "But good sense in another, for unless we can convince him of both our earnestness and character he will refuse us the Kiss of Youth."

"In earnest!" suddenly exclaimed Sylvie and Bruno together. "You don't think he can doubt that?"

"Naturally," pointed out Francis. "Everyone will doubt before you make him believe."

"All of which means," said Sinbad, with the air of wisdom which comes to a man who has seen much and says little, "that we must prove to him his land has places where each of us can live happily and without disturbing its peace."

This wisdom the company accepted as final. Francis was the first to speak as a result of it.

"I should be happy," he said simply, "where there are birds and animals."

"And I where it is very, very quiet, and there are no quarrels," said Joan.

"And I," whispered Nixie, "in the heart of Uncle Paul."

"And I where there are flowers," said Maia.

As if in answer to this a voice from the clouds declared suddenly: "Then steer west of the moon for the Pool of Hippocrine. Fly together. You have the Kiss of Youth on you."

"Fly?" whispered everyone. "But it's not possible!"

"Fly!" repeated the voice, which no one doubted was the voice of Puck.

Thus, almost before any were aware of it Francis and Joan and Maia and Nixie were flying true west of the moon, which means west of the Sea of Dreams and the Never Never Land, over the Valley of Avalon and the Castle of Joyous Gard until you come to the Pool of Hippocrine and the Garden of Proserpine.

When they had disappeared Lirazel said: "I should be happiest in Elfland because my father is king of it."

"And I with her," declared Alveric.

"Then," said the voice without hesitation, "steer south of the Sirius for Elfin City. Fly together! You have the Kiss of Youth on you."

Thus, almost before any were aware of it, Lirazel and Alveric were flying true south of the Sirius, which means south of the Ferlie Firth and the Palace of Oberon, over the Golden Strand and Kelpie Bay until you come to the Elfin City.

So it went until nearly all the company had been admitted to the land they had so long desired; until Sylvie and Bruno had gone to live by the Well of Youth on the shores of Green Harbour, and Aladdin with Gulnarè and Sinbad to dwell near the Gold Caverns which are shining – washed by the Enchanted Sea; and the Mulla-mulgar Nod to dwell in the forests he loved.

To the shadow of the Great Wall went the Duchess and the Cheshire cat, to be neighbours to those queer gentry the Marquis of Carabas and the King of Thule.

All these went openly, all happily and with the Kiss of Youth on them. Only when it came to Ariel and his friends Melmillo and the Pied Piper was there a sign of secrecy; and of these no one can really say when they went or where, or where they are now, for these three were forever restless and mysterious, like the wind which first bore them from the hill-top.

When they had gone, the Happy Prince, the swallow and Taffy – for only these now remained – looked at each other in silence. Then Taffy, being of course a young-person-without-any-manners, set up a great cry as to why her place had not yet been told her, and, when the Prince could not answer her satisfactorily, demanded of the silent clouds from where she imagined Puck to be watching her: "Are you going to keep me waiting forever?"

She shouted petulantly at the swallow, too. She stamped her feet. She beat her fine brown hands on her naked breast. But there was complete silence.

She wept.

At this the Prince, with that kindness which had long ago endeared him to the swallow, said in a consoling whisper: "Remember that the swallow and I were first, and that so far Puck hasn't taken the slightest notice of us."

"But where am I to go?" she pleaded. "Am I to go anywhere?"

"Yes," answered the voice of Puck from the southward, "you are to come with me. Come now – now!"

Taffy turned her wet face to the great still clouds and obeyed. And it is said – though no one will contradict you if you don't believe it – that she went with Puck to the Queen Titania to teach her all those wonderful signs she taught her Daddy, Tegumai Bopsulai, and all the Neolithic ladies and gentlemen who lived on the banks of the Wagai long, long ago.

The Prince and the swallow, left alone, wondered how soon their fate would come, and, calling into the air, asked: "And we, what are we to do?"

Without hesitation the voice came: "You, too, are wanderers. Go where you wish. You have the Kiss of Youth – and if any question as to why you are here, say you have the secret of happiness also."

So the Prince and the swallow were left alone again.

As they flew off, striking out to where they believed the sea to be, great blue armies of cloud came out of the west, and twilight fell. At the same time, the swallow, turning to take one last glance at that hill where he had helped so much to happen, saw a figure standing there. By its stillness and silence it seemed to call to him, so that in a moment he went back to the hill.

There he saw a woman who watched him fly down through the half-darkness, and who, when he asked her name, timidly replied, as if afraid even of him: "I am Mary Rose."

The swallow looked into her face. "You are lonely," he said.

"Yes."

"What are you searching for?" the swallow asked. "For you are searching for something?"

"I can't tell you," she replied. "I can't tell anyone."

"Come with me. We will find what you seek."

Mary Rose smiled. "I cannot fly," she said.

And the swallow saw that this was true, and also that by lingering on the hill he could not only do nothing to help the woman but might also lose the Prince. So he touched her face with his wings as he parted them and whispered again: "Tell me what you are searching for?"

But the woman answered: "I can never tell you. I can never tell you."

"Is it the Kiss of Youth?" he asked. "Is it the Kiss of Youth?"

"Perhaps," she answered sadly, as he flew up. "Perhaps, perhaps."

The Seven Families of
the Lake Pipple-Popple

∾

Edward Lear

Introductory

IN FORMER DAYS – that is to say, once upon a time – there lived in
the Land of Gramblamble, Seven Families. They lived by the side
of the great Lake Pipple-Popple (one of the Seven Families, indeed,
lived *in* the Lake), and on the outskirts of the City of Tosh, which,
excepting when it was quite dark, they could see plainly. The names
of all these places you have probably heard of, and you have only not
to look in your Geography books to find out all about them.

Now the Seven Families who lived on the borders of the great
Lake Pipple-Popple, were as follows in the next Chapter.

The Seven Families

There was a family of Two old Parrots and Seven young Parrots.
There was a family of Two old Storks and Seven young Storks.
There was a Family of Two old Geese and Seven young Geese.
There was a Family of Two old Owls and Seven young Owls.
There was a Family of Two old Guinea Pigs and Seven young
Guinea Pigs.

There was a Family of Two old Cats and Seven young Cats.

And there was a Family of Two old Fishes and Seven young Fishes.

The Habits of the Seven Families

The Parrots lived upon the Soffsky-Poffsky trees — which were beautiful to behold, and covered with blue leaves — and they fed upon fruit, artichokes, and striped beetles.

The Storks walked in and out of the Lake Pipple-Popple and ate frogs for breakfast and buttered toast for tea; but, on account of the extreme length of their legs, they could not sit down, and so they walked about continually.

The Geese, having webs to their feet, caught quantities of flies, which they ate for dinner.

The Owls anxiously looked after mice, which they caught and made into sago puddings.

The Guinea Pigs toddled about the gardens, and ate lettuces and Cheshire cheese.

The Cats sat still in the sunshine, and fed upon sponge biscuits.

The Fishes lived in the Lake, and fed chiefly on boiled periwinkles.

And all these Seven Families lived together in the utmost fun and felicity.

The Children of the Seven Families are sent Away

One day all the Seven Fathers and the Seven Mothers of the Seven Families agreed that they would send their children out to see the world.

So they called them all together, and gave them each eight shillings and some good advice, some chocolate drops, and a small green morocco pocket-book to set down their expenses in.

They then particularly entreated them not to quarrel, and all the parents sent off their children with a parting injunction.

"If," said the old Parrots, "you find a Cherry, do not fight about who shall have it."

"And," said the old Storks, "if you find a Frog, divide it carefully into seven bits, and on no account quarrel about it."

And the old Geese said to the Seven young Geese, "Whatever you do, be sure you do not touch a Plum-pudding Flea."

And the old Owls said, "If you find a Mouse, tear him up into seven slices, and eat him cheerfully, but without quarrelling."

And the old Guinea Pigs said, "Have a care that you eat your Lettuces, should you find any, not greedily but calmly."

And the old Cats said, "Be particularly careful not to meddle with a Clangle-Wangle, if you should see one."

And the old Fishes said, "Above all things avoid eating a blue Boss-Woss, for they do not agree with Fishes, and give them a pain in their toes."

So all the Children of each Family thanked their parents, and, making in all forty-nine polite bows, they went into the wide world.

The History of the Seven Young Parrots

The Seven young Parrots had not gone far, when they saw a tree with a single Cherry on it, which the oldest Parrot picked instantly, but the other six, being extremely hungry, tried to get it also. On which all the Seven began to fight, and they scuffled,

and huffled,
and ruffled,
and shuffled,
and puffled,
and muffled,
and buffled,
and duffled,
and fluffled,

and guffled,
and huffled,
and bruffled, and

screamed, and shrieked, and squealed, and squeaked, and clawed, and snapped, and bit, and bumped, and thumped, and dumped, and flumped each other, till they were all torn into little bits, and at last there was nothing left to record this painful incident, except the Cherry and seven small green feathers.

And that was the vicious and voluble end of the Seven young Parrots.

The History of the Seven Young Storks

When the Seven young Storks set out, they walked or flew for fourteen weeks in a straight line, and for six weeks more in a crooked one; and after that they ran as hard as they could for one hundred and eight miles; and after that they stood still and made a himmeltanious chatter-clatter-blattery noise with their bills.

About the same time they perceived a large Frog, spotted with green, and with a sky-blue stripe under each ear.

So, being hungry, they immediately flew at him and were going to divide him into seven pieces when they began to quarrel as to which of his legs should be taken off first. One said this, and another said that, and while they were all quarrelling the Frog hopped away. And when they saw that he was gone, they began to
chatter-clatter,
blatter-platter,
patter-blatter,
matter-clatter,
flatter-quatter, more violently than ever. And after they had fought for a week they pecked each other to little pieces, so that at last nothing was left of any of them except their bills.

And that was the end of the Seven young Storks.

The History of the Seven Young Geese

When the Seven young Geese began to travel, they went over a large plain, on which there was but one tree, and that was a very bad one.

So four of them went up to the top of it, and looked about them, while the other three waddled up and down, and repeated poetry, and their last six lessons in Arithmetic, Geography, and Cookery.

Presently they perceived, a long way off, an object of the most interesting and obese appearance, having a perfectly round body, exactly resembling a boiled plum-pudding, with two little wings, and a beak, and three feathers growing out of his head, and only one leg.

So after a time all the Seven young Geese said to each other, "Beyond all doubt this beast must be a Plum-pudding Flea!"

On which they incautiously began to sing aloud

"Plum-pudding Flea,
Plum-pudding Flea,
Wherever you be,
O come to our tree,
And listen, O listen, O listen to me!"

And no sooner had they sung this verse than the Plum-pudding Flea began to hop and skip on his one leg with the most dreadful velocity, and came straight to the tree, where he stopped and looked about him in a vacant and voluminous manner.

On which the Seven young Geese were greatly alarmed, and all of a tremble-bemble: so one of them put out his long neck and just touched him with the tip of his bill – but no sooner had he done this than the Plum-pudding Flea skipped and hopped about more and more and higher, after which he opened his mouth, and, to the great surprise of the Seven Geese, began to bark so loudly and furiously and terribly that they were totally unable to bear the noise, and by degrees every one of them suddenly tumbled down quite dead.

So that was the end of the Seven young Geese.

The History of the Seven Young Owls

When the Seven young Owls set out, they sat every now and then on the branches of old trees, and never went far at one time.

And one night, when it was quite dark, they thought they heard a mouse, but as the gas lamps were not lighted, they could not see him.

So they called out, "Is that a mouse?"

On which a Mouse answered, "Squeaky-peeky-weeky, yes it is."

And immediately all the young Owls threw themselves off the tree, meaning to alight on the ground; but they did not perceive that there was a large well below them, into which they all fell superficially, and were every one of them drowned in less than half a minute.

So that was the end of the Seven young Owls.

The History of the Seven Young Guinea Pigs

The Seven young Guinea Pigs went into a garden full of Gooseberry-bushes and Tiggory-trees, under one of which they fell asleep. When they awoke they saw a large Lettuce which had grown out of the ground while they had been sleeping, and which had an immense number of green leaves. At which they all exclaimed:

> "Lettuce! O Lettuce!
> Let us, O let us,
> O Lettuce leaves,
> O let us leave this tree and eat
> Lettuce, O let us, Lettuce leaves!"

And instantly the Seven young Guinea Pigs rushed with such extreme force against the Lettuce-plant, and hit their heads so vividly against its stalk, that the concussion brought on directly an incipient transitional inflammation of their noses, which grew worse and worse and worse and worse till it incidentally killed them all Seven.

And that was the end of the Seven young Guinea Pigs.

The History of the Seven Young Cats

The Seven young Cats set off on their travels with great delight and rapacity. But, on coming to the top of a high hill, they perceived at a long distance off a Clangle-Wangle (or, as it is more properly written, Clangel-Wangel), and, in spite of the warning they had had, they ran straight up to it.

(Now the Clangle-Wangle is a most dangerous and delusive beast, and by no means commonly to be met with. They live in the water as well as on land, using their long tail as a sail when in the former element. Their speed is extreme, but their habits of life are domestic and superfluous, and their general demeanour pensive and pellucid. On summer evenings they may sometimes be observed near the Lake Pipple-Popple, standing on their heads and humming their national melodies: they subsist entirely on vegetables, excepting when they eat veal, or mutton, or pork, or beef, or fish, or saltpetre.)

The moment the Clangle-Wangle saw the Seven young Cats approach, he ran away; and as he ran straight on for four months, and the Cats, though they continued to run, could never overtake him – they all gradually *died* of fatigue and exhaustion, and never afterwards recovered.

And this was the end of the Seven young Cats.

The History of the Seven Young Fishes

The Seven young Fishes swam across the Lake Pipple-Popple, and into the river, and into the ocean, where, most unhappily for them, they saw, on the fifteenth day of their travels, a bright-blue Boss-Woss, and instantly swam after him. But the Blue Boss-Woss plunged into a perpendicular,

       spicular,

          orbicular,

             quadrangular,

                circular depth of soft mud,

where in fact his house was.

And the Seven young Fishes, swimming with great and uncomfortable velocity, plunged also into the mud, quite against their will, and not being accustomed to it, were all suffocated in a very short period.

And that was the end of the Seven young Fishes.

Of what Occurred Subsequently

After it was known that the

> Seven young Parrots,
> and the Seven young Storks,
> and the Seven young Geese,
> and the Seven young Owls,
> and the Seven young Guinea Pigs,
> and the Seven young Cats,
> and the Seven young Fishes,

were all dead, then the Frog, and the Plum-pudding Flea, and the Mouse, and the Clangel-Wangel, and the Blue Boss-Woss, all met together to rejoice over their good fortune. And they collected the Seven Feathers of the Seven young Parrots, and the Seven Bills of the Seven young Storks, and the Lettuce, and the Cherry, and, having placed the latter on the Lettuce, and the other objects in a circular arrangement at their base, they danced a horn-pipe round all these memorials until they were quite tired; after which they gave a tea-party, and a garden-party, and a ball, and a concert, and then returned to their respective homes full of joy and respect, sympathy, satisfaction, and disgust.

Of What Became of the Parents of the Forty-nine Children

But when the two old Parrots,

> and the two old Storks,
> and the two old Geese,
> and the two old Owls,
> and the two old Guinea Pigs,
> and the two old Cats,
> and the two old Fishes,

became aware, by reading in the newspapers, of the calamitous extinction of the whole of their families, they refused all further sustenance; and, sending out to various shops, they purchased great quantities of Cayenne Pepper, and Brandy, and Vinegar, and blue Sealing-wax, beside Seven immense glass Bottles with air-tight stoppers. And, having done this, they ate a light supper of brown bread and Jerusalem Artichokes, and took an affecting and formal leave of the whole of their acquaintance, which was very numerous and distinguished, and select, and responsible, and ridiculous.

Conclusion

And after this, filled the bottles with the ingredients for pickling, and each couple jumped into a separate bottle, by which effort of course they all died immediately, and became thoroughly pickled in a few minutes; having previously made their wills (by the assistance of the most eminent Lawyers of the District), in which they left strict orders that the Stoppers of the Seven Bottles should be carefully sealed up with the blue Sealing-wax they had purchased; and that they themselves in the Bottles should be presented to the principal museum of the city of Tosh, to be labelled with Parchment or any other anti-congenial succedaneum, and to be placed on a marble table with silver-gilt legs, for the daily inspection and contemplation, and for the perpetual benefit of the pusillanimous public.

And if ever you happen to go to Gramble-Blamble, and visit that museum in the city of Tosh, look for them on the Ninety-eighth table in the Four hundred and twenty-seventh room of the right-hand corridor of the left wing of the Central Quadrangle of that magnificent building; for if you do not, you certainly will not see them.

The Seven Ravens

❧

Ludwig Bechstein

As many strange things come to pass in the world, so there was a poor woman who had seven sons at a birth, all of whom lived and throve. After some years, the same woman had a daughter. Her husband was a very industrious and active man, on which account people in want of a handicraftsman were very willing to take him into their service, so that he could not only support his numerous family in an honest manner, but earned so much that, by prudent economy, his wife was enabled to lay by a little money for a rainy day. But this good father died in the prime of life, and the poor widow soon fell into poverty; for she could not earn enough to support and clothe her eight children.

Her seven boys grew bigger, and daily required more and more, besides which they were a great grief to their mother, for they were wild and wicked. The poor woman could hardly stand against all the afflictions that weighed so heavily upon her. She wished to bring up her children in the paths of virtue, but neither mildness nor severity availed anything: the boys' hearts were hardened. One day, when her patience was quite exhausted, she spoke thus to them: "Oh, you wicked young ravens! Would that you were seven black ravens, and would fly away, so that I might never see you again!" and the seven boys immediately became seven ravens, flew out of the window, and disappeared.

The mother now lived with her little daughter in peace and

contentment, and was able to earn more than she spent. And the young girl grew up handsome, modest, and good. But, after some years had passed, both mother and daughter began to long after the seven boys; they often talked about them and wept; they thought that, could only the seven brothers return and be good lads, how well they could all live by their work and have so much pleasure in one another. And as this longing in the heart of the young maiden increased daily, she one day said to her mother: "Dear Mother, let me wander in the world in quest of my brothers, that I may turn them from their wicked ways, and make them a comfort and a blessing to you in your old age."

The mother answered: "Thou good girl! I will not restrain thee from accomplishing this pious deed. Go, my child! And may God guide thee." She then gave her a small gold ring which she had formerly worn when a child, at the time the brothers were changed into ravens.

The young girl set out, and wandered far, very far away, and for a very long time found no traces of her brothers; but at length she came to the foot of a very high mountain, on the top of which stood a small dwelling. At the mountain's foot she sat down to rest, all the while looking up in deep thought at the little habitation. It appeared at first to her like a bird's nest, for it was of a greyish hue, as if built of small stones and mud; then it looked like a human dwelling. She thought within herself: "Can that be my brothers' habitation?" And when she at length saw seven ravens flying out of the house, she was confirmed in her conjecture.

Full of joy, she began to ascend the mountain, but the road that led to the summit was paved with such curious glass-like stones that, every time she had with the greatest caution proceeded but a few paces, her feet slipped and she fell down to the bottom. At this she was sadly disheartened, and felt completely at a loss how to get up, when she chanced to see a beautiful white goose, and thought: "If I had only thy wings, I could soon be at the top." She then thought again: "But can I not cut thy wings off? Yes, they would help me." So she caught the beautiful goose, and cut off its wings, also its legs, and sewed them on to herself; and see! when she attempted to fly, she succeeded to perfection; and when she was tired of flying, she walked a little on the goose's feet, and did not slip down again.

She arrived at length safely at the desired spot. When at the top of the mountain, she entered the little dwelling; it was very small; within stood seven tiny tables, seven little chairs, seven little beds, and in the room were seven little windows, and in the oven seven little dishes, in which were little baked birds and seven eggs. The good sister was weary after her long journey, and rejoiced that she could once again take some rest and appease her hunger. So she took the seven little dishes out of the oven and ate a little from each, and sat down for a while on each of the seven little chairs, and lay down on each of the little beds, but on the last she fell fast asleep, and there remained until the seven brothers came back.

They flew through the seven windows into the room, took their dishes out of the oven, and began to eat; but instantly saw that a part of their fare had disappeared. They then went to lie down, and found their beds rumpled, when one of the brothers uttered a loud cry, and said: "Oh! what a beautiful young girl there is on my bed!" the other brothers flew quickly to see, and with amazement beheld the sleeping maiden. Then the one said to the other: "Oh, if only she were our sister!" Then they again cried out to each other with joy: "Yes, it is our sister; oh yes, it is, just such hair she had, and just such a mouth, and just such a little gold ring she wore on her middle finger as she now has on her little one." And they all danced for joy, and all kissed their sister, but she continued to sleep so soundly that it was a long time before she awoke.

At length the maiden opened her eyes, and saw her seven black brothers standing about the bed. She then said: "Oh happy meeting, my dear brothers; God be praised that I have at length found you! I have had a long and tedious journey on your account, in the hope of fetching you back from your banishment, provided your hearts are inclined never more to vex and trouble your good mother; that you will work with us diligently, and be the honour and comfort of your old affectionate parent." During this discourse the brothers wept bitterly, and answered: "Yes, dearest sister, we will be better, never will we offend our mother again. Alas! as ravens we have led a miserable life, and before we built this hut we almost perished with

hunger and cold. Then came repentance, which racked us day and night; for we were obliged to live on the bodies of poor executed criminals, and were thereby always reminded of the sinner's end."

The sister shed tears of joy at her brothers' repentance, and on hearing them utter such pious sentiments: "Oh!" exclaimed she, "all will be well. When you return home, and your mother sees how penitent you are, she will forgive you from her heart, and restore you to your human form."

When the brothers were about to return home with their sister, they said, while opening a small box: "Dear sister, take these beautiful gold rings and shining stones, which we have from time to time found abroad: put them in your apron and carry them home with you, for with them we shall be rich as men. As ravens we collected them only on account of their brilliancy." The sister did as her brothers requested her, and was pleased with the beautiful ornaments.

As they journeyed home, first one of the ravens and then another bore their sister on their pinions, until they reached their mother's dwelling, when they flew in at the window and implored her forgiveness, and promised that in future they would be dutiful children. Their sister also prayed and supplicated for them, and the mother was full of joy and love, and forgave her sevens sons. They then became human beings again, and were fine blooming youths, each one as large and graceful as the other. With heartfelt gratitude they kissed their dear mother and darling sister; and, soon after, all the seven brothers married young discreet maidens, built themselves a large beautiful house (for they had sold their jewels for a considerable sum of money), and the house-warming was the wedding of all the seven brothers. Their sister was also married to an excellent man, and, at the earnest desire of her brothers, she and her husband took up their abode with them.

The good mother had great joy and pleasure in her children in her old age, and as long as she lived was loved and honoured by them.

Sleeping Beauty

∾

Charles Perrault

THERE WERE FORMERLY a king and a queen, who were so sorry that they had no children; so sorry that it cannot be expressed. They went to all the waters in the world; vows, pilgrimages, all ways were tried, and all to no purpose.

At last, however, the Queen had a daughter. There was a very fine christening; and the Princess had for her god-mothers all the fairies they could find in the whole kingdom (they found seven), that every one of them might give her a gift, as was the custom of fairies in those days. By this means the Princess had all the perfections imaginable.

After the ceremonies of the christening were over, all the company returned to the King's palace, where was prepared a great feast for the fairies. There was placed before every one of them a magnificent cover with a case of massive gold, wherein were a spoon, knife, and fork, all of pure gold set with diamonds and rubies. But as they were all sitting down at table they saw come into the hall a very old fairy, whom they had not invited, because it was above fifty years since she had been out of a certain tower, and she was believed to be either dead or enchanted.

The King ordered her a cover, but could not furnish her with a case of gold as the others, because they had seven only made for the seven fairies. The old Fairy fancied she was slighted, and muttered some threats between her teeth. One of the young fairies who sat

by her overheard how she grumbled; and, judging that she might
give the little Princess some unlucky gift, went, as soon as they rose
from table, and hid herself behind the hangings, that she might speak
last, and repair, as much as she could, the evil which the old Fairy
might intend.

In the meanwhile all the fairies began to give their gifts to the
Princess. The youngest gave her for gift that she should be the most
beautiful person in the world; the next that she should have the wit
of an angel; the third that she should have a wonderful grace in
everything she did; the fourth that she should dance perfectly well;
the fifth that she should sing like a nightingale; and the sixth that
she should play all kinds of music to the utmost perfection.

The old Fairy's turn coming next, with a head shaking more
with spite than age, she said that the Princess should have her hand
pierced with a spindle and die of the wound. This terrible gift made
the whole company tremble, and everybody fell a-crying.

At this very instant the young Fairy came out from behind the
hangings, and spake these words aloud:

"Assure yourselves, O King and Queen, that your daughter shall not die of this disaster. It is true, I have no power to undo entirely what my elder has done. The Princess shall indeed pierce her hand with a spindle; but, instead of dying, she shall only fall into a profound sleep, which shall last a hundred years, at the expiration of which a king's son shall come and awake her."

The King, to avoid the misfortune foretold by the old Fairy, caused immediately proclamation to be made, whereby everybody was forbidden, on pain of death, to spin with a distaff and spindle, or to have so much as any spindle in their houses. About fifteen or sixteen years after, the King and Queen being gone to one of their houses of pleasure, the young Princess happened one day to divert herself in running up and down the palace; when, going up from one apartment to another, she came into a little room on the top of the tower, where a good old woman, alone, was spinning with her spindle. This good woman had never heard of the King's proclamation against spindles.

"What are you doing there, goody?" said the Princess.

"I am spinning, my pretty child," said the old woman, who did not know who she was.

"Ha!" said the Princess, "this is very pretty; how do you do it? Give it to me, that I may see if I can do so."

She had no sooner taken it into her hand than, whether being very hasty at it, somewhat unhandy, or that the decree of the Fairy had so ordained it, it ran into her hand, and she fell down in a swoon.

The good old woman, not knowing very well what to do in this affair, cried out for help. People came in from every quarter in great numbers; they threw water upon the Princess's face, unlaced her, struck her on the palms of her hands, and rubbed her temples with Hungary-water; but nothing would bring her to herself.

And now the King, who came up at the noise, bethought himself of the prediction of the fairies, and, judging very well that this must necessarily come to pass, since the fairies had said it, caused the Princess to be carried into the finest apartment in his palace, and to be laid upon a bed all embroidered with gold and silver.

One would have taken her for a little angel, she was so very beautiful; for her swooning away had not diminished one bit of her complexion: her cheeks were carnation, and her lips were coral; indeed her eyes were shut, but she was heard to breathe softly, which satisfied those about her that she was not dead. The King commanded that they should not disturb her, but let her sleep quietly till her hour of awaking was come.

The good Fairy who had saved her life by condemning her to sleep a hundred years was in the kingdom of Matakin, twelve thousand leagues off, when this accident befell the Princess; but she was instantly informed of it by a little dwarf, who had boots of seven leagues, that is, boots with which he could tread over seven leagues of ground in one stride. The Fairy came away immediately, and she arrived, about an hour after, in a fiery chariot drawn by dragons.

The King handed her out of the chariot, and she approved everything he had done; but, as she had very great foresight, she thought when the Princess should awake she might not know what to do with herself, being all alone in this old palace; and this was what she did: she touched with her wand everything in the palace (except the King and the Queen) – governesses, maids of honour, ladies of the bedchamber, gentlemen, officers, stewards, cooks, undercooks, scullions, guards with their beefeaters, pages, footmen; she likewise touched all the horses which were in the stables, as well pads as others, the great dogs in the outward court and pretty little Mopsey too, the Princess's little spaniel, which lay by her on the bed.

Immediately upon her touching them they all fell asleep, that they might not awake before their mistress, and that they might be ready to wait upon her when she wanted them. The very spits at the fire, as full as they could hold of partridges and pheasants, did fall asleep also. All this was done in a moment. Fairies are not long in doing their business.

And now the King and the Queen, having kissed their dead child without waking her, went out of the palace and put forth a proclamation that nobody should dare to come near it.

This, however, was not necessary, for in a quarter of an hour's time there grew up all round about the park such a vast number of trees, great and small, bushes and brambles, twining one within another, that neither man nor beast could pass through; so that nothing could be seen but the very top of the towers of the palace;

and that, too, not unless it was a good way off. Nobody doubted but the Fairy gave herein a very extraordinary sample of her art, that the Princess, while she continued sleeping, might have nothing to fear from any curious people.

When a hundred years were gone and passed the son of the King then reigning, and who was of another family from that of the sleeping Princess, being gone a-hunting on that side of the country, asked: What those towers were which he saw in the middle of a great thick wood?

Everyone answered according as they had heard. Some said: That it was a ruinous old castle, haunted by spirits; Others, That all the sorcerers and witches of the country kept there their sabbath or night's meeting.

The common opinion was: That an ogre lived there, and that he carried thither all the little children he could catch, that he might eat them up at his leisure, without anybody being able to follow him, as having himself only the power to pass through the wood.

The Prince was at a stand, not knowing what to believe, when a very aged countryman spake to him thus:

"May it please your royal highness, it is now about fifty years since I heard from my father, who heard my grandfather say, that there was then in this castle a princess, the most beautiful was ever seen; that she must sleep there a hundred years, and should be waked by a king's son, for whom she was reserved."

The young Prince was all on fire at these words, believing, without weighing the matter, that he could put an end to this rare adventure; and, pushed on by love and honour, resolved that moment to look into it.

Scarce had he advanced towards the wood when all the great trees, the bushes, and brambles gave way of themselves to let him pass through; he walked up to the castle which he saw at the end of a large avenue which he went into; and what a little surprised him was that he saw none of his people could follow him, because the trees closed again as soon as he had passed through them. However, he did not cease from continuing his way; a young and amorous prince is always valiant.

He came into a spacious outward court, where everything he saw might have frozen up the most fearless person with horror. There reigned over all a most frightful silence; the image of death everywhere showed itself, and there was nothing to be seen but stretched-out bodies of men and animals, all seeming to be dead. He, however, very well knew, by the ruby faces and pimpled noses of the beefeaters, that they were only asleep; and their goblets, wherein still remained some drops of wine, showed plainly that they fell asleep in their cups.

He then crossed a court paved with marble, went up the stairs, and came into the guard chamber, where guards were standing in their ranks, with their muskets upon their shoulders, and snoring as loud as they could. After that he went through several rooms full of gentlemen and ladies, all asleep, some standing, others sitting. At last he came into a chamber all gilded with gold, where he saw upon a bed, the curtains of which were all open, the finest sight was ever beheld – a princess, who appeared to be about fifteen or sixteen years of age, and whose bright and, in a manner, resplendent beauty, had somewhat in it divine. He approached with trembling and admiration, and fell down before her upon his knees.

And now, as the enchantment was at an end, the Princess awaked, and, looking on him with eyes more tender than the first view might seem to admit of: "Is it you, my Prince?" said she to him. "You have waited a long while."

The Prince, charmed with these words, and much more with the manner in which they were spoken, knew not how to show his joy and gratitude; he assured her that he loved her better than he did himself; their discourse was not well connected, they did weep more than talk – little eloquence, a great deal of love. He was more at a loss than she, and we need not wonder at it: she had time to think on what to say to him; for it is very probable (though history mentions nothing of it) that the good Fairy, during so long a sleep, had given her very agreeable dreams. In short, they talked four hours together, and yet they said not half what they had to say.

In the meanwhile all the palace awaked; everyone thought upon their particular business, and as all of them were not in love they were ready to die for hunger. The chief lady of honour, being as sharp set as other folks, grew very impatient, and told the Princess aloud that supper was served up. The Prince helped the Princess to rise; she was entirely dressed, and very magnificently, but his royal highness took care not to tell her that she was dressed like his great-grandmother, and had a point band peeping over a high collar; she looked not a bit the less charming and beautiful for all that.

They went into the great hall of looking-glasses, where they supped, and were served by the Princess's officers; the violins and hautboys played old tunes, but very excellent, though it was now above a hundred years since they had played; and after supper, without losing any time, the lord almoner married them in the chapel of the castle, and the chief lady of honour drew the curtains. They had but very little sleep – the Princess had no occasion; and the Prince left her next morning to return into the city, where his father must needs have been in pain for him.

The Prince told him: That he lost his way in the forest as he was hunting, and that he had lain in the cottage of a charcoal-burner, who gave him cheese and brown bread.

The King, his father, who was a good man, believed him; but his mother could not be persuaded it was true; and, seeing that he went almost every day a-hunting, and that he always had some excuse ready for so doing, though he had lain out three or four nights together, she began to suspect that he was married, for he lived with the Princess above two whole years, and had by her two children, the eldest of which, who was a daughter, was named *Morning*, and the youngest, who was a son, they called *Day*, because he was a great deal handsomer and more beautiful than his sister.

The Queen spoke several times to her son, to inform herself after what manner he did pass his time, and that in this he ought in duty to satisfy her. But he never dared to trust her with his secret; he feared her, though he loved her, for she was of the race of the Ogres, and the King would never have married her had it not been for her vast riches; it was even whispered about the Court that she had Ogreish inclinations, and that, whenever she saw little children passing by, she had all the difficulty in the world to avoid falling upon them. And so the Prince would never tell her one word.

But when the King was dead, which happened about two years afterwards, and he saw himself lord and master, he openly declared his marriage; and he went in great ceremony to conduct his Queen to the palace. They made a magnificent entry into the capital city, she riding between her two children.

Soon after the King went to make war with the Emperor Contalabutte, his neighbour. He left the government of the kingdom to the Queen his mother, and earnestly recommended to her care his wife and children. He was obliged to continue his expedition all the summer, and as soon as he departed the Queen-mother sent her daughter-in-law to a country house among the woods, that she might with the more ease gratify her horrible longing.

Some few days afterwards she went thither herself, and said to her clerk of the kitchen:

"I have a mind to eat little Morning for my dinner tomorrow."

"Ah! madam," cried the clerk of the kitchen.

"I will have it so," replied the Queen (and this she spoke in the tone of an Ogress who had a strong desire to eat fresh meat), "and will eat her with a *sauce Robert*."

The poor man, knowing very well that he must not play tricks with Ogresses, took his great knife and went up into little Morning's chamber. She was then four years old, and came up to him jumping and laughing, to take him about the neck and ask him for some sugar-candy. Upon which he began to weep, the great knife fell out of his hand, and he went into the back yard, and killed a little lamb, and dressed it with such good sauce that his mistress assured him she had never eaten anything so good in her life. He had at the same time taken up little Morning, and carried her to his wife, to conceal her in the lodging he had at the bottom of the courtyard.

About eight days afterwards the wicked Queen said to the clerk of the kitchen, "I will sup upon little Day."

He answered not a word, being resolved to cheat her as he had done before. He went to find out little Day, and saw him with a little foil in his hand, with which he was fencing with a great monkey, the child being then only three years of age. He took him up in his arms and carried him to his wife, that she might conceal him in her chamber along with his sister, and in the room of little Day cooked up a young kid, very tender, which the Ogress found to be wonderfully good.

This was hitherto all mighty well; but one evening this wicked Queen said to her clerk of the kitchen:

"I will eat the Queen with the same sauce I had with her children."

It was now that the poor clerk of the kitchen despaired of being able to deceive her. The young Queen was turned of twenty, not reckoning the hundred years she had been asleep; and how to find in the yard a beast so firm was what puzzled him. He took then a resolution, that he might save his own life, to cut the Queen's throat; and, going up into her chamber, with intent to do it at once, he put himself into as great fury as he could possibly, and came into the young Queen's room with his dagger in his hand. He would not, however, surprise her, but told her, with a great deal of respect, the orders he had received from the Queen-mother.

"Do it; do it" (said she, stretching out her neck). "Execute your orders, and then I shall go and see my children, my poor children, whom I so much and so tenderly loved."

For she thought them dead ever since they had been taken away without her knowledge.

"No, no, madam" (cried the poor clerk of the kitchen, all in tears); "you shall not die, and yet you shall see your children again; but then you must go home with me to my lodgings, where I have concealed them, and I shall deceive the Queen once more, by giving her in your stead a young hind."

Upon this he forthwith conducted her to his chamber, where, leaving her to embrace her children, and cry along with them, he went and dressed a young hind, which the Queen had for her supper, and devoured it with the same appetite as if it had been the young Queen. Exceedingly was she delighted with her cruelty, and she had invented a story to tell the King, at his return, how the mad wolves had eaten up the Queen his wife and her two children.

One evening, as she was, according to her custom, rambling round about the courts and yards of the palace to see if she could smell any fresh meat, she heard, in a ground room, little Day crying, for his mamma was going to whip him, because he had been naughty; and she heard, at the same time, little Morning begging pardon for her brother.

The Ogress presently knew the voice of the Queen and her children, and, being quite mad that she had been thus deceived, she commanded next morning, by break of day (with a most horrible voice, which made everybody tremble), that they should bring into the middle of the great court a large tub, which she caused to be filled with toads, vipers, snakes, and all sorts of serpents, in order to have thrown into it the Queen and her children, the clerk of the kitchen, his wife and maid; all whom she had given orders should be brought thither with their hands tied behind them.

They were brought out accordingly, and the executioners were just going to throw them into the tub, when the King (who was not so soon expected) entered the court on horseback (for he came post) and asked, with the utmost astonishment. What was the meaning of that horrible spectacle?

No one dared to tell him, when the Ogress, all enraged to see what had happened, threw herself head foremost into the tub, and was instantly devoured by the ugly creatures she had ordered to be thrown into it for others. The King could not but be very sorry, for she was his mother; but he soon comforted himself with his beautiful wife and his pretty children.

The Snow Queen

❧

Hans Christian Andersen

Chapter the First
About a hobgoblin

NOW WE ARE GOING to begin. When we have come to the end we shall know a great deal more than we do now. He was a horribly wicked hobgoblin!

He was one of the very worst; indeed, he was the worst of all. One day he was in capital spirits, for he had just invented a looking-glass which, when it reflected anything good or beautiful, made it dwindle almost to nothing, while anything bad and ugly stood out in clear lines, and appeared twice its proper size. The most beautiful landscapes, seen in the mirror, looked like boiled spinach; the best men appeared repulsive, or stood on their heads, with no bodies; every face seen in the glass was distorted, and scarcely to be recognized; and if one had a freckle, one might be sure that it would spread over one's nose and mouth. "That was the beauty of it," said the hobgoblin. If a good, pious thought crossed one's heart, the looking-glass reflected a grin; and the goblin laughed with delight at his invention. Those who attended his school – for he kept a school – said, everywhere, that he had done wonders for them, and that now for the first time they had learned to know the world and men. They went about everywhere with the goblin's mirror, till at last there was not a country or a person that had not been seen through the magic glass. They then wanted to fly up to heaven and hold up the mirror before the angels, but the higher they flew the more the mirror strained and grinned; and at last it fell from their hands and shivered into a million billion pieces, and more besides.

And then it was that the real mischief began, for the tiny bits of glass, no bigger than a grain of sand, flew all over the world; and when one of them flew into a person's eye, there it remained, and the man saw everything distorted or out of drawing, or else he had eyes for nothing that was not false and perverse, for every atom had as much power as the whole mirror. Some men had a piece lodged right in their hearts, and then it was really dreadful – the heart was turned into a lump of ice. A few of the pieces were large enough to be used as window-panes, and it did not answer to look at your friends through that window; other pieces were made into spectacles, and it was a bad case whenever anyone put on a pair of these spectacles in order to see clearly and judge impartially! The hobgoblin laughed till his sides ached again, he was so tickled at his handiwork. But the little pieces of glass kept flying about all over the world, and –

Well, you shall just hear.

Chapter the Second
About a little boy and a little girl

In the large town where there are so many people and so many houses that there is no room for everyone to have a little garden to himself, and most people have to be contented with flowers in flower-pots, there lived two poor children who had a garden not much larger than a flower-pot.

They were not brother and sister, but they loved each other as dearly as if they had been. Their parents lived in two attics exactly opposite each other, and in each house, just where the roof projected and the spouting ran along it, there was a little window; one had but to cross the water-pipe to pass from one window to another.

In each window stood a wooden box, in which garden herbs were growing round a beautiful red rose tree in the centre. The children's parents put the boxes crosswise over the spouting, so that they reached from one window to another, and looked like a wall of flowers. Sweet-peas hung down and hid the sides of the boxes, the roses shot up and climbed round the windows, making a triumphal arch of leaves and flowers. The boxes were very high, and the children knew that they must not climb out upon them without permission; but sometimes they were allowed to carry out their little footstools and sit under the rose trees, and then they used to have a famous game of play.

The winter put an end to their play, of course. The windows were frozen over, and the children could only warm pennies at the stove and hold them against the pane till they had made a round, round peephole, through which their soft, bright eyes looked at each other. His name was Kay and hers was Gerda. In the summer they could meet by just taking a jump out of the window, but in the winter they were obliged to run down the long flight of stairs and through the passage out into the snow.

"Look at the white bees," said the old grandmother; "they are going to swarm."

"Have they a queen-bee?" said Kay, for he knew that real bees have a queen.

"Of course they have," said the grandmother; "she is the largest of them all, and she always flies where they swarm the thickest. But she never lies still upon the ground; her home is in the black cloud. Many a time she flies at midnight through the streets and covers the window-panes with beautiful frosted stars and flowers."

"Yes, we have seen them," said the two children; and then they knew that the story was true.

"Can the Snow Queen come in here?" said the little girl.

"Let her try," said the boy; "I would put her on the stove till she was melted."

The grandmother stroked his hair, and told him some more stories.

That night, when little Kay was going to bed, he climbed on to a chair and looked through the round peephole; a few snow-flakes were still falling, and one of them, the largest of all, settled on the edge of the flower-box. It grew and grew till it changed into a beautiful maiden dressed in white, silvery gauze, sparkling with frosted crystals. She was dazzlingly fair, but cold as ice. Her eyes shone like two stars, but there was neither peace nor rest in their glances. She nodded in at the window and waved her hand. Kay was frightened, and jumped down from the chair. It was as if a large white bird flew past the window.

The next day was a white frost; and in due time the spring came. The sun shone, the leaves came out, the swallows built their nests, the windows were thrown open, and Kay and Gerda sat once more in their little garden, high above the narrow street.

How gloriously the roses blossomed this year! Gerda had learned a hymn all about roses, and when it spoke of the roses she thought it meant hers and Kay's: she taught it to the little boy, and he sang it with her:

> "The roses all must fade and die,
> We shall see Christ the Child on high."

And the children held each other by the hand, and kissed the roses, they looked out into God's clear sunshine, and sang as if the Child Christ stood beside them. What lovely summer days they were! And how beautiful it was out under the crimson roses that seemed as if they never would leave off blooming!

Kay and Gerda were looking at the beasts and birds in their picture-book, when suddenly, just as the church clock struck five, Kay said, "Oh, something has stung my heart and flown into my eye!"

Gerda threw her arms round his neck; he rubbed his eye, but there was nothing to be seen.

"I think it is out now," he said; but it was not out. It was one of the tiny pieces of glass belonging to the magic mirror – you remember the mirror? The goblin's glass which made everything great and good look mean and ugly, and showed up all the bad and evil things, so that if anyone had a fault that was the only thing you saw of him in the mirror? Poor Kay had got a piece in his eye and another in his heart. They did not hurt him, but there they were, and his heart began to turn to ice.

"What are you crying for?" he said to Gerda; "it makes you look so ugly. I am all right. Oh, look at that rose, it is all grub-eaten! And this one is dwarfed and stunted. After all, the roses are ugly things, as ugly as the boxes they grow in." And he kicked at the boxes and began to pull the roses to pieces.

"Kay, what are you doing?" said the little girl; and when he saw how frightened she was, he pulled off another rose and ran in at his window, away from sweet little Gerda.

The next time she brought him the picture-book to look at, he said it was only fit for babies in long clothes; and when his grandmother told him tales he always met them with a "but"; or else he would stand behind her, put on a pair of spectacles, and imitate all she said. He did it very cleverly, and made everyone laugh. Before long he could imitate the voice and walk of everyone he saw; any peculiarity or defect he copied capitally, and people said, "That lad has a clever head on his shoulders." All this came from the glass in his heart; and, by-and-by, he began to tease little Gerda, who loved him with all her heart.

His games and amusements were quite different now from what they were before. In winter, when it snowed, he would hold out a burning-glass, and let the flakes fall on his blue coat. "Look in the glass, Gerda," he cried; and she saw how every snow-flake looked ten times larger and sparkled like a silver flower. "See how regular it is," said Kay; "that is much more interesting than looking at flowers. There is not one fault. All is according to rule. If only they would not melt!"

Soon afterwards Kay came up, wearing thick gloves and carrying his skates over his shoulder. "I am going out to play with the other boys," he said, and away he went.

In the great square where the boys played, the boldest among them used to tie their sleighs to the back of some countryman's cart, and get a good ride behind it. That was fine fun. When they were in the height of their play a large sleigh drove into the square; it was painted white, and inside it sat a figure muffled up in a rough cloak of white fur, and wearing a white fur cap. The sleigh drove twice round the square, and Kay tied his little sleigh behind it. Away it went, faster and faster, right out into the next street. The figure inside nodded at Kay as if they were old friends; every time Kay tried to untie his sleigh the figure nodded again, and Kay sat still.

On they went, out beyond the town gates. It began to snow heavily; Kay could not see his hands before his face; he loosened the string which tied the sleighs together, but it made no difference, on they both went, swift as the wind. He cried aloud, but no one heard him; the snow whirled by, and the sleighs flew faster, sometimes they gave a jolt as if they were flying over hedges and ditches. Kay was frightened. He tried to say the Lord's Prayer, but he could remember nothing but the multiplication table.

The snow-flakes grew larger, till they looked like great white birds; the sleigh suddenly stopped; the figure rose; cloak and hat had vanished, and there stood a maiden in snowy robes, tall and dazzlingly fair – it was the Snow Queen.

"We have ridden well," she cried; "but you are freezing. Creep in under my fur." She drew him into the sleigh and wrapped her cloak round him. He felt as if he were sinking in a snow-drift.

"Are you cold now?" she said, and kissed his brow. Her kiss was colder than ice; it thrilled to his heart. For a moment, he felt as if he were going to die; but after a while he felt better, and did not mind the cold at all.

"My sleigh – don't forget my sleigh!" he cried.

That was the first thing he thought of. It was tied to one of the white birds, who flew away with it. The Snow Queen kissed Kay again; and this time he forgot Gerda and his old grandmother, and everyone he had left at home.

"Now you shall have no more kisses," said the Snow Queen, "or I should kiss you to death."

Kay looked at her. She was very beautiful. He thought he had never seen such a fine, clever face. She did not look now as if she were made of ice, as he thought she was when she stood outside his window long ago. She was perfect in his eyes, and he was not afraid.

He told her that he could do mental arithmetic as far as fractions, and he knew how many square miles there were in the country, and what the population was. She smiled still, and it seemed to Kay that all he knew was not enough. He looked out into the wide space round him; the Queen flew with him high in the air to the black cloud: the storm raged round them, it was as if it sang old melodies. They flew over forest and lake, over land and sea, the cold wind rushed

THE SNOW QUEEN APPEARS TO LITTLE KAY

past below them, the wolves howled, the snow crackled; above them flew black, cawing crows, and the moon shone large and round. Kay looked at it in the long winter nights. By day he slept at the feet of the Snow Queen.

Chapter the Third
About the flower-garden and the woman who could conjure

But what became of little Gerda when Kay did not come back? Where could he be? No one knew: no one could help her. The boys only said that they had seen him tie his sleigh behind another large one, and drive out towards the town gate. No one knew where he was. Little Gerda wept bitterly. Then she said that he must be dead – drowned in the river that runs past the school. Ah, the winter days were long and sad.

The spring came on with the warm sunshine.

"Kay is dead and gone," said little Gerda.

"I don't believe it," said the sunshine.

"Kay is dead and gone," said Gerda to the swallows.

"We don't believe it," said the swallows; and by degrees Gerda began to feel doubtful about it herself.

"I will put on new red shoes, which Kay has never seen," she said, "and go down to the river to ask after him."

It was very early. She kissed her old grandmother, who was still asleep, put on her red shoes, and went out through the town gate to the river.

"Is it true that you have taken away my little play-fellow?" she said. "I will give you my red shoes if you will send him back to me."

It seemed to her that the waves nodded strangely in answer. She took off her red shoes, which were the things she liked best in the world, and threw them in the river. They fell in close to the shore, and the waves bore them back to her feet. It was as much as to say they could not send back little Kay, so they would not keep her shoes. But Gerda thought she ought to have thrown them farther out; so she crept into a boat which lay among the reeds, went to the very end of it, and threw them in from there. Now the boat was not fastened to the shore, and as Gerda threw out the shoes it slipped away from the reeds. The little girl felt it move and ran back as quickly as she could, but by the time she reached the other end the boat was yards away from land, and drifting fast down the stream.

Gerda began to cry. No one heard her except the swallows, and they could not carry her to the shore. All they could do was to fly along the bank by her side, and sing, "Here we are!" The boat flew down the stream; Gerda sat quite still, with nothing on her feet but stockings; the two red shoes came swimming after, but they could not reach the boat.

It was very pretty on both sides of the river; there were beautiful flowers, tall trees, and grassy slopes, with cows and sheep. But there was not a human being to be seen.

"Perhaps the river will carry me on to Kay," said Gerda. She became more cheerful, and watched the green, sunny shores for hours together. At last she came to a large cherry-garden, in the centre of which stood a little cottage, with red and blue windows and a thatched roof. Before the door stood two wooden soldiers, presenting arms.

Gerda called out to them, for she thought they were alive, but of course they did not hear. The current bore straight towards the land, and she called out louder.

At the sound of her voice an old woman came out of the cottage. She walked with a crutch, and wore a large garden bonnet, on which were painted flowers and leaves.

"You poor little child!" exclaimed the old woman; "how have you come down the broad, rushing river? What brings you so far out in the wide world?" She came down to the water's edge, drew the boat to land with her crutch, and lifted little Gerda out.

Gerda was glad to be on dry land again, although she was rather afraid of the old woman.

"Come in and tell me who you are and how you came here."

When Gerda had told her everything, the old woman said, "Hem! Hem!"

"Have you seen Kay? Has he been here?" said Gerda.

The old woman told her that she had not seen him, but that he might yet come. She begged Gerda not to fret, but to come out and eat cherries and look at the flowers. "They were prettier than any picture-book," she said, "for each flower could tell its own story." Then she took the child's hand, led her into the cottage, and shut the door.

The windows were very high, and the panes were yellow, red, and blue, so that the sunshine took the most wonderful colours. On the table stood a plate of cherries, and Gerda ate as many as she liked, for the old woman gave her leave to do so. While she was eating them the old woman combed her hair with a golden comb, and the soft, yellow curls fell round the sweet, fair face which looked so like a rose.

"I have often wished to have a dear little girl like you," said the old woman; "now you will see how happy we shall be together." And as she went on combing Gerda's hair, the child gradually forgot all about Kay, for the old woman was a witch. She was not, however, a wicked witch; she only conjured now and then for her amusement, and she wanted to keep little Gerda. So she went out into the garden and stretched out her crutch over the roses, and they all sank down, just as they were, into the earth; you could not see the place where they had stood. The old woman thought that if Gerda saw the roses she would be reminded of Kay and try to run away.

She called Gerda out into the flower-garden. What fragrance, and what a wealth of colour! There was every imaginable flower growing, and all in full bloom, no matter what the season was. No picture-book could be gayer and brighter. Gerda laughed for joy, and played about till the sun went down behind the tall cherry trees. Then she lay down to sleep in a pretty little bed, with pillows of crimson silk stuffed with violets. No queen upon her wedding night could have had brighter dreams.

The next day she played about among the flowers. Day after day passed by. Gerda knew every flower, and yet, although there were so many of them, it seemed to her that one was wanting, but she could not think what it was. One day, however, she happened to look at the painted wreath on the old woman's bonnet, and among the flowers she saw a rose. The old woman had forgotten to hide the picture when she conjured all the roses into the earth. But that is always the way – one cannot think of everything at once!

"What, are there no roses here?" cried Gerda. She ran among the flower-beds to find one, but she looked in vain. Then she sat down and cried, and her tears fell on the very place where a rose-tree had been buried. The warm tears sank into the earth, and as soon as they touched the roses the whole bush sprang up again in full bloom, just as it sank. Gerda threw her arms round it and kissed the roses. She thought of her roses at home and of little Kay.

"Oh, how I have been hindered!" she cried. "Why, I was looking for Kay. Do you know where he is?" she asked the roses; "do you think he is dead?"

"He is not dead," said the roses. "We have been in the earth where the dead people lie, and Kay was not there."

"Thank you," said little Gerda. She went to the other flowers, looked into their cups, and asked them, "Do you know where Kay is?"

But every flower was dreaming over its own story; Gerda heard plenty of them, but nothing at all about little Kay. The tiger-lily said, "Do you hear the drum? Tum-tum! It has but those two notes, 'Tum-tum!' Listen to the women's funeral chant, and the cry of the priests! Veiled in her long, red cloak, the Hindoo woman stands upon the pile; the flames leap round her and her dead husband; but the woman thinks only of the living – of him whose eyes burn hotter than the fire which will soon consume her body to ashes. Can the heart's flame die out among the ashes of the funeral pile?"

"I cannot understand you at all," said Gerda.

"That is my story," said the tiger-lily.

The convolvulus said, "An ancient castle frowns above the narrow path; evergreens cling to the crumbling walls and twine round the balcony, where a lovely maiden is standing. She looks down the narrow path. No rose upon the spray is lovelier, no apple-blossom stirred by the wind is more graceful than she. Her rich, silken robe rustles. 'Is he not coming?' she cries."

"Do you mean Kay?" said little Gerda.

"I am only telling my story, my dream," said the convolvulus.

The little snowdrop said, "The swing is set up between two tall trees, two pretty little girls – their dresses as white as snow, and long, green ribbons streaming from their hats – are sitting swinging. Their brother, who is taller than they, stands in the swing and winds his arm round the cord to support himself. In one hand he holds a clay pipe, and in the other a little dish. He is blowing soap-bubbles, and as the swing flies through the air the bubbles float round, purple and green and gold. The last one is still hanging on the bowl of the pipe. Down below, the little black dog, light as a bubble himself, tries to jump on to the swing as it falls back; but it rises again, the dog falls and barks furiously. The children tease him as the bubbles burst. A dream of changing colour, lit up by the golden sunlight.

"That is my story."

"And it may be a very pretty one," said Gerda; "but you tell it so mournfully, and you do not even mention Kay."

The hyacinths said, "There were three beautiful sisters, fragile and delicate. One was dressed in red, one in blue, and one in pure white. They danced hand in hand by moonlight, near the silent lake. They were not elves, but human maidens. The scent rose from the forest, rich and strong; the maidens disappeared in the wood, the perfume grew stronger still. Three coffins glided on to the lake from the dark forest and drifted away; within the coffins lay the three lovely maidens. The little glow-worms sparkled round the coffins like wandering stars. Were the maidens dead or sleeping? The scent of the flowers says they are dead; the vesper bell tolls as for a dirge."

"You make me quite sad," said little Gerda. "Your scent is so strong. It reminds me of the three dead maidens. Oh! is Kay really dead? The roses have been in the ground and they say he is not there."

"Cling clang!" rang the hyacinth bells; "we are not chiming for Kay; we do not know him. It is our song; the only song we know."

Gerda went to the buttercup, which shone like gold among its green leaves. "Tell me, you little golden star," she cried, "do you know where I shall find my lost playmate?"

The buttercups shone brighter than ever, and looked at Gerda. What were they going to say? It was nothing about Kay.

"The first spring sunbeams fell into a poor courtyard and gilded the white walls of the neighbour's house. The first yellow flower had just opened, and the old grandmother sat out of doors on her chair. Her granddaughter, a poor servant girl with a pretty face, had just come home for a visit. She kissed her grandmother, and the kiss was rich with the heart's best gold. Gold on the lips, gold in the earth, gold in the early dawn. That is my story."

"Poor old grandmother!" said Gerda. "How she is fretting after me and Kay! But I shall soon go back home and bring him with me. It is of no use asking the flowers; they know nothing but their own story; they can give me no help."

She tied up her dress so that she could run more quickly, but the narcissus caught her foot as she passed. She turned and looked at the tall, yellow flower. "Do you know anything, I wonder?" she thought. She bent over the flower to listen. The narcissus said, "I can see myself! I can see myself! A little dancer stands in the garret-chamber up yonder. She is half-dressed, and she stands first on one leg and then on two. She tramples the world under her feet; she is only an illusion. She pours water out of the teapot on to a piece of stuff which she has in her hand. It is her bodice – cleanliness is a virtue. Her white dress hangs up on a hook. That, too, has been washed in the teapot and dried on the roof. She puts it on, and ties a saffron-coloured scarf round her neck to make her dress look whiter. Out flies her little foot! See how she stands on one stem! I can see myself – I can see myself!"

"What does that matter to me?" said Gerda. "Why do you call me back to listen to such nonsense?" and she ran down to the garden gate.

The gate was shut, but she forced open the rusty latch; it sprang open, and little Gerda ran barefoot out into the world. She looked back three times, but no one was following her; and when she could run no farther she sat down upon a stone to rest. On looking round, she saw that the summer was over, and the autumn far advanced: in the beautiful garden, among the enchanted flowers and sunshine, she had seen no change of season and felt no breath of chill autumnal air.

"How I have hindered myself!" she cried. "Why, it is autumn – I must not rest any longer." And she rose to go.

Oh, how tired and sore her little feet were! It was cold and rough all around her, the long willow-leaves were yellow, and the dew dropped down like rain; one after another the leaves fell from the trees. There were no fruits but sloes, and they were hard and sour. The world looked grey, and bare, and sorrowful.

Chapter the Fourth
About a prince and a princess

Gerda was obliged to rest again. A great crow came hopping across the snow to the place where she sat. He had been standing looking at her for a long time, and moving his head from side to side. At last he said, "Caw! Caw! Good-day, good-day!" He could not pronounce his words very clearly; but he meant well to the little girl, and asked her whither she was going alone in the wide world? Gerda understood the word "*alone*" in a moment; and she told the crow her story from beginning to end, and asked him whether he had seen Kay.

The crow nodded thoughtfully and replied, "It may be so – it may be so!"

"What? You have seen him?" and Gerda almost kissed the crow to death.

"Gently, gently," said the crow. "Be calm. I think so – I believe – it may be little Kay. But he has quite forgotten you; he loves the Princess."

"Does he live with a princess?" asked Gerda.

"Yes. Now listen – but it is so difficult for me to speak your language. Do you understand the crows' language? I could tell you better if you did."

"No, I have not learnt it," said Gerda. "My grandmother understood it and could speak it. What a pity I never learned it!"

"Never mind," said the crow; "I must tell you as well as I can. But I shall not get on very well." And he told Gerda all he knew. "In this very kingdom where we are now sitting there lives a princess so outrageously clever that she has learnt all the newspapers in the world. And she has forgotten them again – she is as clever as that. A short time ago when she was sitting on her throne – and that is not half such a treat as people say – she began to sing. This was the song: 'Why should I not get married?' Now, there is a great deal in that," continued the crow. "And she wanted to get married; but she wanted also to find a man who could speak when he was spoken to, and do more than stand upright and look grand, for one gets tired of that in time. So she ordered the drum to be beat to call up all the Court ladies; and when they heard what she wanted they were extremely delighted.

"You may believe every word I am saying," said the crow. "I have a tame sweetheart who hops about in the palace all day long, and she told me everything."

Of course the sweetheart was a crow. Birds of a feather flock together, and a crow is always a crow.

"The newspapers were immediately published with a row of hearts round the border and the Princess's monogram at the top; and in the leading article it said that every good-looking young man was at liberty to come to the palace and speak to the Princess. Anyone who spoke so as to be heard might make himself at home; but the one who spoke the best would be chosen to marry the Princess. Yes, yes," said the crow, "you may believe me; it is as true as that I am sitting here. Young men came up in crowds; there was quite a tumult and stir in all the land; but nothing was settled, either on the first or second day. They could all speak well enough when they were in the street; but when they entered the palace hall and saw the royal guards in silver, when they went up the stairs and saw the lacqueys all in gold, and the brilliant, lofty rooms, they were quite taken aback. And when they stood before the throne where the Princess sat they could do nothing but repeat the last word she had said, and she had not the slightest desire to hear that over again. It seemed as if all the good folk had drunk off a sleeping-draught, for not a word could they find till they stood in the street again. There was a row of them reaching from the palace entrance to the town gates. I know, for I was among them," said the crow. "They were hungry and thirsty, and they did not get even a glass of water inside the palace. Some of the cleverest had brought some pieces of bread and butter, and they took care not to share it with their neighbours. No! Let him look hungry, and then the Princess won't have him. That was what they thought."

"But Kay, little Kay?" interrupted Gerda. "Was he among the crowd?"

"Wait a little – we are just coming to him. It was on the third day; there came up a youth, without horse or carriage, marching merrily right up to the palace door. His eyes sparkled like yours; he had beautiful hair, but his clothes were poor enough."

"It was Kay!" exclaimed Gerda exultingly. "I have found him again!" and she clapped her hands for joy.

"He had a little bundle on his back," said the crow.

"It must have been his skates," said Gerda. "He had them with him when he went away."

"It may be so," said the crow. "I did not look very closely at it. But I know this from my tame sweetheart, that when he came through the entrance door and saw the royal guards in silver and the lacqueys in gold he was not in the least confused. He just nodded to them, and said, 'You must find it rather tiresome standing perched up there from morning to night. For my part, I would rather go inside.' The halls were ablaze with light, councillors and excellencies were walking about in slippers, carrying golden vessels; it was enough to fill one with awe. And his boots creaked tremendously, but he was not in the least abashed."

"It is Kay; I am sure it is!" cried Gerda. "He had new boots on, and I have heard them creak myself in Grandmother's room."

"Upon my word, they *did* creak," said the crow. "And on he went right up to the Princess, not one whit afraid. She was sitting on a pearl as large as a spinning-wheel: all the maids of honour stood round her, with their attendants behind them, and every attendant had a maid of her own behind her. Then came the courtiers, with their attendants behind them, and the attendants' servants, and every servant had a boy to stand behind him – and the airs of these boys were so overpowering that one hardly dared to look at them, for the nearer they stood to the door the prouder they were."

"It must have been awful!" said little Gerda. "And did Kay win the Princess?"

"If I had not been a crow I would have taken her myself," said the crow, "in spite of my previous engagement. I hear the young man spoke as well as I do when I am speaking my own language: I heard that from my tame sweetheart. She tells me he was most polite and ready-witted: he said he had not come as a suitor, but only to listen to the Princess's wisdom. And the end of it was that they fell in love with each other."

"It must be Kay," said Gerda. "He is so clever: he can work sums up to fractions. Oh, do please take me to the palace!"

"That is easily said," replied the crow, "but how is it to be done? I will talk it over with my tame sweetheart, and she will perhaps advise us. But I must tell you that it is scarcely likely a little girl like you will be admitted into the palace."

"Oh, but I shall be!" cried Gerda. "When Kay hears that I am there he will come out and fetch me."

"Wait for me at the gate," said the crow, nodding; and he flew away.

It was late at night when the crow came back. "Caw! Caw!" he cried. "I am to give you her kind regards; and here is a piece of bread for you. She took it out of the kitchen, where there is enough and to spare; for she said you must be hungry. It is quite impossible for you to be admitted into the palace. You see, you have no shoes and stockings on! The royal guards in silver and the lacqueys in gold would not allow it. Don't cry: you shall go in for all that. My betrothed knows a private staircase which leads to the Prince's room, and she will manage to get the key."

They went into the palace garden, and along the broad avenue where the leaves were falling; and when the lights behind the palace windows had gone out one by one, the crow led Gerda to a back door which had been left unlocked.

Oh, how her heart beat with suspense and longing! She felt as if she were committing an evil deed, and yet all she wanted was to find little Kay. It must be he! She remembered so clearly his long hair and his clever, bright eyes; she could see him smile as he used to do at home under the roses. Surely he would be glad to see her, to hear what a long way she had travelled for his sake, and to learn how sorrowful they were at home when he did not come back! She felt happy, but half afraid.

They went up the private staircase. A small lamp was burning on the landing, and before it stood the tame crow, turning her head from side to side that she might get a good look at Gerda. Gerda courtesied low, as her grandmother had taught her.

"My betrothed has spoken of you so highly to me, my dear young lady," said the tame crow, "that I am delighted to serve you; your life-story is most interesting. Kindly take up the lamp, and I will precede you. We will go straight on, for we shall meet no one here."

"I seem to hear someone behind us," whispered Gerda. A strange sighing sound rushed past her, and things that looked like shadows on the wall – horses with flying manes and thin legs, huntsmen, ladies, and knights on horseback.

"They are only dreams," said the crow. "They are coming to invite the thoughts of all the lords and ladies to the dream-chase. That is all the better for us, because they will be sound asleep. But I hope that when you attain to rank and distinction you will show a grateful heart!"

"That is a matter of course," said the wild crow.

They entered the first room; the walls were hung with rose-coloured satin and brocaded flowers. The dreams followed them and rushed by so swiftly that Gerda could scarcely see the quality, as the tame crow called them. Every room was more splendid than the last; it was enough to dazzle one. At last they entered the bedroom. The ceiling was shaped like a tall palm tree, with leaves of crystal; and from the centre there hung two stems of gold, supporting two beds, formed like the cup of a lily. The Princess's bed was snow-white, the other was red. Gerda went to the bed and pulled aside the crimson leaves. She caught a glimpse of a brown neck. Oh, surely it was Kay! She called him by his name, and held the lamp above his face; the dreams rushed from the room by troops. The Prince awoke, turned round, and – it was not Kay!

The brown neck was the only likeness between them, though the Prince was young and handsome. Then the princess looked out through her white lily leaves, and asked who was there. Gerda wept bitterly as she told them all her story, and what the crows had done for her.

"Poor child!" cried the Prince and Princess, both together. They praised the crows, and said they were not at all displeased with them; but they were never to do it again. In the present instance they should be rewarded.

"Would you like to be set free?" asked the Princess; "or should you prefer a permanent appointment as Court crows, with the perquisites from the kitchen?"

The crows bowed down to the ground, and begged for the permanent appointment. They thought of their old age, and said it would be nice to have something laid by for their latter days.

The Prince rose from his bed and let Gerda sleep in it; and that was all he could do to help her.

Gerda folded her little hands and thought to herself, "How good they all are to me – men and animals alike!" Then she fell asleep, and the dreams came flying back. They looked like happy angels, and they drew after them a little sleigh in which Kay sat smiling. But they were only dreams, and so, of course, when Gerda woke they were gone away.

The next day she was dressed in silk and velvet, and the Princess asked her to stay at the palace and enjoy herself. But Gerda only begged for a little pony-carriage and a pair of boots, so that she might set out again in search of little Kay.

She received all she asked for, and a muff as well; and when she left the palace in her pretty travelling dress, she saw a beautiful golden carriage drawn up before the door, with the coat of arms of the Prince and Princess. Coachman, footmen, and out-riders – for there were out-riders as well – all wore crowns of gold. The Prince himself put her into the carriage, and the Princess came out to wish her all success.

The forest crow, who was now married to his sweetheart, went with her for the first three miles; he sat by her side, because he could not ride with his back to the horses. The other crow stood on the palace steps and flapped her wings; she did not accompany them, for she was suffering from a bilious headache, caused by eating too many good things since her recent appointment as Court crow. Inside the carriage Gerda found a store of sugar-cakes, fruit, and gingerbread-nuts.

"Goodbye, goodbye!" said the Prince and Princess. Little Gerda cried, and the crow cried. At the end of the three miles, the crow had to say goodbye, and that was the hardest parting of all. He flew on to a tree and flapped his wings in the sunshine as long as the carriage remained in sight.

Chapter the fifth
About the little robber girl

They drove on through the dark forest; but the coach shone like a torch, and that dazzled the eyes of the robbers till they could bear it no longer.

"Gold! Gold!" they shouted; and they rushed out, slew the coachman, footmen, and outriders, and pulled little Gerda out of the carriage.

"She is fat, she is tender, she has been fed on nuts," cried the old Robber Queen. She wore a long beard, and her eyebrows hung down over her eyes.

"She is as good as a nice, fat lamb; what a dainty bit she will be!" And she drew out her sharp knife; it was horrible to see how it gleamed.

"Yah!" shrieked the Robber Queen at the same moment. Her daughter, a rough, rude girl, had jumped on her back and bitten her ear. "You –!" said the Robber Queen, and she had no time to kill Gerda.

"She shall play with me," said the robber girl. "She shall give me her muff, and her pretty dress, and sleep in my bed." And she bit her mother again till the old Queen leaped up into the air and wrestled with her daughter. The robbers laughed aloud. "See how she dances with her cub!" they cried.

"I shall ride in the carriage," said the robber girl. And she had her way, for she was dreadfully spoiled and obstinate. She and Gerda sat in the carriage, and away they galloped over stock and stone. The little robber girl was just the same height as Gerda, but stouter and broader-shouldered. Her skin was brown and swarthy, and her eyes black and almost sorrowful. She threw her arm round Gerda's waist. "Nobody shall kill you unless I am angry with you," she said. "I suppose you are a Princess?"

"No," said Gerda. And then she told her story all through, and how dearly she loved little Kay.

The robber girl looked at her solemnly. "They shall not kill you even if I am angry with you," she said; "for then I can do it myself." And she dried Gerda's eyes, and put her hands into the warm, soft muff.

The coach suddenly stopped before the courtyard of the robbers' castle. The building was hardly better than a ruin; ravens and crows flew in and out of the rifts in the halls, and the great bulldogs, each of which looked ready enough to swallow a man, sprang to their full height, but did not bark, for that was forbidden. A clear fire was burning on the stone floor of the lofty, smoke-blackened room. The wreaths of smoke coiled and wound about the ancient rafters; a kettleful of rich soup was boiling over the fire; hares and rabbits were roasting on the spit.

"You shall sleep with me and all my little pet tonight," said the robber girl. Something was given them to eat and drink, and then they went into a corner where straw and carpets were laid down for beds. Above the bed were more than a hundred pigeons on laths and perches; they seemed asleep, but they moved their heads slowly as the robber girl came up.

"Every one of them belongs to me," said the little robber girl. She seized hold of the nearest, held it by its feet and shook it till its wings flapped again. "Kiss it," she said, sticking it against Gerda's face. "Those are the wood gentry up there," she said, pointing to a kind of cage made by a grating of bars placed before a hole in the wall; "if they were not kept very safe they would fly away. And here is my old favourite Baa! She pulled forward a reindeer which was tied up to the wall with a metal ring round his neck. "We have to hold him pretty fast or else he would give us the slip. At night I tickle him with my sharp knife; he is dreadfully afraid of that, I can tell you." She drew a long, sharp knife out of a crevice in the wall and let it slide across the reindeer's neck. The poor animal shivered and plunged wildly, but the robber girl laughed and pulled Gerda into bed with her.

"Do you keep the knife by you while you are asleep?" said Gerda, looking timidly at the glittering blade.

"Always," said the little robber girl. "One never knows what may happen. Now, tell me again about little Kay, and why you came out into the wide world." And Gerda began all over again, while the wood-pigeons moaned in the cage and the tame ones slept. The robber girl put one arm round Gerda's neck and clutched the knife in her other hand. She snored so loudly that Gerda could not close her eyes all night; she did not feel sure whether she was to live or die. The robbers sat drinking round the fire, and their riotous songs filled the little girl with dread.

Suddenly one of the wood-pigeons began to talk. "Curroo! Curroo!" it cried. "We have seen little Kay. A white bird drew his sleigh. He sat by the side of the Snow Queen. They passed through the wood as we lay in our nests. The Snow Queen breathed on us, and all the young ones died but two. Curroo! Curroo!"

"What do you say, up there?" said Gerda. "Where was the Snow Queen going? Tell me all you know."

"Most likely she was going to Lapland, where there is always snow and ice. Ask the reindeer, the one who is tied up by a cord."

"There is ice and snow," said the reindeer. "It is a splendid place. We gallop about unfettered in the glittering plains. The Snow Queen has her summer palace there; but her grandest palace is the one by the north pole, up in Spitzbergen."

"Oh, Kay, my little Kay!" cried Gerda.

"Lie still, or I will plunge my knife into your heart," said the little robber girl.

In the morning Gerda told the robber girl all that the wood-pigeons had said.

She listened gloomily and nodded her head. "It is all one!" she cried. "Do you know where Lapland is?" she asked the reindeer.

"Who should know better than I?" said he, and his eyes sparkled. "I was born and bred there; I have galloped over all its snow fields."

"Look here," said the robber girl to Gerda – "all our men are away; there is only my mother here, and she will stay; but towards midday she will drink out of the great bottle till she falls asleep, and then I will do something for you."

She sprang out of bed, squeezed her mother round the neck, pulled her beard, and cried, "Good morning, my dear old nanny-goat!" And her mother filliped her nose till it was black and blue, and it was all done from pure love.

When the Robber Queen had drunk out of her bottle and was gone to sleep, her daughter went up to the reindeer and said, "I could amuse myself often by tickling you with my sharp knife, for it makes you look so absurd; but, in spite of that, I am going to untie your cord and help you out, so that you may run to Lapland. You must make the best use of your legs and carry this little girl to the Snow Queen's palace, where her little playmate is. I dare say you heard all she said, for she spoke loud enough, and you were listening."

The reindeer bounded with joy. The robber girl lifted Gerda on his back, and had the forethought to tie her firmly on. She gave her her own little cushion for a seat, and her fur boots. "You must have them back," she said, "for it will be dreadfully cold; but I am going to keep the muff; it is so pretty. Not that you need freeze. Here are my mother's driving-gloves; they will come up to your elbows. Come, creep in. And now your hands look like my ugly old mother's."

Gerda wept for joy.

"I can't bear to see you whimper," said the robber girl. "Look merry, this minute! Here are two loaves and a ham, so you won't die of hunger." Everything was tied fast to the saddle; the little robber girl opened the door, called in all the dogs, cut the rope with her sharp knife, and said to the reindeer, "Off with you, and take care of the little girl."

Gerda held out her hands in their great driving-gloves, and said, "Goodbye!" And away went the reindeer over stock and stone, through the dark wood, across marsh and fen, as fast as he could run. The wolves howled and the ravens shrieked.

A light quivered in the sky like fitful flames. "There they are," cried the reindeer, "my old northern lights! How they shine!"

Faster and faster they went; the loaves were eaten up and the ham also, and then they were in Lapland.

Chapter the Sixth
About the Lapland woman and the Finland woman

The reindeer stopped before a squalid, wretched-looking hut. The roof nearly touched the ground, and the door was so low that everyone who passed in and out had to creep on their hands and knees. No one was in the hut but an old Lapland woman, who was boiling fish by the light of a train-oil lamp. The reindeer told her Gerda's story; but not until he had told his own, which seemed to him far more important; and Gerda was so benumbed with cold that she could not speak.

"Poor creature!" said the Lapland woman; "you have a long journey before you still. You must travel a hundred miles farther into Finland, the Snow Queen is living there just now, at her country seat, and burning Bengal lights every evening. I will write a few lines to her on a dried stockfish, for I have no paper; and then all you have to do is to give my letter to the Finland woman. She will be able to advise you better than I can do."

When Gerda had warmed herself thoroughly, and had taken something to eat and drink, the Lapland woman wrote the letter on the dried stockfish, begged her to take care of it, and tied her safely on the reindeer's back.

Away they went once more. The whole air was whizzing and starting with the beautiful blue flashes. The northern lights burned all night long. At last they came to Finland and knocked at the wise woman's chimney, for door she had none.

Inside the hut the heat was almost stifling, and the Finland woman went about half dressed. She lifted little Gerda down from the reindeer, took off her boots and driving-gloves, or she would not have been able to bear the heat, laid a piece of ice on the reindeer's head, and read the letter. She read it over carefully three times, and then, as she knew it by heart, she put the fish in the kettle to boil for dinner – she never wasted anything.

The reindeer told his story, and when he had quite finished he told Gerda's. The old Finland woman blinked her sharp eyes, but did not say a word.

"You are wise and cunning," said the reindeer. "I know that you can tie up all the winds of heaven in a coil of rope. If the sailor unties the first knot he has a favourable wind; but if he unties the second, he is sorry for it before long; and if he unties the third and fourth there comes such a storm as lays whole forests low. Can you not give the little girl a potion which will make her as strong as twelve men, so that she may be able to conquer the Snow Queen?"

"The strength of twelve men would not help her much," said the Finland woman. She went up to her bed and took from it a large roll of parchment, written all over in the most curious characters. This she read and pondered till the perspiration poured down her forehead.

But the reindeer begged so hard for little Gerda, and the child looked at her with such tearful, imploring eyes, that the Finland woman felt her own eyes beginning to twinkle again. She drew the reindeer aside into a corner and whispered something to him while she put fresh pieces of ice on his head.

"Kay is in the Snow Queen's palace," she whispered, "and he finds everything there just to his liking. He thinks it is the best place in the world; but that is because he has a tiny splinter of glass in his eye, and another in his heart. Until they are taken away the Snow Queen will have him in her power, and no one can help him."

"But can you not give little Gerda something which will give her power over the whole thing?"

"I can give her no greater power than she already possesses. Do you not see how great that is? Do you not see how all things, men and animals alike, are forced to help her? And how well she has succeeded already, although she started barefoot in the world? She can receive no spells from us; her power lies in her heart, and consists in her being a dear, innocent child. If she cannot find her own way to the Snow Queen's palace, and to set Kay free, we cannot help her. The Snow Queen's park begins two miles from here, and thither you must carry the little girl. Then set her down by the bush which bears red berries among the snow; don't stay for any foolish chatter, but make haste back to me." And the Finland woman tied Gerda on the reindeer's back, and they set off at full speed.

"Oh, I have left my boots! I have left my gloves!" cried little Gerda. It was the bitter cold which made her find out her loss, but the reindeer dared not stop. He ran on till he saw the bush with the red berries, and there Gerda got down. Great tears fell from the reindeer's eyes; Gerda kissed him; and he turned away without speaking and ran back to the Finland woman's hut. There stood poor little Gerda, barefoot and without gloves, in the bitter Finland ice and snow.

She ran forward as fast as she could among a whole army of whirling snowflakes. They did not fall from the clouds, for the sky overhead was clear and brilliant with the northern lights. The snow-flakes ran along the ground, and the nearer they came, the larger they grew. Gerda remembered how large they had looked when she saw them through the burning glass. But now they were larger and more terrible than ever; they were alive; it was the vanguard of the Snow Queen's army. They were of the most wonderful shapes; some of them like ugly, bristling swine; some like knotted coils of snakes, and some like fat little bears, with ruffled fur; but all were dazzlingly white, and all were alive.

Then little Gerda began to say, "Our Father which art in heaven." It was so cold that she could see her own breath as it came from her lips, like vapour. The vapoury wreaths thickened and grew, and when they touched the ground they took the shape of little angels, with helmets, spears, and shields. Every second their numbers increased, and by the time Gerda had finished her prayer there was a whole legion round her. The angels touched the snowflakes with their glittering spears, and the flakes broke into a thousand pieces. Gerda went bravely forward; the angels stroked her hands and feet till they got back a little warmth, and Gerda reached the palace in safety.

But now it is time to see what Kay was doing. He certainly was not thinking of little Gerda – least of all that she was standing outside the palace door.

Chapter the Seventh
About the Snow Queen's palace, and what happened there

The palace walls were built of drifting snow, and the doors and windows of keen, cold winds. There were more than a hundred chambers in the palace, shaped just as the snow had been blown together; the largest of them was many miles in length. The glittering northern lights gleamed through them all, and showed how empty, cold, and bare they were. Amusements of any kind were utterly unknown in the lofty, brilliant halls; there was never even a juvenile bears' ball, where the young polar bears could dance on their hind-legs and show their polished manners; never a merry game at tic, or a tea-party with bonbons and gossip for the arctic young lady foxes. The great halls were silent, bare, and cold. The northern lights shone so accurately that you could tell when they were highest and when lowest. In the centre of the endless hall was a frozen lake which had cracked in a thousand directions at once. Each piece was like all the rest, and in the centre of the lake sat the Snow Queen, when she was at home. She said the lake was the mirror of reason, the best and most glorious place in the world.

Little Kay was blue, nay, almost black with cold, but he did not know it, for the Snow Queen had kissed him till he was numb, and his heart was a lump of ice. He was busily dragging together sharp, flat pieces of ice, and trying to make them fit into one another. It was just like trying to fit together a Chinese puzzle. He made the cleverest shapes and designs; they were part of the ice puzzle of reason. Kay thought there was nothing in the universe higher or better than these puzzles, but that was because of the piece of glass in his eye. He could place the pieces of ice in written words, but never in the one word he wanted them to make – Eternity! The Snow Queen had said to him, "If you can make out that word you shall be your own master, and I will give you the whole world and a pair of new skates." But he could not make out the word.

"I am going to fly down to the warm countries," said the Snow Queen. "I must look into my black kettles, as people call them" – it was the burning craters of Etna and Vesuvius which she meant – "I must whiten them over a little. It will improve them, and be good for the grapes and lemons." The Snow Queen flew away, and Kay sat alone in the bleak, desolate halls; he bent over his ice-flakes and thought till his limbs cracked again; stiff and silent he sat there; you would have thought that he was frozen.

It was just at that moment that little Gerda entered the palace gate. Keen, bitter winds moaned round her as if they were trying vainly to go to sleep. She walked on through the desolate halls till she saw Kay, and then, with a cry of delight, she rushed forward and clasped him in her arms. "Kay, dear little Kay," she cried, "have I found you at last?" She held him close to her heart; but he remained silent and cold. Then Gerda began to cry, and her hot tears fell on his head and on his breast; they sank into his heart till the ice was melted and the piece of glass washed away. He looked up at her, and she sang:

> "The roses all must fade and die,
> We shall see Christ the Child on high."

Kay burst into tears, and the piece of glass swam out of his eye. Then he knew her again and cried aloud, "Gerda, my sweet little Gerda! Where have you been all this long time? And where am I?"

He looked round him and shivered. "How cold it is here!" he

cried; "how bare and empty!" He clung to Gerda, and she laughed and cried for joy. It was such a pretty sight that even the pieces of ice danced about; and when they were tired they fell of their own accord into the very word which the Snow Queen had bid him make out! There it lay, bright and clear – Eternity. Kay was his own master now, and free to go where he would.

Gerda kissed his cheeks and they glowed red; she kissed his eyes and they shone like her own; she kissed his hands and feet and he felt strong and happy again. The Snow Queen might come home now whenever she liked; there stood his release-warrant written in glittering letters of ice.

Hand-in-hand the children wandered out of the lofty palace, talking of the old grandmother and of the roses on the roof. Wherever they came the winds sank to rest and the sun broke out; and when they reached the bush with the red berries they found the reindeer waiting for them. He had brought with him another young reindeer, whose udders were full of milk; the children drank long draughts of the warm milk and kissed the kind animal. The two reindeers carried Kay and Gerda to the Finland woman first; there they sat till they were warmed and rested and had talked over their homeward journey. They rode next to the Lapland woman, she had made them some clothes and mended their sleigh. The reindeers ran with them as far as the borders of the land; the first green of early spring was beginning to show.

"Goodbye!" said the children to the reindeers.

"Goodbye!" they said all round.

The young birds were beginning to twitter, the delicate green buds were seen on every tree, and out of the forest came a splendid horse which Gerda knew well, for it had been harnessed to the golden coach.

On its back sat a young girl, with a scarlet cap on her head and a pair of pistols in her belt. It was the little robber girl; she had had enough of living at home and was on her way to the North; if that did not suit her, she meant to try some other place. She knew Gerda at once, and Gerda knew her. Both of them were delighted.

"You're a nice fellow to go roving about in this fashion!" she said to Kay. "I should like to know whether you think you deserve that anyone should run all over the world to find you!"

But Gerda patted her cheeks and asked after the Prince and Princess.

"They are travelling abroad," said the robber girl.

"And the crow?" said Gerda.

"Oh, the crow is dead!" answered the robber girl. "His tame sweetheart is now a widow, and hops about with a piece of black crape tied round her leg. She makes a great fuss and to-do, but it is all gammon. But now tell me what has happened to you and how you caught him?"

And Kay and Gerda told her all.

"Snip-snap-snurre-purre-basselurre!" said the robber girl. She shook hands with them both, and promised that if ever she rode through their town she would call and see them. And then she rode away, out into the wide world.

But Kay and Gerda wandered homeward hand-in-hand. The lovely springtide was blossoming round them, the church bells rang, and they saw the tall steeples of the great town where they lived. On they went, through the town gates, up the staircase, into the room where the old grandmother was sitting.

Everything stood in its old place, the clock ticked as before, the pendulum swung to and fro; but as they passed through the doorway they found that they were quite grown up.

The roses peeped in at the window, and there stood the low stools where they used to sit when they were children. They sat down hand-in-hand; the cold, brilliant emptiness of the Snow Queen's palace faded from their memory like a bad dream. The old grandmother sat in the sunshine and read aloud out of her Bible, "Except ye become as little children ye cannot enter into the kingdom of heaven."

Kay and Gerda looked into each other's eyes, and all at once they understood the old hymn:

> "The roses all must fade and did,
> We shall see Christ the Child on high."

There they sat, grown up, and children still. Children in heart and soul.

And it was summer – warm, blessed, glorious summer!

The Story of Nick

~

Christina Rossetti

THERE DWELT IN A small village, not a thousand miles from Fairyland, a poor man, who had no family to labour for or friend to assist. When I call him poor, you must not suppose he was a homeless wanderer, trusting to charity for a night's lodging; on the contrary, his stone house, with its green verandah and flower-garden, was the prettiest and snuggest in all the place, the doctor's only excepted. Neither was his store of provisions running low: his farm supplied him with milk, eggs, mutton, butter, poultry, and cheese in abundance; his fields with hops and barley for beer, and wheat for bread; his orchard with fruit and cider; and his kitchen-garden with vegetables and wholesome herbs. He had, moreover, health, an appetite to enjoy all these good things, and strength to walk about his possessions.

No, I call him poor because, with all these, he was discontented and envious. It was in vain that his apples were the largest for miles around, if his neighbour's vines were the most productive by a single bunch; it was in vain that his lambs were fat and thriving, if someone else's sheep bore twins: so, instead of enjoying his own prosperity, and being glad when his neighbours prospered too, he would sit grumbling and bemoaning himself as if every other man's riches were his poverty. And thus it was that one day our friend Nick leaned over Giles Hodge's gate, counting his cherries.

"Yes," he muttered, "I wish I were sparrows to eat them up, or a blight to kill your fine trees altogether."

The words were scarcely uttered when he felt a tap on his shoulder, and, looking round, perceived a little rosy woman, no bigger than a butterfly, who held her tiny fist clenched in a menacing attitude. She looked scornfully at him, and said: "Now listen, you churl, you! Henceforward you shall straightway become everything you wish; only mind, you must remain under one form for at least an hour." Then she gave him a slap in the face, which made his cheek tingle as if a bee had stung him, and disappeared with just so much sound as a dewdrop makes in falling.

Nick rubbed his cheek in a pet, pulling wry faces and showing his teeth. He was boiling over with vexation, but dared not vent it in words lest some unlucky wish should escape him. Just then the sun seemed to shine brighter than ever, the wind blew spicy from the south; all Giles's roses looked redder and larger than before, while his cherries seemed to multiply, swell, ripen. He could refrain no longer, but, heedless of the fairy-gift he had just received, exclaimed, "I wish I were sparrows eating – "

No sooner said than done: in a moment he found himself a whole flight of hungry birds, pecking, devouring, and bidding fair to devastate the envied cherry-trees. But honest Giles was on the watch hard by; for that very morning it had struck him he must make nets for the protection of his fine fruit. Forthwith he ran home, and speedily returned with a revolver furnished with quite a marvellous array of barrels. Pop, bang – pop, bang! He made short work of the sparrows, and soon reduced the enemy to one crestfallen biped with broken leg and wing, who limped to hide himself under a holly-bush. But, though the fun was over, the hour was not; so Nick must needs sit out his allotted time.

Next a pelting shower came down, which soaked him through his torn, ruffled feathers; and then, exactly as the last drops fell and the sun came out with a beautiful rainbow, a tabby cat pounced upon him. Giving himself up for lost, he chirped in desperation, "O, I wish I were a dog to worry you!" Instantly – for the hour was just passed – in the grip of his horrified adversary, he turned at bay, a savage bull-dog. A shake, a deep bite, and poor puss was out of her pain. Nick, with immense satisfaction, tore her fur to bits, wishing he could in like manner exterminate all her progeny.

At last, glutted with vengence, he lay down beside his victim, relaxed his ears and tail, and fell asleep.

Now that tabby-cat was the property and special pet of no less a personage than the doctor's lady; so when dinner-time came, and not the cat, a general consternation pervaded the household. The kitchens were searched, the cellars, the attics; every apartment was ransacked; even the watch-dog's kennel was visited. Next the stable was rummaged, then the hay-loft; lastly, the bereaved lady wandered disconsolately through her own private garden into the shrubbery, calling "Puss, puss," and looking so intently up the trees as not to perceive what lay close before her feet. Thus it was that, unawares, she stumbled over Nick, and trod upon his tail.

Up jumped our hero, snarling, biting, and rushing at her with such blind fury as to miss his aim. She ran; he ran. Gathering up his strength, he took a flying leap after his victim; her foot caught in the spreading root of an oak tree, she fell, and he went over her head, clear over, into a bed of stinging-nettles. Then she found breath to raise that fatal cry, "Mad dog!"

Nick's blood curdled in his veins; he would have slunk away if he could; but already a stout labouring-man, to whom he had done many an ill turn in the time of his humanity, had spied him, and, bludgeon in hand, was preparing to give chase. However, Nick had the start of him, and used it too; while the lady, far behind, went on vociferating, "Mad dog, mad dog!" inciting doctor, servants, and vagabonds to the pursuit. Finally, the whole village came pouring out to swell the hue and cry.

The dog kept ahead gallantly, distancing more and more the asthmatic doctor, fat Giles, and, in fact, all his pursuers except the bludgeon-bearing labourer, who was just near enough to persecute his tail. Nick knew the magic hour must be almost over, and so kept forming wish after wish as he ran – that he were a viper only to get trodden on, a thorn to run into some one's foot, a man-trap in the path, even the detested bludgeon to miss its aim and break. This wish crossed his mind at the propitious moment; the bull-dog vanished, and the labourer, overreaching himself, fell flat on his face, while his weapon struck deep into the earth, and snapped.

A strict search was instituted after the missing dog, but without success. During two whole days the village children were exhorted to keep indoors and beware of dogs; on the third an inoffensive bull pup was hanged, and the panic subsided.

Meanwhile the labourer, with his shattered stick, walked home in silent wonder, pondering on the mysterious disappearance. But the puzzle was beyond his solution; so he only made up his mind not to tell his wife the whole story till after tea. He found her preparing for that meal, the bread and cheese set out, and the kettle singing softly on the fire. "Here's something to make the kettle boil, Mother," said he, thrusting our hero between the bars and seating himself; "for I'm mortal tired and thirsty."

Nick crackled and blazed away cheerfully, throwing out bright sparks, and lighting up every corner of the little room. He toasted the cheese to a nicety, made the kettle boil without spilling a drop, set the cat purring with comfort, and illuminated the pots and pans into splendour. It was provocation enough to be burned; but to contribute by his misfortune to the well-being of his tormentors was still more aggravating. He heard, too, all their remarks and wonderment about the supposed mad dog, and saw the doctor's lady's own maid bring the labourer five shillings as a reward for his exertions. Then followed a discussion as to what should be purchased with the gift, till at last it was resolved to have their best window glazed with real glass. The prospect of their grandeur put the finishing-stroke to Nick's indignation. Sending up a sudden flare, he wished with all his might that he were fire to burn the cottage.

Forthwith the flame leaped higher than ever flame leaped before. It played for a moment about a ham, and smoked it to a nicety; then, fastening on the woodwork above the chimney-corner, flashed full into a blaze. The labourer ran for help, while his wife, a timid woman, with three small children, overturned two pails of water on the floor, and set the beer-tap running. This done, she hurried, wringing her hands, to the door, and threw it wide open. The sudden draught of air did more mischief than all Nick's malice, and fanned him into quite a conflagration. He danced upon the rafters, melted a pewter-pot and a pat of butter, licked up the beer, and was just making his way towards the bedroom when through the thatch and down the chimney came a rush of water. This arrested his progress for the

moment; and before he could recover himself, a second and a third discharge from the enemy completed his discomfiture. Reduced ere long to one blue flame, and entirely surrounded by a wall of wet ashes, Nick sat and smouldered; while the good-natured neighbours did their best to remedy the mishap – saved a small remnant of beer, assured the labourer that his landlord was certain to do the repairs, and observed that the ham would eat "beautiful".

Our hero now had leisure for reflection. His situation precluded all hope of doing further mischief; and the disagreeable conviction kept forcing itself upon his mind that, after all, he had caused more injury to himself than to any of his neighbours. Remembering, too, how contemptuously the fairy woman had looked and spoken, he began to wonder how he could ever have expected to enjoy her gift. Then it occurred to him that if he merely studied his own advantage without trying to annoy other people, perhaps his persecutor might be propitiated; so he fell to thinking over all his acquaintances, their fortunes and misfortunes; and, having weighed well their several claims on his preference, ended by wishing himself the rich old man who lived in a handsome house just beyond the turnpike. In this wish he burned out.

The last glimmer had scarcely died away when Nick found himself in a bed hung round with faded curtains, and occupying the centre of a large room. A night-lamp, burning on the chimney-piece, just enabled him to discern a few shabby old articles of furniture, a scanty carpet, and some writing materials on a table. These objects looked somewhat dreary; but for his comfort he felt an inward consciousness of a goodly money-chest stowed away under his bed, and of sundry precious documents hidden in a secret cupboard in the wall.

So he lay very cosily, and listened to the clock ticking, the mice squeaking, and the house-dog barking down below. This was, however, but a drowsy occupation; and he soon bore witness to its somniferous influence by sinking into a fantastic dream about his money-chest. First, it was broken open, then shipwrecked, then burned; lastly, some men in masks, whom he knew instinctively to be his own servants, began dragging it away. Nick started up, clutched hold of something in the dark, found his last dream true, and the next moment was stretched on the floor – lifeless, yet not insensible – by a heavy blow from a crowbar.

The men now proceeded to secure their booty, leaving our hero where he fell. They carried off the chest, broke open and ransacked the secret closet, overturned the furniture, to make sure that no hiding-place of treasure escaped them, and at length, whispering together, left the room. Nick felt quite discouraged by his ill success, and now entertained only one wish – that he was himself again. Yet even this wish gave him some anxiety; for he feared that if the servants returned and found him in his original shape they might take him for a spy, and murder him in downright earnest. While he lay thus cogitating two of the men reappeared, bearing a shutter and some tools. They lifted him up, laid him on the shutter, and carried him out of the room, down the back stairs, through a long vaulted passage, into the open air. No word was spoken; but Nick knew they were going to bury him.

An utter horror seized him, while, at the same time, he felt a strange consciousness that his hair would not stand on end because he was dead. The men set him down, and began in silence to dig his grave. It was soon ready to receive him; they threw the body roughly in, and cast upon it the first shovelful of earth.

But the moment of deliverance had arrived. His wish suddenly found vent in a prolonged unearthly yell. Damp with night dew, pale as death, and shivering from head to foot, he sat bolt upright, with starting, staring eyes and chattering teeth. The murderers, in mortal fear, cast down their tools, plunged deep into a wood hard by, and were never heard of more.

Under cover of night Nick made the best of his way home, silent and pondering. Next morning he gave Giles Hodge a rare tulip-root, with full directions for rearing it; he sent the doctor's wife a Persian cat twice the size of her lost pet; the labourer's cottage was repaired, his window glazed, and his beer-barrel replaced by unknown agency; and when a vague rumour reached the village that the miser was dead, that his ghost had been heard bemoaning itself, and that all his treasures had been carried off, our hero was one of the few persons who did not say, "And served him right, too."

Finally, Nick was never again heard to utter a wish.

The Three Bears

∾

Sarah Baker

IN A CERTAIN GERMAN forest near the Hartz mountains there lived three exceedingly domestic bears.

There was the father-bear, the mother-bear, and a little son. They had a nice little house; a chair each to sit on, a bed to sleep in, and a basin each for milk and honey, which was their favourite food.

The father's were the largest, the mother's were a little smaller, the little bear's were the smallest of all.

One day they boiled their milk and honey for breakfast, poured it into their basins, and went out for a walk while it cooled. Now it happened that very near the bear's dwelling lived a woodman's little daughter, all by herself.

She was called Golden Hair. Her father and mother were both dead, so she was quite alone. She kept her small house very neat, made herself a bed of moss and beech leaves, and used to pick berries for her food. Of course the poor little thing had no one to teach her right from wrong, and she lived quite like a little savage in her forest home; only she was a gentle creature, and used to sing like the birds in the trees under which she played.

On the very morning that the three bears went for a walk, Golden Hair also was rambling about the wood.

By-and-by she came to the bears' house, and as the window was open, she peeped in.

Seeing no one there, she lifted the latch and walked into the house. This was very rude of Golden Hair; but then she knew no better.

She saw the three basins, and looked into them, and then, taking up the tiny bear's, she tasted his milk and honey. She thought it very nice indeed; she sat down in the little bear's chair to eat it; but the chair was much too small for her, and she broke the seat and fell through, basin and all.

Now this was certainly stealing, but Golden Hair did not know that she ought not to take that which was not her own. A tiny bear may be only a tiny bear, but still he has a right to his own things.

Then Golden Hair went upstairs, and there she saw three beds all in a row. The first was the father-bear's, the second was the mother-bear's, the last was the tiny bear's.

Golden Hair thought that they looked very comfortable, and as she was a little tired, she got into the tiny bear's, and fell asleep.

By-and-by, the bears came home.

Tiny-bear looked at his chair and basin, and said:

"Somebody has been here."

And Father-bear said gruffly:

"Somebody has been here."

And Mother-bear said, not quite so gruffly:

"Somebody has been here."

Then they went to the table and looked at their basins.

And the Father-bear said gruffly:

"Somebody has touched my basin."

And the Mother-bear said less gruffly:

"Somebody has touched my basin."

And Tiny-bear said in a high, shrill voice:

"And somebody has *broken* mine."

Then they all went upstairs, and looked in their beds.

"There is no one in my bed," said Father-bear gruffly.

"There is nobody in my bed," said the Mother-bear less gruffly.

"There is a little girl in my bed," squeaked Tiny-bear, "and she has eaten up my breakfast, and broken my chair, and cracked my basin."

The shrill voice of Tiny-bear woke up Golden Hair, and she started out of bed.

The window was open, and she was so frightened that she jumped right out of it at once, and ran away; and the bears went to the window and watched her, and saw her disappear in the forest.

And the Father-bear said gruffly:

"The wolves will eat her."

And the Mother-bear said less gruffly:

"The wolves will eat her."

And Tiny-bear squeaked in his shrill voice:

"The wolves will eat her."

But they did not.

Now if you wish very much to know what became of Golden Hair, I will tell you.

As she ran, terrified, through the wood, she fell over the trunk of a tree, and while she lay on the ground, weeping, a bee buzzed up to her and said:

"Little Golden Hair, what has happened?"

And Golden Hair said:

"I went into the bears' house, beautiful bee, and ate up some milk and honey; and then I got into Tiny-bear's bed and fell asleep, and the bears came home and found me; and I was so frightened that I jumped out of the window, and I have just fallen down. If I had not jumped out, I dare say they would have killed me."

"Very likely," buzzed the bee; "I dislike bears very much myself, and never cross their threshold. They eat our honey, and have no manners; and then their figures are so very awkward, and their movements so uncouth! But you had no right to eat Tiny-bear's breakfast ‒ that was stealing, and it is wrong. *I* never take a drop of honey from a flower without asking its leave first."

Golden Hair sobbed out that she did not know it was wrong.

"Well," said the bee, "I don't see how you should, as you have not been taught. We bees have often pitied you. Now I am not rich; I am only an upholsterer bee, and I don't live in a hive, and I have no queen; but if you like to live with me and be my little girl, I will do all I can for you."

Golden Hair was very glad to accept this kind offer, for she thought that honey was very nice; and she had no doubt that it would be her food if she lived with the upholsterer bee.

Then the bee showed the child where she lived, in a hollow tree. And Golden Hair thought it was a very fine dwelling, for the bee had hung it all round with curtains cut from red poppy leaves; and it was so clean that you would have been delighted with it.

"Now, Golden Hair," said the bee, "we cannot endure dirty children. Go and wash yourself in the stream; and wash your frock, and hang it out to dry."

And Golden Hair did as she was told; and when she was nicely dressed again in a clean white frock, and all her golden hair lay on her shoulders glistening in the sun, she looked very pretty indeed.

And she played all day with the butterflies and birds, and when the sun set she fell asleep.

The next day the bee buzzed in her ear as soon as it was light, and woke her up.

"Golden Hair," she said, as the child sat up and rubbed her sleepy blue eyes, "we can't have idle people here. I hate a drone: get up and work."

"I have nothing to do," said Golden Hair; "I can't make honey."

"But you can do a great many other things! I only wish I had your wonderful hands," said the bee.

"What can I do?" asked Golden Hair.

"I will tell you. Get up and take a wooden spade, and dig up the sweetest flowers in the wood, and plant them here close to my cell; and when no rain comes, water them, and don't let the greedy worms eat them all up, but pick them off the leaves."

Golden Hair did as she was told, but not for very long.

For a silly butterfly came and coaxed her to run a race with him, and laughed at her for grubbing in the ground and making her hands dirty.

So she ran races, and did not work.

By-and-by she was hungry, and she said to the butterfly:

"Will you give me some honey for dinner?"

"I have not any honey," he answered; "you could not expect a gentleman like me to provide food. It is quite beneath me. I eat a little bit of leaf here and there."

"Oh! I am so hungry!" sobbed Golden Hair.

"Absurd! How vulgar you are!" sang the butterfly, and he flew away; for, as he told the nearest rose, he hated to see tears; and the rose smiled at his wit, and admired his fine feelings.

Golden Hair went home and found her dinner ready – the purest honey, scented with lilac, and wild thyme, and honeysuckles – and she ate a great deal of it, and thanked the bee.

And the bee said:

"You have not done much work. If I had been as idle as you are, I should have had no dinner to give you."

"It was all the butterfly's fault!" said Golden Hair.

"Nonsense," said the bee, "he could not make you idle unless you chose to be so. Don't tell me! One would get very little done if one could be persuaded to play by every idle insect one saw."

"I will do better tomorrow," said Golden Hair.

"Better begin today," answered the bee. "Who can tell if the sun will shine tomorrow?"

So Golden Hair worked all the afternoon, and when night came she felt happy and satisfied, as everybody does when they have done right.

And a kind nightingale, who had been pleased to see her so

industrious, came and sat on a bough close by, and sang her to sleep.

The next day a robin woke her.

"Get up," he said, "Golden Hair. The lark is singing hymns, and it is a pity you should not join in them; besides, if you don't get up early you will find no worms."

"Thank you," said Golden Hair, "but I don't eat worms; I breakfast on honey."

"That's very well for dessert," said Robin; "but for food I prefer something more substantial."

"I should like a few cherries," sighed Golden Hair.

"There are plenty of strawberries in the wood," said Robin. "If you will come with me, I will show you where they grow."

And he showed Golden Hair a bed of ripe red strawberries growing on a sunny bank. They were quite delicious.

"What a clever bird you are!" said the child, as she ate her breakfast with the robin; "and yet I should not have thought so, judging by your very plain suit, though, to be sure, your breast is a pretty colour."

"We must not judge by outside show," said Robin. "Neither I nor the bee are as gay as the butterfly, but I think I may say, without boasting, that we are worth a dozen of him."

And Golden Hair thought so too.

By-and-by the winter came; the snow fell fast and the bitter wind blew through the trees.

Golden Hair crouched down inside the old tree on the moss, and wept with the cold.

"What a pity it is you have no feathers!" said the robin.

"Go to sleep," said the bee drowsily; "this is the sort of weather for a good nap."

But Golden Hair could not sleep for the cold, and wishing would not give her feathers.

By-and-by the robin said to the bee:

"Golden Hair ought to go home to her own kind. I have had some crumbs today from such good people; I am sure if they knew the child was here, they would help her."

"But how can we let them know?" said the bee. "You

see, their education is so bad that they know nothing of our languages."

"I will tell the dog," said Robin; "he is a great philosopher, and can settle ways and means. I often think he is much wiser than his master. A pheasant told me last autumn that the gentlemen can do nothing without him."

"Do speak to the dog," said the bee. "I don't like to see Golden Hair suffer, and do nothing for her."

So Robin told the dog. The dog said:

"Show me where the child is."

And Robin did so.

And the dog barked and fawned on the little child; and Golden Hair was pleased, and stroked him, and nestled up to him and warmed herself. And the dog lay close beside her, and warmed her with his breath.

And by-and-by he took some meat from his master's plate, and brought it to the hungry child.

And the dog's master said to his wife:

"I wonder where Tray goes every day with a piece of meat?"

And his wife said:

"Why do you not follow him?"

So the next day the gentleman went after his dog, and followed him through the wood till he came to a hollow tree.

And there, inside it, very pale, and cold, and miserable, lay a little child with golden hair. And the dog gave her the meat, while a solitary bee buzzed faintly near, and a robin twittered gratefully from a twig.

The dog's master went in and took the poor babe in his arms, and spoke to her. But Golden Hair had quite forgotten her own language and knew only the dialects of the wood. But she wept, and clasped the gentleman's arm with beseeching hands.

"Poor deserted babe!" he said, embracing her; "I will take you home, and you shall be to me as a daughter."

And the bee buzzed her contentment; and the robin sang a lay of rejoicing, and the dog barked and frisked as if he were wild with delight.

So Golden Hair was taken home by the dog's kind master. And he gave her to his wife, and said:

"I have found a wild child in the forest; let her be our own."

And the lady clasped the babe in her arms, and loved her from that day; and they had her christened "Mary". And thus it happened that no one ever knew what had become of Golden Hair.

The Three Goats Named Bruse; or, The Three Billy-Goats Gruff

~

Peter Asbjørnsen and Jørgen Moe

ONCE ON A TIME there were three goats that were going to the mountain-pasture to fatten, and all of them were called Bruse. On the road there was a bridge across a waterfall, over which they had to pass, and under which lived a great ugly Troll, with eyes as large as tin plates, and a nose as long as a broomstick. The youngest goat came first on the bridge.

"Trip trap, trip trap," said the bridge as he went over.

"Who trips on my bridge?" cried the Troll.

"Oh! it is only the little goat Bruse. I am going to the mountain-pasture to get fat," said the goat in a soft voice.

"Now I am coming to catch thee," said the Troll.

"Oh! no, pray don't take me, for I am so little; but if you will wait, the second goat Bruse is coming this way, and he is much bigger."

"Be it so," said the Troll.

Some time after the second goat came passing over the bridge.

"TRIP TRAP, TRIP TRAP, TRIP TRAP," said the bridge.

"Who trips over my bridge?" cried the Troll.

"Oh! it is the second goat Bruse, who is going to the mountain-pasture to get fat," said the goat, who was not delicate of speech.

"Now I am coming to catch thee," said the Troll.

"Oh! no, pray don't take me, but wait a little while, and then the big goat Bruse will come this way: he is much much bigger than I am."

"Be it so," answered the Troll.

Just at that moment came the big goat Bruse upon the bridge.

"TRIP TRAP, TRIP TRAP, TRIP TRAP," said the bridge, for he was so heavy that the bridge creaked and cracked under him.

"Who goes tramping on my bridge?" screamed the Troll.

"It is I, the great goat Bruse!" said the goat, who was very coarse of speech.

"Now I am coming to catch thee," cried the Troll.

> "Well! come thou then. Two spears I bear,
> With which thy entrails out I'll tear,"

said the goat, and then rushed upon the Troll, thrust out his eyes, broke his bones, and with his horns thrust him out into the waterfall; and then went on to the pasture.

There the goats grew so fat, so fat, that they were hardly able to go home again; and if they have not lost their fat, they are so still; and snip, snap, snout, now is my story out.

The Three Tasks

~

Geraldine Elliot

"Why should that rabbit be the hero of so many stories?" demanded Tandaubwe, the Spider, moodily. "I'm as clever as he is, aren't I? I'm as wise." Privately, Tandaubwe thought that he was far more brilliant. "As for Kamba, the Tortoise, and Nkhandwe, the Jackal, and all those" – a hairy leg was waved in a gesture that included a dozen different creatures – "well, they haven't even got brains. Not what I call brains!"

"I've got brains," asserted Nadzikambe, the Chameleon, a note of indignation in his voice.

"Y-yes," conceded the Spider, reluctantly. "Up to a point, you have. Anyway, there *is* a story about you, and you've only got yourself to blame if you don't come out of it too well!"

"I was unlucky . . ."

"Maybe. That doesn't alter the fact that there *is* a story."

"Come to that," said the Chameleon, "there have been stories about you, and whose fault is it if they are not to your credit?"

Tandaubwe glared at Nadzikambe. It was precisely this point that infuriated him. If he came into a story at all, it was always in some spiteful tale that made him out to be sly, or greedy, or even foolish. And, seeing what a fine fellow he was, and how brilliantly clever, it was obvious to Tandaubwe that everyone was jealous and that the whole thing was a malicious plot. He said so to the Chameleon.

Nadzikambe laughed. "Well, if that's how you feel about it," he said, "why don't you complain to the Chief? Why not ask if you can be the hero of the next story?"

"Not a bad suggestion!" The Spider turned it over in his mind and found it good. He brightened and nodded in a rather condescending way. "I'm much obliged," he said. "Much obliged. Yes, that's what I will do. I don't see that he can refuse so modest a request."

Without wasting more words, Tandaubwe climbed out of his web, let himself down to the ground and scuttled off to the Court of Chief Ngamo.

The Court was in session when he reached it. In the shade of a kindly Fig Tree the old Chief sat with his Councillors, listening to each case in turn; settling claims, giving advice, granting requests, adjusting the differences of his people. The petition of Tandaubwe, the Spider, was the last one of the day to be heard. Thoughtfully stroking his beard, Ngamo listened while the Spider spoke his plea.

"So you want to be the hero of the next story that is told?" The Chief smiled to himself. "Well, why not? If you are as clever as you say, there should be no difficulty. I will give you three tasks to fulfil. If you succeed in them, you shall be the hero."

Tandaubwe beamed with delight. "What, O Chief, are the tasks?" he asked eagerly.

"Bring me a jar of live Bees," said the Chief.

"Yes?" said the Spider, cheerfully.

"Bring me, alive, the Serpent of the Hills."

"Yes?" said the Spider, uncertainly.

"And bring me a live Leopard."

"Y-yes," said the Spider, unhappily. He bowed to the Chief. "The tasks shall be fulfilled," he said. There was more than a touch of bravado in his voice. Ngamo smiled. In a thoughtful silence, Tandaubwe left the Court.

A jar of live Bees . . .

How did one set about that? As he returned to his web, Tandaubwe, the Spider, cudgelled his brain for a solution. Bees, he knew, should be easy. It was the live Serpent and the Leopard that nagged at the back of his mind. Still, it was no good thinking about them until the first task had been accomplished.

If he were to get some bees-wax and put it in a jar, would the Bees think it was their own comb? Unlikely, the Spider decided, though it might be worth trying . . .

His train of thought was interrupted by a ribald voice singing in the clump of aloes that grew not far from his web.

> *Ha! The brave Spider!*
> *See, our hero comes!*

Tandaubwe groaned. He'd hoped the Chameleon would be away for the evening so that he could make his plans without disturbance. Perhaps, if he made a detour, he might escape unobserved. But no. Just as he thought he was safe, the Chameleon hailed him. "Hullo, hero!" Nadzikambe called out. "What did the Chief say?"

"He agreed," replied the Spider, briefly.

"He did? My, that's splendid! I must think up another verse for my song."

The Spider looked at him sourly. He had an uncomfortable feeling that the Chameleon was laughing at him. But Nadzikambe's song was admirable.

> *Spider, the hero*
> *of fable and song.*
> *The Chief has wisdom.*
> *Ha! Ha! Ha!*

"How's that?" he asked, when he had sung it all through twice.

Tandaubwe ignored the question and asked one of his own. "If you wanted a jar full of live Bees, what would you do?"

"A jar of live Bees? Don't be silly. No one wants a jar of live Bees. Most uncomfortable creatures – they sting!" The Chameleon thought the question absurd.

"Yes, yes, I know," said the Spider, testily. "But supposing you *did* want one?"

"Oh, I'd get a jar," replied the Chameleon carelessly, "and I'd think up something – a bet of some sort. Why do you want to know?"

"Never mind."

Nadzikambe grinned at the Spider. There was a speculative look in his eye. "Where are you off to?" he asked. "To find a jar to put your live Bees in? You'd better see that it has a well-fitting lid. And mind you don't get stung!" The Chameleon began to chuckle to himself.

Tandaubwe scowled. "If you want to know, I'm going to my web. I'm tired and I want to sleep. And I'll be much obliged if you will be so kind as to refrain from singing."

"My dear fellow! Of course. I quite understand. A brain like yours needs rest, and no doubt you have some problem on your mind. I won't make a sound."

The Spider frowned, wished the Chameleon a curt goodnight and scurried off to his web.

A good night's rest – that was what he needed. In the morning, he had no doubt, the problem would seem quite simple.

And he was right. In the morning it did. All that was required, as the Chameleon had pointed out, was a jar with a well-fitting lid. Well, a long-necked beer-pot would do admirably, and he could make a wooden bung to fit it. Then he would go and see the Bees.

The Bees lived in a cleft of the rock near the Hunter's Cave. They were more than a little surprised to see Tandaubwe, the Spider, and could not imagine what he was doing, all that way from his home, with a beer-pot by his side. Really, it was most extraordinary! There he sat, obviously deep in thought, and every now and then he would look at the Bees in a puzzled sort of way, and then he would gaze at the jar and shake his head. The Bees could make nothing of it at all. Little hums of conversation rose on all sides.

"What'zz he doing, d'you think?"

"He muzzt be mad!"

"What'zz that jar for?"

"Why'zz he here?"

"Shall we azzk?"

"Yezz, let'zz!"

They came close to the Spider, saw him shake his head again and heard him mutter: "I suppose the Chief is right!" One Bee, bolder than the rest, settled on the lip of the jar and peered inside. He could see nothing but empty blackness. He turned to Tandaubwe.

"What are you doing, if I may azzk? What'zz thizz for?" He indicated the long-necked jar.

"Oh," replied the Spider, "I was talking to the Chief yesterday and he said Bees couldn't fly into a jar like this. I said I was sure they could, but he wouldn't have it. Couldn't be done, he insisted. I suppose he is right, but I must say I'm surprised."

"Why ever should he think that?" The Bee seemed astonished. Of course we could fly into it. What'zz to stop uzz?"

"I don't know. The Chief says it just can't be done – not by Bees. Flies, yes. Bees, no."

More Bees had flown up, and they now began to buzz with indignation.

"Why should the Chief think that Flies can do something that we can't? Of course, we can fly into the jar. Look! We'll show you!"

"Yezz," chorused the Bees. "We'll show you!"

The air quivered with a zooming hum as the leading Bee went in, followed by all his relations. The moment they were safely inside, Tandaubwe clapped the bung into the neck of the jar. Then he gave a sigh of relief.

"Hey! What are you doing? Let uzz out at once!" An angry roar came from the jar. "Let uzz out!"

"I'm sorry," said the Spider, "but I am afraid I've got to keep you there. You won't come to any harm. I have to take you to the Chief."

The roar died down to an indignant grumble and Tandaubwe, the Spider, picked up the jar and set off on his journey to the Court. It was pleasant to think that his first task had been accomplished – and easily, at that. The second task might not be so simple!

Buzz, buzz, buzz!
Bees in a jar
Spider is a hero!
Ha! Ha! Ha!

So sang the Chameleon as Tandaubwe, the Spider, scuttled past his clump of aloes. "Where are you off to today?"

"To the hills to look for Njoka, the Serpent," replied the Spider.

"What in the world do you want with Njoka? Personally, I'd go miles to avoid him!"

"I want to know how long he is, for one thing . . ."

"As long as that stick over there?" The Chameleon pointed to a piece of bamboo that was lying on the ground.

"Longer than that, I think," said the Spider.

"As long as the tallest grass?"

"Longer, I believe."

"Surely not. Like to have a wager on it?"

"No."

"A pity." The Chameleon sounded disappointed. He dearly loved a wager.

"Thanks all the same," Tandaubwe called out. "You've given me an idea."

He continued on his way, trying to work out a scheme for capturing the snake. A stick . . . no, three sticks . . . and a wager . . . yes, the plan was beginning to take shape . . .

Njoka, the Serpent of the Hills, lived somewhere in amongst the boulders of the mountain-side, and it was his custom, each morning, to lie in the sun and watch the world go by. Few people came to visit him, for he was not popular, and this was always a matter for regret, as he liked company and admiration and got little of either. It was, therefore, with pleasure as well as interest that he saw Tandaubwe, the Spider, approaching. Idly he wondered why the Spider had come, and what he could be doing with three sticks of such different lengths . . .

"Good morning," began the Spider, chattily. "Lovely weather we are having. You're looking well!"

"I am well. What are you doing here?" returned the Snake, whose manners were a little uncouth.

"I've come especially to see you."

"Why?" Njoka asked bluntly.

"Well," replied Tandaubwe, "I was talking to the Chief the other day and I said that you were the finest, longest Serpent in Africa, but he wouldn't have it. He said you weren't much longer than this cane." Tandaubwe held up the shortest stick he had.

"What nonsense!" exclaimed Njoka indignantly. "The very suggestion is an insult! I'm much longer than that!"

"That's what I said. I said you were at least as long as this." The Spider held up the second cane.

"Of course I'm as long as that. Longer – much longer!"

"Would you say that? It is difficult to tell, you know, when you are lying in coils. How about straightening out and letting me measure you against the stick?"

"Certainly. You'll soon see that I am much longer than that paltry little cane!" Slowly Njoka began to unwind himself and to straighten out. The Spider laid his cane down beside the Snake and it at once became obvious that Njoka was the longer by many inches.

"My!" exclaimed the Spider excitedly. "You're right! But I'll wager you are not as long as this?" He held up the longest, stoutest stick of the three.

Njoka hesitated. "What'll you wager?" he asked cautiously.

"Two cows to a goat," was the prompt reply.

The Snake's eyes glittered greedily. "Done!" he cried. "Put that stick down!" And he stretched himself out beside it to the fullest extent possible.

Now the surface of the rock was by no means smooth and level, so it was an easy matter for the Spider to pass beneath both the stick and the Snake and, under cover of a spate of chatter and a dozen compliments, Tandaubwe ran from side to side, over and under, over and under, binding the Serpent to the stick by means of a silken thread of his own spinning. The thread was strong but very light, and Njoka was so intent on winning the two cows that he never gave a thought to the Spider's curious antics. Certainly, it did not occur to him that he was being made a prisoner. Realization came when he tried to raise his head to see if his tail reached beyond the end of the stick. He could not do so. Panic seized him.

"What have you done?" he screeched. "Why can't I move? Get me out of this at once!" Njoka strained and writhed, but the thread held and he was powerless to break it. He could not even strike at the Spider and his venomous fangs were of no use to him at all. "Why are you doing this?" he hissed. "I've never done you any harm!"

"And I will not harm you," said Tandaubwe, reassuringly. "I have to take you to the Chief. My children are coming to carry you there."

"What about the two cows? Do I get those?"

"I'm afraid not. You see, you are not quite as long as the stick."

A hiss of bitter disappointment came from the Snake.

"Too bad, isn't it! Still," said the Spider, magnanimously, "in the circumstances, I am prepared to waive my claim to your goat!" Tandaubwe radiated good will and generosity. Now that the second task had been accomplished, he felt he could afford to do so.

> *Hiss, hiss, hiss!*
> *The Serpent of the Hills*
> *now is powerless.*
> *Spider is a hero!*
> *Hiss, hiss, hiss!*

The Chameleon sang gaily and thrummed his *bangwe* – the little stringed instrument that he had made himself. The tinkling noise would, ordinarily, have pleased the Spider, but now he wanted quiet, so that he could give his whole mind to the third task – the capture of the Leopard.

Leopards were vain . . . Leopards were foolish . . . Leopards were very bad-tempered. What else did he know about them?

The Spider's thoughts were again interrupted by Nadzikambe's singing.

> *Where is the Serpent,*
> *the Serpent of the Hills?*
> *Ask Tandaubwe . . .*

"Oh be quiet!" shouted the exasperated Spider. "How can I think if you make such a noise?"

"Don't you like my song?" The Chameleon sounded aggrieved. "I'm very pleased with it, myself. I think it is good."

"Yes, yes," said the Spider, "some other time I've no doubt I'd enjoy it. Just now I want peace and quiet. I need to think."

"Oh? What about?"

"If you wanted to capture a Leopard – alive, mark you – how would you set about it?"

"I wouldn't." The Chameleon grinned. "But then, of course, I have no wish to be a hero!"

Tandaubwe directed a glance of loathing at Nadzikambe. What a maddening creature he was, to be sure. But he was quite clever – sometimes, anyway – and he was full of ideas.

"Supposing you *did*?" insisted the Spider. "What would you do?"

A dreamy look came into the Chameleon's eyes. "I'd take my *bangwe*," he said, "and I'd sing to him."

Tandaubwe groaned. "And what good, do you imagine, would that do?"

"I'd sing him a lullaby – a lovely lullaby. I'd sing him to sleep. And when he was fast asleep, I'd tie a bandage over his eyes and slip a noose over his head and . . ."

"Huh! Your singing wouldn't send a dormouse to sleep!"

"That's what you think!"

"The bandage, though," Tandaubwe was speaking almost to himself now, "that is a good idea. I must think this over."

He moved off, plunged in thought. A strip of bark-cloth would do for the bandage . . . and if he were to . . . yes, yes, that was it! Then, if only . . . but yes, of course! It was a brilliant idea. It could not fail to work!

Delighted with himself, and his plan, Tandaubwe scurried off to fetch the bandage.

Nyalugwe, the Leopard, lived in a cave on the hillside.

The Spider knew that he slept in the day time, but when Tandaubwe reached the cave that afternoon, and peered inside, he saw at once that Nyalugwe was awake and busy with his toilet. Quietly backing out of the cave, the Spider sat down on a rock and tied the bandage over his own eyes. A few moments later the Leopard was amazed to hear cries of wonder and delight coming from outside.

"Oh! Oh, how wonderful! How marvellous! I can't believe it!"

Nyalugwe paused in his grooming and looked up. Whoever could it be?

"Oh! ! ! ! I never dreamed . . ." The sentence tailed off into a delighted chuckle.

What could this mean? Nyalugwe got up, walked to the entrance and had a look round. He saw the Spider.

"What's the matter with you?" he asked. "What d'you think you're doing? Is something wrong with your eyes?"

A cry of ecstasy was the only answer he received.

The Leopard began to lose his temper. "What *is* all this?" he demanded angrily. "What's so wonderful?"

"My bandage. My magic bandage," replied the Spider. "With it, I can see such marvellous things – things you've never dreamed of! Oh! Oh, no! It can't be true!' Clearly, the Spider was seeing yet another exquisite vision.

"Indeed? Then you can give me the bandage," said the Leopard haughtily. "I, too, wish to see these wonderful things."

"Give you my bandage!" exclaimed the Spider. "No fear! I'm not giving it to anyone!"

"I only want to try it. You can have it back."

"Once you've tried it, you'd never let me have it back!"

"Come on. Don't be so selfish. Give it to me at once!" Impatiently, the Leopard stamped his foot.

"No."

"Are you going to give me that bandage? Or do you want me to take it from you?" The Leopard's voice was full of menace and he took a step towards the Spider.

"You great bully! I suppose I'll have to let you have it. Promise you'll give it back?"

"We'll see," said Nyalugwe, darkly.

"It won't do you any good," said Tandaubwe, as he handed the bandage over with every sign of reluctance.

"Now tie it for me!"

Quickly the Spider did as he was told.

"I can't see anything at all," complained Nyalugwe. He sounded peevish.

"You can't expect to, all at once." Hastily, the noose was slipped over the Leopard's head. "See anything yet?" asked the Spider.

"Not a thing."

"Try lying on your back, with your feet in the air. It always works better that way."

Obediently the Leopard lay down and, like lightning, the Spider ran up him and bound his legs together with his own silken thread.

"This thing's no good," grumbled Nyalugwe. "Why won't it work? I don't believe it is magic at all!" Snarling with impatience and disappointment, Nyalugwe decided to tear the bandage off. What was the good of a thing that did not give immediate results? He tried to move his paw . . .

"Hey!" he roared. "What's happened? Why can't I move? What have you done?" He struggled madly, rolled over on his side and tried to rub the bandage off. He did not succeed. Bound and blindfold, he was completely at the Spider's mercy.

"I told you that the bandage would do you no good," said Tandaubwe. "You'd much better lie still. I will not harm you, but I have to take you to the Chief. My carriers will tie you to a pole and bring you there."

The Leopard's bellow of fury died down to a low growl of baffled rage. Gradually he grew calmer. "I wouldn't mind so much," he grumbled, "if your wretched bandage would work! Tell me, what exactly did you see?"

"Aha!" said the Spider. "If I were to tell you, you'd never believe me!"

Drums were sounding in the sapphire night, calling Ngamo's people to a feast in honour of Tandaubwe, the Spider.

The paths leading to the great Chief's village rustled with scuttling forms, and the laughter of happy guests rose up and mingled with the throbbing of the drums. In ones and twos and threes, the people began to arrive. Guapi, the Duiker, and his father, Mphongo, were the first to appear. Kalulu, the Rabbit, and Kamba, the Tortoise, followed close upon their heels. Mwanzi, the Water Monitor, and Kambawa-madzi, the Turtle, reached the village at the same moment as Katumbu, the Otter, and Zonde, the Frog. Mbawala, the Bushbuck, galloped in a little late, for he had overslept.

Last of all came Tandaubwe, the Spider, looking important and very, very proud. Congratulations were showered on him and Chief Ngamo greeted him with much ceremony and bade him sit in the place of honour. Bowls of food and jars of beer were then placed before them and the feasting began.

It was a splendid feast. There was music, there were dancers, there was everything that anyone could desire. And, when the merry-making was at its height, Tandaubwe turned to the Chief and asked if, indeed, he could now be the hero of a story.

"But you are!" exclaimed the Chief. "You have fulfilled the three tasks that I set you. You are the hero of that story. Listen, and you shall hear the tale for yourself!"

Ngamo clapped his hands. A hush fell over the guests and Nadzikambe, the Chameleon, stepped into the centre of the circle.

"Here is the Teller of the Tale, the Singer of the Song. He will give us the story of your exploits."

For a moment the Spider's heart sank. Was Nadzikambe going to make fun of him? He looked anxiously at the Chameleon. Nadzikambe grinned back at him, then slowly closed one eye in a reassuring wink, as if to say: "Don't worry. This is your *day*. You *have* been clever and you *are* a hero. Listen, and enjoy my song!" He plucked a few notes from his *bangwe* and started on the first verse:

> *Hearken, all you people,*
> *hearken to my song,*
> *to the tale of the Spider,*
> *the clever, fearless Spider,*
> *Tandaubwe, the Spider,*
> *the hero of my song.*

Tandaubwe listened, sighed with relief and relaxed. It was going to be all right. This was what he'd dreamed of. This was just what he'd wanted. After all, everyone enjoyed a feast, everyone enjoyed a song, everyone enjoyed a story and – there was no getting away from it – it was delightful to be a hero for once! He closed his eyes and, with a happy smile, settled down to listen to the twenty-five verses of the Chameleon's song.

By the middle of verse nine, Tandaubwe, the Spider, was fast asleep.

The Touchstone

Robert Louis Stevenson

THE KING WAS A MAN that stood well before the world; his smile was sweet as clover, but his soul withinside was as little as a pea. He had two sons; and the younger son was a boy after his heart, but the elder was one whom he feared. It befell one morning that the drum sounded in the dun before it was yet day; and the King rode with his two sons, and a brave array behind them. They rode two hours, and came to the foot of a brown mountain that was very steep.

"Where do we ride?" said the elder son.

"Across this brown mountain," said the King, and smiled to himself.

"My father knows what he is doing," said the younger son.

And they rode two hours more, and came to the sides of a black river that was wondrous deep.

"And where do we ride?" asked the elder son.

"Over this black river," said the King, and smiled to himself.

"My father knows what he is doing," said the younger son.

And they rode all that day, and about the time of the sunsetting came to the side of a lake, where was a great dun.

"It is here we ride," said the King; "to a king's house, and a priest's, and a house where you will learn much."

At the gates of the dun, the King who was a priest met them; and he was a grave man, and beside him stood his daughter, and she was as fair as the morn, and one that smiled and looked down.

"These are my two sons," said the first King.

"And here is my daughter," said the King who was a priest.

"She is a wonderful fine maid," said the first King, "and I like her manner of smiling."

"They are wonderful well-grown lads," said the second, "and I like their gravity."

And then the two Kings looked at each other, and said, "The thing may come about."

And in the meanwhile the two lads looked upon the maid, and the one grew pale and the other red; and the maid looked upon the ground smiling.

"Here is the maid that I shall marry," said the elder. "For I think she smiled upon me."

But the younger plucked his father by the sleeve.

"Father," said he, "a word in your ear. If I find favour in your sight, might not I wed this maid, for I think she smiles upon me?"

"A word in yours," said the King his father. "Waiting is good hunting, and when the teeth are shut the tongue is at home."

Now they were come into the dun, and feasted; and this was a great house, so that the lads were astonished; and the King that was a priest sat at the end of the board and was silent, so that the lads were filled with reverence; and the maid served them smiling with downcast eyes, so that their hearts were enlarged.

Before it was day, the elder son arose, and he found the maid at her weaving, for she was a diligent girl. "Maid," quoth he, "I would fain marry you."

"You must speak with my father," said she; and she looked upon the ground smiling, and became like the rose.

"Her heart is with me," said the elder son, and he went down to the lake and sang.

A little after came the younger son. "Maid," quoth he, "if our fathers were agreed, I would like well to marry you."

"You can speak to my father," said she; and looked upon the ground, and smiled and grew like the rose.

"She is a dutiful daughter," said the younger son, "she will make an obedient wife." And then he thought, "What shall I do?" and he remembered the King her father was a priest;

so he went into the temple, and sacrificed a weasel and a hare.

Presently the news got about; and the two lads and the first King were called into the presence of the King who was a priest, where he sat upon the high seat.

"Little I reck of gear," said the King who was a priest, "and little of power. For we live here among the shadow of things, and the heart is sick of seeing them. And we stay here in the wind like raiment drying, and the heart is weary of the wind. But one thing I love, and that is truth; and for one thing will I give my daughter, and that is the trial stone. For in the light of that stone the seeming goes, and the being shows, and all things besides are worthless. Therefore, lads, if ye would wed my daughter, out foot, and bring me the stone of touch, for that is the price of her."

"A word in your ear," said the younger son to his father. "I think we do very well without this stone."

"A word in yours," said the father. "I am of your way of thinking; but when the teeth are shut the tongue is at home." And he smiled to the King that was a priest.

But the elder son got to his feet, and called the King that was a priest by the name of father. "For whether I marry the maid or no, I will call you by that word for the love of your wisdom; and even now I will ride forth and search the world for the stone of touch." So he said farewell, and rode into the world.

"I think I will go, too," said the younger son, "if I can have your leave. For my heart goes out to the maid."

"You will ride home with me," said his father.

So they rode home, and when they came to the dun, the King had his son into his treasury. "Here," said he, "is the touchstone which shows truth; for there is no truth but plain truth; and if you will look in this, you will see yourself as you are."

And the younger son looked in it, and saw his face as it were the face of a beardless youth, and he was well enough pleased; for the thing was a piece of a mirror.

"Here is no such great thing to make a work about," said he; "but if it will get me the maid I shall never complain. But what a fool is my brother to ride into the world, and the thing all the while at home!"

So they rode back to the other dun, and showed the mirror to the King that was a priest; and when he had looked in it, and seen himself like a King, and his house like a King's house, and all things like themselves, he cried out and blessed God. "For now I know," said he, "there is no truth but the plain truth; and I am a king indeed, although my heart misgave me." And he pulled down his temple, and built a new one; and then the younger son was married to the maid.

In the meantime the elder son rode into the world to find the touchstone of the trial of truth; and whenever he came to a place of habitation, he would ask the men if they had heard of it. And in every place the men answered: "Not only have we heard of it, but we alone, of all men, possess the thing itself, and it hangs in the side of our chimney to this day." Then would the elder son be glad, and beg for a sight of it. And sometimes it would be a piece of mirror, that showed the seeming of things; and then he would say, "This can never be, for there should be more than seeming." And sometimes it would be a lump of coal, which showed nothing; and then he would say, "This can never be, for at least there is the seeming." And sometimes it would be a touchstone indeed, beautiful in hue, adorned with polishing, the light inhabiting its sides; and when he found this, he would beg the thing, and the persons of that place would give it him, for all men were very generous of that gift; so that at the last he had his wallet full of them, and they chinked together when he rode; and when he halted by the side of the way he would take them out and try them, till his head turned like the sails upon a windmill.

"A murrain upon this business!" said the elder son, "for I perceive no end to it. Here I have the red, and here the blue and the green; and to me they seem all excellent, and yet shame each other. A murrain on the trade! If it were not for the King that is a priest and whom I have called my father, and if it were not for the fair maid of the dun that makes my mouth to sing and my heart enlarge, I would even tumble them all into the salt sea, and go home and be a king like other folk."

But he was like the hunter that has seen a stag upon a mountain, so that the night may fall, and the fire be kindled, and the lights shine in his house; but desire of that stag is single in his bosom.

Now after many years the elder son came upon the sides of the salt sea; and it was night, and a savage place, and the clamour of the sea was loud. There he was aware of a house, and a man that sat there by the light of a candle for he had no fire. Now the elder son came in to him, and the man gave him water to drink, for he had no bread; and wagged his head when he was spoken to, for he had no words.

"Have you the touchstone of truth?" asked the elder son; and when the man had wagged his head, "I might have known that," cried the elder son. "I have here a wallet full of them!" And with that he laughed, although his heart was weary.

And with that the man laughed too, and with the fuff of his laughter the candle went out.

"Sleep," said the man, "for now I think you have come far enough; and your quest is ended, and my candle is out."

Now when the morning came, the man gave him a clear pebble in his hand, and it had no beauty and no colour; and the elder son looked upon it scornfully and shook his head; and he went away, for it seemed a small affair to him.

All that day he rode, and his mind was quiet, and the desire of the chase allayed. "How if this poor pebble be the touchstone, after all?" said he: and he got down from his horse, and emptied forth his wallet by the side of the way. Now, in the light of each other, all the touchstones lost their hue and fire, and withered like stars at morning; but in the light of the pebble, their beauty remained, only the pebble was the most bright. And the elder son smote upon his brow. "How if this be the truth?" he cried, "that all are a little true?" And he took the pebble, and turned its light upon the heavens, and they deepened about him like the pit; and he turned it on the hills, and the hills were cold and rugged, but life ran in their sides so that his own life bounded; and he turned it on the dust, and he beheld the dust with joy and terror; and he turned it on himself, and kneeled down and prayed.

"Now, thanks be to God," said the elder son, "I have found the touchstone; and now I may turn my reins, and ride home to the King and to the maid of the dun that makes my mouth to sing and my heart enlarge."

Now when he came to the dun, he saw children playing by the gate where the King had met him in the old days; and this stayed his pleasure, for he thought in his heart, "It is here my children should be playing." And when he came into the hall, there was his brother on the high seat and the maid beside him; and at that his anger rose, for he thought in his heart, "It is I that should be sitting there, and the maid beside me."

"Who are you?" said his brother. "And what make you in the dun?"

"I am your elder brother," he replied. "And I am come to marry the maid, for I have brought the touchstone of truth."

Then the younger brother laughed aloud. "Why," said he, "I found the touchstone years ago, and married the maid, and there are our children playing at the gate."

Now at this the elder brother grew as grey as the dawn. "I pray you have dealt justly," said he, "for I perceive my life is lost."

"Justly?" quoth the younger brother. "It becomes you ill, that are a restless man and a runagate, to doubt my justice, or the King my father's, that are sedentary folk and known in the land."

"Nay," said the elder brother, "you have all else, have patience also; and suffer me to say the world is full of touchstones, and it appears not easily which is true."

"I have no shame of mine," said the younger brother. "There it is, and look in it."

So the elder brother looked in the mirror, and he was sore amazed;

for he was an old man, and his hair was white upon his head; and he sat down in the hall and wept aloud.

"Now," said the younger brother, "see what a fool's part you have played, that ran over all the world to seek what was lying in our father's treasury, and came back an old carle for the dogs to bark at, and without chick or child. And I that was dutiful and wise sit here crowned with virtues and pleasures, and happy in the light of my hearth."

"Methinks you have a cruel tongue," said the elder brother; and he pulled out the clear pebble and turned its light on his brother; and behold the man was lying, his soul was shrunk into the smallness of a pea, and his heart was a bag of little fears like scorpions, and love was dead in his bosom. And at that the elder brother cried out aloud, and turned the light of the pebble on the maid, and, lo! she was but a mask of a woman, and withinsides she was quite dead, and she smiled as a clock ticks, and knew not wherefore.

"Oh, well," said the elder brother, "I perceive there is both good and bad. So fare ye all as well as ye may in the dun; but I will go forth into the world with my pebble in my pocket."

Touk's House

❧

Robin McKinley

THERE WAS A WITCH who had a garden. It was a vast garden, and very beautiful; and it was all the more beautiful for being set in the heart of an immense forest, heavy with ancient trees and tangled with vines. Around the witch's garden the forest stretched far in every direction, and the ways through it were few, and no more than narrow footpaths.

In the garden were plants of all varieties; there were herbs at the witch's front door and vegetables at her rear door; a hedge, shoulder-high for a tall man, made of many different shrubs lovingly trained and trimmed together, surrounded her entire plot, and there were bright patches of flowers scattered throughout. The witch, whatever else she might be capable of, had green fingers; in her garden many rare things flourished, nor did the lowliest weed raise its head unless she gave it leave.

There was a woodcutter who came to know the witch's garden well by sight; and indeed, as it pleased his eyes, he found himself going out of his way to pass it in the morning as he began his long day with his axe over his arm, or in the evening as he made his way homeward. He had been making as many of his ways as he could pass near the garden for some months when he realized that he had worn a trail outside the witch's hedge wide enough to swing his arms freely and let his feet find their own way without fear of clutching roots or loose stones. It was the widest trail anywhere in the forest.

The woodcutter had a wife 'and four daughters. The children were their parents' greatest delight, and their only delight, for they were very poor. But the children were vigorous and healthy, and the elder two already helped their mother in the bread baking, by which she earned a little more money for the family, and in their small forest-shadowed village everyone bought bread from her. That bread was so good that her friends teased her, and said her husband stole herbs from the witch's garden, that she might put it in her baking. But the teasing made her unhappy, for she said such jokes would bring bad luck.

And at last bad luck befell them. The youngest daughter fell sick, and the local leech, who was doctor to so small a village because he was not a good one, could do nothing for her. The fever ate up the little girl till there was no flesh left on her small bones, and when she opened her eyes, she did not recognize the faces of her sisters and mother as they bent over her.

"Is there nothing to do?" begged the woodcutter, and the doctor shook his head. The parents bowed their heads in despair, and the mother wept.

A gleam came into the leech's eyes, and he licked his lips nervously. "There is one thing," he said, and the man and his wife snapped their heads up to stare at him. "The witch's garden . . ."

"The witch's garden," the wife whispered fearfully.

"Yes?" said the woodcutter.

"There is an herb that grows there that will break any fever," said the doctor.

"How will I know it?" said the woodcutter.

The doctor picked up a burning twig from the fireplace, stubbed out the sparks, and drew black lines on the clean-swept hearth. "It looks so —" And he drew small three-lobed leaves. "Its color is pale, like the leaves of a weeping willow, and it is a small bushy plant, rising no higher than a man's knee from the ground."

Hope and fear chased themselves over the wife's face, and she reached out to clasp her husband's hand. "How will you come by the leaves?" she said to him.

"I will steal them," the woodcutter said boldly.

The doctor stood up, and the woodcutter saw that he trembled. "If you . . . bring them home, boil two handsful in water, and give the girl as much of it as she will drink." And he left hastily.

"Husband —"

He put his other hand over hers. "I pass the garden often. It will be an easy thing. Do not be anxious."

On the next evening he waited later than his usual time for returning, that dusk might have overtaken him when he reached the witch's garden. That morning he had passed the garden as well, and dawdled by the hedge, that he might mark where the thing he sought stood; but he dared not try his thievery then, for all that he was desperately worried about his youngest daughter.

He left his axe and his yoke for bearing the cut wood leaning against a tree, and slipped through the hedge. He was surprised that it did not seem to wish to deter his passage, but yielded as any leaves and branches might. He had thought at least a witch's hedge would be full of thorns and brambles, but he was unscathed. The plant he needed was near at hand, and he was grateful that he need not walk far from the sheltering hedge. He fell to his knees to pluck two handsful of the life-giving leaves, and he nearly sobbed with relief.

"Why do you invade thus my garden, thief?" said a voice behind him, and the sob turned in his throat to a cry of terror.

He had never seen the witch. He knew of her existence because all who lived in the village knew that a witch lived in the garden that grew in the forest; and sometimes, when he passed by it, there was smoke drifting up from the chimney of the small house, and thus he knew someone lived there. He looked up, hopelessly, still on his knees, still clutching the precious leaves.

He saw a woman only a little past youth to look at her, for her hair was black and her face smooth but for lines of sorrow and solitude about the mouth. She wore a white apron over a brown skirt; her feet were bare, her sleeves rolled to the elbows, and her hands were muddy.

"I asked you, what do you do in my garden?"

He opened his mouth, but no words came out; and he shuddered till he had to lean his knuckles on the ground so that he would not topple over. She raised her arm, and pushed her damp hair away from her forehead with the back of one hand; but it seemed, as he watched her, that the hand, as it fell through the air again to lie at her side, flickered through some sign that briefly burned in the air; and he found he could talk.

"My daughter," he gasped. "My youngest daughter is ill . . . she will die. I – I stole these" – and he raised his hands pleadingly, still holding the leaves which, crushed between his fingers, gave a sweet minty fragrance to the air between their faces – "that she might live."

The witch stood silent for a moment, while he felt his heart beating in the palms of his hands. "There is a gate in the hedge. Why did you not come through it, and knock on my door, and ask for what you need?"

"Because I was afraid," he murmured, and silence fell again.

"What ails the child?" the witch asked at last.

Hope flooded through him and made him tremble. "It is a wasting fever, and there is almost nothing of her left; often now she does not know us."

The witch turned away from him, and walked several steps; and he staggered to his feet, thinking to flee; but his head swam, and when it was clear, the witch stood again before him. She held a dark green frond out to him; its long, sharp leaves nodded over her hand, and the smell of it made his eyes water.

"Those leaves you wished to steal would avail you and your daughter little. They make a pleasant taste, steeped in hot water, and they give a fresh smell to linens long in a cupboard. Take this as my gift to your poor child; steep this in boiling water, and give it to the child to drink. She will not like it, but it will cure her; and you say she will die else."

The woodcutter looked in amazement at the harsh-smelling bough; and slowly he opened his fists, and the green leaves fell at his feet, and slowly he reached out for what the witch offered him. She was small of stature, he noticed suddenly, and slender, almost frail. She stooped as lithely as a maiden, and picked up the leaves he had dropped, and held them out to him.

"These too you shall keep, and boil as you meant to do, for your child will need a refreshing draught after what you must give her for her life's sake.

"And you should at least have the benefit they can give you, for you shall pay a heavy toll for your thievery this night. Your wife carries your fifth child; in a little time, when your fourth daughter is well again, she shall tell you of it. In seven months she shall be brought to bed, and the baby will be big and strong. That child is mine; that child is the price you shall forfeit for this night's lack of courtesy."

"Ah, God," cried the woodcutter, "do you barter the death of one child against the death of another?"

"No," she said. "I give a life for a life. For your youngest child shall live; and the baby not yet born I shall raise kindly, for I" – she faltered – "I wish to teach someone my herb lore.

"Go now. Your daughter needs what you bring her." And the woodcutter found himself at the threshold of his own front door, his hands full of leaves, and his axe and yoke still deep in the forest; nor did he remember the journey home.

The axe and yoke were in their accustomed place the next morning; the woodcutter seized them up and strode into the forest by a path he knew would not take him near the witch's garden.

All four daughters were well and strong seven months later when their mother was brought to her fifth confinement. The birth was an easy one, and a fifth daughter kicked her way into the world; but the mother turned her face away, and the four sisters wept, especially the youngest. The midwife wrapped the baby up snugly in the birth clothes that had comforted four infants previously. The woodcutter picked up the child and went into the forest in the direction he had avoided for seven months. It had been in his heart, since he had found himself on his doorstep with his hands full of leaves and unable to remember how he got there, that this journey was one he would not escape; so he held the child close to him, and went the shortest path he knew to the witch's garden. For all of its seven months' neglect, the way was as clear as when he had trodden it often.

This time he knocked upon the gate, and entered; the witch was standing before her front door. She raised her arms for the child, and the woodcutter laid her in them. The witch did not at first look at the baby, but rather up into the woodcutter's face. "Go home to your wife, and the four daughters who love you, for they know you. And know this too: that in a year's time your wife shall be brought to bed once again, and the child shall be a son."

Then she bowed her head over the baby, and just before her black hair fell forward to hide her face, the woodcutter saw a look of love and gentleness touch the witch's sad eyes and mouth. He remembered that look often, for he never again found the witch's garden, though for many years he searched the woods where he knew it once had been, till he was no longer sure that he had ever seen it, and his family numbered four sons as well as four daughters.

Maugie named her new baby Erana. Erana was a cheerful baby and a merry child; she loved the garden that was her home; she loved Maugie, and she loved Maugie's son, Touk. She called Maugie by her name, Maugie, and not Mother, for Maugie had been careful to tell her that she was not her real mother; and when little Erana had asked, "Then why do I live with you, Maugie?" Maugie had answered: "Because I always wanted a daughter."

Touk and Erana were best friends. Erana's earliest memory was of riding on his shoulders and pulling his long pointed ears, and drumming his furry chest with her small heels. Touk visited his mother's garden every day, bringing her wild roots that would not grow even in her garden, and split wood for her fire. But he lived by the riverbank, or by the pool that an elbow of the river had made. As soon as Erana was old enough to walk more than a few steps by herself, Touk showed her the way to his bit of river, and she often visited him when she could not wait for him to come to the garden.

Maugie never went beyond her hedge, and she sighed the first time small Erana went off alone. But Touk was at home in the wild woods, and taught Erana to be at home there too. She lost herself only twice, and both those times when she was very small; and both times Touk found her almost before she had time to realize she was lost. They did not tell Maugie about either of these two incidents, and Erana never lost herself in the forest again.

Touk often took a nap at noontime, stretched out full length in his pool and floating three-quarters submerged; he looked like an old mossy log, or at least he did till he opened his eyes, which were a vivid shade of turquoise, and went very oddly with his green skin. When Erana first visited him, she was light enough to sit on his chest as he floated, and paddle him about like the log he looked, while he crossed his hands on his breast and watched her with a glint of blue between almost-closed green eyelids. But she soon grew too heavy for this amusement, and he taught her instead to swim, and, though she had none of his troll blood to help her, still, she was a pupil to make her master proud.

One day as she lay, wet and panting, on the shore, she said to him, "Why do you not have a house? You do not spend all your hours in the water, or with us in the garden."

He grunted. He sat near her, but on a rough rocky patch that she had avoided in favor of a grassy mound. He drew his knees up to his chin and put his arms around them. There were spurs at his wrists and heels, like a fighting cock's, and though he kept them closely trimmed, still he had to sit slightly pigeon-toed to avoid slashing the skin of his upper legs with the heel spurs, and he grasped his arms carefully well up near the elbow. The hair that grew on his head was as pale as young leaves, and inclined to be lank; but the tufts that grew on the tops of his shoulders and thickly across his chest, and the crest that grew down his backbone, were much darker, and curly.

"You think I should have a house, my friend?" he growled, for his voice was always a growl.

Erana thought about it. "I think you should *want* to have a house."

"I'll ponder it," he said, and slid back into the pool and floated out toward the center. A long-necked bird drifted down and landed on his belly, and began plucking at the ragged edge of one short trouser leg.

"You should learn to mend, too," Erana called to him. Erana loathed mending. The bird stopped pulling for a moment and glared at her. Then it reached down and raised a thread in its beak and wrenched it free with one great tug. It looked challengingly at Erana and then slowly flapped away, with the mud-colored thread trailing behind it.

"Then what would the birds build their nests with?" he said, and grinned. There was a gap between his two front teeth, and the eyeteeth curved well down over the lower lip.

Maugie taught her young protégé to cook and clean, and sew — and mend — and weed. But Erana had little gift for herb lore. She learned the names of things, painstakingly, and the by-rote rules of what mixtures did what and when; but her learning never caught fire, and the green things in the garden did not twine lovingly around her when she paused near them as they seemed to do for Maugie. She learned what she could, to please Maugie, for Erana felt sad that neither her true son nor her adopted daughter could understand the things Maugie might teach; and because she liked to know the ingredients of a poultice to apply to an injured wing, and what herbs, mixed in with chopped-up bugs and earthworms, would make orphaned fledglings thrive.

For Erana's fifteenth birthday, Touk presented her with a stick. She looked at it, and then she looked at him. "I thought you might like to lay the first log of my new house," he said, and she laughed.

"You have decided, then?" she asked.

"Yes; in fact I began to want a house long since, but I have only lately begun to want to build one," he said. "And then I thought

I would put it off till your birthday, that you might make the beginning, as it was your idea first."

She hesitated, turning the little smooth stick in her hand. "It is – is it truly your idea now, Touk? I was a child when I teased you about your house; I would never mean to hold you to a child's nagging."

The blue eyes glinted. "It is my idea now, my dear, and you can prove that you are my dearest friend by coming at once to place your beam where it belongs, so that I may begin."

Birthdays required much eating, for all three of them liked to cook, and they were always ready for an excuse for a well-fed celebration; so it was late in the day of Erana's fifteenth birthday that she and Touk made their way – slowly, for they were very full of food – to his riverbank. "There," he said, pointing across the pool. Erana looked up at him questioningly, and then made her careful way around the water to the stand of trees he had indicated; he followed on her heels. She stopped, and he said over her shoulder, his breath stirring her hair, "You see nothing? Here –" And he took her hand, and led her up a short steep slope, and there was a little clearing beyond the trees, with a high mossy rock at its back, and the water glinting through the trees before it, and the trees all around, and birds in the trees. There were already one or two bird-houses hanging from suitable branches at the clearing's edge, and bits of twig sticking out the round doorways to indicate tenants in residence.

"My house will lie –" And he dropped her hand to pace off its boundaries; when he halted, he stood before her again, his blue eyes anxious for her approval. She bent down to pick up four pebbles; and she went solemnly to the four corners he had marked, and pushed them into the earth. He stood, watching her, at what would be his front door; and last she laid the stick, her birthday present, just before his feet. "It will be a lovely house," she said.

Touk's house was two years in the building. Daily Erana told Maugie how the work went forward: how there were to be five rooms, two downstairs and three above; how the frame jointed together; how the floor was laid and the roof covered it. How Touk had great care over the smallest detail: how not only every board slotted like silk into its given place, but there were little carven grinning faces peering out from the corners of cupboards, and wooden leaves and vines that at first glance seemed no more than the shining grain of the exposed wood, coiling around the arches of doorways. Touk built two chimneys, but only one fireplace. The other chimney was so a bird might build its nest in it.

"You must come see it," Erana said to her foster mother. "It is the grandest thing you ever imagined!" She could only say such things when Touk was not around, for Erana's praise of his handiwork seemed to make him uncomfortable, and he blushed, which turned him an unbecoming shade of violet.

Maugie laughed. "I will come when it is finished, to sit by the first fire that is laid in the new fireplace."

Touk often asked Erana how a thing should be done: the door here or there in a room, should the little face in this corner perhaps have its tongue sticking out for a change? Erana, early in the house building, began picking up the broken bits of trees that collected around Touk's work, and borrowed a knife, and began to teach herself to whittle. In two years' time she had grown clever enough at it that it was she who decorated the stairway, and made tall thin forest creatures of wood to stand upon each step and hold up the railing, which was itself a scaled snake with a benevolent look in his eye as he viewed the upper hallway, and a bird sitting on a nest in a curl of his tail instead of a newel post at the bottom of the staircase.

When Touk praised her work in turn, Erana flushed too, although her cheeks went pink instead of lavender; and she shook her head and said, "I admit I am pleased with it, but I could never have built the house. Where did you learn such craft?"

Touk scratched one furry shoulder with his nails, which curled clawlike over the tips of his fingers. "I practiced on my mother's house. My father built it; but I've put so many patches on it, and I've stared at its beams so often, that wood looks and feels to me as familiar as water."

Even mending seemed less horrible than usual, when the tears she stitched together were the honorable tears of house building. Maugie was never a very harsh taskmaster and, as the house fever grew, quietly excused Erana from her lessons on herb lore. Erana felt both relieved and guilty as she noticed, but when she tried halfheartedly to protest, Maugie said, "No, no, don't worry about it. Time enough for such things when the house is finished." Erana was vaguely surprised, for even after her foster mother had realized that her pupil had no gift for it, the lessons had continued, earnestly, patiently, and a trifle sorrowfully. But now Maugie seemed glad, even joyful, to excuse her. Perhaps she's as relieved as I am, Erana thought, and took herself off to the riverbank again.

She wished all the more that Maugie would come too, for she spent nearly all her days there, and it seemed unkind to leave her foster mother so much alone; but Maugie only smiled her oddly joyful smile, and hurried her on her way.

The day was chosen when the house was to be called complete; when Maugie would come to see the first fire laid – "And to congratulate the builder," Erana said merrily. "You will drown him in congratulations when you see."

"Builders," said Touk. "And I doubt the drowning."

Erana laughed. "Builder. And I don't suppose you *can* be drowned. But I refuse to argue with you; your mother knows us well enough to know which of us to believe."

Maugie smiled at them both.

Erana could barely contain her impatience to be gone as Maugie tucked the last items in the basket. This house feast would outdo all their previous attempts in that line, which was no small feat in itself; but Erana, for once in her life, was not particularly interested in food. Maugie gave them each their bundles to carry, picked up her basket, and looked around yet again for anything she might have forgotten. "We'll close the windows first; it may rain," she said meditatively; Erana made a strangled noise and dashed off to bang sashes shut.

But they were on their way at last. Maugie looked around with mild surprise at the world she had not seen for so long.

"Have you never been beyond your garden?" Erana said curiously. "Were you born in that house?"

"No. I grew up far away from here. My husband brought me to this place, and helped me plant the garden; he built the house." Maugie looked sad, and Erana asked no more, though she had long wondered about Maugie's husband and Touk's father.

They emerged from the trees to the banks of Touk's river pool. He had cut steps up the slope to his house, setting them among the trees that hid his house from the water's edge, making a narrow twisting path of them, lined with flat rocks and edged with moss. Touk led the way.

The roof was steeply pitched, and two sharp gables struck out from it, with windows to light the second story; the chimneys rose from each end of the house, and their mouths were shaped like wide-jawed dragons, their chins facing each other and their eyes rolling back toward the bird-houses hanging from the trees. And set all around the edges of the roof were narrow poles for more bird-houses, but Touk had not had time for these yet.

Touk smiled shyly at them. "It is magnificent," said his mother, and Touk blushed a deep violet with pleasure.

"Next I will lay a path around the edge of the pool, so that my visitors need not pick their way through brambles and broken rock." They turned back to look at the water, gleaming through the trees. Touk stood one step down, one hand on the young tree beside him, where he had retreated while he awaited his audience's reaction; and Maugie stood near him. As they were, he was only a head taller than she, and Erana noticed for the first time, as the late afternoon sun shone in their faces, that there was a resemblance between them. Nothing in feature perhaps, except that their eyes were set slanting in their faces, but much in expression. The same little half-smiles curled the corners of both their mouths at the moment, though Maugie lacked Touk's splendidly curved fangs.

"But I did not want to put off this day any longer, for today we can celebrate two things together."

"A happy birthday, Erana," said Maugie, and Erana blinked, startled.

"I had forgotten."

"You are seventeen today," Maugie said.

Erana repeated, "I had forgotten." But when she met Touk's turquoise eyes, suddenly the little smile left his face and some other emotion threatened to break through; but he dropped his eyes and turned his face away from her, and his hand trailed slowly down the bole of the tree. Erana was troubled and hurt, for he was her best friend, and she stared at his averted shoulder. Maugie looked from one to the other of them, and began to walk toward the house.

It was not as merry an occasion as it had been planned, for something was bothering Touk, and Erana hugged her hurt to herself and spoke only to Maugie. They had a silent, if vast, supper around the new-laid fire, sitting cross-legged on the floor, for Touk had not yet built any furniture. Maugie interrupted the silence occasionally to praise some detail she noticed, or ask some question about curtains or carpeting, which she had promised to provide. Her first gift to the new house already sat on the oak mantelpiece: a bowl of potpourri, which murmured through the sharper scents of the fire and the richer ones of the food.

Into a longer silence than most, Erana said abruptly, "This is a large house for only one man."

The fire snapped and hissed; the empty room magnified the sound so that they were surrounded by fire. Touk said, "Troll. One troll."

Erana said, "Your mother −"

"I am human, yes, but witch blood is not quite like other human blood," said Maugie.

"And I am my father's son anyway," said Touk. He stretched one hand out to the fire, and spread his fingers; they were webbed. The firelight shone through the delicate mesh of capillaries.

"Your father?"

"My father was a troll of the north, who −"

"Who came south for the love of a human witch-woman," said Maugie gravely.

Erana again did not ask a question, but the silence asked it for her. "He died thirty years ago; Touk was only four. Men found him, and . . . he came home to the garden to die." Maugie paused. "Trolls are not easily caught; but these men were poachers, and trolls are fond of birds. He lost his temper."

Touk shivered, and the curling hair down his spine erected and then lay flat again; Erana thought she would not wish to see him lose his temper. She said slowly, "And yet you stayed here."

"It is my home," Maugie said simply; "it is the place I was happy, and, remembering, I am happy again."

"And I have never longed for the sight of my own kind," said Touk, never raising his eyes from the fire. "I might have gone north,

I suppose, when I was grown; but I would miss my river, and the birds of the north are not my friends."

Erana said, "My family?"

"You are a woodcutter's daughter," Maugie said, so quietly that Erana had to lean toward her to hear her over the fire's echoes. "I . . . did him a favor, but he, he had . . . behaved ill; and I demanded a price. My foster daughter, dearer than daughter, it was a trick and I acknowledge it . . ."

She felt Maugie's head turn toward her, but Touk stared steadfastly at the hearth. "You always wanted a daughter," Erana said, her words as quiet as Maugie's had been, and her own eyes fixed on Maugie's son, who swallowed uncomfortably. "You wish that I should marry your son. This house he has built is for his wife."

Maugie put out a hand. "Erana, love, surely you −"

Touk said, "No, Mother, she has not guessed; has never guessed. I have seen that it has never touched her mind, for I would have seen if it had. And I would not be the one who forced her to think of it." Still he looked at the flames, and now, at last, Erana understood why he had not met her eyes that afternoon.

She stood up, looked blindly around her. "I − I must think."

Maugie said miserably, "Your family − they live in the village at the edge of the forest, south and east of here. He is the woodcutter; she bakes bread for the villagers. They have four daughters and four sons . . ."

Erana found her way to the door, and left them.

Her feet took her back to the witch's garden, the home she had known for her entire life. She had wondered, fleetingly, once she understood that Maugie was not her mother, who her blood kin might be; but the question had never troubled her, for she was happy, loving and loved. It was twilight by the time she reached the garden; numbly she went to the house and fetched a shawl and a kerchief, and into the kerchief she put food, and then went back into the garden and plucked a variety of useful herbs, ones she understood, and tied the kerchief around them all. She walked out of the garden, and set her feet on a trail that no one had used since a woodcutter had followed it for the last time seventeen years before.

*　　　*　　　*

She walked for many days. She did not pause in the small village south and east of the witch's garden; she did not even turn her head when she passed a cottage with loaves of fresh bread on shelves behind the front windows, and the warm smell of the bread assailed her in the street. She passed through many other small villages, but she kept walking. She did not know what she sought, and so she kept walking. When she ran out of food, she did a little simple doctoring to earn more, and then walked on. It was strange to her to see faces that were not Maugie's or Touk's, for these were the only faces she had ever seen, save those of the forest beasts and birds; and she was amazed at how eagerly her simple herbcraft was desired by these strangers. She found some herbs to replace the ones she used in the fields and forests she passed, but the finest of them were in the garden she had left behind.

The villages grew larger, and became towns. Now she heard often of the King, and occasionally she saw a grand coach pass, and was told that only those of noble blood rode in such. Once or twice she saw the faces of those who rode within, but the faces looked no more nor less different from any of the other human faces she saw, although they wore more jewels.

Erana at last made her way to the capital city, but the city gates bore black banners. She wondered at this, and enquired of the gate guard, who told her that it was because the King's only son lay sick. And, because the guard was bored, he told the small shabby pedestrian that the King had issued a proclamation that whosoever cured the Prince should have the King's daughter in marriage, and half the kingdom.

"What is the prince's illness?" Erana asked, clutching her kerchief.

The guard shrugged. "A fever; a wasting fever. It has run many days now, and they say he cannot last much longer. There is no flesh left on his bones, and often he is delirious."

"Thank you," said Erana, and passed through the gates. She chose the widest thoroughfare, and when she had come some distance along it, she asked a passerby where the King's house lay; the woman stared at her, but answered her courteously.

The royal gate too was draped in black. Erana stood before it, hesitating. Her courage nearly failed her, and she turned to go, when a voice asked her business. She might still have not heeded it, but it was a low, growly, kind voice, and it reminded her of another voice dear to her; and so she turned toward it. A guard in a silver uniform and a tall hat smiled gently at her; he had young daughters at home, and he would not wish any of them to look so lost and worn and weary. "Do not be frightened. Have you missed your way?"

"N-no," faltered Erana. "I − I am afraid I meant to come to the King's house, but now I am not so sure."

"What is it the King or his guard may do for you?" rumbled the guard.

Erana blushed. "You will think it very presumptuous, but − but I heard of the Prince's illness, and I have some . . . small . . . skill in healing." Her nervous fingers pulled her kerchief open, and she held it out toward the guard. The scent of the herbs from the witch's garden rose into his face and made him feel young and happy and wise.

He shook his head to clear it. "I think perhaps you have more than small skill," he said, "and I have orders to let all healers in. Go." He pointed the way, and Erana bundled her kerchief together again clumsily and followed his gesture.

The King's house was no mere house, but a castle. Erana had never seen anything like it before, taller than trees, wider than rivers; the weight of its stones frightened her, and she did not like walking up the great steps and under the vast stone archway to the door and the liveried man who stood beside it, nor standing in their gloom as she spoke her errand. The liveried man received her with more graciousness and less kindness than the silver guard had done, and he led her without explanation to a grand chamber where many people stood and whispered among themselves like a forest before a storm. Erana felt the stone ceiling hanging over her, and the stone floor jarred her feet. At the far end of the chamber was a dais with a tall chair on it, and in the chair sat a man.

"Your majesty," said Erana's guide, and bowed low; and Erana bowed as he had done, for she understood that one makes obeisance to a king, but did not know that women were expected to curtsey. "This . . . girl . . . claims to know something of leechcraft."

The whispering in the chamber suddenly stilled, and the air

quivered with the silence, like the forest just before the first lash of rain. The King bent his heavy gaze upon his visitor, but when Erana looked back at him, his face was expressionless.

"What do you know of fevers?" said the King; his voice was as heavy as his gaze, and as gloomy as the stones of his castle, and Erana's shoulders bowed a little beneath it.

"Only a little, your majesty," she said, "but an herb I carry" – and she raised her kerchief – "does the work for me."

"If the Prince dies after he suffers your tending," said the King in a tone as expressionless as his face, "you will die with him."

Erana stood still a moment, thinking, but her thoughts had been stiff and uncertain since the evening she had sat beside a first-laid fire in a new house, and the best they could do for her now was to say to her, "So?" Thus she answered: "Very well."

The King raised one hand, and another man in livery stepped forward, his footsteps hollow in the thick silence. "Take her to where the Prince lies, and see that she receives what she requires and . . . do not leave her alone with him."

The man bowed, turned, and began to walk away; he had not once glanced at Erana. She hesitated, looking to the King for some sign; but he sat motionless, his gaze lifted from her and his face blank. Perhaps it is despair, she thought, almost hopefully: the despair of a father who sees his son dying. Then she turned to follow her new guide, who had halfway crossed the long hall while she stood wondering, and so she had to hasten after to catch him up. Over her soft footsteps she heard a low rustling laugh as the courtiers watched the country peasant run from their distinguished presence.

The guide never looked back. They came at last to a door at which he paused, and Erana paused panting behind him. He opened the door reluctantly. Still without looking around, he passed through it and stopped. Erana followed him, and went around him, to look into the room.

It was not a large room, but it was very high; and two tall windows let the sunlight in, and Erana blinked, for the corridors she had passed through had been gray, stone-shadowed. Against the wall opposite the windows was a bed, with a canopy, and curtains pulled back and tied to the four pillars at its four corners. A man sat beside the bed, three more sat a little distance from it, and a man lay in the bed. His hands lay over the coverlet, and the fingers twitched restlessly; his lips moved without sound, and his face on the pillow turned back and forth.

Erana's guide said, "This is the latest . . . leech. She has seen the King, and he has given his leave." The tone of his voice left no doubt of his view of this decision.

Erana straightened her spine, and held up her bundle in her two hands. She turned to her supercilious guide and said, "I will need hot water and cold water." She gazed directly into his face as she spoke, while he looked over her head. He turned, nonetheless, and went out.

Erana approached the bed and looked down; the man sitting by it made no move to give her room, but sat stiffly where he was. The Prince's face was white to the lips, and there were hollows under his eyes and cheekbones; and then, as she watched, a red flush broke out, and sweat stained his cheeks and he moaned.

The guide returned, bearing two pitchers. He put them on the floor, and turned to go. Erana said, "Wait," and he took two more steps before he halted, but he did halt, with his back to her as she knelt by the pitchers and felt the water within them. One was tepid; the other almost tepid. "This will not do," Erana said angrily, and the man turned around, as if interested against his will that she dared protest. She picked up the pitchers and with one heave threw their contents over the man who had fetched them. He gasped, and his superior look disappeared, and his face grew mottled with rage. "I asked for *hot* water and *cold* water. You will bring it, as your king commanded you to obey me. With it you will bring me two bowls and two cups. Go swiftly and return more swiftly. Go *now*." She turned away from him, and after a moment she heard him leave. His footsteps squelched.

He returned as quickly as she had asked; water still rolled off him and splashed to the floor as he moved. He carried two more pitchers; steam rose from the one, and dew beaded the other. Behind him a woman in a long skirt carried the bowls and cups.

"You will move away from the bed, please," Erana said, and the man who had not made room for her paused just long enough to prove that he paused but not so long as to provoke any reaction, stood up, and walked to the window. She poured some hot water into one bowl, and added several dark green leaves that had once been long and spiky but had become bent and bruised during their journey from the witch's garden; and she let them steep till the sharp smell of them hung like a green fog in the high-ceilinged room. She poured some of the infusion into a cup, and raised the Prince's head from the pillow, and held the cup under his nostrils. He breathed the vapor, coughed, sighed; and his eyes flickered open. "Drink this," Erana whispered, and he bowed his head and drank.

She gave him a second cup some time later, and a third as twilight fell; and then, as night crept over them, she sat at his bedside and waited, and, as she had nothing else to do, she listened to her thoughts; and her thoughts were of Touk and Maugie, and of the King's sentence hanging over her head like the stone ceiling, resting on the Prince's every shallow breath.

All that night they watched, and candlelight gave the Prince's wan face a spurious look of health. But at dawn, when Erana stood stiffly and touched his forehead, it was cool. He turned a little away from her, and tucked one hand under his cheek, and lay quietly; and his breathing deepened and steadied into sleep.

Erana remained standing, staring dumbly down at her triumph. The door of the room opened, and her uncooperative guide of the day before entered, bearing on a tray two fresh pitchers of hot and cold water, and bread and cheese and jam and meat. Erana brewed a fresh minty drink with the cold water, and gave it to the Prince with hands that nearly trembled. She said to the man who had been her guide, "The Prince will sleep now, and needs only the tending that any patient nurse may give. May I rest?"

The man, whose eyes now dwelt upon her collarbone, bowed, and went out, and she followed him to a chamber not far from the Prince's. There was a bed in it, and she fell into it, clutching her herb bundle like a pillow, and fell fast asleep.

She continued to assist in the tending of the Prince, since it seemed to be expected of her, and since she gathered that she should be honored by the trust in her skill she had so hardly earned. Within a fortnight the Prince was walking, slowly but confidently; and Erana began to wonder how long she was expected to wait upon him, and then she wondered what she might do with herself once she was freed of that waiting.

There was no one at the Court she might ask her questions. For all that she had been their prince's salvation, they treated her as distantly as they had from the beginning, albeit now with greater respect. She had received formal thanks from the King, whose joy at his son's health regained made no more mark on his expression and the tone of his voice than fear of his son's death had done. The Queen had called Erana to her private sitting room to receive her thanks. The Princess had been there too; she had curtseyed to Erana, but she had not smiled, any more than her parents had done.

And so Erana continued from day to day, waiting for an unknown summons; or perhaps for the courage to ask if she might take her leave.

A month after the Prince arose from his sickbed he called his first Royal Address since his illness had struck him down. The day before the Address the royal heralds had galloped the royal horses through the streets of the King's city, telling everyone who heard them that the Prince would speak to his people on the morrow; and when at noon on the next day he stood in the balcony overlooking the courtyard Erana had crossed to enter the palace for the first time, a mob of expectant faces tipped up their chins to watch him.

Erana had been asked to attend the royal speech. She stood in the high-vaulted hall where she had first met the King, a little behind the courtiers who now backed the Prince, holding his hands up to his people, on the balcony. The King and Queen stood near her; the Princess sat gracefully at her ease in a great wooden chair lined with cushions a little distance from the open balcony. It seemed to Erana, she thought with some puzzlement, that they glanced at her often, although with their usual impassive expressions; and there was tension in the air that reminded her of the first time she had entered this hall, to tell the King that she knew a little of herbs and fevers.

Erana clasped her hands together. She supposed her special presence had been asked that she might accept some sort of royal thanks in sight of the people; she, the forest girl, who was still shy of people in groups. The idea that she might have to expose herself to the collective gaze of an audience of hundreds made her very uncomfortable; her clasped hands felt cold. She thought, It will please these people if I fail to accept their thanks with dignity, and so I shall be dignified. I will look over the heads of the audience, and pretend they are flowers in a field.

She did not listen carefully to what the Prince was saying. She noticed that the rank of courtiers surrounding the Prince had parted, and the King stepped forward as if to join his son on the balcony. But he paused beside Erana, and seized her hands, and led or dragged her beside him; her hands were pinched inside his fingers, and he pulled at her awkwardly, so that she stumbled. They stood on the balcony together, and she blinked in the sunlight; she looked at the Prince, and then turned her head back to look at the King, still holding her hands prisoned as if she might run away. She did not look down, at the faces beyond the balcony.

"I offered my daughter's hand in marriage and half my kingdom to the leech who cured my son." The King paused, and a murmur, half surprise and half laughter, wrinkled the warm noontide air. He looked down at Erana, and still his face was blank. "I wish now to adjust the prize and payment for the service done me and my people and my kingdom: my son's hand in marriage to the leech who saved him, and, beside him, the rule of all my kingdom."

The Prince reached across and disentangled one of her hands from his father's grip, so that she stood stretched between them, like game on a pole brought home from the hunt. The people in the courtyard were shouting; the noise hurt her head, and she felt her knees sagging, and the pull on her hands, and then a hard grip on her upper arms to keep her standing; and then all went black.

She came to herself lying on a sofa. She could hear the movements of several people close beside her, but she was too tired and troubled to wish to open her eyes just yet on the world of the Prince's betrothed; and so she lay quietly.

"I think they might have given her some warning," said one voice. "She does have thoughts of her own."

A laugh. "Does she? What makes you so sure? A little nobody like this − I'm surprised they went through with it. She's not the type to insist about anything. She creeps around like a mouse, and never speaks unless spoken to. Not always then."

"She spoke up for herself to Roth."

"Roth is a fool. He would not wear the King's livery at all if his mother were not in waiting to the Queen . . . And she's certainly done nothing of the sort since. Give her a few copper coins and a new shawl . . . and a pat on the head . . . and send her on her way."

"She did save the Prince's life."

A snort. "I doubt it. Obviously the illness had run its course; she just happened to have poured some ridiculous quack remedy down his throat at the time."

There was a pause, and then the first voice said, "It is a pity she's so plain. One wants a queen to set a certain standard . . ."

Erana shivered involuntarily, and the voice stopped abruptly. Then she moaned a little, as if only just coming to consciousness, and opened her eyes.

Two of the Queen's ladies-in-waiting bent over her. She recognized the owner of the second voice immediately from the sour look on her face. The kindlier face said to her, "Are you feeling a little better now? May we bring you anything?"

Erana sat up slowly. "Thank you. Would you assist me to my room, please?"

She easily persuaded them to leave her alone in her own room. At dinnertime a man came to enquire if she would attend the banquet in honor of the Prince's betrothal? She laughed a short laugh and said that she felt still a trifle overcome by the news of the Prince's betrothal, and desired to spend her evening resting quietly, and could someone perhaps please bring her a light supper?

Someone did, and she sat by the window watching the twilight fade into darkness, and the sounds of the banquet far away from her small room drifting up to her on the evening breeze. I have never spoken to the prince alone, she thought; I have never addressed him but as a servant who does what she may for his health and comfort; nor has he spoken to me but as a master who recognizes a servant who has her usefulness.

Dawn was not far distant when the betrothal party ended. She heard the last laughter, the final cheers, and silence. She sighed and stood up, and stretched, for she was stiff with sitting. Slowly she opened the chest where she kept her herb kerchief and the shabby clothes she had travelled in. She laid aside the Court clothes she had never been comfortable in, for all that they were plain and simple compared with those the others wore, and dressed herself in the skirt and blouse that she and Maugie had made. She ran her fingers over the patches in the skirt that house building had caused. She hesitated, her bundle in hand, and then opened another, smaller chest, and took out a beautiful shawl, black, embroidered in red and gold, and with a long silk fringe. This she folded gently, and wrapped inside her kerchief.

Touk had taught her to walk quietly, that they might watch birds in their nests without disturbing them, and creep close to feeding deer. She slipped into the palace shadows, and then into the shadows of the trees that edged the courtyard; once she looked up, over her shoulder, to the empty balcony that opened off the great hall. The railings of the ornamental fence that towered grandly over the gate and guardhouse were set so far apart that she could squeeze between them, pulling her bundle after her.

She did not think they would be sorry to see her go; she could imagine the King's majestic words: *She has chosen to decline the honor we would do her, feeling herself unworthy; and, having accepted our grateful thanks for her leechcraft, she has withdrawn once again to her peaceful country obscurity. Our best wishes go with her* . . . But still she walked quietly, in the shadows, and when dawn came she hid under a hedge in a garden, and slept, as she had often done before. She woke up once, hearing the hoofs of the royal heralds rattle past; and she wondered what news they brought. She fell asleep again, and did not waken till twilight; and then she crept out and began walking again.

She knew where she was going this time, and so her journey back took less time than her journey away had done. Still she was many days on the road, and since she found that her last experience of them had made her shy of humankind, she walked after sunset and before dawn, and followed the stars across open fields instead of keeping to the roads, and raided gardens and orchards for her food, and did not offer her skills as a leech for an honest meal or bed.

The last night she walked into the dawn and past it, and the sun rose in the sky, and she was bone-weary and her feet hurt, and her small bundle weighed like rock. But here was her forest again, and she could not stop. She went past Maugie's garden, although she saw the wisp of smoke lifting from the chimney, and followed the well-known track to Touk's pool. She was too tired to be as quiet as she should be, and when she emerged from the trees there was nothing visible but the water. She looked around and saw that Touk had laid the path around the shore of the pool that he had promised, and now smooth gray stones led the way to the steep steps before Touk's front door.

As she stood at the water's edge, her eyes blurred, and her hands, crossed over the bundle held to her breast, fell to her sides. Then there was a commotion in the pool, and Touk stood up, water streaming from him, and a strand of waterweed trailing over one pointed ear. Even the center of the pool for Touk was only thigh-deep, and he stood, riffling the water with his fingers, watching her.

"Will you marry me?" she said.

He smiled, his lovely, gap-toothed smile, and he blinked his turquoise eyes at her, and pulled the waterweed out of his long hair.

"I came back just to ask you that. If you say no, I will go away again."

"No," he said. "Don't go away. My answer is yes."

And he waded over to the edge of the pool and seized her in his wet arms and kissed her; and she threw her arms eagerly around his neck, and dropped her bundle. It opened in the water like a flower, and the herbs floated away across the surface, skittering like water bugs; and the embroidered silk shawl sank to the bottom.

The Tree's Wife

❧

Jane Yolen

THERE WAS ONCE A young woman named Drusilla who had been widowed longer than she was wed. She had been married at fifteen to a rich old man who beat her. She had flowered despite his ill treatment, and it was he who died, within the year, leaving her all alone in the great house.

Once the old man was dead, his young widow was courted by many, for she was now quite wealthy. The young men came together, and all claimed that she needed a husband to help her.

But Drusilla would have none of them. "When I was poor," she said, "not one of you courted me. When I was ill treated, not one of you stood by me. I never asked for more than a gentle word, yet I never received one. So now that you ask, I will have none of you."

She turned her back on them, then stopped. She looked around at the grove of birch trees by her house. "Why, I would sooner wed this tree," she said, touching a sturdy birch that stood to one side. "A tree would know when to bend and when to stand. I would sooner wed this tree than marry another man."

At that very moment, a passing wind caused the top branches of the birch to sway.

The rejected suitors laughed at Drusilla. "See," they jeered, "the tree has accepted your offer."

And so she was known from that day as the Tree's Wife.

To keep the jest from hurting, Drusilla entered into it with a

will. If someone came to the house, she would put her arms around the birch, caressing its bark and stroking its limbs.

"I have all I need or want with my tree," she would say. And her laugh was a silent one back at the stares. She knew that nothing confounds jokers as much as madness, so she made herself seem very mad for them.

But madness also makes folk uneasy; they fear contagion. And soon Drusilla found herself quite alone. Since it was not of her choosing, the aloneness began to gnaw at her. It was true that what she really wanted was just a kind word, but soon she was so lonely almost any word would have done.

So it happened one night, when the moon hung in the sky like a ripe yellow apple, that a wind blew fiercely from the north. It made the trees bow and bend and knock their branches against Drusilla's house. Hearing them knock, she looked out of the windows and saw the trees dancing wildly in the wind.

They seemed to beckon and call, and she was suddenly caught up in their rhythm. She swayed with them, but it was not enough. She longed for the touch of the wind on her skin, so she ran outside, leaving the door ajar. She raised her hands above her head and danced with the trees.

In the darkness, surrounded by the shadow of its brothers, one tree seemed to shine. It was her tree, the one she had chosen. It was touched with a phosphorescent glow, and the vein of each leaf was a streak of pale fire.

Drusilla danced over to the tree and held her hands toward it. "Oh, if only you *were* a man, or I a tree," she said out loud. "If you were a man tall and straight and gentle and strong then – yes – then I would be happy."

The wind died as suddenly as it had begun, and the trees stood still. Drusilla dropped her hands, feeling foolish and shamed, but a movement in the white birch stayed her. As she watched, it seemed to her that first two legs, then a body, then a head and arms emerged from the bark; a shadowy image pulling itself painfully free of the trunk. The image shimmered for a moment, trembled, and then became clear. Before her stood a man.

He was tall and slim, with skin as white as the bark of the birch and hair as black as the birch bark patches. His legs were strong yet supple, and his feet were knotty and tapered like roots. His hands were thin and veined with green, and the second and third fingers grew together, slotted like a leaf. He smiled at her and held out his arms, an echo of her earlier plea, and his arms swayed up and down as if touched by a passing breeze.

Drusilla stood without movement, without breath. Then he nodded his head, and she went into his arms. When his mouth came down on hers, she smelled the damp woody odor of his breath.

They lay together all night below his tree, cradled in its roots. But when the sun began its climb against the farthest hills, the man pulled himself reluctantly from Drusilla's arms and disappeared back into the tree.

Call as she might, Drusilla could not bring him out again, but one of the tree branches reached down and stroked her arm in a lover's farewell.

She spent the next days under the tree, reading and weaving and playing her lute. And the tree itself seemed to listen and respond. The branches touched and turned the pages of her book. The whole tree moved to the beauty of her songs.

Yet it was not until the next full moon that the man could pull himself from the tree and sleep away the dark in her arms.

Still Drusilla was content. For as she grew in her love for the man of the tree, her love for all nature grew, a quiet pullulation. She felt kin to every flower and leaf. She heard the silent speech of the green world and, under the bark, the beating of each heart.

One day, when she ventured into the village, Drusilla's neighbors observed that she was growing more beautiful in her madness. The boldest of them, an old woman, asked, "If you have no man, how is it you bloom?"

Drusilla turned to look at the old woman and smiled. It was a slow smile. "I am the Tree's Wife," she said, "in truth. And he is man enough for me." It was all the answer she would return.

But in the seventh month since the night of the apple moon, Drusilla knew she carried a child, the tree's child, below her heart. And when she told the tree of it, its branches bent around her and touched her hair. And when she told the man of it, he smiled and held her gently.

Drusilla wondered what the child would be that rooted in her. She wondered if it would burgeon into a human child or emerge some great wooden beast. Perhaps it would be both, with arms and legs as strong as the birch and leaves for hair. She feared her heart would burst with questions. But on the next full moon, the tree man held her and whispered in her ear such soft, caressing sounds, she grew calm. And at last she knew that, however the child grew, she would love it. And with that knowledge she was once again content.

Soon it was evident, even to the townsfolk, that she blossomed with child. They looked for the father among themselves – for where else *could* they look – but no one admitted to the deed. And Drusilla herself would name no one but the tree to the midwife, priest, or mayor.

And so, where at first the villagers had jested at her and joked with her and felt themselves plagued by her madness, now they turned wicked and cruel. They could accept a widow's madness but not a mother unwed.

The young men, the late suitors, pressed on by the town elders, came to Drusilla one night. In the darkness, they would have pulled her from her house and beaten her. But Drusilla heard them come and climbed through the window and fled to the top of the birch.

The wind raged so that night that the branches of the tree flailed like whips, and not one of the young men dared come close enough to climb the tree and take Drusilla down. All they could do was try and wound her with their words. They shouted up at her where she sat near the top of the birch, cradled in its branches. But she did not hear their shouts. She was lulled instead by the great rustling voices of the grove.

In the morning the young men were gone. They did not return.

And Drusilla did not go back into the town. As the days passed, she was fed by the forest and the field. Fruits and berries and sweet sap found their way to her doorstep. Each morning she had enough for the day. She did not ask where it all came from, but still she knew.

At last it was time for the child to be born. On this night of a full moon, Drusilla's pains began. Holding her sides with slender fingers, she went out to the base of the birch, sat down, and leaned her back against the tree, straining to let the child out. As she pushed, the birch man pulled himself silently from the tree, knelt by her, and breathed encouragements into her face. He stroked her hair and whispered her name to the wind.

She did not smile up at him but said at last, "Go." Her breath was ragged and her voice on the edge of despair. "I beg you. Get the midwife. This does not go well."

The tree man held her close, but he did not rise.

"Go," she begged. "Tell her my name. It is time."

He took her face in his hands and stared long into it with his woods-green eyes. He pursed his lips as if to speak, then stood up and was gone.

He went down the path toward the town, though each step away from the tree drew his strength from him. Patches of skin peeled off as he moved, and the sores beneath were dark and viscous. His limbs grew more brittle with each step, and he moved haltingly. By the time he reached the midwife's house, he looked an aged and broken thing. He knocked upon the door, yet he was so weak it was only a light tapping, a scraping, the scratching of a branch across a window pane.

As if she had been waiting for his call, the midwife came at once. She opened the door and stared at what stood before her. Tall and thin and naked and white, with black patches of scabrous skin and hair as dark as rotting leaves, the tree man held up his grotesque, slotted hand. The gash of his mouth was hollow and tongueless, a sap-filled wound. He made no sound, but the midwife screamed and screamed, and, screaming still, slammed the door.

She did not see him fall.

In the morning the townsfolk came to Drusilla's great house. They came armed with clubs and cudgels and forks. The old midwife was in the rear, calling the way.

Beneath a dead white tree they found Drusilla, pale and barely moving, a child cradled in her arms. At the townsfolk's coming, the child opened its eyes. They were the color of winter pine.

"Poor thing," said the midwife, stepping in front of the men. "I knew no good would come of this." She bent to take the child from Drusilla's arms but leaped up again with a cry. For the child had uncurled one tiny fist, and its hand was veined with green and the second and third fingers grew together, slotted like a leaf.

At the midwife's cry, the birches in the grove began to move and sway, though there was not a breath of breeze. And before any weapon could be raised, the nearest birch stretched its branches far out and lifted the child and Drusilla up, up toward the top of the tree.

As the townsfolk watched, Drusilla disappeared. The child seemed to linger for a moment longer, its unclothed body gleaming in the sun. Then slowly the child faded, like melting snow on pine needles, like the last white star of morning, into the heart of the tree.

There was a soughing as of wind through branches, a tremble of leaves, and one sharp cry of an unsuckled child. Then the trees in the grove were still.

The Ugly Duckling

~

Hans Christian Andersen

IT WAS BEAUTIFUL IN the country; it was summer-time, the wheat was yellow, the oats were green, the hay was stacked up in the green meadows, and the stork paraded about on his long red legs, talking in Egyptian, which language he had learned from his mother. The fields and meadows were skirted by thick woods, and a deep lake lay in the midst of the woods. Yes, it was indeed beautiful in the country! The sunshine fell warmly on an old mansion, surrounded by deep canals, and from the walls down to the water's edge there grew large burdock-leaves, so high that children could stand upright among them without being seen. This place was as wild and unfrequented as the thickest part of the wood, and on that account a duck had chosen to make her nest there. She was sitting on her eggs; but the pleasure she had felt at first was now almost gone, because she had been there so long, and had so few visitors, for the other ducks preferred swimming on the canals to sitting gossiping with her.

At last the eggs cracked, and one little head after another appeared. "Quack, quack!" said the duck, and all got up as well as they could, and peeped about from under the green leaves.

"How large the world is!" said the little ones.

"Do you imagine this to be the whole of the world?" said the mother. "It extends far beyond the other side of the garden, to the pastor's field; but I have never been there. Are you all here?" And then she got up. "No, I have not got you all; the largest egg is still here. How long will this last? I am so weary of it!" And then she sat down again.

"Well, and how are you getting on?" asked an old duck, who had come to pay her a visit.

"This one egg keeps me so long," said the mother, "it will not break; but you should see the others! They are the prettiest little ducklings I have seen in all my days."

"Depend upon it," said the old duck, "it is a turkey's egg. I was cheated in the same way once myself, and I had such trouble with the young ones; for they were afraid of the water, and I could not get them to go near it. I called and scolded, but it was all of no use. But let me see the egg – ah yes! To be sure, that is a turkey's egg. Leave it, and teach the other little ones to swim."

"I will sit on it a little longer," said the duck. "I have been sitting so long that I may as well spend the harvest here."

"It is no business of mine," said the old duck, and away she waddled.

The great egg burst at last. "Tchick, tchick!" said the little one, and out it tumbled. But oh! how large and ugly it was! The duck looked at it. "That is a great, strong creature," said she, "none of the others are at all like it. Can it be a young turkey-cock? Well, we shall soon find out; it must go into the water, though I push it in myself."

The next day there was delightful weather, and the sun shone warmly upon all the green leaves when mother-duck with all her family went down to the canal. Plump! she went into the water. "Quack, quack!" cried she, and one duckling after another jumped in. The water closed over their heads, but all came up again, and swam quite easily. All were there, even the ugly grey one.

"No! It is not a turkey," said the mother-duck; "only see how prettily it moves its legs, how upright it holds itself. It is my own child, and it is really very pretty when one looks more closely at it. Quack, quack! Now come with me, I will take you into the world; but keep close to me, or someone may tread on you, and beware of the cat."

When they came into the duck-yard, two families were quarrelling about the remains of an eel, which in the end was secured by the cat.

"See, my children, such is the way of the world," said the

mother-duck, wiping her beak, for she too was fond of roasted eels. "Now use your legs," said she, "keep together, and bow to the old duck you see yonder. She is the most distinguished of all the fowls present, and is of Spanish blood, which accounts for her dignified appearance and manners. And look, she has a red rag on her leg; that is considered extremely handsome, and is the greatest honour a duck can have."

The other ducks who were in the yard looked at them and said aloud: "Only see, now we have another brood, as if there were not enough of us already. And fie! how ugly that one is; we will not endure it," and immediately one of the ducks flew at him, and bit him on the neck.

"Leave him alone," said the mother, "he is doing no one any harm."

"Yes, but he is so large, and so strange-looking."

"Those are fine children that our good mother has," said the old duck with the red rag on her leg. "All are pretty except one, and that has not turned out well; I almost wish it could be hatched over again."

"Certainly he is not handsome," said the mother, "but he is a very good child, and swims as well as the others, indeed rather better. I think he will grow like the others all in good time, and perhaps will look smaller." And she scratched the duckling's neck, and stroked his whole body. "Besides," added she, "he is a drake; I think he will be very strong, so he will fight his way through."

"The other ducks are very pretty," said the old duck. "Pray make yourselves at home, and if you find an eel's head you can bring it to me."

And accordingly they made themselves at home.

But the poor duckling who had come last out of his egg-shell and who was so ugly was bitten, pecked, and teased by both ducks and hens. And the turkey-cock, who had come into the world with spurs on, and therefore fancied he was an emperor, puffed himself up like a ship in full sail, and marched up to the duckling quite red with passion. The poor thing scarcely knew what to do; he was quite distressed because he was so ugly.

So passed the first day, and afterwards matters grew worse and worse. Even his brothers and sisters behaved unkindly, and were constantly saying: "May the cat take you, you ugly thing!" The mother said: "Ah, if you were only far away!" The ducks bit him, the hens pecked him, and the girl who fed the poultry kicked him. He ran through the hedge; the little birds in the bushes were terrified. "That is because I am so ugly," thought the duckling, and ran on. At last he came to a wide moor, where lived some wild ducks; here he lay the whole night, so tired and so comfortless. In the morning the wild ducks flew up, and perceived their new companion. "Pray who are you?" asked they; and our duckling greeted them as politely as possible.

"You are really very ugly," said the wild ducks; "but that does not matter to us, if you do not marry into our families."

Poor thing! He had never thought of marrying; he only wished to lie among the reeds, and drink the water of the moor. There he stayed for two whole days. On the third day there came two wild geese, or rather ganders, who had not been long out of their egg-shells, which accounts for their impertinence.

"Hark-ye," said they, "you are so ugly that we like you infinitely well; will you come with us? On another moor, not far from this, are some dear, sweet, wild geese, as lovely creatures as have ever said 'hiss, hiss'. You are truly in the way to make your fortune, ugly as you are."

Bang! A gun went off all at once, and both wild geese were stretched dead among the reeds. Bang! A gun went off again, whole flocks of wild geese flew up, and another report followed.

There was a grand hunting party. The hunters lay in ambush all around; some were even sitting in the trees, whose huge branches stretched far over the moor. The hounds splashed about in the mud, bending the reeds and rushes in all directions. How frightened the poor little duck was! He turned his head, thinking to hide it under his wing, and in a moment a fierce-looking dog stood close to him, his tongue hanging out of his mouth, his eyes sparkling fearfully. He opened wide his jaws at the sight of our duckling, showed him his sharp white teeth, and, splash, splash! he was gone – gone without hurting him.

"Well! Let me be thankful," sighed the duckling. "I am so ugly that even the dog will not eat me."

And now he lay still, though the shooting continued among the reeds. The noise did not cease till late in the day, and even then the poor little thing dared not stir. He waited several hours before he looked around him, and then hastened away from the moor as fast as he could. He ran over fields and meadows, though the wind was so high that he could hardly go against it.

Towards evening he reached a wretched little hut, so wretched that it knew not on which side to fall, and therefore remained standing. He noticed that the door had lost one of its hinges, and hung so much awry that there was a space between it and the wall wide enough to let him through. So, as the storm was becoming worse and worse, he crept into the room.

In this room lived an old woman, with her tom-cat and her hen. The cat, whom she called her little son, knew how to set up his back and purr. The hen had very short legs, and was therefore called "Cuckoo Shortlegs"; she laid very good eggs, and the old woman loved her as her own child.

The next morning the cat began to mew and the hen to cackle when they saw the new guest.

"What is the matter?" asked the old woman, looking round. Her eyes were not good, so she took the duckling to be a fat duck who had lost her way. "This is a capital catch," said she. "I shall now have duck's eggs, if it be not a drake. We must try." So the duckling was put to the proof for three weeks; but no eggs made their appearance.

Now the cat was the master of the house, and the hen was the mistress, and they used always to say, "We and the world," for they imagined themselves to be not only the half of the world, but also by far the better half. The duckling thought it was possible to be of a different opinion, but that the hen would not allow.

"Can you lay eggs?" asked she.

"No."

"Well, then, hold your tongue."

And the cat said: "Can you set up your back? Can you purr?"

"No."

"Well, then, you should have no opinion when wise persons are speaking."

So the duckling sat alone in a corner, and was in a very bad humour. He happened, however, to think of the fresh air and bright sunshine, and these thoughts gave him such a strong desire to swim again that he could not help telling it to the hen.

"What ails you?" said the hen. "You have nothing to do, and therefore brood over these fancies; either lay eggs, or purr, then you will forget them."

"But it is so delicious to swim," said the duckling; "so delicious when the waters close over your head, and you plunge to the bottom."

"Well, that is a queer sort of pleasure," said the hen; "I think you must be crazy. Not to speak of myself, ask the cat – he is the most sensible animal I know – whether he would like to swim, or to plunge to the bottom of the water. Ask your mistress; no one is wiser than she. Do you think she would take pleasure in swimming, and in the waters closing over her head?"

"You do not understand me," said the duckling.

"What, we do not understand you! So you think yourself wiser than the cat and the old woman, not to speak of myself! Do not fancy any such thing, child, but be thankful for all the kindness that has been shown you. Are you not lodged in a warm room, and have you not the advantage of society from which you can learn something? But you are a simpleton, and it is wearisome to have anything to do with you. Believe me, I wish you well. I tell you unpleasant truths, but it is thus that real friendship is shown. Come, for once give yourself the trouble to learn to purr, or to lay eggs."

"I think I will go out into the wide world again," said the duckling.

"Well, go," answered the hen.

So the duckling went. He swam on the surface of the water, he plunged beneath, but all animals passed him by, on account of his ugliness. The autumn came, the leaves turned yellow and brown, the wind caught them and danced them about, the air was very cold, the clouds were heavy with hail or snow, and the raven sat on the hedge and croaked. The poor duckling was certainly not very comfortable!

One evening, just as the sun was setting, a flock of large birds rose from the brushwood. The duckling had never seen anything so beautiful before; their plumage was of a dazzling white, and they had long, slender necks. They were swans; they uttered a singular cry, spread out their long, splendid wings, and flew away from these cold regions to warmer countries, across the open sea. They flew so high, so very high! And the ugly duckling's feelings were very strange; he turned round and round in the water like a mill-wheel, strained his neck to look after them, and sent forth such a loud and strange cry, that it almost frightened himself. Ah! he could not forget them, those noble birds! Those happy birds! The duckling knew not what the birds were called, knew not whither they were flying, yet he loved them as he had never before loved anything. He envied them not; it would never have occurred to him to wish such beauty for himself; he would have been quite contented if the ducks in the duck-yard had but endured his company.

And the winter was so cold, so cold! The duckling had to swim round and round in the water, to keep it from freezing. But every night the opening in which he swam became smaller and smaller; the duckling had to make good use of his legs to prevent the water from freezing entirely. At last, wearied out, he lay stiff and cold in the ice.

Early in the morning there passed by a peasant, who saw him, broke the ice in pieces with his wooden shoe, and brought him home to his wife.

The duckling soon revived. The children would have played with him, but he thought they wished to tease him, and in his terror jumped into the milk-pail, so that the milk was spilled about the room. The good woman screamed and clapped her hands. He flew thence into the pan where the butter was kept, and thence into the meal-barrel, and out again.

The woman screamed, and struck at him with the tongs; the children ran races with each other trying to catch him, and laughed and screamed likewise. It was well for him that the door stood open; he jumped out among the bushes into the new-fallen snow, and lay there as in a dream.

But it would be too sad to relate all the trouble and misery he had to suffer during the winter. He was lying on a moor among the reeds when the sun began to shine warmly again, the larks sang, and beautiful spring returned.

Once more he shook his wings. They were stronger than formerly, and bore him forward quickly, and, before he was well aware of it, he was in a large garden where the apple trees stood in full bloom, where syringas sent forth their fragrance and hung their long green branches down into the winding canal. Oh! everything was so lovely, so full of the freshness of spring!

Out of the thicket came three beautiful white swans. They displayed their feathers so proudly, and swam so lightly, so lightly! The duckling knew the glorious creatures, and was seized with a strange sadness.

"I will fly to them, those kingly birds!" said he. "They will kill me, because I, ugly as I am, have presumed to approach them; but it matters not. Better be killed by them than be bitten by the ducks, pecked by the hens, kicked by the girl who feeds the poultry, and have so much to suffer during the winter!" He flew into the water, and swam towards the beautiful creatures. They saw him and shot forward to meet him. "Only kill me," said the poor duckling, and he bowed his head low, expecting death. But what did he see in the water? He saw beneath him his own form, no longer that of a plump, ugly, grey bird – it was that of a swan!

It matters not to have been born in a duck-yard, if one has been hatched from a swan's egg.

The larger swans swam round him, and stroked him with their beaks, and he was very happy.

Some little children were running about in the garden. They threw grain and bread into the water, and the youngest exclaimed: "There is a new one!" The others also cried out: "Yes, a new swan has come!" and they clapped their hands, and ran and told their father and mother. Bread and cake were thrown into the water, and everyone said: "The new one is the best, so young, and so beautiful!" and the old swans bowed before him. The young swan felt quite ashamed, and hid his head under his wing. He was all too happy, but still not proud, for a good heart is never proud.

He remembered how he had been laughed at and cruelly treated, and he now heard everyone say he was the most beautiful of all beautiful birds. The syringas bent down their branches towards him, and the sun shone warmly and brightly. He shook his feathers, stretched his slender neck, and in the joy of his heart said: "How little did I dream of so much happiness when I was the ugly, despised duckling!"

The Ugly Unicorn

~

Jessica Amanda Salmonson

IN A GARDEN IN China five hundred years ago, there was a maiden whose eyes were so pretty, it was difficult to believe she was blind.

The blind girl's name was Kwa Wei. She was befriended by the Liu-mu, a homely silver-haired creature like a one-horned jackass. As Kwa Wei was blind, she had no idea the Liu-mu was ugly.

It came the first time in spring. Kwa Wei had been smelling orange blossoms and plums. On hearing the beast's hoofs upon the lawn, she thought it was a pony broken loose from Uncle Lu Wei's stables.

It was friendly, so she petted its head, and felt the single horn, blunt at the end.

At once she thought it had to be a young Poh, the strongest and most beautiful unicorn of the many kinds that live in China. She clapped her hands and giggled.

"It's a Poh! Have you come to visit me in my darkness? I'm glad!"

The Liu-mu was too embarrassed and ashamed to say, "I am not the strong, good-looking Poh, but only an unfortunate Liu-mu." He had never been mistaken for anything beautiful until now. So all he said was, "Yes, I have come to visit you."

"Oh! How I wish I could see you with these useless eyes!" said Kwa Wei, and giggled anew.

The Liu-mu lowered his broad head until the blunt horn touched the ground. His eyes were as sad as a deer's.

"Would you like a ride through the garden?" asked the Liu-mu. Kwa Wei clapped her hands delightedly and climbed upon the ugly unicorn. "Hold on to my mane," he said, then trotted off through a maze of hedges.

Such creatures as the Liu-mu are able to run through more than one world. Kwa Wei knew at once that the garden had changed. The air was thicker with perfume. Grander flowers pressed around her as she rode around and about Fairyland.

"Where!" exclaimed Kwa Wei, feeling the gentle wind in her hair. "Faster!" she said, laughing. "Faster!"

"Not too fast," said the Liu-mu. "I'll get worn out."

Such was the first meeting of Kwa Wei and the ugly unicorn.

The girl's uncle was a famous general under the rule of Duke Ling. Such important families live sad and violent lives.

On the day of Kwa Wei's birth, it had been arranged that she would marry Hah Ling Me, Duke Ling's grandson. When the girl was two years old, she became ill and lost her sight. She hardly remembered what it was like to see.

It was difficult to dissolve a marriage agreement between important families. Year after year, Duke Ling wished that Kwa Wei would die, so that his favorite grandson needn't be burdened with a blind wife. If the marriage agreement were cancelled, there might be war between Duke Ling and his own general.

As for Uncle Lu Wei, he knew it was a painful situation. Over the years he had sought the aid of famous physicians from all over China.

"Her eyes are so beautiful," he said. "Why can't you make them work?"

The physicians could do nothing.

When his niece approached the year of marriage, Uncle Lu sent in desperation for the wizard-woman of Mount Tzu.

The wizard-woman was thin and tiny and wrinkled. She looked like an old fairy, that's how small she was. She had no teeth and her nose was so small you could hardly see it. She looked into Kwa Wei's face and in her eyes and finally said, "She can be cured."

Lu Wei was delighted. "How can she be cured?" he asked.

"It requires only the rind of an orange and the pit of a plum, ground together with the horn of a Liu-mu."

Uncle Lu's spirits fell. "I have oranges and plums in my garden. They will bear fruit soon. But as to the horn of the Liu-mu; who has ever seen one?"

To Kwa Wei the little old wizard-woman said, "Pretty girl, would you like to be able to see through those eyes?"

"I cannot remember what it was like to see," she said. "The world is very nice even so." Then wistfully she added, "But I would like to see my friend the Poh, the most beautiful unicorn in China."

"Have you the Poh as your friend?"

"Yes, I do."

"Well, you may go now. I must speak to your uncle in private."

When the blind girl left the hall, the wizard-woman said to Lu Wei: "There were silver hairs on her dress. They are the hairs of the Liu-mu. It may have represented itself as a glorious Poh, being ashamed of its ugliness."

From her bag of medicine, the wizard-woman retrieved two cubes of sugar. She said, "This is Liu-mu poison. The Liu-mu is intelligent and will not eat from the hand of anyone it doesn't know. Kwa Wei herself must feed the Liu-mu the poison. Then you can tear out the horn from its brow and grind it with the orange peel and plum pit. When Kwa Wei eats biscuits made of this mixture, her eyes will be cured."

When the wizard-woman returned to her mountain retreat, Uncle Lu sat in his high-backed wooden chair and sighed. He said to himself, "I must let Kwa Wei believe the Liu-mu is a Poh. I must trick her into believing these poisonous cubes are sugar for her pet Poh. When the Liu-mu is dead, I will take its horn to make the curative biscuits. But Kwa Wei must never know how it happened, or she will be unhappy. It is a sad thing, but if I do not do it, there will be war with Duke Ling."

Uncle Lu was not a bad man. Nevertheless, he planned to do this bad thing. Kwa Wei would have her sight; she would be able to marry her betrothed; no one would be offended, so there would be no war. What was the life of the Liu-mu, which after all was ugly, compared to all these good outcomes? Even so, Uncle Lu felt terrible.

The following afternoon, Kwa Wei once more rode the Liu-mu in and out of Fairyland. "I smell a flower unlike anything in my uncle's garden!" she said excitedly. "What does it look like; oh most beautiful and strong Poh?"

"It looks like a persimmon tree, but its flowers are lacy hollow balls that glow in the middle."

"Oh! And I smell something like a tulip tree, but it's different!"

"Its leaves are purple and red, but its flowers are emerald-green."

"Is it true?" Kwa Wei asked. "Fairyland is a beautiful place for a unicorn as beautiful as you."

The Liu-mu felt guilty not to admit it was not a Poh-unicorn. To make amends for his lie, he said to the rider on his back: "I would like to take you to visit the Vale of the Unicorns."

"Is there such a Vale?" asked Kwa Wei enthusiastically.

"The Vale of the Unicorns is terrifyingly beautiful, so much so that mortals go blind if they see it. As you are already blind, it will be perfectly safe. Even without your sight, you will feel the beauty, and smell the beauty, and hear the beauty of the Vale of the Unicorns."

Therefore the Liu-mu took his rider toward two stone lanterns. The lanterns began to grow until they were as large as temples. Then Kwa Wei and the ugly unicorn were in the Vale of the Unicorns. The first unicorn they met was the fierce Hiai-chi. It was humming to itself a primitive chant in a deep voice. If birds were as big as dragons, they might sound like the humming Hiai-chi.

"What is making such a deep song?" asked Kwa Wei, clinging tightly to the Liu-mu's curly mane.

"It is my friend the Hiai-chi. You can say hello to it."

"Hello, Hiai-chi. I have come to the Vale of the Unicorns riding the beautiful, strong Poh."

The Hiai-chi was a unicorn twice the size of an elephant. Its horn sprouted between the eyes of its dragon head. It had a tail like a hundred brooms and a mane like a lion. When this wonderful animal heard Kwa Wei say she was riding on a Poh, the Hiai-chi began to laugh in its bass voice. It said, "Are you riding on a Poh? Ha ha ha! You're a funny maiden!"

"Yes, I am the Poh-unicorn," said the Liu-mu sternly, and the Hiai-chi stopped laughing.

"You have a marvelous voice to chant with," said Kwa Wei. "Will you chant sutras for my Uncle Lu, who has been unhappy for several days?"

"I will chant sutras for your uncle," said the Hiai-chi. Then Kwa Wei and the ugly unicorn went elsewhere in the Vale. The next beast they encountered was the Kio-toan tiger-unicorn. It had striped fur and three pairs of legs. Its horn was like a licorice-and-orange candy stick. It was purring like a big kitten.

"What a pleasant sound," said Kwa Wei. "What sort of unicorn is it?"

"The tiger-unicorn, Kio-toan," said the Liu-mu. "If you reach over to one side, you can scratch behind one of its ears."

Kwa Wei scratched behind the Kio-toan's ear. The beast purred louder. "Such gentle hands!" said the Kio-toan. "Scratch a little to the left."

"I'm glad to meet you," said Kwa Wei as she continued to scratch behind the ear. "As I am blind, the beauty of the Vale cannot hurt me. Even without sight, I can tell that it is a splendid place. And the tiger-unicorn is almost as lovely as the Poh that I am riding."

The Kio-toan laughed. "So that is a Poh you are riding? Well, thank you for the nice rub behind my ear."

The next unicorn they met was the Pih Sie, a little goat-unicorn with long white fur, golden eyes, and sweet pink lips. It made a sound like a gentle lamb and Kwa Wei guessed at once, "It's the Pih Sie! Oh, sweet little goat-unicorn, am I glad to meet you, riding as I am on China's most beautiful unicorn, the Poh!"

"That is very funny," said the Pih Sie in a musical voice. "That is funny indeed. This is the most beautiful Poh, is it?"

"Yes I am," said the Liu-mu. "Don't pretend you don't know me."

"I know you very well, Master Poh, O Most Beautiful Among

Us. But that ugly fellow over there among the peony flowers knows you better."

Among the peony flowers stood the actual Poh, a graceful horned horse with strength to devour lions. Suddenly the Liu-mu began to tremble.

"What's wrong?" asked Kwa Wei, feeling her friend shake.

The Poh spoke with the voice of an angelic being. "The Poh that you are riding is afraid because I am the vicious Kutiao, the leopard-unicorn. I am usually dangerous. But here in the Vale of the Unicorns, I am harmless. Don't worry about me, strong and beautiful Poh-unicorn, Ruler of the Vale of Unicorns. But as you leave, take care not to run into the ugly face of the Liu-mu, or your friend might not think the Vale is excellent after all."

Then the Poh, pretending to be a leopard-unicorn, leapt across the hedge of peonies and was gone.

The Liu-mu, ashamed of itself, took Kwa Wei back toward the temple-sized lanterns. The two stone lanterns began to shrink until they were ordinary garden decorations. Then Kwa Wei recognized the sounds and smells of her uncle's garden.

"I am glad you took me to that place," said Kwa Wei as she climbed down from the back of the ugly unicorn. "The biggest surprise was the Kutiao. I never would have guessed a leopard-unicorn would sound like an angel instead of a grouchy old leopard."

"Kwa Wei," said the Liu-mu. "What if I weren't the most beautiful unicorn in China, but only an unfortunate Liu-mu that looks like a silly old donkey."

"Ha ha!" laughed Kwa Wei. "It could never be true, so why think about it? You are gentle and the best friend anyone could have. What could you be but the strong and gorgeous Poh? Anyway, you are the most beautiful to me."

Then, remembering something, Kwa Wei opened the pouch dangling from her belt, and removed two sugar cubes. She said, "Uncle Lu gave me these candies and said they would be a nice treat for my friend the Poh. Here, this one's your reward for taking me through the Vale of the Unicorns."

"Thank you, I accept," said the Liu-mu as it ate the sugar.

Kwa Wei laughed musically and said, "I'm a selfish girl, so I'll eat the other one myself." She put it right in her mouth. It was tasty but it made her head swim. She said goodbye to the ugly unicorn and started away through the familiar garden.

When it was time for the day's last meal, Kwa Wei did not show up at the table. Servants went to find out what she was doing. They found her on the ground outside the mansion, unable to get up. She was carried to bed and the local physician was sent for. Uncle Lu Wei arrived to see what was wrong. Kwa Wei said, "Oh, Uncle, I don't feel very well. Do I have to eat my dinner?"

"Not if you don't want to," said Uncle Lu.

The doctor said, "It is something in her stomach. What did you eat today, young mistress Kwa Wei?"

The girl replied, "Nothing since lunch, except a piece of candy."

Lu Wei became pale when he heard this. He backed out of the room, stumbling. When the doctor came out, Kwa Wei's uncle said, "She has eaten Liu-mu poison prepared by the wizard-woman of Mount Tzu. What can we do?"

"She must have the antidote in two or three hours or she will die," said the doctor.

Soldiers employed by Uncle Lu Wei, along with everyone else available in and around his mansion, were sent immediately to Mount Tzu to search for the wizard-woman. Lu Wei himself went, it was so important.

Every afternoon, Duke Ling's favorite grandson, young master Hah Ling Me, visited the old ruler for a game of checkers. But today the old man's favorite grandson hadn't come. When a servant went to check on Hah Ling Me and find out why he was tardy, they discovered, stretched out on the floor in the young man's house, an ugly unicorn too sick to stand up. Soldiers came and surrounded the sick animal and pointed spears at him. "What have you done with Hah Ling Me!" demanded one of the soldiers.

The sick unicorn said, "I am none other than Hah Ling Me, too sick to return to my human shape."

The soldiers weren't sure they believed it, but took the sick Liu-mu to the palace on the back of a cart. Duke Ling came out into the yard to talk to the Liu-mu. He recognized Hah Ling Me's sorrowful eyes and gentle voice. "Grandfather," said the ugly unicorn, "as I was never allowed to see my betrothed, General Lu Wei's niece, I took this other form to see her in her uncle's garden. Now I am sick and cannot change back."

Duke Ling looked around at the members of his household, who were gathered in the yard to see the ugly unicorn. Then the Duke announced the long hidden secret:

"My son, Prince Ling, who died in brave battle ten years ago, had three wives. His favorite was Princess Chu, who vanished after the death of my son. It was often rumored that the beautiful woman was a fairy princess, and that she returned to Fairyland after the death of her husband. She left behind their only child, young master Hah Ling Me, a homely boy, but so gentle and kind that everyone loved him. As you can see, he is a fairy-boy after all, and has fallen ill in his other shape as a Liu-mu. There is only one person with the skill to nurse a Liu-mu: the wizard-woman of Mount Tzu. All my soldiers and even the scullery maids and servants must go at once to Mount Tzu to find the wizard-woman in order to save my fairy grandson.

Everyone from Lu Wei's mansion had already rushed into the mountains to seek the wizard-woman. The exception was one nurse, who remained at pitiful Kwa Wei's side, mopping her brow with a silk rag. The girl moaned. Suddenly there was a commotion against the outside wall of the bedroom, as though something were trying to knock the mansion over.

The nurse hurried to a place beside the door to the hallway and grabbed a long wooden pole. She stood ready to fight. But when the wall crumbled, the nurse saw a big animal, China's most beautiful unicorn, its one horn as long as a spear, its nostrils flaring, its four hooves like big hammers pounding the floor of the bedroom.

The nurse dropped her fighting-stick and fell down in a swoon.

Kwa Wei sat up slowly and asked, "Is it an earthquake? Why has the wall fallen in?"

Then Kwa Wei heard the huge footsteps and asked, "Who is it?"

"You have met me once before," said the Poh, and Kwa Wei recognized the angelic voice.

"You are the leopard-unicorn! You said you were dangerous outside the Vale of the Unicorns. Will you eat me?"

"I am not the leopard-unicorn, but the ruler of unicorns, the Poh that all call beautiful. I said I was the Kutiao because your friend the Liu-mu pretended to be me."

"My dear friend is not the Poh but the Liu-mu?"

"Now you know the truth. He is the ugliest of unicorns. He is also sick, just like you, because you both ate poison. Come quickly! Ride upon my shoulders! I will take you to the only one that can save your life!"

Kwa Wei struggled from beneath the covers and went to the Poh's side wearing her silk nightgown. The Poh-unicorn knelt so that Kwa Wei could climb wearily onto the strong white shoulders. Then the Poh leapt through the hole in the wall and ran across the tops of trees.

Duke Ling's soldiers and servants and Duke Ling himself were all in the mountains looking for the wizard-woman, leaving behind one elderly gardener to stand over the sick Liu-mu. When the gardener saw the fiercely beautiful Poh running toward the castle, right across the tops of trees, what could the old man do but hide in the bushes?

The Poh and its rider, Lu Wei's blind niece, landed gracefully in the yard. The elderly gardener trembled as he saw the Poh snatch up the Liu-mu in its mouth as a mother cat snatches up a kitten. Then the Poh ran off in the direction of a small stone garden ornament, where the Poh, the Liu-mu, and General Lu Wei's blind niece, disappeared.

Just like Kwa Wei's nurse, Duke Ling's gardener fainted.

Goodness! What a strange story! Does anyone know what is likely to happen next? The most beautiful unicorn in China, with the most ugly unicorn held by the scruff, and the beautiful blind maiden riding on its back, hurried into Fairyland where the Poh deposited its cargo before the throne of the Fairy Queen.

The Queen lived in a crystal palace. She was more beautiful than mortal eyes can tell. She kept at the side of her throne a small bag that looked exactly like the bag owned by the wrinkled old wizard-woman of Mount Tzu. Was it possible that the withered-up mountain hag and this beautiful queen were the same woman? Who knows! In any case, the Fairy Queen was instantly able to cure Kwa Wei and the Liu-mu of the poison.

When the Liu-mu opened its eyes, it turned into the homely but sweet young master Hah Ling Me, Duke Ling's grandson. He looked up at the Queen of Fairyland and exclaimed, "Mother! I haven't seen you in so long! I thought you must have died. I was sad!"

"You were meant for the mortal world, Hah Ling Me and you were meant for this mortal girl. But your grandfather Duke Ling didn't want you to marry her because she is blind. Due to my tricks, I have gotten you together. Now you will be married in Fairyland, where no one can stop you. You will be sent home with many wedding presents to start your own house and be independent of the families Ling and Wei. You can do what you please from now on."

"And will you cure my bride of blindness?" asked Hah Ling Me.

"I will gladly die for Kwa Wei!" said Hah Ling Me.

"Wait a minute," said Kwa Wei. "Have I complained because I'm blind? If I had my vision, you could never again take me to the Vale of the Unicorns, because in the first place you'd be dead, and second of all, if I saw the Vale with my eyes, it would blind me! I want to marry you, Hah Ling Me, oh most beautiful boy in China!"

"I am not beautiful, Kwa Wei, but you are very beautiful. Can you really marry such an ugly fellow?"

Kwa Wei laughed as though it were a joke. "Anyway," she said, "let's get married right now."

Up on the side of Mount Tzu, the soldiers and household members of Duke Ling's palace had come to blows with the soldiers and household of Lu Wei's mansion. Scullery maids and stable workers and soldiers used their kung-fu to give each other black eyes and bloody noses. After a while, they were all worn out. Their bones were sore. The fighters were scattered on the ground, sweating and puffing and unable to move. Duke Ling and General Lu Wei shouted for both sides to get up and fight some more. They finally did get up, but not to fight. Instead, a wonderful thing began to happen, and everyone stood to see it.

Coming down from the highest part of the mountain was a wedding-parade of a startling kind. Riding on the back of the Poh were a groom and a bride. Hah Ling Me and Kwa Wei were both dressed in fabulous costumes and wore bright opera paint on their faces. Behind them came a whole train of animals with carts full of useful and valuable objects.

The Pih Sie or goat-unicorn pulled a cart laden with gold coins.

The purring Kio-toan or tiger-unicorn's cart was full of fine lacquered furniture, bolts of cloth that shimmered like precious stones and metal, and swords encrusted with gems.

The Hiai-chi or dragon-unicorn was humming the wedding song. It pulled a gigantic cart on which sat a big house with prettily carved doors and windows and roofs.

Walking alongside this procession was the old wizard-woman of the mountain. She had married them herself. When the procession stopped, the wizard-woman said, "Hah Ling Me and Kwa Wei have been married in Fairyland. These gifts will set them up in their own house. It is for Duke Ling and Lu Wei to decide where the newly-weds' house will be."

"I will give my north acres, closest to Duke Ling's palace," said Uncle Lu Wei happily.

"I will give my south acres, closest to Lu Wei's mansion," said Duke Ling, equally glad.

Then the beat-up and bruised members of the two households began to dance and sing together. They followed the wedding procession down from the mountain.

For five hundred years this story has waited to be told. Now it has been.

The Unhappy Princess

❧

Richard Cowper

ONCE UPON A TIME there lived a Princess. She was an only child and her parents spoiled her disgracefully. They gave her beautiful toys to play with and let her wander as she liked through the lovely gardens that surrounded the palace. But in spite of the birds that sang in the trees and the coloured fountains that played on the lawns, she was unhappy. When her mother asked her what was the matter she could not say, for in truth she did not know herself. She just felt that somehow, somewhere, there was a certain something that would make all her days delightful and her nights be as the days. And yet she did not know what it was.

Her old governess, who was the only person allowed to reprimand her without being thrown into the dungeons, said she wanted a husband. The King thought this must certainly be the case and sent heralds to the courts of all the neighbouring countries to publish the news that he would not look unfavourably upon suitors for his daughter's hand. And, because the dowry was handsome and the Princess beautiful, the suitors came flocking in.

There were fair ones and dark ones, thin ones and fat ones, in fact every conceivable build of prince imaginable came – and went away disappointed, for the Princess was quite certain that being married would *not* make her happy even though she did not know what would. So she just went on playing with her toys and walking in the garden and feeling that the world was treating her abominably.

Then one day, when she could not walk in the garden because it was raining and she had played with her games until she could beat herself every time even though she gave herself a start, for want of something better to do she wandered into the palace library. She did not go there very often because reading bored her, and on the rare occasions when she did, it was usually to ask the palace librarian for a reference book for the King, who spent his spare time writing a study of different forms of government.

She walked beside the shelves idly pulling books out and looking at the pictures, but they were not particularly interesting so she decided to get the stepladder and try the top shelves. Having climbed up, she opened the first book on the topmost shelf. It was written in a language she could not understand, but this did not bother her because she was interested only in the pictures. And what pictures there were! Never, she thought, had she seen anything so lovely. Pictures of desert islands rising like emeralds out of the blue sea. Pictures of castles clinging like *edelweiss* to the sheer walls of frowning gorges. Pictures of strange ships and finally – most wonderful of all – a picture of a tree!

Such a tree she could never have imagined. It was growing on the top of a great rock in the middle of a limitless sandy waste. Around the base of the rock were leaping tongues of flame and growing on the tree, whose highest branches were crowned by a wreath of filmy cloud, was a single golden apple. As she feasted her eyes upon this extraordinary fruit the Princess knew that she was gazing upon the only thing that could ever make her happy.

She tucked the precious book under her arm, climbed down the steps and hurried off to find the palace librarian. She discovered him writing out a new index for the poetry section. Carefully laying down the book, she opened it at the picture of the mysterious tree and asked what it was.

The old man took off his glasses, wiped them carefully on his sleeve and put them back. He bent over the inscription. "That, Your Highness, is the Tree of Life," he said.

"And the fruit? What is the golden fruit?" asked the Princess.

"The fruit, Your Highness, is the Golden Apple of Wisdom that ripens once every thousand years."

"But where is it? Can I find it? Is the apple still there? Is it ripe now?" cried the Princess, tears starting to her eyes.

"That I cannot say, Your Highness," replied the old man, and bent purposefully over his index.

Realizing that she could expect no further help from him, the Princess picked up the book and went to find her friend the Court Magician.

Taking great care not to offend him, she first enquired politely about his rheumatism and, having found herself favourably received, asked him what he knew of the Tree of Life and the Golden Apple of Wisdom. She could hardly have chosen a more inappropriate subject. The old man squinted at her narrowly, grunted, and lapsed into an obstinate silence. All her cajolery and threats were of no avail, and she was beginning to despair of ever finding out where the wonderful tree grew when she had an idea.

"All right," she said slowly, "since you won't speak I shall have to tell Mother that it was you transformed her favourite corgi into a blue guinea pig and then, when you were trying to turn it back, changed it into a cockroach by mistake and trod on it. Won't she be cross?"

She did not really intend to say anything, because she was very fond of the old magician, but as a threat it served its purpose. He paled visibly under his grey whiskers, blew his nose twice and said: "All right, then, but don't say I didn't warn you."

"You old darling!" cried the Princess. "I knew you would. And I promise I'll never mention that beastly little dog ever again. Now tell me about it."

"Well," said the old man slowly. "What exactly do you want to know?"

"Where it grows! How you can get to it! Whether it's ripe now! What it tastes like!" said the Princess all in one breath.

"One at a time! One at a time!" cried the old man, flapping his hands in the air. Then he shuffled slowly across to a bookshelf and lifted down a great leather-bound tome. Laying it out on the table, he licked his finger and began turning over the pages, muttering to himself as he did so. At last he found what he was looking for and grunted with satisfaction.

"Here you are," he said, cracking his ancient bony knuckles. "This ought to satisfy you."

The Princess peered over his shoulder. "Why that's the same as my picture!" she said. "Except that it's not coloured. What does it say about it?"

"It says, Your Highness, that the Tree of Life which grows on the Mountain of Sorrow lies beyond the Seventh Sea in the middle of the Desert of Forgetfulness."

"Well, where's that?" asked the Princess, and then, when the old man seemed about to launch himself into a long and detailed explanation, hurriedly added, "But it doesn't matter now. Tell me if the apple's ripe."

The old magician was a little piqued at being cut off, but since he couldn't afford having the corgi disaster being made public just yet he only said: "Pass me my crystal and I'll try to find out." Then he draped his head in a black velvet cloth and peered into the cloudy depths of the glass ball while the Princess hopped from one foot to the other and waited impatiently for his verdict.

At last he lifted back the cloth and beckoned her over, signing her not to make a noise. She lowered her head and gazed into the hitherto murky depths of the crystal. Lo and behold! In place of the milky mist that had obscured the interior of the ball she saw the mountain of her picture, while above, far more splendid than any artist could hope to portray them, rose the tree bearing the Golden Apple. "Oh! It's *lovely, lovely!*" she cried, clapping her hands. Too late! As she uttered the words the mountain faded slowly before her eyes and in its place appeared the old impenetrable mist. But she had seen the Golden Apple and knew that until she had tasted it she would never be happy again.

Turning to the old magician, who stood smiling at her enraptured face, she said thoughtfully: "Now the thing is to find someone who'll go and get it for me."

Such conviction was there in her voice that the old man was quite taken aback: "Do you mean you *want to taste the Golden Apple of Wisdom, my child?*" he asked incredulously.

"Of course," said the Princess, turning on him in surprise, "Why not?"

"But do you realize what you will be doing – just supposing for one moment that you ever do get the fruit?"

"What do you mean, what I will be doing?"

"Why, my poor child, whoever tastes of the Golden Apple knows not only all there is to know in this world but in the next as well. No one has ever eaten one."

"Then I shall be the first," said the Princess firmly. "I shall know just what everybody is thinking about me and where we all go to when we die and – oh, hundreds of things. I shall be the wisest person the world has ever known. Nothing shall be hidden from me."

"But will you *want* to know what everyone thinks about you? Just imagine, if you taste that Golden Apple you will never be able to enjoy anything again because you will know everything that ever was. Why, before somebody speaks to you you'll know what they're going to say. You'll even know when you're going to die – think of that! Every day you'll say 'Only another so many days' and then the next day it will be one less and so on. Oh, it won't be a joke then." But it was no use. The Princess had made up her mind that she would taste the Golden Apple of Wisdom and nothing the old man could say would dissuade her.

She went straight to her father the King and told him she would marry any man who would bring her the Golden Apple from the Tree of Life.

At first many volunteers came forward, all eager to win the hand of the Princess. But as the months rolled by and they failed to return the others became discouraged, and at, last it appeared that there was no one left who would undertake the task of searching for and bringing back the Golden Apple of Wisdom. The Princess became more and more unhappy.

Then one day she was wandering in the garden, crying to herself because she had nearly lost all hope of achieving her heart's desire, when she heard a voice behind her say: "What's the matter? Have you lost something?"

She looked round and saw a young man in a very ragged suit sitting on the wall of the palace garden, swinging his legs and grinning down at her. Before she had time to ask him what he was doing up there he dropped down and walked across the lawn to her, explaining as he did so that his name was Damon and that, hearing someone crying while he was strolling past outside, he had climbed up to see if there was anything he could do to help.

In the normal way the Princess would have called the palace guard and had him put in chains, but just now she felt so miserable that she was glad of anyone to talk to. So, instead of asking him what he was doing in the Royal Gardens, she told him about the Golden Apple and how so many people had gone to find it but no one had come back. When she had finished Damon looked very thoughtful and asked her if she had any idea where the Tree of Life grew, and the Princess told him what the magician had said. Then Damon said: "Are you quite certain that you *want* the Golden Fruit? *Really* want it, I mean?"

The Princess replied: "I want it more than I want my own life; more than I've ever wanted anything else in the whole world. I think I shall die if I don't get it."

"Well," said Damon, "you certainly seem to mean it all right, and because I like you and you are obviously very lovely, even though you are spoiled, I'll see what I can do."

The Princess blushed prettily and said that he should remember she was still a Princess, but she thought he was really rather a nice person in spite of his shabby clothes.

He said goodbye and climbed swiftly back over the wall, pausing only to wave before he dropped down out of sight on the other side. The Princess thought he was quite one of the nicest people she had ever met, and began almost to wish he had not been in quite such a hurry to seek the Golden Apple after all, because she was fairly certain that she would never see him again.

Next morning at daybreak Damon saddled his horse and set out to seek the Golden Fruit. Since no one had any idea where it grew he decided that it did not matter particularly which way he went, so he took the first road he came to, shook his horse into a jingling trot, and rode along whistling to himself. He asked several travellers whether they could tell him where he might find the Desert of Forgetfulness, but they either looked at him queerly and rode swiftly on or said they didn't know. So after a while he stopped enquiring and just trotted along enjoying the countryside.

After three days he entered a great forest. The trees rose like huge cliffs on either side and only a faint light penetrated through the branches that twined in a thick canopy high above his head. The forest was so gloomy that Damon wondered whether it would not perhaps be better to turn round and go back, but he decided he might just as well go on, since by now he was probably in the middle and either road would be as long as the other. But as he rode on and on and the end never seemed to get any nearer he began to wish he *had* turned back before, for he realized it must be close on nightfall and there was no sign of an inn or anywhere to put up for the night.

Just as he was beginning to despair of ever getting out, he saw a glimmer of light through the trees and, gripping his sword hilt tightly in his hand, he turned his horse towards it, in the hope that he might be able to obtain a lodging.

The light was coming from the window of a hut that stood in a clearing entirely surrounded by a great wall of darkness. High above, Damon could see a small circle of sky already pinpointed with stars. Hemming him in, as if they were watching and only waiting for a suitable moment to pounce, stood the silent trees. Leading his horse by the bridle, he walked up to the door and knocked.

There was no answer. Only the melancholy cry of a hunting night bird sounded in the depths of the forest. He knocked again, this time calling aloud, but still there was no reply and so, with a fast-beating heart, he tried the latch. The door swung inwards on silent hinges and, to his astonishment, instead of the rough table and bed he had expected, he beheld a great corridor illuminated by row upon row of gleaming candles stretching away before him.

Amazed, he looked about him, wondering at the thick carpets and the beautifully panelled walls and trying to imagine why anyone should have built such an extraordinary dwelling in the centre of a dense forest. He decided to tether his horse and then see if he could find a bed, but just as he was turning to go out a sweet voice said very softly, almost in a whisper: "Don't go away, Damon."

He swung round, his hand darting to his sword hilt, but the corridor stood just as it had before. Not a soul was there to be seen.

"Who's that? Where are you? Does anybody live here?" he called, getting ready to run.

The same voice, seeming to come from right beside him, murmured: "Of course somebody lives here. I do!" And then as though to set his mind at rest added: "And your horse is being looked after."

"Where are you? Why can't I see you?" demanded Damon of the empty air, but the only answer was a silvery laugh and the command: "Come with me. I know all about you, Damon. You needn't be afraid."

Damon was not so sure about that, but, deciding it was better to risk anything rather than spend a night in that forest, he followed the voice down the corridor.

A door at the end opened before him and he stepped through into a great hall which appeared to be illuminated solely by a fountain of pure light that bubbled up into a transparent basin. Great columns supported the ceiling which was so high as to be almost invisible. In the centre of the hall stood a table laden with food. "You may eat," said the voice, "and I will talk to you."

The food was delicious and to Damon, who had not eaten since early that morning, the meal presented an opportunity that must be grasped before it slipped from between his fingers. While he ate the voice said: "You are the young man who has fallen in love with the Unhappy Princess and now goes to seek the Golden Apple of Wisdom."

Damon nodded, for by this time he was past surprise.

"Yet do you think she will bother about you once she has tasted that wonderful fruit? Of course she won't! Why don't you give up the whole idea and stay here with me? I could make you very happy."

"But how *could* I stay with you when I can't even see you?" said Damon pointedly.

"Well, you could become invisible too," said the voice, "then you would be able to see me."

But Damon thought of the Unhappy Princess and of how lovely she had looked with her eyes full of tears and decided it was not worth it. "I'm sorry," he said, "and I really am very grateful for all you have done for me, but I've sworn to go on with this search until I either find the Golden Apple of Wisdom or perish in the attempt. So there's no use trying to dissuade me."

"I think you're being very silly," said the voice with a sigh, "but since you are determined I suppose I'd better give you some advice."

Damon thanked it and the voice continued sadly: "When you leave me tomorrow you will find a green star shining before you. Follow it and it will lead you to the shore of the Seventh Sea. When you reach it, wade into the water up to your waist and beat the waves with your hands three times. A boat will appear and carry you across to the far shore. Take some of the silver sand you will find and put it in your satchel. You will need it later. I am afraid that is all I can tell you, but it should help."

Damon said he was sure it would, and thanked the voice again. Then he rose to his feet and asked whether he could be excused as he was very tired and would like to go to bed.

For answer the voice said: "Come this way," and set off down another corridor leading from the hall. It paused at a great door and said: "This is where you shall sleep."

Damon was about to open the door when the voice spoke his name very softly. He turned towards it and felt a pair of soft lips brush his cheek, but when he stretched out his arms they encountered nothing but air, and from down the corridor he heard the voice mournfully wish him a good night. He lay down on the silken bed and within less time than it takes to tell was fast asleep.

Time passed, and the Unhappy Princess found herself thinking less and less about the Golden Apple and more and more about Damon until, when he had been absent for over three months, she realized that she must have fallen in love with him. This made her more unhappy than ever, for she knew the chances were that she would never see him again, and she had practically given up all hope of anyone ever getting the wonderful fruit. Feeling more miserable than ever, she went to her old friend the Court Magician to see if he could help her. Carefully she explained the circumstances and, feeling sorry for her, he said he would have a look into the crystal and see whether he could find the young man.

For a long while he peered into the cloudy depths, apparently with no satisfaction, and the Princess began to fear that perhaps Damon was already dead. Biting her lip to keep back the tears, she tiptoed round behind him and peered underneath his arm.

A greenish glow was lighting the crystal from within, and by its sickly light she could just discern the shore of a strange sea. Gradually the green light faded until it was the merest hint in the sky and in its place came a purple gleam of dawn. As the light grew stronger she could discern a figure lying on the beach. With a start of horror she realized that what she had at first taken to be smooth round stones were in fact human skulls that the wind and the waves had bleached until they gleamed along the shore like clots of yellow cream.

The tired sea heaved itself forward to fall silently and without foam, in waves as regular as they were lifeless, and she knew without being told that she was gazing upon the torpid waters of the Seventh Sea. Pulled by some unimaginable tide, the water crawled up the beach, lapping its thousand tongues around the scattered skulls, until at last one wave, a little stronger than the rest, trickled itself against the outflung hand of the fallen man. Slowly the fingers closed and then opened again, exploring what they found, until, with movements as slow as the sluggish tide, the man rose to his knees and turned his face towards her.

There was no recognition in his eyes, he seemed to stare straight through her and beyond, but it *was* Damon, and he was alive. For the moment she cared about nothing else. Wearily he climbed to his feet and stood staring out over the pale waters, then with a gesture of resignation he walked resolutely forward into the advancing waves, until the water rose about his waist. Three times he raised his arms and let them fall, scanning the horizon as if he were looking for some object that was not there, then he waded wearily back to the beach.

The Princess could scarcely contain her curiosity, but she could hardly have been prepared for what followed.

Across the water, down a blazing purple channel made by the reflection of that extraordinary sun, came a black barge. Swiftly it drove onwards, the oars rising and falling in perfect unison, yet no one stood at the helm to guide it and no visible hands were pulling at the oars. Right up to the beach it sailed, coming to rest gently on the shelving sand at Damon's feet while the invisible crew held their oars aloft in readiness for the departure.

As soon as he had stepped aboard the oars dipped and the barge turned and set off whence it had come, bearing its passenger out of sight. The waves slid back sullenly, obliterating the tracks in the sand.

Although the Princess had been reassured by the fact that he was still alive, Damon himself felt far from happy. Since leaving the palace in the forest he had ridden night and day in the track of the green star. It had led him through strange lands in which the grass grew red instead of green and the trees bore fruit shaped like human hands; through mountain passes in which the snow never melted and the sound of a voice was sufficient to start an avalanche; across foaming torrents and to the margins of unbelievable lakes, where the fish appeared to swim in the very air itself, so clear was the water.

The journey was so difficult that at last his exhausted horse had been able to carry him no further, and for the past two days he had been obliged to follow the star on foot, until finally he had stumbled and fallen by the shore of the Seventh Sea.

Now, as the strange barge approached the farther shore, his mind dwelt on the possible dangers that awaited him. Why had he been advised to gather the sand he would find? Why had the invisible girl been unable to help him farther? Even as he turned these things over in his mind the barge drew in towards the shore, and, pausing only to thank his unseen friends, he leapt ashore while the boat turned swiftly and vanished into the distance.

Kneeling, he filled his satchel with the silver sand, then, turning his back on the strange sea and its barren shore, he set out towards the range of hills that rose before him.

By midday he had reached the first slopes, and after filling his flask from a little stream he began the ascent. The hillside was covered in thick rough grass which pulled at his ankles and made progress difficult, but he kept on, and, reaching the summit at last, peered down over the other side.

Beneath him, spreading outwards like some petrified yellow sea, was the Desert of Forgetfulness, and rising from its centre like a huge and solitary finger pointing up towards the sky was the mountain he had come so far to climb. Round its rocky base leapt a barrier of flame, seemingly impassable. Yet having come this far he could not now turn back, and, trusting that good fortune would continue to aid him, he scrambled down the hill towards the gleaming tract of sand.

He reached the margin, tentatively put forward a foot to test the surface, and, finding it held no apparent traps, stepped forward.

The hot air rose around him, stroking his face like a caressing hand. The farther he advanced towards the quivering mountain the faster it appeared to recede, and gradually he felt a gentle drowsiness creeping over him, an almost irresistible desire to lie down on the soft, yielding sand and drift off into sleep. More and more insistent became this craving until he began to wonder why he was walking at all; then the soft dunes seemed to whisper to him to rest his tired limbs and his beating heart sounded like the sweetest music to his enchanted ears.

Somehow he kept going, and at last, thinking to lighten himself a little, he decided to get rid of some of the heavy sand in his satchel. Seizing a handful, he cast it ahead of him.

No sooner had the scattered grains fallen than in their place blades of grass sprung up. Stepping forward upon this extraordinary carpet, he felt his weariness vanish as though a cool breeze had blown the mists from his memory. He started forward once more, casting the magic sand before him, until the path reached out like a thin green ribbon all across the surface of the desert.

Proceeding in this way, he soon came within the shadow of the strange mountain and could feel the heat of the surrounding flames scorching his face. Finding no break in the fiery cordon, he decided to try the effect of the last of the magic sand. Holding his arm before his face to shield his eyes from the heat, he ran forward and cast the remaining handful into the very centre of the furnace. At once the roar diminished, the flames died away, and on opening his eyes he saw that a narrow green path was dividing the fiery barrier. With a prayer on his lips he ran swiftly forward over the slender green bridge.

Now he saw before him the strange mountain towering upwards into the dark sky, but he saw too that instead of being completely smooth, as he had at first supposed, the glassy slope was pocked with countless shallow crevices. Removing his now empty satchel, he laid it beside his jacket at the foot of the rocks. Then he took a deep draught of water from his flask and began to climb.

Up and up he went, higher and higher, until from a distance he resembled a tiny fly clinging to the blank black surface of the rock wall. No longer by looking down could he see the bright square of colour that was his jacket, and the path across the desert was now little more than an emerald thread drawn across the aching expanse of yellow sand. Each breath he drew was a gasp of pain; his fingers and knees were raw and bleeding, and his legs felt as heavy as if each foot were encased in a boot of lead.

Just when he had decided that he could climb no higher and was on the point of letting go his hold and slipping backwards into space and the merciful oblivion of certain death, his bruised and bleeding hands groped over a ledge. Summoning up the last of his strength, he hauled himself over the edge and toppled forward unconscious.

How long his swoon lasted he had no means of telling, but when he next opened his eyes the violet-coloured sun had crept across the sky and was now shining directly down upon his upturned face.

Groaning with pain, he moved his limbs and became at once aware of the sickening drop that lay beneath his outflung feet.

With infinite deliberation he drew his knees up to his chest and paused, crouching, his cheek resting against the sun-warmed rock-face. Very slowly he turned his head and craned his neck upwards. The black stone appeared to continue in an unbroken plane for as far as he could see. Beneath him lay the abyss.

The pain tugged sharply at his legs and arms as he rose to his feet and turned, facing outwards, with arms stretched wide for balance on either side. To go down was impossible and above lay who knew what? Releasing one hand, he unclipped the flask from his belt and let the last drops of water trickle down his parched throat.

The water revived him. He clipped the empty flask back on to his belt and commenced the second half of his terrible climb.

He soon found that through some trick of light or eyesight the second slope, though still very steep, was far less difficult to climb than he had supposed. He moved on steadily upwards, trying not to think of the awful drop that awaited him should he misplace foot or hand.

The higher he climbed the gentler the slope became until, glancing back, he discovered that the edge of the rock completely obscured his view of the desert, and he was now able to scramble forward monkey-fashion.

As he topped the ridge that he felt must surely be the last he saw, rising before him, first the spreading branches and then the trunk of the Tree of Life.

Throwing caution to the winds, he stumbled forward over the boulder-strewn summit of the mountain and reached the bole of the great Tree.

Between the enormous roots was a huge block of white marble, and engraved upon it in gold letters each a span high was the following legend:

*He Who Eats Of My Fruit Shall Have Wisdom Beyond Belief.
But Also He Shall Know That Which Is Not Meet For Him
To Know. He Shall Know Neither Joy Nor Sorrow — Death
Nor Life.*

Damon read the daunting inscription and tried to puzzle it out, but the more he puzzled the more obscure the meaning seemed. At last he shrugged his weary shoulders, took a deep breath and began to climb the Tree.

The Tree itself presented few problems to a climber such as he had shown himself to be, and soon he was groping towards the Golden Apple.

As his fingertips touched it the whole Tree sighed, and the leaves began to tremble so violently that for a moment Damon feared he might be pitched to the rocks below. However, the trembling only lasted for a few seconds, and after edging his way carefully along the topmost branch he came within reach of the Golden Apple of Wisdom.

His fingers curled round it and at a tweak of his wrist the great Fruit settled into his palm. In one movement he had slipped it inside the neck of his shirt, where it rested cool and heavy and safe against his chest.

At that moment there was a clap of thunder and a great voice boomed:

"Who is he that dares to pluck the Fruit from the Tree of Life?"

Damon was mightily alarmed at this odd turn of events, but he managed to identify himself without too noticeable a tremor in his voice.

"Impudent mortal! How came you to cross the Seventh Sea and the Desert of Forgetfulness?" roared the voice.

Damon thought for a moment, then said; "Well, if you'll be so good as to let me climb down, I'll be only too happy to tell you all about it."

No sooner had these words left his lips than he found himself sitting beside the slab of white marble. But the Apple was still cold and comforting against his chest, and he guessed that his possession of the marvellous fruit had something to do with the fact that he had not been dashed to the ground and killed outright. It made him feel a little happier.

"Well?" thundered the voice.

"I do wish you wouldn't shout so," said Damon. "How

do you expect me to tell my story when you're making my ears ring?"

"Speak!" said the voice again, but this time it was hushed, musical and low.

Damon sighed with relief. "Well, it happened like this," he said, and proceeded to give an account of all that had befallen him since he had left the palace garden.

"So the Princess intends to eat the Golden Apple of Wisdom, does she?" was the only comment the voice made when Damon had concluded.

Damon admitted that that was the general idea. "And who are you," he enquired, "if you don't mind my asking?"

"I am the Guardian Spirit of the Tree of Life," said the voice.

"Well, it's not really for me to say so," said Damon, "but to be candid I don't think you've done your job very well."

The voice sighed: "Do you know that you are the only person who has made the attempt for five thousand three hundred and forty-two years? Is it surprising that I should doze off?"

"Well, speaking personally, you understand," said Damon, "I'm very glad you did. And believe me when I say that for me it's been a great privilege to talk to you like this. But I'm sure you'll understand when I remind you that I've got a very long journey ahead of me, and so, with your permission, I think I had better begin the climb down."

"Oh, that won't be necessary," said the voice. "Now you've got the Apple you'll find all the hazards will have disappeared. Look behind you."

Damon turned his head and saw that where hitherto there had been only scattered boulders there was now a golden staircase leading down into the heart of the mountain. "How do I know it's not some trick?" he demanded.

"You need have no fear," said the voice, sadly. "Now you possess the Golden Apple no one has any power to harm you – neither man nor beast nor spirit."

"Oh, well, in *that* case – " said Damon cheerfully, and walked across to the head of the golden staircase. Just as he was about to begin the descent he turned and enquired: "What will happen to you, now that someone has taken the Apple you were meant to guard?"

"I wish I knew," said the voice mournfully, and it began to weep softly to itself.

Damon murmured something sympathetic, then shrugged his shoulders and started down the stairs. He could still hear the muffled sobs long after the Tree had disappeared from his view.

The staircase ended at a hole in the rock-face just beside his jacket and satchel and he emerged into the light to find that the fire had now died away completely.

All was as the voice had predicted. No longer was the Desert of Forgetfulness a thing to be feared and he crossed it as though the sand were the King's own highroad. Likewise the barge was awaiting him at the shore of the strange sea, and he disembarked to find his horse, already saddled, awaiting him on the farther strand. The numerous difficulties that he had encountered on the journey no longer existed now that he was the possessor of the Golden Apple, and, riding hard and fast, it was a matter of two short weeks before he galloped under the stone-arched gateway of the city and rode up the cobbled street to the palace.

So great had been his hurry that he had not paused to equip himself with a new suit and his rags were now even more unsightly than they had been when he had set out. People stared in astonishment at the sight of the wildly galloping boy who reined up his horse so violently before the palace gates and cried in a loud voice:

"Take me at once to the Princess!"

The spectators were even more surprised when the guard, instead of laying violent hands on him, meekly opened the gates and led him in. But then they knew nothing of the strange properties of the Golden Apple.

Once inside the palace courtyard he seemed to change his mind. "No," he said, "it will do the Princess good to come to me for a change. Go and fetch her." Obediently the Junior Footman told the Senior Footman, who told the Butler, who told the Major-Domo, who whispered in the ear of the Grand Vizier that the Princess was urgently required in the palace courtyard.

The Grand Vizier hurried off and found the Princess.

"Your Royal Highness is required in the palace courtyard," he panted.

Never before in her life had the Princess been "required" to do anything. Nevertheless she went.

Damon was standing beside his horse's head, waiting for her. As soon as he caught sight of her he put his hand down his shirt and took out the Golden Apple of Wisdom. Not a blemish showed on its dusky skin. It glowed like a globe of fire in his hands.

"The Golden Apple from the Tree of Life, Your Highness," he said with admirable nonchalance, while the surrounding courtiers gasped in amazement.

But, to Damon's great surprise, the Princess, instead of seizing the Apple and sinking her white teeth into its juicy flesh, ran forward and, flinging her arms round his neck, cried as if her heart would break.

Without a second thought Damon dropped the Golden Apple and took her in his arms while the whole court stood and gaped in horror at the sight of a young vagabond embracing *their* Princess.

In the excitement no one noticed Damon's horse. The poor animal had come a long way and been ridden extremely hard, moreover it was a long time since he had seen anything as tempting as the juicy Golden Apple. So, without so much as a "by your leave" he opened his mouth and in three bites all that was left of the fabled Fruit of Wisdom was a tiny piece of the stalk and one solitary pip. And that was later eaten by a sparrow.

Fortunately horses cannot have been included in the inscription on the marble slab at the mountain top, for, after a solitary whinny of pleasure, he stood patiently waiting for a command from his master.

But Damon had other things to think of. They tell me he made a very good king eventually, and as for the Tree of Life, well, if my arithmetic is right the next Golden Apple isn't due to ripen for another six hundred and seventy-two years, so there's no sense in worrying about *that*.

The White Cat

❧

Marie-Cathérine d'Aulnoy

THERE WAS ONCE UPON a time a king who had three brave and handsome sons; he was afraid that the desire to reign should take possession of their minds before his death; certain reports were even in circulation that they were endeavouring to acquire supporters to assist them in seizing the government of the kingdom. The King felt that he was old, but, his sense and his capacity for government not being at all diminished, he did not feel inclined to yield them a place he filled so worthily; so he thought that the best way for him to live in quiet would be to amuse them with promises, the fulfilment of which he would always find a means to elude.

He had them summoned to his closet; and, after having spoken to them with great kindness, he said: "You will agree with me, my dear children, that my great age cannot permit me to attend to the affairs of state with so much care as formerly: I am afraid that my subjects will suffer in consequence, and wish to place my crown on the head of one of you; but it is very just that in return for such a gift you should find some means of pleasing me. My intention is to retire into the country, and it appears to me that a well-trained little dog, pretty and faithful, would be pleasant company in my walks; therefore, without choosing either my eldest on account of his seniority, or my youngest for love, I declare to you that he of you three who shall bring me the prettiest little dog, shall be my immediate successor." The princes were all much surprised at their father's desire for a little dog; but as the two youngest saw that they thus stood as good a chance for the throne as their eldest brother, they joyfully acceded to the proposal: the eldest was either too timid or too respectful to represent his rights. They took leave of the King, who gave them money and jewellery, and told them that that day twelve months, without fail, they were to return, bringing with them their little dogs.

Before their final departure they went to a castle which was situated three miles from the town. They invited their most confidential friends and gave a sumptuous entertainment, at which the three brothers vowed eternal friendship, agreeing to have no jealousy or animosity against each other in this affair, but that the successful candidate should share his fortune with the two others; finally they separated, agreeing to make that castle their rendezvous on their return, and thence to proceed together to the King; they did not wish to be followed by anyone, and changed their names that they might not be known.

Each of them took a different road: the two eldest encountered many adventures, but my intention is to relate only those that befell the youngest. He was a young prince of graceful demeanour, and of a cheerful and lively temper; he was of a noble figure, had a well-shaped head, regular features, handsome teeth, and was very skilful in all the exercises suitable to a prince. He sang agreeably, and played on the lute and mandolin with much taste and delicacy. He understood painting, and, in a word, was very accomplished; with regard to his courage, he was brave to intrepidity.

Not a day passed without his buying dogs, large and small, grey-hounds, mastiffs, bloodhounds, staghounds, spaniels, water-spaniels and lap-dogs; when he met with one which he preferred to those he already had, he let the others go and kept that; for it was impossible for him to keep thirty or forty thousand dogs, and he did not wish for gentlemen, valets or pages in his suite. He continued to pursue his road, not having decided on taking any particular direction, when he was surprised by night and a storm of thunder and rain in a forest, with the roads of which he was unacquainted.

He struck into the first he came to, and after proceeding some distance he perceived a light, which induced him to think that there was a house not far distant, where he might obtain a shelter till the next day. Proceeding in the direction of the light, he presently arrived at the gate of the most superb castle that could be imagined. This gate was of massive gold, studded all over with carbuncles, the clear, bright rays of which illumined all around. It was, indeed, their lustre which the Prince had perceived from afar; the walls were of transparent china of various colours, and on these were represented the histories of all the fairies from the creation of the world until that day; the famous adventures of Ass's Skin, of Finetta, of the Orange-tree, of Graciosa, of the Sleeping Beauty in the Wood, of Green Serpentine, and many others were not omitted. He was charmed to find that Prince Lutin had a place there, for that prince was his uncle. The rain and bad weather prevented his making a longer observation of the place while he was fast getting wet through; besides, he could only examine those places which the light shed by the carbuncles rendered visible to him.

He returned therefore to the golden gate: and observed a roebuck's foot fastened to the end of a diamond chain. He could not forbear admiring its magnificence, and the security in which the inhabitants of the castle seemed to dwell: "For what," said he, "is there to prevent thieves from cutting off this chain and wresting off those carbuncles? They would enrich themselves for ever."

He pulled the roebuck's foot and immediately heard a bell ring, which from the sound it returned he judged to be either of gold or of silver; in a moment the door opened, without his perceiving anything but a dozen hands in the air, each holding a flambeau. He was so astonished that he hesitated to advance, when he felt other hands pushing from behind, with a little violence. He then entered rather uneasy, and, as he thought, in some danger, so he kept his hand on the hilt of his sword; but, entering a vestibule, the walls of which were encrusted with porphyry and lapis-lazuli, he heard two almost celestial voices singing this stanza:

"With unconcern behold each hand,
    And dread no false alarm,
If you are sure you can withstand
    The force of beauty's charm."

He could not believe that he was invited so kindly to suffer any injury; so that, feeling himself gently pushed towards a large coral door which opened of itself as he approached, he entered a large hall of mother-of-pearl, and subsequently several chambers, each ornamented in a different taste, and so enriched with paintings and jewellery, that he was like one enchanted. Vast quantities of lights, disposed regularly from the ceiling of the hall downwards, contributed to illumine some of the other apartments, which were besides filled with lustres, branch-candlesticks and sideboards covered with wax lights; in a word, the magnificence was such that its detail would almost be incredible.

After having entered sixty chambers, the hands which conducted him stopped, and he observed a large elbow-chair making its way towards him from the chimney. The fire kindled of itself at the same time, and the hands, which seemed to him very pretty, small, plump and well-proportioned, undressed him, for, as I have already said, he was very wet, and it was to be feared he would take cold. Without his seeing anyone, a shirt fine enough for a wedding-day was handed to him, with a dressing-gown of gold brocade, embroidered with little emeralds which formed cyphers. The trunkless hands placed a table within his reach, on which his toilette was arranged. Nothing could be more magnificent: they combed out his hair with a lightness and dexterity which gave him great pleasure. Presently they dressed him, but not in his own clothes; a much richer suit was provided for him. He silently admired all that he observed, and occasionally little fears, of which he could not entirely divest himself, obtruded themselves on his mind.

When his hair was curled and powdered, his clothes finally adjusted and ornamented, and his person sweetly perfumed, he looked more handsome than Adonis, and the hands conducted him to a superb saloon, rich in gilding and furniture. Around it were to be seen paintings representing the histories of the most celebrated cats: Rodillardus hanging by his feet at the Council of the Rats; the Master Cat, or Puss in Boots; the Marquis of Carabas; the Writing Cat; the Cat metamorphosed into a woman; witches in the shape of cats, their ceremonies and nightly meetings – such were the subjects of some of these pictures, than which nothing could be more odd and curious.

Two tables were laid in this saloon; each of them was garnished with gold plate; the buffet was surprising on account of the vast number of vessels, all of rock-crystal or precious stones, arranged therein. The Prince did not know for whom these two cloths were laid, and while he was considering he observed cats enter the saloon and arrange themselves at a little orchestra, placed expressly for them; one held the most extraordinary music-book that was ever seen, another a little roll of paper wherewith to beat time, and the others carried little guitars. Of a sudden they all began mewing in different tones, and scraping on the strings of the guitars with their claws; it was the strangest music that ever was heard. The Prince would have thought that he was in the infernal regions, if the palace had not been too wonderfully fine to allow him to encourage a thought so degrading; but he stopped his ears, and laughed with all his heart at witnessing the various attitudes and grimaces of these novel musicians.

He was pondering on the curious things that had already happened to him in the castle, when he noticed a little figure, not two feet in height, enter the saloon. This large doll was enveloped in a long black crape veil. Two cats were leading her, clothed in mourning; they wore cloaks, and swords by their sides; a numerous *cortège* of cats formed her train; some of them carried traps full of rats, and others mice in cages.

This sight did not decrease the Prince's astonishment; he knew not what to think. The little figure in black walked up to him; and raising her veil he saw the most beautiful white cat that was ever or will ever be seen. She looked very young, and very sad withal; she said to the Prince: "Son of a king, you are welcome; my feline majesty sees you with pleasure."

"Madam Puss," said the Prince, "you are very generous to receive me with so much hospitality, but you do not seem to be an ordinary cat; your gift of speech and your superb castle are very evident proofs to the contrary."

"Son of a king," replied the White Cat, "I request you to forbear paying me compliments; I am simple in my manners and discourse, but I have a good heart. Come," continued she, "let supper be served, and let the musicians cease to play, for the Prince does not understand their music."

"And do they sing anything, madam?" asked he.

"Undoubtedly," she resumed; "true we have poets of infinite imagination, of which, if you remain a short time with us, you will have opportunities of being convinced."

"It is only necessary to hear you affirm it to believe it," said the Prince gallantly; "for, madam, I look upon you as an exceedingly rare cat."

Supper was brought up, the trunkless hands being the only attendants. Tureens of rich soup were first placed on the table, one being made of young pigeons, and another of fat rats. The sight of the second tureen prevented the Prince from eating any of the first, he fancying that the same cook had dressed both; but the little cat, who divined from his looks what was passing in his mind, assured him that her own kitchen was apart from that in which the pigeon soup was prepared, and that he might partake of what was presented to him with certainty of there being neither rats nor mice in it.

The Prince gave her no occasion to repeat her assurance, for he did not believe that the pretty little cat would deceive him. He remarked that she held in her paw a tablet containing a miniature portrait, which surprised him. He entreated her to let him see it, thinking that it was the picture of Minagrobis, or some favoured feline lover. He was very much astonished to see the countenance of a young man, so handsome that it was almost doubtful whether nature could form one to match it, had not the features borne so strong a resemblance to his own, that a better likeness of himself could not have been painted. She sighed, and, becoming still more sorrowful, kept a profound silence. The Prince plainly saw that there was something extraordinary in the affair; however, he dared not inform himself on the subject for fear of displeasing or grieving the cat. He entertained her with all the news he possessed, and found her well acquainted with the different interests of princes, and with the various events that were passing in the world.

After supper the White Cat invited her guest into a large hall which contained a stage, on which twelve cats and twelve apes were dancing a ballet. The cats were dressed as Moors and the apes as Chinese. It may easily be imagined how agile they were in their movements, and how high they leaped; and how, from time to time, they gave one another cuffs with their paws; with this entertainment the evening closed. The White Cat bade her guest goodnight; the hands which had conducted him thither resumed their guidance and led him to an apartment attached to that in which he had performed his toilette. It was furnished with less magnificence than good taste; the walls were hung with tapestry made of butterfly-wings, the colours of which were disposed in the shape and resemblance of various beautiful flowers. There were also feathers of very rare birds which most likely were never seen except in that place. The bed furniture was of gauze, looped up with many bows of ribbon. There were besides noble looking-glases reaching from the ceiling to the floor; the frames were of gold, chased to represent thousands of little cupids.

The Prince went to bed without saying a word; for there was no means of holding a conversation with the hands in attendance upon him; he did not sleep much, and was awakened by a confused noise. The hands immediately took him out of bed, and dressed him in a hunting suit. He looked into the courtyard of the castle and observed more than five hundred cats, some of them leading greyhounds in couples, and others winding horns; the day being a great festival. The White Cat was going to the chase, and wished the Prince to go also. The officious hands presented to him a wooden horse that was very swift and very steady; he made some objection to mounting it, alleging that he had no desire to turn knight-errant like Don Quixote; but his resistance was unavailing; they mounted him on the wooden horse. His horse-cloth and saddle were embroidered with gold and diamonds.

The White Cat mounted an ape, the handsomest and most superb that was ever seen; she no longer wore her long veil, but a hat and feather, which gave her so fierce an air that all the mice that saw her were quite terrified. Never was there a more pleasant chase; the cats ran faster than the rabbits and hares, so that they took plenty of game, the White Cat having them fed in her own presence, and encouraging them; for the birds, they were in no greater safety; the cats climbed the trees, and the ape carried the White Cat to the eagles' nests, to dispose as she thought fit of their little highnesses the eagles.

When the chase was over she took a horn which was as long as a man's finger, but which yielded so clear and loud a sound that it was distinctly audible thirty miles off. After sounding two or three flourishes, she was surrounded by all the cats in the country; some appeared in the air mounted on chariots, others came by water, in boats; in a word, a similar sight was never before seen. They were nearly all differently dressed; she returned to the castle with this pompous suite, and requested the Prince to accompany her. He was very willing, though all this seemed to him to savour a little of witchcraft and sorcery; but the fact of the White Cat's being able to speak surprised him more than all the rest.

When she arrived at home, she resumed her large black veil; she supped with the Prince, who was hungry and ate with a good appetite; rich liquors were brought, of which he drank with pleasure, and they had the effect of immediately obliterating from his mind all thoughts of the little dog that he had to take to the King. He only thought of listening to the White Cat's mewing, and keeping her good and faithful company; he spent the days in the most agreeable manner, sometimes fishing or hunting, at others dancing and feasting, with a thousand other diversions of the most pleasant kind; the beautiful cat frequently composed songs and verses in so impassioned a style that he thought she must have a tender heart, and that no one could express herself as she did, who was insensible to love; but her secretary, an aged cat, wrote so bad a hand that at the present day, although her works are still preserved in the hands of our publisher, it is impossible to decipher them.

The Prince had forgotten his country. The hands so often mentioned continued to attend on him. He sometimes regretted that he was not a cat, that he might pass the remainder of his life in such good company.

"Alas!" said he to the White Cat, "how sorry I shall be to leave you; I love you so dearly! Either become a woman or change me into a cat."

She was mightily pleased with this request, but only gave him obscure answers, of which he could not at all comprehend the meaning.

A year quickly passes away when one has neither anxiety nor

trouble, and enjoys good health and spirits. The White Cat knew the time when the Prince should return, and, as he no longer remembered it, recalled it to his recollection. "Are you aware," said she, "that you have only three days to find the little dog that the King your father wishes for, and that your brothers have got some very fine ones?"

The Prince, thus reminded, and much astonished at his negligence, exclaimed: "By what secret charm can I have forgotten that thing of all others which to me is the most important in the world? There goes my glory and my fortune; where shall I find a little dog beautiful enough to gain a kingdom, and a horse fleet enough to take me to the King my father within the prescribed time?" He then began to feel uneasy and to afflict himself very much.

The White Cat said to him soothingly: "Son of a king, do not grieve, I am your friend; you may remain here one day longer, and, although your country is one thousand five hundred miles from hence, the good wooden horse will carry you thither in less than twelve hours."

"Many thanks, beautiful Cat," said the Prince; "but I not only want to return to my father; I must take him a little dog."

"Here," said the White Cat, "take this acorn: in it you will find one more beautiful than the dog-star itself."

"Oh," said the Prince, "Madam Puss, your majesty is pleased to be facetious with me."

"Put the acorn to your ear," continued she, "and you will hear it bark." He did so; immediately the little dog barked "Bow-wow-wow," at which the Prince was in ecstasies, for a dog which was capable of being contained in an acorn must of necessity be very small.

So great was his desire to see it that he had a mind to open it; but the White Cat told him that the little dog might take cold on the road, and he had better wait till he was in the King his father's presence. He thanked her a thousand times, and, after bidding her a tender adieu, he added: "I assure you that the days have passed so pleasantly in your company, that I regret very sincerely to leave you here; and though you are a queen, and all the cats who compose your court have more wit and gallantry than can be found in ours, I cannot forbear inviting you to accompany me." The Cat only answered this proposal with a profound sigh.

They parted. The Prince arrived first at the castle which had been agreed upon as the rendezvous of himself and brothers. They made their appearance shortly after him, and were not a little surprised to see in the courtyard a wooden horse that leaped better than any in the academy.

The Prince went out to meet them. They embraced several times and told each other their adventures; but our prince disguised his from his brothers, and showed them a vile cur of a turnspit, telling them he thought it was so pretty that he had decided on taking it as his present to the King. However great the friendship between them, the two eldest felt a secret joy at the wretched choice their brother had made, and when they were seated at table they trod on each other's feet, as much as to say that there was nothing to fear in that quarter.

The next day they set out together in the same carriage. The two elder sons carried their little dogs in baskets so fine and delicate that one hardly dared to touch them. The youngest led his miserable turnspit in a string, and it was so dirty no one could touch it. When they had entered the palace, everybody crowded round them to bid them welcome; they passed on to the King's apartment. He knew not in whose favour to decide, for the little dogs presented him by his two elder sons were so nearly of equal beauty; and they were already arguing their rights to accession when the youngest settled the difference by taking from his pocket the acorn that the White Cat had given to him. He immediately opened it, when everybody saw a little dog lying on some cotton. He was so small that he would pass through a ring without touching it. The Prince put him on the floor, where he immediately began dancing a saraband with castanets, as lightly as the most practised dancer at Madrid. He was of many different colours, his ears and long silky hair reaching to the ground. The King was very much confused, for it was impossible to find any fault with Toutou's beauty.

However, he had no wish to get rid of his crown, the smallest gem of which was dearer to him than all the dogs in the universe. So he told his sons that he was satisfied with the trouble they had taken to gratify his wish, but that they had been so successful in the first thing he had desired of them that he wished to make further trial of their abilities before keeping his word; he accordingly gave them twelve months to search by land and sea for a piece of cloth of so fine a texture that it would pass through the eye of a cambric needle. All three of them were very much afflicted at being obliged to set out on a new search. The two princes whose dogs were not so fine as that of their youngest brother consented, however, with a good grace. Each of them went his way, without their bidding the youngest or one another nearly so friendly an adieu as they had done on the first occasion, for the turnspit had a little alienated their affections.

Our prince remounted his wooden horse, and, without seeking other assistance than what he hoped for from the White Cat's friendship, he departed with all diligence, and returned to the castle where she had before so kindly entertained him. He found all the doors open; the windows, the roofs, the towers, and the walls were illuminated with a hundred thousand lamps, which had a marvellous effect. The hands which had before so well attended on him advanced to meet him, taking the bridle of the excellent wooden horse and leading him to the stable, while the Prince entered the White Cat's chamber.

She was lying in a little basket, on a very neat white satin mattress. She wore her cap *négligée*, and seemed in low spirits; but when she saw the Prince she made a thousand skips and jumps to express her joy. "Whatever reason I may have had," said she to him, "to wish for your return, I confess, son of a king, that I dared not flatter myself with that hope; for I am generally so unfortunate in the result of my wishes that I am surprised at your reappearance."

The grateful Prince caressed her a thousand times; he informed her of the success of his journey, which she perhaps knew better than he did himself, and that the King required a piece of cloth so fine that it might be passed through the eye of a needle; he added that, for his part, he thought the thing was impossible, but that he had resolved to search for such a piece of cloth, relying on her friendship and assistance. The White Cat, assuming a grave look, said: "It is an affair that requires consideration. By good fortune I have in my castle some cats who spin pretty well, and I will superintend this work myself and see it advanced: thus you can remain in quietness, without going farther in search of what can be procured here, if at all, more easily than at any other place in the world."

The hands appeared, bearing flambeaux, and the Prince, accompanied by the White Cat, following them, entered a magnificent gallery that looked on to a large river, on which most surprising artificial fireworks were exhibiting. Four cats, who had been condemned in all due form to be burned, were about to suffer the execution of their sentence. They had been accused of eating the roast meat prepared for the White Cat's supper; of having stolen her cheese and milk; and of having conspired against her person with Martafax and Heremita, two famous cats of that country, and spoken of as such by that veracious author, La Fontaine; but, though there was sufficient evidence against them, it was thought that there had been much caballing in the business, and that most of the witnesses had been bribed. However that may have been, the Prince obtained their pardon. The fireworks did no one any harm, and the sky-rockets were as beautiful as any ever seen.

A very nice repast was then served up, which was more agreeable to the Prince than the fireworks, for he was very hungry, his wooden horse having brought him with so much expedition that it had given him a good appetite. The succeeding days passed, as the former ones had done, in a thousand agreeable entertainments, with which the White Cat diverted her guest. The Prince was perhaps the first mortal who had been so well entertained by cats, without any other company.

Indeed, the White Cat was very ready-witted, complaisant, and well informed. She had more learning than is usually the lot of cats. The Prince, in astonishment, would sometimes say to her: "No! All that I observe in you so remarkable cannot be natural. If you love me, charming Puss, inform me by what prodigy you are able to think so accurately and to speak so justly, that you might be admitted into the most learned academies?"

"Forbear your questions, son of a king," she would answer, "I am not permitted to reply to them; but you are at liberty to push your conjectures to what extent you please, without my opposing them; let it suffice that for you I have always a velvet paw, and that I interest myself tenderly in all that concerns you."

Insensibly as had the first, the second year rolled away; the

Prince wished for nothing that the diligent hands did not bring to him immediately; whether he desired books, jewellery, pictures, or antique medals; in a word, if he only formed a wish for a certain jewel in the Mogul's cabinet, or in that of the King of Persia, for such a statue in Corinth or other part of Greece, he immediately saw it before him without knowing who had brought it, or whence it had come. This was certainly a source of pleasure to him, for, to relax occasionally, it must be an agreeable thing to be in possession of the finest treasures of the world.

The White Cat, who always watched the Prince's interests, warned him that the time for his departure had arrived, and that he might make himself easy on the score of the piece of cloth of which he was in want, as she had had a wonderfully fine one made; she added that she intended this time to give him an equipage worthy of his birth, and requested him to look into the courtyard of the castle. He there observed an open chariot of gold and enamel, embossed in flame-colour with a thousand tasteful devices, as pleasing to the mind as to the eye. Twelve snow-white horses, placed four deep, drew it, their harness being of flame-coloured velvet embroidered with diamonds and decked with plates of gold. The lining of the chariot was of the same material as the harness; and a hundred carriages, each drawn by eight horses, and filled with noble lords richly dressed, followed it. It was attended besides by a thousand body-guards, whose clothes were so covered with embroidery that the cloth was entirely hidden; what was very singular was that the White Cat's picture was everywhere visible, both in the devices on the chariot, on the guards' regimentals, or attached by a ribbon to the coats of those who composed the *cortège*, as the badge of a new order with which they had been recently invested.

"Go," said she to the Prince, "and appear at the King your father's court in so sumptuous a style that your magnificent appearance may so impose upon him that he may no longer refuse you the crown that you deserve. Here is a walnut, be careful to crack it in his presence, and you will find in it the piece of cloth that you asked me for."

"Lovely White Cat," said the Prince to her, "I must acknowledge to you that I am so penetrated with your kindness that, if you will consent to it, I prefer to pass my life with you to all the greatness that I may reasonably expect elsewhere."

"Son of a king," replied she, "I am persuaded of the goodness of your heart; it is a rare commodity with princes, who would be loved by everybody, but would love no one themselves; you, however, show that the general rule has exceptions. I set great store by the attachment you testify for a little White Cat, who after all is only fit to catch mice."

The Prince then kissed her paw and departed.

The speed with which he travelled would be hardly credible, were we not acquainted with the fact that the wooden horse had on the former occasion carried him in less than two days a distance of upwards of 1,500 miles on the same road; but the same power which had animated the horse urging forward his present conveyance still more strongly, he achieved the same distance in twenty-four hours! They stopped for nothing until they had reached the King's palace, where the two elder brothers had already arrived. Not seeing their youngest brother there, they congratulated each other, saying in a low voice: "This is very fortunate, for he is either dead or ill, and will not be our rival in the important business now about to be transacted." They then displayed their pieces of cloth, which in truth were so fine that they would pass through the eye of a large needle, but by no means through that of a small one; the King, glad to find this pretext for evasion, showed them the needle he had proposed, which was brought from the treasury, where it had been carefully guarded by the magistrates.

This dispute caused a great deal of murmuring. The friends of the princes, and particularly those of the eldest, for his piece of cloth was the finest, said that the whole was a piece of arrant chicanery and evasion, managed very artfully and to good purpose. The King's creatures maintained that he was not obliged to keep conditions he had not made. At last, to put an end to the difference, a charming concert of trumpets, hautboys and kettledrums was heard: it was our prince arriving in pompous style. The King and his two sons were equally astonished at so magnificent a spectacle.

After respectfully saluting his father, and embracing his two brothers, he took the walnut out of a box covered with rubies. He

cracked it, expecting to find in it the piece of cloth so much boasted of;
but saw nothing but a hazelnut. He cracked this, and was astonished
to find only a cherry-stone. All the by standers looked at each other,
and the King slightly smiled in ridicule that his son should have been
so credulous as to believe he had a piece of cloth in a walnut: though
he had no occasion to doubt its possibility, seeing that the Prince
had already brought him a little dog in an acorn. The prince cracked
the cherry-stone which contained only the kernel, when a buzz arose
in the chamber, and nothing was audible but whisperings that the
Prince was duped. He made no reply to the courtiers' bitter jests,
and opened the kernel; he found in it a grain of wheat, and in that
a grain of millet. At the sight of this last he actually began himself
to doubt, and muttered between his teeth: "White Cat, White Cat,
you have deceived me."

At this moment he felt a cat's paw on the back of his hand, which
scratched him to such purpose that it fetched blood. He knew not
whether this scratch was inflicted to encourage or to dismay him.
However, he opened the grain of millet, and not a little astonished
everybody present by drawing from it a piece of cloth four ells long, of
such marvellous workmanship that all kinds of birds, beasts, and fishes
were represented on it as naturally as life; there were also representa-
tions of the different kinds of trees, fruits and plants, rocks, shells, and
other wonders of the deep, with the sun, the moon, the stars, and the
planets of the heavens: there were besides the portraits of all the kings
and emperors who had ever reigned until then in the world; those of
their queens, their children and all their subjects, the most vagabond
of their dominions not being omitted: they were all dressed according
to their various conditions, and each of them in the costume of his
country. When the King saw this piece of cloth he turned as pale as
the Prince had turned red in looking for it so long. The needle was
produced and it was passed and repassed through it six times. The
King and the two elder princes kept a sullen silence, although the
beauty and rarity of this piece of cloth constrained them to say from
time to time that it was not to be matched in the whole world.

The King fetched a deep sigh, and, turning to his children:
"Nothing," said he to them, "can give me so much consolation in
my old age as the gratification of knowing that I have such dutiful

sons; which, however, makes me desirous of putting you to a new trial. Travel for another twelve months, and he who at the end of that period shall bring with him the most beautiful damsel shall marry her and be crowned king at the same time; it is quite certain that my successor must marry. I promise, I swear, that I will then no longer defer the reward."

All the injustice of this sentence fell on our Prince. The little dog and the piece of cloth were worth ten kingdoms, rather than one; but he was of so sweet a temper that he had no wish to oppose his father's will; so he got into his chariot without delay; his equipage followed him, and he returned to his dear White Cat. She knew the day and hour when he was destined to arrive, and had had flowers scattered on his road, and thousands of pastilles lighted in all directions, particularly in and near the castle. She was reclining on a Persian carpet in a pavilion of cloth of gold, whence she could witness his return. He was received by the hands which had hitherto waited on him. All the cats climbed to the battlements and greeted him with joyous mewing.

"Well, son of a king," said she to him, "you have once more returned without your crown."

"Madam," replied he, "your kindness placed me in a condition to gain it, but I am persuaded that the King would have had more pain in divesting himself of it than I should have had pleasure in putting it on."

"No matter," said she, "nothing must be neglected to deserve it, and I will be of some service to you on this occasion: since you must take a beautiful maiden with you to the King your father's court, I will look for one who shall gain you the prize; meanwhile let us make merry and rejoice, for I have ordered a naval battle between the terrible rats of this country and my cats. The latter may be a little embarrassed, for they dread the water; however, they are much the better fighters, and the combatants ought to be as nearly equal as possible."

The Prince admired Madame Puss's prudence. He praised her for it, and they walked together to a terrace which looked on to the sea.

The cat's vessels consisted of large pieces of cork, on which they floated very commodiously. The rats had constructed their vessels of several ostrich half egg-shells. The fight was very obstinate and cruel; the rats threw themselves into the water and swam much better than the cats, by which means they were conquerors and conquered twenty times; but Minagrobis, admiral of the feline fleet, reduced the rattish tribe to the utmost despair. He ate, at a mouthful, their admiral, an old experienced rat, who had thrice sailed round the world in very good ships, in which he had been neither captain nor sailor, but only an interloper.

The White Cat had no wish to exterminate these unfortunate rats. She was politic enough to foresee that if there were no rats or mice in the country, her subjects would live in a state of idleness that might operate to her prejudice.

The Prince passed this year as he had passed the others, in hunting, fishing, and at play, for the White Cat was very fond of chess. He could not forbear from time to time asking her again by what miracle she was able to speak. He asked her whether she were a fairy, or whether she had been metamorphosed into a cat, but as she never said more than she chose to say, she only answered him by a few little insignificant words, whence he easily inferred that she was not willing to communicate her secret to him.

Nothing passes so quickly as happy days, and if the White Cat had not been so careful as to remember the time when he should return to Court, it is certain that the Prince would have entirely forgotten it. She warned him of it the day before, and told him that it remained with him only to procure one of the most beautiful princesses in the world; that he might do so (the time for destroying the fatal work of the fairies having at last arrived), he must make up his mind to cut off her head and tail and throw them promptly into the fire.

"What," cried he, "lovely White Cat, I! And shall I be barbarous enough to kill you? Ah! you would doubtless try my heart, but rest assured that it can never fail in the friendship and love it owes you."

"No, son of a king," continued she, "I do not suspect you of ingratitude; I am acquainted with your merit, but neither you nor I can prescribe in affairs of our destiny. Do as I bid you, and the happiness of both of us will be the consequence, and you will know, on the word of a Cat of truth and honour, that I am truly your friend."

Tears stood two or three times in the young Prince's eyes at the bare thought that it was necessary for him to cut off the head of his pretty little cat who had been so good to him. He said all that he could imagine of the most tender description to induce her to dispense with the terrible service she required of him, but she obstinately answered that she wished to die by his hand, and that it was the only means of preventing his brothers from obtaining the crown – in a word, she pressed him with so much warmth that trembling, and with an unsteady hand, he drew his sword and cut off the head and tail of his good friend the Cat. Immediately, however, that he had done so, he saw the most charming metamorphosis imaginable. The White Cat's body increased in size and changed suddenly into a young lady, so handsome and accomplished as to mock all description. Her eyes must have captivated all hearts, and her sweetness retained them; her shape was majestic; her air noble and modest; her wit ready and universal; her manner engaging – in a word, she was beyond everything that is most lovely in conception.

At the sight of her the Prince was so surprised, so agreeably surprised, that he thought himself enchanted. He could not speak, his eyes were not large enough to look at her, and his tongue was so tied that it could not give vent to his astonishment, but it was much augmented when he saw an extraordinary number of gentlemen and ladies enter, all of them having cat-skins thrown over their shoulders, and prostrate themselves at the Queen's feet, and express their joy at seeing her restored to her natural state. She received them with demonstrations of kindness which sufficiently manifested the character of her heart. After listening for some time to their congratulations, she requested to be left alone with the Prince, whom she addressed as follows:

"Do not think, sir, that I have always been a cat, or that I am of obscure birth. My father was king of six kingdoms. He was tenderly fond of my mother, and allowed her to follow the bent of her own wishes. Her prevailing inclination was a wish to travel, so that while I was yet unborn she set out to visit a certain mountain of which she had heard surprising things. On her road, she was informed that there was situated near to where she was passing an ancient fairy castle, the finest in the world, at least it was so believed from an old tradition which related thereto, for as no one ever entered the castle it could not be judged of with certainty; it was, however, well authenticated that the fairies had in their garden some most excellent fruit, the finest flavoured and most delicious that was ever eaten.

"Thereupon the Queen my mother conceived so violent a longing to eat of this fruit that she immediately turned her steps towards the fairy castle. She reached the door of a superb edifice, which was resplendent with gold and azure, but although she knocked repeatedly it remained unopened; no one appeared, and it would seem as though all the inhabitants were dead; her desire increasing by reason of this difficulty, she sent for ladders to scale the garden walls, and would have succeeded in so doing but that the walls rose of themselves as she advanced and mocked her efforts; ladders were tied together until they broke under their own weight, added to that of those who were sent up them, killing some and maiming others.

"The Queen was in despair. She saw large trees loaded with delicious fruit, but beyond her reach; she resolved to eat of it or die, and accordingly had rich tents pitched before the castle and remained there six weeks with all her court. She neither slept nor ate, but continually sighed, speaking of nothing but the fruit of the inaccessible garden; at last she fell dangerously ill, and no remedy could be found for her, for the inexorable fairies had not even shown themselves since she had been residing near their castle. All her officers were plunged in the deepest affliction; nothing was heard but tears and sighs; the dying Queen asking her attendants for fruit, while she would eat of none because it came not from the fairies' garden.

"One night, after falling into a slight doze, she saw on awakening a little, decrepit, ugly old woman, seated in a cushioned armchair near her bed. She was surprised that her women had allowed a stranger to come so near her, when the old woman said: "We find your majesty very importunate in your desire so stubbornly to eat of our fruit; but, since your precious life is in danger, my sisters and I consent to let you have as much of it as you can carry away, and to let you eat of it as long as you stay here, provided you make us a gift."

"'Ah! my good mother,' cried the Queen, 'speak, I will give you my kingdom, my heart, my soul to have some of your fruit, which I shall not think too dear at any price.'

"'We desire,' said she, 'that your majesty give us the daughter you will presently have; when she is born we will come to fetch her; she shall be brought up amongst us, and there are no virtues or charms that she shall not be possessed of, no accomplishments with which we will not endow her; in a word, she shall be our child, and we will make her happy; but your majesty must observe that you are not to see her again until she is married. If this proposal suit you, I will immediately cure you, and take you to our orchards; notwithstanding that it is night, you will see well enough to choose what you want. If what I say does not please you, goodnight to your majesty; I must go to sleep.'

"'Hard as are your terms,' answered the Queen, 'I accept of them, rather than die; for it is certain that I have not otherwise a day to live. Cure me, wise fairy,' continued she, 'let me not be debarred for a moment from the enjoyment of the privilege you have just granted to me.'

"The fairy touched her with a little golden wand, saying: 'Be your majesty free from all the illness that confines you to this bed.' The Queen immediately felt as if a very heavy and coarse garment with which she had been overwhelmed were removed from her; she was even better than she had been before the attack, particularly in all respects in which the disease had been most severe. She summoned all her ladies, and told them gaily that she was wonderfully well, and intended to rise, for at last the long-bolted and barricaded doors of the fairy palace would be opened to admit her to eat of the beautiful fruit and to carry away as much as she pleased.

"All the ladies thought that the Queen was delirious, and that at that moment she was dreaming of the fruit for which she had had so violent a longing; so instead of answering her, they began to cry, and had all the physicians awakened to see how she was. This delay put the Queen into the utmost despair; she quickly asked for her clothes, and they were refused her; she flew into a passion, and was becoming very red in the face; all this was thought to be the effect of her fever. At this juncture the physicians came, and, after feeling her pulse, looking at her tongue, and making sundry enquiries, they could not deny that she was in perfect health. Her women, seeing the error into which their zeal had led them, tried to repair it by dressing her quickly. They all asked her pardon, and were forgiven, and she hastened to follow the old fairy, who had been waiting for her all this time.

"She entered the palace, where nothing was wanting to make it the finest in the world. You will have no difficulty to believe that, son of a king, when I tell you that it was this in which we now are; two other fairies, not quite so old as the one who had conducted my mother, received them at the door, and gave her a very favourable reception. She begged them to conduct her immediately to the garden, and to the trees which bore the best fruit.

"'It is on all equally good,' said they to her, 'and were it not that you desire to have the pleasure of gathering it yourself, we should only have to call the fruit, in order to make it come here of itself.'

"'I entreat you, ladies,' said the Queen, 'to indulge me with this extraordinary sight.' The senior fairy put her fingers in her mouth, and whistled three times, and then called out: 'Grapes, apricots, peaches, nectarines, cherries, plums, pears, melons, currants, apples, oranges, citrons, gooseberries, strawberries and raspberries, come all at my bidding.'

"'But,' said the Queen, 'all the fruits you have named are not ripe at the same season.'

"'The case is different in our orchards,' said they; 'we have all sorts of fruit, always ripe, always good, and which never spoil.'

"In an instant they came rolling and tumbling in, without spoiling or even acquiring a single bruise; and the Queen, impatient to satisfy her longing, fell upon them and took the first that came to her hand; which she devoured rather than ate.

"When she had in some degree satisfied her appetite, she begged the fairies to let her go to the trees, and enjoy the pleasure of gathering the fruit for herself.

"'We willingly consent,' said the fairies; 'but bear in mind that the promise you have made to us cannot be recalled.'

"'I am persuaded,' replied she, 'that to live with you would be so pleasant, and this palace appears to me so fine, that if I did not tenderly love my husband, I would offer to remain here myself also; therefore you need not fear that I shall forfeit my word.'

"The fairies, very well satisfied, opened all their gardens and enclosures to her; she remained in them three days and three nights, without wishing to stir, so delightful did she find them. She gathered fruit for her provision; and, as it never spoiled, she carried away four mule-loads of it with her. The fairies added to their fruit gold baskets of exquisite workmanship to keep it in, and other rarities of enormous value; they promised so to educate me as to make me a perfect princess, and to choose for me a proper husband: adding that they would inform her of the wedding, and trusted that she would attend it.

"The King was in ecstasies at his queen's return; all the courtiers expressed their joy at the event, nothing was thought of but balls, masquerades, ring-races and feasts, at which the Queen's fruit was served up as a delicious regale. The King ate of it in preference to anything that the attendants could offer him. But he knew not of the bargain that had been made for it with the fairies, and often asked the Queen to what country she had been, to bring thence such good things; she answered that they grew on a nearly inaccessible mountain; at another time she said that they grew in valleys; then that she had found them in the middle of a garden, or in a forest. The King was surprised at so many contradictions. He questioned those who had accompanied her, but she had so expressly forbidden them to relate to anyone her adventure, that they dared not mention it. At last the Queen grew uneasy about her promise to the fairies; and fell into a frightful melancholy, sighing every moment and continually changing countenance. The King was alarmed, and pressed the Queen to impart to him the subject of her sorrow; after much difficulty she informed him of all that had passed between the fairies and herself, and that she had promised them the daughter that was soon to be born to them. 'What,' cried the King, 'having no children, and knowing how anxious I am for some, were you capable of promising your daughter in exchange for the gratification of eating a few apples? You cannot possibly have any love for me.'

"Thereupon he overwhelmed her with upbraidings, which made the poor Queen nearly ready to die with grief; but he did not stop at that, for he confined her in a tower, and placed guards all round it, to prevent her from holding intercourse with anyone but her attendants, taking care to remove those who had been with her to the fairies' castle.

"This misunderstanding between the King and Queen plunged the Court into the utmost consternation: they laid aside their rich clothes, and dressed in garments suited to the general grief. The King, for his part, appeared inexorable, and would not see his queen; directly I was born he had me brought to his palace to be nursed, while she was detained a prisoner, and in a bad state of health. The fairies were ignorant of nothing that was passing; they were provoked at it, and wanted to have me, looking on me as their property and considering it as a robbery to withhold me from them. Before seeking revenge commensurate to the injury thus done to them, they despatched a celebrated embassy to the King, desiring him to set the Queen at liberty and to restore her to his favour; they entreated him also to send me with the ambassadors, to be nourished and brought up among them. The ambassadors were so small and deformed, for they were hideous dwarfs, that they could not prevail with the King. He refused them rudely, and, if they had not hastened their departure, he might have used them worse.

"When the fairies were made acquainted with my father's proceedings, they were as indignant as possible, and after visiting his six kingdoms with all imaginable evils, to desolate them, they let loose a terrible dragon which ate men and children, filling with venom every place he passed through, and killing plants and trees with the breath of his nostrils.

"The King, finding himself reduced to the last extremity, consulted with all the wise men of his kingdom as to what he should do to relieve his subjects from the misfortunes with which they were so oppressed. They advised him to have a search made all over the world for the best physicians and most excellent remedies, and on the other hand to promise their lives to all criminals condemned to death, who were willing to fight the dragon. The King, satisfied with this advice, put it into execution, but received no benefit from so doing, for the mortality continued, and everyone who fought with the dragon was devoured; he then applied to a fairy who had protected him from his most tender years. She was very old, and hardly ever rose from her seat; he went to her, and overwhelmed her with reproaches for allowing fate to persecute him without giving him any assistance.

"'What would you have me do?' said she to him; 'you have

provoked my sisters; they are as powerful as I am and we rarely act in opposition to each other. Try to appease them by giving them your daughter; the little Princess belongs to them. You have confined your queen in a close prison; what has that amiable woman done to deserve such ill-treatment? Determine on keeping the word she pledged, and I assure you that all will end happily.'

"The King my father loved me tenderly; but, seeing no other means of saving his kingdoms, or of being delivered from the fatal dragon, he told his old friend that he would confide in her; and that he was willing to give me to the fairies immediately, as she assured him that I should be taken care of, and treated as became a princess of my rank; that he would also release the Queen, and that she had only to tell him to whom he was to entrust me, that I might be carried at once to the fairies' castle.

"'It is necessary,' said she, 'to carry her in her cradle to the Mountain of Flowers, and you must yourself remain thereabouts to see what takes place.' The King told her that in a week from that day he would go with the Queen, and that she must acquaint the fairies, her sisters, with his intention, that they might take their measures accordingly.

"On his return to the palace he had the Queen brought from the tower with as much pomp and tenderness as he had placed her in it with anger and passion. She was so fallen away and altered that he could hardly have recognized her, if his heart had not told him she was the same person of whom he had once been so fond. He entreated her with tears in his eyes to forget the ill-treatment she had suffered, assuring her that it should be the last she should receive at his hands. She modestly replied that she had drawn it on herself by her own imprudence in promising her daughter to the fairies, and that if anything could plead in excuse for her, it was the condition to which she was then reduced. At last he declared to her that he was willing to place me in the fairies' hands. The Queen in her turn opposed this design; it seemed as though, through some fatality, I were always destined to be a cause of discord between my father and my mother. After much groaning and crying, without obtaining what she desired (for the King saw but too surely the fatal consequences that had already followed the breach of her promise, and his subjects continued to die as though they had participated in their sovereign's faults), she consented to his wishes, and preparations were made for the ceremony.

"I was put into a cradle of mother-of-pearl, adorned as much as possible by art and good taste. Garlands and festoons of flowers were hung all about it, the flowers being composed of precious stones, the different colours of which reflected the sun's rays so brilliantly that it was impossible to look at them. The magnificence of my attire surpassed, if possible, that of my cradle. All the bands and rolls of my swaddling-clothes were buckled with large pearls; four-and-twenty princesses of the blood-royal carried me in a kind of light litter; their clothes were all of precious materials; they were allowed to use no colour but white, as emblematical of my innocence. All of the Court accompanied me, each according to his rank.

"As the procession was ascending the mountain, a melodious symphony was heard approaching; and presently the fairies appeared, thirty-six in number, the three having invited their friends to come with them; each of them was seated in a pearl shell, larger than that in which Venus had risen from the sea; marine horses, which cannot usually travel well on land, drew them more pompously than the first queens in the world; yet they were old and ugly to excess. They carried an olive branch in their hands, to signify to the King that his submission had gained their favour; and when they had me, their caresses were so extraordinary that it seemed as if they only wished to live to make me happy.

"The dragon which they had made their instrument of vengeance against my father followed, confined in diamond chains. They took me in their arms and caressed me a thousand times, endowed me with numerous gifts, and immediately commenced dancing the fairies' hornpipe. This is a very lively dance, and it is almost incredible how the old women skipped and leaped about; then the voracious dragon, who had eaten so many people, drew near, crawling. The fairies to whom my mother had promised me seated themselves on his back, placing my cradle between them, and, striking the dragon with a wand, he immediately outspread his large scaly wings, which were finer than crape, and intermixed with a variety of colours, and they were immediately borne to the castle. My mother, seeing me

in the air, exposed on this furious dragon's back, could not forbear
uttering loud cries. The King comforted her by the assurance his
friend had given him, that no accident should befall me, and that I
should be taken as much care of as if I were in his own palace. She
was pacified, though she was much grieved to part with me for so
long a period, and especially as she herself had been the cause of it;
for if she had not longed to eat some fruit from the fairies' garden, I
should have remained in my father's kingdom, and should not have

undergone all the misfortunes the history of which I am about to relate to you.

"You must know, son of a king, that my guardians had built a tower expressly for me, in which there were a thousand beautiful apartments for all the seasons of the year, with magnificent furniture and agreeable books; but there was no door to this tower, and entrance was obtained through the windows only, which were at a prodigious height. Attached to the tower were beautiful gardens, ornamented with flowers, fountains, and groves of verdure, which excluded the heat on the hottest dog-day. In that place did the fairies bring me up, with care that outdid all their promises to the Queen. My clothes were made in the last fashion and of such magnificent materials that anyone seeing me would have thought that it was my wedding-day. They taught me all that befitted my age and birth: I did not give them much trouble, for there was nothing that I did not comprehend with great facility; my gentle disposition was very agreeable to them, and if I had seen no one but them, I should have been content to have remained there all my lifetime.

"They were continually visiting me, mounted on the furious dragon of which I have already spoken; they never mentioned the King or Queen to me, and always addressed me as their daughter, and I believed that I was really so. No creature lived in the tower with me, excepting a parrot and a little dog, which they gave me for my amusement, and endowed with the faculties of reason and speech.

"One side of the tower was built on a hollow road, planted thickly with elms and other trees, which shaded it so much that up to the time of which I am about to speak I never saw anyone pass through it while I was confined there. But, as I was gazing from the battlements one day, I heard a noise in that direction. I looked all round, and observed a young gentleman, who was stopping to listen to our conversation. I had never seen one before but in pictures. I was not sorry that accident had placed this opportunity in my way; so that, not suspecting the danger that attends the satisfaction of contemplating a lovely object, I advanced to look at him, and the longer I looked the more pleasure I felt. He made me a low bow, fixed his eyes on me, and seemed to be troubled as to how he should communicate with me; for as my tower was very high, he was fearful of being overheard, and he knew very well that it was the fairies' castle that I was in.

"Night came on suddenly, or, more properly speaking, came on without our perceiving it; he sounded his horn two or three times, and played a few airs on it to divert me; and he then departed, without my being able to distinguish which way he went, it was so dark. I remained very thoughtful; I ceased to feel the pleasure I had hitherto taken in conversing with my parrot and my dog. They said the prettiest things in the world to me, for fairy beasts are very witty; but my thoughts were otherwise engaged, and I knew not the art of dissembling. My parrot observed it; he was cunning, and said nothing of what was passing in his head.

"I did not fail, the next morning, to rise at daybreak. I hastened to my window, and was agreeably surprised to see the young gentleman at the foot of the tower. He wore a magnificent dress; I flattered myself that I had had a little share in his choice of it, and was not mistaken. He spoke to me through a kind of speaking-trumpet, and, assisted by it, he told me that till then he had been insensible to the charms of all the beauties he had seen; but that when he saw me, he was so violently smitten with mine that it would be impossible for him to live without constantly seeing me. I was mightily pleased with this compliment, and very uneasy at not daring to make him any reply; for I must have called out with all my might, and have run the risk of being better heard by the fairies than by him. I threw him a few flowers that I had in my hand, and he received them as so signal a favour that he kissed them over and over again: he afterwards asked me if I approved of his coming every day at the same hour under my window, and added that if I did I was to throw him something. I had a turquoise ring, which I hastily pulled from my finger, and threw it precipitately to him, making him a sign to hasten his departure; for I heard in another direction the fairy Violenta, who was coming on her dragons back to bring me my breakfast.

"The first words she said on entering my apartment were these: 'I smell here the voice of a man; search, dragon.' Alas! what a condition was I in! I was dreadfully terrified lest it should go out of the other window and follow the young gentleman, for whom I was already much interested. 'Indeed,' said I, 'my good mamma' (for the old fairy wished me to call her so), 'you must be joking to say that you smell a man's voice here: can a voice be smelt? And if it should be so, what mortal were daring enough to venture coming up into this tower?'

"'What you say is true, my daughter,' answered she, 'and I am delighted to hear you argue so clearly. I fancy it is the hatred I bear men that sometimes persuades me that they are near when they are not.' She gave me my breakfast and my distaff. 'When you have finished your breakfast, do not fail to spin, for you did nothing yesterday,' said she to me, 'and my sisters will be angry at it.' In fact, I had been so taken up with the stranger that I had been quite unable to spin.

"When she was gone, I threw the distaff on one side, in a rather refractory manner, and ascended to the terrace to take a distant view of the country. I had a most excellent perspective glass; nothing escaped my rigid scrutiny on all sides, and I discovered my lover on the summit of a mountain. He was reclining under a rich pavilion of cloth of gold, and was surrounded by a numerous court. I had no doubt that he was the son of some king in the neighbourhood of the fairies' palace. Being fearful that if he returned to the tower he would be discovered by the terrible dragon, I sought my parrot, and told him to fly to that mountain, and that he would find there the person who had spoken to me; I instructed him to beg the Prince on my part to return no more to the tower, as I was fearful that the vigilance of my guardians would discover him and would prompt them to do him an evil turn.

"My parrot acquitted himself of his commission like a parrot of wit. All the Court was surprised to see him perch on the King's shoulder, and whisper in his ear. The Prince felt both joy and sorrow at hearing the subject of his errand. My care flattered his passion, while the difficulties which opposed his speaking to me overwhelmed him, without deterring him from his design of pleasing me. He asked the parrot a hundred questions, and the parrot, in his turn, asked him quite as many, for he was naturally curious. The King charged him with another ring, in return for my turquoise; this was a turquoise also, but much finer than mine, being shaped like a heart and surrounded with diamonds. 'It is right,' added he, 'that I should treat you as an ambassador: here is my portrait, of which I make you a present; show it only to your charming mistress.' He tied the portrait under his wing, and carried the ring in his bill.

"I awaited the return of my little green courier with an impatience that I had never known till then. He told me that the person to whom I had sent him was a great king, that he had received him in the handsomest manner in the world, and that I might rest assured that he would only live for me; that, though it was very dangerous for him to come to the foot of my tower, he was resolved to risk everything rather than renounce seeing me. This news so perplexed me that I began crying. My parrot and Toutou, my dog, consoled me as well as they were able, for they loved me tenderly, and then my parrot presented me the prince's ring and showed me the portrait. I confess that I had never been so overjoyed as I was at contemplating near me a person whom I had only seen at a distance. He appeared to be still more lovely than he had seemed at first; and so many thoughts crowded into my mind, some agreeable and others sad, that they gave me an unusually anxious look. The fairies who came to see me perceived it. They said one to another that I must be troubled at something, and that they must think of providing me with a husband of the fairy race. They named several, and presently pitched upon the little king Migonnet, whose kingdom was situated five hundred thousand leagues from this palace, but that was not of much importance. My parrot, who overheard this agreeable consultation, related the whole of it to me, and said: "Alas! my dear mistress, how much I pity you, if you should become Queen Migonnetta! He is a frightful baboon, I am sorry to tell you, and I am sure that the King who loves you would scorn to have such a person for his foot-boy."

"'Have you seen him, my parrot?'

"'I think, if I am not mistaken,' continued he, 'that I have been perched on the same branch with him.'

"'How on a branch?' replied I.

"'Why, he has the feet,' said he, 'of an eagle.'

"I was much grieved at receiving this account; I looked at the charming portrait of the young King, and fancied that he had only given it to the parrot that I might have opportunities of seeing it, and when I made a comparison between him and Migonnet I no longer wished to live, and resolved rather to die than marry the latter. I slept not during the night, but conversed with my parrot and Toutou; I slept a little in the morning, and my dog, who had a very good nose, smelt the King, who was at the foot of the tower. He awakened the parrot. 'I will engage that the King is there, below,' said he.

The parrot answered, 'Silence, prattler; being always watchful and on the alert yourself, you are envious of the rest of others.'

"'But I will engage,' said the good Toutou, "that I am right, for I am certain that he is there.'

"The parrot answered, 'And I am certain that he is not there; did I not, in our mistress's name, forbid him to come here?'

"'Ah, truly you talk finely about your forbidding him!' cried my dog; 'a man in love only consults his heart;' and thereupon he began pulling the parrot's wings so roughly that the bird got angry. They awakened me with their cries; they told me the subject of their dispute, on hearing which I ran, or rather flew, to the window: I saw the King, who stretched his arms to me when he saw me, and told me through his trumpet that he could not live without me, and conjured me to discover a means of quitting the tower, or of admitting him to me, invoking the gods and all the elements to witness that he would marry me and thus make me one of the greatest queens in the world.

"I bade my parrot go and tell him that what he wished appeared to me almost impossible; that, however, on the word he had pledged and the oaths he had sworn to me, I would apply myself to what he wished; that I conjured him not to come every day, lest he should at last be discovered, in which case the fairies would show him no quarter. He went away, overjoyed with the hope that I had given him, while I was in the utmost embarrassment when I reflected on what I had just promised. How was I, so young, so inexperienced, and so timid, and with no one to assist me but my parrot and Toutou, to quit a tower in which there were no doors? I came to the resolution of not attempting a thing in which I could never succeed, and despatched my parrot to inform the King of my determination. He was for killing himself on the spot; but he finally charged my parrot with the task of persuading me either to come and see him die or bring him some comfort. 'Sire!' cried the winged ambassador, 'my mistress is sufficiently disposed to console you; she only wants the power.'

"When he gave me an account of all that had passed, I was more afflicted than ever. The fairy Violenta came; she observed that my eyes were swollen and inflamed; she said that I had been crying, and that if I did not tell her the cause of my grief she would burn me; for her threats were always terrible. I replied, trembling, that I was tired of spinning, and desired to have some nets to entrap the little birds which came to peck at the fruit in my garden.

"'What you desire, my daughter,' said she, 'shall cost you no more tears, for I will bring you as much twine as you are in want of,' and in fact she did so that same evening; but she advised me to think less of working than of setting off my beauty, for King Migonnet was expected to arrive in a few days. I shuddered at this sorrowful news, and made no reply.

"When she was gone I began two or three rows of my nets; but I presently applied myself to making a rope ladder, in which I succeeded very well, though I had never seen one. The fairy had not supplied me with as much twine as was necessary, and said continually, on my asking her for more: 'My daughter, your work is like that of Penelope; it does not advance, yet you do not cease to ask for fresh materials.'

"'Oh, good mamma,' I would say, 'you may say what you please; but can you not see that I do not know how to manage it, and that I burn all that does not please me? Are you not afraid that I shall ruin you in twine?' My air of simplicity satisfied her, although she was in a very disagreeable and cruel humour.

"I desired my parrot to tell the King to come one evening under my window, where he would find a ladder, and that he should know the rest when he arrived. In fact, I had made it very secure, resolved to make my escape with him; but when he saw it, without waiting for me to descend, he hastily mounted by it himself, and threw himself into my chamber, where I was getting everything in readiness for my flight.

"His presence so overjoyed me that I forgot the danger we were in. He renewed all his vows, and conjured me not to defer my marriage with him. We made my parrot and Toutou the witnesses of our contract; never did a wedding take place between persons of so high a rank with less splendour and bustle, and never were hearts more contented than were ours.

"At daylight the King left me, but not before I had informed him of the dreadful design the fairies had of marrying me to the little Migonnet. I described his figure to him, which he held in as much aversion as myself. When he was gone the hours seemed as long as years; I ran to the window, and followed him with my eyes, notwithstanding the darkness; but how great was my astonishment to see in the air a fiery chariot, drawn by winged salamanders, accompanied by guards mounted on ostriches.

"I had no leisure to consider whether it was the baboon Migonnet that was thus traversing the air; but I concluded that it must be a fairy or an enchanter.

"Shortly afterwards the fairy Violenta entered my chamber. 'I bring you good news,' said she; 'your intended husband has arrived some time; here are fine clothes and jewellery; prepare to receive him.'

"'But who told you,' said I, 'that I wanted to marry? I am sure that nothing is farther from my thoughts; therefore send back King Migonnet, for I will not add a single pin to my dress; whether he think me handsome or ugly, I am not for him.'

"'Heyday! heyday!' said the fairy again; 'you little rebel, you empty pate, I do not understand your raillery, and I will –'

"'What will you do to me?' said I, enraged at the names she had called me; 'can anyone be worse treated than I am, shut up in a tower with a parrot and a dog, and visited every day by that terrible dragon?'

"'Ha! Little ingrate!' said the fairy; 'is this all we deserve for our cares and pains? I have but too often told my sisters that we should have but a sorry recompense.'

"With that she went to find them, and related to them our dispute, which not a little surprised the whole of them.

"My parrot and Toutou made me many remonstrances, representing that, if I continued refractory, they foresaw that bitter misfortunes would befall me. I felt so proud of possessing the heart of a great king that I despised the fairies and the advice of my humble companions. I would not dress at all, and affected to be slovenly in my head-gear, that Migonnet might think me disagreeable. Our interview took place on a terrace; he came in his fiery chariot. Of all dwarfs he was certainly the smallest that was ever seen. His feet were like an eagle's, and close to his knees, for he had no leg bones, and walked with the assistance of two diamond crutches. His royal mantle was only half an ell in length; and the third part of it trailed upon the ground. His head was the size of a bushel, and his nose was so large that a dozen birds roosted on it, whose warbling pleased him; he had so strong a beard that canaries built their nests in it, and his ears reached a foot above his head; but this latter circumstance was rendered less perceptible by the high pointed crown he wore to make himself look more grand. The flame of his chariot roasted the fruit, withered the flowers, and dried up the fountains in my garden. He came up to me with open arms to embrace me, but I remained standing quite upright, which obliged his first esquire to hold him up; but as soon as he came near me I fled to my chamber, and secured the door and windows. Migonnet retired to the fairies, very much enraged against me.

"They asked him a thousand pardons for my rudeness, and to appease him, for he was powerful, they resolved to bring him to my chamber in the night while I was asleep, and, having bound my hands and feet, to place me in his burning chariot with him; that he might take me away. This course being decided on, they scolded me for the rudeness I had been guilty of, and desired me to think about repairing it. My parrot and Toutou were surprised at such mildness on their part.

"'Depend upon it, dear mistress,' said my dog, 'that it bodes no good; these fairies are strange personages, and especially Violenta.'

"I ridiculed his fears, and awaited my dear husband's arrival with the last impatience – a feeling too much shared by him to permit delay on his part. I threw him the rope-ladder, resolving to make my escape with him; he lightly ascended it, and said a thousand such tender things that I dare not recall them to my remembrance.

"While we were talking together with the same tranquillity as if we had been in his palace, we saw all of a sudden the windows of my chamber broken in, and the fairies enter on their terrible dragon, followed by King Mignonnet, in his fiery chariot, and attended by his guards on their ostriches. The King, quite undaunted, clapped his hand to his sword, thinking only of securing and protecting me in this cruel pass; and immediately – how shall I tell it you, sir? – these barbarous creatures set their dragon at him, and though he defended himself long and bravely with his sword, yet the dragon at last prevailed, and devoured him before my face.

"Desperate at his misfortunes and my own, I threw myself in the horrible monster's jaws, hoping that he would devour me, as he had just devoured all that was dear to me in the world. He wished it likewise; but the fairies, more cruel than he was, would not allow him. 'She must,' said they, 'be reserved for more lasting torment; a speedy death is too good for this worthless creature.' They touched me, and I found myself changed immediately into a white cat; they conducted me to this superb palace, which belonged to my father; they metamorphosed all the lords and ladies of the kingdom into cats; and for the remainder of the subjects left the hands only of them visible, thus reducing me to the deplorable condition in which you found me, not without first informing me of my birth, of the death of my father and mother, and that I should only be delivered from my feline figure by a prince exactly resembling the one of whom they had deprived me. It is you, sir, who bear this resemblance," continued she, "both in figure, features and tone of voice. I was immediately struck with the resemblance on seeing you, and was informed of all that has since happened, and of all that is about to occur; my troubles will soon be over."

"And will mine, beautiful Queen," said the Prince, "be of long duration?"

"I already love you more than my life, sir," said the Queen; "we must depart for the King your father's palace, and learn his sentiments towards me, and whether he will consent to what you desire."

She went out, and the Prince handed her into a chariot, seating himself by her side: it was much more magnificent than either of those he had previously used. All the rest of the equipage matched so well with it that the horses' shoes were of emeralds, and the nails of diamonds. In all probability the like was never seen before. I shall say nothing of the agreeable conversation the Queen and Prince held together. She was unique with respect to beauty, and equally so for wit, nor was the young Prince less perfect than she; so that all their thoughts were bright and agreeable.

When they came near the castle where the Prince's two elder brothers were to meet, the Queen entered a little crystal cage, set with gold and rubies. Curtains were drawn closely round it, that she might not be seen, and it was carried by very handsome and superbly-dressed young men. The Prince remained in the chariot, and saw his brothers each walking with a charming princess. On seeing him, they immediately advanced to receive him, and asked him if he had brought a mistress with him: he told them that he had been so unfortunate throughout his journey as to meet only with very ugly ones, but that he had brought a much greater rarity in the shape of a little White Cat. They began to laugh at his simplicity. "A cat," said they to him; "were you afraid that the mice would eat up our palace?" The Prince replied that in truth he was not very wise to make such a present to his father; and thereupon they all took the road to the city.

The elder princes, with their princesses, went in carriages of gold and azure, the horses' heads being decked with aigrettes and plumes of feathers; nothing could exceed the brilliancy of this cavalcade. The young Prince preceded them, and he was followed by the crystal cage, which everybody admired.

The courtiers hastened to tell the King that the three princes were approaching.

"Are they bringing fair ladies with them?" asked the king.

"Fairer are not to be found," was the answer, at hearing which he seemed to be displeased. The two princes made haste to show their beautiful princesses. The King received them very graciously, and did not know in whose favour to decide: he looked at their brother, and said: "This time, then, you are come alone?"

"Your majesty," said the Prince, "will see in this cage a little White Cat, who mews so sweetly, and plays so prettily, that you cannot but be pleased with her." The King smiled, and went to open the cage himself; but directly he came near it, the Queen, with a spring, broke it in pieces, and appeared like the sun showing himself after being obscured by a cloud. Her fair hair was spread over her shoulders, and hung in large curls down to her feet; her head was adorned with flowers; her gown of thin white gauze was lined with rose-coloured taffety; she courtsied low to the King, who could not, in the excess of his admiration, forbear crying: "This is the matchless beauty who deserves my crown."

"Sire," said she, "I am not come to deprive you of a throne which you fill so worthily: I was born heiress to six kingdoms; allow me to offer you one of them, and also one to each of your two sons. The only recompense I ask is your friendship and this young prince for my husband: three kingdoms will be quite enough for us." The King and all the courtiers gave vent to their joy and astonishment in loud and repeated shouts. The marriages of all the three couples were immediately solemnized, and the court spent several months in rejoicings and pleasures. They then set out, each for his own dominions, the White Cat having immortalized herself as much by her bounty and generosity as by her rare merit and beauty.

For Those who Want to Know More

∾

IN THIS SECTION I'd like to tell you a little about the writers who produced all of these stories and something about fairy tales themselves. After all fairy tales, or folk tales, which most of them are, are amongst the oldest writings in the world. Stories just like fairy tales have been found amongst the ruins of ancient Egypt as far back as 2500BC, and there are similar stories to be found amongst the writings in other ancient civilizations like China, India and, of course, Greece and Rome. In fact there isn't a culture anywhere in the world which doesn't have some kind of folk tales, all the way from Eskimos to the Maori, from the ancient Maya to the Romanies of today.

So why do we call them fairy tales? To answer that we have to go back over three hundred years to the time when the fairy tale in the form we know now became fashionable.

There was a lady living in Paris called Marie-Cathérine d'Aulnoy. She was a bit of a character. In her teens she had married a man in his mid-forties and the marriage was very unhappy, even though she had six children. Along with her mother, young Marie-Cathérine tried to find a way of getting rid of her husband, but she was found out and had to flee the country. She may have spent some time in a convent and, if her own stories are to be believed, she travelled throughout the courts of Europe, especially Spain and maybe even England.

In 1690 she wrote a long adventurous and romantic novel called *L'Histoire d'Hypolite Comte de Duglas*, or *The Story of Hypolitus, Count Douglas*, and in one chapter the hero tells a story about a man who is taken by the wind Zephir to an island where he lives in happiness with a fairy for what feels like only a few weeks but which is, in the real world, several centuries. Eventually Father Time catches up with him. The story is sometimes reprinted as "The Isle of Happiness" and was one of the first "modern" fairy tales – that is, a story deliberately written in that form rather than a retelling of an old traditional folk story.

Because of her stories and adventures Marie-Cathérine d'Aulnoy became a celebrity in France, and her home became a literary salon where the scholars and nobility of France came to gossip and entertain. Madame d'Aulnoy published some of her stories as *Contes des fées* in 1697, and when the book was published in England two years later it was translated as *Tales of the Fairys* (that spelling is right). Because of their popularity, this type of story very rapidly became called fairy tales. And that name stuck, even if the story did not contain fairies. It more or less became synonyous with children's stories or nursery rhymes, which is a shame, because Madame d'Aulnoy composed her stories for adults. Not only her stories, but many fairy tales can be enjoyed equally by young and old alike. I'll return to Madame d'Aulnoy under the entry for "The White Cat", below.

One of the regular visitors to Madame d'Aulnoy's *salon* was a French civil servant called Charles Perrault. Unlike some of the stuffy-nosed men in French government, Perrault was good-humoured and delighted in making fun of pomposity. He ended up having an argument with his colleagues about which was of higher quality – the stories and books of antiquity, or stories of the present day. Perrault preferred modern stories, and began to write his own as a way of ridiculing the establishment. He chose Madame d'Aulnoy's fairy tale approach, though his were initially written as poems, with the deliberate intention of lampooning the nobility. The satire wasn't always that evident – you have to read between the lines, something Perrault suspected his peers would not have the wit to do – so he was able to have a go at them without them realizing it.

Perrault's first true fairy story was "The Sleeping Beauty", which first appeared in 1696. Unlike Madame d'Aulnoy, who more or less wrote new stories based only on a thread of legend or folk tradition, Perrault based his much more firmly on stories he had heard recounted throughout his life – after all, he was in his sixties when he started writing these stories. Some of these tales had been captured by two earlier writers – both Italian – Giovanni Straparola and Giambattista Basile, who were amongst the first to write down folk tales that they had heard. I'll come back to them in my comments upon "Cinderella" and "Sleeping Beauty" below.

Charles Perrault gave rise to another popular character. The frontispiece to the French edition of his fairy tales depicted an old lady telling stories to a group of children; behind them, a plaque on the wall stated "CONTES DE MA MÈRE L'OYE". This was translated in the first English-language edition as "MOTHER GOOSE'S TALES". By 1768 the title *Mother Goose's Tales* had superseded Perrault's original, and the character of Mother Goose entered the language.

Because of the popularity of fairy tales in France, the French read anything they could get their hands on. So when the Oriental scholar Antoine Galland began translating ancient Persian and Arabian stories as *Mille et une Nuits*, or *The Thousand and One Nights* in 1704, his book became a bestseller – not just in France but all over Europe. Many of our favourite fairy tales and Christmas pantomimes are based on the Arabian Nights – Aladdin, Ali Baba, Sinbad – all names and tales that have passed into our language.

By the start of the nineteenth century the fairy tale had become a standard part of story-telling. The Victorians would start to adapt it from a moral tale often with two levels of interpretation into stories strictly for children, essentially nursery tales. But many of these stories could still be enjoyed by adults. The story of the development of the nursery rhyme can be followed further in the story notes set out below. These follow the same sequence as the stories are presented in the anthology, but if you follow the notes through, you'll be able to trace the history of the fairy tale from the earliest times to the modern day. All of the main writers of fairy stories are covered below.

A BAG OF POETRY and **THE FOREST OF DREAMS** by **Lawrence Schimel** (born 1971). Schimel is a new writer who in a short time has produced a lot of very short-short stories which place new twists on old ideas. Although only a few hundred words long, "A Bag of Poetry" says a lot about the power of the imagination.

BEAUTY AND THE BEAST by **Jeanne-Marie Leprince de Beaumont** (1711–1780). Some authorities say this is one of the most popular of all fairy tales, although my bet goes on either "Cinderella" or "Sleeping Beauty", both of which are reprinted in this book. Either way, "Beauty and the Beast" must be the best known story by the least well-known writer. Jeanne-Marie had much in common with her predecessor Madame d'Aulnoy (see "The White Cat"), because she too had an unhappy marriage and ended up running away from France to live in England in 1746, where she worked for several years as a governess. She stayed in England on and off for the next twenty years before settling in Switzerland. A prolific writer, she had a particular affinity with children, and her collection of stories, translated as *The Young Misses Magazine* in 1757 but first published in French in 1756, was very popular in her day. Nothing from it is remembered nowadays except for "Beauty and the Beast". Madame Leprince de Beaumont had adapted this story from a much longer work also called "La Belle et la Bête" by Gabrielle-Suzanne Barbot de Gallon de Villeneuve (1695–1755) which had first appeared in 1740. That earlier version is rather tedious and pedestrian. It was Madame Leprince de Beaumont who found the secret of the story and told it in the form remembered today. Just where the story came from is less clear. There are many stories of young girls marrying an ugly or deformed man who turns out to be enchanted and is released from the spell by the girl's love. In fact elements of it can be found as far back as the Roman story of "Cupid and Psyche", written in the second century AD. Perhaps that is the reason for the story's appeal. Its theme is as old as time itself.

THE BELLS OF CARILLON-LAND by **Edith Nesbit** (1858–1924). If you're reading this book from beginning to end rather than dipping about, then Edith Nesbit must be the first well-known name you'll have encountered. She wrote many books for children, the best known being *The Railway Children* (1906). She was very prolific in the quarter-century from 1891 to 1916, and most of her children's fantasies are still in print. These include *Five Children and It* (1902), *The Phoenix and the Carpet* (1904), *The Story of the Amulet* (1906) and *The Enchanted Castle* (1907). She also wrote lots of short stories for children, though these are less well known. This story is taken from the collection *The Magic World*, first published in 1912.

THE BIRTHDAY BATTLE by **Louise Cooper** (born 1952). This is a new story written especially for this anthology. Louise Cooper has been a writer of magical fantasies since 1973, when her first book, *The Book of Paradox*, appeared. After fifteen years of writing for adults she began to write for younger readers with *The Thorn Key* (1988) and *The Sleep of Stone* (1991), and she is one of the regular contributors to the Dark Enchantments series of books. This story was inspired by a visit to the beautiful but still mysterious Forest of Dean on the Welsh/English border, one of the likely hunting forests of King Arthur.

BLUE ROSES by **Netta Syrett** (*c*1870–1943). Known as Netta from her childhood, although baptized Janet, Netta Syrett was a popular writer of children's stories and plays at the turn of the century. Forgotten now, she was instrumental in establishing a children's theatre in 1913 and wrote and produced many plays for children following the popularity of *Peter Pan* by J.M. Barrie. Although she wrote some longer works, she was best known for her short stories which appeared in such volumes as *The Garden of Delight* (1898) and *The Magic City and Other Fairy Tales* (coll 1903). "Blue Roses", which was sub-titled "A Fairy Tale for Impossible Women" – so it's worth reading between the lines – first appeared in the *Pall Mall Magazine* in December 1903.

THE BOY WHO PLAITED MANES by **Nancy Springer** (born 1948). Since her first book, *The Book of Suns* (1977), Nancy Springer has been a prolific writer of fantasy novels, mostly for adults. Her collection *Chance and Other Gestures of the Hand of Fate* (1987) contains a number of stories which verge on the fairy tale, including this rather sinister one which first appeared in *The Magazine of Fantasy and Science Fiction*, October 1986.

THE CASTLE by **George MacDonald** (1824–1905). MacDonald is one of the greats of fantasy fiction. He was the first to write seriously adult fantasies with *Phantastes* (1858) and *Lilith* (1895), as well as producing two of the best known Victorian children's novels, *At the Back of the North Wind* (1871) and *The Princess and the Goblin* (1872). He also wrote what many regard as the single most perfect Victorian fairy story "The Golden Key" (1867). His work has influenced countless writers since, not least C.S. Lewis and J.R.R. Tolkien. A Scottish minister, MacDonald utilized his fiction not to moralize but to stimulate the emotions and abilities locked within us. Some of his stories are quite deep, and though they can be read superficially as delightful tales they clearly have something else to say – though quite what, MacDonald chose not to explain. You'll find something of this in "The Castle", which first appeared in his rather episodic novel *Adela Cathcart* (1864). Incidentally, MacDonald was a close friend of Charles Dodgson, better known as Lewis Carroll, and it was MacDonald who recommended that Dodgson should seek publication of what was then called *Alice's Adventures Under Ground*. See below under "The Mad-Hatter's Tea Party" for more information.

CINDERELLA, OR THE LITTLE GLASS SLIPPER by **Charles Perrault** (1628–1703). Here's my contender for one of the best known of all fairy tales. If not the best known then it certainly must hold the record for the number of versions – apparently there are around seven hundred! This must say something for the antiquity of the tale for it to turn up in so many cultures. The earliest known version comes from ninth-century China. It includes a wicked stepmother, though the fairy godmother in this case is a fish! When I first planned this book I considered including the earliest known European version of the story, which is "La Gatta Cennerentola" or "The Cat Cinderella". This was included by the Italian Giambattista Basile (1575–1632) in a collection of stories now known as the *Pentamerone*, which was first published in Naples in 1634. However, I finally decided that a story in which Cinderella murders her stepmother by smashing her head with the lid of a trunk and gets away with it was perhaps a bit too much. It shows, though, that stories from folk tradition don't necessarily promote good Christian values. The version of the story we know best today is that written by Charles Perrault, which he called "Cendrillon", and included in his collection of fairy tales *Histoires, ou Contes du Temps Passé,* or *Stories or Tales of Past Times,* first published in France in 1697 and translated into English in 1729. At the same time that his story appeared, his friend Madame d'Aulnoy (see under "The White Cat"), published her own version as "Finetta the Cinder-Girl", and you'll find yet another version in the fairy tales of the Brothers Grimm as "Aschenputtel". Incidentally, those who are used to the pantomime version of *Cinderella* may be a bit surprised to find that in Perrault's tale the Prince is not known as Prince Charming. That name was invented by Madame d'Aulnoy for her story "The Blue Bird".

THE FORTRESS UNVANQUISHABLE SAVE FOR SACNOTH by **Lord Dunsany** (1878–1957). Here is one of my favourite stories by one of my favourite writers. I sincerely believe there was no more imaginative writer on this Earth than Lord Dunsany. For over fifty years his imagination remained alive and vibrant and he created some of the most brilliant fantasies ever written. Most were intended for adult readers, but many can equally be enjoyed by younger ones. This story comes from Dunsany's collection *The Sword of Welleran,* first published in 1908, but could easily have been written yesterday. It contains all that is best about stories of heroic fantasy which are still being written by such currently popular writers as David Eddings, Terry Brooks and Terry Goodkind. They all owe their debt to Lord Dunsany. He has been a huge influence on twentieth-century fantasy, almost as much as J.R.R. Tolkien, yet most of his work has been long out of print. If you want to enjoy some of the greatest fantasy written this century, then search out the boks of Lord Dunsany.

THE CLOAK OF FRIENDSHIP and **THE GREEN BIRD** by **Laurence Housman** (1865–1959). Housman's reputation has become somewhat lost in the shadow of his elder brother, the poet A.E. Housman, renowned for his work *A Shropshire Lad* (1896). Laurence probably didn't help himself either, by frequently having his plays banned because of their rather indiscreet references to religion and the Royal family. Housman was definitely a man after my own heart, though — not afraid to say what he thought, and prepared to follow his own course regardless of the consequences. He had a remarkably long career, not only as an author and playwright but also as an artist and illustrator, stretching over sixty years. All of his works are worth tracking down, though the only one I know to be still in print is his own adaptation of *The Arabian Nights*, which appeared in 1907. Housman's fairy tales take on a variety of forms. "The Cloak of Friendship" is clearly a Christian allegory, whilst "The Green Bird" is much more like a fable. They both have a delightful atmosphere of far lands and other days. A collection of his best stories is long overdue.

THE COTTON-WOOL PRINCESS by **Luigi Capuani** (1839–1915). Capuani was an Italian folklorist with a particular interest in the folk tales of Sicily. He collected these, and other fairy tales, in several volumes, of which the most popular was *C'era una volta* (1882) translated into English as *Once Upon a Time* (1892).

THE DRAWING SCHOOL by **J. Muñez Escomez** I've had little success in finding out any details of Señor Escomez. Many years ago I acquired a copy of his stories translated as *Fairy Tales from Spain* (1913), which caught my sense of the absurd since the first story in set in China and another is set in Persia. Clearly Escomez, like Andrew Lang and others, was a collector of folk tales from all over the world, including many from Spain. "The Drawing School" has always appealed to me because it shows that graffiti is not a modern phenomenon.

THE DUTCH CHEESE by **Walter de la Mare** (1873–1956). De la Mare is probably best remembered today for his poems for children, as well as his adaptation of various *Stories from the Bible* (1929), but he was a prolific and varied writer. In addition to many stories and novels for adults he produced one of my favourite children's fantasies, *The Three Mulla-Mulgars* (1910), a book that took so long to find a publisher that, by the time it was published, he'd almost regretted writing it. De la Mare not only retold many well-known fairy tales in *Told Again* (1927), but wrote several of his own. The best, including this one, were collected as *Broomsticks and Other Tales* (1925).

THE ELVES by **Ludwig Tieck** (1773–1853). One of the things I wanted this anthology to do was to rectify the common belief that fairy tales began with the Brothers Grimm. They certainly didn't. I've already mentioned Charles Perrault and Madame d'Aulnoy several times as antecedents from France, but the Grimms had predecessors in Germany as well. Amongst these was Johann Ludwig Tieck, who was one of the primary movers in German romantic fiction at the time of Goethe. He began producing a series of stories based on old folk tales and legends starting with "Der Blonde Eckbert" or "Eckbert the Fair" in 1796, which is one of the earliest tales of modern fantasy. "The Elves" or "Die Elfin" first appeared in 1811 and is regarded in Germany as one of the classics.

THE ENCHANTED WATCH by **Charles Deulin** (1827–1877). Deulin was a French folklorist whose stories were very popular in their day. "The Enchanted Watch" is based on a Bohemian folk tale which has also been suggested as the source Antoine Galland used for "Aladdin". The version used here is that translated by one of Andrew Lang's colleagues for *The Green Fairy Book* (1892).

THE ENCHANTED WHISTLE by **Alexandre Dumas** (1802–1870). Dumas was almost a one-man industry, and remains one of the most prolific of all writers in the world before the invention of the typewriter. He is most famous for *The Three Musketeers* (1844) and for my own favourite amongst his books, *The Count of Monte-Cristo* (1846), but he also wrote several volumes of children's stories. So prolific was Dumas that it was believed he collaborated with others who ghost-wrote work under his own name. Primary amongst these was Dumas's illegitimate son, Alexandre Dumas *fils* (1824–1895), and it is possible that the son wrote the following story, as I have seen it attributed to him. Dumas *père* wrote most of his children's stories in the 1840s, although the majority of them were not collected together or translated until after his death, which may well account for the confusion with his son. *The Dumas Fairy Tale Book* was not published in Britain until 1924.

THE FAIRY GIFT by **Charlotte Brontë** (1816–1855). Here's a rare and forgotten story. In their teens, Charlotte Brontë and her sisters wrote many stories set in imaginary and faraway worlds. None of these was published during their short lives and were eventually discovered over sixty years later amongst papers kept by Charlotte's husband following his second marriage after her death. He had several times come close to burning them, but they were saved from destruction by Brontë's biographer Clement Shorter, who eventually published them in *The Twelve Adventurers and Other Stories* (1925). This story appeared earlier as "The Four Wishes" in *The Strand Magazine* for December 1918.

THE FOREST FAIRY by **Lord Brabourne** (1829–1893). Created Lord Brabourne in 1880, and a politician and junior minister from 1857 to 1880, Edward Knatchbull-Hugesson was a cheerful man who loved to lampoon the stodginess of his fellow parliamentarians and enjoyed the pleasures of storytelling probably more than he did being an MP. As a devoted father, he used to tell stories to his children, and after these became a success, when published as *Stories For My Children* in 1869, he proceeded to write a new fairy story collection almost every year for the next twenty years, most of them set in Brabourne's home county of Kent. This story comes from that first collection.

THE GIRL WHO LOVED THE WIND and **THE TREE'S WIFE** by **Jane Yolen** (born 1939). Yolen has been called the twentieth century's Hans Christian Andersen, and that is praise indeed, but well deserved. Her stories are able to capture the real essence of the fairy tale and deliver it in only a few hundred words. She has published over a hundred books, many of them picture books, but you'll find the best of her fairy tales and fantasies in *Tales of Wonder* (1983) and *Dragonfield and Other Stories* (1985).

THE GLASS DOG by **L. Frank Baum** (1856–1919). Almost certainly the most famous contribution by an American to children's fantasy has got to be *The Wizard of Oz*, originally *The Wonderful*

Wizard of Oz (1900), which was already perenially popular before Judy Garland starred in the even more popular film version in 1939. Baum's early career was dogged by a weak heart, though he spent some time as a travelling salesman and as a window dresser before the success of his picture book, *Father Goose, His Book* (1899), allowed him to consider writing as a possible career and to turn the bedtime stories he used to tell his children into *The Wonderful Wizard of Oz.* Sales of the book were so phenomenal that it still remains one of the bestselling children's books of all time. Although Baum turned to writing other books, including *American Fairy Tales* (1901) from which this story is taken, and *The Life and Adventures of Santa Claus* (1902), the success of the Oz book demanded sequels, which came with *The Marvellous Land of Oz* (1905) followed by many more. The Oz books so dominated Baum's life thereafter that he had no time to return to other fairy tales, But he didn't need to. He left a legacy which has made him immortal.

THE HAPPY PRINCE by Oscar Wilde (1854–1900). Wilde had a natural affinity with children – he loved his own two and it broke his heart when, after the Alfred Douglas court case, he was not allowed to see them again. There was always a melancholic side to Wilde. Whilst his plays brought out that wonderfully witty and acerbic Wilde, his fairy tales allowed him to indulge in an inner sadness. Wilde's fairy tales are clearly modelled on those by Hans Christian Andersen, who had the same view that fairy tales were for all age groups. When this story was first published in *The Happy Prince and Other Tales* (1888), Wilde said that the stories were "for child-like people from eighteen to eighty."

HOW WRY-FACE PLAYED A TRICK ON ONE-EYE by Agnes Grozier Herbertson. A prolific writer, Agnes Herbertson produced books and stories for children for over thirty years, starting with a book about the heroes of old, such as St George and Robin Hood, whose tales she retold in *Heroic Legends* (1908). This story comes from the same year, from a collection called *Cap o' Yellow* (1908). Other stories for children will be found in *The Book of Happy Gnomes* (1924) and *Stories from Elfland* (1924).

JACK AND THE BEANSTALK This is one of those stories whose origins are lost in the mists of time, although not so historic that we shouldn't have some idea who wrote it. The story is more on the side of "Anonymous" than "Traditional". A version of it was apparently already a folk tale at the end of the seventeenth century, though that version involves no giant but tells of a luckless youth whose mother was a witch who lost her power when Jack found her magic bean and planted it. The giant beanstalk became a home for families and Jack became its sovereign lord. Somehow, by the end of the eighteenth century, that story had metamorphosed into the one we all know and which is printed here. This was part of the *Popular Stories* series of chapbooks published by Benjamin Tabart, and the earliest known copy appeared in 1807. Tabart was a publisher's name, but may not have been a real person. Behind the Tabart insignia lurked Sir Richard Phillips (1767–1840), who later became Sheriff of London and who was something of a political revolutionary. He was a hack writer for years and it's quite possible that he wrote this version, using it to satirize the government of the day. See what you can read in between the lines. The beanstalk, reaching up into the sky (or heaven) is probably derived from the old Nordic belief of the Tree of Life, the World Tree, called Yggdrasil, under which the Norns spun the fates of mankind.

THE KNAVE AND THE FOOL by **Juliana Horatia Ewing** (1841–1885). Juliana Ewing was one of the leading Victorian writers of children's fantasies and fairy tales. Her mother, Margaret Gatty (1809–1873), also wrote for children and started the children's periodical *Aunt Judy's Magazine* in 1866, to which her daughter frequently contributed. This story, under the title "Knave and Fool", first appeared in the June 1872 issue. Mrs Ewing's story "The Brownies" (1865) was so popular that it was used as the name for the junior division of the Girl Guides in 1918. Her most popular collections were *The Brownies and Other Tales* (1870), *Lob Lie-By-the-Fire* (1874) and *Old-Fashioned Fairy Tales* (1882). Her works had an influence upon Rudyard Kipling and in particular Edith Nesbit, who always felt her own work inferior to that of Ewing's. Probably Juliana Ewing's most realistic novel of childhood is *Daddy*

Darwin's Dovecote (1884), which draws on her own memories of a Yorkshire upbringing. It tells of the relationship between a boy from the workhouse and an old smallholder who races pigeons and takes the boy in.

LITTLE RED RIDING HOOD by Laura Valentine (1814–1899). The original story of Little Red Riding Hood seems to have been invented by Charles Perrault, and first appeared in his collection of fairy stories in France in 1697. His story is the basic one that we remember, and ends with the wolf devouring the little girl. However, the version that appears in the tales of the Brothers Grimm, called "Little Red Cap", had an altered ending in which two huntsmen kill the wolf and when they slit it open find Little Red Riding Hood and her grandmother alive inside. Somehow neither of these versions best satisfied Victorian writers. The first was too abrupt and unhappy an ending, but the second was rather too absurd. Several writers came up with alternatives. The one I like best was by Mrs Valentine in *The Old, Old Fairy Tales* (1889) which not only seemed eminently sensible, but also gave the story a purpose. See what you think.

LITTLE SNOWDROP; OR, SNOW WHITE AND THE SEVEN DWARFS by Jakob and Wilhelm Grimm Probably thanks to the Walt Disney animated feature film, this story is now amongst the best known of all fairy tales. Disney gave the seven dwarfs names but, as you'll find, the original did not. The story comes from "Sneewitchen" ("Snowdrop") from the first major volume of folk tales gathered together by Jakob Grimm (1785–1863) and his brother Wilhelm (1786–1859) called *Kinder- und Hausmärchen* (1812), or *Nursery and Household Tales.* They heard the story from two sisters, Jeannette and Amalie Hassenpflug, but it was clearly already a popular tale. Something very similar to it had been written by Johann Karl Musaeus in "Richilde", a story included in his massive collection of German Folk Tales, *Volksmärchen der Deutschen,* published only thirty years earlier. And elements of it, including the poisoned comb and the glass coffin, appear in "The Young Slave", one of the stories in *The Pentameron* by Giambattista Basile, published in 1634. One has to ask why the stories by the Grimm Brothers are remembered and revered to this day while the earlier versions are forgotten, at least in Britain (they are much better known in Germany). One reason has to be Britain's moralistic attitude to folk tales and fairy stories at the start of the nineteenth century. Any story which was not seen as morally improving was frowned upon and shunned. However, what the Grimm Brothers did was assiduously collect and attribute the sources to their stories, which therefore became of academic propriety – in other words they seemed respectful. Even though the more lofty establishment still frowned upon them, when the Grimms' stories were first published in Britain in 1823 as *German Popular Stories* they created a storm of interest and a flurry of fascination with our own folk and traditional tales. They consequently set the trend, and have remained in the forefront of our memories ever since. In fact, it's likely that we attribute most popular fairy tales to the Grimm Brothers first, or perhaps to Hans Christian Andersen, and forget everyone else.

THE MAD-HATTER'S TEA PARTY by **Lewis Carroll** (1832–1898). Under his real name, Charles Lutwidge Dogson was a lecturer in mathematics at Oxford, and he kept this persona entirely separate from that of Lewis Carroll, under which name he wrote comic verse and stories and two of the best known works of children's fantasy in the world: *Alice in Wonderland* (1865) and *Alice Through the Looking-Glass* (1871). Actually, neither of these is the original title to the books. *Alice in Wonderland* began life as a totally different book, *Alice's Adventures Under Ground*, which is the version that Dodgson told to the daughters of the Reverend Henry Liddell, Lorina, Alice and Edith, during boat trips along the Thames in 1862. When Dodgson eventually came to write these down the story changed somewhat and became *Alice's Adventures in Wonderland*. He showed the manuscript to his friend George MacDonald, with whose children Dodgson was also a great story-telling companion, who recommended it for publication. It is difficult to emphasize the impact of the book. After a century or more of very stuffy, moralistic stories, children's books were at last giving way to more fantastic tales, but their appearance was slow and experimental. Dodgson, however, jumped right in at the deep end, producing a piece of nonsense which hung together with the paradox of children's logic. The book remains as fresh today as ever. It wasn't quite an overnight success, but within a few years sales were mounting, and by the time of Dodgson's death the book was one of the best-selling of all children's fantasies. *Through the Looking-Glass, and What Alice Found There*, which is the proper title to its sequel is, if anything, more entertaining and original than the first volume, and certainly is quoted more frequently. Although Dodgson wrote other books for children, somehow these books never captured the public imagination as the two Alice books. They aren't really fairy tales in the strict sense, but who cares? You'll find everything that's in a fairy tale in these books and a lot more besides. I couldn't compile this volume without something from Alice, and what better than "The Mad-Hatter's Tea Party"?

THE MISTREATED FELLOW and **THE UGLY UNICORN** by **Jessica Amanda Salmonson** (born 1950). Jessica Salmonson is an American writer who established herself with a series of adult fantasy novels set in a world of Japanese myth, starting with *Tomoe Gozen* (1981). She is fascinated with the legends and folk tales of all nations, and a variety will be found in her collections *A Silver Thread of Madness* (1989), *The Mysterious Doom* (1992) and *Phantom Waters* (1995). Her stories here draw upon Nordic and Chinese folklore respectively. "The Ugly Unicorn" was further inspired by Salmonson's reading of the stories of Laurence Housman, who is also represented in this anthology (see "Cloak of Friendship" and "The Green Bird").

MOTHER-OF-ALL by **F. Gwynplaine MacIntyre** (born 1947). Scottish by birth, raised in Australia and now resident in the United States, MacIntyre is a talented writer who draws upon a mass of cultural traditions for his stories. "Mother-of-All" is a new story. The title is the name of one of the components of a spinning wheel. MacIntyre took as its basic premise the Grimm Brothers' story "The Three Spinners" and wove into it elements of "Rumpelstiltskin" (which will also be found in this volume). The three spinners represent the Fates from Greek and Roman mythology – Clotho, Lachesis and Atropos – who controlled the birth, life and death of every person. The Three Fates are also represented in Nordic mythology as the three Norns, who represent past, present and future, and who spin their threads at the base of the world-tree or Yggdrasil. This same tree, as I mentioned earlier, is believed to be the origin of the beanstalk in "Jack and the Beanstalk".

THE NECKLACE OF TEARS by **Mrs Egerton Eastwick**. I'm afraid I can tell you very little about Mrs Egerton Eastwick (or, for that matter, Mr Egerton Eastwick), other than that her maiden name was Mary Nott and that she wrote a handful of books and several children's stories around the turn of the century. She also wrote under the name Playdell North. She may have lived for some of her life in Singapore. "The Necklace of Tears" first appeared in *The Strand Magazine* for December 1896.

THE NIGHT THE STARS WERE GONE by **Joan Aiken** (born 1924). Joan Aiken is one of the most accomplished and most respected of writers for children writing today. You may well have read (or seen or heard, in various film, television and radio adaptations) her stories set in an alternate Britain where the Stewart kings continued to rule. The two best known of these books are *The Wolves of Willoughby Chase* (1962) and *Black Hearts in Battersea* (1964). She's written many stories (for children and adults), but to my mind her supreme collection of fairy tales and fantasies is *The Faithless Lollybird* (1977), from which this story is taken.

OLD PIPES AND THE DRYAD by **Frank R. Stockton** (1834–1902). Although very popular in his day, the American writer Frank R. Stockton is remembered now (if at all) for just one story, "The Lady or the Tiger?" (1882), which is memorable because its ending is unresolved and you have to guess which choice the hapless hero takes. It has kept people guessing for over a century. It's a shame that so many of his other stories have been forgotten, as he was a clever writer. One collection which does surface from time to time is *The Bee Man of Orn* (1887) from which this story is taken. The title story is still in print in a booklet illustrated by Maurice Sendak. Stockton, wrote many children's stories for magazines, but somehow these did not outlive them and their work for children became forgotten once L. Frank Baum's *The Wonderful Wizard of Oz* became all the rage. You may find in some books Stockton's story "The Griffin and the Minor Canon", but I much prefer this story, "Old Pipes and the Dryad", because it has more that atmosphere of the fairy tale.

THE PIPED PIPER OF HAMELIN by **Charles Marelles** (1827–?). The story of the Pied Piper of Hamelin is best known to us today from the poem of the same title by Robert Browning (1812–1889). He heard the story from his father, and it had probably passed down the generations for hundreds of years. There is a legend that in the year 1284 a young piper came to Hamelin and lured all the children away (the story of the rats came later). The story may also owe something to the Children's Crusade, which started in 1212 and saw the exodus of many young men from France and Germany on their own expedition to the Holy Land. Most never returned. The version presented here was one collected by the French folklorist Charles Marelles in his collection *Affenschwanz* (1888) – the title means *The Monkey's Tail.* Marelles called the story "The Ratcatcher", and in his version the man plays a form of bagpipes, but otherwise the story is exactly the same.

THE POT OF GOLD by **Horace E. Scudder** (1838–1902). The legend that at the end of the rainbow is a pot of gold is so old that its origins are lost in antiquity. Of course anyone who has tried knows that you never do reach the end of the rainbow, and the search for the pot of gold is a fruitless quest. The idea has been used in many stories, and the one I most like is "The Pot of Gold" by Horace Scudder. Scudder was an American writer and editor who was extremely influential in raising the standard of fiction for children in the various magazines that he edited, especially the *Riverside Magazine,* which he began in 1867. His books for children include *Dream Children* (1864), *The Children's Book* (1881) and *The Book of Folk Stories* (1887). Scudder's elder brother was a missionary in India, which I imagine instilled a wanderlust for foreign lands in young Horace, hence the reference to India at the start of the story and that urgent desire to travel which carries the story along.

PRINCESS CRYSTAL; OR, THE HIDDEN TREASURE by **Isabel Bellerby**. I confess I know nothing about Isabel Bellerby, and can find no other books or stories by her. Maybe this was a one-off. It appeared in the March 1896 issue of *The Strand Magazine*.

PRINCESS SANSU by Tanith Lee (born 1947). Since the publication of *The Birthgrave* in 1975, Tanith Lee has become better known for her adult fantasy and supernatural stories, but she began by writing for children. Her first book, *The Betrothed* (1968), was a short story printed privately by a friend. This was followed by *The Dragon Hoard* (1971), a rousing adventure fantasy, *Animal Castle* (1972), a picture book, and the collection *Princess Hynchatti and Some Other Surprises* (1972), from which this story is taken. The story was written when Tanith Lee was about nineteen, though it wasn't published till six years later. The story contains a strong measure on the consequences of parental pressure and false expectations.

THE RAT THAT COULD SPEAK by **Charles Dickens** (1812–1870). Dickens loved fairy stories. He was writing at the time that they came into vogue and he contributed to their popularity, writing several of his own like "The Magic Fishbone" and this story. Dickens firmly believed that fairy tales were a much better form of children's fiction than the highly moral stories of the previous generation. He was a great champion of the work of Hans Christian Andersen, although he rather cooled on Andersen when that master came to stay at the Dickens household in 1847 and rather overstayed his welcome. Most of Dickens's best known children's stories are those which make up the sequence *A Holiday Romance* published in 1868, but he wrote several earlier ones. "Prince Bull" appeared in *Household Words* in 1855 and this one, which is also sometimes called "The Devil and Mr Chips", appeared alongside "Captain Murderer" in *All the Year Round* in 1860, as stories remembered by Dickens from his nursery.

RUMPELSTILTSKIN by **Jakob and Wilhelm Grimm.** This is the best known version of a story which may be found in many European cultures, including Britain, where the little man is variously called Tom

Tit Tot or Terrytop. What's interesting about it is the long-held belief that if you let a person know your real name they will have power over you, and thus you should have a public name and a private real name. The concept is central to several modern fantasy stories, and you'll find it working at its best in Ursula K. Le Guin's Earthsea series, especially the first book, *A Wizard of Earthsea* (1968).

THE SEEKERS by **H.E. Bates** (1906–1974). Now here's a forgotten little gem. Herbert Ernest Bates is, of course, well known for his Pop Larkin stories, *The Darling Buds of May* (1958), as well as for some of his books drawn from wartime experiences, such as *Fair Stood the Wind for France* (1944). Much of his earlier works, including many stories for children, have become forgotten. *The Seekers* is one of those, written while Bates was in his late teens and published as a small booklet in 1926. It carries the dedication "To All Children Who Ask WHY?" In describing the land of Faerie, Bates draws upon all his favourite childhood books. See how many you can identify. Some are less obvious than others, but you'll find some that are elsewhere in this book. The references to Sylvie and Bruno refer to the books which Lewis Carroll wrote after his Alice books; Nod, the Mulla-Mulgar, is from the novel by Walter de la Mare, *The Three Mulla-Mulgars* (1910); while Nixie and Uncle Paul refer to *The Education of Uncle Paul* (1909) by Algernon Blackwood (1869–1951), a popular writer of supernatural stories whose children's stories have been unjustly forgotten. This story is a real celebration of fantasy. Other children's fantasies by Bates will be found in *Seven Tales and Alexander* (1929).

THE SEVEN FAMILIES OF THE LAKE PIPPLE-POPPLE by **Edward Lear** (1812–1888). Lear was one of those rare breaths of fresh air that blew away some of the dust of pomposity from Victorian society and allowed everyone to laugh. There wasn't really anyone else like him – Lewis Carroll came closest – and his legacy continues to this day, most especially in the humour of Spike Milligan and Terry Jones. His first *Book of Nonsense* appeared in 1846 and he added to it over the years, bringing out other volumes, including *More Nonsense* in 1872. His most famous poem is "The Owl and the Pussy-Cat", written in

1867 and published in *Nonsense Songs, Stories, Botany and Alphabets* in 1870, the same book from which this much lesser known story comes. Lear was a lonely man all his life. He suffered from epilepsy, which caused him to remain solitary, though he would have loved the companionship of marriage and would have loved even more to have had children, in whose company he came alive.

THE SEVEN RAVENS by **Ludwig Bechstein** (1801–1860). Totally forgotten today, during his lifetime Bechstein's collections of folk tales were even more popular than the Grimms'. These volumes began to appear in 1823, but the grand omnibus is *Altdeutsche Märchen, Sagen und Legenden* (*German Folk Tales, Sagas and Legends*), published in 1863. "The Seven Ravens" comes from *Deutsches Märchenbuch* (*The Book of German Folk Tales*), published in 1848.

SLEEPING BEAUTY by **Charles Perrault** (1628–1703). "Sleeping Beauty", or "The Sleeping Beauty in the Wood", to give it its full title, was Perrault's first fairy tale in prose and was written in 1695, appearing in a newspaper early in 1696. As with most of Perrault's stories, there are earlier sources. For instance, the story of "Sun, Moon and Talia" by Giambattista Basile in *The Pentameron* (1634) has much in common with it, though, in that story, the King who finds and wakens Sleeping Beauty is already married, and his wife becomes the equivalent of the wicked stepmother in her desire to kill the girl and her later children. There's an even earlier story, "Troylus and Zellandine", from the fourteenth-century French romance *Perceforest*, that contains the basic elements. Perrault's story has some of the less seemly elements toned down, but it is still longer than most people recall because it continues the story after the Prince awakens Sleeping Beauty, which was the point where the Victorians preferred to end it. You may be a little surprised at the violence of the ending.

THE SNOW QUEEN and THE UGLY DUCKLING by **Hans Christian Andersen** (1805–1875). In my opinion Andersen is the world's greatest storyteller. I don't believe anyone has bettered his stories before or since. What's more, unlike the stories of Perrault or Grimm, which were based upon traditional folk tales, almost all of Andersen's stories are original, drawn from his own imagination. Only his very earliest stories relied upon tales he vaguely remembered from his childhood. Like Edward Lear, Andersen was a lonely child, which arose partly from his family poverty but also because of his ungainliness – "The Ugly Duckling" is modelled on Andersen's own childhood. He was remarkably clumsy. It meant that when he made friends he went overboard in showing his affection for them. As a consequence Charles Dickens – who greatly admired him – soon grew tired of him when Andersen overstayed his welcome at the Dickens household during a prolonged visit in 1847. Andersen's first collection of stories was *Eventyr Fortalte for Børn* (*Tales Told for Children*), a small booklet which appeared in 1835 containing just four stories. Thereafter he produced a new booklet almost every year, changing the title to *New Fairy Tales* in 1845 and to *Stories* in 1852, demonstrating that they were intended to appeal to all ages. "The Ugly Duckling" was printed in the first of the *New Fairy Tales* volumes in 1845 and "The Snow Queen", one of Andersen's longest stories, came in the second volume in 1846.

THE STORY OF NICK by **Christina Rossetti** (1830–1894). Christina Rossetti was the brother of the poet and painter Dante Gabriel Rossetti, but she was no mean writer and poet herself. She is best known today for her long children's poem *Goblin Market* (1862), but she wrote several other fairy poems and stories including "The Story of Nick", first published in 1857, which is a variant on the three-wishes theme.

THE THREE BEARS by **Sarah Baker** (1824–1906). Although better known as "Goldilocks and the Three Bears" the name of Goldilocks is a comparatively recent addition, being first used in an edition published in 1904. In the original story, by the poet Robert Southey (1774–1843), which he published in 1837, the intruder to the bears' house is a nosy old woman who is chased out. When reprinting the story, in *Treasury of Pleasure Books for Young Children* (1850), Joseph Cundall (1818–1895) changed the old woman to a young girl and renamed her Silver-Hair. In subsequent reprintings over the next few years, this changed to Silverlocks, Golden Hair and finally Goldilocks. The version reprinted here is the one by Sarah Baker, who was known as Aunt Friendly and revised the story for *Aunt Friendly's Nursery Keepsake* (1870), where we find the girl Golden Hair.

THE THREE GOATS NAMED BRUSE; OR, THE THREE BILLY-GOATS GRUFF by **Peter Asbjørnsen and Jørgen Moe**. This story is better known as "The Three Billy-Goats Gruff", the title used by Sir George Dasent (1817–1896) when he reprinted it in *Popular Tales from the North* (1859). The original story, though, was collected by the friends Peter Asbjørnsen (1812–1885) and Jørgen Moe (1813–1882), the Norwegian equivalent of the Brothers Grimm, who issued their own *Norske Folkeeventyr* (*Norwegian Folk-Tales*) in 1842, which they regularly updated. That volume also includes one of the stories which, in translation, has the most evocative title of all fairy tales: "East of the Sun and West of the Moon".

THE THREE TASKS by **Geraldine Elliot** (born 1899). Born in India but raised and educated in Somerset, Geraldine Elliot joined the BBC in 1923, and soon found herself telling stories on the radio as Aunt Geraldine. She married in 1927, and in 1928 her husband, then in the Colonial Service, was stationed in East Africa, where Geraldine began collecting African folk tales. Her first anthology of these, *The Long Grass Whispers*, appeared in 1939. Three other volumes followed, *Where the Leopard Passes*, *The Hunter's Cave* (from which this story is reprinted) and *The Singing Chameleon*. Most of the stories I have reprinted in this anthology are of the standard fairy tale tradition, from Western Europe, but I wanted to include at least one African fairy tale to show that such stories are not confined to Europe. Geraldine Elliot's stories are wonderfully alive and vibrant and have been far too long out of print.

THE TOUCHSTONE by **Robert Louis Stevenson** (1850–1894). Stevenson was perhaps the greatest of all Victorian writers of children's adventure stories, of which *Treasure Island* (1883) and *Kidnapped* (1886) are the peak. It's easy to overlook the fact that he also wrote a number of fables and fairy tales, some of them rather misanthropic, reflecting Stevenson's general pessimistic view of the world. "The Touchstone", written in 1888, was one such story, though is perhaps rather more optimistic than most.

TOUK'S HOUSE by **Robin McKinley** (born 1952). Robin McKinley is one of the current generation of writers who have rediscovered the merits of the fairy story and have adapted them to a new readership. She presented her own version of "Beauty and the Beast" in *Beauty* (1978), and retold several other stories in *The Door in the Hedge* (1981). "Touk's House" was first published in 1985 and will be found in her collection *A Knot in the Grain* (1994).

THE TRIUMPH OF VICE by **W. S. Gilbert** (1836–1911). Yes, this is the same Gilbert of Gilbert and Sullivan fame. A great humorist and a devotee of fairy fiction, Gilbert combined the two in a number of fairy comedies which he wrote for the stage (before his association with Sullivan), and in various stories which he wrote for popular humour magazines, like *Fun* during the 1860s. Gilbert took advantage of the rent caused in moralistic fiction by Lewis Carroll and others to write stories which turned Victorian morals on their heads. This is one such utterly shameless story, written entirely for fun and with no redeeming features at all!

THE UNHAPPY PRINCESS by **Richard Cowper** (born 1926). Richard Cowper is the pen name of John Middleton Murry, usually known as Colin to distinguish him from his father, the critic and publisher John Middleton Murry (1889–1957), who was the friend and supporter of D. H. Lawrence, Virginia Woolf and others. Cowper established himself as an author of science fiction and fantasy in the 1970s, especially with his Bird of Kinship trilogy, *The Road to Corlay* (1978), *A Tapestry of Time* (1982) and *A Dream of Kinship* (1981) which, though set in the future, has all the atmosphere and feel of a fairy tale. Cowper has written several fairy stories, but all of these have appeared in small press limited editions and so are scarcely known at all. They include *The Missing Heart* (1982), *The Story of Pepita and Corindo* (1982) and the stories in *The Magic Spectacles* (1986), as well as *The Unhappy Princess* (1982).

THE WHITE CAT by **Marie-Cathérine d'Aulnoy** (*c*1650–1705). I have already mentioned Madame d'Aulnoy at the start of this appendix. Her collection *Contes des fées* (1697), and subsequent volumes, really began the modern vogue for fairy stories. Unlike the stories of her colleague Charles Perrault, Madame d'Aulnoy's were longer and more complicated, and as a result their full versions have not survived or remained as popular. The Victorians edited them down to their bare essentials, and in so doing lost the original thrill and delight that d'Aulnoy created. A few survived relatively untouched, and amongst them "The White Cat" is perhaps the best. It combines all the elements that we have long since come to know, love and expect in fairy tales – quests, magical enchantments, impossible tasks, beautiful ladies and kings fearful of their crown! The version printed here is that adapted by Laura Valentine, otherwise known as Aunt Louisa, for her collection *The Old Old Fairy Tales* (1889). With another two hundred years of fairy tale tradition since the story had first appeared, Laura Valentine wove into the tale references to other stories to make it all the more familiar. I think they improve the story, so I've left those references in.

If you are interested in reading the stories in the order in which they were first written or published, the following is a chronological index:

1696 *Sleeping Beauty*, Charles Perrault
1697 *Cinderella*, Charles Perrault; and *Little Red Riding Hood*, Laura Valentine
1698 *The White Cat*, Madame d'Aulnoy
1757 *Beauty and the Beast*, Jeanne-Marie Leprince de Beaumont
1807 *Jack and the Beanstalk*
1811 *The Elves*, Ludwig Tieck
1812 *Little Snowdrop* and *Rumpelstiltskin*, The Brothers Grimm
1838 *The Fairy Gift*, Charlotte Brontë
1842 *The Three Goats Named Bruse*, Peter Asbjørnsen and Jørgen Moe
1845 *The Ugly Duckling*, Hans Christian Andersen
1845? *The Enchanted Whistle*, Alexandre Dumas
1846 *The Snow Queen*, Hans Christian Andersen

1848　*The Seven Ravens*, Ludwig Bechstein

1857　*The Story of Nick*, Christina Rossetti

1860　*The Rat That Could Speak*, Charles Dickens

1864　*The Castle*, George MacDonald

1865　*The Mad-Hatter's Tea Party*, Lewis Carroll

1869　*The Forest Fairy*, Lord Brabourne

1870　*The Three Bears*, Sarah Baker

1871　*The Seven Families of the Lake Pipple-Popple*, Edward Lear

1872　*The Knave and the Fool*, Juliana H. Ewing

1879　*The Enchanted Watch*, Charles Deulin

1882　*The Cotton-Wool Princess*, Luigi Capuani

1887　*The Pot of Gold*, Horace E. Scudder; and *Old Pipes and the Dryad*, Frank R. Stockton

1888　*The Pied Piper of Hamelin*, Charles Marelles; *The Touchstone*, Robert Louis Stevenson; and *The Happy Prince*, Oscar Wilde

1896　*Princess Crystal; or the Hidden Treasure*, Isabel Bellerby; *The Necklace of Tears*, Mrs Egerton Eastwick

1901　*The Glass Dog*, L. Frank Baum

1903　*Blue Roses*, Netta Syrett

1905　*The Cloak of Friendship*, Laurence Housman; and *The Bells of Carillon-Land*, Edith Nesbit

1906　*The Fortress Unvanquishable, Save for Sacnoth*, Lord Dunsany

1908　*How Wry-Face Played a Trick on One-Eye*, Agnes G. Herbertson

1913　*The Drawing School*, J. Muñez Escomez

1925　*The Dutch Cheese*, Walter de la Mare

1926　*The Seekers*, H.E. Bates

1932　*The Green Bird*, Laurence Housman

1951　*The Three Tasks*, Geraldine Elliot

1972　*Princess Sansu*, Tanith Lee; *The Girl Who Loved the Wind*, Jane Yolen

1977　*The Night the Stars Were Gone*, Joan Aiken

1978　*The Tree's Wife*, Jane Yolen

1982　*The Unhappy Princess*, Richard Cowper

1985　*Touk's House*, Robin McKinley

1986　*The Boy Who Plaited Manes*, Nancy Springer

1987　*The Forest of Dreams*, Lawrence Schimel

1991　*The Ugly Unicorn*, Jessica Amanda Salmonson

1997　(all new) *A Bag of Poetry*, Lawrence Schimel; *The Mistreated Fellow*, Jessica Amanda Salmonson; *Mother-of-All*, F. Gwynplaine MacIntyre; *The Birthday Battle*, Louise Cooper.

Index to stories by author

⌒

624

Copyright and Acknowledgements

◆

I would like to thank Richard Dalby, Lawrence Schimel and Jessica Amanda Salmonson for their help in compiling this anthology, in particular for their suggestions of stories and the provision of some rare and hard to find texts.